W9-BRF-959

. . . and what she can't remember could kill her.

"A DEFINITE MASTER OF SUSPENSE."
—*A Romance Review*

Praise for the Novels
of Karen Robards

Pursuit

"Robards's fans will enjoy this fast-paced and action-packed romantic thriller."   —*Publishers Weekly*

"Cleverly written, intense, and riveting . . . best saved for a day devoted to reading, because once you start you will not want to put it down. Karen Robards has become a master at blending romance and suspense, offering readers pulse-racing drama. Robards once again keeps us enthralled. [*Pursuit* is] riveting, spellbinding, enthralling, captivating, mesmerizing, and any other *–ing* that means it grabs your attention and keeps it."   —*The Monitor* (McAllen, TX)

"A tense and erotic political thriller sure to be as popular as Robards's previous novels."   —*Booklist*

"A fast-paced romantic-suspense political thriller . . . a thrilling tense tale."   —*Midwest Book Review*

Guilty

"Karen Robards is emerging as one of the top romance suspense authors, one whose name means 'read this book.' And she doesn't disappoint with *Guilty*."
          —*The State* (Columbia, SC)

"[A] scintillating romantic thriller. . . . Robards once again shows her flair for coupling first-rate suspense with multi-dimensional characters."   —*Publishers Weekly*

"*Guilty* is truly a pleasure as the ever-popular and prolific Robards gives her readers an especially exciting top-notch tale of romantic suspense."   —*Booklist*

"An exciting urban thriller . . . strong, entertaining romantic suspense."   —*Midwest Book Review*

continued . . .

"Will keep readers turning the pages."

—*Publishers Weekly*

Superstition

"Fans of Tami Hoag, Iris Johansen, and Kay Hooper will love *Superstition*." —*Midwest Book Review*

"[*Superstition*] is another winner from . . . Robards. A classic edge-of-the-seat read." —*Booklist*

"When you see Karen Robards's name on a new book, *grab it*! . . . [She] is . . . guaranteed to deliver an entertaining, must-read, can't-put-down story. And she does it again with *Superstition*. This has all the earmarks of a Robards story: a compelling mystery, an engaging cast of characters, and a strong hero and heroine with amazing chemistry."

—*The State* (Columbia, SC)

Bait

Romantic suspense at its absolute best. I didn't want *Bait* to end." —Janet Evanovich

"Veteran romance/crime bestseller Robards delivers another hold-your-breath drama, this time starring FBI agent Sam McCabe and advertising executive Maddie Fitzgerald. Her pacing is excellent, and regular infusions of humor keep the story bouncing along between trysts and attacks. This one is sure to please fans." —*Publishers Weekly*

"Robards returns once again with a pulse-pounding novel. Nonstop suspense amidst sensual romance heats up the pages of this captivating novel. Top-rate suspenseful action and sizzling romance form the backbone of this spectacular read, one of Robards's all-time best." —The Best Reviews

ALSO BY KAREN ROBARDS

PURSUIT

Karen Robards

A SIGNET BOOK

SIGNET
Published by New American Library, a division of
Penguin Group (USA) Inc., 375 Hudson Street,
New York, New York 10014, USA
Penguin Group (Canada), 90 Eglinton Avenue East, Suite 700, Toronto,
Ontario M4P 2Y3, Canada (a division of Pearson Penguin Canada Inc.)
Penguin Books Ltd., 80 Strand, London WC2R 0RL, England
Penguin Ireland, 25 St. Stephen's Green, Dublin 2,
Ireland (a division of Penguin Books Ltd.)
Penguin Group (Australia), 250 Camberwell Road, Camberwell, Victoria 3124,
Australia (a division of Pearson Australia Group Pty. Ltd.)
Penguin Books India Pvt. Ltd., 11 Community Centre, Panchsheel Park,
New Delhi - 110 017, India
Penguin Group (NZ), 67 Apollo Drive, Rosedale, North Shore 0632,
New Zealand (a division of Pearson New Zealand Ltd.)
Penguin Books (South Africa) (Pty.) Ltd., 24 Sturdee Avenue,
Rosebank, Johannesburg 2196, South Africa

Penguin Books Ltd., Registered Offices:
80 Strand, London WC2R 0RL, England

Published by Signet, an imprint of New American Library, a division of Penguin
Group (USA) Inc. Previously published in a Putnam edition.

First Signet Printing, February 2010
10 9 8 7 6 5 4 3 2 1

Copyright © Karen Robards, 2009
Excerpt from *Shattered* copyright © Karen Robards, 2010
All rights reserved

Ⓤ REGISTERED TRADEMARK—MARCA REGISTRADA

Printed in the United States of America

AS ALWAYS, THIS IS FOR
DOUG, PETER, CHRIS, AND JACK,
WITH LOVE.

Acknowledgments

First of all, I want to thank my wonderful editor, Christine Pepe, who has done such a great job with this book. I also want to thank my agent, Robert Gottlieb. More thanks go to Leslie Gelbman, Kara Welsh, and everyone at Signet, and to Stephanie Sorensen in Publicity. Finally, to Ivan Held and the rest of the Putnam family, many thanks for your continued support.

I couldn't do it without any of you!

Chapter 1

"IS SHE THERE? Do you see her?"

As Jessica Ford pushed through the smoked-glass door in front of her, cell phone clamped to her ear, urgency sharpened John Davenport's voice to the point where the alcohol-induced slurring of his words almost disappeared.

"Yes," Jess answered, her hand tightening around the phone as the door swung shut behind her, because the lady was and she did.

On the fringe of a raucous crowd intent on watching a televised basketball game, the First Lady of the United States was sitting alone at a table for two in a dark, secluded corner of the hotel bar, knocking back a shot of some undetermined golden liquid with the stiff wrist and easy gulp of a practiced drinker. Wearing a generic black tracksuit with white stripes down the sides and white running shoes. With her trademark short blond hair tucked up beneath a baseball cap pulled low over her eyes. The sheer unlikelihood of her presence in this mid-priced hotel just a few blocks from the White House at ten minutes past midnight on a Saturday night, plus a strategically placed leafy potted ficus near her elbow, was all that stood between her and a Texas-size scandal.

Jess felt butterflies at the realization.

"Thank God." Davenport's tone was devout. "Tell her ..."

A cheer from the basketball fans made it impossible for Jess to hear the rest. Grimacing, fearing disaster with every way-too-fast beat of her heart, she hurried toward the corner.

Even knowing what she did, her mind boggled at what she was being asked to do. She was not the First Lady's handler.

"I couldn't hear you. It's kind of crowded in here," Jess said into the phone as the cheering died down.

"Shit." Davenport added a few more choice words under his breath. "Just get her out of there, would you?"

"Yes." Jess had already learned not to say "I'll do my best" to her formidable boss. He would snap that he wasn't paying for her to do her best, he was paying for her to *do it.* End of story. The phone disconnected with a click in her ear. Okay, the problem was now officially hers.

Where the hell is the Secret Service when you need them?

Casting another glance around, she had her answer: Nowhere useful, obviously. There wasn't a black suit in sight.

Davenport had said the First Lady would be alone. Silly of her to have doubted the all-knowing one.

"Mrs. Cooper?" she asked in a low voice as she reached the table, mindful of possible listening ears. Besides the First Lady and the basketball fans, there were only a few other patrons in the small, wood-paneled room. No one seemed even remotely interested in the solitary woman in the corner.

Still, it never paid to take chances. She needed to get her newest problem out of there fast.

The First Lady continued to stare at her now-empty

shot glass. If she'd heard Jess speak to her, she gave no indication of it. Clearing her throat, Jess tried again.

"Mrs. Cooper? Mr. Davenport sent me."

That did it. The brim of the baseball cap tilted up. The look Mrs. Cooper gave her was tense, wary.

"Who're you?"

Jess attempted a reassuring smile. It felt tight.

"Jessica Ford. I work for Mr. Davenport."

The blue eyes that seemed so soft and gentle on TV and in magazine spreads narrowed. Tonight they were red-rimmed and puffy, devoid of obvious makeup, and hard. The attractive, round-cheeked face was puffy, too, and pale, but still instantly familiar in the way a fuzzy copy of an iconic photograph is familiar. The lines seemed blurred, the angles less defined, the features indistinct, but the subject was definitely recognizable.

It was impossible to miss that Mrs. Cooper had been crying.

They fight a lot. She and David. All you need to do is hold her hand and nod sympathetically until she gets it out of her system, Davenport had said.

David being the President. Of the United States. And before she could get busy with the hand-holding, Jess first had to coax his wife—one of the most recognizable women in the world—out of a packed hotel bar she had no business being in. Without anyone recognizing the icon in their midst. Jess could already almost feel a posse of gossip-hungry reporters panting at her heels.

FIRST LADY FLEES WHITE HOUSE, the headlines would scream.

Oh, jeez. If she screwed this up, she would probably lose her job. For sure, her boss would go crazy. The *world* would go crazy. The image of the weepy, sweats-clad, run-away First Lady would be plastered on every TV screen and on the front page of every newspaper and magazine in the world. The political fallout would be incalculable.

The personal fallout would be incalculable. And hers would be the first head on the chopping block.

This was way too much responsibility. Jess felt her palms grow damp. She clasped them in front of her. *Do not wring them.*

She didn't, but she still must have looked less than reassuring because the First Lady's expression turned hostile.

"I don't know you. I want John."

Perfectly manicured pink nails drummed the table. Then Mrs. Cooper's well-tended hand curled around the cell phone lying beside the shot glass. Davenport was the First Lady's old friend and personal lawyer. Jess was a lawyer, too, junior grade, who had been working for the filthy-rich megafirm of Davenport, Kelly, and Bascomb, the most prestigious and powerful of the giant legal firms operating in the shadow of the U.S. Capitol, for just under a year. Although officially known as an associate, Jess sometimes thought her main duty consisted of asking "How high?" when Davenport said "Jump." When Davenport had hired her part-time during her second year at George Mason School of Law, which catered almost equally to older night-schoolers wanting to change careers and hardscrabble kids with crippling student loans and no money, such as herself, Jess had been giddy with excitement over her good fortune. This was her big chance, an opportunity to grab the golden ring for herself and her family, and there was no way she was going to blow it. If she had to work a hundred hours a week, she would work a hundred hours a week. If she had to put up with crap from the Ivy League blue bloods in the corner offices, she would put up with crap. If she had to be more efficient, more knowledgeable, and more determined than everybody else to get where she wanted to go, then that's what she was going to do.

That was the game plan. And so far it was working.

She'd been offered a full-time position upon graduation, and she did the prep work on many of Davenport's most important cases. The drudge behind the star, that was her. For now. Not forever.

Jess definitely knew who Annette Cooper was. Not surprisingly, although the First Lady had been in the office a number of times while Jess had been there and Jess had once been sent to hand-deliver some papers to her, Mrs. Cooper didn't remember her.

Wallpaper, that's what I am, she thought as Mrs. Cooper punched a single button on the phone and lifted it to her ear while running suspicious eyes over Jess. Jess took quick mental inventory in conjunction with Mrs. Cooper's sweeping look: twenty-eight years old but younger-looking; chin-length mahogany hair pushed haphazardly behind her ears; square-jawed, even-featured, ivory-skinned face with a hastily applied minimum of makeup imperfectly concealing a scattering of freckles; hazel eyes complete with contacts; five-two, slim, regrettably flat-chested; dressed in her favorite go-to black pantsuit with a black tee and, unfortunately, well-broken-in black sneakers (she usually wore heels when working because she needed the height). She was wearing the sneakers because her new roommate, her college-student sister, Grace, had apparently "borrowed" her good black heels without asking and had scattered the rest of her meager shoe wardrobe around the walk-in closet they now shared.

"You sent a *flunky*?" Mrs. Cooper spoke in an outraged tone into the phone. Davenport presumably had answered. There was a pause, and then Mrs. Cooper swept another condemning look over Jess. "Are you sure? She looks fifteen years old."

Jess tried to shut her ears and keep her face impassive even as she positioned herself between her new charge and one of the couples. Luckily, the noise level in the bar made it extremely unlikely that they could hear a thing.

Jess only wished she were so lucky. That she had not yet succeeded in impressing Mrs. Cooper was excruciatingly clear.

"Not when you do something like send over a teenage stand-in. This is *it*, do you hear? *I mean it*. I need *you*."

Whether fighting with her husband was a regular feature of Mrs. Cooper's life or not, she sounded both angry and desperate. Her voice was low but increasingly shrill. She blinked rapidly. Her cheeks had flushed a deep, distressed pink.

Uncomfortable, Jess glanced away.

I'm counting on you for this, Davenport had said in the phone call that had interrupted Jess's sleepy viewing of a Lifetime movie from the cozy comfort of her bed and sent her scrambling out of her pj's and into the car he had sent to pick her up. From the way Davenport had slurred his words, it was obvious he'd been imbibing pretty heavily.

In no shape to babysit Annette tonight, was how he had unapologetically put it. *Anyway, I'm not home. It'd take me an hour or more to get there. While you . . .*

Her apartment was maybe ten minutes away.

As she had scrambled into her clothes she'd thought, *This is a chance to get to know the First Lady.* It's inner-circle stuff, the kind of thing that any newbie lawyer would kill for. It could lead to a promotion. It could lead to a whole lot more . . . everything. Responsibility. Prestige. Money. Always, in the end, it came down to money.

The story of her life.

"But I *need* you. This is an *emergency*. Do you hear? This is *it*," Mrs. Cooper told Davenport again, louder than before, drawing Jess's attention back to her. To Jess's horror, big tears started to leak from the First Lady's eyes and roll down her cheeks. Her face crumpled, her mouth shook, and so did the hand holding the phone. Jess shot a sideways glance at the next table, then tensed at the sound of a footstep behind her. Pivoting, using her body to block the sight line to her illustrious charge as best she could, she confronted a waiter who was clearly intent on checking in with the customer at the corner table.

Yikes.

"I tell you, it's *true*," Mrs. Cooper continued in what was almost a sob, growing louder with every word. Sight lines she could block, Jess thought despairingly. Voices, not so much. "It's a nightmare. You have to help me."

"We don't need anything else, thanks," Jess said brightly to the waiter.

"You sure?" The waiter was maybe midtwenties, a slight guy with dark hair and eyes. His gaze slid past Jess, seeking Mrs. Cooper, who was—thank God—silent again, apparently listening to Davenport now. Jess could only hope that the woman's head was once again down, with the baseball cap obscuring her face.

Taking a sliding step to the left with the intention of more completely blocking the waiter's view, Jess nodded.

"I'm sure."

"That'll be twelve dollars, then."

Twelve dollars. Okay, Jess, pay the First Lady's bar bill.

Jess opened her shoulder bag, felt around in the zipper compartment where she kept her money, came up empty, looked down and suffered a split second of horror as she discovered that Grace had "borrowed" her cash along with her shoes. She didn't really want to hand over a credit card, because she had some sort of barely coalescing idea that it would be better if there was no hard evidence that she—and, ergo, Mrs. Cooper—was ever in this bar. Besides, the object was to break land speed records getting the First Lady out of there and waiting for her card to be returned would not facilitate that. Before she could completely panic, she remembered the emergency twenty-dollar bill she kept folded away at the bottom of the zippered compartment of her purse from force of habit now, although it had begun at her mother's insistence when she had gone to her first—and only—high school dance.

Honey, believe me, you don't want to have to count on any man for anything, not even a ride home.

Words to live by, Mom.

Jess handed the twenty over, and the waiter hurried away.

Enjoy the tip. A tinge of regret about forking over money she didn't even owe colored the thought. The whole twenty was gone, of course. Because she couldn't wait for change.

"As quick as you can," Mrs. Cooper said, her tone urgent. "Hurry."

Jess turned back to the table in time to see the phone snap shut. Mrs. Cooper lowered it, holding it clenched tightly in her hand. Then she looked up at Jess. Her jaw was hard and set. Her eyes were still damp, but tears no longer spilled over. Instead, the soft blue glinted with—what? Anger? Determination? Some combination of the two?

"I can't believe that bastard sent you instead of coming himself."

Jess blinked. The reality of the woman in front of her juxtaposed with the First Lady's saccharine image was starting to make her head spin.

"Mr. Davenport was afraid he couldn't get here quickly enough." The calmness of Jess's tone belied the hard knot of tension forming in her stomach. "I brought a car. It's waiting outside. We should go, before . . ."

A small but comprehensive gesture finished her sentence: *before somebody figures out who you are and the shit hits the fan.*

"Don't give me that. He's drunk as a skunk." Mrs. Cooper abruptly stood up, the legs of her chair scraping loudly back over the wood floor. Despite the potentially attention-attracting sound, Jess breathed a silent sigh of relief. It had just occurred to her that if Mrs. Cooper didn't want to move, she had no way of budging her. Tugging the brim of her cap lower over her face, and tucking an envelope-size, absolutely gorgeous, and totally inappropriate crystal-studded evening bag beneath her arm, Mrs. Cooper stepped away from the table. "All right, let's go."

Without another word, braced for the possibility of discovery with each step, Jess turned and led the way to the door. As she skirted their tables, the basketball fans leaped to their feet, cheering in deafening unison and nearly causing her heart to leap out of her chest. She stopped dead. A glance over her shoulder showed her that Mrs. Cooper, likewise clearly startled, had stopped in her tracks as well, her mouth dropping open, her eyes shooting fearfully to the celebrating crowd. But their noisy exuberance had nothing to do with her, and, indeed, the rowdy focus on the TV provided some much-needed cover for their hastily resumed exit. Walking quickly once the initial shock had passed, they made it safely out of the bar without anyone noticing them at all.

At least, so Jess hoped. But with cell phones being as ubiquitous as they were, all it took was one vaguely curious onlooker to snap a picture and . . .

I am so out of my league here.

The dim, old-fashioned lobby was about twenty feet wide and three times that long, with the reception desk and bell stand opposite the bar and an adjacent restaurant that was now closed and dark. Only a single female clerk in a red blazer stood behind the reception counter, talking on the phone and paying no attention to the two women newly emerged from the bar. The bell stand, located a dozen wide marble steps down from the reception desk, at street level, was deserted. A red-jacketed doorman waited beside the triple glass doors, holding one open for—whom? Jess couldn't see who was on the way inside, but someone definitely was, and as a consequence she felt more exposed than ever.

Keep moving.

"This way." Keeping her voice low, she indicated the main entrance with a gesture. Mrs. Cooper nodded and fell in beside her.

Jess was just thankful that Mrs. Cooper finally seemed to be aware of just how vulnerable to discovery she was and how disastrous that discovery could be. Keeping her head down, the woman took care to stay between Jess and the wall. Striding along beside her, Jess held her breath, her heart pounding, her gaze fixed on that open door. *Anyone could walk through it, glance up, and . . .*

Just as they reached the top of the steps, a pair of middle-aged men, low-level executives from the quality of their suits, brushed through the open door one after the other, each dragging his own battered suitcase on wheels, which clattered along behind them like noisy, overweight black dogs.

"Can I take those for you?" the bellman asked. The businessmen brushed him off with curt shakes of the head and began lugging the suitcases up the steps themselves while the doorman, deprived of his hoped-for tip, scowled after them. Hugging the paneled wall on the opposite side of the stairs, Jess and Mrs. Cooper hurried on down. As far as Jess could tell, neither the businessmen nor the doorman even so much as glanced their way.

I'm not qualified for this. Scandal Quashing 101 wasn't even on the course list in law school.

"Where's the car?" On the last step now, Mrs. Cooper

looked out at the street through the plate-glass doors that were just ahead. She seemed tense, on edge—just about as tense and on edge as Jess felt.

"Out front." Jess hadn't thought to tell the driver to wait anywhere else. A screwup, probably, she realized now. She probably should have looked for a side entrance, but she had been in such a hurry at the time that she had just told the driver to stop at the entrance and scrambled out. She could only hope that in the end it wouldn't matter.

"We need to hurry. They'll be looking for me."

"Who?" Jess asked before she thought, although the answer was almost instantly clear: most of official Washington. The press corps. Her husband.

"The Secret Service."

Oh, yeah. Them, too. Although, come to think of it, Mrs. Cooper could probably use a bodyguard about now. And I could certainly use some backup.

As she pushed through the thick glass door at the far end of the trio from the one the businessmen had used, the knot in Jess's stomach twisted tighter. For the first time it really dawned on her what she was doing: spiriting away an unprotected, emotionally overwrought, on-the-lam First Lady. *On Davenport's instructions,* she reminded herself, but the sensation that she was getting in way over her head here persisted.

Next time the phone rings at midnight, I don't answer it, she promised herself as the cold, fresh air of the early April night blew her hair back from her face and plastered her jacket against her body. The smell of car exhaust notwithstanding, its briskness was a welcome antidote to the overly warm mustiness of the aging hotel. *You don't have to be at Davenport's beck and call twenty-four hours a day, you know.*

But the sad truth was that she did, if she wanted to keep collecting her nice fat paycheck. Which, thanks to her always-good-for-a-complication family, she now needed more than ever.

"So, where is it?" Mrs. Cooper meant the car. She stopped on the sidewalk beside Jess, who had paused, too, briefly taken aback. The car was not parked where it had been when she had exited it some ten minutes before, which was just to the left of the front entrance, mere steps from where they now looked for it in vain.

Good question, Jess thought as she glanced swiftly around. The white glow of the hotel's marquee was too bright for comfort. She felt like they were standing under a spotlight. Other nearby businesses—a sushi bar, a liquor store, a pharmacy—spilled light out over the sidewalk, too. A steady stream of vehicles cruised the street in both directions, their headlights providing even more illumination. There were people everywhere, strolling the sidewalk, entering and leaving stores, exiting a car that had just parked in front of the sushi bar. Their noise rose over the steady hum of the traffic. Anyone could glance their way and . . .

"Can I get you ladies a cab?" the doorman asked, making Jess jump. He was right at her shoulder, and she hadn't heard him approach at all.

"N-no, we're fine, thanks." With a shake of her head she fobbed him off, then, without thinking about the whole breach of protocol such a gesture probably constituted until it was too late, caught Mrs. Cooper firmly by the arm. Heart thudding, desperately scanning both sides of the street for the errant car, she pulled the First Lady away from the bright lights of the hotel. *Please let it be here some . . . Hallelujah. There it is.* Her breath expelled in a sigh of relief. "The car's right up there."

The black Lincoln that Davenport had sent waited at the end of the line of cars parked bumper to bumper at meters almost to the intersection. It had pulled over to the curb in the no-man's-land between the legally parked cars and the traffic light. Red parking lights glowing at them through the darkness told Jess that the driver had, as instructed, kept the engine running.

"Oh, shit, there's Prescott." Ducking her head, Mrs. Cooper picked up the pace. She moved quickly between Jess and the buildings on her right, her shoulders hunched now as she sought to deflect the casual glances of passersby.

"Who's Prescott?" Voice hushed, Jess cast a hunted look over her shoulder.

"One of my detail."

"Secret Service?" Jess perked up. At least the responsibility for keeping this woman safe would no longer be hers alone. Yes, there he was, a tall, well-built man in a tailored dark suit talking to the doorman in front of the hotel. White shirt, dark tie. Short, neat, dark hair. Handsome, clean-shaven face. Lifting his hand to his mouth to say something into his fist. He might as well have been wearing a flashing neon sign.

Reinforcements at last. Thank God.

"What are you doing?" Mrs. Cooper grabbed her hand when Jess started to wave at Prescott to signal their location.

"You need protection and . . ."

"Protection?" Mrs. Cooper's laugh was bitter. The hand holding Jess's tightened until Jess's fingers hurt. "They're more like wardens." Her eyes blazed into Jess's. "Don't you understand, you stupid little girl? *I'm a fucking prisoner.*" Her gaze shot past Jess's shoulder. *"Get back in the car."*

By this time they had reached the Lincoln. Mrs. Cooper's fierce command was hurled at the driver, a burly redhead in a black chauffeur's uniform who was at that moment coming around the front of the car, presumably to open the door for his passengers.

As she spoke, Mrs. Cooper jerked open the rear passenger door and ducked inside. With one hand on the open door, Jess exchanged glances with the startled driver. He shrugged and obediently reversed directions. Her gaze slid toward the Secret Service agent, who was looking their way.

Jess hesitated. The First Lady was way more upset than a simple fight with her husband should dictate, and . . .

"Get in," Mrs. Cooper barked.

The driver was already sliding behind the wheel.

His eyes fixed on the Lincoln, now clearly suspecting that his principal was inside, the Secret Service agent turned, waved, and started to jog their way.

"Go. Now," Mrs. Cooper shrieked. Jess looked down just in time to watch as the First Lady's hand slapped the back of the front seat hard.

There was no time. The driver put the car in gear. Heart thudding, Jess flung one more doubtful glance back at the man who was now racing toward them. Then, throwing herself into the backseat with the woman she'd been sent to collect, she slammed the door just as the Lincoln screeched away from the curb.

Chapter 2

THE CRASH SCENE was horrific. Smoke roiled in thick gray coils from the overturned car. Having blazed so hot that the tires had exploded and the pines in which the vehicle had come to rest had gone up like torches, the fire, courtesy of the multitude of orange-coated fire-fighters who were still wetting down the surrounding areas, was now out. Shortly after the crash, the flames had blazed so high that he had been able to see the bright red glow from ten miles out as he had raced to the scene. The smell on the wind—Secret Service Agent Mark Ryan didn't want to think about that. It reminded him of charred meat.

Word was, three people had died in the overturned black Lincoln at the bottom of the ravine. Officially, the identities of the dead had not yet been confirmed, but unofficially he knew that one of them was Annette Cooper, the First Lady of the United States. Mark thought of the thousands of threats against the First Family that poured into the White House monthly, of the hairy foreign tours to hostile regions they'd shepherded the First Lady through, of the dozens of protesters waving signs and shouting slogans at nearly all her official engagements, at the constant threat of the lone nut job of whom they lived in fear because it was the hardest to prepare for, and thus defend against. He thought of the bomb-sniffing dogs and bulletproof limos and rooftop snipers and legions of police and military types and, yes, the best personal protection agency in the world, the U.S. Secret Service, deployed for the First Family's protection everywhere they went.

There was no other security apparatus to equal it anywhere in the world.

And yet the First Lady of the United States had just died in a fiery car crash.

Already, at one-thirty-five a.m. Sunday, a little less than an hour after the crash, the news was starting to reverberate around the world. And all hell was breaking loose.

As the head of her security team, or, as he was officially known, special agent in charge of detail, he was responsible. The unthinkable had happened on his watch. The knowledge rode like a stone in his gut. His throat felt tight, like someone was gripping it hard. He was sweating buckets even though the temperature had dropped during these predawn hours to the midforties.

How the hell had it happened?

"Halt! This is a protected area. You'll have to go back."

One of the marines whose unit guarded the site belatedly became aware of Mark's presence as he slid the few remaining feet to the bottom of the steep, brushy slope, and stepped forward to confront him. About a hundred feet beyond the marines, a circle of klieg lights had been set up to illuminate the crash site in a merciless white glow. To Mark's left, at the edge of the flat area at the base of the slope, tall pines swaying in the wind blocked much of the star-studded sky. A rain-swollen creek rushed past, gleaming black through the thicket of tree trunks. It was dark and hazy where he came to an obedient stop just outside the reach of the bright blaze of the rescue

lights, and the equally bright blaze of the TV crews setting up shop on the roadway and bridge above. Having
already penetrated the first level of protection designed
to keep reporters and camera crews and everyone else at
bay, Mark had his ID in hand.

"Secret Service." He flashed his gold shield and was
allowed to pass. The final circle of protection, the FBI,
swarmed near the car. Over the snap, crackle, and pop of
the superheated metal, the hiss of the settling foam, and
the *thump-thump-thump* of the helicopters circling overhead, he could hear them shouting at one another through
their transmitters. Closer still, a forensics team in orange
coveralls was already setting up shop. Clenching his jaw,
he picked his way carefully through the knee-high brush,
eyeing the flattened bushes and shorn-in-half trees that
marked the car's death roll from the highway forty feet
above. Finally, his gaze settled on the smoking hulk of
the car, which rested on its crushed roof.

Fury, disbelief, shock, all combined to send adrenaline
surging through his system. Uselessly. Because it was too
late. There was nothing he could do.

*What was she doing outside the White House? What
was she doing in that fucking car?*

A stretcher was being carried up the slope toward
one of the half-dozen ambulances that waited, silent but
with strobe lights flashing, on the highway above. Mark
didn't know the identity of the body-bagged victim, but
he knew who it wasn't: Mrs. Cooper was already gone,
having been taken away first in the medevac helicopter
that had been rushed to the scene. He'd been en route
when the word had come that she was dead, killed in the
crash, her body so badly burned that she was almost un-
recognizable. But he had continued on, driven by a fierce
need to see the site of the impossible for himself.

What the hell had gone down here?

When he had left the White House at eleven p.m., just

over two and a half hours earlier, the First Lady had only moments before excused herself from a dinner for the president of Chile. Pleading a headache, she stepped into the East Wing private quarters' elevator that would whisk her up to the family residence. He had watched the doors close on the slim figure in the glamorous white evening gown, said a few words to Will Prescott, the agent on post in front of the elevator, and proceeded on down to the Secret Service White House command post in the basement. Once inside, he had spoken briefly with the agents covering the monitors streaming real-time, full-color views of all hallways and rooms except the most private areas of the residence. At the large electronic board that displayed color photos of every member of the White House Secret Service detail, he'd punched a button to transfer his name to the off-duty column. Then he'd glanced at the digitized protectee locator board that tracked each member of the First Family from room to room, and noticed that only Mrs. Cooper was in the residence, and she was in her bedroom.

Safe and secure for one more night. Or so he had thought.

Now she was dead.

What the hell had gone wrong?

"Who the—oh, it's you." The speaker was FBI Special Agent Ted Parks, whom Mark had known for the twelve years he'd been with the Secret Service and disliked for at least half that time. Of average height, wiry and bald as an egg at forty, making him four years Mark's senior, Parks had his hands thrust deep in his trouser pockets as he surveyed the scene. His narrow face looked ghastly in the harsh glare of the rescue lights. Shock or grief, Mark supposed. Annette Cooper had been wildly popular—at least with those who didn't know her personally. "This is un-fucking-believable."

Mark didn't even grunt in reply. He just kept on walking toward the car. The chemical smell of the foam they'd used to put out the flames was almost stronger than the burned smell. Almost.

"Hey, sorry about Prescott," Parks called after him.

Prescott. The name hit him like a blow to the stomach. It confirmed something he'd been told but still didn't want to believe: Secret Service Agent Will Prescott, his subordinate and a good guy, had been in that car. Last time Mark had seen him, Prescott was settling in for a long, boring eight-hour shift in front of the elevator. The job was like that: endless hours of routine punctuated by the rare few minutes of excitement. God save them all from those few minutes.

Prescott and the First Lady in a car of unknown origin speeding away from the White House to an unknown destination. What the hell had happened while he'd been picking up his belated dinner at a McDonald's drive-thru and heading home through the Virginia countryside to the house he now shared solely and reluctantly with an emotionally needy cat?

The third victim was reported to be the driver. A professional chauffeur. He'd been IDed, but Mark couldn't remember his name. All he knew at this moment was that whoever the guy was, he had no business driving Annette Cooper. She had official vehicles with highly trained drivers and full-bore protection to take her anywhere she needed to go. No way should she have been in that car.

"I'm sorry, sir. No one's allowed past this point." Another marine blocked his path. Just beyond him, an official barricade of sawhorses and police tape was being set up around the destroyed car. Now that the last of the bodies had been removed, emphasis was shifting to investigating the crash. He stopped, because there was nothing to be gained by going any nearer. He was already so close that he could feel the residual heat of the burned-out wreckage on his face. There was no brush here where the car had landed, and the dry thicket of last year's grass beneath his feet was short. Short and crisp and black because it had been charred in the fire.

"Fucking press." FBI agent Jim Smolski stopped at his elbow, taking a deep drag on a cigarette as he glanced up the slope. Following his gaze, Mark became aware of a TV crew still filming avidly as a contingent of marines herded them back to the narrow blacktop road, where a barricade manned by the Virginia State Police had been set up to contain them. At least half a dozen TV vans were on the scene, unmistakable because of their logos and antennas, and another one, rooftop antenna rotating wildly, arrived even as he watched. A growing throng of reporters crowded the barricade, jockeying for position and attention as they shouted questions down at rescuers.

"Was the First Lady killed instantly?" "Who else was in the car?" "Where was Annette going?" "Where's David?" "Any idea what caused the accident?" "Who was driving?" "Is the President okay?"

Luckily, the questions weren't directed at him. Mark shut the reporters' voices out as he focused on more important matters. Debris was strewn along the path the tumbling car had taken, scattered among the mutilated greenery as if it had been shaken out of a giant salt shaker. A hubcap, bits of taillight, a shoe . . .

His eye was caught by something that glittered silver in the bright beam of the camera crew's retreating light.

"Somebody's going down big-time for this." Smolski cut his eyes toward Mark. "I'm glad I'm not you guys."

Mark's gut tightened.

On my watch.

"I thought you quit smoking." He turned away, the better to pinpoint the location of the silver thing as he spoke. It was lodged in a bush, an uncrushed bush three-quarters of the way up the slope that was about twenty feet to the right of the car's path.

"I started up again."

Mark grimaced. "After this, I might, too."

Walking away from the perimeter that was now almost fully established around the smoking hulk of the car, Mark picked his way up the slope toward the flash of silver. More helicopters circled overhead now, search beams playing down over the wreckage like dueling Jedi lightsabers. Air swirled like a mini-tornado around him as a particularly aggressive chopper swooped in low. Glancing up, Mark saw the familiar NBC peacock logo on its door.

Goddamn vultures.

Without the TV crew's light, the silver thing became almost impossible to see. Mark kept his eyes trained on the bush, which, he saw as he grew closer, was some sort of scrubby evergreen. There was a whole thicket of them, about waist high, with branches like hairy tentacles that swayed in the wind kicked up by the choppers. Up here, courtesy of the snapped-off trees, the scent of pine was strong, reminding him of the Christmas tree–shaped air freshener his now fifteen-year-old daughter Taylor had hung from the rearview mirror of his car when he'd still been a pack-a-day smoker.

When had those become the good old days?

He couldn't see the silver thing anymore: It was too dark. But he remembered where it was. Reaching in among the prickly branches, he touched it almost at once, felt the cold bumpiness of the surface, and instantly suspected what it had to be: the First Lady's elegant evening bag. He had last seen the sparkling bauble clutched in her right hand as the elevator doors had closed on her. Leaving her, as he'd thought, safe and sound for the night.

Wrong again.

Pulling it out, looking down at it, experiencing the weight of it in his hand, he suddenly felt the urge to puke. It drove home with brutal finality the hard truth that the impossible had happened: Annette Cooper was dead.

He glanced back down at the accident scene. Pictures were now being taken of the blackened car from every angle and what looked like survey equipment was being set up to, if his memory of accident investigation techniques served him correctly, measure the distance the car had traveled from the road above before coming to rest on its roof. Several members of the forensics unit were down on all fours to, presumably, take a look at the inside of the car. He opened his mouth to yell at investigators, announcing his find.

Then he looked down at the small, crystal-studded rectangle and shut his mouth again.

After only a split second of indecision, he flipped open the clasp and reached inside. Along with the various assorted cosmetics and small brush she customarily carried, there were a number of credit cards held together by a rubber band and a good-size roll of cash. As surprising as those items were—the First Lady never paid for anything herself and, therefore, as far as he was aware, never carried credit cards or money— they were not his target. Just as he had been sure it would be, the brown plastic bottle of tablet-style artificial sweetener the First Lady supposedly favored and took with her everywhere was tucked down at the bottom, nestled against the smooth satin lining. Only, as he had learned to his dismay, the pills inside the bottle weren't aspartame. They were painkillers—Vicodin, Percocet, you name it, including, most recently and disastrously, OxyContin, to which Mrs. Cooper was—had been—hopelessly addicted.

Mark's hand closed over the bottle, which he removed

and stuffed in his jacket pocket. The pills inside rattled insistently.

Serve and protect.

She was dead, but he meant to do what he still could to honor that vow. No way was he letting that bottle fall into the wrong hands.

"Yo, up here!" he yelled, and as a couple of FBI heads craned his way, he waved at them. Then, realizing that the bright lights blazing in their faces coupled with the darkness of where he stood prevented them from seeing him, he turned to go back down the slope, the purse now ready to be turned over to the investigation.

He'd taken no more than a step when the sound came out of the darkness to his left. It was the merest breath of a whimper. But it caught his attention, stopping him in his tracks. He looked sharply in its direction.

Something lay curled on the ground just beyond the bush where he'd found the purse. He could just make out the dark shape of . . . what?

Frowning, moving cautiously toward it, Mark at last realized what it was and caught his breath.

It was a body. A girl's small, slender body, lying crumpled and broken among the swaying evergreens.

Chapter 3

"LIE STILL. Help's coming."

Those words penetrated the darkness Jess was lost in. It was a horrible darkness, riven with screams and pain and an explosion of hot, leaping flames. Warm, strong fingers touched her neck, her cheek, and she swam even closer to full consciousness.

My God, my God...

"I need some help over here! There's an injured woman!"

The shout, uttered in the same deep, drawling male voice that had told her to lie still, sent terror stabbing through her.

No, no...

"Shh," she breathed, because that was the best she could do. He was crouched beside her, bending over her, she realized, and realized too in that moment when she saw stars swirling through the ink-black sky beyond the dark shape of his head that her eyes were now open.

Not dead, then.

The reality of his large body looming so close caused her heart to leap. Her stomach cramped with fear. She sucked in air.

The pungent smell of something burning filled her nostrils. It stung her throat, curled down into her lungs.

Please, God, no.

"Hey! We need help!"

"Be quiet," she whispered, clutching desperately at his trouser leg. She tried to make the caution urgent, sharper and louder, but it came out sounding more like a sigh. A deep, pain-racked sigh. With reason: She hurt. All over.

Cold. So cold. Freezing cold.

"It's gonna be okay. There's an ambulance here."

The man stood up. Her grip on his trouser leg tightened. He'd made no move to hurt her—he couldn't be one of the demonish wraiths from her dream. Could he? Her instincts said no. He felt safe, somehow. Like she could trust him. Her hand made a tight fist around the cloth near where it broke over his shoe. Conviction coalesced inside her: Whatever happened, he mustn't leave her here in the dark alone.

"We had a wreck." The words hurt her throat as they emerged. She remembered it now, the tires screeching, the car skidding then leaving the road. . . .

What car?

Slow-motion flip-flops, end over end . . .

The others. Where were they?

She started to shake.

"Damn it, move your asses! Get a medical crew over here *now*!"

That wasn't a shout, it was a roar. Loud enough to shatter the night. Loud enough to pull her head out of the terrible vision she seemed to be watching from a distance. Loud enough to make her cringe. Loud enough to penetrate the sounds—the deep, rhythmic thumping overhead, the jumble of voices, the clang of metal, the hum of motors, of which she was just becoming fully aware. Loud enough to be heard. Thanks to him, they would know where she was now without any possibility of concealment.

They?

Her pulse pounded. Panic shot through her veins.

Have to escape, have to escape, have to . . .

She was, she realized, curled on her side on damp, cold ground. Her cheek rested on something that both cushioned and prickled—dead grass? Something large and sharp that she guessed had to be a rock jabbed into her hip. Her head felt like it was lower than her legs because she lay twisted like a discarded doll on a hillside. She had only to push herself up and . . .

Gathering all her force, she tried to get to her feet, to scramble away, to run until the darkness swallowed her up and hid her and she was safe once more. Pain shot everywhere, zigzagging along her nerve endings like white-hot lightning bolts, making her want to scream at the intensity of it—only she couldn't. It hurt too much.

I can't move.

The realization stunned her.

Only her head moved, and her arms, with a great deal of effort. Getting them beneath her, she found she could push her torso a few inches from the ground—and that was all. She was trapped, immobilized in her own body. As she fell back, terror turned her insides icy. Her thoughts went fuzzy. All she knew for sure was that she was in pain, quickly intensifying pain. Her ribs, her legs, her head—they all hurt. She couldn't get away. And she was afraid.

I should be dead.

Certainty laced the thought. The crash had been bad. Flying out into darkness, into nothingness, the car rolling over and over, end over end . . . and screams, multiple screams. Soul-shattering screams. She was screaming, too. She could still hear the screaming in her head.

Are the others dead?

That's what she tried to ask him when he crouched

beside her again. Either she was making no sense or he
didn't hear. She clung to his trouser leg. The material was
smooth and cool and sturdy. A lifeline.

"Help's coming. Try not to move."

He must have felt her grip on him, or maybe he sensed
her desperation through the darkness, because he patted
her hand in clumsy comfort. *If he wanted to hurt you, he's
had plenty of time to do it by now.* Instead she felt protected. *Thank God.* Letting go of his trousers, she clutched
his hand instead.

Warm, strong fingers . . .

"Don't leave me," she begged, her voice a hoarse, dry
rasp in her throat. "They . . . they . . ."

But her mind fogged up again, and all of a sudden she
couldn't remember who "they" were. Wasn't even sure
she had ever known in the first place.

They?

*Dark shapes rushing through the darkness, silhouetted
against the flames . . .*

"What?" He leaned closer, clearly having heard her
voice but not understanding what she was trying to say.
"Who are you? Were you in the First Lady's car?"

*The First Lady. Annette Cooper. Oh, God, oh, God,
oh . . .*

She could hear a flurry of movement not too far away:
the crunch of dried grass, the shuffle of footsteps, a frag-
ment of conversation. People approaching.

Jess caught her breath. Terror grabbed her heart and
squeezed.

"Please . . ." she begged.

"Over here," he called, releasing her hand with a
quick compression of her fingers and standing up. Jess
guessed that the forest of swaying bushes surrounding
her probably blocked her—both of them—from the view
of whoever was approaching.

Until now.

Desperation sent her heart pounding against her rib cage like it was trying to beat its way to freedom.

"Gotcha," a man called back.

Her rescuer crouched beside her again. Jess caught his hand.

"The paramedics are almost here," he said before she totally panicked.

Of course. Paramedics were coming. He wouldn't be yelling like that at anyone else.

But her thundering heart wouldn't be calmed.

More footsteps, drawing closer and closer. Rustling branches. Crunching grass. As a spotlight found her in the darkness she couldn't help it: She cringed. Half-blinded, she felt like a small animal in a trap, helpless to save herself. All of a sudden she was ruthlessly exposed, visible to everyone, vulnerable. Her pulse pounded. Her heart raced. Her hand tightened on her rescuer's fingers. He glanced down at her. She saw the dark gleam of his eyes shift so that they were once again focused on her. Though the spotlight was on *her,* the glaring white beam pinioned *her*, the shadows enshrouding him receded slightly so that he was more visible, too. Her vision was all blurry—her contacts, she must have lost them—and he was still mostly in darkness, but she was able to absorb the broad strokes. He was a big guy, wide chest, broad shoulders, thick neck, short, thick, fair hair. White dress shirt, no tie. Black suit coat . . .

One of them.

Recognition flew through her consciousness with the swift, fierce speed of an arrow. She gasped—gasping hurt—and dropped his hand.

"So, what've we got here?" It was a new voice, another man, and, contrary to the terror she'd felt a moment before at the idea of being discovered by anyone else, Jess welcomed it now. Welcomed him. There was safety in numbers—right?

Safety from what?

"She's conscious. She must have been in the car."

He moved back, out of her line of vision, as paramedics bustled around.

"Hi, there, what's your name?" Another man crouched beside her. Fingers found her pulse.

"Jessica." She closed her eyes against the light. "Jessica Ford."

"We're going to take good care of you."

"Get a cervical collar on her," someone else said.

Then she stopped listening, stopped thinking, stopped doing anything, really, except feeling, or trying not to feel, the pain that came in waves. Her attitude was fatalistic: Whatever happened happened, and there was nothing she could do to change any of it now. There were two men, both EMTs, she thought, both seeming dedicated to making sure she would survive. The man who had found her stayed back, mostly just out of her sight, although she caught the occasional glimpse of him with her peripheral vision as the EMTs stabilized her, then loaded her onto the stretcher and carried her up the hill.

"Keep her away from the press." The drawl in his voice was unmistakable. He had found her, and stayed with her. He was with them still, walking near the stretcher. She was afraid of him now. *One of them.* That was the thought that kept darting through her mind. But she couldn't quite justify the fear.

He hadn't hurt her. And he didn't feel like a threat.

But still she was afraid.

Waking up in the ambulance as they were threading an IV into her vein, Jess realized that she must have lost consciousness sometime during the latter part of the ascent.

Not that it mattered. Now that she was out in the open, now that *they* knew where she was, now that she was hurt and helpless and trapped in her own body, there was nothing she could do to help herself even a little bit. Except maybe . . .

"Call my boss." With what she feared were her last few seconds of clarity before sedation claimed her, she summoned every bit of strength and determination left to her and spoke to the paramedic securing the needle to her arm with tape. At first her voice was a mere thread of sound. She strained to make it louder. The paramedic heard, because he met her gaze with a questioning look. "John Davenport. And my mother. The numbers are in my phone. . . ." Which had been in her jacket pocket. She remembered feeling the solid shape of it bumping against her thigh as they put her on the stretcher, but she wasn't wearing the garment now and—there it was, her jacket, in pieces on a shelf; they must have cut it off her. . . . "Which is in my jacket pocket. Over there."

She tried to cut her eyes toward the remnants of her jacket, but already her lids had grown heavy. With a rush of panic so strong it almost countered the effect of whatever drug was now being pumped into her system, she realized she was going under.

Helpless . . .

But there was nothing she could do to save herself. Even as darkness overwhelmed her, even as she sank bonelessly into the void, she found herself back in the speeding black Lincoln as it shot off the roadway, and screams, her own included, once again echoed in her ears.

Chapter 4

MARK DROVE STRAIGHT BACK to the White House. Although most of the country, and the world, still slept, he knew that the news of Annette Cooper's death would be sweeping through official and unofficial channels like wildfire. Already the Eighteen Acres, as the White House complex was known, was surrounded by an ever-growing crowd of media. The bright glare of klieg lights as various TV stations reported the First Lady's death packed enough kilowattage, he was sure, to be visible from the International Space Station. The guard who waved him through the Northeast Guard Booth was ashen. Mark parked his car, then went straight to the basement, to the Secret Service command center. He was tapping in the six-digit code when the door was jerked open from the inside.

Harris Lowell, the White House chief of staff, stood in the aperture, one hand still on the knob, his expression changing to a glare as he realized who he was looking at. Stocky and florid-faced, with thinning ginger strands of hair arranged in a classic comb-over and bulging blue eyes, the fifty-four-year-old Lowell resembled nothing so much as a bulldog. A bad-tempered bulldog in a two-thousand-dollar pin-striped suit.

"What the hell happened?"

Mark shook his head. "I don't know."

"It's your fucking job to know."

"Something got screwed up."

"Ya think?" Lowell made a sound that could have been a snort or a bitter laugh. Over Lowell's shoulder, Mark could see that the command post was surprisingly full for just past two o'clock in the morning. Of course, the team that was supposed to be guarding the First Lady now had nowhere to be, so they obviously had assembled there. There were others, too, besides his people, some who were supposed to be working that shift, some who he could only assume had been brought in by the news. Some were standing, some were sprawled in chairs watching the monitors that streamed what was, for the time of night, a tremendous amount of activity going on in the halls and rooms they guarded. A few walked around, seemingly aimlessly. All were chalky-faced. All had the stunned looks of disaster victims. All were silent. And all had at least one eye on him and the confrontation taking shape in the doorway.

"The President wants to see you. He wants to ask you some questions." Lowell brushed past him. Mark caught the door before it could close, and held it open while he turned to look at Lowell.

"I don't have any answers for him right now."

"Your funeral." Lowell seemed to realize the infelicitousness of his choice of words, because his expression changed. His cheeks quivered, and the bellicose glare lost a little of its brio. The reality of the First Lady's death was just beginning to sink in for him, too.

Funny how the world can change in an instant.

"Give me a minute, would you?" Mark still felt like he could puke, and he'd had to pull over to pee by the side of the road twice on the ride in, but he was functioning. And he still had a job to do.

"A minute."

Whether it was meant to be or not, Mark chose to take Lowell's growl as assent. Stepping inside the brightly lit room with its windowless, steel-reinforced walls, gleaming silver banks of monitors, computers bristling with state-of-the-art technology, hanging tapestries that concealed safes holding enough hidden weaponry to fend off a small army, and rows of recharging radios, he shut the door firmly behind him. The scent of coffee from the machine in the corner was strong. It made the gorge rise in his throat.

"Is it true about Prescott?"

The question came from the back of the room. Mark looked at the speaker—Susan Wendell, an attractive, thirtysomething blonde who'd had kind of a thing for the single, good-looking Prescott—and nodded curtly. *No good beating around the bush.* Her face tightened. She swallowed once. Other than that, and a certain whiteness around her mouth, she betrayed no sign of emotion.

Secret Service agents don't cry.

With a gesture, Mark gathered his people around him. Not counting himself, there were seven of them on-site: Wendell, Paul Fielding, Steve Matthews, Michael Varney, Spencer Hagan, Janelle Tandy, and Phil Janke. The first three, along with Prescott, had been on duty when he had signed out for the night. The others had apparently come in as word of the tragedy had spread.

"Anybody know why FLOTUS and Prescott were in that car?" Mark's voice was low. No point in airing dirty laundry in front of everybody in the room. There had been a screwup, and he wanted to know the details first. His own ass might be swinging in the wind about now, but he would do what he could to cover his team.

Lowered eyes. A couple of head shakes. Tense expressions all around.

"The first we knew that anything went wrong was when Prescott radioed in," Wendell said. "He said he'd

gone with Mrs. Cooper and Folly"—the Coopers' spaniel—
"to the Rose Garden, and Mrs. Cooper had gotten out
of his sight and he couldn't find her. He was panicking
because she'd given him the slip, but it wasn't like she'd
been abducted or anything. She hadn't been gone but a
few minutes, and we didn't want to make it into a big
deal if it wasn't, so we all rushed out and started looking
for her. About the time we got the call about the"—her
voice faltered—"the crash, we were in the process of setting up a massive search effort." She winced. "Too
late."

Mark's shoulders tightened. There was a lot he wanted
to say, but it was too early to start the blame game. Hell,
ultimately the blame was his, anyway: These were his
people. This was his job.

"I want to know how this happened." Mark's voice
was grim. "I want to know every single, solitary detail of
what went down. Like, yesterday." Glancing around, he
jerked his head at Paul Fielding. Like all of them, thirty-
nine-year-old Fielding was in excellent physical condition. But at six-two, with his chubby cheeks and mild
blue eyes, his balding head and easygoing air, he always
made Mark think of Buddha. A blond Buddha bobble-
head in a Secret Service suit. At the moment, Fielding
was sweating slightly although the room was cool. He
knew the feeling; he also knew Fielding, considered him
a friend as well as a colleague. More to the point, he
trusted Fielding. He and Fielding had gone through the
Academy together. Mark's star had risen higher and
faster, mainly because he put more into the job. His life,
in fact.

Fielding hadn't made that mistake. He was still married to his first wife, and he had kids who loved him.

"When I come back, I want to watch replays of the
surveillance tapes from ten p.m. on," he said to Fielding
as the man moved to stand beside him. A sharp rap on

the vaultlike door behind him made Mark grit his teeth:
Lowell, impatient as always. "Not just Mrs. Cooper but
everything. I want to see every single move anybody
made in or around the residence. Anybody who entered.
Anybody who left. Anybody who so much as sneezed in
front of the elevator. And I want video from the Rose
Garden. And from every exit out of the Eighteen Acres.
Every one, you understand? I want to know when she
left, I want to know how she left, I want to know who she
was with, and *I want to know why she was in that fucking
car.*"

Fielding nodded. "You got it."

"You realize we're going to take the heat for this,
people. It's imperative we get some answers fast."

Fielding nodded again, along with the rest of them.
Mark knew they all understood the point he was making:
Not only their asses but the Secret Service's reputation
was on the line.

Whatever had occurred to put Mrs. Cooper in that
crash, the bottom line was they had failed.

Now that the knowledge had well and truly sunk in,
it was starting to eat at him. He felt as jumpy as a frog
leg in a frying pan.

Failure is not an option.

Another rap on the door, louder than before.

Fucking Lowell.

"I also want to know everything there is to know
about Jessica Ford." Her name had lodged in his memory, along with her bloodied face and small, crumpled
form. If he hadn't stumbled across her, would she have
lain out there until she died?

More to the point, who was she to Annette Cooper?
And what was she doing in that damned car?

Thanks to the press, the world would know the answers soon enough. He wanted to know first.

"Isn't she the survivor?" Wendell, always quicker than

the rest, met his gaze with sharpened interest. Ever the professional, she was keeping any personal-level grief she felt at Prescott's passing well hidden.

"Survivor?" Mark frowned.

"That's what they're saying on CNN. That there were four people in the First Lady's car, and one survived."

Mark felt surprised, then felt stupid for feeling surprised. He'd seen the reporters on the scene for himself, seen the trucks and cameras circling the White House. Why hadn't he realized that every tiny detail they could scratch up would be broadcast instantly around the world?

"Jesus." He'd known it, of course, but the reality was just now hitting home: The scope of this thing was going to be huge. Global. An international convulsion that would play out in the media for days, possibly weeks, maybe even months to come. And everybody in the world who was in the least bit interested was going to know every tiny dredged-up detail about Annette Cooper's life and death—unless some things could be kept hidden. He hoped to God they could be kept hidden. "Yeah, she's the survivor. And I want to know who the hell she is, and what the hell she was doing in that car. In about fifteen minutes, tops."

"I'm on it," Wendell said.

"Okay, everybody keep your mouths shut on this subject until further notice. No talking to anybody—and I mean anybody—outside this group."

With a nod of dismissal, he turned to open the door. Lowell was standing there, hand raised to knock again, glaring at him. Behind him, the long corridor was filling with people. More Secret Service agents coming in, heading for the room he was just exiting. Medical personnel bound for the in-house clinic. FBI agents. Housekeeping staff. Some military types. More than a few were openly weeping. Others were pale, grim. Most looked to be in the first disbelieving stages of shock.

Hell, he was still in that stage himself. But he was being forced out of it fast. Survival mode was kicking in.

"You got no room for error here, Ryan," Lowell warned under his breath as they stepped across the hall to the elevator that would take them up to the family residence. "The President wants an explanation. Where the hell were you guys?"

"I don't know what happened yet. I will."

Lowell grunted. After that they rode up in silence. At its heart, the White House is a vast, impersonal office building with a small, ultraluxurious hotel inside where the First Family lives. Now he was headed up to the equivalent of the presidential suite. Mark stared at his reflection in the shiny brass wall. For the first time he became aware that he was sweaty and dirty-looking, his jaw dark with stubble, still wearing the black suit he'd worn to work on Saturday—he'd taken off his jacket and tie when he'd gotten home, sat on the couch, clicked on the TV, and been in the middle of eating his Big Mac when he'd gotten the call about the accident, grabbed his jacket again, and headed out—with his white shirt stained and limp and no tie. Not exactly Secret Service regulation. Well, it couldn't be helped, and under the circumstances he guessed it didn't matter.

Right now he had bigger problems than being on the wrong side of the Secret Service dress code.

When the elevator opened, the hush was what he noticed first. It was thick and heavy, palpable as fog. The scent of fresh cut roses from a huge crystal bowl opposite the elevator made the whole place smell like a damned funeral parlor. He tried not to think about that as he followed Lowell into a small anteroom and through the double doors that led to the elegantly furnished foyer of the family residence. Price Ferris of the presidential Secret Service detail met them inside the foyer. They exchanged the briefest of greetings. Beyond Ferris, he could see that the Yellow Oval Room was already full of people. Some important—he spotted popular Vice President Sears and his wife and the Secretary of State and his—and some not, like the First Nephew. They were milling around, drinks in hand, talking in near whispers that combined to roll out into the hallway like the steady hum of traffic. The somber mood was palpable from where he stood. Nodding at his fellow agents as he passed them—and getting the distinct feeling from the looks he received in return that he was about to get his balls nailed to the wall—Mark followed Ferris and Lowell down the long hall to the President's bedroom.

And tried to ignore the knots in his gut.

Ferris knocked at the door. Another agent, Donald Petrowski, opened it. Mark followed Lowell into the room.

David Cooper was sprawled on his back on the big mahogany four-poster in the bedroom that had served every president since Calvin Coolidge. He wasn't a big man—maybe five-ten, one sixty-five—but, thanks to the workout room on the third floor, he was exceptionally fit for a fifty-eight-year-old. Mark knew from personal experience on Cooper's security detail that his healthy tan owed more to some kind of spray than to the great outdoors, and his famous mane of silver hair got a little help from the dye bottle, but, hey, the guy had cameras trained on him twenty-four-seven, and in the dog-eat-dog political arena image was important. He and fifty-two-year-old Annette had made an attractive, photogenic, popular couple. With their now grown son and daughter, they had been the picture-perfect all-American family.

Only those closest to them got to see behind the facade. Right about now, Mark found himself wishing he hadn't ever gotten that close.

"... at Bethesda?" It was the tail end of a question, uttered in a voice that was unmistakably that of the President of the United States.

"That's right."

The reply, Mark saw as he continued on into the room, came from the First Father, Wayne Cooper. The octogenarian Texas oilman stood near the fireplace with another man Mark didn't recognize. Built like the President except for a slight paunch, his hair gone now except for a feathery white fringe, Wayne was a widower who adored his only son. He was also a billionaire, which, to Mark's mind, explained a lot about how that son had made it to the White House. His other child was a thrice-married daughter, Elizabeth, who was pampered and protected but otherwise ignored. All Wayne's hopes and dreams were bound up in his son.

"I told you, I'm not taking any damned pill," the President snapped.

"But sir . . ."

Except for his dinner jacket, David Cooper was still dressed up in the tux he'd worn to wine and dine the president of Chile. His shoes rested on the tufted gold bedspread of a bed that had not yet been turned down. John Downes, the President's personal physician, leaned over him, his back to Mark. Leonard Cowan, his valet, hovered on the far side of the bed, a tray holding what appeared to be the President's favored scotch and soda in his hands.

"Here's Ryan," Lowell announced.

The President sat up. All eyes focused on Mark. All conversation suspended. Taking a deep breath, he felt his jaw tighten and hoped to hell it was the only outward sign of tension they could see.

"God in heaven, you want to tell us how this terrible

thing happened?" Wayne Cooper's booming voice was punctuated by an audible clink as he put his glass down on the marble mantel.

"I can't answer that yet, sir."

"Well, by damn . . ."

"Dad, everyone, could you excuse us a minute, please?" His customary courtesy back in place despite the slight wobble that was barely detectable in his voice, David Cooper swung his legs over the side of the bed. His face was haggard, his skin pale, his eyes red. Meeting his gaze, Mark felt the knot in his gut twist tighter.

The zinger was, David Cooper had loved his wife.

My watch.

"Davey . . ." Wayne protested. Anguish over his son's obvious pain quivered in his voice.

"Please," the President said again. Wayne Cooper frowned, but he, like everyone else, slowly filed out. The click of the door closing behind them was loud as a gunshot to Mark's ears.

The President came to his feet. Their eyes met. It was all Mark could do not to flinch at the accusation he saw in the other man's face.

"I trusted you, Mark. You knew what was going on with her. You were supposed to watch her. You were supposed to keep her safe."

Making excuses wasn't his style, so Mark didn't. "I'm sorry, Mr. President."

Cooper took a hasty turn about the room. Watching him, Mark felt a burning inside his chest. He knew what it was like to love a woman who didn't give a shit about you. It hurt like hell. Right at that moment, his sympathies were with David Cooper.

The President stopped in front of him, ran his hands through his hair. "Just tell me this: Was she out there trying to score drugs?"

The million-dollar question.

"I don't know. Maybe." Mark withdrew the artificial sweetener bottle from his pocket and held it out. "I went to the crash site. This was in her purse. Along with a roll of cash and some credit cards."

Since the First Lady almost never carried cash, the implication was plain: A drug rendezvous was a definite possibility. The credit cards—who the hell knew what was up with the credit cards? He hadn't had time yet to even begin to think that through. Although as far as he knew, drug dealers still didn't accept them.

Sucking in his breath, the President took the bottle and stared down at it. "Damned pills." Then he looked up at Mark. His eyes were dark with pain. "This can never get out. Her reputation . . ." His mouth shook, and then his face crumpled like a collapsing building. "Oh my God, my God, I can't believe this has happened. I can't believe she's dead. *Annette . . .*"

His voice spiraled into a ragged wail. Even as the door burst open and the room filled with people and he was nearly shoved back out into the hall, Mark could not escape the terrible sounds of the President's keening. Again, he felt a stab of guilt.

My watch.

Lowell caught up to him as he headed for the elevator.

"That woman." Falling in beside him, Lowell glanced all around as if to make sure no one was close enough to overhear. "The woman who was in the car. The one who survived."

They were in the foyer now, walking fast past a group of new arrivals being shepherded into the Yellow Oval Room. Mark recognized a famous singer along with some friends of the First Family. Throat tightening, he wondered when the Coopers' two adult children, Laurie Donaldson and Brad Cooper, would arrive.

He really didn't want to be here for that one.

"What about her?" he asked.

"What do you know about her?"

"Nothing except her name. Yet." The implication that he soon would know everything there was to know about Jessica Ford was understood by Lowell, who nodded.

"Yeah, well, we hear that she's a lawyer who works for John Davenport. We're trying to get hold of him now, but he's not at home and he isn't answering his cell phone. The information we have—and it's preliminary, but we think it's good—is that the First Lady called Davenport, and he sent the car."

"Why?" But at least that probably meant Annette Cooper wasn't out there chasing the drugs she was being slowly, forcibly weaned off of after all. Or maybe she was, and Davenport had found out and sent a car and a subordinate to get her off the streets.

"Who the hell knows?" Lowell looked grim. "Look, you go to this Ford woman, and you keep her the hell away from the press. Stay with her until you find out what she knows. And if she knows anything, anything at all, that could in any way be harmful to the First Lady or the President, you get her to keep her damned mouth shut." The glint in Lowell's eyes reminded Mark just how ruthless the Chief of Staff could be. "You fucked up, now you clean up the mess."

Mark's mouth compressed. Then he nodded and stepped into the elevator.

Chapter 5

SOMETHING WOKE HER.

What?

Jess didn't know. All she knew was that she was breathing hard. Feeling weird. And instantly uneasy. Even as her mind came to full awareness her senses were alert, spurred by a kind of edgy sixth sense that told her something was wrong.

Where am I?

Her eyes blinked opened on—nothing. A blur of darkness. The feeling of being inside, with four walls around her and a ceiling she could not see not too far above her head.

Cold, so cold.

Biting down on her lower lip, she tried to control the violent shivers that claimed her. She felt groggy, disoriented. As if she were floating, almost. Her head throbbed. Her mouth felt like it was stuffed with cotton balls. Her body was one big dull ache that, paradoxically, did not hurt as much as she knew it should have. She had the feeling that she was alone, although earlier, she was almost certain she had heard her mother's voice. Others she knew, too. Her sister Sarah's, maybe.

There were no voices now. No sounds, except a steady mechanical beeping and a dull hum and the slightest of drawn-out creaks. She didn't know how it was possible that she could be so cold; she seemed to be swaddled to the armpits in layers of cloth. Against her body, the texture of the cloth was tightly woven and smooth, while the cloth her hands, which were on top of the pile, rested on was coarser and fuzzy. That, plus the firm resilience of the surface upon which she lay and the mounded softness beneath her head, led her to conclude that she was in a bed. A sharp, distinctive smell—antiseptic?—defined it further: She was in a bed.

In a hospital.

Annette Cooper. The wreck.

Horror washed over her in an icy wave. Her stomach turned inside out. She felt a surge of dizziness so strong she almost sank back into the blackness again.

Something's wrong.

That was the thought that kept her present. It was strong enough to beat back the wooziness that threatened to carry her away again.

What?

The darkness was not absolute, she discovered, as her eyes adjusted: There was the faintest of bluish glows to her right. Slowly she turned her head—moving required so much effort—to find that the bluish glow emanated from a cluster of free-standing machines near the bed. One showed what appeared to be a zigzagging line; it was the one producing the steady beep, and she thought it might be a heart monitor. If so, hers seemed to be beating right on track, with a good, steady rhythm. The deep hum seemed to come from somewhere overhead, possibly from the ventilation or heating system. The narrowing crack of light outlining the door beyond the machines pinpointed the source of a creaking sound: Someone was slowly, carefully closing the door to the room where she lay.

Even as she discovered it, the sliver of light disappeared. The faintest of clicks announced that the door was now securely shut. The area behind the instruments had gone completely dark. But a blur of movement in the shadows where the sliver of light had been told her that she was not alone. A cold frizzle of wariness tingled along her spine.

Who?

Her heartbeat quickened as she heard light, quick footsteps. Her eyes widened as someone stepped around the machines. Then she got a blurred look at a tall form in blue scrubs.

A doctor, then. Or a nurse. Someone medical, anyway.

Her breath released in a near-silent whoosh. It was only then that she realized she had been holding it.

Who were you expecting?

"Are you awake?"

The question was soft, so as not to disturb her if the answer was no. Although the darkness coupled with her bad eyesight kept her from getting a good look at him, it was obvious that the speaker was a man. A stranger. Could he see her eyes glinting at him through the darkness? She didn't know. She knew only that the soporific tone of his voice contrasted oddly with his movements, which were swift and sure as he strode toward the head of her bed.

"Yes."

Her voice was a mere thread of sound, creaky and tired. Her mouth was so dry that it was hard to form even that one short word.

Swallowing to moisten her throat, she followed him with her eyes. She wanted to ask for information, for the conditions of the others in the car, but she didn't have the strength. Her tongue felt thick and heavy, and pushing words out past it required more effort than she could summon at the moment.

"Do you remember what happened?"

He took hold of the tall metal pole standing at the head of her bed. When she saw the plastic bag swinging from it, saw the tubing, she realized that it was an IV pole. And she was attached to it, by a long, clear tube that ran down into the back of her hand.

The liquid in the bag was emptying into her vein. Tape on her hand secured the needle in place.

"Wreck," she managed.

"That's right."

He was holding a syringe, she saw, and fiddling with her tubing, right there where it joined the bag.

"What are you doing?"

The vague sense of unease she had felt since opening her eyes intensified. He was lifting the syringe toward the tubing—which, since he was a doctor, shouldn't have alarmed her at all.

But it did.

Why?

"This will help you go back to sleep, sugar. Just close your eyes."

Again with the soft, soothing voice. Her lids drooped as his suggestion tempted her. To just close her eyes and drift into unconsciousness . . . How good would that feel? And how easy would it be to do?

All of a sudden she remembered the nightmare shapes. But they belonged to the wreck. Not the hospital. She'd been found, rescued, and now she was safe. She could sleep if she wanted to.

So tired . . .

The light from the machines cast a blue glow over the floor. Jess found herself noticing it as her eyes drifted downward and he moved again, his feet shuffling in and out of the light. She forced her lids wide open and her gaze up and watched as he tugged impatiently on the tubing.

Despite her best efforts, her lids felt as heavy, as if her lashes were made of concrete. She wanted to close her eyes in the worst way. But still that prickly sense that something was wrong would not leave her.

"Are you . . . a doctor?"

"Mm-hmm."

The tone of the murmur was comforting. The tubing was cooperating now, and he was, she saw, holding a port and positioning the syringe so that he could send its contents down the tubing into her body with a single quick depression of the plunger.

Not good.

The disturbing thought made her frown even as her eyes slid down his body toward the floor again. Where he was standing now, the blue glow spilled over his legs, illuminating them to the knees. The scrubs were too short for him, their legs ending some three inches above the hem of his black pants, black suit pants. Worn over shiny black wing-tip shoes marred by just a few stray bits of ... what? Her vision was too fuzzy to be certain, but it could have been dead grass.

Prickly grass cushioning her cheek ...

Jess's heart gave a great leap and her eyes shot wide open. She sucked in air.

"No! No, stop! Wait!"

But he didn't stop. He didn't even glance her way. Instead, his thumb clamped down on the plunger. Jess couldn't see clearly enough to watch it happen, but she imagined liquid shooting out of the needle into the tube that emptied into her vein.

What liquid?

The question exploded in her mind even as she grabbed for the needle in her hand. Her nails scraped at the tape and she yanked at the tube right where it met her tender skin. The needle—no, a small, clear plastic tube—ripped free of her flesh with a sharp, burning sensation that was as nothing compared to the terror rocketing through her veins.

WHAT LIQUID?

"What the ... ?" The man snatched at the tubing, caught it, and stared at it in stupefaction for a split second as he saw that it swung free.

He dove for her. She screamed. The bed, on wheels that apparently hadn't been locked, careered toward the far wall as his body slammed against it.

His hand, sweaty and warm, clamped around her wrist just as the front-left corner of the bed smacked into the wall and bounced away. As more screams tore out of her throat, she yanked her arm free.

Run.

Every instinct she possessed shrieked it, but to her horror she discovered she couldn't run: Her legs just would not obey her brain's urgent command. Desperate, Jess kicked violently, but the "kick" message somehow got scrambled on its way down to her legs and she ended up bucking on the hospital bed like a landed fish, screaming and fighting him off with flailing blows that missed more than they landed while the bloodied catheter she had torn from her arm swung behind him, spewing tiny drops of a cold viscous liquid that made her shudder with horror when they sprayed over her arm, her neck, her leg.

He'd put something terrible in the bag. . . .

"Shut up, you!" It was a hoarse growl.

The empty syringe came flashing down toward her. With a burst of horror, she saw that he was wielding it like a knife now, meaning to stab her with it. Then a glimmer of light caught it and she realized that it wasn't empty at all, or perhaps it was another, backup syringe, because it was full of liquid. His aim, she realized in that frozen instant in which she watched the clear tube with its glinting needle drive toward her body, was to plunge the needle into her, to release whatever liquid was in that syringe into her flesh directly, and never mind the IV now.

Black shapes circling the flaming car . . .

"No! Help! Help!"

Screaming like a siren, Jess threw herself violently to one side just in the nick of time—and toppled off the side of the bed.

Chapter 6

TIRED TO THE BONE but so wired he couldn't have slept even if he had ignored Lowell and gone home, Mark pushed through the metal door that led from the hospital's emergency staircase to the third floor. According to an ER nurse who had been extraordinarily cooperative from the moment he had flashed his badge—and smile— at her, Jessica Ford had arrived on that floor some fifteen minutes earlier. As they'd talked, he'd seen a plump blond woman the nurse had confidentially identified as Ms. Ford's mother leaning over a desk and filling out paperwork. He wanted to reach Ms. Ford before her mother did, just in case she might be conscious and feeling chatty. He'd chosen to take the stairs rather than the elevator because the press was already on the trail of the story and had gathered in a seething, amorphous, ever-growing pack in the hospital lobby. The difficulty lay in the fact that some of them might recognize him, and then his presence at the hospital would become part of the story, leading to all kinds of speculation. No doubt at some point the harassed-looking security guards would force them outside, but he didn't have the time to wait for that. It was easier to take the stairs and avoid the problem.

If Ms. Ford had anything to say, he wanted to hear it first. There was nothing else he could do for Annette

Cooper now except try to keep her all-American-mom image intact.

He pushed the stairwell door shut behind him with an elbow and was striding down the hall toward Ms. Ford's room when a blood-curdling shriek froze him in his tracks.

It was a woman's terrified scream, so shocking in this hushed, overcooled, sterile environment that it made the hairs on the back of his neck spring to attention. A cold, hard fear seized him even as a terrible premonition jolted his world, even as his gaze shot down the long hallway that right-angled out of his sight just beyond the nurses' station.

For as far as he could see, the hall was dim and nearly empty and utterly incompatible with the explosion of sound that filled it as the woman screamed again and again, raw, jagged screams of pure fear that covered the pounding of his heart—and of his footsteps as he catapulted into a dead run.

Jesus Christ, it wasn't possible. . . .

Mark didn't finish the thought as he raced down the hall toward room 337, the room where Ms. Ford had been taken, where he knew with every bit of gut instinct he possessed that she was screaming like a crazy woman now.

Why?

It was useless to speculate. He didn't want to speculate. He wanted the suspicion that oozed like venom through his brain to be wrong.

Passing a frightened-looking nurse who had apparently paused to ring the security button before going to her patient's aid and shoving aside an orderly, Mark burst into Ms. Ford's room with his Glock at the ready and his heart pumping like a six-cylinder engine.

"Freeze!"

As the door bounced open he was through it, assuming firing stance, the echoes of her shrieks ringing in his ears as his eyes scanned the blue-tinged darkness for her—and whoever might be threatening her.

Only she wasn't screaming now. No one was. Except for the thundering of his pulse in his ears and the *blip-blip-blip* of some damned machine, the room was quiet as a cemetery at midnight.

No one was there.

No one that he could see, anyway.

"Jessica!" he called.

It was a two-person room, complete with two beds and two TVs and a number of chairs and what appeared to be enough medical instruments to keep half the hospital alive. The partially drawn curtain separating the halves of the room fluttered slightly, but despite that small movement, the room did indeed appear empty: Certainly both beds were unoccupied. They were out of place, though, with the nearer one much closer to the door than it should have been and the far one catty-corner against the window wall.

Careful.

His left hand hit the light switch as he advanced into the room on high alert, continuing to scan his surroundings although there wasn't a soul in sight. The sudden brightness made him blink. Including the bathroom, the door of which was ajar, there were only a few places that he couldn't immediately see, which meant there were only a few places for an intruder to hide.

"Jessica?"

Someone had been there, he could sense it, feel the energy of a recent presence. Despite the current silence, there was also no doubt in his mind that he had followed the screams to their source.

So where the hell was she?

"Jessica?"

Coming warily around the foot of the far bed, the one that was pushed out of position, the one with the askew pillows and missing covers that the glowing machines facing it indicated had seen recent use, he found her. Swaddled in blankets, looking small and fragile, she lay facedown on the slick, gray floor, one delicate bare leg and foot curved toward the door, the other concealed by the bedcoverings that were twisted around her. Part of her back was bared, too, by the green hospital gown that imperfectly covered her. Her bare right arm stretched toward the bed. The other must have been tucked up under her body. Her tangled dark brown hair concealed her face, but still he had no doubt that it was her.

"Jessica?"

Mark crouched beside her, cautious still, keeping one eye on his surroundings, not quite ready yet to holster his gun. She was breathing, he saw at a glance, and as far as he could tell had no obvious new injury. There was no pool of blood, no knife protruding from her back, nothing like that. His fingers closed around her wrist: She definitely had a pulse. He could feel it beating fast and strong.

"Jessica, can you hear me?"

Her head moved, and she murmured something that he couldn't understand. She resisted his touch, trying to pull her wrist away, and he let go.

"It's okay. I've got you. You're safe now."

As he glanced swiftly around the apparently empty space around them, suspicion continued to niggle at the edges of his mind. But so far suspicion was all it was; the truth was that he had no idea in hell what had happened to her. Maybe he'd get lucky and find that she'd just fallen out of bed.

He prayed to God that was all it was.

In the circles he moved in, the circles of loosely connected spooks and spies and personal protection officers and government agents who were all to differing degrees ready, willing, and able to do the dirty work of the powerful, the name of the hospital where she had been taken would be common knowledge by now. . . .

Even as that thought arose to bug him, the orderly, several nurses, a couple of security officers, and who knew how many others burst through the door in a big, untidy knot.

"Miss Ford . . ." It was a male voice.

"Oh my God, he's got a gun!" one of the women cried, and then they all practically fell over themselves as they tried to reverse or otherwise get out of harm's way.

"Secret Service." Mark stood up, flashing his badge, and holstered his gun. Reassured, the security guards—a pair of retired cops from the look of them—stopped fumbling with their weapons and the rescue party resumed its mission, crowding around the woman on the floor.

"Miss Ford? What happened?"

One of the nurses, a thirtyish blonde, smoothed the hair back from the patient's face. Mark caught a glimpse of a smooth, white cheek and a full, pale mouth. Her lashes flickered, but there was no reply.

Superfluous now, he stepped back out of the way and set himself the task of discovering what had befallen her. Checking out the bathroom was tops on his list, so that's where he headed.

"She must have tried to get up," another of the nurses said as he came back out of the bathroom, sure now that no one was in there. All he could see of the group huddled over Jessica was the tops of their heads as they crouched around her. Except for the security guards, who were standing back out of the way, frowning as they watched. "Maybe she was trying to get to the bathroom or something. It looks like she's knocked herself out."

"She's catheterized."

"Well, maybe she didn't realize."

"Think she hit her head on a corner of the table?"

"Possible. Or the floor."

"Yup, there's a bump back here. No cut or anything. It's swelling, though."

"Look, she pulled out her IV."

A round of tongue-clucking followed this discovery.

"Help . . ."

Faint and panicky, it was Jessica's voice. Weak as it was, Mark recognized it instantly through the sea of chatter.

Abandoning his quick turn around the perimeter of the room just to see if there could possibly be someone concealed in a corner somewhere that he could have missed—there wasn't—Mark moved in closer to hear what she had to say.

"It's all right, you fell out of bed. We'll just get you back up and . . ."

"There was . . . a man. He tried to put something in my IV."

A brief silence greeted this. While Mark frowned— this was emphatically not what he wanted to hear—a couple of the nurses exchanged significant looks. It was clear from their expressions that they didn't put much stock in what she was telling them.

"I was in here earlier." The orderly stood up. He was a skinny twentysomething in blue scrubs. Medium brown hair pulled back in a short ponytail. Traces of acne on his chin and cheeks. He held up both hands as if to deflect blame. "But I just checked the fluid level. I didn't put anything in the bag."

"He had . . . a needle. He tried . . . to stab me with it." Jessica's voice was faint and shaky, and it was clear that speaking cost her considerable effort. But the urgency underlying it carried the ring of truth—as far as Mark was concerned, at least.

Shit. Shit, no.

"Well, that settles it. Definitely not me." With a humor-the-poor-fool smile, the orderly shook his head.

"I tried to run—I couldn't move my legs." Jessica's

voice was shriller now, and stronger. "Why can't I move my legs?"

Jesus, was she paralyzed?

"You need to try to calm down." The nurse's tone was soothing. "Can you roll onto this? No?" There was the briefest of pauses and a kind of shuffling sound. "Okay, everyone, one, two, three."

A moment later, Jessica was lifted back onto the bed and positioned so that she lay flat on her back. She was shivering violently, Mark saw, as they straightened out her limbs. The green hospital gown covered her from her neck to midthigh. Her legs were slender and pale and well-shaped, and her feet were narrow with unpainted toes.

As the orderly positioned her legs carefully side by side, she lifted her head a few inches off the mattress and looked down at them with obvious horror.

"My legs aren't working."

She sounded frightened. He couldn't blame her.

"Could you look straight at me, please? I need to check your pupils."

The blond nurse leaned over the bed, shining a penlight into each of Jessica's eyes in turn. For a moment Jessica cooperated, seeming bemused as she stared into the light.

"Looks fine," the nurse said.

"I need to sit up." Jessica moved her head restlessly. "Please."

Someone pressed the remote control, and the head of the bed rose with a whirr until she was in a semireclining position.

"Get her vitals."

The light was withdrawn, the bed rail snapped back into place, and she was situated more comfortably on the bed, the pillows adjusted under her head, the covers smoothed and tucked into place, all in a flurry of organized movements. As they finished, Jessica lay limply back against the big white pillows, looking absolutely exhausted and about as vigorous as a rag doll.

"Why can't I move my legs? Why doesn't anyone care that somebody just attacked me? Are any of you even listening to what I'm saying?" Sounding both frightened and angry, she clenched her fists around folds of the blue blanket as if she was holding on to it for dear life.

As her gaze swept her caretakers, Mark got his first real look at her face: squarish, with a high forehead, high cheekbones, and a determined jaw. A gash over her right eyebrow was closed by a neat line of perhaps six stitches. A purpling bruise darkened on her right cheekbone. Another one angled up her neck to her ear, also on the right side. Otherwise, her skin was white as chalk. A distraught expression widened her eyes. Her hair was chin-length, the color of chocolate syrup, and badly tangled on the right side, where most of her visible injuries were located. He recalled that she had been lying on her right side when he had found her. Disregarding the effects of the crash, he would describe her as kind of cute rather than pretty, not the type to attract looks in a bar or at a party or anywhere else. The generic kid-sister type, which might explain why she also seemed vaguely familiar. Freckles, which made her look way too young to be the lawyer Lowell claimed she was, dusted her nose and cheeks. She looked like a kid, like a teenager. What she definitely did not look like was a junkie, or a drug dealer, or anyone who had dealings with junkies or drug dealers.

So what the hell was she doing with Mrs. Cooper?

"You're not helping yourself by getting hysterical." The oldest of the nurses, the one with the short salt-and-pepper hair, sounded stern as she withdrew a thermometer from Jessica's mouth and looked down at it. "Hopefully, some of this you're experiencing is just the side effects of all the medication you're on."

"My legs?" Jessica's voice cracked.

"You'll have to speak to your doctor about that. I don't want to say anything that might be wrong. But the hallucination is almost certainly from the medication."

"Not a hallucination! *Someone attacked me.*"

It was then that Mark caught a glimpse of her left hand. The back of it was torn and bright red with oozing blood. It took him a second to realize that the wound had resulted from the IV being torn from her flesh. His gaze shifted to the tall silver pole resting cockeyed against the wall between the two beds, where it had clearly been shoved with some force.

If what she claims is true, the evidence to prove it is right there.

"One time when they had me on morphine after surgery I imagined I was surrounded by a pack of wolves," the orderly said. "Scariest thing that ever happened to me."

Mark was on the move. His target was the bag of fluid that still hung from the IV pole. And the tubing that was attached to it. Whatever had happened in that room, those items would tell the tale. But even if she was right on the money and there had been a man in her room—in other words, if an attempt on her life really had been made—he couldn't let anyone outside of their own small group know it. It was something he meant to explore— and deal with, if it proved to be true—privately.

But he didn't think it was true. In his judgment, such a thing was almost impossible.

"Him! It was him!" Jessica's voice, high-pitched and panicky, made him turn his head sharply. She had apparently been giving him a once-over, because her gaze flew up his body to his face even as he looked at her. Luckily, because every eye in the room was instantly trained on him, the bag and tubing were now stowed safely out of sight in his jacket pocket.

She meant him, Mark realized with some surprise. She was staring at him, fear plain in her face.

Chapter 7

"YOU'RE WRONG, YOU KNOW." Keeping his tone deliberately gentle, Mark moved to stand beside the bed, one hand curling around the cold silver bed rail while the other steadied the squishy, half-full bag of fluid stuffed in his pocket. Her eyes were a clear greenish hazel framed by a thick sweep of black lashes, he saw, as they bored into his. Her brows were straight dark brown slashes that at the moment nearly met over her nose because of the intensity of her frown. "It wasn't me. I was outside in the hall heading for your room when I heard you scream. My name's Mark Ryan. I'm a Secret Service agent. I was there at the crash site, remember? I found you."

Her shoulders, which had been rigid with tension, slumped. Her features softened fractionally as some of the fear that had sharpened them seemed to ease. She blinked and collapsed back against the pillows, although her gaze didn't leave his face and she still frowned.

"I remember."

"We all saw him running down the hall while you were screaming," said the nurse who'd been pushing the security button as he had blown past her. She was of Asian descent, with short, smooth hair and a shapely figure. Using a gauze pad, she wiped the blood from Jessica's hand as she spoke. The scent of alcohol hit Mark's nostrils, and he made a face at the strength of it. It had to sting, but if it did she wasn't reacting. The tear wasn't long, and it didn't look deep. But it was jagged and still oozed blood.

For whatever reason, the IV needle had definitely parted from her flesh in a violent fashion.

"Yeah, he couldn't have been in here doing bad things to your IV," the orderly agreed, passing a blue plastic ice pack to the oldest nurse, who with a quiet word to Jessica applied it to the back of her head. "I saw him, too. I think that means he's got a quadruple alibi."

"What made you think it was me?" Mark eyed her curiously. Did he have a twin running around somewhere that he didn't know about? Or had it really been just a hallucination after all, with maybe her subconscious plugging in his face because he had found her and she therefore associated him with the crash?

She didn't answer. Her eyes seemed unfocused suddenly, as if she were no longer really seeing him, although she continued to look right at him. After a long moment she inhaled deeply, then winced as if breathing in like that had hurt. Her eyes regained their awareness, narrowing on his face, and her body tensed. Her hands clenched tight around the blanket she still gripped.

"Mrs. Cooper?" Her voice was scarcely louder than a whisper.

Mark hesitated. His instinct was not to add to her distress by giving her more bad news so soon, but the impression he got was that she knew the answer even as she asked the question. What exactly had she seen? Why was Mrs. Cooper—why were any of them—in that car? He needed to know the answers like yesterday, so backing off was not an option, whether he wanted to or not. This was the perfect opening—his cue to find out how much she knew about the circumstances surrounding the

First Lady's death, and to shut her up if the answers weren't what they should be. What she knew would determine what he did about it, of course. Buying her silence was always an option, and pointing out to her how unpleasant things could get for an up-and-coming lawyer who stepped on the toes of some of the most powerful people in the country was the unfortunate corollary to that, the stick to the carrot, as it were. A job, a really good job paying really good money, could be found for her locally or far from Washington, whatever and wherever she wanted. He was in the position to grant her a number of things. All she needed to do was "forget" whatever she knew, if indeed she knew anything at all, and refuse to talk to the press. The Coopers and their loyalists had many ways of rewarding those whom they considered their friends—and just as many ways of punishing their enemies.

Which was the part that was bothering him.

Under the circumstances, though, he really didn't think that was what was going on here. He couldn't believe anybody in the Texas mafia, as the President's mostly homegrown ring of closest advisers was informally known, would resort to trying to have her killed. To conceal the First Lady's drug addiction, which would certainly be embarrassing and hurtful to the family if revealed but would probably, ultimately, win sympathy for the President who had tried to deal with it? Nah. Anyway, at this point, this girl just wasn't a threat: Nobody had a clue whether she was aware of Annette Cooper's problems at all. And even if she was, he was ninety-nine-point-nine percent sure that buying her off would be the solution of choice. The fact that Jessica had thought *he* was her attacker boded well for the hallucination theory. Anyway, Lowell at least hadn't sent anyone to kill her, because if so he wouldn't also have sent Mark to deal with her. As Lowell was well aware, Mark was many things, but he wasn't one to condone a cold-blooded murder, especially when it happened practically under his nose. And he didn't go in for violence against women under any circumstances.

"Could you give us a minute here, please?" he asked, sweeping a meaningful look around the room. The implication was that he simply wanted privacy in which to break the bad news about Mrs. Cooper's death—which in a way he did, although that wasn't all of it, and he didn't think what he had to say was going to come as a surprise to her.

Jessica's eyes widened, and for a moment he thought she meant to protest. Mark realized that she was probably alarmed at the prospect of being left alone with him, which, if she really thought he'd tried to put something in her IV, he could certainly understand.

"You don't have to worry; you're safe with me," he told her in his best reassuring tone, to head her off before she could protest. "I'm on your side. I'm here strictly to make sure you're taken care of."

She looked at him hard, but she didn't object.

"Well . . ." The oldest nurse frowned at him. So did the blond one, looking across the bed at him as, with a loud zip of releasing Velcro, she unwrapped the blood-pressure cuff she had applied to Jessica's arm a moment before. The security guards shuffled uneasily. Mark had the feeling that if he hadn't been Secret Service, there was no way in hell he would have gotten her alone. As it was, though, it was clear that none of them quite had the guts to come right out and say no.

"It's all right." Jessica clenched the matter.

"We'll be right outside the door," the oldest nurse promised. With a glance at Jessica, the blond nurse stepped away from the bed. Then all of them, security guards included, left the room. There was a soft *whoosh* and then a click as the door closed behind them.

Mark looked at Jessica.

"Well?" Her voice was flat. Her eyes held his. She looked small and fragile lying there. She also looked kind of like she'd been hit by a Mack truck, which when he thought about it wasn't too far from what had actually happened to her. Mind-boggling that this nondescript girl, rather than the First Lady of the United States, or fit, strong Will Prescott, or even the adult male driver, had survived. Either she was a lot tougher than she looked or lucky as hell, and he didn't think she was very tough. What surprised him, though, was how calm and in control of herself she seemed. Pretty remarkable, he reckoned, under the circumstances. She had already suffered a lot both physically and emotionally, and she was probably in pain.

But still she had the moxie to scowl at him.

"The First Lady was killed in the crash," he said. There was no way to sugarcoat it, so best just get it out there.

Her eyes flickered, and she glanced down and away. Her lips shook, then firmed, as if she was refusing to let the emotion she was clearly feeling gain the upper hand. She took a breath, carefully shallower than before. Then, as he weighed what to say next, she was suddenly looking straight at him again. Her eyes blazed.

"Where the hell were you?" There was accusation in her voice.

"What?" She'd taken him by surprise. He almost blinked at her.

"I know you—you're the SAIC of the First Lady's security detail. Why weren't you there with her at the hotel? Or why wasn't somebody? Why was she alone? If you'd done what you were supposed to do, none of this would have happened."

"She was at a hotel?"

He latched on to the one piece of solid information and ignored the rest. He had to, because the guilt that her accusation stirred up was something he couldn't deal with right now. The thing that killed him was, she was right. One hundred percent totally correct.

"Isn't it your job to know that?"

Now she was starting to bug him. Whatever he'd been expecting, to have his balls busted by this girl who didn't look much older than his daughter wasn't it.

Anger bubbled. It was fueled by guilt, he knew. Mark told himself to chill.

"What do you know about my job?" He kept his voice even and his gaze level on her face. "For that matter, how do you know who I am?"

She didn't ease up. "I'm an associate with Davenport, Kelly, and Bascomb, Mr. Ryan. Mrs. Cooper has been to our offices on several occasions, and you've been with her. And I've seen you at the White House, when I delivered some papers to her."

It was all Mark could do not to blatantly look her over again, which he figured would not be politic. The thing was, he didn't remember ever seeing her, not in Davenport's office and not in the White House. Not that he meant to say so.

"That's right," he said, as if he recalled the occasions perfectly. "So, would you mind telling me what hotel Mrs. Cooper was in, and what she was doing there?"

"Are you asking out of idle curiosity, or in an official capacity?"

Keep it cool, keep it easy. "Part of my job."

A beat passed. Then she said, almost sulkily, "It was the Harrington. And I have no idea why she was there."

"So why were you there?"

"Mr. Davenport sent me to meet Mrs. Cooper there because he couldn't go himself."

"The First Lady was meeting Davenport at a hotel?"

"In the bar. Apparently, she called him and asked to meet, but he couldn't make it. He sent me instead."

"Why?" He couldn't fathom a circumstance in which the First Lady's close friend and trusted confidant would need to meet her in a bar, or would send a stranger—and he was as sure as it was possible to be under the circumstances that Mrs. Cooper hadn't known Jessica from Adam before tonight—to meet with her in his stead. Unless, as Lowell had speculated, a drug deal of some sort was involved. Or maybe the heading off of one.

"Because I live close by. Because I could get there quickly. Because Mr. Davenport trusts me."

"Ah." Mark still didn't get it, but why Davenport had sent a subordinate in his place really wasn't the most important point he needed clarity on at the moment, so he let it go. "So you met Mrs. Cooper in a hotel bar. Then what happened?"

"We left."

Mark stifled a glimmer of annoyance. The antagonistic vibes she was sending his way were starting to get old.

"Care to elaborate?"

"We walked out together to the car I had come in— Mr. Davenport had arranged for it—and drove away."

She stopped, closing her eyes. He waited. Her dark hair fanned out against the pillow as she turned her head away from him, showing glints of red amid the deep brown. Under the unforgiving glow of the harsh overhead lighting, her face looked almost as white as the pillowcase. Taking in just the damage to her that was visible, he felt bad for even questioning her. But time was of the essence here. He might—thank Jesus—be the first, but he wouldn't be the only one to ask all this and more. He had to know what she was going to say.

"So," he finally said when it became clear she wasn't going to resume talking anytime soon, "you and Mrs. Cooper are in the car, it drives away, and . . . ?"

Her head turned back toward him, and her eyes

opened again with a slow sweep of thick lashes. It seemed to cost her some effort to focus on his face. "That's the last thing I remember. Getting into the car and pulling away from the hotel."

Mark made his voice even gentler. "What about the crash?"

"I don't remember it. I don't remember anything from the time the car left the hotel until you found me. Nothing. At all."

She said the last "at all" as if for emphasis.

There was a pause as Mark processed that. She'd been through a terrible trauma just hours before. Trauma often erased the events immediately preceding it from the mind, as he knew from experience. Therefore, it made sense that she wouldn't remember, he decided. And it also made things easier.

For him. And for her.

"You said Mrs. Cooper was alone in the bar. You mean really alone? There wasn't a Secret Service agent with her?" He was thinking of Prescott, who had clearly hooked up with the First Lady at some point before the crash.

Jessica shook her head.

"One of our agents, Will Prescott, was killed in the crash along with Mrs. Cooper and the driver. If he wasn't with Mrs. Cooper at the bar, how was it that he was in the car with you all?"

She seemed to think about that.

"I don't know. I don't remember," she said at last. "Wait—he may have been outside in front of the hotel, on the street. When we came out."

"So he joined you in the car."

"I don't know. I remember being in the car with Mrs. Cooper and the driver, and no one else, as we pulled away from the curb. After that—it's a total blank."

Mark decided to let the logistics of Prescott's presence in the car go for the moment, too. She seemed increasingly exhausted, a nurse or anyone else could come in at any moment and interrupt, and he had other, more urgent, fish to fry while the frying was good. Finding out what she knew without letting her in on anything she didn't already know about the First Lady required a delicate balance. Unfortunately, he wasn't sure he was up to it. Even under the best of circumstances, delicacy had never been his strong suit.

"So what did Mrs. Cooper do in the bar? What was she doing? When you got there."

"Finishing her drink. She was alone at a table in the corner. I told her Mr. Davenport had sent me and a car to pick her up. So she left with me."

"Where were you going?"

She hesitated. There was a new tension around her eyes and mouth that made him wonder if she was in pain. He hadn't had that impression before, but he supposed that if she had been on painkillers, they would have been delivered via the IV, which obviously was no longer happening. It wasn't too big a stretch to assume the painkillers she'd already received might be starting to wear off.

"I . . . don't know. I was supposed to call Mr. Davenport for instructions once I had the First Lady safely in the car. But . . . I can't remember if I did."

"Safely?" The word tugged at him.

She wet her lips. Her eyes opened wide again to focus on him. It seemed to cost her considerable effort just to lift her lids.

"You know, I was only with the First Lady for about ten minutes, tops. At least, that I remember. I walked into the bar, told her Mr. Davenport had sent me to get her, and walked out with her. We got in the car. And that's it. That's everything. That's all I know. I don't remember anything else. So could you please just go away and leave me alone? I'm really not up to this."

He looked at her consideringly. If possible, she was even paler than before, so colorless her skin appeared almost translucent, and the bruises on her face and neck stood out like zebra stripes. She was shivering now, where she hadn't been before, her hands curled into the blanket. He felt a quick stab of compassion. She was injured, perhaps terribly, and she'd survived a gruesome car crash that had left the three others involved dead. He'd gotten the answers he needed from her, or at least most of them. The important one, which was that she knew nothing and remembered little. So probably it was time for him to back off and turn her back over to the medical personnel who were caring for her.

"The President would appreciate it if you didn't talk about his wife or the crash or anything related to any of that to the press." He evoked the power of the office almost reluctantly. He hadn't said anything about the President earlier, in case one of the others in the room at the time later blabbed to the media the details of his visit to Jessica, which, the principles of medical privacy be damned, he figured they were highly likely to do. He didn't want anyone saying that he was at the crash survivor's bedside at the direction of the President until the way the spin on this was going to be handled had been worked out. Maybe they would decide he had rushed to Jessica's bedside at the President's behest, and maybe they would decide he hadn't. Hell, for all he knew he might not even have officially seen her at all. "I recommend . . ."

That was as far as he got. A plump blond woman— Jessica's mother; he recognized her from the lobby and assumed she had finally finished with the hospital admission paperwork—pushed through the door, high heels tapping, beringed hands fluttering in agitation as she spoke over her shoulder to the younger, slimmer blond woman following her. They looked enough alike that it was obvious that they were mother and daughter, although one was about fifty and the other was maybe in her midtwenties. Both were round rather than angular, and tall, with the kind of bleached-out platinum hair that was clearly the result of multiple home dye jobs. The mother wore hers in short curls; the daughter's was shoulder-length with bangs. Both had round, apple-cheeked faces, snub noses, and dark brown eyes that gave the lie to their hair color. Both wore tight jeans and V-neck pullover sweaters. The mother's was baby blue. The daughter's was pink. Neither looked anything at all like Jessica.

"Honey, you're awake." The mother barely glanced at Mark as she rushed, heels clacking, toward her daughter's bedside. "Oh, my goodness, Jess, you just about scared us to death."

"Mom." Jessica's chin wobbled, and Mark realized to his horror that she was going to cry. She looked past her mother at her presumed sister. "Sarah. Guys, I can't move my legs."

"Oh, Jess." The younger woman rushed to the bedside, too, and they both leaned over their relative. Mark didn't know if they all engaged in a group hug or what because he was busy backpedaling away from the lovefest just as fast and unobtrusively as he could. "What matters is that you're alive."

"The doctor down in the emergency room said it was probably temporary," her mother soothed. "He said the X-rays didn't show anything, so it's probably just . . ."

The door flew open again as if propelled by great force. Two little towheaded boys, maybe four and six years old, wearing Batman and Incredible Hulk pajamas respectively, tumbled into the room, the older one shoving the younger one so that he nearly fell flat on his face.

"He pushed me!" Recovering his balance, Batman

ran toward the sister—Sarah—who had turned upon their entrance. His arms wrapped tight around her legs. "Mom! He pushed me!"

"Is Aunt Jess dead?" Hulk skidded to a halt near the foot of the bed and peered up at Jessica, whose face Mark could no longer see because of the screen provided by her family. "Nah, she's just crying. Why are you crying, Aunt Jess?"

"'Cause she's hurt her face, stupid. See all the places?"

"Boys," their mother—at least, Mark presumed Sarah was their mother—warned sharply. "Behave."

"... have anybody to leave them with," another female voice said apologetically, and Mark's gaze swung toward the door. It was opening again. The speaker was talking over her shoulder to someone—the older nurse, Mark saw as they entered one after the other and headed toward the bed. This blonde was a bombshell, slim yet curvy and tall like the other two, with long, straight hair that swung as she walked. Maybe twenty-one or -two, dressed in a killer black miniskirt and heels that made her tanned bare legs look a mile long. She was wearing a jacket, too, a black leather bomber, but Mark barely noticed that. It was all he could do to look away from the legs.

"I'm sorry, but children aren't allowed on this floor." The nurse sounded like she'd said this more than once and was fast running out of patience.

"Their dad's coming for them," Sarah told the nurse. "It'll just be a little while. They'll be real quiet."

"You said you were going to watch TV and go to bed," the bombshell said accusingly to Jessica. "What happened?"

"A lot." Jessica's voice sounded thick. Mark, who still couldn't see her, took this to mean she was still weepy. "I'm so glad to see you guys."

"Believe me, not as glad as we are to see you."

Group hug again, during which the boys, clearly revolted, crawled under Jessica's bed. Nobody except the nurse—who gave them an evil look—paid the slightest attention.

"One of you could wait with the children in the lobby," the nurse suggested, in the kind of stern tone that made it more of an order than a suggestion.

"It's full of reporters," the bombshell said, glancing around at her relatives. "They were taking the kids' pictures. I don't know how the subject came up, but apparently Hunter told them Jess was their aunt. After that, we had to go."

"They were talking 'bout some lady being killed in a car wreck," Hulk said from beneath the bed. "I told 'em my aunt was in a wreck too. Then they just started asking all kinds of questions and taking pictures."

"And Aunt Grace made us leave," Batman chimed in. "I got to push the elevator button, though."

"Oh, no." Their mother voiced the dismay apparent in the faces of everyone Mark could see.

"What could they have said?" Jessica's mother made an excusing face. "They're just little kids."

"Nobody should say anything to anybody." Jessica's tone was urgent. "Mom, Mrs. Cooper was killed in the wreck."

"Honey, I know. It's a terrible, terrible thing. She seemed like such a nice lady, too."

"I'm just glad it wasn't you," the bombshell said fiercely. "What would we do without you?"

"Well, we'll just get your IV hooked up again." Giving up on banishing the kids, the nurse went for the pole, obviously noticed the missing bag, stopped dead, and frowned. Mark could feel the thing practically burning a hole through his pocket.

"No! No IV!" Jessica protested in agitation. Not that

Mark minded, because her reaction distracted the nurse's attention from the missing bag. "Look, I'm a lawyer, and I know I have the right to refuse to have one. And I refuse! Do you hear? I refuse!"

The nurse shook her head at her. "You have to have an IV. Your medications are administered through it and ..."

"*No*. What part of 'someone just attacked me' did you miss?"

"Wait a minute." Jessica's mother frowned. "Someone *attacked* you?"

"We're sure it was a hallucination brought on by the medication," the nurse said wearily.

"It was *not* ..."

While the standoff continued, Mark judged his principal perfectly safe for the time being and slipped from the room.

It had to be a hallucination. That was the only thing that made sense. Yes, there were others, known variously as cleaners, plumbers, repairmen, whatever, covert operatives that routinely dealt with problems to the powerful like the one Jessica potentially presented. But to employ them on a woman who might very well know nothing of the First Lady's secrets, who might very well present no problem at all, would be the ultimate in overkill. He'd known the Coopers long, and he knew the Coopers well. They would never be party to such a thing.

But under the circumstances, and just in case, he meant to keep tabs on Jessica until he could be absolutely, positively certain he was right.

Because one thing he'd learned over the years was that you could be absolutely, positively certain you were right about something—and still be dead wrong.

Nodding at the security guards, who still hovered in the hall, he walked over to one of the three pay phones on the wall behind the nurses' station—a phone that he was pretty damned sure wasn't tapped and wouldn't be monitored, because nobody would ever figure on anything sensitive going out over it—and placed a call to Harvey Brooks, a lab guy he knew, all while keeping an eye on the door to room 337.

When that was completed to his satisfaction, he pulled his encrypted phone—which he hadn't used to call Brooks because, cynical bastard that he was, he figured that somewhere in the coils of the government he worked for there was somebody who could break through the encryption at will—out of his pocket and called Lowell.

Chapter 8

I'M SCARED.

That was the thought that popped into Jess's brain as her eyes opened, slowly and reluctantly, on what proved to be the shadowy, whisper-quiet world of her hospital room. Like the desperate hand of a drowning person going down for the last time, it shot out of the black void of the already almost forgotten dream she'd been caught up in, breaking the surface of her consciousness and grabbing hold. She blinked, trying to be rid of it, but still it held on.

Oh, God, we've got to get out of here....

That voice, shrill with terror, swirling up out of the darkness, was more residue from the dream. It was a woman's, but it wasn't hers; she didn't recognize it.

Or maybe she did.

As she contemplated that, a cold little frisson of dread made her shiver. Her heart pumped like she had been running for miles.

In self-defense, she dismissed the other swirling images trying to take shape in her mind before they could solidify, and instead focused determinedly on the immediate, on the here and now.

Instinctively, she knew it was safer that way.

The walls were white, the curtains green. They were

closed, with slivers of dull light glowing around their edges and, mysteriously, what looked like a stripe of duct tape running down the center line holding them together. The monitoring machines stood silent beside her bed; she hadn't allowed them to be hooked up again because the idea of machines being attached to her body freaked her out now. Her mother stood between her bed and the machines, looking tired and frazzled in the soft, gray shadows of the heavily curtained room as she reached for something on the stand beside the bed. There were bags under her eyes that were not normally there, the creases running from her nose to her mouth and in between her eyebrows seemed deeper than usual, her lipstick had worn off, and her short cap of blond hair was straight and flat, as though it had not seen a curling iron in some time. Judy Ford Turner Whalen always had immaculate makeup and always curled her hair, world without end; for her to have neglected either showed just how extremely stressed out she was.

The phone was ringing. Her mother was reaching for the ringing phone. Probably, Jess decided, the sound was what had awakened her.

Just looking at her mother made her thudding heart start to slow. Judy was many things, not all of them totally positive, but one thing she definitely was was a tigress in defense of her young. No harm could come to her with her mother in the room—no harm that Judy could prevent, anyhow.

The certainty calmed her. Jess took a steadying breath. Whatever had come before or would come after, for now, for this moment in time, in this gloomy cocoon of a room, she was safe.

"Hello," her mother said cautiously into the receiver. It wasn't like her mother to be cautious, so Jess immediately knew something was up. She felt herself tensing again. Their eyes met. It was hard to read the nuances of her mother's expression through the gloom, but Judy's widened eyes and slight smile acknowledged the fact that Jess was awake.

It also made her think that whatever was going down on the phone couldn't be so terribly bad. Judy wouldn't be smiling at her like that if it was anything bad.

"You think I don't know my own sister's voice? This sure as hell is *not* Jessica's Aunt Tammy." Her mother slammed the receiver back down with enough force to make the phone jump. Jess would have jumped, too, if she'd had the strength. She winced instead, which hurt. "Damned reporters."

"Mom?" Jess frowned at her in surprise.

"They've been trying every which-a-way to get information about you," Judy informed her. "Ron"—Sarah's possibly soon-to-be-ex-husband; their separation had led to Sarah, boys in tow, moving back in with Judy three weeks ago, which in turn had led Grace, who had been living with their mother, to flee to Jess's apartment for sanctuary—"couldn't even take the kids to school this morning. There was a TV truck out in front of his house! He had to call the police to run them off."

"A TV truck?" Realization hit Jess like a bucket of cold water to the face. *The wreck . . .* She shivered. Her stomach clenched. "Mrs. Cooper's death is all over the news, isn't it?" It occurred to her that, as someone who had been in the accident and survived, the *only* one who had survived, she was a very obvious focal point for the media. "Are there reporters here at the hospital, too?"

Her mother nodded.

"They've been camped out around the place since before I got here, and it seems like more of 'em just keep coming. It's a nightmare just trying to get to the car. We had to tape the curtains in here closed because one of them got up in a room in the wing across the way and was trying to take pictures of you lying there in that bed through the window. They've even tried to sneak up here a couple of times. If there wasn't security at the door, I don't know what we would have done."

"Security?"

"There's two Secret Service agents outside the door right now. They change shifts every eight hours or so."

Judy's voice was hushed with respect. Jess knew she was impressed that her daughter rated notice from the White House, no matter how horrific the circumstances. To Judy, a president was somebody you saw on TV. The fact that her daughter's job brought her into daily contact with people who knew people in the White House had been a source of tremendous pride. When Jess had told her that her boss was the First Lady's lawyer and personal friend and that she herself had actually been in the same room as the First Lady and been introduced to her by name and shaken her hand and talked to her, Judy's awe had been palpable.

"You're kidding, right?"

But even before Judy shook her head, Jess knew she was not.

Jess wet her lips. The thought of Secret Service agents outside her door made her blood run cold. *Why?* She didn't know, precisely, she realized. The idea of it just made her feel—panicky.

"Can you believe it? The White House sent them. 'Cause they want to help us out until you're back on your feet, they said." Judy's expression changed as she focused on her oldest child. "How you feeling, honey?"

Jess thought about that. She was anxious. She was dizzy. She hurt all over, with special emphasis on her head and ribs. And her back ached, right down at the base of her spine, with a continuous, deep, throbbing pain that had her arching this way and that in a futile effort to relieve it.

"My legs . . ."

Fighting a rush of fear as she remembered how they had refused to work before, she tried to move them.

Her right leg slid sideways maybe a couple of inches. The toes curled on her left foot. The pain in her back turned excruciating, shooting up her spine, freezing her in place. She grimaced, and would have groaned, except she didn't want to worry her mother.

"When the doctor came in to see you this morning, he said the X-rays didn't show any sign of permanent damage. No fracture or anything like that. He thinks you must have bruised your spine. They've been giving you painkillers, and steroids to help with the swelling, and he said when that goes down you should be able to move better. He said you'll be stiff and sore for a while, but everything'll heal sooner or later. It's just going to take some time."

Hearing that made Jess feel like a humongous stone had just been lifted from her chest.

"Thank God." She took a deep breath. Until that moment she hadn't realized just how frightened she had been that she might have lost the use of her legs for good. If she wasn't going to die or be paralyzed, then she was going to live and eventually be fine, so she might as well get on with it. "I want to sit up."

Her mother nodded and hit the remote. Jess felt the head of the bed slowly rising beneath her.

"How's that?"

"Better."

Filled with renewed determination, gritting her teeth with effort, Jess concentrated on moving her legs. Her right knee rose off the mattress high enough to tent the covers. She was less successful with her left leg but managed to at least shift it sideways. The effort sent another sharp pain shooting up her back and electric tingles coursing down both legs, causing her to squirm in protest, but still she felt a wave of relief. At least that was proof she could move.

"You're doing good," her mother encouraged as Jess, frozen in place now, waited for the pain to recede. Which, somewhat to her surprise, it did.

Breathing easier, she concentrated again, and managed to get her left knee off the mattress, too. Then she cautiously wiggled the toes on both feet and turned her feet from side to side at the ankle. The pain was bad but not nearly as bad as the thought of her legs being paralyzed had been, so she persevered until she was sure everything still worked. Finally, using her hands for leverage, she scooted farther up in the bed until she was propped up against her pillows, and brushed her hair back from her sweaty face with both hands. Moving hurt. So did lifting her arms and scrunching up her face, which she did in reaction to the other pain, but she kept on. She figured that if she did only what didn't hurt, she would basically just lie there and breathe. Shallowly.

"I need a shower."

"How about I get a bowl of water and some soap and you make-do with washing your face and hands for now?"

Jess thought about the effort required to move at all, extrapolated that to the far greater effort to get out of bed and somehow make it to the shower, then stand, sit, or lie there beneath the steaming-hot water for long enough to get clean, and made a face. With the best will in the world, she couldn't do it. A bowl of water and some soap was not what she wanted, but clearly it was what she was going to have to settle for.

"Fine," she said with a sigh.

Her mother headed for the bathroom, flipping on the overhead light as she passed the switch. Jess flinched at the unexpected assault of so much brightness. While her eyes were adjusting to the near-blinding fluorescent glow, she cast a quick look at the bedside clock. The numbers were blurry since she wasn't wearing her contacts, but by squinting and tilting her head and shading her eyes with her hands she was able to read them. The time was five-twenty-three, and from the light filtering in around the curtains she knew it wasn't a.m., because at this time of year at almost five-thirty in the morning it would still be dark outside. Therefore, it was late Sunday afternoon; ordinarily, she would be finishing up briefs to be presented in court on Monday. Apparently, whatever they'd put in the shots they'd given her—no way was she ever having another IV for as long as she lived, as she'd finally made crystal clear to the bevy of hospital personnel who had taken turns trying to bully her into it—must have been something potent to make her sleep for a little more than twelve hours. Her mother had said they'd given her painkillers; she was still feeling pain, so they weren't doing so great with that, but at least she'd gotten plenty of sleep.

Her glasses, the ones with the big black frames that she kept as backup to the contacts, rested on the table beside the clock. They were a little fuzzy around the edges but unmistakable, and she guessed that someone— Grace, most likely—must have fetched them from her apartment. Reaching for them greedily, sliding them on and experiencing the instant relief of seeing the world around her in focus again, she noticed something else: the TV remote beside the clock.

The temptation proved irresistible. She didn't want to know, she was better off not knowing, but she couldn't help herself: She picked up the remote, clicked it at the ceiling-mounted TV just beyond the foot of her bed, and . . .

A close-up of Annette Cooper smiling as she shook hands with someone an unseen narrator identified as Chilean president Jorge Peres de Toros blinked to life. The camera pulled back, and Jess saw that the First Lady looked beautiful in a floor-length white evening dress that shimmered with sequins. Her trademark short blond hair gleamed in the light of the overhead chandelier. Her skin was smooth and tan and glowing. Her eyes were bright.

Jess had expected it, of course, when she had turned on the TV. Still, the shock of seeing Annette Cooper was overwhelming. She caught her breath. As agonizing as it was to watch, she couldn't look away as the First Lady said something over her shoulder to her tuxedo-clad husband, who laughed and nodded in response.

". . . such a short time ago Mrs. Cooper was at the President's side as he . . ."

Biting down hard on her lower lip, Jess changed the channel.

A shot of the White House filled the screen. A crowd, an enormous sea of people that seemed to stretch all the way to the Mall, had gathered around it, and the camera panned dozens upon dozens of weeping faces. It seemed to be a live shot, taken in real time, because the sky that formed the backdrop was streaked with sunset colors of orange and purple and gold, and the White House itself cast a long shadow across the lawn.

". . . thousands gathering in the capital to pay tribute to First Lady Annette Cooper, who this evening is lying in state in the Capitol Rotunda. Mrs. Cooper was killed in a car crash shortly after . . ."

Punching the button with far more force than was necessary now, Jess changed the channel again. She was breathing hard, she realized, and her palms were sweaty. Her stomach churned. She felt gorge backing up in her throat.

It was night, and a car, blackened and crushed and flipped over on its roof, filled the screen.

Jess's eyes widened. She was instantly bathed in cold sweat. The shot seemed to have been taken from above, and it showed the still-smoking undercarriage, the flattened tires, the circle of charred grass in which the vehicle rested, the dozens of firefighters and rescue workers and police officers and military personnel and plainclothes investigators moving around the scene. Make and model were impossible to determine because of the car's burned-out state, but she knew instantly that it was the black Lincoln that Davenport had sent her to pick up Mrs. Cooper in. It was a night shot, lit up by big orange klieg lights focused on the scene and the bright beams of spotlights crisscrossing the wreck from above—helicopter searchlights, she realized, and realized, too, that the shot had been taken from a helicopter soon after the accident.

So soon that she might still have been lying semiconscious on the dark slope that fell away from the road on the right side of the shot.

Jess started to shake.

"... preliminary investigation indicates that the vehicle was traveling at excessive amounts of speed—one estimate suggests as much as ninety miles an hour in a forty-five-mile-an-hour zone—when the driver, identified as Raymond Kenny of Silver Spring, Maryland, who had worked for the company that owned the car, Executive Limo, for fourteen years, lost control and the car went off the side of Brerton Road and rolled down an embankment, killing three of the four people inside, including First Lady Annette Cooper. She was said to be on her way to visit a dying friend at the Sisters of Mercy Hospital in Fredericksburg and ..."

Dear God.

Closing her eyes, feeling like the world was tipping sideways and she was clinging on by her fingernails in an effort not to fall off, Jess hit the power button, hit it without even consciously making the decision to do so. It was as if her body, reacting in its own defense, just said no to exposure to anything else that might cause her distress. But even with her eyes closed, even with the voices from the television silenced and the screen gone black, it still felt like she was tumbling down into nothingness as images from the accident chased one another through her mind.

Chapter 9

*SPEEDING THROUGH THE NIGHT, going faster
and faster until the rolling hills and dark pastures and a
narrow fence line of tall trees outside the window became
nothing more than a black blur and her heart was pumping with alarm, feeling a hard jolt that sent the car skidding sideways, the terrible squeal of brakes drowned out
after a single terrified moment by screams . . .*

"Jess, are you all right?"

Jess opened her eyes. She was drenched in sweat and
drawing deep, shuddering breaths, and she realized from
her mother's expression that she was probably as pale as
a piece of angel food cake.

*"She was said to be on her way to visit a dying friend
at the Sisters of Mercy Hospital in Fredericksburg . . ."*
That's what they'd said on TV.

Only it was a lie. They were telling lies.

Why?

"Jess?"

Frowning, Judy walked toward her carrying a blue
plastic basin filled with water that sloshed softly with
every step, a small unwrapped bar of soap, a blue washrag, and a matching towel.

"Jessica Jane? Do you hear me talking to you?"

It occurred to Jess that she was staring at her mother as if she had been poleaxed. She willed herself to focus.

Think it through later. Shake it off.

"Oh, sorry. I was just . . . I'm fine."

That is, other than the fact that she was dizzy and limp with dread. Which she didn't mean to share with her mother. Which she didn't even totally understand herself. Taking a not-too-deep breath, she fought to get her emotions under control, to seem like her normal self, so her mother wouldn't guess that something was majorly wrong. She didn't know why she felt this was so important, but she did.

Dark figures rushing past her down the slope . . .

Jess realized she was breathing way too fast.

"You don't look fine. You look worse than you did when you were unconscious, for pete's sake."

"I have a little headache."

That was true, as far as it went. Also, her palms were sweaty. Her mouth was dry. Her pulse was racing. Disoriented, that's how she felt. Almost as if she could see—no, she didn't want to see.

Who were the dark figures? Were they even real?

She didn't want to think about it. She didn't want to know.

Her mother's frown deepened. She was looking at her hard.

"Maybe I should call the nurse."

"No. No, don't."

You can't go there now. Snap out of it.

Every instinct Jess possessed screamed that she had to keep her mother—keep her family, keep everyone—from knowing that her memory wasn't totally wiped out where the crash was concerned after all. Instead, it was throwing up weird images like puzzle pieces that didn't quite fit. No, make that terrifying images.

Fire ... It started as a tiny orange burst and then—boom!—it exploded, pillars of flame enveloping the car, shooting toward the ink-black sky. . . .

Jess closed her eyes. She clenched her fists. She bit down hard on the tip of her tongue. The pain did what it was supposed to do—it cleared the hideous pictures from her mind.

"Jess?"

Jess opened her eyes. "It's just a headache ... I'm better now."

"It's been a while since they last gave you anything for pain—maybe we ought to ask for something."

"It's okay. It's gone."

Her mother was still looking at her with concern. Jess took a deep breath and managed a weak smile for her mother as Judy settled the basin on her stomach.

"Thanks." Jess felt limp, as if the pictures in her head had taken a physical toll on her body. "And thanks for staying with me, by the way."

"Are you kidding? It'd take wild horses to get me out of here. After you thought somebody attacked you?" Judy made a *tsk-tsk* noise. "Here, let me help you with that."

"I can manage."

Making a conscious effort to keep her hands steady and her head in the present, Jess summoned another perfunctory smile and tucked her hair behind her ears and dipped the washrag in the warm water.

"Maybe the attack *was* a hallucination." Careful to keep her voice free of any inflection, Jess wrung out the rag without looking at her mother.

The attack was real. It happened.

But even though she was almost completely convinced of it, she didn't say so. After listening to the TV, she was beginning to get her mind around the true enormity of what Annette Cooper's death meant. The global scope of it. The interest in it. And the possible ramifications. Through no fault of her own, she was caught up in a world-class tragedy. As the only living witness, in fact. Not a comfortable spot to be in. And, she was becoming increasingly afraid, not a safe one.

Whatever was going on—and she was almost positive that something she'd really rather not know about was going on—she didn't want to get her mother—her family—involved.

That was the thing about family, she was discovering. Having them, having people you care about, makes you so damned vulnerable.

Annette Cooper fled the White House.

"Whether it was a hallucination or not"—Jess, mindful of her injuries, carefully dabbed at her cheeks and chin, as Judy retrieved a hairbrush from her purse, held it up so Jess could see it, and set it on the bedside table next to the remote—"I'm not leaving this place until you do."

That was her mother—loyal to the bitter end. For better or for worse.

"I love you, Mom." It was something she almost never said anymore. None of them did.

Her mother's face softened. "I love you too, Jessica Rabbit."

It was a nickname from when she'd been a little girl, funny, so her sisters said, because their Jessica was the polar opposite of her cartoon namesake. Not sexy, not a man-eater, just plain, skinny, blind-as-a-bat bookworm Jess.

Thanks for the confidence builder, guys. She could almost hear them answering, *You're welcome, Wabbit.*

"Look what else I've got." The crinkle of tearing plastic wrap was followed by her mother waving a cheap pink toothbrush at her, then placing it and a small tube of Crest beside the hairbrush. "It's been in my purse since the dentist gave it to me."

Jess's eyes lit up. "Fantastic."

Judy poured her a glass of water from the yellow plastic pitcher beside the bed, and Jess quickly brushed her teeth. The minty tang of the toothpaste was so normal, so much a part of her regular, everyday life, that the very ordinariness of it felt special.

She was suddenly, overwhelmingly, thankful to be alive. The idea of never seeing her mother and sisters again, of their grief if she had been killed along with everyone else in that car, made her throat tighten. They were a mess, every single one of them—herself included, she supposed. They could be, and frequently were, a giant pain in her ass. But in the end, she was just now discovering, none of that really mattered.

What mattered was that they were a family.

Annette Cooper had a family, too.

Jess's throat tightened again. Leaning over the basin, she splashed her face, the better to conceal incipient tears, and discovered that in some places her skin was so raw it stung.

Ironically enough, the small discomfort banished the sudden urge to cry.

Mrs. Cooper ran away from the Secret Service agent who came looking for her.

"You've got to be exhausted," Jess said to her mother in an effort to banish the torturous thoughts that just wouldn't stay out of her head. Wiping the water from her eyes, she looked at Judy. Her mother really did look tired. "Have you gotten any sleep at all?"

Judy nodded. "Maddie came in this morning, so I lay down on the other bed and slept while she was here. She and Grace went out about an hour ago to pick up some things from the house." Maddie was Jess's youngest sister, a just-turned-eighteen-year-old high school senior. The previous weekend, Maddie had precipitated a family crisis—and when weren't they ever in some kind of crisis?—by telling Grace, who told Sarah (because Jess was working all weekend and Grace had to tell somebody, and Sarah possessed the closest ear), who told their mother, who then told Jess, that she was pregnant.

At the time, having National Merit Scholarship–winning, valedictorian-candidate Maddie confess that she was pregnant had seemed like the family-size equivalent of an atom bomb.

Now it seemed manageable. A small pothole in the road of life. One of those things that you end up making the best of, maybe even laughing about in twenty years. When the kid-to-be was a beloved member of the family.

Nothing like almost dying to provide a little perspective, Jess reflected with an inner grimace as she worked the soap into bubbly lather, which she then carefully spread over the parts of her face that weren't either stinging or stitched together.

Mrs. Cooper said her Secret Service agents were more like wardens. She was upset, way more upset than she should have been from something as ordinary as a fight with her husband. She was running away.

"I hate for you to stay with me again tonight—you've got to work tomorrow," Jess said. "You'll wear yourself out."

Her mother operated a small day-care center out of her home. Both Maddie and Grace, who was a junior at University of Maryland, worked there part-time. It was her mother's latest moneymaking venture after she lost her job as a shift supervisor at the Red Cross shoe plant three years ago, when Jess had been in her first year of law school and working at Davenport, Kelly, and Bascomb as a research assistant at night. Since then, Judy had been a temp, a waitress, a veterinary assistant, a sales associate at Macy's, and a pizza delivery person, and sometimes two or three at once. None of which, singly or in multiples, paid enough to support her family. Even with Grace and Maddie holding down part-time jobs, and Jess contributing every penny she could, there was never enough. Until Jess had graduated law school and gotten the fat-salaried job with Davenport. With what she was now able to contribute to the family kitty, everyone was comfortable for the first time that Jess could remember.

Do I even still have a job? Probably the last thing I should be worried about now, but . . . I need the money. We need the money. She grimaced inwardly. *Face it, doesn't everybody always need the money?*

"We didn't open today, and we're not opening tomorrow. Probably not the rest of the week, either. I called all the parents—they understand. Lots of businesses around here are shut down out of respect for Mrs. Cooper anyway, and they all know that you're my daughter and what happened to you."

It took Jess a second, but then she caught it.

"Is this *Monday*?"

"Sure is. What did you think?"

"I thought it was Sunday." Jess rinsed her face and reached for the brush, which she pulled carefully through her hair: *Ouch.* She'd been out of it for almost forty-eight hours: unbelievable. And oh my God, it was a workday and she'd missed it. The first one ever. Then she remembered, and realized that it was almost certainly *not* a workday. Not for a firm so closely associated with the First Lady. "Has Mr. Davenport called? Or anyone from work?"

"There were so many calls the hospital switchboard's only been putting family through."

So many calls—because everyone wanted her to talk about the accident.

The panic that had been slowly building just below her precariously maintained calm started to bubble to the surface.

They—she wasn't quite sure who was to blame—had it wrong about where Mrs. Cooper was going when the car crashed. Jess's memory of what had transpired during the accident might be spotty, but her recall of what had happened before was unimpaired. Mrs. Cooper had been running away from the White House, and Davenport had sent Jess and a car to pick her up and take her—somewhere. Those were facts. Admittedly, Jess didn't remember where they were headed, but for sure it wasn't to visit a dying friend in a Fredericksburg hospital. Maybe that was an honest mistake, maybe it was a deliberate lie, or spin, as Davenport would probably put it, but the discrepancy made her uneasy. Couple that with the images in her mind of dark figures rushing down the slope past where she lay and surrounding the burning car, add in Mrs. Cooper's upset and her claim that she was a prisoner in the White House (more facts), as well as the near certainty that she herself had been attacked right here in this very room just hours after the First Lady's death, and what did you get?

Either something really bad—or a whole lot of vivid imagination mixed with a little bit of truth that added up to nothing much at all.

Her imagination had never been that vivid. Therefore, she was going with something really bad.

You gotta tell somebody. You can't keep this to yourself. It's too big—too important.

"Mom, could you get rid of this stuff, please? I'm finished with it."

"You look better." Giving her a critical once-over, her mother gathered up the bedpan and glass, etc., and headed for the bathroom with it. "Still a little the worse for wear, but better."

"Wonderful. Oh, and you might want to wash your face while you're in there. You've got mascara smudges under your eyes."

"Oh, my."

That, Jess figured, had just bought her a good ten minutes. She barely managed to wait until Judy disappeared
into the bathroom and closed the door before snatching
up the phone by the bed and punching in Davenport's
number—not the office but the private cell phone number he had given her on Saturday night when he had sent
her out to retrieve Mrs. Cooper. It was his direct line, the
only number, home or office, that wasn't routed through
Marian Young, his longtime secretary.

It was recorded in her cell phone's memory, but her
cell phone was nowhere in sight. But she remembered
it.

Perfectly, as it turned out. Because he answered on
the second ring.

Chapter 10

"WHO IS THIS?" Davenport demanded, instead of giving his name or any identifying information. Jess realized that the hospital name and number must have come up on his caller ID, but nothing that would tell him specifically it was her. The thing was, only a few people had this number, which was normally reserved for very special clients like Annette Cooper, so there weren't a whole lot of choices. Unless he'd thought the number had been discovered by the press.

"Jessica Ford, Mr. Davenport."

She heard him catch his breath.

"God in heaven, Jessica, you're a living, breathing miracle. Do you realize that? Do you appreciate it?"

"Yes." Brushing over that impatiently, she spoke in an urgent whisper with one eye on the bathroom door. "Mr. Davenport, listen, I think something may be wrong about this. For one thing, a man attacked me not long after I was admitted to the hospital. He tried to put something in my IV. I think he might have been trying to kill me. And . . ."

"How did such a terrible accident happen? Annette, everybody else—" Davenport's voice shook as he broke in on her hurried recital. Jess was pretty sure he hadn't listened to a word she had said. Because it was obvious that just like he had been the last time she had talked to him, he'd been drinking pretty heavily. "Well, I'm just glad you're alive. Just so glad. It just seems so impossible...."

He made a choking sound, and Jess realized it was a sob.

"Mr. Davenport. They're saying on TV that Mrs. Cooper was on her way to visit a dying friend and we both know that's not—"

"Wait! Stop!" Davenport's normally deep and authoritative voice was high-pitched and wobbly. "Don't say it. Not anything. Not on the phone. Anybody could be listening."

Jess's heart skipped a beat. Her eyes widened, and she had an absurd impulse to glance around the room even though she absolutely knew it was empty.

"Who? Who do you think is listening?"

"Anybody. Everybody. Bad people."

"Bad people?" Her heart speeded up. It sounded like he harbored some of the same suspicions she did, when what she'd really wanted was for him to tell her that they couldn't possibly, no way, uh-uh, be true.

"The dark forces. They're dangerous, you know."

She was pretty sure the gulping sound she heard was him knocking back another long swallow of whatever it was he was drinking. It certainly wasn't her swallowing. She wasn't that loud.

"I don't know who else to go to with this. You're the only one I can trust and—"

"No, no, no! Not on the phone!"

Jess was feeling desperate. She got the impression that he might hang up on her at any second. "Could we talk in person, then?"

"Maybe." Another gulp. "Yes, that would probably be a good idea."

"Are you at the office? I could come there—" She

thought of her physical condition. She was pretty sure she couldn't even walk. "No, on second thought, I can't. Can you come here?"

"No. Not possible. It would cause too much of an uproar. The media's knee-deep around that hospital. They've already traced the car back to me, you know, and they're calling every number they can find for me practically non-stop. If I showed up there they'd jump on me like fleas on a dog, and I'm just not up to dealing with that yet. Anyway, I'm out of town." She heard him take a deep breath. There was a pause before he continued in a voice that suddenly sounded almost normal. "I'll be coming in for Annette's funeral on Thursday. I could meet you Thursday night."

Annette's funeral. Oh, God.

"Where?" She kept her voice carefully steady.

"The condo."

In addition to his elegant Georgetown mansion and sumptuous Virginia estate, Davenport quietly maintained a two-bedroom suite in the Watergate Apartments. He said it was for the overnight use of out-of-town clients, but Jess suspected that he did some personal entertaining of the extramarital sort there as well. Not that it was any of her business. She'd been there twice, both times to drop off paperwork for her boss, once in the evening and once in the early morning before heading to work. The first time, the dining table had been set for two, a bottle of wine or champagne or something had been chilling in an ice bucket beside the table, and fresh flowers perfumed the air.

She had noticed all this accidentally, just from glancing past Davenport as he'd come to the door in his robe. Poker-faced, she'd handed him the documents she'd brought him, turned around, and left.

Because that's what junior lawyers who wanted to rise in the ranks did: exactly what they were told. Without asking any questions.

"You remember where it is?"

"Yes." She noticed that he wasn't mentioning the address, realized it was deliberate, and felt a cold chill. She could almost feel unseen ears listening in.

If she was paranoid, then he was, too. The knowledge was the opposite of comforting.

"I hear you're going to be released from the hospital in the next couple of days. When you get out, that's where you go. You just call the office when the time comes, and I'll send Marian over to get you. You won't be able to go home anyway. There'll be media everywhere. The next few weeks are going to be a damned circus."

It was the first time Jess had really, truly comprehended how much her life had been altered. Reporters would be after her; she couldn't go home. . . .

She had to fight to keep her voice steady. "All right."

"And, Jessica . . ."

"Yes?"

"Anything you may have seen or heard while you were with Annette, just forget it, understand? Forget it."

"Okay."

Then Jess remembered the Secret Service agent talking to the hotel doorman before he spotted them and came running toward the Lincoln: Prescott, that was his name. And she realized that simply forgetting what little she knew wasn't going to wipe the First Lady's trail clean. Not by a long shot. There was that doorman, for instance, and . . .

"They're going to find out she was at the hotel," she warned. "Mrs. Cooper—"

"Don't say another word," he interrupted, his voice suddenly fierce. "Not over the phone. Not anywhere. Not to anybody about anything, do you understand? Not to investigators. Not to the press. Not to your family. Not to *anybody*. Nothing. Say nothing. You don't know anything. You don't remember anything."

"Yes, all right." There was real fear in his voice, she realized. And that scared her worse than almost anything else so far. For Davenport, the rich and well-connected power player, to be afraid was huge.

Over the phone, she heard the muffled sound of a doorbell.

"Look, somebody's here. I've got to go. I'll be back in D.C. on Thursday. We'll talk then. In the meantime, you just sit tight and *keep your mouth shut*. About everything, and I mean *everything*."

He disconnected, and not a moment too soon. Jess was in the act of restoring the receiver to its cradle when a quick knock sounded on the door to her room.

In a guilty panic, she dropped the receiver, which fortunately landed on the phone but jangled. Her eyes widened, riveting on the door. Who would knock, instead of just walking in? Not her family, or the nurses . . .

A reporter maybe, having snuck past security? Or somebody else? Somebody sinister . . .

Jess's pulse shot into overdrive.

The knob turned . . .

Her breathing suspended. Her fight-or-flight response kicked in, but unfortunately under the circumstances flight was not an option.

The conclusion she came to as she watched the door start to open made her sick: *Whoever this is, I'm a sitting duck.*

She was just opening her mouth to yell for her mother when Judy walked out of the bathroom.

"Mom . . ." Jess said. Before she could continue, Judy, oblivious to the possibility of any kind of threat, simply caught hold of the edge of the door and pulled it the rest of the way open.

For a moment Judy said nothing, just stood there looking at whoever was on the way in that Jess couldn't quite see. Then she smiled, and Jess's pounding heart began to slow. She took a deep, calming breath. She knew that expression. Whoever was standing there, it was someone Judy knew. Someone she liked. Someone who was welcome.

That's why the name that came out of her mouth shocked Jess so.

"Why, hi there, Mark. Come on in."

Mark Ryan walked into the room. Beyond him, through the open door, Jess got a glimpse of the hospital corridor, a nurse hurrying past, a woman in street clothes walking in the opposite direction, and a huge, bald-headed, dark-suited Secret Service agent leaning against the opposite wall and watching with unsmiling intensity as Ryan entered the room.

An icy little shiver ran over her at the sight.

Were they there to keep people out—or her in?

She didn't want to think about it.

"I've got some information for you." Ryan bestowed an easy smile on her mother. Then his gaze went past Judy to seek out Jess. "You, too, Ms. Ford, since you're awake."

She looked at him warily.

Judy said, "Oh, you can call her Jess. We're not fancy."

Her mother, bless her man-eating little heart, was sucking in her stomach and beaming and fluttering her hands so that her rings flashed and doing everything but batting her lashes at him, which wasn't surprising. Judy had always been an absolute idiot when good-looking men were concerned. And Ryan was nothing if not good-looking. He was in his late thirties, with thick, light brown hair that had probably been white-blond when he was a kid, cut ruthlessly short. His face was lean and angular, with the kind of outdoorsy, baked-in tan that would send a woman racing for the Retin-A before the wrinkles could set in. His brows were sandy above eyes that were a clear ocean blue. His face wasn't perfect: His nose was a little thick. His lips were a little too thin, a little too crooked. There were creases around his eyes, and deeper ones running from his mouth to his nose. But on the plus side, he was a hair north of six-foot-two, with wide shoulders and an athlete's toned physique that the navy suit, white shirt, and navy-striped tie he was wearing served only to emphasize.

Taken all together, it added up to sex on the hoof.

Jess had noticed him the first time he'd walked into Davenport's office at the First Lady's heels. He hadn't spared her so much as a glance.

She had remembered him when he had accompanied Annette Cooper on a second visit. At his request, she had handed him a glass of water, which he had passed on to the First Lady. He had thanked her with a nod and a smile that had sent a disorienting little thrill shooting through her solar plexus clear down to her toes.

By the First Lady's third visit, she had been anticipating seeing him again, even though she would have died before she admitted it to anyone. Standing behind Davenport's desk while Davenport and Mrs. Cooper talked, she had given him a little smile.

He had smiled back with enough charm to make her catch her breath.

On his fourth visit, he had smiled at her as soon as he had walked through the door. Her reaction? Basically, *Be still my heart.*

When Davenport had needed someone to hand-carry some papers over to the White House's East Wing for Mrs. Cooper's signature, she had actually volunteered to go despite a punishing workload that already promised to keep her in the office until after ten that night. Because she had hoped to see Mark Ryan there. Because, much as it irked her now to acknowledge it, she'd been nursing a little bit of a crush—oh, all right, a great big giant crush—on him.

Sure enough, he'd been there, standing right beside the door to the First Lady's office as Jess had approached. It had been obvious from his unsmiling glance, from his brusque tone as he'd asked her her business, from his entire demeanor, that he hadn't the slightest clue that he had ever seen her before.

Humiliatingly obvious.

After getting the required signatures from Mrs. Cooper, she had slunk back to her office while vowing never to let herself be so stupid as to have her head turned by a handsome face and a practiced smile again.

And now here she was, stuck in a hospital bed, wearing an ugly green gown that everybody knew meant she was naked underneath, her hair a dirty mess, her face bruised and stitched, which, if you wanted to look on the bright side, at least probably meant that the makeup she wasn't wearing wouldn't have been an improvement anyway.

Wearing the same kind of big black glasses that had led to her high school classmates calling her Four Eyes.

So what? she challenged herself. *Why do you even care?* Then she added firmly, *I don't.*

Ryan had found her lying injured and barely conscious after the crash, and had stayed with her until she'd been loaded into an ambulance. He'd come to the hospital that same night, from all accounts running into her hospital room like the Terminator on a mission to save Sarah Connor. From the way her mother beamed at him now and called him Mark like it was something she was used to doing, Jess assumed he'd been in her room more than once since.

And he still didn't remember her from before. That was all too clear.

Bottom line was, she was getting tired of being wallpaper.

"That okay with you?" He was looking at her, and

Jess realized he was referring to her mother's invitation for him to call her *Jess.*

She was tempted to say, "Ms. Ford works," but didn't want to listen to the flak from her mother later.

"Sure."

"I'm Mark."

Well, golly gee. I get to use your first name. What an honor.

"You said you had some information?" She couldn't help it. Her tone was frosty.

The sad thing was, despite everything, she was itching to whip off her glasses, even though she was practically blind without them. She glared at him through the embarrassingly thick lenses as he walked right up to her bedside, with her clueless mother—who'd clearly spent the hours while her injured daughter had been at death's door happily working on making the hunk's acquaintance—sashaying along behind.

Judy only ever wiggled like that in the presence of an attractive man.

Jess gave her a look. *Give it a rest, Mom.*

Judy didn't even notice. She was too busy ogling Ryan's butt.

Ryan asked, "Remember thinking somebody tried to tamper with your IV the night they brought you in here?"

Oh, yeah. "I remember."

"Well, just to be on the safe side, just so we could know for sure what we were dealing with, I took the bag of fluid that was in your room that night and had some lab tests run on it. The results just came back, and it's good news—there was nothing harmful in it at all. Nothing that shouldn't have been in there."

Judy said, "That was so *smart* of you. What a relief."

Jess's lips compressed. She would have glared at her mother if she'd thought Ryan wouldn't have noticed.

"So you're saying I imagined that attack?"

"It's pretty clear it was a hallucination, yes."

"He never actually put anything into the bag itself, you know. He was emptying the syringe into a port in the tubing when I figured out what was going on."

"I remembered you said that, so I had the tubing checked, too. No sign that it had been tampered with. No trace of anything that shouldn't have been in there in the fluid or on the sides of the tubes or on the bag. Absolutely nothing out of the way at all."

Jess didn't say anything for a moment. A million thoughts chased one another through her mind. Chief among them was *It was* not *a hallucination.* Followed closely by *I don't think.*

In the end, what it boiled down to was, there were three possibilities: Her instincts to the contrary, it indeed had been just a very real hallucination. Or the lab that had examined the bag and its contents had made a mistake. Or Ryan was lying.

Why would he do that?

Three inches of dark suit pants beneath too-short scrubs. Shiny black shoes in a pool of blue light.

"Isn't that wonderful?" Judy enthused, giving her daughter a look that meant *Be enthusiastic or die.* "We don't have to be afraid somebody was trying to kill you anymore."

"Oh, yay," Jess said.

"I just thought knowing that might make you sleep a little easier." Ryan smiled at her. The same charming, eye-crinkling, you're-somebody-special smile he had used on her in Davenport's office weeks before. That she, to her everlasting shame, had believed was actually genuine and meant for her.

She did not smile back, and pretended not to notice that her mother was practically salivating over the man.

Who wears dark suits and shiny black shoes? Who had

*Mrs. Cooper described as being more like wardens than
protectors? Who was now parked outside her door giving
her the willies with the knowledge that she couldn't go
anywhere without their knowledge?*

Secret Service agents.

"It will," she said.

Like she believed him. Like she trusted him.

She didn't. Not for a minute. Maybe he was telling the
truth, and maybe he wasn't. Maybe he'd had that bag
tested, and maybe he hadn't. Maybe he was her friend—
and maybe he was her enemy.

He was a Secret Service agent, too.

If the Secret Service was somehow involved in this—
and she still couldn't quite get her mind around what she
thought "this" was—he was very likely involved, too.

In Mrs. Cooper's death.

Jess felt as though a giant hand had just grabbed her
heart and squeezed. *There. That's what you've been
pussyfooting around.* She suspected . . . that it wasn't an
accident at all.

Oh, God, I can't think about this now.

Too late: Her heart picked up the pace. Her mouth
went dry. She only hoped that none of what she was trying not to think about was showing on her face.

Because Ryan was watching her. Carefully. Like he
was trying to read her mind. His baby blues bored into
her eyes like information-seeking tractor beams.

For the first time in her life, Jess found herself thankful for her glasses. Superman himself with his X-ray vision couldn't read much through *her* lenses.

"You doin' okay?" Ryan asked in a confidential tone, as
if the question was for her ears alone and her mother wasn't
even in the room. That Southern drawl of his—she wouldn't
be surprised to learn he practiced it just to make it sexier—
was more pronounced than usual. It was *intimate*. Just like
his smile. Which he probably practiced, too.

"I'll live."

Giving her a hard sideways glance that was mom code for *What's the matter with you?* her mother added, "She's doing so well; the doctor who came in this morning said they'll probably release her in the next couple of days. He said all she needs now is some time to heal, and maybe some rehab. Because she's still having trouble with her legs, you know. And . . . other things. And she's in some pain."

Mo-ther. Do you always have to tell everybody everything you know? Answer, arrived at with silent, groaning resignation: *Yes, you do.*

"I'm sorry to hear she's in pain. But I'm glad she's doing so well otherwise." Ryan flashed one of those smiles at Judy, then looked again at Jess, who gave him a quick little—grim—smile of her own. "You remembering any more about what happened? About the crash?"

His voice was gentle. His eyes were sharp.

Dream on, pretty boy. That stupid I'm not.

Jess shook her head. "Where the accident's concerned, my mind's a complete blank."

"And let's hope it stays that way." Judy shuddered and shook her head. "Why on earth would you even want to remember? It's just so horrible I hate thinking about it. You're better off not having any kind of images of it in your head, honey. Just let it go."

"Yes, Mother." Jess's tone was so sweetly obedient that Judy gave her another of those hard looks. Okay, so she was going to hear it from her mother later. It was worth it.

"If it does start coming back to you, I hope you'll let me know. We're still trying to figure out exactly what happened. And the press—well, they'll make your life hell if you let them. Better to let any new information come out through official channels."

She knew what he meant: *official channels like him.*

"You'll be the first person I tell if I remember anything," she promised. *Liar, liar, pants on fire.*

"I know it's early days to be talking about this, but the Cooper family wants to ..." he began, but then the door opened without warning and he broke off. Which was too bad: Jess would have been interested in hearing his version of what the Cooper family wanted just so that she could be sure to avoid it.

Chapter 11

"JESS, YOU'RE AWAKE," Grace said happily as she entered. She was carrying a pizza and looking hot, as usual, in jeans, boots, and her favorite black leather motorcycle jacket. Behind her, Maddie had an arm wrapped around a brown paper bag. Her other arm hung by her side, weighted down by the big red plastic tote bag her mother had used for her beauty essentials for as long as Jess could remember. Despite everything, the sight wrung a slight smile out of Jess.

What was the first sure sign I was going to live? My mom had her beauty bag brought to the hospital.

"Hey, guys," Jess said.

"Hi, Jess. Hi, Mark." Grace, who liked good-looking men every bit as much as Judy did, smiled at Ryan as she put the pizza box down on the empty extra bed. Men fell for Grace by the boatload and always had, but Ryan's answering smile was no different than the one he'd bestowed on Judy—or, for that matter, Jess.

In other words, it dazzled with practiced charm. Grace's animated expression made it clear that despite her umpteen past and present boyfriends, she was no more immune than the rest of them.

What Ryan's reaction was to Grace, Jess couldn't tell. The eyes behind the smile were unreadable.

"You would not believe how bad it is out there. They know who we are now—we practically had to fight our way through." Grace tossed her hair—for Ryan's benefit, Jess knew—and opened the pizza box.

"Who are you talking about?" Jess asked.

"The press. They're, like, lying in wait out there in the parking lot. They keep asking us how you're doing, and who's called, and if you've said anything about the accident. Of course, we don't tell them anything." She cast Ryan a smiling glance. He acknowledged it with another slight smile of his own, which Jess interpreted to mean her family was keeping silent on his orders. Grace's gaze shifted back to Jess. "Oh, and I ran into Bruce Minsky and he asked me to give him a call and let him know when he can stop by the hospital to see you. He said he'd been trying to call you here in the room and on your cell, too, but not getting any answer. Which, after I told him you've been unconscious, he perfectly understood, of course."

Bruce Minsky was a junior accountant employed by the giant accounting firm that did work for Davenport, Kelly, and Bascomb. He and Jess had been on exactly four dates, three for coffee and once for dinner—actually, fish sandwiches eaten at her apartment while they went over some financial records for a case Davenport wanted Bruce's boss to testify about. Bruce seemed smitten. Jess was less so. Probably because they were so much alike. Both nose-to-the-grindstone types. Both total straight arrows. Both a little uncomfortable with the opposite sex. When the two of them got together, it was, in her opinion, kind of like a geek-o-rama.

"I don't want visitors. And I don't know where my phone is."

"But Bruce is so cute. With those little glasses and all."

Jess started to make a face at her sister, but it hurt too much. Which was probably just as well. Ignoring her was the dignified thing to do. And the only thing that worked in the long run.

"I told Grace we should try to sneak in through one of the side doors, but she wouldn't do it." Maddie plopped the grocery sack on the bed beside the pizza box and started rummaging through it. "I think she just likes being on TV."

"You can get on TV by just walking into the hospital?" Jess asked, bemused, as Maddie pulled out a package of paper plates.

Grace nodded. "You won't believe how huge this is. The whole city—the whole country—the whole world, even, probably—is practically shut down. Actually, you're lucky you're in the hospital so you don't have to deal with it. You're the one they really want to talk to. You're the survivor."

"Grace, don't worry your sister." Judy's tone was stern.

Mother and third-oldest daughter exchanged a look. Jess was left wondering what wasn't being said. She decided she didn't want to know.

"Anyway, we brought dinner." Sliding a slice of pizza onto a paper plate, Grace advanced on Jess's bed with it. "Your favorite: thin-crust pepperoni."

The smell reached Jess's nostrils, and she felt the faintest stirring in her stomach: hunger.

It felt good to be hungry. The last time she had been hungry was around eight on Saturday, when she'd made a grilled cheese sandwich while she'd read over some back cases in hopes of finding additional support for a position Davenport, Kelly, and Bascomb had taken on a pleading that had been overturned on appeal.

Just hours before the crash.

"I have Cherry Coke," Maddie added.

Her youngest sister was nowhere near as head-turningly beautiful as Grace, but Maddie was still very pretty in her own quieter way, with delicate features and a fresh-scrubbed look that didn't depend on makeup for its allure. Her natural dark-blond hair was pushed back from her face by a narrow purple headband so that it fell straight and shining to her shoulders, and her school uniform of white shirt, navy blazer, and khaki skirt looked almost stylish on her slender figure. She stood five-foot-six in her white ankle socks and sneakers. She looked like what she was, a wholesome, high-achieving, all-American high school girl with a bright future.

Jess had spent the entire previous week sick to her stomach at the thought that Maddie was pregnant. But now she was just glad to see her sister.

"Thanks," Jess said.

She smiled at Maddie, who was heading toward her with the can of soda extended temptingly. The Cherry Coke had been purchased especially for her and was a peace offering, she knew, because Maddie was the only one who knew she liked it. Last summer, with Judy tied down by the day care and unable to get away, she and Maddie had discovered it together when Jess, on her precious one week of vacation before starting full-time at Davenport, Kelly, and Bascomb, had driven her around the Northeast on a whirlwind tour of possible colleges—colleges that Jess hoped and prayed Maddie would get a scholarship to. They'd been full of big plans for Maddie's future—or at least, as Jess had realized when she thought back over it, she had been full of big plans for Maddie's future. Maddie really hadn't said much. The last time Jess and Maddie had been together, it had been over at Judy's house the weekend before the crash and the whole family had ended up shouting at one another over the ramifications of Maddie's pregnancy. Maddie had capped off the festivities by running from the house in a flood of tears. Then she'd spent the following week shacked up with the twenty-year-old auto-mechanic boyfriend no one had even known she had. She'd been with him the night of the crash, too, as it had turned out, and thus had been the last of the family to find out what had happened to Jess.

But that was then. This was now.

"You're welcome." Maddie handed the soda to Jess. Jess's slice of pizza already waited on the table beside the bed, courtesy of Grace. "There's plenty," Maddie added, smiling shyly at Ryan. "Just help yourself."

Jesus, he'd charmed her, too.

Ryan shook his head.

"Thanks, but I've got to go." He looked at Jess. "If you remember anything, or you need anything . . ."

"I'll be sure to let you know."

"Your mother has my number."

Jess nodded.

"I don't know if you should be eating pizza and a Cherry Coke just yet," Judy worried aloud, frowning at Jess as she carried her own slice of pizza toward the chair in the corner and sat down. "We should probably ask one of the nurses first."

"I'll be fine, Mom."

Judy frowned still, but her gaze left her daughter to follow Ryan as he headed toward the door.

"Bye, Mark."

"Bye, Mark," Grace and Maddie chorused.

He responded with a wave as he left the room.

"Yum," Grace said as the door clicked shut and she plopped down on the corner of Jess's bed. From her tone, she wasn't referring to the pizza she was nibbling on. "I could eat him for supper."

"He's too old for you," Judy said reprovingly.

Grace snorted. "Well, I hate to be the one to break this to you, but he's too young for you."

"Then it's a good thing I'm not interested in him, isn't it?" Judy bit into her pizza with dignity. "I'm just real grateful to him for everything he's done for Jess." Her gaze shifted to her oldest daughter. "Not that you seem to be very grateful yourself. You were downright snippy, missy."

Jess chose that moment to pick up her slice of pizza and take a cautious bite. Since she couldn't tell her mother the truth, the best thing would be not to tell her anything at all. And she couldn't talk with her mouth full, could she?

"You know, I think he likes you," Grace said to Jess. "He's been coming by to see you a lot."

Yes, because he's scared to death I'm going to remember something about the accident and tell somebody.

Right out of nowhere, that was the thought that popped into Jess's head.

It was followed almost immediately by another: *What happens if I do remember something? What if it's bad? As in, it provides evidence that Mrs. Cooper's accident was no accident?*

Jess felt cold sweat prickle to life around her hairline at the thought.

There it was again, that thing she hadn't wanted to face.

I don't think it was an accident.

She swallowed convulsively, and the tiny bit of pizza she was chewing caught in her throat and nearly choked her. It was suddenly as tasteless as a mouthful of rocks, and as hard to get down.

Now that the thought had taken form and shape in her mind, it was impossible to dislodge.

She couldn't prove it, of course. And she didn't want to. Didn't even want to have the idea taking root like an impossible-to-eradicate weed in her mind.

Because she knew what would happen if she did remember something that blew the whole accident scenario out of the water, knew it with the kind of conviction that no amount of evidence to the contrary was ever going to be able to change.

If I remember, they'll kill me.

Chapter 12

HE'D TOLD THE TRUTH.

At least, every word he'd said had been the truth.

That was the same thing, wasn't it?

No. Hell, no. Mark knew that was the answer even as he asked himself the question. What he'd said, while absolutely factual, was actually a pathetic lie.

And the need to tell such a lie was still worrying him.

The lab results had come back clean, just as he'd said. Everything that had been tested had checked out perfectly. There had been no traces of anything that shouldn't have been in that IV bag anywhere on it or in it. Nothing that shouldn't have been there in the tubing, either.

As for the catheter, the soft little tube that had actually delivered the contents of the IV into her vein, it was missing by the time the apparatus got to the lab and Brooks got his hands on it.

Given the chain of custody, it almost certainly hadn't been attached when he'd stowed the bag in his pocket. Because if it had become dislodged in his pocket, or in the transfer to Brooks—who had been horrified by Mark's less-than-protocol handling of the evidence and had promptly plastic-bagged everything—in the grocery store parking lot where they had agreed to meet, one of them would have found it.

Yep, everything had been clean. Every test Brooks had run had revealed nothing except the standard saline solution.

Which was the problem.

Mark had obtained Jessica's medical file. The one that started with her arrival in the emergency room, where the IV line had been placed.

According to the file, there was a whole raft of medications that should have been in that IV fluid.

They weren't there.

None of them. Not one. No trace.

Just plain old saline solution. Generic. Standard.

No trace of her blood or DNA on the tubing, although usually when an IV was inserted there was a little bit of a backflow as the nurse made sure she or he had a vein.

Not in this case. Nada.

No catheter, either. Nothing at all to connect the unit to her.

If the thing had ever been used, Brooks said he couldn't tell it.

Which meant what, exactly?

That the IV unit he'd removed from her room and had tested was not the one that had been used on Jessica Ford.

There were other possibilities, of course, because there were always other possibilities, but in this case they were so convoluted he got a headache trying to work them all out. The bottom line was, the most likely explanation under the circumstances was that the IV units had been switched, probably in the brief period that had elapsed from the time she had pulled it from her arm to the time he'd burst into the room.

Which meant she almost certainly had been attacked right there under his nose in her hospital room, just as she had claimed.

And the attacker, upon realizing that he'd failed in his

objective, which Mark was going to assume was Jess's murder, knew that the doctored bag could provide solid evidence of what had gone down, grabbed the incriminating IV bag, put up a fresh one, which he would have brought with him for just that purpose, and somehow made it out of the room without being seen by him or anyone else.

Mark tried for what must have been the hundredth time to visualize the room as it had looked when he had barreled into it. He'd been on high alert, looking all around, ready to take down an intruder—but in thinking back on it, the room never quite became clear to him. He remembered it being filled with shadows and distracting things, including a dividing curtain that swayed in the breeze of the opened door, a bed that moved as he went past it, and that damned open bathroom door.

At the time his primary focus had been on locating Jess.

Someone could have slipped out.

While he'd knelt beside her. No, wait, wouldn't the hospital personnel racing toward the room have noticed someone coming out the door? So the next window of opportunity would have been in the mass confusion after everyone else had arrived in the room.

The simple thing to do, of course, would be to check the security tapes and see who was in the vicinity around the time of the attack who shouldn't have been there. There were two cameras in each corridor, filming everything that went down in them. Spotting a suspicious individual should have been a piece of cake.

But the cameras for the third floor had mysteriously turned up without film in them, an oversight on the security staff's part—or something more ominous?

Mark's vote went to something more ominous.

"Goddamn it, Lowell, don't tell me nothing went down in that hospital."

Despite the accusation in it, Mark's voice was hushed as he slid into the red vinyl corner booth where the Chief of Staff was already sipping a cup of coffee while he looked over the menu.

They were meeting at the IHOP on the fringes of Anacostia, a troubled D.C. neighborhood where the press would not expect anybody to turn up.

"God Almighty, are you still going on about that?" Lowell shook his head in disgust. "I already told you, whatever did or did not happen there had nothing in the world to do with us."

Mark's eyes narrowed as they fastened on Lowell, but before he could reply he saw the waitress, a tiny gray-haired grandma-type in IHOP's trademark uniform and sensible shoes, bearing down on them. Only three of the other booths were occupied. Two guys who looked like truckers plowed through an enormous breakfast in one, an AARP-type couple who probably went with the RV parked outside nibbled doughnuts and read the paper in another, and the third was occupied by an old street guy with grimy fingers nursing a cup of coffee.

"Can I get you some coffee?" the waitress asked. When they nodded, she poured each a cup.

Caffeine was something he desperately needed at the moment. He had spent most of the previous night at Quantico, where the death car, as the press were now calling it, had been taken via flatbed truck after the accident and where it was now being held in a warehouse to keep the telephoto lenses of the press from getting any more ghoulish shots of it. Officially, he didn't have clearance to look at it, but unofficially he had friends in the Bureau who gave him access to the car and to the files that went with it. The official cause of the crash—an overcorrection made at a high rate of speed, possibly because of an animal of some sort on the road, although that last was pure speculation—had already been determined. It had been trumpeted all over the world, and given that the world supposed Mrs. Cooper to have been rushing to a dying friend's bedside when the crash occurred, it even made sense.

Since Mark had been around when that particular bit of spin had been decided on (because Mrs. Cooper did indeed have a friend in the named hospital that night), he knew damned well it wasn't true. Which once again begged the question: What the hell had the First Lady of the United States been doing in that car?

Mark knew that he would never pass another peaceful night until he had the answer.

The waitress left. Mark fixed Lowell with a grim look.

"Jessica Ford doesn't know squat about the First Lady's habits, and doesn't remember anything about the accident. Nothing, you understand? She's no threat to anybody. I want to make that crystal clear."

Lowell took another sip of coffee and met his gaze over the rim of the cup.

"You sure about that?"

The waitress returned, asking if they were ready to order.

"I'm ready," Lowell said, and told her what he wanted.

For the sake of not attracting attention, or at least Mark assumed that was his motive, Lowell had clapped an Orioles cap on his head, and removed his expensive suit jacket. His blue shirt and rep tie were generic enough in appearance to go unnoticed. Mark was similarly attired, minus the baseball cap, although his white shirt and gray tie were genuinely generic, bought on sale at Macy's. Lowell's round, ruddy face was well known in government and political circles but unlikely to be recognized here. Unless they were very unlucky, knowledge of this meeting would stay between the two of them, which was how they both wanted it.

The waitress looked at Mark.

"You?"

He ordered, too, bacon and eggs and toast and orange juice. He figured he needed the energy. Just like he hadn't been sleeping, he hadn't been eating well since the crash. His stomach was too tense; he felt like if he swallowed more than a few bites, it would come right back up.

It didn't help that everywhere he looked, from TV to the front page of newspapers and magazines to black-bordered "in memoriam" billboards looking down over the expressways, he saw Annette Cooper's face.

My watch. He couldn't get the guilt out of his system.

The waitress left.

He eyeballed Lowell.

"Yeah, I'm sure."

"Really? Then why did she call Davenport last night and tell him she thinks there's something wrong with what's being said about the accident?"

Mark blinked. He didn't know why he was surprised, but he was. He knew how this worked: broken legs and arms, burglarized offices, "accidental" fires—those were all in a day's work in the high-stakes world of politics. An illegal wiretap or two was hardly even worthy of mention.

"You monitoring her phone calls?" He kept his voice carefully even.

"What do you think? Of course we are. The funeral's in two days' time, and nobody wants any kind of crap about Mrs. Cooper getting out to spoil it. The lady—and the family—deserves to be allowed to rest in peace."

Mark couldn't argue with that. But he sure as hell could raise a stink over the method of containment he was becoming increasingly convinced someone had tried to employ. He decided to call Lowell's bluff and see what reaction he got.

"So somebody did try to kill Jessica Ford that night in the hospital."

"No. Hell, no." Lowell glared at him. "I already said that, all right? As far as I know, nobody did anything to little Miss What's-her-name in the hospital or anywhere else. What do you think I am?"

While Mark debated about whether or not to tell him, the waitress arrived, bringing their food. She slapped it down in front of them, asked if she could get them anything else, and took herself off when they declined.

"You get the word out to whoever's interested that Jessica Ford is not a threat," Mark said. The thing was, Mark knew that Lowell might be telling the absolute truth and still somebody in the big, amorphous, interconnected circles of shadow people who protected the President and his family might have targeted her in the panic following the First Lady's death. "I'm taking care of it. You tell them that."

"I tell you what you need to do." Lowell dumped ketchup on his eggs. Mark had to look away. His stomach was bothering him again, knotted so tight he knew he wouldn't be able to choke down so much as a bite of the triangle of buttered toast he'd picked up. He put it back down on the plate without even making the attempt. "You need to get her to sign a secrecy agreement—offer her whatever money you have to—and get her the hell out of town until this blows over. I've checked into her background—she doesn't have a pot to piss in, and never has. Comes from nothing. She'll be glad to get the money. And to keep her mouth shut for it."

"The problem with a secrecy agreement," Mark pointed out in measured tones, "is that it exists. If she doesn't know anything, it clues her in that there just might be something to know. And if it somehow goes public, it makes it look like there's a conspiracy. Like somebody has something to hide."

"Hell, we do have something to hide. There's no reason in the world for anybody to know that Mrs. Cooper had a problem, or that she was out there trying to score drugs when she died."

"You sure that's what she was doing?"

"It's looking like it. Why else would she sneak off like that? With that amount of money in her purse?" Lowell shoveled down his doctored eggs with enthusiasm. Watching was making even the coffee turn sour in Mark's stomach.

"I don't know."

There was a lot he didn't know, Mark reflected—like what state Mrs. Cooper had been in when she left the residence that night, or if anybody besides Prescott had been with her when she'd headed out to the Rose Garden. One reason he was having so much trouble figuring out those things was that he'd been put on official leave: Just as he had suspected, his had been the first head on the chopping block. He was still on the payroll, still in the loop; he was still working, as was evidenced by his careful coordination of the babysitting of Jess Ford. But all that was on the QT, at the behest of Lowell and the rest of the President's inner circle. Because they knew he was loyal, knew he'd keep his mouth shut, knew he'd get the job done for them. For the record, though, he was in deep shit, complete with all the media finger-pointing that came with it. The worst thing about it was being denied access to the very things he needed to use to get answers. Answers to the questions about that night that were eating him up. The White House surveillance tapes, for example, were not available to him; they'd been turned over to the investigative arm of the Secret Service. Between them and the FBI, the crash probe was being conducted at the highest levels, as his boss had assured him when he'd pressed for access. Lowell had refused to intervene.

Your job is to handle the survivor, Lowell had said. *Let the trained investigators handle the investigation.*

The trained investigators who didn't know anything about Mrs. Cooper, and thus had no clue what to be on the lookout for. Which, maybe, was the point.

Or maybe he was just growing increasingly suspicious with age. And experience.

"So what do you suggest?" Lowell stabbed a sausage link with his fork and took a huge bite.

"We pay her off, but we channel the money through someone else. If it comes from us, she's immediately suspicious about why, right? What we don't want is for her to start asking herself that. We just want her to take the money, keep her mouth shut, and fade out of the picture."

"Amen to that. You sure you can fix it?"

"I'm sure."

"So we're good?" Lowell polished off the last of his meal and took a quick last swallow of coffee as he stood up.

Mark looked up at him. "As long as nothing else happens to Miss Ford."

"Nothing *did* happen to her."

The waitress had seen Lowell stand up and was heading their way with the check. Mark stood up, too, his stomach as tight as a clenched fist, his breakfast uneaten. What he needed, and he hated to admit it, was a cigarette. He'd quit four years ago, gone cold turkey since, and now he was craving nicotine in the worst way.

The truth was, as he'd discovered about himself before, he really didn't handle stress all that well.

"Was there something the matter with the food?" the waitress asked as she handed him the bill. Lowell was already on his way out the door. Mark understood: Mark had requested the meeting, so breakfast was on him.

"Turns out I wasn't hungry after all." Mark put a couple of twenties down on the table, more than enough to cover the food and a tip, and followed Lowell.

Who was already gone.

Funny, he reflected as he pushed through the door into the gray bleakness of a cold April dawn and felt the chill of the rushing wind bite into him, he didn't feel any better about things now than he had before the meeting.

The day was just getting started, and it was already on its way downhill. And he still had Prescott's funeral to attend.

Chapter 13

IN THE END, avoiding the media had been surprisingly easy, Jess reflected as she looked out the concave glass window of the helicopter that was at that moment carrying her toward D.C. Avoiding Mark Ryan, who'd been hovering around her and her family like a hungry bat with a cluster of mosquitoes in its sights, had been equally simple: She'd simply waited to go until he wasn't around. Leaving the hospital by helicopter had worked like a charm; apparently, no one had expected it. Of course, it also helped that her exodus had been carefully timed to coincide with Annette Cooper's funeral service.

The thought made her queasy. Or maybe it was the motion of the helicopter, swooping up and down like a hawk riding the gusting air currents as they followed the twisty path of the Potomac past Reagan National Airport and into D.C. As Davenport's assistant, Jess was no stranger to helicopters, but seeing the Capitol laid out before her like a sparkling miniature village was something that never failed to awe her.

Even today.

"Mr. Davenport wants you to feel free to use the condo for as long as you need. He anticipates that it will be for at least several weeks," Marian said.

"That's nice of him."

Davenport's longtime personal secretary was buckled into the cushy leather seat next to Jess. She was sixty-one, unmarried, and totally devoted to Davenport and, to a lesser extent, the firm. Tall, lean, and elegant, with coarse iron-gray hair that she wore in an elaborate chignon, she was dressed in a pale gray skirt suit and a lavender blouse. Her features were strong rather than attractive, her makeup was minimal but well done, and she was very good at blending into the woodwork until Davenport needed her.

Which he constantly did. As far as everything that wasn't connected to legal research (Jess's department) was concerned, Marian was Davenport's right hand. She knew him better than his young third wife, sent the gifts, made the reservations, fielded his phone calls, set up his meetings, and then sat in on them taking notes. If Davenport had a secret that Marian didn't know, Jess would be surprised. No, she would be shocked. But Marian kept Davenport's secrets, too.

Besides the pilot, who was sitting up front and was separated from the passenger compartment by a partition, she and Jess were alone in the helicopter. According to Marian, Davenport had decided that the fewer people who knew where they were going today, the better.

The safer. But Jess filled that in for herself.

The million-dollar question was, did Marian know what was going on? That Davenport was afraid of something concerning Annette Cooper's death, concerning the crash? Or was this one secret Davenport had kept from her?

Jess didn't know, and she couldn't ask. She wasn't going to say a word on the subject to anyone until after she had talked to her boss.

Davenport would know what to do, where to go with her suspicions, to whom it was safe to tell them. Because right now, she didn't feel like she could trust anybody else.

Not the cops, not the FBI, and certainly not the Secret Service, all of which had sent representatives to question her about the crash once they learned she was conscious and coherent. She had said the same thing to each of them: *I don't remember.*

They had gone away.

She had been on pins and needles, fearing they would come back. Which was why she'd been so glad to leave today, twenty-four hours ahead of schedule.

The Secret Service agents outside her room, all of whom had become accustomed to her comings and go-ings inside the hospital over the last few days as she'd suffered through more tests and X-rays and treatments and had worked with physical therapists to regain her mobility, had followed her at a discreet distance as she'd headed for the elevator some thirty minutes earlier. Their faces were vaguely familiar because they'd been around, but she didn't know either of them and they didn't know her in any kind of personal way, which made telling them that she needed a few minutes alone with her companion—Marian—and then closing the elevator doors in their faces all the easier. After that, it was a piece of cake: a trip up to the hospital's helipad, bundling into the chopper, and taking off. She was free.

Just like that. After tossing and turning through a sleepless night and then suffering butterfly-inducing anticipation all morning, the ease of her escape— because that was how she thought of it—was almost anticlimactic.

Maybe Ryan wasn't at the hospital because he was attending Mrs. Cooper's funeral. If he'd been there, she had a feeling that getting away wouldn't have been quite so simple.

She hadn't even told her mother and sisters where she

was going. Just that her boss was sending someone for her, and she would be staying in one of his houses for a while until media interest died down. Grace had packed her a suitcase and brought it to the hospital that morning. Jess had parted from her and Judy and Sarah and Maddie with a round of weepy hugs. Judy had wanted her to come home with them, but Jess, with Marian backing her up, had been adamant: Davenport was a pro at handling crises of all sorts, and she would do what he wanted her to do. Reluctantly, Judy saw the sense of that: Like the hospital, her house and Jess's apartment were still under siege, and some reporters had even started waving fat checks around in hope of procuring an interview.

"I'll be fine. I'll call you," she promised her mother. The truth was, she was desperate to get away from them, terrified that somehow what she knew, or suspected, would be conveyed to them and then they would be in danger, too. Or maybe they didn't even have to really know or suspect anything. Maybe just being in her vicinity was enough to make them targets.

And maybe she was just totally paranoid, too.

But she didn't think so.

"Mr. Davenport wanted me to assure you that you're still drawing your salary, by the way," Marian said. "I made the arrangements for it to be direct-deposited into your account yesterday. It will continue until you're able to come back to work. And he said to tell you that you'll be getting a large settlement soon."

Jess couldn't help it. Even under the circumstances, the prospect of obtaining a substantial amount of money made her heartbeat quicken. It was a result, she was sure, of having spent almost her whole life never being sure that she and her family would have enough groceries to last out the week, or a roof over their heads from month to month.

Lifting her eyebrows with what she hoped looked like only polite interest, she said, "A large settlement?"

Marian looked impatient. "You were badly injured in a car wreck. The limousine company and its driver are liable, among others. Ordinarily it would take months, possibly years, to negotiate just compensation. Given the circumstances, though, Mr. Davenport was able to do very nicely for you. All you have to do is sign the papers."

Clearly, working around lawyers for so many years had an effect on people, because Marian was sounding like one herself.

"What papers?" If Jess's tone was faintly wary, well, she guessed she had reason. One thing she had learned for sure over the years was that if it sounded too good to be true, it usually was. "And how large a settlement are we talking about?"

"Mr. Davenport will explain. He'll go over everything with you when you talk to him later."

Fair enough. "What time is he coming?"

The look Marian gave her was withering. "When it's convenient for him."

"I'll be sure and be ready, then." If there was a smidgen of dryness to her tone, Marian didn't appear to notice.

The two of them were publicly cordial, but they were not friends. Jess sometimes wondered if Marian, jealous of her own position in Davenport's life, didn't resent Davenport's increasing reliance on Jess.

Jess said nothing else, and the conversation ended. Her gaze drifted down to the scene below. For the first time in her memory, nothing was moving on the Beltway or 295 or any of the other arteries into and around the city. Cars had pulled over to the side of the roads; the expressways were clear. Seeing the flashing blue and red strobe lights at the entrance ramps, Jess realized that police had them blocked off. Instead of cars, D.C.'s center was filled with people. Hordes of them, tens of thousands of them, stretching from the Lincoln Memorial to Capitol Hill in a near-solid carpet, massing in Constitution Gardens, surrounding the Vietnam Veterans Memorial and the White House and the Washington Monument, crowding around the Tidal Basin and the Reflecting Pool and filling the Mall, filling the downtown, filling the whole of D.C. for as far as she could see, packing the streets and the public spaces so that everywhere you looked they were all you saw, eclipsing the buildings and monuments, the variegated colors of their clothing putting to shame even the intense pinks of the cherry blossoms for which D.C. was famous.

She remembered that Congress had declared today a national day of mourning.

A motorcade, composed of vehicles that from this height appeared no bigger than the Hot Wheels cars her nephews loved, caught her eye. It moved slowly down Constitution Avenue. From the tiny flags flying on the lead cars and the number of long black vehicles involved, Jess knew what it had to be: Mrs. Cooper's funeral cortege transporting her body from the Capitol Rotunda, where it had been lying in state, to the National Cathedral for her funeral service.

Of course. It was just after one-thirty. The funeral was scheduled to begin precisely at two p.m. The dolorous tolling of church bells all over the city—that was the sound that was barely audible over the thumping of the helicopter's rotors; she only just identified it—rang out in long peals of collective grief.

Throat suddenly tight, Jess leaned back in her seat, unable to watch further. Remembering the sweats-clad woman who'd done shots in the bar, who had been obviously frightened of something but was nevertheless determined to escape, whose arm she had taken and flight she had so disastrously shared, she ached inside. Closing her eyes, she said a silent prayer for the souls of Annette Cooper, and the Secret Service agent and the driver who had died with her. Then she added her own fervent thanks for being allowed to live.

When she opened her eyes, it was to discover that Marian was watching her, a sour twist to her mouth.

"Mr. Davenport is sick with grief about this." Marian clasped her hands tightly in her lap. "He seems to feel that if he'd gone himself that night instead of sending you, Mrs. Cooper wouldn't be dead now."

The unspoken subtext was that she'd screwed up. The hard gleam in Marian's eyes made the message unmistakable. Did Davenport share Marian's view? Jess hadn't thought of that. But her conscience was clear. Whatever had happened, she knew in her heart she could not have prevented it. She was as much a victim of the accident as the other three. The only difference was that she had survived.

So far.

That thought made her go cold all over. She tried to ignore it.

"If Mr. Davenport had gone that night instead of me," Jess pointed out, "he might very well be dead now, too."

That shut Marian up, just as Jess had intended. The other woman pressed her lips together and stared straight ahead.

Instead of looking down again, Jess carefully concentrated on the bright blue sky and cottony white clouds all around them. Though crisp, it was a bright, sunny spring day, with a brisk wind that blew the clouds around like feathers. The air, as she knew from her quick journey across the hospital rooftop to the helicopter, smelled sweet and fresh with scents of new grass and blossoming baby leaves and just-blooming flowers.

The day was too beautiful for a funeral.

Her phone began to ring. Jess's eyes widened. The sound was so *normal,* so much a part of her ordinary, everyday existence before the accident, that in the context of what was happening to her now it was almost bizarre. It took her a second to realize what it was, and then she unzipped her purse, which the hospital had given to her mother along with a bundle containing the now-ruined clothes she had been wearing when the accident had occurred. Judy had brought the purse to the hospital that morning in anticipation of Jess's departure later in the day. Fishing her phone out, she saw the number and name on her caller ID: Laura Ogilvy, one of her lawyer friends from work. No doubt calling to ask how she was and to glean all the gossip she could.

A glance at Marian, who looked on with way too much interest, made her initial reaction certain: She wasn't going to take the call.

"You're not going to answer?" Marian asked with disapproval when the call went over to voice mail to join the other forty-seven messages she had waiting.

"My battery's low. Anyway, I don't really feel like talking right now."

Which was the truth: She didn't. She was physically much stronger, although the outward signs of her injuries—the bruises, the stitches—were still apparent. Face it: Mentally, she was all over the place. She knew what she knew, she suspected what she suspected.

And she remembered . . . more than she wanted to.

The Watergate complex, famous for its explosion into the national conversation when it was the site of the notorious burglary that had torpedoed Richard Nixon's presidency, was actually a semicircular grouping of upscale skyscrapers overlooking the Potomac that housed a hotel, apartments, and condominiums along with a variety of pricey restaurants and shops. As the helicopter set down atop one gleaming silver tower, Jess got a glimpse of a sparkling fountain set in a green lawn surrounded by neatly clipped hedges in a courtyard below. Then the runners settled, the motor was cut, and the rotors slowed. Jess unbuckled her seat belt just as the pilot opened the door.

He lifted the wheelchair from the cabin. Marian got out first, and Jess followed, climbing down into a cold, stiff wind that belied the day's sunny brightness. Her back ached with every movement, and she was as stiff as cheap new jeans, but she was able to walk the few steps to the wheelchair, which the pilot held for her, without feeling like she was going to collapse. Still, she sank into it thankfully, and was glad that it was motorized so that she could get to the elevator without relying on Marian's help. The other woman's expression was unyielding as she carried Jess's suitcase.

It took just a few minutes to reach the apartment.

"Now that we're here, I can tell you that Mr. Davenport will be busy for the rest of the afternoon. He'll call me with further instructions sometime after six."

Marian spoke behind her as Jess rolled across the spacious, gray-carpeted living room with its white leather couches and chairs and black Lucite tables toward the big picture window. Jess noticed that she was careful to subtly stress the *me* in that last sentence, thus confirming her impression that in Marian's own mind at least, the woman was battling to retain the supremacy of her position in Davenport's life.

Jess just nodded in reply. They were on the twelfth floor, so she had a panoramic view of the Georgetown Channel of the Potomac curving around Roosevelt Island below. There were no boats on the river below her, not even the big commercial barges that seemed to run continuously, and even as she wondered at it, it hit her that it was because the entire country, and especially

D.C., was shut down in a paroxysm of grief over the terrible tragedy that was reaching its culmination at that exact moment.

Marian sank down on the couch and flipped on the TV.

The slow, sad notes of a military dirge caught Jess by surprise. She turned around. Her gaze was riveted by the pale stone and soaring Gothic arches of the National Cathedral filling the big TV. Her breathing suspended, her hands clamped around the edges of the wheelchair's arms, and her throat threatened to close up.

She was watching the event live.

A military honor guard carried a flower-draped coffin up the wide front steps. Marines in dress blues stood at attention on either side. Behind the coffin came the President of the United States, his face as white and still as if it had been carved from marble, his two adult children and their families close behind him. They were followed by Wayne Cooper, the President's father; his sister, Elizabeth; and a gaggle of other family members Jess didn't recognize. A contingent of Secret Service agents glancing cautiously from side to side and receiving instructions via earbuds formed a moving wall of protection that fanned out on either side of the family party and brought up the rear. The hearse and the long black motorcade surrounding it waited at the curb. In the opposite lane from the motorcade, boxy white news vans with satellite feeds formed a nucleus around which a heaving mass of reporters, held at bay by stern-faced lines of uniformed cops manning sawhorse barriers, narrated the proceedings for their various audiences. Other than the motorcade and the media, the street was empty, obviously having been cleared in anticipation of the arrival and eventual departure of the funeral cortege. Hundreds of mourners lined the sidewalk across the street from the cathedral, pressing up against more sawhorses controlled by more somber-looking cops. The camera panned the crowd, and suddenly thousands of ordinary citizens, dressed in everything from jeans and sweatshirts to business suits to the ethnic attire of many cultures, packed the shot for as far as the eye could see.

"... sensational story reaches its tragic culmination now, as the First Lady of the United States is carried in her coffin into the National Cathedral. Annette Wiley Cooper first appeared on the national scene five years ago, when her husband became Vice President upon the death of then Vice President Thomas Haynes. This past November, David Cooper won the presidency, and in the brief months since his inauguration, Annette Cooper cemented her hold on the affection of a nation. The causes close to her heart were education and literacy, and ..."

"Mr. Davenport is there in the cathedral, you know." Marian cast an evil look Jess's way as she spoke over the TV. "I was invited to attend, too, but he asked me to stay with you instead."

"I'm sorry you had to miss it." Jess's careful politeness was an attempt to neutralize Marian's barely veiled venom. She didn't think it worked, but at least the other woman shifted her gaze back to the TV.

Jess did, too, to find that on the screen now it was night, with the flashing strobe lights of an ambulance painting bright bursts of blue and red across the small, dark-haired figure on a stretcher that was being loaded into its open back.

With a shock Jess realized she was looking at a taped shot that had been filmed in the immediate aftermath of the crash, and that the victim on the stretcher was her.

She swallowed hard.

"... sole survivor of the accident, attorney Jessica Ford. So far investigators say she has been unable to remember any of the details of what happened that night, although it is believed that she was accompanying Mrs.

Cooper on her doomed dash to the hospital at the request of Mrs. Cooper's longtime friend and personal lawyer, and Miss Ford's boss, John Davenport, who sent the car. . . ."

Suddenly Jess found herself watching another taped shot, of Davenport walking up the steps of the National Cathedral with his tall, blond, ex-model wife, Brianna, at his side. Fit and trim at fifty-eight, with thinning white hair and a thick white mustache set off by a tan that Jess knew was carefully maintained, he looked nothing if not distinguished. Both he and his wife, with whom he had two young children, were clad in black, both wore sunglasses, and both emanated Washington-insider glamour. It was clear that the scene had taken place only a short time ago, while the mourners filed into the church prior to the casket's arrival.

"I hate to interrupt, but they're getting ready to take Mrs. Cooper inside now." Katie Couric broke in on the reporter's recitation, and the shot turned live again as the coffin was carried into the sanctuary to the strains of *Ruffles and Flourishes*. Still walking behind it, President David Cooper bowed his head. One on either side of him now, his children clasped his hands.

Jess couldn't watch any longer. Chest tight, throat burning, she thought of Annette Cooper as she had last seen her and felt a dreadful, tearing grief for the woman and her family. Tears springing to her eyes, she fled to the nearest bedroom.

And cried until she had no more tears left to shed.

She wasn't prone to crying. In fact, she almost never cried. She was the stoic, practical oldest child who kept her head in any crisis and who everyone looked to for a solution to any problem. Ms. Fix-it, her mother called her. But since the accident—well, *Cry Me a River* wasn't only the title to a song.

By the time she emerged into the living room again,

it was nearly nine p.m. She had slept, been awakened by
Marian with the news that Davenport would be there at
nine, refused an offer of carryout for supper, then slept
some more. Finally she had gotten up, taken a long
shower, and dressed in anticipation of the meeting with
Davenport. Restoring her glasses to her purse, she
popped in a new pair of contacts for the first time since
the accident. She blow-dried her hair into its usual no-
nonsense style, and did what she could with what little
makeup she possessed to cover the now yellowing
bruises. Fortunately, Grace had packed one of her favorite work outfits, a black Armani skirt suit that she'd gotten on major sale at Filene's Basement and wore with a
white silk blouse, which, since Jess kept the entire outfit
on a single hanger in her closet, her sister had included.
Her good black heels, the expensive ones Grace had borrowed, were in there, too, and Jess had to fight off an instant, automatic flashback to last Saturday night as she
slid her feet into them. Her favorite old sneakers, just
like the ruined clothes she'd been wearing at the time of
the crash, were presumably in the bundle that had been
given to her mother. She had worn brand-new sneakers
with a sweatsuit in the helicopter earlier, fearing that any
departure from what she normally wore around the hospital would alert the Secret Service agents outside her
room to her pending escape. But tonight, because she
was meeting Davenport, she dressed as she would for
work; looking professional was part of getting ahead.

The TV was still on when Jess rolled into the living
room. So was a lamp beside the couch. The rest of the
apartment was dark. The curtains were closed. Marian
sat in a corner of the couch, her jacket discarded so that
she wore only her lavender blouse and gray skirt, shoes
off, slender legs drawn up beside her, the remote control
in her hand.

Home movies of Annette Cooper growing up were

playing on the screen. Jess took one look and refused to look again.

"Have you heard from Mr. Davenport?" she asked. It was obvious that he was not yet there.

Marian nodded and stood up, clicking the remote to turn off the TV.

"He asked me to bring you to meet him. Your appointment is at nine-thirty sharp." Marian stuck her feet in her shoes as she spoke, then pulled on her suit jacket.

Jess frowned. "Where are we going?"

Marian scooped up a set of keys from the bowl on the coffee table and headed toward the door. Jess turned—she was getting really good at working the wheelchair—to keep her in sight.

"*We* aren't going anywhere." There was an unmistakable edge of bitterness to Marian's voice. Her eyes were cold as they raked Jess. "He wants to meet with *you*. On your own. Tonight, I'm just your driver."

"Oh." Jess wasn't sure she liked the idea of that. Just the thought of getting in a car again gave her the willies. Kaleidoscopic memories of the accident crowded in on her without warning, and a shiver of dread slid over her skin. Then she gritted her teeth and forced them away. She couldn't spend the rest of her life afraid to ride in cars, for goodness' sake. This had to be overcome, and now was the time to start. Still, the sense of discomfort persisted. She didn't even know for certain that this arrangement had been made by Davenport. Maybe Marian had come up with it on her own, as part of a plot to eliminate someone she seemed to persist in seeing as her rival.

Now you really are getting paranoid, Jess scolded herself. If she had to trust somebody, and she did have to, because this was way too big to deal with on her own, then that somebody would be Davenport. And if there was anything that was certain in life, it was that Marian was absolutely loyal to him.

In other words, Marian would connive in Jess's murder only if Davenport asked her to.

Comforting thought.

"So are you coming?" Holding the door open, Marian looked back at her with obvious impatience.

Jess put the wheelchair in motion. "Right behind you."

They didn't speak again until they were in the elevator, heading down to the parking garage. Marian stood stiffly beside her, her arms folded over her chest, her attention focused on the door in front of her, refusing to look at Jess.

"So I'm meeting with Mr. Davenport where?" Jess tried rephrasing her earlier question. She was growing increasingly nervous, and a little conversation would be nice to keep the bad thoughts at bay.

"What, don't you like surprises? Wait and see." The nastiness in Marian's tone was unmistakable now. The glance she shot Jess was openly unfriendly.

Okay, the hostility was getting old. "Tell me something, Marian: What did I ever do to make you dislike me?"

Marian stiffened.

"You think you're more important to him than I am because you're a lawyer, don't you? Well, you're not. He only hired you out of that nothing law school you went to because you're a little worker bee who'll do the drudge work none of the other associates want to do."

There was a reason why one of the first things they taught you in law school was to never ask a question unless you're sure you want to hear the answer. Now the other woman's enmity, instead of being hidden, was right out there in the open.

"You know what? I'm fine with that," Jess said. And she was. She'd known all along what her role in the firm was. And she also knew that she was determined to work hard enough to rise above it.

Marian snorted. The elevator stopped and they got out.

The drive into the heart of the city was brief, uneventful, and largely silent. Traffic was heavy now that the funeral was over and the masses of people who'd poured into D.C. to mourn had started moving around, heading for places to eat, places to sleep. Likewise the sidewalks were packed, and the parks, and just about every available space where people could crash. Flags at every public building hung at half-mast. Funeral wreaths, black ribbons, and every imaginable religious symbol from crosses made out of twigs to carved-soap Buddhas adorned trees and lampposts and mailboxes by the hundreds. Other than that, D.C. was its vibrant self, alive again with light and sound and movement and the smells of food and car exhaust and the water surrounding the city.

Jess figured out where they were going only minutes before Marian drove into the parking garage at the side of the building that served the law offices of Davenport, Kelly, and Bascomb. There was no attendant on duty, so she used her pass card to get in, then drove straight to the elevator that was available only to building employees who had a special key.

Jess was too junior to have one.

"Mr. Davenport said you were to meet him in his office." Marian handed over the key. "I'll be down here waiting when you're ready to leave."

Chapter 14

AN OFFICE SKYSCRAPER at night is just naturally spooky, Jess decided as she rode the elevator up to the twentieth floor, the highest of the four floors that the law firm she worked for occupied—the floor that, naturally, contained Davenport's expansive private office, along with the expansive private offices of the firm's other partners and the less expansive but still impressive offices of a select few top associates. Jess's closet—which was how she thought of her own tiny, interior private office—was on the seventeenth floor, the firm's very lowest level. Just like she herself was at the firm's lowest level.

Down at street level, the building was brightly lit. Its impressive two-story bronze-and-glass entrance would be staffed by a doorman or two, who could summon security at the touch of a button. On the same block, retailers such as Burberry and Brooks Brothers drew window-shoppers who then went on to dine at such fashionable eateries as Michael's or The Inn at Farragut Park. Up here, the long halls were dimly lit and deserted, so deserted that the hum of the wheelchair's motor seemed to echo off the faux-finished tortoiseshell walls and the slick marble floors. The offices and conference rooms lining either side of the halls were dark. Their doors were closed and locked. Usually a few gung-ho souls—herself

included—would be still working at this hour, and the
janitorial staff was always around, cleaning floors and
bathrooms and the like, and thus there would be light
and sound and the impression of energy and warmth.
But on this particular Thursday, this National Day of
Mourning when the First Lady had been laid to rest, nobody was at work. The halls felt empty and cold.

Davenport's office was at the front of the building
overlooking Connecticut Avenue. The private elevator
that connected directly to the parking garage was at the
rear. Therefore, it required a journey of several anxiety-
compounding minutes to reach her target. Using the
wheelchair felt odd, but since as recently as this morning
her legs had threatened to give out on her when she had
done no more than walk to the bathroom and back on
her own, she was afraid that walking all the way from the
elevator to Davenport's office and back would be more
than she could handle. Plus, he never asked junior associates to sit down in his presence, and she was sure she
couldn't stand for any extended period. Of course, under
the circumstances, she *could* sit down, and of course he
wouldn't mind, but . . . it was less complicated all around
to use the wheelchair.

Jess's palms grew damp as she turned the final corner
and found herself in the last of the long halls that ended
at Davenport's office. This one was wide as well as long,
with a deep gold carpet running down the center. The
ceiling was high and coffered, and the walls were lined
with huge, expensive modern paintings that filled the
space between discreet mahogany doors with their polished brass plates announcing the names of the favored
associates who occupied them. Behind Jess was a bank
of gleaming brass client elevators that connected to the
lobby. In front of her, at the far end of the hall, was a reception area where supplicants—no, make that clients—
waited to see Davenport himself, and a long mahogany

desk where receptionists Denise Caple and JoAnne Subtelny politely repelled all but the favored few with automatic access or coveted appointments to see the great man. To the right was Marian's office.

Jess paused at the top of the hallway to take a long, wary look.

No one was there. The desks, the offices, the halls—the whole damned place—took on a completely different atmosphere when no people were around. The silence was absolute.

Okay, stop it. You're creeping yourself out.

She started moving again.

Jess had almost reached the reception desk when she saw that Davenport's door was ajar. Just a few inches, enough so that she could see that the office itself was dark inside.

Not good.

She let up on the wheelchair's controls. The thing stopped cold. She looked at that open door for a minute, considered the possibilities, weighed her options.

Her heart, which was already beating faster than normal, picked up the pace again. Her breathing quickened, too.

"Jessica?"

Jess almost jumped at the sheer unexpectedness of it. But the voice was Davenport's. No doubt about that, even if it was muffled a bit.

He was talking to her through the intercom on the reception desk, of course. Which meant that he was at his desk. That's where his end of the intercom was, and he had a little monitor on the credenza to his left, which, when turned on, allowed him to view the reception area.

Her shoulders slumped with relief. Then she realized that if he was talking to her, he could see her, and she sat taller in the chair and put her game face on.

"Hello, Mr. Davenport."

"Come on in."

Yeah, okay. Just as soon as my insides stop shaking.

Taking a deep breath, she rolled forward again, skirting the reception desk, pushing the door to his office open wide enough so that the wheelchair could get through.

His office was really a two-room suite with an opulently furnished sitting room complete with twin couches, a quartet of chairs, a wet bar, and all kinds of impressive accoutrements. That was the room she found herself in. The lights were off and the thick drapes were tightly drawn, which was why it had appeared dark from the hallway. To the left were doors leading into Davenport's private bathroom and a small kitchenette. To the right, an open door led into his actual office. Light streamed through its door, although not the bright light of artificial lighting. As she reached it and entered the huge corner office, Jess saw why.

All the lights were off, but the curtains were open to the max. Both outer walls were floor-to-ceiling windows, and the luminescence from the thousands of sparkling lights that lit up the city like a Christmas tree at night was bright enough to cast a lovely, otherworldly radiance over the entire office. Jess stopped abruptly, able for the moment to do nothing but absorb the breathtaking view. There was the glowing dome of the Capitol, the shining white obelisk of the Washington Monument, the White House itself. Then her attention was drawn by a movement inside the office to her left, and she realized there was someone behind the desk. Davenport, of course. Silhouetted against the background of the luminous windows, the desk appeared as no more than a long, black rectangle. Seated behind it, Davenport himself was a silhouette against the city he loved so much.

A sudden prickling at the back of her neck, as if her instincts were alerting her to another, unseen presence, made her catch her breath. The sensation was so strong that she felt compelled to glance behind her into the dark sitting room and then around the office to make sure they were completely alone.

They were. At least, as far as she could tell.

Still she felt tense. Uneasy.

"Drink?" Davenport turned on his desk lamp. Now she could see him properly—a big man sitting in a big chair behind a big desk. His always perfectly groomed white hair was disheveled, as though he had run his hands through it more than once. He wore a white shirt and solid black tie, probably the same ones he had worn to the funeral earlier, only now the shirt was rumpled and unbuttoned at the neck, and the tie was askew. She could also see the empty glass on his desk, and the bottle of Chivas he held up invitingly.

"No, thanks."

He tipped the bottle, poured some into the glass. Jess could tell—from many things, like the slight unsteadiness of his hand, the ruddiness of his face, the twitch in his cheek near his mouth—that he'd been drinking before she got there. Heavily, she feared. The bottle was more than half empty, and there was whisky residue already in the glass when he started to pour. A small puddle of liquid around the glass gleamed in the yellowish lamplight.

"I don't think Mrs. Cooper's death was an accident."

There it was; she'd put it right out there on the table before she could lose her nerve, have second thoughts, chicken out, however you wanted to put it.

He heard her; she could tell he did because his eyes narrowed and he frowned a little. But he barely checked in the act of swallowing about half the glass of booze.

"She had problems, Annette."

As he spoke he lowered the glass, swirling the golden liquid that remained in it and watching it as it sloshed against the sides, then looked at Jess sadly. She sat just outside the circle of light cast by the lamp, probably about twelve feet from the desk, not having moved since she'd been stopped upon entering by the sheer beauty of the view. On the wall behind her and to her left, surrounding the door to the sitting room, were the custom-built floor-to-ceiling bookcases that held everything from his law books to photos of Brianna and their children, taken on the previous summer's safari in Kenya. To her right the wall was covered with pictures of Davenport with nearly every VIP who had passed through D.C. during the last fifteen years, including this President and his two predecessors.

As Jess had already learned under his tutelage, impressing clients was the name of the game. And that wall was very impressive.

"As soon as I spoke to her at the hotel, I could see that she was upset, even frightened. She ran from her Secret Service detail. She told me she was, to use her exact words, a 'fucking prisoner.'" Talking fast, Jess ticked off the points she wanted to make in chronological order. "She—"

"I should have taken her seriously," he interrupted, shaking his head. "But she wasn't happy. Never happy. Fighting with David all the time. All the other things. The last few months, she just bitched and bitched and bitched. I just thought it was more of the same."

If he wasn't already drunk, he was close, Jess realized with a sinking sensation in the pit of her stomach. She wasn't entirely sure that what she was saying was even registering with him.

"Mr. Davenport. I think Mrs. Cooper may have been murdered," she tried again, spelling it out as plainly as she could in case he wasn't getting the point.

He downed the rest of the Chivas in his glass.

"Doesn't matter." Then he slammed the glass back down on the desk hard enough so that Jess jumped. "None of it matters anymore. God, I hate that 'dust to dust, ashes to ashes' crap. Who the hell"—his voice cracked—"who the hell wants to be dirt?"

He's losing it. The thought was terrifying.

"I think whoever did it also tried to kill me in the hospital." To hell with what Ryan had said about the tests on the IV equipment coming up negative. Either he was lying or the tests were wrong, because she knew she wasn't. Desperation made Jess lean forward as she tried to hammer her point home; she gripped the wheelchair arms tightly. Her eyes fought to hold his, hoping to keep his attention focused on what she was telling him rather than whatever inner demons he was currently battling. "I think they're trying to cover up what they did to Mrs. Cooper. They tried to kill me because they're afraid I'll remember something."

"I told you to keep quiet, didn't I?" He poured more whisky into his glass. Jess watched with dismay.

"I have kept quiet. All I've said to anybody is that I don't remember. But that isn't entirely true. I do remember some—"

He broke in on her before she could finish. "She wanted me. She said, 'I need you, John.' And this time she did. She really did. And I didn't go. I was tired of dealing with her, to tell you the truth. So I sent you."

He chugged from the glass. It was such an inelegant gesture, complete with gurgling sounds as he sucked the booze down, that Jess's eyes widened as she watched. In all the time she had known Davenport, she had never seen him behave like anything other than a very cultured gentleman. He was either far more drunk than she had supposed or in far worse emotional straits.

She continued doggedly, "Somebody was chasing us. Another car. I remember that, and—"

"I tried to protect you. I tried. I did. You can't say I didn't." He drank more whisky, drank it so fast that when he set the glass down again his mustache was wet and a little golden rivulet trickled from one corner of his mouth. He wiped his mouth on his sleeve. "I tried to help Annette, too. I always listened to her. I always advised her to the best of my ability. One time, one time only, she calls me and I don't go running to her as fast as I can. And now she's dead. Dead. Annette. My old friend Annette."

His mouth shook. Jess realized that tears were seeping from his eyes. She sat bolt upright in the wheelchair now, watching him with dismay. This meeting in which she had put so much stock, in which she had planned to tell everything she knew and thus place the whole nightmare in his hands, letting this far more experienced, connected, respected lawyer deal with the mess he had gotten her into in the first place, was turning into a debacle.

Desperate, she tried one more time to get through to him.

"Mr. Davenport, please, I know you're grieving, but this can't wait. I came to you tonight because I don't know who else to tell these things to. I can't go to the Secret Service—I think the man who attacked me in the hospital might have been a Secret Service agent. And Mrs. Cooper was running from her own Secret Service detail when she died. And . . . and . . . I just don't think it's safe. Which means I can't go to the FBI or the local police or any other kind of law-enforcement agency, either, because they all know each other. They all stick up for each other. They all talk. Somebody will tell somebody, and then whoever is behind this will find out that I've remembered something and they'll kill me. And I can't just keep quiet because it's *murder*, the murder of the First Lady of the United States and two other people, and anyway, I don't think just keeping quiet is going to help, because they're afraid I might remember something that will incriminate them and they're going to kill me anyway just on the off chance. You know those 'dark forces' you warned me about? I think it's somebody in the government. I don't see—"

"No, you don't," Davenport interrupted fiercely, his voice thick, his eyes wet. Tears trickled down his cheeks. "You don't see anything. You haven't had time to get married or have kids or build any kind of career that matters, any kind of legacy. You don't know anything about power, about actions and consequences. You don't know anything about how things work, or the kinds of things people sometimes have to do."

He sobbed, then clamped his lips tightly together as if ashamed that the sound had escaped through them.

Jess stared at him, appalled.

"You're right, I don't." She worked to keep her voice very, very steady. If he wouldn't—or couldn't—help her, what would she do? Her stomach twisted at the thought. If she was right about what she suspected—and she was almost sure she was—the perpetrators would hunt her down and kill her without compunction. They were big and bad and relentless, and in the end she would have nowhere to go, nowhere to hide. "But I know I'm in danger, and I'm pretty sure so do you. You obviously think something's wrong about Mrs. Cooper's death, too. So who do we contact? Who do we tell? *We've got to tell someone that she was murdered.*"

Panic curled through her insides as she searched his face. If there was anything there except sodden grief, she couldn't see it.

"I always thought I was a brave man." His eyes dropped away from hers as he poured the last of the Chivas into his glass. "Now I know I'm not. I'm a coward. A *damned* coward."

He picked up the glass and drank thirstily, noisily. When he set the glass down, his mustache was wet, and he swiped his arm across his mouth again.

Jess watched despairingly.

"Maybe you could go directly to the President," she suggested. "Tell him."

He made a sound that might have been a scornful laugh. It was only then, as she tried to figure out what that laugh meant, that it occurred to her that if, indeed, the Secret Service was involved, then the President himself might very well be, too.

Because who else did the Secret Service take orders from?

"There has to be somebody we can tell," she said. "Somebody who can launch an investigation and . . ."

Her voice trailed off as he swallowed the last of his whisky.

The press, she thought, as she frantically sought some other way to get what she knew and remembered and suspected out there and thus do her moral duty and also, she hoped, remove any motive for anyone to kill her at the same time. She would go to the media and tell them everything. It was obvious Davenport wasn't going to be able to help her; even if he wanted to—maybe when he was sober and in a different frame of mind—it might be too late.

By that time, the dark forces might already have found her and shut her up permanently, with no possibility of mistake.

Maybe they'd just been waiting for her to get out of the hospital before they tried again.

Jess's heartbeat quickened at the thought.

Maybe the Secret Service wasn't involved in this after all. Maybe they had been all that was keeping her safe. And she'd just run away from them. . . .

A slithering sound caught her attention. Frowning as she tried to figure out what it was, she realized after a couple of seconds that Davenport had just opened one of his top desk drawers.

"This is the only thing I can do." Davenport stood up, swaying a little on his feet. "This is the only thing left for me. I have to save what I can for my kids."

Jess had only just registered that he was holding a gun in his hand when he whispered, "God forgive me."

Jess's eyes widened. Her stomach contracted. Her heart leaped.

"Mr. Davenport . . ."

Hand shaking visibly, he pointed the gun at her and fired.

Chapter 15

THREE THINGS HAPPENED SIMULTANEOUSLY.

There was a tremendous *bang,* and the bullet passed so close to her left cheek that she could feel it brush past.

She screamed, throwing herself from the chair.

And something hit her in the back with the force of a freight train. Still screaming, she landed facedown on the antique Oriental rug that covered the center of the floor as an enormous weight smashed violently to earth on top of her, stopping her forward momentum dead, crushing her, forcing the air from her lungs.

It hurt so much that she went dizzy with it.

"Davenport! Drop it!"

The shout sounded almost in her ear. She understood in that split second that what lay atop her was a man, a man who had dived on her hopefully with the intent of saving her life, and then another shot exploded, the sound muffled this time by the bulk of the man whose body covered hers. It was followed almost instantaneously by the sound of shattering glass, then a shower of almost musical notes as if it were suddenly raining tinkling wind chimes.

Cringing, wheezing as she fought to draw air into her flattened lungs, tucking her chin into her chest and wrapping her arms around her head, Jess tried to become one with the carpet, overwhelmingly grateful for the body atop hers. Terror turned her blood to ice as every nerve ending she possessed went wild in anticipation of the impact of a bullet—the next bullet—that would hit her protector's body and even, possibly, tear through it into her own shrinking flesh.

"Jesus God," the man on top of her said. His tone made it a prayer.

There was no other sound. No more bullets. No more wind chimes. No more voices. Nothing.

Just the pounding of her own heart in her ears.

"You okay?" the man asked as he rolled off her.

Jess barely even had to look at him to know who he was: Ryan. She realized that some part of her had recognized him as soon as he spoke. Much as she hated to admit it even to herself, she would now know his deep, drawling voice anywhere. For just a moment he lay on his side on the carpet facing her, looking her over carefully, his face hard, his normally light eyes dark with some emotion she couldn't put a name to.

He was holding a gun, a big black pistol, in his right hand. It was, she was relieved beyond words to see, not pointed at her.

She realized that in that case she was profoundly thankful to see him.

Their gazes met. She sucked in air.

"Fine," she wheezed.

A corner of his mouth twisted up in the smallest of involuntary smiles. "Good to know."

Then, in a horrifying instant of clarity, she realized if he was facing her that meant his back was turned to the source of the danger.

Her eyes widened. "Mr. Davenport . . ."

Fear sharpened her voice. Her gaze flew past Ryan toward the desk, toward the place where Davenport had so unbelievably stood up and pointed a gun at her, shot at her, terrified of what she might see, what might be happening at that very second, only to find that she couldn't see Davenport anywhere. Had Ryan fired that second shot, then, and had Davenport been hit by it and taken down?

"He's gone."

Ryan rolled to his feet with surprising grace for such a big man. He seemed slightly out of breath, which, as a matter of fact, she was herself. He was wearing a black suit and tie with a white shirt, as if he, too, was still dressed for Annette Cooper's funeral, and he looked much better than any man who had just thrown himself into the line of fire to save another's life had any right to. He kept the pistol at his side and pointed down.

"Gone?" Jess frowned in incomprehension.

"He shot out the window. Then he jumped." Ryan spoke over his shoulder as he walked across the room and looked down.

Horror hit Jess like a blow to the chest. "Oh my God."

Pushing herself up into a sitting position, she stared at the far wall where Ryan stood looking down, where, she realized with a combination of disbelief and shock, only a few shards of glass continued to cling to the metal frame. Otherwise, the window was gone. The office was open to the night. The roar she heard wasn't in her ears at all but was some combination of wind, traffic, and shouts and screams from the people below. Fresh air blew in, sharp and clean-smelling, lifting the edges of the heavy curtains, sending some of the papers on Davenport's desk swirling out and skyward on an upward spiral like dueling kites.

"Can you get up?" His voice surprisingly gentle, Ryan came back from the edge and held a hand out to her. "We need to get out of here. Right now. Security will be on the way. And the police. And there might be—hell, who knows. Somebody else."

"Mr. Davenport tried to kill me."

"Yeah, I caught that."

Jess was still stunned, but fear made her move. She put her hand in his and let him pull her to her feet. As she straightened, a sharp pain in her back caused her to wince, and she realized she was shaking all over. His eyes slid over her again to check for a new injury. Except for a laddered stocking and a scraped knee, she was okay.

He dropped her hand. "Where's that damned chair?"

It was on its side a few feet away.

"He killed himself." Okay, that was obvious, which made it a stupid thing to say. But she was feeling stupid or, rather, stupefied, as she stared out at the star-studded night where all of D.C. continued to glow while Davenport had just died in its midst. She had to be in the early stages of shock. Her heart palpitated. She was finding it hard to breathe. She took a halting step forward, then another and another, drawn by an almost irresistible urge to look down into that black void. Impossible to believe that Davenport had just stepped out the window, fallen twenty stories, and was now lying broken and bloodied on the sidewalk below.

"Trust me, you don't want to do that." Ryan caught her by the arm before she reached the edge. "Sit down."

Having fetched the chair, Ryan practically pushed Jess into it and thrust her purse into her lap. She shivered and swallowed hard.

"Don't freak out on me. We don't have that kind of time."

"I'm not freaking out." Her voice was surprisingly steady. "What are you doing here, anyway?"

"You mean besides saving your life? That's something

we probably need to talk about. You want to settle in for a chat now or you want to get the hell out of here?"

By way of a reply, she shot him a withering look.

"Then let's go."

He headed toward the door as he spoke. Her hand moved to the controls, turning the chair to face the door, leaving Davenport and everything she thought she had known about him behind. The whirr of the motor sounded as loud as a jet engine to her ears, but she knew that was just because she was so on edge she was ready to jump out of her skin.

"You all set?" Weapon in hand, he stuck his head inside the dark sitting room and looked cautiously all around.

"Yes." She rolled to join him.

"Kick that thing into high gear. We need to *move*. And stay close."

He kept in front of her, his pistol at the ready, moving fast but cautiously toward the hall, glancing back to make sure she was keeping up. With one last disbelieving look at the open air panel that just minutes ago had been the front wall of Davenport's office, Jess rolled into the thick, gray shadows of the sitting room, following Ryan as closely as she could.

That sense she'd had of someone behind her when she'd entered Davenport's office—it almost certainly had to have been Ryan.

She'd already come close to dying tonight. That made it twice in a week. What was it they said about the third time being a charm?

"Can't you speed that thing up?" Ryan frowned at her over his shoulder as they emerged into the relative brightness of the reception area.

"If I could, I would."

They passed the reception desk. She rolled down the center hall, going as fast as she could, putting the pedal to the metal in wheelchair terms, while a fast walk was all that was required for Ryan to keep pace with her. The fact that Davenport was dead and had tried to kill her was more than Jess could take in for the moment. She did her best to push all thoughts of what had just occurred out of her head. Just getting out of there had to be her first priority. The dim lighting, the closed doors on either side, the enormous paintings with their abstract slashes of black—everything felt different now. Her workplace had suddenly become a place of fear. So had the rest of the world.

A bullet could come out of nowhere. . . .

"Security's probably watching us right now." It came out in a horrified exclamation as Jess suddenly remembered the building's elaborate camera system. Heart in her throat, she searched wide-eyed for any cameras protruding from the ceiling.

"Davenport knew you were coming, right?"

"Yes."

"Believe me, when somebody gets around to checking they'll find the cameras up here aren't working for some reason or another."

Jess blinked. *Right.* Davenport would have made preparations. He had planned this. He had told her to come up here planning to kill her.

Davenport's first shot had missed, but if they'd been alone, a second one almost certainly wouldn't have, because after throwing herself out of the chair she had just run out of options. If it hadn't been for the man striding along beside her, she would be dead right now. She looked up at him. He was eye candy as always, but that wasn't what she cared about right then. His jaw was taut, his mouth grim. He scanned the area ahead of them with cold precision. He held the gun like he knew what to do with it, which of course he did. He looked like somebody who could be counted on to keep them both alive.

"I have a key to the private elevator," she told him. "That's how I came up."

"The problem with elevators is that if anybody figures out you're in one, they can trap you in it."

As they reached the end of the hall, Jess was still digesting the mind-boggling thought that somebody might want to trap her in an elevator. Something, a sound, an instinct, pulled her gaze to the elevator bank with its gleaming brass doors. And the numbers above it. One was lit up. The car on the left was on the second floor, no, now the third. It was on its way up.

One look, and she thought her heart might leap right out of her chest.

"Ah, shit." Ryan saw it, too. "Okay, stop."

"What?"

He shoved his pistol into its holster and, when she didn't immediately do what he told her, grabbed the handles at the back of her chair to stop her himself.

"This thing is too damned slow. We've got to *go*. Here, put your arms around my neck."

Jess realized he meant to pick her up at just about the time he scooped her out of the chair. She barely managed to hang on to her purse as she was swung up into his arms.

"What? What are you doing?"

"Picking up the pace."

He was already running with her, racing down the hall away from whoever was coming up on that elevator, heading toward the north end of the building, where she had come up in the private elevator. She wrapped her arms around his neck and held on for dear life. His arms were hard with muscle and strong around her, and he was carrying her in the most comfortable way possible for her, high and close against his chest as one would carry a cherished child. She guessed that he was mindful of her injury and didn't want to hurt her, and she appreciated that.

Still, comfortable this was not. She was bouncing all over the place.

"If you don't want to use the elevator, how do you suggest we get out of here?" she gasped out.

"The stairs."

"Stairs?"

"Yep."

"They'll be here soon," she warned. She knew from experience that the elevators in the building were fast.

"Figured." He was running flat out, his hard-soled shoes pounding on the slick marble floor.

"They'll see the wheelchair."

"Can't help it."

Seconds later they had nearly reached the end of the long hall. It was a good distance from where whoever was coming up on the elevator would emerge but still within their sight if they looked left.

A tiny *ping* sounded in the distance.

"They're here," she whispered in a panic.

"Hang on."

Another bound, and he skidded to a stop in front of the door marked EMERGENCY EXIT. Jess felt one arm shift as he grabbed the knob and jerked the metal door open. Then they were through, and he was holding her tight again. The narrow chute of steel-reinforced concrete had been designed to be fire- and blast-proof, but it looked surprisingly low-tech, beige walls and gray metal stairs with iron-bar railings. Jess could do nothing but hold on tight as Ryan clattered down the stairs with her.

"If you're . . . heading toward the parking garage, you should know that there's somebody down there . . . waiting for me. At street level. Near the private elevator, which means . . . near the building." The ride had just gotten a whole lot rougher, which was why she was talking in bursts. Her grip on him tightened exponentially as her fear of falling or being dropped skyrocketed.

"Who?"

"Davenport's secretary, Marian Young. She drove me here." Jess suddenly felt sick. Had Marian known what Davenport intended? Maybe, but she didn't think so. On the other hand, before tonight she would never have believed that Davenport might try to kill her, either.

"She alone?"

"She was when I left her."

"Okay."

His replies were clipped and brief for good reason. He was in great shape, there was no doubt about that. But she could feel his body heat increasing with each flight of stairs. By the time he burst out through another exit door onto the second floor of the parking garage, he was practically panting.

The scream of sirens hit her even before the door closed behind them, proof that the stairwell was soundproof as well as everything-else-proof. The flashing lights of some kind of an emergency vehicle burst through the large rectangular openings in the top half of the concrete walls to carom around the parking garage in disorienting bursts of blue. She could hear shouts, jumbled voices, the sounds of a crowd on the street just below.

That was good, right? Because there was safety in numbers, and all that?

But as far as she could tell, this level of the parking garage was deserted. If anybody wanted to attack them, this was the place. The walls were gray, the floor was gray, the high, concrete-beamed ceiling was gray. The lights set deep into the ceiling provided circles of distilled illumination in the areas directly below them and cast the rest of the vast space into shadow. Add in the revolving emergency lights, and it became almost mind-blowingly psychedelic. Jess thought they were alone, that no one was following them, but given the constantly changing nature of their surroundings, it was impossible to be sure.

"Do you have a car?" Her narrowed eyes continually scanned the shadows behind him, just in case.

"Across the street."

She realized that he was heading toward the door at the far end of the garage. One flight down, and another door just like it would open onto Connecticut Avenue, at the opposite end of the garage from where Marian was parked. Jess felt a quick welling of pity as she pictured the other woman waiting in her car for Jess to reappear, with no idea that her world had just been smashed to smithereens. Marian would be sick with grief when she found out that Davenport was dead.

Ryan pulled open another door, and then they were in another stairwell, going down.

When he reached the bottom one short flight later, he pushed open the door. They had to cover only a few more yards through a shadowy corner of the garage before exiting through the door out into the street.

"Maybe we should go tell Marian what happened." She spoke practically in his ear, her voice hushed.

"Yeah. No."

He said it like that was that. Like it was entirely his decision to make. Which, since he was the legs of the operation at the moment, she guessed it was.

Her eyes straining through the darkness, she searched for Marian's car. There were a couple of others, parked and left for the night or however long—but, yes, there it was, right where Jess had gotten out, waiting beneath the neon elevator sign which shed just the tiniest amount of light on the Volvo's navy blue roof. All the lights inside and outside the car were off, but the elevator light above illuminated the interior just a little bit. Jess frowned. She couldn't see Marian. In fact, if Jess hadn't known better, she would have sworn the car was empty.

She was still craning her neck toward it when Ryan shouldered through the door to the street.

They emerged into a growing, jostling crowd, with people packed together on the sidewalk. Most people were barely moving. They were gawking. At something lying in the street.

Jess felt her stomach turn inside out. She couldn't see anything, which was probably a good thing, but she knew what they had to be looking at. Multiple sirens, most still at a distance, filled the air, drowning out the noise of the crowd. About five blocks down, Jess saw the flashing lights of an ambulance as it fought to reach the scene.

"You can put me down now. I couldn't manage the stairs, but this is flat," she whispered in Ryan's ear. Her voice took on an urgent undertone as she noticed a few glances directed their way. "We're starting to attract attention."

Ryan grunted in acknowledgment and set her on her feet, keeping a hard arm around her waist for support. Her legs felt rubbery, but she gritted her teeth and wrapped her arm around him and started walking when he did, responding to his assessing glance with a nod that said she was all right. Using his shoulder as a buffer, taking her with him, he wove through the crowd clogging the sidewalk with single-minded purpose. Against her body, she could feel the solid strength and heat of him.

"Duck your face down. I don't want anybody getting a good look at you."

Of course. She'd been plastered all over TV. People might recognize her. She had forgotten that. It occurred to Jess in a lightning burst of awareness that if she still harbored any doubts about Ryan and his intentions toward her, this was her moment to scream some variation of "This man is not my daddy!" and enlist the power of the many people surrounding them to get away.

The question boiled down to this: Was she safer with him or without him?

On the negative side, he was a Secret Service agent.

And she was pretty sure he'd lied about having tests done on her IV.

But then he'd saved her life tonight, and in the hospital. He was a trained protection officer with a gun.

She was pretty sure he didn't want to kill her, or want anyone else to kill her. Otherwise, she'd be dead.

So she was going with, *with*.

Shaking her head so that her hair covered most of her face, she lowered her head so that she was looking at the ground.

"Careful of the curb," he warned in an undertone.

Then they stepped off the sidewalk and into the street, heading, she assumed, toward wherever he had left his car, dodging the vehicles that were still trying to force their way past and that would occasionally shoot free of the congestion like a cork from a champagne bottle.

The view was better as they crossed the street, because the bulk of the crowd stayed on the sidewalk. For the moment only a single police car was on the scene. The two officers were out of the car. One was trying single-handedly to redirect the honking traffic that was already backed up for blocks. The other was standing in the street, looking down.

Jess couldn't help it. She followed his gaze. She caught just a glimpse of black dress pants and a white shirt, realized that it was Davenport lying sprawled on his stomach on the pavement, felt the gorge rise in her throat, and hastily looked away.

She was suddenly breathing hard. Her pulse pounded in her ears. She felt light-headed, woozy—and then she saw Marian.

Unmistakable with her upswept hair and gray suit, the woman burst through the crowd about two hundred feet away.

"John!" Marian screamed. Her face twisted into a

mask of hysterical grief, she ran frantically into the street toward Davenport's body.

In the space of a heartbeat, Jess saw what was about to happen but was helpless to do anything about it.

A small tan car shot past the cop trying to stop traffic and hit Marian dead-on. She flew up in the air, slammed back down on the car's roof, and then was thrown to the ground as the car streaked away.

Chapter 16

"MARIAN!" JESS SHRIEKED, pulling away from Ryan. Horror grabbed her heart like a fist and squeezed.

A couple of heads turned in her direction.

"Shut up," Ryan growled, tightening his grip on her at the same time as he quickened his step. "Jesus, don't draw attention to yourself."

Jess didn't fight him, but she couldn't look away. Other people in the crowd were gasping, yelling, surging forward, crowding around the accident site. The cops abandoned what they were doing to run toward where Marian now lay crumpled in the street. One knelt beside her while the other held back traffic, which had now ground to a total halt because the street was completely, hideously blocked. Jess had eyes for nothing but Marian. The woman lay unmoving, her left leg bent at an unnatural angle. A pool of dark liquid was forming beneath her head.

Blood, black as oil as the streetlights hit it.

"I got the license plate number!" a man shouted, elbowing his way through the crowd toward the cops.

"Let the ambulance through!" someone else cried.

"Keep your head down." Ryan pulled her up on the curb with him just as the ambulance rolled past. Behind it came two more police cars, strobe lights flashing, sirens screaming a warning into the night as cars nudged onto the sidewalk and wedged into a single lane to let them pass.

"Oh my God." Jess could hardly talk. Her teeth chattered. Her breathing was suddenly way too fast and shallow. "I've got to go to her."

"Like hell." There was a brutal edge to Ryan's voice that she had never heard in it before. With his arm clamped around her, he shouldered deep into the crowd, clearly intent on putting as much distance between them and the accident as he could. Suddenly, Jess could see nothing but a forest of people. "Anyway, there's nothing you can do."

His arm was like iron around her now, as though he feared she might struggle to escape. She didn't. Too many terrible things had happened too quickly, and all she knew for sure was that she was afraid. They were on the edges of the crowd now, and he was moving faster, propelling her with him as he plunged past others rushing toward the scene, leaving it behind as quickly as he could. More police cars slowly forced their way through the stopped traffic. Cars moved aside to let them pass.

It started to rain, a slow sprinkle that hit her exposed skin like cold tears.

"The car just drove away." Scarcely able to believe what she had just witnessed, Jess looked back, tried to see what was going on with Marian but could not. "It just hit her and drove away."

"That's what it did, all right."

Jess's heart clutched. Her head was up now, and he wasn't saying anything about it, so she guessed it was safe enough. The rain was making her blink in an effort to keep it out of her eyes. "Do you think she's—dead?"

"Hard to say. Believe me, everything that can be done for her is being done."

They rounded a corner into near darkness. The wind caught her hair, whipping it back, driving a cold drizzle against her skin. The smell of booze and garbage mixed with the wet-earth scent of the rain. Jess realized that they had left the crowd behind. The thought scared her. Shivering, she looked carefully all around. Tall buildings rose up on either side; they were in an alley now. A starless and rainy alley lined with trash cans and Dumpsters and mounds of things she preferred not to think about. Rows of dark windows looked down on them like sightless eyes.

Ducking her head against the rain, Jess instinctively leaned closer into Ryan, taking comfort from the solid warmth of his body. Watching what had happened to Marian had stripped the last of her illusions from her. This was big, it was real, and it was not going away. She felt exposed, like danger was closing in from all sides.

Like there was nowhere left that was safe.

Could someone be following us even now?

She looked fearfully back. A white plastic grocery bag tumbling toward them like a pale ghost in the wind made her jump. A sound—a rattle—rain on the trash-can lids, maybe—made her catch her breath. At the mouth of the alley, the flashing blue lights from the rescue vehicles pulsed, giving weird life to everything they touched.

Then the alley opened up, and they turned right into a parking lot filled with vehicles. There were lights, two tall halogen lamps at either end that emitted a foggy yellow glow, and row upon row of cars. *It would be easy for someone to hide.* Jess's heartbeat quickened, but before she could look around more than once he stopped beside a small, dark-colored RAV4, said, "Hang on a minute," and pressed the button to unlock the doors. Then he opened the passenger door and bundled her inside. A moment or so later he slid in behind the wheel.

As soon as he was inside, he locked the doors. The click as he did so was enough to make her jump. Even as she realized what the sound was, Jess wondered if he feared being followed as much as she did.

"Was that an accident?" Jess burst out, still looking warily all around as he started the car. She was wet, cold, and shaking like a leaf, and she folded her arms over her chest for warmth. The parking lot was filled with shapes and shadows, and she was on pins and needles in case someone should suddenly spring at them out of the darkness. "That wasn't an accident, was it?"

"I don't know. Maybe."

He backed the car out in a fast swoop, then shifted into drive. A moment later they pulled out onto M Street. Jess felt a little safer because they were now moving targets.

"Put your seat belt on."

He was wearing his, she saw. Hands trembling, Jess did as she was told.

"Where are we going?"

He glanced at her. "My house. It's just outside of Dale City. You can stay there until we get this thing figured out."

Jess wasn't in any state of mind to argue. Without a better suggestion, she didn't even bother to reply.

As a result of what was happening on Connecticut Avenue, traffic was already clogging up throughout downtown. He headed away from the congestion, driving fast but not too fast, making good time through the interconnected grid of streets, glancing just a little too often in his rearview mirror for her to think they were now safe. Rain fell steadily, and the constant rhythm of the windshield wipers provided a numbing counterpoint to the swish of the tires on wet pavement. She was shivering, which, she suspected, had very little to do with the fact that she was cold and wet and had a whole lot to do with the fact that she had just witnessed two violent deaths and nearly suffered one herself. He must have noticed because he cranked the heat. A moment later, the smell of damp clothes circulated throughout the car.

"Why would Mr. Davenport try to kill me? Why would he kill himself?" The questions that had been tumbling through her mind spilled over as he braked for a red light. "If there was anybody I thought I could trust, it was him."

"Babe, outside of your family, I'd say there's nobody you ought to be trusting right about now." He gave her a quick, grim smile. "Except me, of course."

Jess looked at him and frowned. Some of the shock was receding, and her brain was slowly regaining its ability to function. *Okay, time to focus here.* Before she fell hook, line, and sinker for the whole "trust me" thing, he had some explaining to do.

Her eyes narrowed at him. "About that. What were you doing in Mr. Davenport's office again?"

"Let's just say I was monitoring the situation."

"Situation?"

"Yeah."

"You know, I don't mean to be ungrateful or anything, but I think I'm going to need a little bit more of an explanation than that."

The light turned green, he accelerated and turned left, and they joined a long line of cars heading up onto the Beltway.

"Just out of curiosity, what happens if you don't like what you hear?"

Good question. Jess was already asking herself that. She was in his car traveling at around seventy miles an hour on an expressway filled with other cars going equally fast. They were alone. He was a highly trained federal agent; she was a highly trained lawyer. He was big, she was small. Plus, he had a gun. If it came down to a fight for her life, she didn't like her chances.

She made a face. "I'll cross that bridge when I come to it, I guess."

He laughed, a small, amused sound that went a long way toward making her feel safer, and shot a look at her.

"I was following you, okay? To make sure you were safe. Which obviously you weren't."

Jess frowned. "How did you even know where I was? I deliberately left the hospital when you weren't around. No one outside Mr. Davenport and Marian was even supposed to know where I was going."

"Piece of cake."

Now that Jess thought about it—Davenport's secretary, Davenport's helicopter, probably easy enough to find out where the helicopter had landed—she guessed it was, and felt stupid for feeling as safe as she had in the condo. Ryan—and no telling who else—had known where she was all along. What was the word she wanted to apply to herself? *Oh, yeah: thick.*

"So how did you get into the building?"

"I'm good at things like that."

"Up to the twentieth floor?"

"Those damned stairs. I watched you roll into Davenport's office, and I followed you."

"You heard everything I said to him." Jess had only just realized that. Quickly she reviewed the conversation in her mind and stiffened with alarm.

"Pretty much, yeah."

He knew—and he hadn't killed her. Or let Davenport kill her, which would have been way too easy. That had to weigh heavily on the *trust him* side.

"I don't think Mrs. Cooper's death was an accident." She threw it out there like a challenge.

"So I heard you tell Davenport. You want to tell me why?"

Jess wrapped her arms tighter around herself. Despite the blasting heat, she was bone cold. It was all she could do to keep her teeth from chattering.

"She was running away from something. She was nervous, afraid, even." If Jess hesitated, it was because she suddenly remembered once again that he was a Secret

Service agent. And a lot of the evidence that she'd pieced together in her mind pointed to Secret Service involvement in Mrs. Cooper's death and in the subsequent attack on Jess in the hospital, which Ryan had almost certainly lied about. And in Davenport's suicide? She didn't see how the Secret Service could have orchestrated that, but she was starting to feel that anything was possible. And what about Marian? An accident, or something far more sinister? At this point, she just didn't know, but she was prepared to assume the worst. "She tried to get away from the agent— Prescott—who was chasing her, but he caught up with us at the corner and managed to jump into the car."

She paused, watching him for a reaction. There was none. His face was impassive. His eyes stayed on the road. A semi rolled past on the right, rattling the SUV. He eased into the lane behind it.

"Go on," he said.

She took a deep breath. "That put him in the front passenger seat, with me behind him and Mrs. Cooper behind the driver. Mrs. Cooper was screaming at him, telling him to get out, to not call anybody, that what she did was none of his business. He told her that if she wanted to go somewhere, she was going to have to take him, too, or he would call backup to come and collect her and take her back to the White House whether she wanted to go or not. He said he was just staying with her to keep her safe, and they kind of agreed that as long as he didn't call anybody or interfere with her, he could do that. And so she calmed down. Then we got off 95 onto this two-lane road, and she was making phone calls until she lost the signal. So she got mad and threw the phone, which ended under the front passenger seat down by my feet. She wanted me to get it, and I had to unbuckle my seat belt and slide down into the footwell and stick my hand way up under the seat to try to find it. So I was doing that when headlights from behind us flashed through the car. I don't know what happened next—I was down on the floor—but Mrs. Cooper screamed, 'We've got to get out of here,' and then she yelled something at Prescott—something like, 'You called them, you bastard,' something like that. He was swearing that he didn't while she was screaming at the driver to go faster, and the driver did. He booked it, started speeding up, and then we were just flying. I managed to get back in my seat and was grabbing for my seat belt when something slammed into the back of the car. It felt like something hit us; it was this tremendous jolt, but I could still see the other car's headlights, and they were close but not close enough, you know? So I don't know what it could have been. But like I said, we were going really fast, and there was this jolt, and the back end of the car slewed around like we were on ice, and I think the driver hit the brakes—and the car just shot off the road. I remember ... I remember ..."

Jess broke off, shuddering, as a slide show of terrible images flashed one after the other through her mind. Trying to make sense of them, trying to sort them out, she stared silently out through the windshield at the now pouring rain. They were on the bridge, she could see the lights reflected in the black waters of the Potomac beneath them, and the sound of the tires changed subtly to reflect the fact that the surface they gripped had changed. It only occurred to her that they were probably going to be following the exact same route the car Davenport had sent had taken that night when she saw the big green sign for I-95 flash past overhead. She was still absorbing the implications of that when the RAV4 trailed the semi down the ramp onto 95. The sudden sense of déjà vu was so strong she felt light-headed.

"You gonna tell me the rest, or am I supposed to try to guess?" Ryan's voice snapped her back to the present.

Swallowing hard, Jess looked at him. The tall lights

illuminating the spaghetti-like junction with I-95 shone brightly inside the car, and headlights from cars going in the opposite direction slashed directly across his face. Internally, she juggled seared-into-her-psyche images of the sexy Fed who hadn't known she was alive despite her cringe-worthy efforts at getting him to notice her against what she now knew of him. His face was shiny and damp, his hair and clothes were wet, he had tired lines around his eyes and mouth, and he managed to look hot anyway. But he also looked tough, competent, and, yes, dammit, trustworthy.

She was going to trust him. God help her if she was wrong.

Taking a deep breath, she continued.

"We were all screaming, and the car just started flipping over, and then all of a sudden I was out of the car, sailing through the air kind of doing somersaults, but I could still see the car rolling down the hill and I realized I must have been thrown clear. Then I hit and . . ."

"You blacked out?" he supplied when she hesitated.

She nodded, relieved to have been offered such an easy out. "Yes."

"So that's it?"

Wetting her lips, she shot him a wary glance. Her mouth had gone dry. This was the part that frightened her the most. It was also the part that she most needed to tell.

"Jess?" he prompted. Something in her silence must have told him there was more.

I could always say, "Then I woke up and you were leaning over me." It would be so easy. She was tempted. Then she shook her head at herself. *No, finish it.*

"Okay." She swallowed. "I did black out, but not for long. I remember opening my eyes and thinking how dark the night was, and wondering what I was doing lying outside where I could see the stars, and why I hurt so much. Then I saw these small, round lights coming down the hill.

Flashlights, I realized. There had to be people carrying them. I tried to call out to the people with the flashlights—I knew something was wrong by that time, knew I needed help—but I guess the breath had been knocked out of me because I couldn't make a sound. I lay there gasping for air, watching these dark figures holding flashlights rushing—they were moving as fast as they could with the ground so steep—past me down the hill. And then I realized that somebody was screaming. I hadn't noticed it before, maybe because my ears were ringing. I don't know."

Closing her eyes as the memory took on life in her mind, she raised her hands to her temples, where her pulse pounded ferociously. She had to remind herself to breathe, and deliberately took in a couple of slow, careful sips of air.

Still, she could almost hear the screaming.

"Jess?"

Once again, his voice brought her out of it.

Her eyes opened. Her hands dropped to twine in her lap. Unable to look at him, she stared out through the windshield without seeing anything of the closed-for-the-night strip malls and car repair shops and apartment complexes they passed.

"I looked down, toward where the screaming was coming from, and I saw the car. One of the headlights still worked, kind of marking where it was, so I saw it as soon as I looked, lying on its roof with its tires still spinning." She swallowed. "The people with the flashlights reached it right about then. They shined their lights on it. Someone . . . someone was moving inside, trying to get out. And there was still that screaming."

Her fists clenched. Her eyes slid toward him. He glanced her way at the same time, and for the briefest of moments their gazes met. His expression was impossible to read.

Get it out there. All of it.

He was watching the road again. Her eyes stayed glued to his face. She took a steadying breath.

"There was this small burst of flame. Just a little *poof.* About the size of a tiki torch, or something like that. It burned for a couple of seconds—I watched it. And then the whole car just exploded into flames." Her heart clutched as she remembered. "Everybody was still inside. The people with the flashlights didn't even try to get anybody out. They stood there and watched it burn. The screaming . . . it got worse, and then it stopped." By then, she was having so much trouble getting the words out through her dry throat that her voice was scarcely more than a hoarse whisper. "I'm almost sure it was a woman screaming. I'm almost sure it was Mrs. Cooper I heard."

A violent shudder racked her. The others had burned alive. That was the knowledge that she had to share, that was the knowledge that she couldn't live with. The horror of it made her sick, made her want to vomit, made her want to push it out of her mind forever and never think of it again. Everything seemed to spin. Dropping her head back against the headrest, she closed her eyes, wrapped her arms around herself for warmth, and breathed.

In, out. In, out. Slow and steady, not too deep.

"Okay, hang on." The car seemed to slow, and then there was a bump, and then they rolled forward for a minute before stopping altogether.

Jess opened her eyes. She was still nauseated, still light-headed, still haunted by the images she couldn't shake. Bright light bathed the inside of the vehicle now, and she saw they were at a McDonald's. In the drive-thru line, to be precise. Just as she made the connection, a tinny voice came over the intercom asking to take their order.

"You drink coffee?" Ryan asked.

Jess nodded.

"Two large coffees. Cream and lots of sugar." He glanced at Jess again. "You had supper?"

Jess shook her head.

"You like hamburgers? Big Macs? What?"

Actually, she wasn't a real big fan of McDonald's. But she felt so bad, so weak and shaky and drained, that she was willing to try anything that might make her feel a little more normal.

"A hamburger," she said. "Plain."

He repeated her order into the intercom, added a Big Mac and two large fries, and rolled on around to the pickup window. Moments later a white bag was passed through the driver's-side window, along with two coffees in foam cups.

He didn't stop, just took the food and pulled back onto the road, and Jess was glad. Everything around the McDonald's was closed, and even though the surrounding parking lots and businesses had their night lighting on, she still felt exposed. Somebody could be following them. Somebody could be watching them. Somebody could be just waiting for a chance.

To do what? *To kill her*, Jess thought, and shivered.

Clearly hungry, Ryan ate while he drove, taking big bites out of his sandwich and shoveling in fries by the bunch. Jess couldn't choke down more than a couple of bites of her hamburger and she flat-out couldn't stomach the fries, but the coffee helped. She was still nursing it, savoring each hot, sweet sip, when he finished his meal, passed her the trash so that she could stuff it down in the bag with her own, then shot her an assessing look.

"Better?" he asked.

"Better," she agreed.

"You feel like talking anymore?"

Actually, she didn't. She never wanted to speak of it again. She never wanted to think about it again. She just wanted it all to go away.

Not gonna happen.

She faced the bitter truth. And she looked out at the

road unspooling before them, at the rolling hills and fields that were cloaked in darkness now, and tried not to remember the last time she had driven this way.

"I guess," she said.

"You were pretty woozy when I found you on that hillside, you know. Are you sure you actually saw everything you just described to me? I'm asking if you're positive it really happened, or if there's any possibility that you could have imagined or dreamed some of it?"

Suddenly the few bites of hamburger Jess had managed to get down felt like billiard balls in her stomach.

"Like the attack in the hospital, you mean?" Sarcasm laced the question.

He didn't so much as twitch an eyelash. "Yeah, like that."

Jess let it go for the moment. "I can't be totally sure, of course, because I was in a terrible accident and I did get knocked unconscious." She reasoned it out for him just as she had for herself when the memories had first come flooding back, and she had hoped and prayed they *were* just a really bad dream. "But I am as certain as it is possible to be that they're real."

"You think that the car you were riding in was struck by something unspecified and forced off the road, and then unknown subjects with flashlights, presumably from the car behind you, ran down the hillside past you, surrounded the crashed car with at least one screaming survivor still inside it, and either set it on fire or watched it burn without doing anything to help?"

Jess clenched her fists and tried not to let the memories in again. "Yes. That's exactly what I think."

"Then you were attacked later that same night in the hospital by someone who presumably had not realized you had been thrown clear of the car at the time and wanted to silence the only living witness to the murder of the First Lady?"

"Yes," she said again. Then she took a deep breath and looked at him steadily. "You were lying about the tests on the IV equipment coming back negative, weren't you?"

"Nah."

Jess felt herself tensing. "I know I did not imagine that. I—"

"Hold on a minute." He glanced at her. "I did not lie. I told you the truth. But what I didn't tell you was that the equipment tested negative for everything except standard saline solution. None of the medications that should have been in there according to your chart were there. Which means that either the tests were wrong or somebody switched the bags."

Jess felt a thrill of horror at having her suspicions confirmed, followed by a rush of indignation.

"So you knew I was telling the truth. You knew somebody attacked me. Is that why you were following me?"

He didn't reply. They had reached Dale City by that time, and traffic had picked up again. She allowed him a few minutes of concentration time as he drove past exits for the Potomac Hills Mall, which Jess knew from her own personal shopping experiences was the second-largest outlet mall in northern Virginia, and the Waterworks Water Park. But when they pulled off onto the exit for Clearbrook, stopped at an intersection that boasted a 7-Eleven and a liquor store, then turned onto a two-lane road devoid of traffic and he still didn't answer, she narrowed her eyes at him.

"That's why you followed me to Davenport's office, isn't it? Because you knew I'd told the truth about what had happened in the hospital." The headlights swept over a strip of golden, waist-high grass. Ahead the road gleamed pale, curving away into the night.

He glanced her way. He still looked abstracted, as though he was having a hard time leaving behind whatever thoughts occupied him.

"I followed you as a precaution," he said at last. "Just to make sure you were all right."

Before she could reply he hit the brakes, pausing briefly before continuing through an intersection onto a narrow asphalt lane. It was only then, as the tires swooshed over the smooth ebony surface and her attention shifted to her surroundings, that Jess realized they had well and truly left Dale City behind. Thanks to the still-falling rain, the night was dark as pitch. Woods crowded in close, and the headlights flashed past what seemed like an endless stockade of enormous trees on both sides. She was just opening her mouth to ask where they were when he turned into a driveway and a two-story house came into view. It was a clapboard farmhouse, painted dark gray with white trim. It had an outbuilding off to the side.

His house. Of course, this had to be his house.

There was not a single light on in the place.

It occurred to her that, aside from the RAV4's headlights, there was not a single light in sight.

This was not a neighborhood. There were no other houses around, no other buildings of any description that she could see. Just dark, dark, and more dark.

Apprehension tightened her muscles. Her pulse quickened. She sat up a little straighter, looking all around.

"Is this your . . . ?" she was asking just for clarification as he braked in the small paved area to the right of the house. That was as far as she got because, just as he slid the transmission into park and killed the headlights, she caught a glimpse of two tall figures stepping out from behind the outbuilding and moving swiftly toward them.

That was when she quit talking, because fear closed her throat.

Chapter 17

"YO," MARK CALLED OUT to Wendell and Fielding as he stepped out of the SUV. They replied in kind. Mark immediately started breathing easier. With what had gone down with Davenport and his secretary, it was clear that the situation was out of control. At least, out of his control. He had no doubt that somebody was pulling the strings. He just wasn't sure who it was yet, or exactly what was going on. And while he found out, he meant to do what he had to do to keep Jess alive and well. Thus he'd texted Fielding as soon as he had put Jess in the RAV4 and before he had gotten in himself, and told him to round up Wendell and Matthews and meet him at his house. They were pulling bodyguard duty for the next few hours, or until he figured something else out, whichever came first.

If Davenport had been coerced by some means or another to first kill Jess and then commit suicide, as Mark suspected, and his secretary had then been run down by a vehicle that, he was almost certain, would turn out to be stolen, then the safest thing was to assume he was dealing with a sophisticated assassin or team of assassins operating under a scorched-earth policy.

One who either had orchestrated the murder of the First Lady, as Jess suspected, or was pulling cleanup duty in the aftermath of her death. Either way, it didn't bode well for Jess.

The thing that was proving the biggest obstacle for him in believing that the First Lady was murdered was motive. Annette Cooper's drug addiction was a problem but not a killing one. First, the President and his people had already put a plan in place to handle it. Second, no one outside a tight little circle knew about it. Third, other politicians and their spouses had confessed to various drug-related problems in the past, and the fallout had not been catastrophic. In fact, in the case of spouses in particular, it had even made them seem more sympathetic to the public.

If the First Lady had been murdered, there had to be another reason, a motive he was missing or knew nothing about. Alternatively, the whole thing, from Annette Cooper's fleeing the White House to her death to the purported attack on Jess in the hospital to Davenport's attempt to kill Jess and subsequent suicide to what happened to Marian Young, was all a series of unfortunate events that had occurred one after the other like falling dominoes. Connected but not premeditated, as it were. Kind of like a butterfly's wings causing a hurricane halfway around the world.

Yeah, Mark concluded reluctantly, and he believed in Santa Claus, too.

"That the survivor?" Meeting him at the front of the car, Wendell nodded toward Jess, who appeared as just a small, dark shape huddled in his front passenger seat.

"Yeah." Mark walked around the car and opened her door. He meant to reach in for her, but she was already sliding her legs out. The rain had lightened up, and the cold sprinkle that was currently falling was barely heavy enough to be felt. He ignored it, and apparently she was planning to as well, because she made no effort to shield her head from the drizzle as it emerged next.

"I take it you know these people."

It was too dark to see her expression, but her voice had an edge to it. Having strangers pop up unexpectedly had probably scared her.

"Yeah. I guess I should have given you a heads-up."

"That would have been nice."

Her shoes—black high heels, which seemed an idiotic choice for a woman who was having trouble walking—made a gritty sound as they planted on the rough concrete of his parking area. He leaned in to help her out, but she shook her head at him.

"I can manage."

As if to prove it, she stood up, one hand holding on to the door for balance.

"Okay." He stepped back, willing to let her do her thing. Wendell and Fielding immediately closed in, providing a human barrier between her and anyone who might be out there watching.

If this was scorched earth, a sniper's bullet was always a possibility. Although he didn't mean to tell Jess that. No need to scare her unnecessarily.

"Jessica Ford," he said to Wendell and Fielding by way of an introduction. He looked at Jess. "Susan Wendell and Paul Fielding, Secret Service."

"Nice to meet you," Fielding said.

Wendell, as befitted her more taciturn nature, merely nodded. Jess nodded back. The five-eleven Wendell towered over her even in the no-nonsense flats Wendell favored. And with Fielding and himself rounding out the group, Jess made him think of a sapling in the midst of a stand of oaks.

He felt a sudden surge of protectiveness toward her. She was under his wing now, and he meant to see to it that she got out of this in one piece, whatever it took.

"Where's Matthews?" he asked.

By this time, Jess had let go of the door and was walking

with slow, careful steps toward the house. Mark stayed close, ready to catch her if she needed catching. She didn't so much as glance his way. Yeah, she was ticked.

Women.

"Checking the perimeter," Fielding replied.

Mark unlocked the side door, pushed it open, and stood back for Jess to precede him into the house. There was only one small step onto the stoop, and then another into the house itself, and she managed both with no apparent difficulty. He followed her inside, flipping on the switch beside the door as he passed it so that warm yellow light suffused the kitchen from the old-fashioned fixtures overhead. Wendell and Fielding entered behind him, and he shut and locked the door.

Like all his locks, it was a good one: a nearly unbreachable dead bolt. It was the most up-to-date thing in the kitchen. Everything else, the harvest-gold appliances, the faux-wood floor, the fruit-print wallpaper, the red-and-gold-checked curtains, was left over from the previous owner. He'd thought about remodeling it a couple of times but didn't see the need. He almost never cooked, and he was hardly ever home. Even when Taylor stayed with him, they mostly ate out.

He turned to discover Jess, with one hand leaning against the round oak table in the center of the room, looking big-eyed and pale and sort of like a half-drowned kitten as she gave comparative rottweilers Wendell and Fielding a once-over.

"So what's the plan?" she asked, her eyes sliding to meet his. He was, he realized, beginning to know her well enough to detect, beyond her annoyance at him, an edge of wariness in her expression. *Well, fair enough.* After all she'd been through over the last few days, she had every reason in the world to be wary. And Wendell, with her slicked-back blond hair, chiseled, square-jawed face, and tall, athletic figure encased in a snug black pantsuit, and

Fielding, in a navy suit, his cherubic cheeks notwith-standing, were a formidable-looking pair based on size alone. Add in the fact that Wendell was standing in such a way as to reveal part of the holstered gun at her waist, and he could see why Jess might be intimidated by them.

She was a very small woman, after all. Even in her power suit and high heels, which she must have donned in honor of her meeting with Davenport, it was hard to remember that she was twenty-eight years old.

"We hole up here, get some sleep, try to work out what's going on," he told her. "The key is, we've got enough firepower now to keep you safe from whatever while we figure this thing out."

Fielding and Wendell both nodded in agreement. There was the faintest of crackles, and Wendell seemed to listen intently. Then she said something into her sleeve.

"Matthews says the perimeter is clear. He's on his way in," she announced, and Mark nodded.

"Could I talk to you, Ryan?" Jess asked, straightening away from the table.

Clearly, she meant alone.

"Sure. Make yourselves at home, guys," he said to the others, both of whom had been to his house before on social occasions and both of whom also knew exactly why they were there: to keep Jess alive. With a gesture, he indicated to Jess that she should precede him through the rectangular doorway that led into the dining room. Like the other rooms in the Victorian-era farmhouse, it was smallish and square, finding its charm in narrow mullioned windows and high ceilings. He never used the dining room, either, which was why there were cobwebs in the corners and a fine layer of dust on the table, so he followed Jess on into the living room, which was comfortably furnished with a big flat-screen TV, a big couch, and

two overstuffed chairs. The curtains were drawn. The
door—the front door to the house, the second of three
entrances that included a door in the basement—was
closed and locked. To the right, just beyond the entrance
to the dining room, were stairs to the second floor.

Only the faintest amount of light from the kitchen
penetrated here. Mark bent and turned on a lamp.

As the small pool of light enveloped her, Zoey, the
orange tabby cat, looked up from where she had been
napping in a corner of the couch, meowed a greeting,
and stood up, stretching and kneading the brown leather
that was ragged with her claw marks.

A few feet ahead of him, Jess jumped like she'd been
shot and whirled to face him, catching the back of the
nearest recliner for balance when the sudden movement
was almost too much for her.

"What . . . ?" she gasped.

Mark realized that Zoey's small sounds had spooked
her, and he had to smile. He gestured at Zoey, who
headed his way as usual, finally balancing on the rolled
arm of the couch as she butted her head against his thigh,
wanting attention.

The cat operated under the delusion that she was
his.

"You have a cat?" Jess looked at him with obvious
surprise.

He scratched behind Zoey's ears. True to form, the cat
started purring and shredding leather at the same time.
The sad thing was, when he'd bought the couch he'd paid
a lot for it because he had expected it to last forever.

"She belongs to my daughter."

"You have a daughter?"

He nodded. "Taylor. She's fifteen. She's not here right
now. She lives with my ex-wife in McLean. I get to keep
my daughter's cat because her mother has allergies."

Or so Heather claimed. The truth was that Heather

didn't want a cat in her house—a McMansion she shared with her banker third husband and Taylor—clawing her furniture and shedding on her rugs. So when soft-touch Mark hadn't had the heart to make Taylor return the kitten she'd brought home from a neighbor's one sunny Saturday two summers ago, he got sole custody. Of the cat, not the kid.

Which worked. At least it gave Taylor a reason to want to come and visit. With her busy social life, she was ducking out of their weekends more and more. Who needs a dad when you've got the mall?

For a moment Jess looked like she wanted to ask more questions. Then she frowned, straightened away from the chair, and looked past him toward the dining room.

Mark realized that she was checking to see if Wendell or Fielding were in sight.

He quit scratching the cat and immediately moved away from the couch, thus evading Zoey's attempt to climb him like a tree. Stopping just a short distance from Jess, he stuck his hands in his pockets and met her gaze. "So what did you want to talk to me about?"

Jess looked tense all over again. Reaching out, she caught his arm, pulling him closer.

"Why did you call them?"

He realized she was referring to Fielding and company. Her voice was scarcely louder than a whisper. The top of her head barely reached his shoulder, so he had to tilt his head toward her just to hear her properly.

"Because I need backup. I can protect you from a lone killer, maybe even two—as long as I'm awake. But I have to sleep. And what if there are more than two? What if they take me by surprise?" He watched her brows fold into a forbidding V above her eyes and added, "Hey, it's your ass I'm thinking of here."

"Nobody knows where we are." Even as she said it, she

looked unsure. Then she looked waspish. "Or at least, they didn't until you called in the cavalry in there."

His eyes narrowed at her. "We could have been followed. I—or we—could have been caught on video somewhere in or around that building. I was keeping an eye on you while you were in the hospital, so somebody could make a good guess as to where you are from that. Let me put it to you this way: I wouldn't have brought you here unless I knew I had the personnel in place to keep you safe."

Her lips compressed. "Yeah, well, who keeps me safe from your 'personnel'?"

"What?"

"You heard me."

"That's ridiculous."

"Is it?"

There was a commotion in the kitchen. Mark frowned, glancing around, only to feel the flare-up of reflexive adrenaline caused by the sudden noise die down as he heard Matthews say, "So what's up with this chick again?"

Wendell replied—he recognized her voice—but in too low a tone for him to make out the words.

Clearly, Matthews had been admitted to the kitchen. Nothing any more alarming than that. He looked back at Jess.

She started talking at him before he could so much as get his mouth open to attempt to reassure her some more.

"Do not tell those people what I told you. About the wreck. About what I remember. Any of it." It was a low but fierce command. Her eyes—looking more green than hazel at the moment, thanks to, he supposed, some combination of the dim lighting in his living room and how mad she was—blazed up into his.

They were really pretty eyes, he registered. Feminine,

flirty eyes. Or at least, they would be if they weren't glaring at him.

"I wasn't going to." His tone was mild. She was scared, and with good reason, so he wanted to be sensitive to that. "Look, you're safe here. You don't have to worry about anything. I'll take care of this."

She looked skeptical.

"Ryan?" Wendell called from the kitchen before Jess could say whatever it was she looked like she wanted to say. "We're not doing you a whole lot of good stuck here in a clump in the kitchen. We need to spread out."

She was right, he knew.

"We good?" he asked Jess.

"Oh, yeah."

She didn't mean it, which her sarcastic tone made clear. Too bad. He was taking her response at face value anyway. The bottom line was, he didn't have time for this right now. Keeping her alive was his number one priority. Keeping her happy fell further down the list.

"We're done here," he called back. "Come on in."

Jess's glare got downright ferocious.

"I don't remember anything after the car pulled away from the hotel," she hissed as footsteps headed their way. Her hand tightened on his arm. If she'd been any bigger, her grip might actually have hurt. "You got that? Nothing. That's what you tell them."

"Jess . . ."

"Got it?"

With what he considered a truly heroic effort, he managed not to roll his eyes. "Fine. I got it."

Her hand dropped away from his arm. Her expression changed as if by magic, the frown vanishing, the tension transforming itself into vaguely pleasant nothingness.

Wendell walked into the living room right on cue, followed by Matthews, who was about six-one with medium brown hair, wearing a dark suit like the rest of them. Typical Secret Service agent. Mark nodded at him, introduced him to Jess. Perfunctory greetings were exchanged.

"Do you think I could take a shower?" Jess's tone was considerably sweeter now as she looked at him. "And maybe get some dry clothes?"

He remembered that she was wet. And had been shivering. And had had a hell of a bad day. All things considered, she was hanging in pretty well. Actually, damned well.

"There's a bathroom and bedroom upstairs you can use," he told her, even as he watched Matthews go over and test the front door, then push the curtain aside to take a peek out the window.

Wendell settled down in one of the chairs, her eyes on Jess as she headed for the stairs. Jess's back, which was turned to them, was ramrod straight. Her head was held high. She walked slowly, but her gait was surprisingly steady under the circumstances. He was guessing that it cost her to keep it that way.

"You have an alarm system?" Matthews turned away from the window, attracting his attention. Mark caught just a glimpse of the obsidian blackness beyond the glass. At just after eleven p.m., there was still a lot of night to go. A lot of hours in which anything could happen. The thought made him antsy.

"No," he answered.

"That would be us." Wendell's voice was dry.

"Any other means of egress?" Matthews asked.

"Basement door."

Matthews said something back, but Mark missed it, following Jess with his body as well as his eyes now over to the stairs, which were narrow and steep. Mark came up behind her as she paused with one hand on the newel post before attempting the ascent.

"Want some help?" he asked in her ear.

She shook her head, didn't give him so much as a glance. "Nope."

Okay, she was clearly still feeling waspish.

Squaring her shoulders, she started to climb. Mark stayed where he was in case he was needed, watching her plant one foot after the other on the treads with steely determination. The effort it cost her was apparent in her tight grip on the handrail and her slight hesitation between each step. His instinct was to run up behind her, pick her up despite what he was sure would be her protests, and carry her to the top of the steps, but he resisted. She would be angry. And embarrassed. While he didn't mind making her angry—she was cute when she was angry—he didn't like the idea of embarrassing her in front of the others.

But his eyes never left her.

Despite the businesslike suit, she looked delicate. Fragile even.

Narrow shoulders, tiny waist, slim calves above the idiotic high heels.

The thing that struck him most though, hit him as kind of a revelation.

She had a nice ass.

High and tight and round as a basketball. With just enough of a feminine sway as she climbed the stairs to really catch his attention.

Sexy.

That was the thought that was ping-ponging through his surprised brain when Fielding walked into the room and said, "So, Ryan, you want to give us an overview of what's happened?"

"Yeah," Mark answered, even as Jess paused and stiffened. What was going through her head was as plain as if she had turned around and yelled it at him: *Don't tell them what I told you.* Which he had no intention of doing, if for no other reason than she'd asked him not to. Anyway, he believed in erring on the side of caution. He trusted these guys, but . . .

There was always a *but.* Always.

"Bathroom's first door on the right," he called up to Jess. "You can use the bedroom beside it."

"Great. Thanks." She started moving again, still without looking at him. In female-speak, this meant he was still in the doghouse with her, as he knew from long and sometimes bitter experience with the species. "I should be down in a little while."

"Don't come back down. Go to bed. Try to sleep. Unless something changes, we're fixed here until at least morning."

"All right. Good night, then."

Mark didn't realize he was still watching her until she gained the top of the stairs and walked out of sight, still without so much as a glance over her shoulder. Then, collecting himself, he turned to find three pairs of eyes looking at him. Wendell's, at least, were bright with speculation. He wondered if she was just more observant than the others, or if there really was such a thing as feminine intuition and if he was witnessing it at work. Frowning, hoping his little mental digression on the state of Jess's posterior had not been obvious, he moved back into the center of his living room and put Jess out of his mind. With Zoey weaving in and out around his ankles, he got back to business, giving them a carefully edited account of the evening's events. They listened intently, which was what he expected. As part of the team that had been on duty that fateful Saturday night, Wendell, Fielding, and Matthews had all suffered in the backlash of the tragedy, remanded to desk duty by the director for the duration of the investigation. Above and beyond providing firepower if needed, they were thus more than ready, willing, and able to help him try to figure this thing out.

They were eager. Their careers had been damaged, too.

"Wendell, I need you to check on Marian Young's condition," he concluded, looking at her as she sprawled out in the chair. *Ladylike* was not in Wendell's vocabulary, and he kind of liked that about her.

"Will do, boss." She got to her feet, running her hands over her hair, and headed for the kitchen, presumably to make the necessary calls.

"If somebody really wants to kill her"—Fielding straightened away from the wall he'd been leaning against and jerked his head upward to indicate Jess—"she's not going to be hard to find. It's kind of an open secret in the Service that you've been keeping an eye on her."

"Fielding's got a point." Matthews rose from the couch. "This house is bound to be a target."

"That's why you're here," Mark said. "Tomorrow we'll move her. We just need to keep her safe for tonight."

"No worries, then." Fielding grinned and patted the Glock holstered at his waist. "Bring it on. I even brought an extra clip."

That was actually pretty funny, considering that Fielding was notorious for running short on ammunition during training exercises.

"Marian Young's dead," Wendell announced, returning from the kitchen. "Arrived DOA at University Hospital."

The tension immediately ratcheted up again.

JUST BECAUSE HE WAS a suspicious bastard at heart, Mark waited until he was alone to make a quick phone call. It was to a friend at the FBI; it was made on Wendell's phone, which he filched from her pocket when she removed her jacket and hung it in the hall closet (he didn't want to use his in case it was being monitored, and he figured Wendell wasn't likely to check her own outgoing call history anytime soon); and his request was quick and to the point: He wanted somebody to check the rear of the burned-out Lincoln for any kind of collision or other damage that might have forced it off the road.

That done, he returned the phone to Wendell's pocket. Grabbing a bottle of water out of the refrigerator, he exchanged a few words with Wendell and headed upstairs.

There was one more quick question he needed to ask Jess before she went to sleep.

Chapter 18

SHE WAS SHIVERING WHEN she stepped into the shower, from fear and delayed reaction and God knew what else. Plus, her back ached. Her legs ached. Her head pounded. Collapsing where she stood was starting to feel like a real possibility.

Only she wasn't going to let that happen. If ever there was a time to be strong, this was it. Gritting her teeth, she turned on the taps and stepped under the spray.

What she wanted more than anything in the world was just to be able to go home. To take a shower in her own bathroom, crawl into her own bed, and pretend that none of this had ever happened.

If she could only turn the clock back to last Saturday night, she would never, ever, in a million years have picked up that phone.

But she couldn't turn back time, she had picked up that phone, and here she was.

Taking a shower in the bathroom of a hunky Secret Service agent she wasn't even sure she could trust.

While jumping at every stray flutter of the shower curtain or unexpected sound in mortal terror that somebody might be trying to kill her again.

Besides Ryan, there were three other Secret Service agents downstairs. Which, on the face of it, might seem like a good thing. Jess was unconvinced. Maybe these three were, as Ryan seemed to think, good Secret Service agents.

And maybe they weren't.

And that didn't even factor in Secret Service agent number four, Ryan himself. *He* didn't want to kill her, she was almost sure.

So why, in that case, hadn't she told him that she suspected the Secret Service itself was involved in this?

The answer was dismally apparent: She might trust Ryan, but not enough. She still harbored that wiggly little smidgen of doubt where he was concerned. Maybe he was just pretending to help her while setting her up for something big; maybe, if he knew she suspected the Secret Service was part of what had happened, he would stop pretending and get on with the something big, which presumably would include her death.

You're paranoiding yourself out here.

She was so tired that trying to figure anything out was useless, so she quit. In an attempt to empty her mind, she deliberately focused on the here and now. The hot water helped, chasing away the shivers and calming the worst of her nerves. In fact, it felt better to Jess than anything had in ages. She stayed under the steaming cascade for a long time, washing her hair, soaping herself from head to toe, then letting the hot water run over her until the worst of the stiffness in her back and legs had washed away.

Two pain pills from the prescription that had been given to her in the hospital, which was now in a small bottle in her purse, taken before she had gotten into the shower and finally kicking in, helped, too.

When she got out at last, she wrapped herself in a threadbare orange towel from the linen closet beside the sink, wrapped another around her hair, then wiped the worst of the steam off the mirror. Having taken her contacts out preshower, her reflection was pleasantly blurry. Fishing her glasses out of her purse, she put them on and immediately made a face at herself as she came into focus.

Still the same old ordinary four-eyed Jess, plus a few yellowing bruises and a line of stitches above her eye.

What, had she been hoping for something different?

If she was, it was because of Ryan, and that could stop right now. She wasn't dumb enough to start fantasizing about him again, even if she did get a little thrill from just remembering what it felt like to be held against that big, strong, muscular chest in those big, strong, muscular arms.

He was holding you in his arms because somebody's trying to kill you, fool.

The thought served as a figurative slap in the face. She kicked Ryan out of her head. She needed to try to come up with a plan to survive, not moon over some hot guy.

Maybe I should just tell everything to the media and get it all out there. If everybody knew what I know, no one would have any reason to want to kill me. Would they?

Unwrapping the towel from her head, Jess turned that thought over in her mind and arrived at no definitive solution. Like everything else, the matter was best left to be mulled when she wasn't so tired. Accordingly, she put her efforts into getting ready for bed. The bathroom was clearly used frequently by a female, most likely his daughter. There was a hair dryer in the closet beside the sink and she got it out, retrieved a brush from her purse, and started blow-drying her hair. The process was short and simple, a blast of hot air here, a few twirls of the brush there, and it was done: presto, chin-length bob. Then she brushed her teeth with the travel toothbrush she always carried in her purse and some of Ryan's Crest toothpaste, applied a little cherry ChapStick, rubbed on a little lotion, rinsed out her undies, wrapped them in a towel and tucked them under her arm along with her suit to be hung in the bedroom to dry, and headed out the door.

The hall was dark. The only illumination was a yellowish glow from the living room below. She could hear people talking—the Secret Service on the job. The thought made her shiver. Fortunately, the door to the bedroom was only a yard or so to the left. Too bad she hadn't thought to leave on the light.

"Hey."

Coming unexpectedly out of the dark just as soon as she walked into the bedroom, Ryan's voice made her jump. Luckily, she recognized the deep, drawling timbre of it before her body could go into full crisis mode. She recognized him, too, in the solid long shape sprawled out on the still-made bed.

"What are you doing in here?" She glared at him, which was, of course, a waste of a good glare because he couldn't see it properly. He reached out a long arm and switched on the lamp beside the bed, revealing the boxy bedroom with the headboard-less double bed pushed into the corner beside the single, heavily curtained window.

Then the glare worked.

"Waiting for you. Look, I brought you some water." He held up an unopened plastic bottle, then put it back down on the bedside table. He'd lost his jacket, and his shoes, and his white shirt had come untucked. The sleeves were rolled up almost to his elbows. "And some pj's."

He got to his feet as she eyed the new-looking pink flannel pajamas that lay across the foot of the bed. They had a high neckline and a ruffle down the front, and were covered with dancing black poodles. In tutus.

These had to be his daughter's, although they were awfully childish for a fifteen-year-old.

"I'm not sure your daughter would like me wearing her pajamas."

"Don't worry about it. She's never worn them. I bought them for her for Christmas, and she took one look and practically gagged. She made it pretty clear she'll never wear them in this lifetime."

The man was clearly clueless. His daughter's bedroom was just across the hall, and the door was open. Unlike the rest of the house, which was done in soothing if uninspired earth tones, it was painted deep purple and decorated with Day-Glo band posters taped to the wall. Having glimpsed that, and the picture on the living-room mantel of the pretty blond girl on horseback wearing jeans and a black skull-and-bones tee, Jess could see how the pink pajamas might not be quite to the teen's taste.

"Well, thank you." She stepped aside in clear indication that he was now free to leave the room.

He didn't move. "I actually had a reason for coming in here other than pj's and water."

"What?" If her tone was a little abrupt, it was because she was feeling distinctly uncomfortable. Just as she had finished taking in the full glory of the pink pajamas, it had hit her with all the force of a two-by-four between the eyes that she was wearing an orange towel. Period. A skimpy orange towel that covered all the pertinent parts but left her shoulders and most of her legs bare.

The thing was, he'd noticed. That's what had alerted her, the way his expression had changed. He had blatantly checked her out, his eyes sliding over her, while he had thought she was busy examining the pajamas. She'd caught the whole long look out of the corner of her eye. It was an entirely masculine look, an unmistakably sexy look, and her heart was beating faster as a result. Now, as their gazes met, she curled a hand around the top of the towel right where it overlapped between her breasts, just to make sure that the flimsy thing stayed where it was supposed to.

Jeez, am I blushing?

It was then, as she frowned in pure flustered self-defense at the hard, handsome face that was in such perfect focus that she could see every tiny line around his eyes and bristle in the stubble darkening his cheeks and chin, that she remembered she was wearing her glasses. That was worse by far than being caught in a towel. It was all she could do not to whip them off.

Don't be a complete idiot. This is not about you and him. It's about . . .

"Close the door," he directed in a low voice.

She couldn't help it. Her eyes widened a little on his face. Her mouth went dry, and her pulse picked up the pace. If naughty thoughts sprang instantly into her mind, it wasn't because she thought they were going to leap into bed the moment she complied. It was, rather, because the room was small and he was close and she was next to naked.

And she'd had dreams like this. Actually, too many to count.

How embarrassing is that?

"Why?"

"Because I don't want anyone else overhearing this conversation."

Okay, then. She was so near to the door that all she had to do was reach out and close it, which she did.

Suddenly, the room seemed even smaller.

"So, what?" she asked defensively, pressing the top of the towel more firmly against her chest.

"First off, Marian Young's dead. I'm sorry."

Her heart gave a sad little thump, even though the news wasn't a surprise. Jess realized she'd known it all along.

"Poor Marian. She didn't deserve that."

"Nobody deserves that." His expression changed subtly, his eyes narrowing, his mouth tightening, and Jess realized that the face she was now looking at belonged to the Fed. "I've got a question for you: Where were you going? In the car that night, you and the First Lady and the others?"

"What?" Given the change of subject, the question took her a moment to process.

"You told me that Davenport was going to call and tell you where the First Lady was going once you got in the car. Did he call? Where were you going?"

It took her a moment to remember.

"Mr. Davenport didn't call. He was drinking that night, just like he was drinking earlier, and he didn't want to deal with Mrs. Cooper. It was Marian who called. She called the driver directly, and then she called Mrs. Cooper, which made Mrs. Cooper furious, because she didn't like dealing with a secretary. She wanted to talk to Mr. Davenport. Presumably, Marian told the driver where we were going. I'm pretty sure she told Mrs. Cooper, too, because Mrs. Cooper was trying to call somebody to make sure all the arrangements had been made when she couldn't get a signal and got mad and threw her phone. But I don't know who that somebody was, and I don't know where we were going."

Ryan frowned at her for a moment, his expression thoughtful. He was so near she could have closed the distance between them in a single step.

Not that she wanted to, of course, or was even thinking about doing anything like that.

Anyway, he now appeared about as aware that she was nearly naked as he did that she was wearing glasses. Which was to say not at all.

Wallpaper, that's what she was once again.

Which was probably a good thing, even though it might not feel like it at the moment.

"The First Lady never said a name?"

"Nope."

"Didn't say anything about what she planned to do when she got there?"

"Nope."

"You sure? She must have said something that would provide some kind of clue."

"Not that I can remember."

"You're not being much help here."

"I can't tell you what I don't know."

"You know, to end this thing and get you back to your normal life, we've first got to figure out what exactly is happening."

"Actually," Jess said, "I may have thought of another way to get myself out of this."

"Such as?"

"What if I went to the media? I know a reporter who works at the *Post*. What if I contacted him and told him everything I know and he published it? Or what if I went on TV and told the whole thing to the entire country? There wouldn't be any point in anyone killing me after that. Everything I know or suspect would be out in full public view."

Ryan shook his head. "Go to the press? Without any kind of proof? That would be the worst thing you could do."

"I don't see why." She put up her chin. "In fact, the more I think about it, that's just what I may do. I'm ready to end this."

He took the step needed to close the distance between them and caught her by the arm. Just like the rest of him, his hand was big. His fingers felt warm and strong curling into the soft skin just above her elbow. His grip was firm, almost hard.

She was very aware of it—and him. Whether she wanted to be or not.

"Don't even think about doing that." There was an intensity to his gaze that told her he meant every word. "If you go public with the stuff you told me, without any kind of proof to back you up, then it will be just you accusing some very dangerous people of murdering the First Lady of the United States and a bunch of other people, too. That would cause them a problem. What's the best way to take care of that problem? Take care of you. No more witness? No more problem. Poof! The whole thing just goes away when you do."

"People would still investigate. . . ."

"They might, but you wouldn't know anything about it because you'd be dead." He must have realized that his grip on her was getting too hard, because he let go. "You do want to get out of this alive, don't you?"

The look she gave him was answer enough.

"Then just hang tight. I've got people looking into it. If we get some proof, then you can think about going public. But not until then."

"Fine."

He studied her. His expression softened fractionally. "Look, I'm handling this, okay? Everything's going to be all right."

"Are you going to pat me on the top of my head now?"

For a moment he looked surprised. Then he grinned. "I would, but you look like you might break my arm if I tried."

"Just so we're clear."

"Clear as glass. Go to bed, Jess." He walked past her, opened the door, and paused, looking back at her. "By the way, you look damned good in a towel."

Before she could react, he closed the door and was gone, leaving her heart to flutter like the poor foolish thing it was.

By the time she put on the fuzzy pink pajamas and crawled into bed, she was so tired her head was spinning, so tired she couldn't think straight.

Which was good. Because she didn't want to think at all.

Because if Ryan wasn't filling her head, worse things were: images of Davenport pointing the gun at her and firing, of the big window wall suddenly shattering so that the office was open to the night, of Davenport lying lifeless in the street below, of Marian flying up into the air.

Followed by memories of the crash itself.

Ryan wouldn't tell anyone that she had remembered. He'd promised, and anyway, he was on her side, and ...

Annette Cooper was buried today.

Okay, enough. Jess started counting sheep, picturing the woolly little things leaping a fence in a spring-green meadow.

One little sheepie, two little sheepies ...

The next thing she knew, she was waking up. Which meant, of course, that she had been asleep. So deeply asleep that it took her a minute to get reoriented, to recall whose bed she was sleeping in and where she was.

The room was so dark that she knew where the door was only because of the thin line of light seeping beneath it. There was a clock beside the bed, the kind that glowed if you touched it, so she did. The glow happened, but the numbers were blurry. Putting on her glasses, she saw that it was four-forty-nine a.m. She'd been asleep for about five and a half hours.

She had to go to the bathroom.

Jess remembered the bottle of water she'd chugged before going to sleep and grimaced. She should have known better.

Getting up reluctantly, she headed for the bathroom without bothering to turn on the light.

The house was quiet. The upstairs was dark, while a glance down the stairs told her that below some lights were still on. The good Secret Service agents below were acting as her bodyguards, and thus had stayed awake all night to protect her. Or maybe they were sleeping in shifts.

Coming back out of the bathroom, she found herself looking toward the master bedroom at the far, dark end of the hall and wondering if Ryan was in there, asleep.

The picture that she conjured up awoke a little pulse of heat deep inside her body.

You look damned good in a towel.

Just remembering him saying that made the flicker of heat get a whole lot hotter.

He . . .

Voices from below distracted her.

". . . feel like breakfast?" The voice was muffled so that she couldn't really identify the speaker, except that it wasn't Ryan. It was obvious that whoever it was had just walked into the living room, which was why she had heard only the last part of what was said.

"Kind of early for that, isn't it?" Jess thought that might be Wendell talking. It kind of sounded like a woman, but without seeing the speaker it was hard to be sure.

"It's never too early for breakfast, sugar."

Jess stopped walking, like she'd been poleaxed. She stood in the middle of the hall, with the pool of light from below ending just in front of her bare feet. Unable to help herself, she looked down the stairway toward the living room. She could see nothing but the newel post and a rectangle of wood floor at the bottom. The sudden tightness in her chest was accompanied by an awful sinking sensation in the pit of her stomach.

The roaring in her ears was so loud that if they were still talking, she couldn't hear it.

But she'd heard enough: that one word, *sugar.*

With a certainty so intense it was sickening, she knew where she had heard it before.

Chapter 19

THIS WILL HELP YOU go back to sleep, sugar.

That's what the person in the too-small scrubs with the suit pants and shiny black shoes showing below them had said just moments before he tried to kill her.

She'd just heard the same endearment again, in the same voice with the same intonation.

As Jess faced the truth of that, her heart pounded so hard it felt like it was trying to beat its way out of her chest.

The person who wanted to kill her was here. He was, as she had suspected from the beginning, a Secret Service agent, one of Ryan's supposedly "good" Secret Service agents who were downstairs right now with a mandate to protect her.

The ringing in her ears subsided enough so that her hearing came back.

"...two scrambled eggs, then. With sausage."

"If you're cooking, I'm eating. I'll have the same thing."

"'Fraid I'm all out of sausage." That voice was Ryan's. She would recognize it anywhere. He was down there, too. With them.

One of them. He'd lied about the results of the testing on her IV bag. At least, until she had called him on it.

"You got bacon, then?"

"Should have." Ryan again. "Check the fridge and see."

There was a reply, but it was muffled so that she couldn't quite make out the words. Probably the speaker was heading for the kitchen.

Jess didn't wait to hear anything more. Moving very, very quietly, she headed back to the bedroom and shut the door. Curse the luck, it didn't have a lock.

For a long moment, she simply stood in the pitch dark with her back pressed to the door, trying to slow her breathing, trying to calm her pounding heart, processing what she'd heard while panic surged icy cold through her veins.

What do I do?

Going running to Ryan was obviously out. First, the scale had again dipped drastically in favor of not trusting him. And second, he was down there with the others.

Every instinct she possessed shrieked that she needed to get out of that house as soon as possible. Before Shiny Shoes, as she was going to call him, got a chance to try to kill her again.

Maybe they were all in on it. Even Ryan.

At the thought, she broke out in a cold sweat and her breathing grew ragged.

She didn't know. She had no way of knowing. All she knew was that she recognized that "sugar"—and that was enough.

I have to get out of here.

The thought brought another surge of panic with it.

The good news was, they all thought she was asleep. It would be an hour, maybe an hour and a half, until dawn, so she'd have darkness to cover her escape. Probably no one would even consider checking in on her before eight at the earliest. At the minimum, she had about three hours to put as much distance between herself and them as possible.

Where do I go?

Her mouth went dry as she realized she had no idea. She couldn't go back to her apartment: Even if Grace wasn't there, it was the first place anyone would look. She couldn't go to her mother's and put her family in danger. Friends and coworkers were out, too, and for the same reason: How awful would it be to visit on them the fate that seemed to befall everyone who got caught up in this?

I've got to find a place to hide out.

But where? Given everything that had happened, she had to assume that whoever this was could track her anywhere. That they *would* track her anywhere. That they would be relentless in trying to find her, and ruthless when they did.

The bottom line was that she needed to disappear. But how?

The window of darkness she would need to get away from the house unseen was rapidly shrinking. She was going to have to work out on the fly the details of what she was going to do once she was out of there.

Jess took a deep breath. First things first: She had to get dressed. She had to collect the belongings she meant to take with her. Then she had to get out of the house.

If I could get to my car ...

She owned a gray Acura TL. It should still be in the parking garage next to her apartment. The keys were in her purse.

The car's in D.C.

Turning on a light was a bad idea. Probably everyone was inside the house. Probably they wouldn't notice. But she wasn't willing to take that chance, because the only advantages she had was that, one, they imagined she was sound asleep, and, two, they had no idea she had discovered that the person who had previously tried to kill her was in their midst.

Probably they'll be able to put some kind of all-points bulletin out on my car. Once they realize I've taken it.

There was a tiny flat flashlight attached to her key chain, the kind that's supposed to last forever. Jess remembered it, crossed to the night table where her purse rested, extracted her keys by feel, and pushed the flashlight's button.

Presto, a narrow beam of white light.

I should be able to get at least a few hundred miles away before they even know I'm missing. Then I can ditch the car, switch the license plates, something. Trade it in, maybe.

Her underwear hung from the windowsill weighted by a book. The silky nylon wasn't quite dry, but she gathered it up. Her suit was damp, too, and so was her shirt. And her shoes—she groaned when she remembered them.

Why did I have to wear heels?

There were possibly items she could use in Mark's daughter's closet, but there was no way to be sure, and she was afraid someone might hear her in there and come up to investigate. It wasn't worth the risk.

How to get to the car?

A quick check inside the closet in the room she was in came up empty. Not so much as a hanger.

Okay, then.

She got dressed as quickly as she could in her damp clothes, threw her purse over her shoulder, and, picking up her shoes so that the heels wouldn't clatter on the hardwood floor, padded barefoot over to the window. The curtains were some kind of thick slubby material lined in white, she saw as she shoved them aside. Immediately, pale moonlight flooded in through the multi-paned, double-hung window. The rain had passed, which was both good and bad. Once outside, she would be able to see what she was doing without the flashlight. On the other hand, she would be easier to spot, too, if anyone happened to be looking.

Jess saw the lock, shined her flashlight on it. Surprisingly, it was bright brass and looked brand-new. Unlocking it was easy. The window itself, however, was old. The only encouraging sign was that the handles set into the bottom of the frame were, like the lock, bright new brass. Somebody had replaced the hardware in the recent past, which meant they had probably opened the window, too.

Stowing the flashlight in her purse, grasping the handles in the window frame, she pulled upward.

Please let the window open.

It did, with the most earsplitting screech imaginable.

Her heart going wild, Jess froze with the thing only partway up, looking over her shoulder as if she expected a bad guy to pop up behind her instantly.

Did they hear?

Nothing happened. No shouts. No footsteps as someone came upstairs to check out the screech. Just the same hushed house sounds as before, plus the soft moaning of the wind outside. Through the open window, cold, damp air poured in around her, causing the curtains to billow, making her think about needing a coat. Which there was no way in hell she was going to take the time to look for.

Go. Now.

There was a screen in the window blocking her exit. Putting a cautious hand through the opening, Jess felt rather than saw it. She was afraid to use the flashlight now unless she absolutely had to. The bright beam could give her away. So she ran her fingers over the cold roughness of the screen, feeling it, testing it out. It was thin wire mesh, designed to foil insects while letting air into the house. She tried to raise it. It was stuck fast.

Cut it.

Pulling her keys from her purse, she did just that, using her apartment key (she was afraid of damaging her car key, because she needed it so desperately) as a blade and sawing through the screen from bottom corner to bottom corner, then up on both sides. The sound reminded her of ripping cloth. Only if someone was right outside would they hear.

By the time she finished, her nerves were so on edge she felt ready to jump right out of her skin.

Go.

The path was now clear. She had about two feet of space between the sill and the window frame. Given the sound it had made the first time, she didn't dare try to raise the window further. Taking a deep breath, Jess stuck her head out and looked carefully all around. It was a straight drop down, with nothing beneath the window but grass. The earthy scent in the aftermath of the rain was strong. The wind blew past the house with a soft whooshing sound, making the tops of the nearby trees sway back and forth as if they were doing the wave. It was cold, maybe midforties. The bedroom was located at the back near the middle of the house, and the window looked out over a small, neat yard with some kind of patio to her right and woods encroaching on the unfenced lawn just a few feet beyond the patio's end. Her immediate goal was to make it to those woods.

I can see light from the kitchen.

Panic surged through her all over again as she spotted the square of yellowish light spilling out over the grass and realized what it was. It wasn't bright, which meant it was probably filtered through a thin curtain or something—she remembered the kitchen's unfortunate gold-and-red-checked curtains and nodded to herself— but it was definitely there.

All anybody in the kitchen would have to do is look out into the backyard . . .

They're probably in the kitchen right now. Cooking. Eating.

Jess visualized the kitchen, the placement of the table, the stove, the refrigerator. None of it was situated in such a way as to give anyone sitting, cooking, or opening the refrigerator a view of the backyard. She didn't think.

If she dropped straight down, she wouldn't land in the light. She would land right in the dense bank of shadows directly below. Even if they heard something and looked out, they shouldn't be able to see her. The bottom of the window was, perhaps, ten feet up. The ground beneath looked clear. If she held onto the windowsill with both hands, she would fall less than five feet. She hoped she wouldn't hurt herself, or make much noise.

Then she could run like hell.

Experimentally, Jess dropped her shoes, aiming them a little to the side so that she wouldn't land on them, and heard nothing as they hit. *Good.* Obviously the ground was soft from the rain. She had one final thought, and lightly touched the bottom of the screen's frame. It was, as she had feared, sharp and ragged enough to scratch her up pretty badly as she squeezed out.

The towel.

The orange one she had been wrapped in earlier. It now hung from the closet doorknob. Retracing her steps, she grabbed it, folded it over the ruined screen, pressed down to flatten the sharp edges as much as possible, then left it in place as a barrier between her skin and the wires.

This is as good as it's going to get.

Luckily, she was small. Hiking her skirt, throwing one leg over the windowsill and feeling the cold breath of the wind on her bare skin, she slithered out, then hung awkwardly from her hands before letting go. The towel fell with her—good thing; it was bright orange and to anyone looking at the rear of the house, it would have given her away as soon as dawn broke. She landed on her bare feet in smushy wet grass, the jolt of it shuddering through her, the towel fluttering down beside her. Her glasses were knocked askew. Shoving them back into place, she immediately went into a crouch, looking all around like a hunted small animal, heart pounding.

There were no shouts of discovery, no sounds other than the normal ones of a rural predawn. A quick glance at the lighted square on the grass, then up at the kitchen window itself, showed no change: The lights were still on in the kitchen, and as far as she could tell no one was looking out.

She reached for her shoes, picked them up, then grabbed the towel so its brightness wouldn't give her away.

Run.

Throwing herself forward, she made a dismal discovery: She couldn't. Running was beyond her.

But still she moved, lurching toward the questionable protection of the woods with an unsteady gait that sent needles of pain shooting up her spine. *Maybe I'm doing myself damage, maybe my injury's not healed enough for this. . . .* The thought brought a surge of panic with it. But what was the alternative? There was none, so she forced herself on, glancing wildly over her shoulder and all around as her bare feet sank into the icy wet grass and she clenched her teeth to keep them from chattering for fear someone might hear.

It was still night, still dark with thick, shifting shadows dancing across the ground from the clouds that played hide-and-seek with the pale sickle moon overhead. To her right she could see the parking area, Ryan's RAV4, and the outbuilding, which she could clearly tell now was a detached two-car garage. With a bicycle leaning against the side of it and another car—presumably having been used by the other agents—parked in another small paved area behind it.

Jess practically leaped into the blacker darkness at the base of the woods even as the presence of that bicycle imbedded itself in her mind. Already, her feet were so wet and cold that they were next to numb, which was probably a good thing because of the slippery leaves and sharp twigs and other debris piled beneath the trees. Small, prickly branches from the heavy undergrowth scratched at her legs, and in the near distance a pair of round, golden eyes stared unblinkingly down from what had to be the lower limbs of a tree. She could hear rustling as if the owl—she hoped it was an owl—was ruffling its wings. The insect chorus was louder now that she was away from the house. The scent of wet earth was stronger. The air felt colder.

As she paused to quickly dry her feet on the towel and slip on her shoes—any protection from the cold, treacherous ground was better than none—she realized that she was shaking all over. Gritting her teeth, she tried to will the tremors away. Having finished with the towel, she dropped it and kicked leaves over it until she was as certain as it was possible to be that it would stay hidden from view once the sun came up.

Straightening, looking fearfully back at the house, she realized that her escape was tenuous at best. They could miss her at any moment. Then they would come looking. . . .

Her heart thundered at the thought.

I've got to get a plan. No way can I walk from here to my car. No way can I ride a bicycle that far. I can't steal Ryan's car. She distinctly remembered him taking the keys. *Or the other car, either. What am I going to do?*

Unless she could put miles between the people in that house and herself first, they would be on her like a pack of wolves on a doe as soon as they discovered she was

gone. On her own, on foot, how far could she possibly
get in just a few hours?

The answer clearly was, not to her car. Not even into
D.C.

Her choices, then, came down to this: hide or find a
ride.

The woods were out. They were too close. They would
be searched. Jess had a hideous vision of herself running
(lurching) away from pursuers following her trail with
packs of baying bloodhounds. If she were caught, by
whatever means, she had little doubt she would be killed.
Shiny Shoes had tried it once before, and there would be
nothing to stop him from trying again, and probably
succeeding.

Nothing except Ryan. But she couldn't count on that.
She couldn't count on him. To do so would be to risk her
life.

The previous plan—which was, basically, trust Ryan
to get her out of this alive—obviously had to be scrapped,
too.

Which brought her back to the *previous* previous
plan. Go to the media. More specifically, to the reporter
she knew at the *Post*. During the last year, she had dealt
with Marty Solomon on at least a dozen occasions when
Davenport had met with him to provide deep background on certain stories, or had her call him with judi-
cious, client-favoring "leaks." Presented with the scoop
of a lifetime, Solomon would be ecstatic. He would also
be prepared to roll instantly out of his warm bed and
drive like a bat out of hell to pick her up.

Did she remember his number? Jess thought for a
second, then felt a glimmer of triumph. Yes, she did.

The back door opened. Just like that, with no warning
whatsoever. Jess jumped at the suddenness of it, then
took a couple of silent steps back into the inky black
protection of the nearest tree as Ryan came out onto the

stoop. All she could see of him was his tall form silhouetted by the light pouring out around him, but she knew
with no possibility of mistake who it was. She could hear
voices—whoever else was in the kitchen talking—and as
another gust of wind hit her she could smell, just faintly,
bacon. Eyes widening, heart slamming against her ribs,
Jess flattened herself against the rough bark of the tree
trunk and watched as Ryan closed the door behind him
and headed toward the RAV4.

He was alone.

*I could run to him, tell him that the person who tried
to kill me in the hospital is one of his friends in there. We
could jump in the car and get out of here together. We
could . . .*

No.

She could not run to him, although she realized dismally that she wanted to with every fiber of her being.
She realized, too, that the crush was alive and well and
possibly in the process of morphing into something
more.

Something dangerous, considering that Ryan had
summoned to his house the person who had tried to kill
her in the hospital. For the purpose, perhaps, of setting
her up for another attempt on her life.

It would be stupid to assume he wasn't in on it, too.

Trusting him could cost her her life.

So she pressed closer against the tree and watched
him open the door of the RAV4, watched the light inside
the vehicle come on and illuminate his fair hair, his
handsome face, his broad shoulders, watched him close
the door again and start to walk away before clicking the
lock shut over his shoulder. He was carrying something,
she saw before the interior light in the car went out,
something small that he could hold in one hand. Then he
reached the stoop, knocked, and was let in by someone
she couldn't see. The door closed and he was gone.

Alone again in the chilly darkness, still staring at the now closed door, Jess was disgusted to realize she felt totally bereft.

Get a grip.

Wasting time mooning over Ryan was nothing short of idiotic. Any one of them could go upstairs at any moment and discover that she was missing. The bedroom door didn't lock. The window was open. Figuring that she had gone out of it would not require much of a mental stretch. Then the chase would be on.

Icy prickles of fear raced over her skin at the thought.

I've got to get out of here.

She wasn't going to get far on foot. At this point, her legs were totally unreliable.

Her gaze went to the bicycle. Could she pedal? The driveway had a gentle downward slope. As far as she remembered, the road was pretty much downhill, too. Certainly there was no big hill she would have to pedal up that she could remember. Under those circumstances, yes, she thought she could.

Keeping a wary eye on the house—and mindful, too, that there might be danger from another source lurking unseen anywhere around, behind her, on the other side of the garage, crouched in any shadow or hidden behind any tree—she made her way through the woods until she was even with the garage. Then, heart pounding, she crept across the cursedly moonlit yard.

This was the most dangerous part, she realized as she reached the bicycle, which leaned in deep shadow against the garage's clapboard wall. If there was anyone at all around, anyone to see, she would be caught now. Pulling it out with clumsy haste, turning it to face down the driveway, trying to be as quiet as a little mouse, she slid her purse over the handlebars, hitched up her skirt, and hopped on, casting scared little glances around all the while. There was, simply, no place to hide.

It was a girl's bike, a ten-speed, presumably his daughter's. Taking a deep breath, knowing that anyone coming out the back door or who happened to be in the vicinity (what if one of them had gone out to check the perimeter again, for example?) would spot her instantly, she took off, her shoes slippery on the pedals as she forced her still-dodgy legs to pump as best they could.

It was enough to get her going.

There was no outcry, no rush to stop her, nothing. She rolled silently down the driveway with the crisp, rain-scented wind nipping at her cheeks and her hair flying behind her and her bare legs and hands already tingling with cold and threatening to quickly grow as numb as her feet. Her back ached. Her head throbbed. Her breathing came in short, frightened pants. Still she pedaled doggedly, hating the rattle of the chain, the whisper of the tires, battling the urge to look over her shoulder and thus possibly upset her balance. If anyone was back there, she would find out soon enough. The thought was terrifying.

Shoulder blades tensing, she leaned closer to the handlebars, half expecting to be stopped by a bullet in the back at any moment.

It didn't happen. Nothing happened. The night remained calm and cold, its peace undisturbed. The road, when she reached it, unfurled in front of her like a silver ribbon in the moonlight. On it, she discovered with a quick upsurge of fresh fear as she turned out of the driveway, she was hideously exposed. She could only pray that no one would come looking for her until she'd had time to meet up with Solomon and be whisked away.

Putting her head down, she coasted, occasionally pedaling to keep up her speed, thankful for the momentum the downward slope of the driveway had given her, concentrating on putting as much distance between herself and the house as she could.

Much as she hated to, though, as soon as she judged she had gone far enough to make immediate discovery unlikely, she braked, pulling over to the side of the road. She could not place the call she had to place while racing away. She had too much to lose if she crashed trying to juggle the phone and handlebars while keeping the bike on the road. Finding herself at the top of a gentle slope, she decided that this was the place. As she slid off the seat, straddling the bike and stretching her aching back, the woods on either side of the road suddenly seemed to close in. Darkness settled over her like an all-enveloping blanket. She felt very small, very alone. Very scared.

Aware of her surroundings with every nerve ending she possessed, pulse pounding so loud in her ears that she could barely hear the night sounds all around her, she fished her phone out of her purse, opened it, and punched in Solomon's number with shaking hands.

What if he doesn't answer? What if I get his voice mail?

The call seemed to take an inordinately long time to go through. She listened to it ringing with her heart in her throat. The glow from the phone unnerved her. It undoubtedly could be seen for a long way. Plus, she knew that using a cell phone was a risk in and of itself, that the signal could act as a tracking device, giving her position away. But she was counting on the fact that no one was looking for her yet, and by the time they started looking for her she would be so far away from here that the problem would be moot. The hard truth was that sooner or later Ryan and the others in the house were going to discover that she was gone. Then they were going to come after her. At least one, if not more of them, wanted to kill her. In her opinion, her best chance at survival lay in getting as far away as possible before they missed her. Calling Solomon and having him pick her up and drive her to her car was her best chance of making that happen.

After placing this one call, she would not use her cell phone again. She would throw it away. She would . . .

"Jessica? Jessica Ford?"

Solomon's voice in her ear made Jess jump. Of course, her name had popped up on his caller ID. She was so rattled she hadn't thought of that. No wonder he'd answered so quickly. Right now she had to be the flavor of the month among journalists.

"Yes, Marty, it's me." Although there was no one around to hear, she kept her voice low, glancing around apprehensively. Overhead, the sky was vast and black and lightly sprinkled with stars. The woods rose up on either side of the narrow road like tall black walls. *Eerie* was a word that came to mind. *Terrifying* was another. "Listen, this is urgent. I need you to—"

"I don't fricking believe this. Where are you? Did you hear about Davenport?" he interrupted, sounding surprisingly alert considering that she must have woken him up. She pictured him, probably sitting up in bed, his bald head with its fringe of black hair shining in the light from a bedside lamp he'd switched on, thrusting his wire-rimmed glasses onto his beaky nose. He was maybe fifty, short and stocky, and she'd seen the outline of a wife-beater beneath his dress shirt on more than one occasion. He probably slept in that and—never mind. She didn't want to go there. "He killed himself last night. Jumped out his office window."

"Yes. I was there. That's why I'm calling. There's something—" she broke off, debating how much information she should give him over the phone. After all, once he had the story he would no longer need her. And every instinct she possessed screamed that she needed to get off this dark and potentially deadly road fast. What she had to do was entice him to come for her as quickly as he could. "Can you come and pick me up? Right now? I'll tell you everything then. An exclusive.

About Mr. Davenport and the crash and everything. But you have to hurry."

"Baby girl, I'd come to the ends of the earth to pick you up right now." Jess could practically hear him salivating at the prospect of the story he was hoping to get. "Just give me directions."

Jess recalled the exit Ryan had taken and told him how to get there. Then she asked what kind of car he would be driving.

"A blue Saturn." He gave her the plate number: EGR-267.

"I'll be looking for it. Pull in at the 7-Eleven that's right there as you get off." It was maybe six miles from where she was at that moment, she guessed. How long did it take to bicycle six miles? She had no idea. "Park and wait. If I'm not at your car in five minutes or so, come looking for me. I'll be somewhere down a little two-lane road that's"—she tried again to recall the route she and Ryan had taken; coming up with the name of the road was impossible because she'd never known it—"to the left of the intersection. Head northeast."

"I'll find you," he promised, and she knew he would. Davenport had always said that Solomon was a pit bull in the pursuit of a story. "I can be at the 7-Eleven in, say, half an hour."

"Okay." Jess had a momentary qualm. Once he knew the story, his life might very well be in danger, too. Until it became public knowledge. Then they'd both be safe. "Marty, there's a lot going on here. Dangerous stuff. Be careful."

"I live for this shit," he said happily. "I'll be there as quick as I can."

He disconnected. Jess looked down at the still glowing phone, then turned it off and stuck it back in her purse. Time enough to throw it away once she connected with Solomon. Until then, there was no way to know if she might need to make another call. In case he didn't show, or—well, who knew.

They couldn't track her if they weren't looking for her, Jess reminded herself when her pulse started racing out of control as various horrifying scenarios of triangulating cell phones flashed through her mind. Deliberately dismissing them, she took a deep breath and climbed back on the bike again. Gripping the handlebars hard, she pushed off and started to pedal. Her legs felt weak, her back hurt like crazy, but she gritted her teeth and kept going.

Some ten minutes later, just as she was resting her aching legs, coasting as she sailed around a curve, something caused her to glance back over her shoulder. What she saw nearly caused her to run off the road.

A car was coming toward her fast, its headlights slashing through the dark like twin white laser beams.

Jess's blood ran cold.

Dear God, is it them?

Chapter 20

BRAKING, PRACTICALLY FALLING OFF the bike, Jess realized she had no chance of making it to the woods. The car was coming too fast, swooping down toward her like a bird of prey, already at the top of the curve she'd just coasted around. Thank God for the tall grass! Half running, half stumbling, her heels catching in the soft ground, pushing the bike with her because she was afraid to leave it, afraid it might be spotted and give her away, she plunged into the nearly waist-high weeds, covering just a few measly yards before she realized, with a quick, terrified glance over her shoulder, that the car was almost upon her. Dropping the bike, throwing herself down in the grass, she covered her head with her arms so that the paleness of her face wouldn't give her away and peeked out as the headlights swept over the wheat-colored grass, over her, just a flash and then they moved on. The car itself—the RAV4, Jess was almost sure—followed with a whoosh of tires. Then it was gone.

Jess wasn't aware she was holding her breath until she let it out. Her heart pounded so hard in her chest that she could actually feel it beating against her ribs. Her stomach had knotted tight.

It's okay. The car's gone.

Taking a deep breath in an effort to calm herself, trying to figure out just how far she was from the 7-Eleven—probably not more than two miles, a walkable distance if she could only walk properly—Jess realized that taking to the road again verged on suicidal. As much as she wanted to believe that the vehicle that had just passed wasn't the RAV4, she couldn't. The only smart thing to do was assume she had been missed far sooner than she had expected and they were now looking for her.

Oh God, what do I—

Jess never finished the thought. She was still staring dry-mouthed down the road after the SUV when she saw the red flash of its brake lights.

She froze.

The thing was stopping—turning a wide, fast U-turn, its headlights sweeping the woods—and coming back.

Coming back for what?

Jess was horribly afraid she knew. Whoever was driving had seen something to tell them she was there.

What? It didn't matter.

Heart thumping, hands flattening on the cold, wet weeds on which she lay, she scrambled up into a crouch as the SUV barreled back toward her. Careful to keep below the top of the grass, bending almost double, she turned and scurried toward the woods, her shoes sliding on the slippery grass, her heels sinking in the mud, catching herself with her hands when it seemed she might fall. Wet stalks slapped her in the face. Insects rose buzzing around her. It was so dark she couldn't see anything except the pale curtain of grass directly in front of her eyes—and, in her peripheral vision, the bright blaze of headlights closing fast behind her.

A screech of brakes. The slam of a car door. Heart thundering, Jess dared a quick, hunted look back over her shoulder.

The SUV had pulled off onto the soft gravel shoulder just yards away, and was now stopped with its headlights still slicing through the dark, pointing back the way it had come. A man walked around the hood, a tall man, moving fast. The headlights gave her a glimpse of black dress pants and a blue shirt with the sleeves rolled up.

"Jess!"

Oh, God, she'd known it was Ryan as soon as she'd seen the car. Sucking in a quick gulp of air, she dropped to her knees, afraid that the movement of the grass as she plunged through it would give her away.

"Jess!"

Cringing, making herself as small as possible, she turned just enough so that she could watch him easily and then held very still, like a rabbit in the presence of a dog. What did he want with her? Her stupid heart urged her to run to him, to trust him, but her head told her she dared not. If she was wrong about him, it could cost her her life.

A small circle of white light appeared out of nowhere like an unblinking eye. A flashlight. He was holding it, looking around, scanning the area where she had left the road. How was he able to pinpoint it so precisely? She didn't know. It didn't matter. Somehow it seemed he just knew.

A moment later, her heart leaped into her throat as she realized he'd found the bicycle.

"Goddamn it, Jess! Answer me!" It was a roar that seemed to echo off the trees. He looked up again, scanning the darkness, the flashlight beam skimming the feathery tops of the grass. "Jess!"

The flashlight lowered, circled, paused, then moved in her direction with uncanny accuracy. Jess realized to her horror that he was following the trail she'd left through the grass. He would find her in a matter of minutes. If she ran, he would catch her. He was bigger and stronger and faster and in her present state she had no hope, no prayer, of getting away.

Plus, he had a gun.

At the thought, she broke out into a cold sweat.

Maybe you can trust him. . . .

"Jess!" He headed toward her unerringly, the flashlight beam leading the way. Her pulse thundered in her ears. Her chest tightened.

He's done everything he can to keep you alive so far. . . .

He was still coming and was now just a few yards away. She could hear the crunch of grass beneath his feet above the pounding in her ears.

"Ryan? Is that you?" She stood up on rubbery legs.

"Jess?"

He closed the distance between them in two long strides, caught her elbows, and pulled her against him, wrapping her tightly in his arms, hugging her close. She allowed herself to rest against him because there was no other choice, then found herself taking momentary insane comfort in the solid warmth of his body, in the muscular strength of his arms around her. If she hadn't been leery about trusting him, she realized she would have been so glad to see him she would be dizzy with it. Much as she hated to acknowledge it, his arms felt right around her. Despite everything, she discovered that in them was just exactly where she wanted to be.

"You scared the absolute shit out of me! Are you all right?"

Her heart still pounded like a trapped bird's. Her cheek nestled into his wide chest and her arms circled his firm waist while her mind raced a mile a minute, trying to decide what to do. His gun was in its holster at his waist; she could feel the hard protrusion of it hidden beneath his shirt. Comforting—or scary? She breathed in the scent of him—powder fresh, a hint of musk—as she realized that choice had been taken from her. Since she had no reasonable hope of getting away, she had to trust him . . . or at least pretend to.

God, she wanted to be able to trust him.

"Where are your friends?" she asked, her voice only slightly unsteady.

Grasping her upper arms, Ryan pushed her away from him a little and looked down at her. If she hadn't been wearing her heels he would have towered over her, and she still had to tilt her head back to see up into his face. She couldn't read his expression: The night was too dark. She doubted that he was having any more success with hers.

"Where do you think? Out looking for you." There was a definite edge to his voice. "Wendell went upstairs to take a shower and felt cold air blowing out from under your door. She checked on you, and guess what? The window was open. You were gone. I take it you left voluntarily? Nobody dragged you out by your hair or anything?"

"Could we talk about this somewhere else, please?" He was alone in the car, she was almost positive. Still, she was having hideous visions of one of the others showing up at any second. Driving away in his car with him felt a whole lot safer than standing here in the great outdoors waiting for that to happen.

"That's probably the best idea you've had all night."

Grabbing her hand, he started walking back toward the RAV4. Considering that her legs felt about as sturdy as rubber bands and her back ached like a sore tooth and she was so tired she felt wilted, keeping up was hard to do.

"You okay?" He glanced back as she stumbled.

"Yeah. They're not, like, right behind you or anything, are they?" She kept walking even though it required a major effort of will, looking back up the road for any sign of another vehicle.

His grip on her hand tightened. "Something about that make you nervous?"

"I don't trust them."

"Is that why you . . . ? Never mind. We'll have this conversation in a minute. Get in the car."

They had reached the SUV by that time. He opened the passenger-side door and watched her sink into the seat with more relief than she hoped showed. She hurt in places she hadn't known she could hurt.

"Stay put." He shut the door on her. Shivering from some combination of cold and nerves, Jess cast a quick glance at the ignition—no keys. Not that she had expected to get that lucky. Would she really have driven away and left him there beside the road anyway? She didn't even have to think about that: Yes, she would.

Her life was on the line here. And just whose side he was on was still very much up in the air. The question was, how much did she tell him when he got back in the car? If she went with the truth, the whole truth, told him how deeply she felt the Secret Service was implicated in this, would he openly turn into the bad guy she feared he secretly might be?

The interior light flashed on as he opened the back cargo door, making her jump. He lifted the bicycle inside and closed it again. A moment later the driver's-side door opened and he slid in beside her, tossing her purse into her lap. By the car's interior light, she could see that he was looking tired, stubbly, and decidedly grumpy. Angry, even.

"Thanks."

"So talk." He gave her an assessing look as he closed the door and thrust the key into the ignition.

"Like I said, I don't trust your friends."

"I kind of gathered that."

It was once again dark inside the car. That didn't stop her from admiring the clean, classical lines of his profile.

She was just like her mother, she realized dismally: a fool for good-looking men. Getting a glimpse of herself in the sideview mirror, she was reminded that she was still wearing her glasses. *Well, so be it.*

"You didn't tell them what I told you?" Not that she supposed it mattered now. At least one of them clearly already wanted to kill her, and giving him an additional motive wouldn't make her any more dead. Ryan shot an unsmiling glance at her.

"Did you think I would?"

"I wasn't sure."

Hesitating, Jess thought frantically. Should she tell him the rest? Of course, if he was a bad guy, she had already talked way too much and he already knew enough about what she knew to seal her fate. But she felt the opposite of threatened by him. In fact, she realized that somewhere deep inside, she was glad he had found her. Whether it was foolish or not, she *felt* safe with him.

"Good to know." There was a definite edge to his voice. The RAV4 had already pulled back onto the pavement and was starting to pick up speed as it headed back around the curve. With another glance at her, he turned on the heat and cranked it up, and she realized he must have noticed the fine tremors that shook her. "So, you want to tell me what you were thinking to do something as stupid as climbing out a window and deliberately running away from a protected environment?"

"Just so you know, I wasn't feeling all that protected."

"You think you're safer out here? On your own? You've got to be nuts." He sounded like his patience was wearing thin. "Just for the record, I about had a heart attack when Wendell told me you were missing. You know why? Because there may very well be a killer out here somewhere who's just waiting his chance to take you out. If you're right about the First Lady's death, then you know what that makes you? The only thing standing in the way of somebody getting away with it." He glanced at her. It was too dark to see his expression, but his tone left no doubt that he was getting angrier by the minute. "Jesus, I thought somebody had gotten to you."

He was driving too fast, handling the car like a weapon. The distance that she had covered on the bicycle was, she realized as the tires ate it up, really ridiculously short. Her heart started to speed up as they passed the place where she had made the phone call to Solomon. Another few minutes and Ryan's driveway would come into view.

She wrapped her arms around herself in an effort to banish the shivering, and saw his mouth tighten. Maybe she was making a mistake, but she was going to go with her gut and trust him. He'd had ample opportunity, after all, and she wasn't dead yet. And he'd cranked the heat. You didn't crank the heat for a woman you were preparing to kill. She thought.

"Okay, you want to know why I went out the window? Because I think one of the agents you brought in might be the person who attacked me in the hospital."

"What?" He cast an incredulous glance at her. A shaft of moonlight spilling in through the car window allowed her to see that he was frowning, disbelieving, and, yes, angry—but not suddenly self-conscious or guilty-looking, as she would have expected him to be if he had some kind of prior knowledge that what she was telling him was the truth.

The hard knot in her stomach relaxed a little. The shivers started to ease. Trusting him just might have been the right thing to do.

"I'll tell you the whole story, but you've got to turn around first. I can't go back to your house."

"You're not serious."

"Turn around."

There was a moment of silence during which Jess

could feel the issue hanging in the balance. Then, thank God, he braked, turning the car around in another wide U-turn so that the tires crunched on the gravel berm. His driveway couldn't have been more than a few minutes ahead.

She let out a sigh of relief.

"Okay, cut the crap." He was still driving too fast, but at least it was in the right direction. This time Jess was thankful for the speed that ate up the distance. "Why would you think something like that?"

"Because in the hospital, just as he started to put whatever was in that needle in my IV line, the person who attacked me said, 'This will help you to go back to sleep, sugar.' And tonight I heard that same voice say 'sugar' again. I woke up, had to go to the bathroom, and when I came out I was standing at the top of the stairs and heard him downstairs saying something like 'It's not too early for breakfast, sugar.'"

"You heard a *man* saying that? We're talking Fielding or Matthews here?"

"I'm not clear on the names. It was somebody who was downstairs in your house about twenty minutes ago. And I'm almost positive it was a man."

"I didn't hear anybody say anything like that. Of course, I wasn't with them all the time."

"I know what I heard." Her tone dared him to doubt her.

"Fielding or Matthews, then." He paused, seeming to think it over, then shook his head. "That's not possible."

"What do you mean it's not possible? It's *true.*"

"Do you know how many guys go around calling women 'sugar'?"

"It was exactly the same. Same voice, same intonation. What, do you think I'm imagining things again?" She put some bite into her voice on that last.

They had passed the place where she'd hidden from

him now and were swooping on down in the direction of the 7-Eleven. Jess spared a passing thought for Solomon, who was undoubtedly barreling in their direction at that very moment. She still meant to give him his exclusive, although she was sure that Ryan was going to hit the roof when he found out she'd called a reporter despite his warning. Still, she had to rely on her own best judgment, and going public was the only thing she could think of that might have any chance of making this whole thing just go away. But maybe, after talking to Solomon, she would stay with Ryan until she felt safe again.

If he would let her, that is.

"If you believed that, why the hell didn't you come tell me?"

"Oh, I don't know, maybe because you were downstairs with the person I heard saying 'sugar' and you're a Secret Service agent, too?"

"You thought it was a better idea to jump out a window and run away into the dark?"

"I was kind of short on options."

"You should have come to me." They were rounding another bend, and Jess saw, just faintly, the lights of I-95 glimmering in the distance. Soon they would be off the dark country road and heading toward—where? Time to work that out when she'd convinced him of this. "You know, I've known those three back there for years. They're good people."

"One of them isn't." Jess realized she was no longer shivering. The heat was working—and so was the idea, however wrongheaded it might be, that she was safe with him. "Why are you having such a hard time believing me?"

"There's never been a traitor in the Secret Service. Never."

"So this is something new. Get your mind around it. I'm telling the truth."

"I'm not saying you're not. I'm just saying that maybe

you're mistaken. If one of those guys tried to kill you in the hospital, the reason would have to be to perpetuate some kind of cover-up of the First Lady's death, which means they would have to be involved in that. I don't buy it. I can't."

To Jess's ears, it sounded like he was trying to convince himself.

"There's something else," she said. "After the crash, those people I told you about who went rushing down past me with flashlights? The ones who surrounded the car and either set it on fire or watched it burn?"

"Yeah?"

"I think they were Secret Service agents, too."

Dead silence greeted that. Jess looked at him, trying to read his expression in the shifting darkness. All she could see was his profile, and all of a sudden it looked like it had been carved from stone.

"Why would you think—?"

Jess jumped as the "William Tell Overture" blared out of nowhere, interrupting. It took her a moment—and the sight of him digging his cell phone out of his pants pocket—to realize that it was his ringtone. It seemed to her that after looking at the caller ID he hesitated for a moment before he flipped the thing open and pressed the connect button.

"Yeah?" he said into the phone.

"You got your problem fixed yet?" The voice on the other end belonged to a man. It was faint and crackly and unknown to her, but Jess could hear every word.

"Taken care of."

"You found her?"

"Yeah."

"She with you now?"

"Yeah."

Jess didn't need the glance Ryan slanted at her to realize that she was the topic of conversation. She stiffened, watching him intently. From the brevity of his responses, Jess gathered that he didn't realize she could hear both sides of the conversation.

The voice continued. "She's been talking. To a reporter."

Jess went cold with horror. How could anyone know that?

"I don't think so," Ryan replied. They were nosing into a sharp curve, and Ryan tapped the brakes, slowing the car. Now she could almost see the individual trunks of the tall pines as they whipped past the window. Pale gray moonlight filtered in through the windshield, dappling the interior of the car. The changing light made him look like a stranger.

"It's true. He's on his way to meet with her now."

The look Ryan directed at Jess was sharp. *"What?"*

"Yep. There's more going on here than you know. It stinks, but we've got to take care of this."

"I am taking care of it."

There was a stop sign at the bottom of the curve. She remembered it now: Stop at that sign, cross an intersection, and then they were on the road that led to I-95 and the 7-Eleven.

The voice crackled again. "She can't talk to any reporters."

Another glance came her way from Ryan, this one unmistakably grim. "She won't. You have my word."

Jess thought she heard a sigh through the phone. "I'm afraid that's not good enough anymore. Why don't you go on and take her back to your house? I'll meet you there."

"How do you know I'm not at my house?" Ryan's voice suddenly had an edge to it.

There was the briefest of pauses. "I think you know the answer to that. You've always been a team player, Ryan. We appreciate it, too. Don't think we don't. And we'll remember this."

Jess watched Ryan's hand tighten on the phone.

"You have anything to do with what happened to Davenport and his secretary?" His voice had an ugly undertone now.

Jess couldn't help it. Her eyes widened on his face. She could feel her heart slamming against her rib cage. Her palms turned clammy and she wiped them on her skirt in response. They were almost at the stop sign, she saw out of the corner of her eye. The RAV4 was slowing down.

"No. Hell, no. Look, just bring the woman back to your house. I'll meet you there, and we'll talk this out."

Ryan glanced her way once more. His face was in shadow again, and she couldn't read his expression at all.

Oh, God, please let me be able to trust him. She was suddenly terrified that she'd made a mistake, that she couldn't, that she'd let her attraction to him cloud her judgment. Her mouth went dry at the thought.

"Yeah, okay." The ugliness was gone. He sounded perfectly normal again. "As long as we're both clear that talking is all we're going to do."

Jess took a deep breath. Her stomach plummeted clear down to her toes. She wasn't letting him take her back to his house. No way in hell. She would be killed. She was as certain of that as she was that the sun would come up in about forty-five minutes.

And Ryan was in on it. That thought was almost more horrifying than anything else.

"Absolutely." The man sounded relieved. "It'll take me maybe half an hour to get there."

"All right."

"Keep her with you. Don't let her out of your sight."

Ryan wasn't looking at her now, but the new tension she could feel emanating from him in waves spoke volumes. "You got it."

His answer struck fear into her soul. There was absolutely no emotion in his voice at all. Coupled with the suddenly fraught atmosphere in the car, that told her everything she needed to know. Swallowing, she pulled her gaze away from him to their surroundings with real effort. A four-way stop. A small slope leading to a strip of tall grass like the one she had just hidden in, leading to a strip of woods. The woods couldn't be very deep because of the road cutting through them that intersected this one in a T. Pass through the intersection, and you were on the road leading to the 7-Eleven. Solomon was waiting there, or would be soon. If she could just get to the 7-Eleven ...

All that went through her mind in a flash as Ryan disconnected. At the same time, the RAV4 rocked to a halt at the stop sign—and she grabbed the door handle and shoved the door open.

"Jess!" Ryan grabbed at her and missed.

"Leave me alone!"

"Damn it to hell, Jess!"

This time his grab caught the tail end of her jacket. She just managed to yank it free as she catapulted from the car.

Her feet in the cursed high heels struck the gravel shoulder hard. She staggered and almost fell, barely managing to catch herself before she hit her knees. One shoe came loose, and she kicked it off, then kicked off the other to match and went plunging barefoot down the slope. Darkness immediately cloaked her, but she knew that wasn't going to be enough. Behind her the RAV4's interior light glowed yellow, lighting her path at the same time as it ruthlessly exposed her. Gravel cut into her soles. The strawlike grass was slippery underfoot and whipped around her legs. Her heart raced and adrenaline surged through her like rocket fuel as she launched herself through the waist-high grass, stumbling frantically toward the woods. Her legs felt as heavy as if she were wearing concrete boots, and she knew escaping from him was going to be all but impossible—but she had to try. The tone of the conversation had made it perfectly clear—Ryan was one of them after all. Maybe reluctantly, maybe halfheartedly, but still a team player just as the other man had said.

The hard truth was, she was a danger to them. A danger that could only be fully eliminated by her death.

Ryan had agreed to bring her back to his house. Even as she reeled at the knowledge that he was involved, that she was just as foolish as she had suspected, Jess shuddered at the thought of what they might be planning to do to her. An accident—would they want to make it look like an accident, like Marian's death? Or a suicide like Davenport? Or would they . . .

There was the smallest of sounds behind her, a funny little metallic click. It was such an insignificant sound that she didn't know what made her glance over her shoulder in an attempt to identify it.

But she did, and was just in time to watch as the RAV4 exploded with a hollow-sounding boom accompanied by a fireball the size of a house.

Chapter 21

JESS WHIRLED TO FACE the explosion, both hands flying to cover her open mouth. For a moment she just stood there, dumbfounded, as a whoosh of heat blasted past her and a geyser of debris shot skyward. A split second later, car parts rattled down on the road and the area surrounding it, although none reached as far as where she stood frozen in the tall grass perhaps thirty feet away. The blaze completely engulfed the RAV4, lighting up the night like a giant bonfire. Black smoke billowed toward the sky. The smell of burning hit her, bringing back instant hideous memories of another burning car....

"Mark!" she screamed, as the past was wiped out by a rush of brand-new horror. "Mark!"

He had been in that car.

Moving like she had never believed she would be able to move again, she raced toward it, adrenaline giving her dicey legs a strength and purpose that carried her back through the grass toward the car faster than she had run away from it. Heart thundering, pulse pounding, gasping with emotion, she watched the flames devouring the vehicle and knew already that there was nothing she could do, no help she could give.

Too late, too late, too late—the thought beat through her mind like the desperate pounding of a drum.

Scrambling up the slope, feeling the heat as intense as a furnace on her face and exposed skin, she heard the crackling of the fire, smelled burning rubber and gasoline and she refused to think what else, and saw that the asphalt on which the vehicle sat was already melting and bubbling from the intense heat of the flames.

Then she was on the road, running around the front of the RAV4 to the driver's side, her eyes stinging, her throat aching, knowing it was useless but . . .

Even as she tried to absorb the reality of the total conflagration that made any attempt at rescue both impossible and pointless, she spotted him. Her heart gave a great leap.

He wasn't in the car. He lay sprawled on his stomach on the pavement on the opposite side of the road. The leaping flames that lit up the night bathed him in a flickering orange glow so that the dark bulk of him was just visible against the glittering blacktop.

Oh, God, thank God, he'd been thrown clear.

"Mark!" She flew toward him. *Is he hurt? Is he dead?* "Mark!"

Dropping to her knees beside him, she ran her eyes over him, put her hands on his shoulders, and felt the solid, intact strength of them, slid her hand to the center of his back to see if she could detect the rise and fall of his rib cage that would indicate he was still breathing, checking the extent of his injuries as best she could by the uncertain light of the blazing fire behind them.

Please, God, please, God, please, God . . .

He groaned and rolled over, then sat up, blinking at her.

"Mark!"

Throwing her arms around him, she hugged him, pressed her face to his, kissed his warm, bristly cheek a couple of times, so glad he wasn't dead that she completely forgot everything else. One hard arm came around her, and she felt him clumsily patting her back. That brought her back to reality a little, and she let go of him, sinking back on her haunches to frown at him, her freezing toes curling into the rough pavement. He quit patting her, but his arm still curved loosely around her waist, casually intimate.

He was looking past her at the burning car, his expression as astounded as hers must have been moments earlier.

"Holy shit," he said.

"Are you hurt?" Her voice was sharp.

He frowned, then shook his head. "I don't think so. A little dazed, maybe. Jesus Christ, if you hadn't gone jumping out of the car like an idiot and I hadn't gotten out to go chasing after you, we'd both be toast right now."

That brought everything rushing back in a reorienting burst of memory. *He was going to take me back to his house to be killed.* Her widening eyes met his narrowing ones for a pregnant instant of shared knowledge, and then she pushed his arm aside and surged to her feet.

Lunging forward, he grabbed her wrist, his long fingers circling it like a manacle.

"Oh, no you don't."

She did her best to yank her arm free. "Let me go, you son of a . . ."

"What the hell is the matter with you, anyway?" He held on tight. "Are you *trying* to get yourself killed?"

"What, do you think I'm stupid? Do you think I'm deaf? I *heard* that phone call. I heard that man telling you to take me back to your house, and you agreeing to do it!"

Grimacing, he rolled to his feet without letting go of her wrist. "I was just agreeing with him to buy a little time. Jesus, we don't have time for this. I'm on your side, okay?"

Your side.

"You need convincing, take a look at my car. That bomb would have gotten me, too."

Bomb. That was the first time that exactly what had happened really registered with her. The RAV4 had been blown up with a *bomb*.

She stopped struggling to look at the burning husk of what had been his SUV. The fire was consuming the RAV4 at a furious clip. Hot and orange, it popped and crackled and hissed, putting out incinerator-like heat intense enough to shimmer in the air and warm the pavement beneath her feet. If either one of them had been inside, they would have been cremated by now.

"Give me your purse." Apparently feeling he had convinced her, or else figuring it just didn't matter because there wasn't anyplace she could run to that he couldn't catch her easily, Mark released her wrist, grabbed her purse off her arm, and opened the small zipper compartment at the side.

"What're you doing?" His action so completely surprised her that she actually felt indignation, and tried futilely to snatch her purse back without even thinking about attempting to get away.

"There's a homing device in here. How the hell do you think I found you?" He tore something from the zipper compartment and, taking a step forward, hurled it into the fire. Speechless, Jess watched the button-size device arc into the flames. "Where's your phone?"

He was already pawing through the larger compartment.

"What? No . . ."

Too late. He tossed her phone into the fire, then followed it with his own.

"We can be tracked anywhere with those." He thrust her purse back at her. "Here. Let's go. We need to get out of here before they show up."

They. The word was even more galvanizing than the idea of a bomb. It made her heart jump.

He grabbed her hand and was pulling her across the pavement in the direction she had been going to begin with when she happened to glance past the flames up the road in the direction of his house.

What she saw sent a stab of terror through her.

Round white lights flickered through the trees, small because they were still distant but moving toward them far too quickly.

A car.

Jess stared, electrified.

Of course, it doesn't have to be them....

At this time in the morning? Who are you kidding? Who else would it be?

"Headlights," she gasped, tugging on his hand and pointing. "A car's coming."

"Shit." His gaze followed hers. He was just starting down the slope while she still stood at road level close enough to the fire to feel its heat radiating through her jacket to warm the skin on her back. Plunging on, he pulled her down to the bottom of the slope with him. She barely felt the sharpness of the gravel on her cold, bare feet this time. With what she considered great presence of mind, she grabbed her shoes as she passed them. The heels were a problem, but she had already figured out the hard way that bare feet were worse. "Come on."

At the bottom she stumbled and would have fallen to her knees if he hadn't caught her. Making an impatient sound, he snatched her up in his arms and bolted toward the woods with her.

"You don't have to carry me."

"Baby, I want to live."

Okay, he had a point. Clearly, in this moment of emergency, he was going to be far faster at getting them both out of the reach of danger than if she tried to run on her own. Her shoes were useless, and the ground was tearing up her feet. Her legs already ached from her previous efforts, and her lower back throbbed. She spared a momentary longing thought for the pain pills in her purse, but there was no time. Tucking her shoes in close to his body, balancing her purse on her stomach, Jess gave in to expediency, twining her arms around his neck and curling close to his chest and hanging on for dear life, watching dry-mouthed over his shoulder as the approaching headlights closed in.

He was just bounding from the grass into the deeper darkness of the woods as the headlights slowed and then stopped a few yards behind the burning car.

An icy shiver of fear shot up her spine.

"Mark." It was an urgent whisper delivered almost into his ear. She could just see the denser outline of his profile against the backdrop of tree trunks and hanging vines. Glancing back, she saw a quick flash of light as the interior light came on, but then as he kept going more trees obscured her view before she could see anything else, like someone emerging from the stopped vehicle, which she guessed was what was happening. "There they are. At the car."

The tangle of undergrowth beneath the trees had caused him to slow down. He was no longer running but, rather, forcing a path through prickly branches that reached as high as her bent legs and hanging vines that occasionally smacked her face like cold, damp hands. The earthy smell of vegetation gone wild was strong. Here in the trees, the insect chorus was loud enough to all but block out the now-distant roar of the fire. Holding her higher against his chest in a near-futile attempt to protect her from the scratchy things all around them, turning to maneuver through a particularly dense patch of undergrowth, he cast a quick look back, but he didn't stop, or even slow down. He couldn't see anything any-

way, she realized as she followed his gaze, except two
frosty white beams of light pointing toward the bright
orange glow that had been his SUV.

"If we're lucky, for the next fifteen minutes or so
they'll think we're inside the car."

"What happens if we're not lucky?"

"They'll come looking sooner."

Jess's stomach knotted. She took a deep breath to try
to stay calm.

Plan. Plan. What's the plan? Aha, she had one.

"Whoever you were talking to on the phone was right:
I did call a reporter. Marty Solomon from the *Post*. I'm
supposed to meet him at the 7-Eleven just up the road.
He should be there now. If we can get to him
before . . ."

She let her voice trail off, because the "before" was
obvious. Before they were caught.

"Didn't I tell you going to the press was a bad idea?"
He was starting to sound breathless. She could feel his
body growing progressively warmer through the thin
cotton of his shirt. Good thing the guy was muscular,
because no matter how petite she was, she was still a
solid armful under the circumstances. Her calves began
to cramp, and she unobtrusively tried to stretch. "I bet
you used your own phone, didn't you?"

"I sure wasn't going to use the phone in your
house."

"Well, guess what? Your calls were being monitored.
When you called this reporter, somebody was listening
in. They heard every word you said."

"And you knew about this?" Jess's voice, though still
scarcely louder than a whisper, went shrill with indignation.

He didn't answer. Instead, his mouth twisted. And
that, for her, was answer enough.

"You did. You knew!"

"Yeah, I knew."

"You put a tracking device in my purse! You knew they were listening to my phone calls! You lied about the results of the IV testing! You agreed to take me back to your house where you know as well as I do I was going to be killed! And I'm supposed to believe you're on my side?"

"In case it's escaped your notice, I'm also lugging your ass through a fucking jungle and my car just got blown up with me almost inside it. I think you're pretty safe in assuming I'm trying to keep you alive."

Okay. Good point.

"Anyway, I think you're missing the important thing here," he continued. "That being that if you made the arrangements to meet your reporter friend at the 7-Eleven on your cell phone, anybody listening in heard that, and if they have half a brain they'll guess that's where we're headed."

Jess felt her stomach tighten.

"I did," she said in a small voice.

"Figured." He sounded more disgusted than alarmed. "The good news is, we've got a little time. Whoever's calling the shots is still hoping the bomb worked. When the people on the ground figure out it didn't, they still have to call the bad news in, and whoever's listening to your conversations has to remember about the 7-Eleven. So if the reporter's there and we're quick, we've got a shot at getting away before they put it all together."

Jess digested that.

"Who were you talking to, anyway?"

There was a pause, as if he were debating answering. "Harris Lowell."

Jess's jaw dropped. "The White House Chief of Staff?"

"That's the guy."

"Oh my God." Her world rocked on its axis. "At least

tell me you believe me now about the Secret Service being involved."

"Looking that way."

"And one of your agent friends from the house attacking me in the hospital."

"That way, too."

It wasn't a ringing endorsement of everything she'd told him, but for the moment it would have to do, because just then they reached the outer edge of the woods. The terrain before them was awash in moonlight. It seemed hideously open compared to the darkness and heavy cover they were leaving behind. Jess realized that she could see it all clearly: another strip of tall grass about thirty yards wide, a narrow ditch, and then the road that intersected the one the RAV4 was still burning on. On the other side of the road was more tall grass leading into more woods. The intersection was up to the left. Jess couldn't see it from where they stood. The road that led to the 7-Eleven—a continuation of the road the RAV4 was on—could be just glimpsed as a solid black strip cutting through the trees across the road.

Moonlight wasn't the reason she could see so much, Jess realized about as soon as Mark went plunging into the grass, and suddenly she had to work a little harder to breathe. Cold little curls of fear twisted through her insides. It was no longer quite as dark as it had been. The deep charcoal of night was slowly fading into a paler shade of gray. Dawn would break soon....

Jess's breath caught as a terrible thought occurred.

"If they don't know it already, they'll know we're not in the car as soon as it gets light. They'll be able to see our trail through the grass."

"Yeah." Mark didn't sound like this revelation came as a surprise. Clearly, it had already occurred to him. "As much as I think your little chat with the reporter was a bad idea in principle, that's what we're banking on now.

You better pray he's there, because we're running out of time."

"What happens if he's not?" she asked, anxiety making her voice catch as he reached the ditch and, gathering himself, jumped across. She hung on, her arms tightening around his neck even as his grip tightened on her, then cast a scared glance back the way they had come. Through the trees, she realized she could still see the orange glow of the fire—but not the dark outline of the car parked behind it. Should she be able to see it? Had she ever been able to see it? God, she couldn't remember.

It was difficult to draw air into her suddenly constricted lungs.

"We go to plan B." Climbing the slope, he looked both ways, then sprinted across the road.

"Plan B?" The echo was surprised out of her. She hadn't known they had one.

"Yeah." His answer was short as he leaped another ditch, then forged through more tall grass. His body was growing warmer, the soap-tinged scent she was starting to associate with him more intense.

Her reply was polite. "I'd love to know what that is."

"Would you, now?" A fleeting grin accompanied the glance he gave her. Even as tense as she was, the sight of it warmed her. This guy—Mark, and as his given name came automatically to mind she realized that the attempt she had been making to mentally keep him at arm's length by continuing to think of him by his last name had just abysmally failed—was risking his life for her. It was kind of starting to make up for the fact that he had never so much as noticed her before the crash.

"Yes, I would."

"We wing it."

Jess gave him a withering look, which she doubted that he saw.

"You know, whoever that is back there might not have stayed with the RAV4," she pointed out as they cut catty-corner through the woods and emerged at another road. This one, she realized, was the one the 7-Eleven was on. The one the RAV4 was on. They were on the other side of the intersection now. "They could be driving around looking for us. They could come this way."

"They could." His tone told her that he'd already thought of that, too. "That's why I want you to keep a lookout for their headlights. We'll make better time if we take the road."

Jess's heart lodged in her throat as he leaped the ditch and took to the pavement, his shoes slapping the asphalt loudly enough to make her cringe. Could anyone hear? Only if they were close enough, she told herself, which wasn't exactly comforting. But they had worse problems. While they were in the woods, she realized, it had been growing lighter by the minute. The trail they had left in the grass wouldn't be hidden by darkness much longer. Once it was seen, the hunt would be on for real. Clearly aware, Mark was moving faster, picking up the pace, jogging down the road toward the 7-Eleven, which, she judged, was just around the next bend. She kept a wary eye on the road behind them, but it remained deserted.

So far.

But they were getting close. If she listened hard she could hear the distant hum of traffic on 95—and a siren. Yes, she could definitely hear a siren. Make that multiple sirens. Were they heading their way?

A sudden spurt of hope leaped inside her.

"Do you hear that siren?" She didn't wait for an answer. Clearly, if she could hear it he could, too, despite his heavy breathing. "Maybe somebody called the fire department. Or the police. About the burning car. If they come, we could—"

"No, we couldn't." He cut her off, his speech a little

ragged now. The gloom had faded enough so that she could see the color infusing his face and the fine sheen of sweat popping out on his forehead. But his arms around her were still sturdy and strong, and he was moving at a surprisingly fast pace. Of course, he could see that dawn was breaking, too. Heart hammering, Jess cast another searching glance back down the road. Still nothing. Which didn't mean someone couldn't already be following their path through the trees ... "I could flash my badge and demand protection, and they would probably do their best, but the truth is they can't protect you from these guys. They're lethal. They're playing for keeps, and they're serious about making you dead. Now that they know we know they're coming after us, they're going to go at it full-throttle. Our best chance—hell, just about our only chance—is to hide until we figure out who's involved. Then we'll know who isn't, and that will be who we go to for help."

Jess felt a quick upsurge of nausea. "What if we guess wrong?"

He didn't answer, but his expression did. They would be dead.

Jess looked at the tense, determined face so close to her own. "You know, they're not really after you. They're after me. You could leave me."

He gave a derisive huff. "Babe, I'm not leaving you. No way, no how. Put the thought out of your head."

"I'm just sayin'," she said. But, reassured and more thankful than she even wanted to think about, she tightened her grip on his neck and curled a little closer into his warm chest as they rounded the bend that brought the 7-Eleven into view at last.

"Did you happen to ask your reporter friend what kind of car he would be driving?"

"A blue Saturn." They were within shouting distance of the 7-Eleven now. Screaming distance, if it came to that.

Feeling a rush of relief so strong she nearly went limp with it, Jess eagerly scanned the mix of vehicles parked in front of the store and refueling at the gas pump.

It wasn't hard. There were only four of them.

"He's not here." Ryan had just completed the same visual scan she'd been engaged in.

Having already come to the same sickening conclusion, Jess looked around again.

"He'll be here," she promised a little desperately, casting another quick, precautionary look over his shoulder as she spoke. At what she saw, a thrill of pure fear shot through her.

A car swept up the road from the intersection they had just skirted around. It was still too dark to tell a lot about it at that distance, but she could see the approaching headlights clearly through the trees.

Chapter 22

"MARK. *MARK.*" Jess's stiffening like a board and stuttering his name almost in his ear gave him a split-second's warning that more bad news was headed his way even before she laid it on him. "A car's coming. I think it might be them. We've got to hide."

"Shit."

Casting a quick glance back, he took off, sprinting toward the store through the shadows blanketing the edge of the parking lot. Desperate to find an alternative solution, he scanned the parking lot as he ran. A 1990s maroon Escort, a gray '05 or '06 Jetta, and a green '08 PT Cruiser were parked in front of the store, an open-twenty-four-hours type with a well-lit interior that allowed him to see customers and a single bored male clerk at the cash register inside. A white '86 Silverado pickup with a long bed sat at the gas pumps. Just sat there, no gas hose connected to it. Nobody in any of the vehicles, nobody watching anywhere as far as he could tell. In a snap decision, he looked back at the Silverado. Already making the call in his mind, he veered toward the truck even as he continued to visually check it out. A couple of ladders bungeed together and some equipment sheltered by a blue tarpaulin were stowed in the back. The black plastic bed liner was worn and scarred. Clearly a work truck.

Bingo. Just what they needed: a way out.

The other choice, which involved hiding in the woods and waiting for the reporter to show up, had just gotten a whole lot riskier. As he'd told Jess, Lowell and company knew the guy was coming to the 7-Eleven, which might be why the car, if it was indeed a pursuing vehicle, was heading their way. Whoever was in it—much as he hated to think it, there was a good chance it was Fielding, Wendell, or Matthews, or some combination thereof—would park and wait for Jess and him to show up to meet the reporter. Letting Jess connect with a representative of the media was the very last thing they wanted to happen. They would stop it however they could.

Under those circumstances, the best-case scenario would be if he and Jess were nowhere in the vicinity when the reporter showed up.

"What are you *doing*?" Jess was trying to keep her cool, but her face was whiter than the truck in the purpling light of daybreak. She'd obviously expected to take shelter inside the store.

"Getting us out of here. Grab your stuff." Mark skidded to a stop at the back of the truck, cast a final searching look all around—clear—and heaved Jess, shoes, purse, and all, over the side of the bed. "Get under the tarpaulin. Fast."

"What?" She sounded stunned. The truck rocked slightly as she landed. Despite her question, Jess apparently got the idea, because as soon as he let her go she dropped out of sight. There was the smallest of clatters, as if she had dropped something, probably one of her stupid-ass shoes.

Mark sprang up himself. A foot on the bumper and a hop and then he was in, crouching low, glancing around. Just as he'd suspected, her stray shoe was almost at his feet. He grabbed it. Couldn't leave anything so obviously out of place to be found by the owner or anyone who might happen to look into the bed. The area around the pumps was relatively brightly lit, and a high-heeled shoe appearing out of nowhere was the kind of thing somebody might notice. Having already lifted the edge of the tarpaulin and currently in the process of scooting feet-first beneath it, Jess looked at him wide-eyed. Her glasses were slightly askew, her lips were parted, her bare feet were pale against the black plastic, and the slim-cut skirt of her businesslike suit was riding interestingly high on her slender, bare thighs. He was just noticing that when both of them saw the slice of headlights through the lightening gloom at the same time as a new vehicle—almost certainly the one they'd seen coming—bumped into the parking area. Mark felt his gut clench and forgot all about her skirt.

Innocents arriving by chance, his buddies from the house on a search-and-destroy mission with him and Jess as targets, or the far deadlier possibility of a team of unknown assassins on their trail: The car could contain any of the three.

"What happens if somebody looks in the truck?" Almost undercover now, Jess sounded panicky as the lights flashed over the truck bed before moving on toward the store.

"We deal."

Lips tightening at what he had to admit wasn't an especially helpful response, Jess slithered the rest of the way beneath the tarpaulin without another word.

Keeping his head low, Mark reached for his holster as he crawled to join Jess. Unsnapping his Glock, he thrust Jess's shoe at her, then shoved his legs under the tarpaulin, sliding in on his side beside her on the hard plastic so that they were lying chest-to-chest, the top of her head level with his chin, and her shoes and purse digging into his stomach. Pulling the tarpaulin over them both, breathing in the smell of paint—there were cans of house paint and various tools stored in an open plastic container behind Jess, and her back was pressed up tight against the container—he eased his pistol free. For the moment he kept it pressed against his thigh. The familiar smooth metal of the gun in his hand provided a modicum of reassurance. If push came to shove, he could shove back.

"What do you think they're doing?" she tilted her head back to ask. Her voice was a mere breath of sound.

"I don't know. Parking."

Hunting was the real answer, but no need to say that. The fact was, if the people looking for them found them, a firefight would ensue. Cornered now, with no place left to run, shooting it out with them was his only choice.

As he contemplated plugging a bullet into Fielding, or Wendell, or even Matthews, his mind reeled. Could he do it? He felt Jess shiver against him. For her? Oh, yeah. He could.

Just like they could plug a bullet into him.

The whoosh of tires on pavement as the arriving vehicle passed nearby made Mark go tense with anticipation. Whatever was going to happen would happen very soon. His hand tightened on the Glock.

Jess clearly heard the arriving vehicle, too. She shuddered and pressed so close against him that he could feel the pounding of her heart. Or maybe it was his own heart that was thumping away. Hard to tell.

Straining to hear, he listened carefully, trying to pick up any and all sounds beyond the truck bed. He'd rarely felt so helpless in his life. With his field of vision confined to the blue cocoon in which he and Jess were wrapped, his ears were all he had left to use.

The muffled one-two slam of car doors was his reward. The sound made Jess start. He could hear the hiss of her breath as she inhaled.

There were at least two of them, then.

He badly wanted to look out, to free himself from the damned constricting, blinding tarpaulin, to see what was going on with his own eyes. If this was one or more of the guys from his house, he wanted to confront them, to look them in the eye and ask them point-blank what the hell they thought they were doing, but he didn't. He couldn't. He had Jess to consider.

If they were here, they were no longer his friends. They were her enemies, and that's how he had to think of them.

A team of assassins was what he most feared. They would be black ops, under the radar, paid to handle problems like Jess, no fuckups, no mercy, cold as ice.

He'd made his choice, thrown his lot in with Jess, so whoever was out there was his problem, too. The bomb—and damn Lowell or whoever for blowing up his car, which still had two years' worth of payments to run on it—had made it clear they knew whose side he was now on. There was no going back for any of them: This was going to be a fight to the death.

"How are we going to know when Solomon—the reporter—gets here?" Jess whispered.

"We won't. Shh."

He heard—or thought he heard—something nearby. A shuffle of footsteps, a rustle of clothing . . .

Going still as a stone, barely breathing, his senses so attuned to what was going on beyond the tarpaulin that he felt like a single exposed nerve, he moved the hand holding the Glock to rest, very lightly, on Jess's shoulder.

If he was fast, he could spring up and snap off a few shots, maybe take one or more of them out before they realized what was happening.

Yeah, and maybe he could walk on water, too.

Silently he watched as Jess spotted the gun with a

downward flick of her lashes and froze. Then she wet her lips.

The gesture made his heart constrict. He knew she was terrified, knew by how still and stiff she was, by the rapid rise and fall of her chest against his, by the uneven-ness of her breathing, by the way her hand that was rest-ing on his waist clenched into a fist. But she glanced up at him then and he saw that she was okay, keeping her head, keeping her composure, just as she had throughout this whole ordeal, and he realized he admired her a lot for that.

The girl definitely had game.

A click near at hand made them both quit breathing. The truck tilted and swayed. A door slammed.

The driver had returned to the truck. He was in the cab. Even as Mark realized that, the sound of the engine turning over confirmed it.

His whole body slumped with relief.

"What about Solomon?" Jess's whisper was urgent as the truck, with a couple of sputters just to ratchet up his anxiety level, slowly got going, curving around the gas pumps.

"We can't hook up with him here. It's too late. They're already watching for us. That's why they showed up here so fast."

The ride came complete with so many rattles and squeaks and bangs that at least they no longer had to worry about being overheard. Jess acknowledged the probable truth of what he said with a silence that lasted until the truck left the parking lot with a hard bounce that made the tailgate drop open. Mark knew that was what the sudden loud clang was because he had lifted the edge of the tarpaulin just a couple of inches at about the same time to let in some badly needed air—and see if he could spot who was waiting at the 7-Eleven.

The newcomer to the parking lot was a black BMW,

Virginia tag BCW-248. Not Fielding's Saab, which he had last seen parked behind his garage. Not a vehicle that he'd ever seen before. Which, he realized, didn't mean a thing.

First chance he got, he needed to check the tag. For now, speculating was all he could do.

The paint smell was suffocating. His eyes were already starting to water. He figured Jess had to be about ready to expire, since she was snuggled so close up against him that he could feel her warm breath on his neck as well as the sharp heel of one of her shoes digging into his stomach and every curve and hollow of her sweet little shape that wasn't displaced by the driver's equipment.

"At least no one's following us." Jess's whisper was reedy. She craned her face toward the opening, too, clearly welcoming the influx of oxygen. He made it as large as he dared, then tucked the edge of the tarpaulin beneath his body so he wouldn't have to hold it in place. The truck was on the ramp leading up to I-95 now. With the tailgate down, he could clearly see the road behind them almost all the way back to the 7-Eleven. The good news was, there was not a vehicle in sight.

"Where do you think we're going?" Jess was looking out, too.

The truck was heading north, picking up speed. The jolting was picking up, too. Mark plucked Jess's shoes and purse from between them after a particularly vicious stab in the gut and shoved them down behind his legs out of harm's way. "I don't know. Toward D.C. We'll see where we end up."

"They're not going to give up, are they?"

"No."

Restoring his gun to its holster now that, in his judgment, the immediate danger had passed, Mark did what he could to make himself and Jess as comfortable as possible. As soon as they were out of the truck, they would be on the run, probably on foot, and since he'd gotten no sleep at all, grabbing a few minutes' rest while he could would probably be wise. Not wanting to shift around too much lest the truck's driver should spy suspicious movement in his rearview mirror and stop to check under his tarpaulin, or even call the police so they could check under his tarpaulin, he ended up whispering to Jess to roll over. Then when she complied he simply wrapped his arms around her so his body could maybe cushion her from the worst of the jarring ride, which he had no way to brace them against. With both their faces turned up toward the air, her back to his front, her head resting on his upper arm and her body plastered as close to his as peanut butter to jelly, he was surprised to find himself feeling any number of things. Comfortable, however, was not one of them. He had a quick flashback to how hot she had looked wearing nothing but a towel, then had to work hard to try to force the image from his head. She kept moving, kind of wriggling as if she was trying to get comfortable, which didn't help. He distinctly remembered her kissing him repeatedly right after she'd thought he'd been blown up. At the time, shell-shocked as he had been, the soft little pecks she had planted on his face had barely registered, but now, in retrospect, they registered.

"Mark." The husky quality of the whisper stirred his blood.

"Hmm." Her skirt was riding up again. He could feel it, feel the cloth bunching up high on her thighs. He was reminded of how sexy her legs looked with the skirt riding up on them. Then he caught himself taking it further, trying to imagine what kind of underwear she wore. Granny panties? A bikini? A thong?

No. He fought to banish the tantalizing images.

"My left leg is cramping. I have to turn over."

She wriggled against him again, and he realized that what she was actually doing was trying to straighten her legs. With a wry inner grimace, he obligingly loosened his hold on her waist.

She turned over, sighing with relief as she stretched out her leg.

Discovering with some dismay that his body was acutely attuned to her now, he felt the small, soft globes of her breasts flattening against his chest, and tried to force his thoughts elsewhere—with, unfortunately, indifferent success, especially since the jolting of the truck kept bouncing her against him.

"We need to come up with a plan," she said, sliding her arm around his waist and squirming again, this time, he thought, to escape the ridges of the plastic bin that had to be cutting into her back. Her head was still on his arm, and he could feel the warm tickle of her breath against the underside of his chin. Glancing down, he saw that her face was turned up to his. The glasses made her look like a librarian, but when you looked past them you saw wide eyes the color of sweet tea, plus soft, full lips and creamy skin that he already knew was silky to the touch, and a tangle of chocolaty dark hair that looked damned sexy spilling across his arm.

Her glasses were crooked again. He straightened them out for her in a gesture that even he recognized was really kind of tender, took in the sudden surprise in her eyes, and put his itching-to-wander hand right back where it belonged: flat on her back.

"We've got a plan." If his voice was a little gruff, well, it was a small price to pay for exercising some self-control.

"Oh, yeah? What?"

"Survive."

He glanced away from her just to break the sexual tension, which as far as he could tell was all on his part.

Dawn was breaking for real now, and the sky was slowly turning from deep purple to lavender. Visibility was improving by the minute, which under the circumstances wasn't a good thing. Even so early in the morning, traffic was heavy. Mindful of the snarl of traffic that the expressways became during rush hour, a great many people were already heading in to work. A swaying eighteen-wheeler cast a shadow over the truck bed as it rumbled past. The breeze of its passing rattled the tarpaulin and sent a blast of exhaust-scented wind swirling beneath it. Even that was better than the smell of paint. Mark realized to his dismay that he was starting to feel faintly nauseated.

The good news was, feeling sick to your stomach was a great way to get your mind off the woman in your arms. The bad news was, when you had a government-authorized death squad after you, wanting to barf could not be considered a plus.

"Not funny." Jess poked him in the ribs, which caused him to look back down at her. She was frowning censoriously at him. Either her stomach was stronger than his, or she was doing a better job of hiding what was going on with it. "I think the best thing to do is call Solomon from a pay phone the first chance we get."

Mark shook his head.

"You can't contact him again. They'll be watching him now, and if you call him they'll be on us like a duck on a june bug. See, they look for you where you've been. Rule number one of hiding out: You can't contact anybody you've ever known. That's how they find people."

He would have continued, but he needed air. Turning his head toward the opening and breathing deeply, he missed whatever she said in reply. All he knew was that it started with "*But . . .*"

Of course she was going to argue with him: That, he was learning, was Jess. But he was feeling too queasy to listen. He tried concentrating on the horizon—which, unfortunately for him, was obscured by moving cars that wove in and out and emitted a hell of a lot of exhaust.

"... has to be the President," she said, her tone letting him know those were the concluding words of a lengthy statement.

"What?" He glanced back down at her. "Sorry, I missed that."

She gave him an impatient look. "We've got to seriously consider that the President himself might be behind this. Lowell's his Chief of Staff, and that's who phoned you to make sure we were both in the car right before it blew up. And who else could order the Secret Service around like this?"

Mark knew he wasn't quite hitting on all cylinders at the moment, but two things he was sure of even through the worsening waves of illness: David Cooper had loved his wife, and the Secret Service had never had a traitor.

"Assumptions are dangerous things." He spoke to himself as much as to her. "They can blind you to the truth. For example, just because Lowell called me right before my car blew up doesn't mean he blew it up. Necessarily."

He had to break for air again before he could arrive at any more profound insights. Figuring out who was behind all this was a necessity, he knew, if they wanted to come out alive on the other side, but he just wasn't up to mental gymnastics right now. At the very least he required fresh air and terra firma. A double line of vehicles all barreling in the same direction clogged the road behind them for as far as he could see. They were weaving in and out like the line down the middle was some kind of maypole. The truck driver was booking it now. The old truck rattled and banged and shook like a hoochie dancer.

Jess said something he didn't hear.

Mark would have closed his eyes, but he had the feeling that doing so would prove fatal—to his stomach, not his life.

Then, suddenly, thankfully, traffic started slowing down.

The truck braked, lurched, and merged into the right lane, where other cars quickly joined it, and slowed to a crawl. An almost smooth crawl. As pleased as he was that they were now inching forward, Mark started to get a bad feeling that wasn't centered in his stomach, which was actually a good thing because it was an indication that his stomach might be starting to settle down. The traffic tie-up probably wasn't related to them at all, but still his thoughts ran along the lines of a driver with a cell phone reporting suspicious movement beneath a tarpaulin in the back of a pickup truck. Almost as bad would be a roadblock for drunk driver checks, or . . .

". . . something the matter? You've gone white as a sheet." Jess's whisper penetrated again at last, and he took a risk and looked down at her, pleased to discover that he no longer felt like upchucking the instant he inhaled paint smell. "Is there something you're not telling me?"

She was looking tired, anxious, and way too pale herself. With her face tilted toward his and her head resting on his upper arm, she was so close that he could have counted every tiny individual freckle on her nose and cheeks.

"Nope."

Frowning, she looked more anxious still. "I don't believe you. You haven't been listening and you haven't been talking. There has to be a reason." She wet her lips and her body tensed. He could feel the hand that had been resting on his back clenching. "So what don't I know? If there's something, please tell me. I don't care what it is, I would just rather know."

Apprehension radiated from her like heat. Her eyes searched his, looking for some awful truth she seemed to suspect he was hiding.

"Look, don't worry about it."

"Mark, please."

His mouth twisted wryly.

"The paint smell and the motion haven't been bothering you at all?"

"What?" Her frown deepened as she stared at him in incomprehension. Then her eyes lit up with sudden understanding. "Are you saying you're carsick?"

"No," Mark said, revolted at the wimpy image that conjured up. "No, I am not saying that. I'm just saying that the paint smell was kind of getting to me for a minute there."

"You're *carsick.*" She grinned, then chuckled outright at the expression on his face.

"Maybe." Mark started to frown her down, but she looked so delighted, so bright-eyed and twinkly with amusement suddenly that he didn't have the heart. Smiling a little sourly at her instead, he realized that it was the first time he had ever seen her laugh. "Funny, huh?"

"Just a little."

Watching her enjoying the moment, he decided that making a fool of himself was worth it.

"You know something? You're beautiful when you laugh," he told her, and when that made her quit laughing and look suddenly serious and self-conscious and kind of shy, he was so struck by the way she was looking at him that he leaned forward the required six inches and kissed her.

Chapter 23

MARK WAS KISSING HER.

Mark was kissing her.

It took Jess's stunned brain a second or two to absorb the fact, and by then her heart was pounding and her pulse was racing and her body had already caught fire. The warm, firm pressure of his mouth had caused her lips to part and her head to tilt so their mouths fit together perfectly, and the hand that wasn't trapped between them slid sensuously up his back, reveling in the feel of the taut muscles beneath his shirt—and that was before she even truly realized what was happening.

When she did, she went all light-headed and shivery inside. Closing her eyes, she kissed him back like he was the culmination of every erotic dream she'd ever had—which he was. Slanting her mouth across his, she took the previously gentle kiss to a whole new level, returning it with a heat and hunger that she'd never felt before, not even once in the whole twenty-eight years of her life.

I want you so much. But she didn't utter the shattering confession aloud. Instead, her body spoke for her, quaking and burning and yearning against him while her mouth explored his with a blistering urgency that made her bones dissolve. Her heart thumped so hard she could hear its fierce beat against her eardrums. Her blood turned to steam.

He tasted, faintly, of coffee. It suddenly became her favorite flavor in the world. She absolutely could not get enough. Pressing herself against him, she discovered proof positive that he was turned on, too—and the knowledge made her wild.

"Jesus God," he muttered against her lips when he pulled back a moment later to grab a quick breath.

"This is crazy." She saw that his eyes were dark and hot.

"So maybe crazy's good." His lips curved in the smallest of smiles, and then his mouth was on hers again. Sliding his hand around behind her nape, he shifted so that he was leaning over her. Pressing her head down into his hard-muscled triceps, he kissed her so expertly and so thoroughly that she forgot everything, the danger they were in, the rickety, rocking truck, the paint fumes and tarpaulin, all of it. Everything except Mark.

She was kissing *Mark*.

Dizzy at the knowledge, she wrapped her arms around his neck.

She could feel the heat of him, the hard strength of his body against hers, the weight of his chest pressing against her breasts, their urgent, swelling response. Her bare toes curled. Her fingers threaded up through the short, crisp hair at the back of his head. Deep inside, her body tightened into an intense rhythmic throbbing that was the most delicious thing she had ever felt.

I'm in love with Mark.

The truck stopped with a jolt.

It took a moment for that to register. Actually, it probably wouldn't have registered at all if Mark hadn't torn his mouth away from hers to, she presumed, check things out. For a moment she blinked up at him in befuddled incomprehension before she noticed that they were no longer moving. Although his mouth was still scant inches from hers, he wasn't looking at her. He was looking out through the opening at the back of the tarpaulin. And his face was, just briefly, tinted blue.

Revolving blue, she corrected herself, as the color came back, receded, and came back again in split-second rotations.

Jess's eyes widened, and with a quick indrawn breath she shifted so that she could look out.

What she saw was a police car parked in the passing lane, an empty police car with the siren off. Its flashing blue lights were going strong, though, lighting up the still-grayish dawn. As the truck started moving again, she saw that another police car was parked in front of it, empty and silent, but with its strobe lights going as well. Jess never even considered that they might be there on account of her and Mark.

What she thought, even before she saw the ambulance, before she saw the stretcher being lifted into its open rear doors with a white sheet covering the figure strapped to it, before she saw the crushed car that rested diagonally across the grassy median, was that there had been an accident.

The line of traffic was being waved forward past the accident site when she learned that she was right. Only one car was involved, as far as she could tell.

Jess barely saw the cop who was doing the waving, or the other police cars and the fire truck they rumbled past.

Her attention was all on the crushed car.

It was a blue Saturn. It was still too dark and the distance was too great to allow her to read the entire plate, but she was almost sure the first two letters were EG.

The realization felt like a blow to her solar plexus.

"Mark."

He was up on an elbow, looming above her, still taking in the scene. Even as the truck trundled clear of the accident site and started picking up speed again, she continued to stare back. Her heart beat in slow, thick strokes. The tinny taste of bile was bitter in her mouth.

"Yeah."

"That was Marty Solomon's car. The reporter."

"Yeah." His tone told her he'd already realized that.

Jess took a deep breath. "You were right: They were listening to my calls. They got to him. They *killed* him. Because of me."

Her voice shook at the end.

"*Not* because of you." Mark lowered himself down beside her and pulled her into his arms. When her gaze continued to seek the tarpaulin's opening in order to keep visual faith with that mangled car, drawn by guilt and shock and fear and a whole jumble of other churning emotions, he caught her chin and made her look at him instead. "Not because of you, do you hear? Because of whatever sick thing that's happening here. He's a victim just like Mrs. Cooper and the rest. Just like you."

Her eyes clung to his. He let go of her chin to stroke gentle fingers over her cheek.

"You hear?"

"Yes, okay, I know." She tried to get a grip, but she was too shaken. "Oh my God, I talked to him just a little while ago. He was asleep. He'd probably be waking up about now, getting ready to go into work. Instead he's *dead*."

She was breathing way too fast and too shallowly, maybe getting close to hyperventilating, and she tried to consciously deepen her breathing and slow it down.

"There's nothing we can do for him." Mark's jaw looked tight. His eyes were dark and hard in the uncertain light. "Except stay alive to figure this thing out, and bring these bastards down."

"I hate this." Despite its fierceness, her voice was a mere breath of sound.

"I know."

He pulled her close, wrapping his arms around her, silently offering what comfort he could. Resting her head against his chest, she soaked up his warmth and listened to the steady beat of his heart. Closing her eyes, clutching his shirtfront with both hands and holding on as if for dear life, she tried to calm herself, to force her emotions back. *I should never have called Solomon.* That was the thought that kept running through her mind. But *should've*s and *would've*s and *could've*s were wasted: What was done was done, and there was no undoing it. If she hadn't overheard that "sugar," she would probably be dead now, too. Or if she hadn't leaped from Mark's car, or if Mark hadn't followed her to Davenport's office—there were a dozen *or*s. She—and Mark, too—could still die at any time. The killers on their trail were probably only a step or so behind. As she faced that, fear, cold and solid as a block of ice, settled in her stomach.

I don't want to die. I don't want Mark to die. Especially not now that I've figured out I'm in love with him.

The anguished thought was both ridiculous and true.

For God's sake, get a grip.

Holding on to Mark as if one of them would vanish if she let go, she did her best. Finally, her natural determination asserted itself. If the key to her survival—and Mark's—lay in identifying who was behind all this, then that was just exactly what she was going to try to do.

Blocking out everything else, she started turning pieces of the puzzle over in her mind.

By the time the truck rattled over the skeleton-like scaffolding of the 14th Street Bridge into D.C., she was feeling calmer. She also had a plan.

"We need to check the phone records." Loosening her hold on Mark's shirt, resisting the urge to smooth out the wrinkles her desperate grip had made in the cloth, Jess tilted her head back to look up at him. If she felt self-conscious about the heated kiss they had so recently shared, well, she'd be damned if she would show it. *Hey, I kiss big, studly guys like you all the time.* That was the attitude she needed to cultivate. If she'd been stupid enough to fall head over heels for the hottest guy around, at least she was smart enough not to let him know it. Accordingly, the look she gave him was her lawyer look, businesslike and cool.

"Phone records?" He frowned slightly as his eyes slid over her face.

Jess nodded. "Mrs. Cooper's, Davenport's, maybe Harris Lowell's. We should be able to tell from them where Mrs. Cooper was heading that night and who the others were talking to. Maybe that'll give us a direction to start looking in."

"Great idea—except I've got a nasty feeling I've lost my clearance to access things like that."

The truck slowed slightly as it bounced around a downward sloping curve, and with a quick glance out the opening Jess realized they were on an access ramp.

"I can do it," she said.

He looked surprised. "For real?"

"I checked phone records for Mr. Davenport all the time. All I need is a computer."

Mark gave her a slow-dawning grin. "Baby, where've you been all my life?"

Before she could reply—the truthful answer was "For the last few months, I've been right under your nose"—their attention was distracted by the truck coming to a shuddering stop. Another glance out through the tarpaulin's opening confirmed that they were at the bottom of a ramp, presumably waiting at a traffic light.

"First thing we've got to do is get off this truck," Mark said as the truck started moving again, clattering through the intersection and picking up speed. "Sooner or later the driver's going to stop for real. Or someone is going to spot us."

Jess nodded.

They were in a mixed residential and commercial neighborhood, she saw as the truck stopped again, hopefully one with a number of stop signs. They probably wouldn't get a better opportunity. Apparently, Mark thought so as well, because he thrust her purse at her.

"I'm going to crawl to the back." He was holding her shoes, presumably intending to carry them himself. "You follow me. Next time the truck stops, we jump."

"What happens if the driver sees us?"

"That's a chance we'll just have to take. What's he going to do, call the police? By the time they get here we'll be long gone."

He extracted himself from under the tarpaulin and crept to the tailgate, crouching there at the corner, staying low, looking back at her. Jess realized that she could see him quite clearly even as she forced her increasingly stiff legs to work, and she crawled laboriously to join him. Dawn was breaking in earnest. Bright bands of pink and gold streaked the eastern sky, and the rising sun limned the roofs of the two- and three-story brick buildings, surrounding them with a shimmering gold. The air was crisp and cold, particularly after the stifling warmth under the tarpaulin. A quick glance around as she reached Mark told her that they were driving through a block of small restaurants and shops, none of which were open yet, as far as she could tell. The sidewalks were, thankfully, deserted. Even as she swept a nervous look around, the truck slowed again. Mark jumped off while it was still moving, then reached up for her as it shuddered to a halt, grabbed her under the armpits and lifted her down at the corner, where it was possible to avoid the tailgate.

Her knees were shaky and the concrete was cold as

ice, but with his arm hard around her waist they made it onto the sidewalk. A wary glance back at the truck found the driver, a man in a baseball cap, still looking forward as he got under way again, pulling on through the intersection. If he had any idea he had been carrying stowaways, he gave no indication of it.

"I don't think he saw us," Jess said.

"Just in case, we're out of here."

Mark kept his arm around her as they hurried along the sidewalk before ducking into an alley.

"I need my shoes," Jess reminded him once they were out of sight of the street. Her poor bare feet were freezing.

"Oh, yeah." Stopping, he handed them to her, waiting while she slid her feet into them. Glancing up once she had her shoes on, she saw that he was looking at them with disfavor.

"When I decided to wear heels, I didn't know I was going to be running for my life," she said defensively.

He snorted. "I'm surprised you can even walk in those things."

"My legs are a little unsteady," she admitted. Which was an understatement. They felt stiff and unwieldy and her knees were weak and her lower back throbbed.

"I'm not surprised." His eyes met hers. The smallest of smiles touched his mouth. "I can always carry you again."

"Not necessary. Come on, let's go." She started walking. She could feel him watching her critically.

"Let me know if you change your mind."

Catching up, he offered her his arm for support in a gesture that would have been almost courtly under different circumstances. Jess slid her hand into the crook of his elbow, grateful for the support. Leaning against him, moving carefully as she tried to work some of the stiffness out of her legs, she realized something: She would be perfectly happy to snuggle up against his side for the rest of her life.

I'm in love with him. The thought wasn't a joyous one. Rather it filled her with dismay. *Think it hurt when he didn't remember you in Mrs. Cooper's office? Wait till this is over and he gives you a chuck under the chin and walks away.*

Of course, that cheerful image was predicated on the idea that one day this *would* be over, that the two of them would come through it and survive, which was looking iffy at best. Reminded of how much danger they were in, Jess pushed the awful truth about her feelings for Mark to the back of her mind. Before it became a problem that she had to deal with, they had to get out of this alive.

"They have public-access computers at the library. That's where we need to go," she said. Jess spared a quick, longing thought for her own laptop, which would be waiting on the desk in her living room right where she had left it. More than anything else in the world, she wanted to go home to her apartment, which, she guessed, was not an option.

"Later. The first thing we want to do is get out of this area as fast as we can." Mark cast a quick, assessing glance back over his shoulder, and Jess felt a corresponding nervous chill.

"We weren't followed"—she was almost sure—"so how could they know where we are?"

"By now they've probably realized they missed us at the 7-Eleven. Sooner or later, I'm guessing they'll either remember the truck or check the store's security cameras and find it and have a eureka moment. There's lots of ways they can trace it, from something simple like running the tag and going to talk to the owner to zeroing in on the route it took this morning with satellite imagery."

"Satellite imagery?" Jess felt sick.

"Baby, we've got eyes in the sky that can spot a mosquito on the roof of a building. Whoever this is, you can bet they have access. The problem is knowing where to look. And in the District, there are a lot of people to look at."

They reached the end of the alley and emerged onto 2nd Street, according to the sign. She was vaguely familiar with the area, which was a mix of fifties-era boxy concrete rectangles and older restored brick buildings. It was home to a plethora of federal agencies, including the FAA, the Department of Education, and the Department of Health and Human Services. None of them were open to tourists, and, more important, none of them were open this early. Up the street, there was an old woman walking a dog. Just beyond her, a homeless man pushed his belongings in a shopping cart. The rattling of the wheels on the uneven pavement jangled Jess's nerves. Other than that, this street, too, was deserted.

So much for his assertion that because there were lots of people in D.C., finding them would be harder. There weren't lots of people *here*. And the idea that a satellite might be recording their every move right at that very moment gave her the willies.

Jess's toe caught on something and she stumbled.

"You okay?" Mark stopped to steady her. Regaining her balance, she nodded, and he added, "I vote we head for the metro and put some distance between us and where we got off the truck as quick as we can."

"Just a minute," she said. Mark was scruffy, but then he looked hot scruffy. She had a strong feeling that she was scruffy, too, and she knew from experience that she definitely did not look hot that way. Unzipping her purse, she dug into it even as she spoke. "It would be better if we looked as normal as possible. Let me brush my hair."

"Now?" He looked at her with disbelief, but she was

already dragging a brush through her hair. Finishing, she ran her brush over his.

"Hey."

"Your hair was sticking up."

"Nobody's going to notice *me.*"

"They might."

"If people are gonna be looking at us that close, you probably ought to know that you have dirt on your face."

"Really?"

"I was kidding." He groaned as she dug through her purse for the wet wipes she carried and carefully wiped her face. Then she pulled out a tube of the neutral pink lipstick she always wore and slicked that over her lips. Since she never wore much makeup anyway, Jess calculated that she now probably looked pretty close to normal. Except for the bruises and stitches, of course.

"You all done?" he asked.

Jess ignored the too polite tone. "Yes."

"Good." Taking her arm, Mark started walking, and she, perforce, went with him. "Look, I know this area. There's a metro station two blocks over. It would be nice if we could get there before the people who want to kill us catch up."

The reminder made her shiver. A few minutes later Jess spotted the brown pole with the M sign on it that indicated a metro station. So close to the metro there were numerous people around. Nervously her gaze slid over a couple of college-age men in hoodies and jeans wearing backpacks, a blond middle-aged woman in the kind of bright polyester uniform that a dental assistant or pediatrician's assistant might wear, an older guy in a suit carrying a briefcase, a woman about her own age in a Denny's uniform. All were hurrying toward the metro. None spared so much as a glance for her or Mark. None looked like a threat.

Mark stopped dead. Glancing at him in surprise, she

discovered that he was staring at the intersection directly
ahead of them as if he'd seen a ghost. A red light was
holding up cross traffic, while a taxi sped through to
zoom past them with a rattle and a whoosh of air.

"What?" she demanded. His expression was enough
to make her stomach tighten without his even having to
say a word.

"See that black BMW?" His voice was very quiet. His
hand tightened on her arm, and he started walking again,
urging her toward the metro station. His eyes were on the
intersection that was maybe a quarter of a block away.

Following his gaze, she saw that there were three vehicles lined up waiting for the light to change: a red
Honda or something similar, a white Econoline van with
some sort of writing on the side, and the black BMW.
Shiny and new-looking, it had tinted windows and bright
chrome wheels.

"What about it?" she asked, as the light changed and
those vehicles got under way in turn, crossing in front of
them.

"It was at the 7-Eleven." They were almost at the
steps that led down to the station. "I think it's a Dark
Car."

Chapter 24

"A DARK CAR? You want to tell me what that is?"

The answer was going to be bad news, Jess knew as she asked the question. She could tell from the rigidity of his jaw, the tightness of his mouth, and the sudden deepening of the lines around his eyes as he shot a look at her. She swallowed hard. Her heart, which was already beating too fast, began to race.

"It's a special-ops vehicle."

Jess hesitated at the top of the long flight of concrete steps that led to the metro platform, glancing down them with dismay. Making a sound under his breath, Mark scooped her up and started down with her. Jess grabbed his shoulders and hung on. The truth was, the stairs were a problem for her for the moment, and they both knew it.

"They always use black, foreign-made cars. The tags, registration, all that will turn out to be attached to some sham company. Untraceable."

"Does it belong to the Secret Service? The CIA? What?" It was all Jess could do to keep the squeak out of her voice. They were on the platform now, and he set her on her feet. While not crowded, it was fairly well populated even as early as it was. Her gaze shot around, looking for—what? Men in dark suits? If so, there were a few, but none who looked threatening. Jeez, was she making a possibly fatal mistake by assuming that all government operatives wore dark suits and were as big and buff as Mark? But he was scanning the crowd, too, and didn't appear to find any fresh cause for alarm. The ubiquitous smell of subways everywhere, the stale air and exhaust mixed with notes of body odor, urine, and alcohol, wasn't too bad. D.C. was known for its clean stations. Jess could see that the train was already rushing toward them. The roar echoed off the concrete walls.

"Way more off the grid than that. Black ops. We're basically talking government-authorized hit men."

"Oh my God."

The train pulled into the station with a wheeze. As far as Jess could tell, nobody was paying them the least bit of attention. Just to be safe, she shot a nervous glance back toward the entrance: a college-age girl bumping a bicycle down the stairs, a middle-age woman in a red dress in a hurry to catch the train. Nobody threatening.

"You good by yourself for a minute?" he asked.

That caught her attention.

"Where are you going?"

"Right over there. Don't move."

Giving the newcomers a once-over as they reached the bottom of the steps and joined the milling group of waiting riders, Mark wove through the swelling assemblage to a vending machine half a platform away. Shooting continual wary glances at the eddying tide of people around her, Jess watched as he put in a few dollars and procured two fare cards. Returning, he handed one to her.

"I have a fare card," she told him as she accepted the one he gave her. Most residents of D.C. did; the metro was the easiest, most economical way to move around inside the District.

"I have one, too, and neither of us can use ours." His expression turned flinty again. "They're hoping we'll do something that dumb. We can't use credit cards, or debit cards, or anything else like that, either, without them pouncing on us. We're strictly cash-and-carry from here on out."

Jess ran a fingertip along the edge of the fare card. Her stomach was now knotted so tight it actually hurt.

"I have about twenty-four dollars in my purse." That was including the emergency twenty, which her mother had replaced, showing the folded bill to her before tucking it into the zippered compartment.

"Well, I have a hundred and twelve, so that gives us a kitty of . . ."

"A hundred and thirty-six dollars." Jess's tone was glum. That wouldn't last long. She faced the terrifying truth. "We can't run forever, Mark."

"We don't have to run forever. We just have to keep a step ahead of them until we come up with some way to bring them down."

"Oh, is that all?" Jess shot him a look. "If that was supposed to make me feel better, I should probably tell you it failed miserably."

He smiled.

"Keep your head down. You've been on the news a lot lately." His hand slid around her elbow, urging her into motion. "The last thing we need is somebody recognizing you."

A thrill of alarm shot out along her nerve endings at the thought as she obediently ducked her head. Probably because she'd watched almost none of the coverage, she'd forgotten she had just been all over TV in connection with Annette Cooper's death.

"Do you think they will?" Her shoulders rose defensively as her head sank between them. She moved closer to his side.

"I don't think so. The glasses are good. Every time I've seen you on TV, you haven't been wearing them."

"That's because I hate them."

"Do you?" He sounded surprised. "You look cute in them. Brainy. Hot."

If she hadn't been scared out of her mind, Jess thought she might have blushed. She flicked a quick sideways look up at him.

"If you're after my twenty-four dollars, you can just forget it," she said tartly.

He laughed. "I'm serious. Brainy *and* hot. The combination's killer."

She didn't answer. Instead, she secretly hugged his words close as they fell in with the queue of people boarding the train. Oh, God, how idiotic was it that even while she was running for her life, just getting a compliment from him could make her go all warm and fuzzy inside? Unbidden, she had a sudden flashback to that blazing kiss. *Mark . . .*

"Careful." His hand tightened on her elbow as she reached the train and stepped aboard, and the necessity of quickly vetting all the people already sitting in the upholstered seats was as effective at banishing romantic yearnings as a bucket of cold water to the face.

Forget being in love. What you want to do here is survive.

Her legs were more unsteady than she'd hoped, and she was relieved to find a seat. Mark dropped down beside her, eyeing the people around them before apparently deciding they were all as harmless as they looked.

The train groaned and jerked as it got under way.

"So what you're telling me is that somebody's decided your Secret Service buddies aren't getting the job done, and now they've sent in the real professionals?" Jess asked under her breath. The situation was now so bad it was almost funny. *Not.*

"It's because of me." His eyes were harder and colder than she had ever imagined they could be. His mouth was tight, his expression unreadable. She was reminded that he was a federal agent, with a gun holstered on his belt. *Thank God.* "Last night, or rather early this morning, whoever's behind this apparently realized that if they killed you I wasn't going to be fine with it, and they were going to have to deal with me. So now they're out to eliminate us both."

"The bomb," Jess said, appalled.

"Yeah."

She tried to think logically despite the panic that was welling up inside her as irrepressibly as fizz in a shaken soda bottle.

"You realize this means I've been right all along. No-body would send out a government hit squad if they weren't trying to cover up something as big as"—her voice, which had been scarcely louder than a whisper before, dropped even lower, although an anxious glance around reconfirmed that no one seemed to be paying the least bit of attention—"the First Lady's murder."

"I got that."

"In other words, we're in trouble."

He gave a curt little nod.

"Bigger trouble than I was in before."

"Oh, yeah." His eyes cut toward her. There was a sud-den glint of wry humor in them. "Of course, now they're trying to kill me, too. They probably feel the job's going to be a little harder."

"So call out the big guns, *hmm*?" As her grip tight-ened convulsively on the armrest, Jess took a deep breath. Panicking was useless. What she needed to do was stay calm so she could think. "Who do you think is behind this? Who could order out a black-ops team? To hunt people down and murder them?"

Despite her best efforts, her voice shook. To think that this could possibly be happening to *her,* in the United States of America, was mind-boggling.

Mark was slouched down in the seat, his arms crossed over his chest, his long legs sprawled out in front of him.

To the ordinary observer, his posture would look casual, even careless. Until they got a good look at his eyes. There was a cold watchfulness in them that reminded her of steel. They were the eyes of a man who had been trained to protect the lives of those he shielded by dying—or killing. Whichever it took.

Jess took heart.

"Not more than a handful of people." He seemed unwilling to go on.

"The President?"

He nodded curtly. "Along with a small group of his top advisers. The Secretary of State. The Secretary of Defense. The Secretary of Homeland Security. People like that."

"Harris Lowell?"

"Not on his own. Only if it was presumed he was acting on the order of the President."

Mark's expression had grown increasingly thoughtful. By the time he finished that last sentence, he was frowning into space as if he were turning something over in his mind. Jess was just about to demand to know what that something was when the brakes squealed and the train shuddered into another station.

Mark immediately stood up. She looked at him questioningly. Unless there was something she was missing, this definitely wasn't their stop.

"Before we do anything else, we've got to muddy the waters." Mark reached for her hand and pulled her up beside him. The doors opened, and riders started exiting the car as more filed in. Glancing nervously out through the windows, she realized that this station was much busier than the last, so busy that after only a moment she gave up on trying to scan every face and hunt for every dark suit. Seven a.m. marked the start of rush hour and, according to the big clock on the opposite wall, it was twelve minutes after that now. Maneuvering her so that she stood in line in front of him, Mark rested his hands lightly on her waist to give her some support and spoke in her ear as they filed out of the car. "It's obvious that they were able to identify the truck and track it into town. We can't take a direct route anywhere anymore. It's too easy to follow."

THE MAIN BRANCH of the library was a modern four-story glass-and-steel cube located on G Street NW at 9th. By the time Jess slid into a seat in front of one of its computers, it was after two p.m. She was wearing new-to-her jeans and a white Hanes T-shirt straight from a really new three-pack along with her own jacket, a pair of black Converse sneakers, and a D.C. United baseball cap. Mark was still in the blue dress shirt and black suit pants he'd been wearing all along. The only change was the addition of a newly acquired Redskins cap. At his insistence, they'd gone shopping at a Goodwill outlet that morning. Their purchases, which included a three-pack of cheap cotton panties for her and a pair of boxers for him, had mostly come from the clearance bin and had totaled seven dollars and twenty-two cents. Mark had insisted the wardrobe change was necessary to make them harder to spot, and Jess was glad for the fresh clothes, especially the sneakers, but she regretted spending the money. After eating lunch at Taco Bell, which had cost an alarming four dollars and ninety-eight cents for both of them, their kitty had shrunk to one hundred twenty-three dollars and eighty cents.

Just thinking about it gave her palpitations.

But at the moment, she'd filed it, along with a whole boatload of other terrifying things, under the category of something to worry about later. The first thing she did, upon sitting down at the computer, was e-mail her mother, who she knew would be frantic with worry as soon as she heard about Davenport's death, especially considering the fact that Jess was no longer answering her cell phone. Using Grace's account to make it less obvious in case anybody was monitoring her mother's incoming e-mails, Jess left a message that she was fine, under Secret Service protection, and would be in touch as soon as she could. Then, she checked out a license plate number Mark gave her—BCW-248. It was registered to a chain of local dental clinics, which made Mark snort, "Yeah, right," when she told him. After that, she concentrated on gaining access to the phone records that, she hoped, would provide the information they needed. Ordinarily something like this was a snap. She knew how to bypass the access codes and passwords, how to worm her way into the phone company's or the Internet service provider's or the IRS's or whoever's information systems, how to zero in on the individual in question and pull up the appropriate data: It was part of what had made her so valuable to Davenport.

But almost immediately she ran into a problem.

"What?" Mark whispered as she quit tapping and frowned. He was leaning on the back of the open, shoulder-height cubicle, scanning the screen along with her. The screen that was, unfortunately, blank except for a code that she'd seen only once before.

Not good.

"*Shh.* It looks like somebody's pulled the records." There were maybe a dozen other users scattered among the terminals that lined the room. All of them looked harmless and appeared to be totally engrossed in their own work, but the last thing they needed was to attract any attention.

"Whose?"

"*Shh.*"

Annette Cooper's, Davenport's, Marian's, Prescott's, the driver's—she hadn't known his name but Mark supplied it when asked. As the pattern became alarmingly clear, she checked Marty Solomon's. Same code. Same blank screen.

She faced the truth with a thrill of fear. The speed of

it, the thoroughness of it, the power it would take to do such a thing, was terrifying.

"They've pulled them all. Everybody who's been killed. There's nothing here."

"Shit."

"*Shh.*"

Okay. The next step was to try to access the records of likely suspects. Like Harris Lowell. Jess wasn't optimistic, and her lack of optimism was rewarded: His records were unavailable, too. Ditto the President's, of course, and the Secretaries of State, Defense, and Homeland Security—those whom Mark had mentioned as having enough clout to send out a government hit squad—as well as a few random shots of her own, like the Vice President and the Speaker of the House.

All blanks.

Fingers poised on the keyboard, Jess stared at the blinking code on a screen that should have been crawling with phone numbers, and thought. With no way to determine who any of the victims had spoken to in their last hours, it seemed they were well and truly stymied. They would have to find some other means. . . .

Wait.

Just like hacking into computer files, the key to getting the information they needed was to go in through the back door.

The records of high-level officials clearly were too protected to be accessed by a skilled amateur at a public computer. And whoever was behind this was smart enough to have pulled the pertinent records for those who had been killed. No one was getting to those.

But had they pulled the records of the people still in the game? The minor players, the foot soldiers, the extras?

To start off with, how about the limo company? Aztec Limos: Jess knew the name because that was the company Davenport always used.

Jess smiled, a satisfied little curl of her lips brought on by a flash of, if she had to say so herself, absolutely brilliant insight.

"What?" Mark must have seen the smile, because he moved to stand beside her, thrusting his hands into his trouser pockets as he leaned forward to peer at the screen.

"I'm going to check the limo company."

Pulling up the records was a snap. No attempt had been made to make them inaccessible. Jess paged to the night in question and found Davenport's cell phone number. It was the calls that came in immediately afterward that interested her most.

"Anything?"

"Maybe. That's Davenport's number." She pointed. "See those calls that came in to the company after that? The three of them right after Davenport's are from the same number. I'm guessing they're from wherever the limo was heading, checking to see why it didn't arrive as scheduled. You notice they were all placed between one and one-fifteen, and then they stopped."

"Because word of the accident was getting out."

"Yes." She pointed to the calls that started arriving nearly every minute right after the last of the three. Hundreds of calls, one right after the other. "Those are probably reporters and news agencies. But we need to check them, too, just to be sure."

"Can you print that out?"

Jess hit print. The distant hum of the printer going to work sent Mark off to retrieve the papers.

Annette Cooper had accused Prescott of calling someone, presumably backup, right before the Lincoln had been forced from the road.

"Give me the full names of the Secret Service agents who were at your house last night." Jess scooted a pad and pencil, thoughtfully provided by the library and left in the cubicle for the use of its patrons, toward Mark when he returned. "Also their phone numbers and addresses, if you know them. And Prescott's, too."

"Why?"

"Mrs. Cooper accused Prescott of calling for backup. If he did, it's possible that whoever he called either was in the car behind us or sent the car."

"I know their names, partial addresses, and Fielding's number." He bent over, writing. "The other numbers were in my phone."

Which meant they were lost. But as long as she had the names, she could work it out.

Fielding's records came up beautifully. Scrolling quickly through them, working without Prescott's cell phone number, Jess realized that knowing the date and approximate time of the call would be enough.

Bingo.

Elated, she almost called out to Mark and stopped there. But then, just to make sure, she decided to check Matthews's phone records.

Another bingo. Same number, presumably Prescott's, two minutes later.

Frowning, she went into Wendell's.

Bingo again. Same number again, four minutes earlier than Fielding's hit. And then a second one, ninety seconds after Matthews's.

"So what've you got?"

"Prescott texted Fielding, Matthews, and Wendell separately in the ten minutes before the crash. Actually, he texted Wendell twice."

"He contacted all three? You're shitting me."

"Nope."

The problem was, the fact that Prescott had contacted all three agents made the information practically useless. It did nothing to pinpoint a traitor in the ranks. As they both silently absorbed that, Jess hit print so they could comb through the records more thoroughly later.

Mark again went to fetch the printouts before anyone else could pick them up.

Prescott would have been in the Lincoln with them at the time. Jess realized that the picture of him frantically texting his fellow agents fit with what she remembered. That's why he had been so quiet in the front seat and had paid so little attention to the histrionics in the back. The First Lady had been right on the money: Prescott had contacted backup. Actually, when Jess thought about it, she had been right on the money about everything so far.

I'm a fucking prisoner. The words echoed through Jess's mind. Annette Cooper had been referring to her Secret Service detail, Jess was almost sure.

Of which Mark had been special agent in charge.

Just because of that, and because she was now a charter member of Paranoids-R-Us, and because she wanted to make absolutely certain that none of her really sick residual suspicions weren't so, Jess keyed in Mark's information.

His cell phone records popped right up. *No problemo.*

Jess's eyes widened and her heart started beating faster as she paged through them. Before the crash, nothing jumped out at her. But in the days after the crash, a familiar number occurred with increasing frequency: Davenport's.

In fact, Mark's last call to Davenport had been placed some two hours before he had fired a shot at Jess and then stepped out the window.

"Jess. We gotta go." Mark was back, thrusting the folded printouts into his pants pocket as he spoke. She barely had enough presence of mind to push the quit button to exit the file before she looked up at him.

Blindly.

"Get up. We're leaving." He hit the power button on the computer, turning it off as he grabbed her arm and pulled her to her feet. She must have looked as stunned as she felt, because he gave her arm a little shake. "Jess. They're here."

Chapter 25

"WHAT?" THAT GOT HER adrenaline going. What-ever he may or may not have done, she discovered that at her core, she did not fear Mark. However, she feared those who were chasing them to the point of teeth-chat-tering terror.

"I checked out the window when I was coming back with the printouts." Mark grabbed her purse and the plastic bag with their old clothes and the new purchases from Goodwill as he spoke. "I saw the Dark Car drive past. If they're in the vicinity, you can bet your sweet life it's because they know we're here."

They were moving as he spoke, Jess managing to keep up with Mark's long strides because of the sheer juicing power of abject fear. Her heart pounded. Her pulse hammered in her ears. Her stomach—well, the poor thing had almost forgotten what if felt like *not* to be twisted into a pretzel.

"Somebody must have tagged the files." Jess had been afraid of that. Of course, if somebody went to all the trouble of pulling the information, tagging the files so they would be notified if someone tried to access them would be the next logical step. She had at least hoped to have a little more time before anybody noticed and took action. "When I tried to access them, it sent out an alert."

"Which they were able to trace back to the computers here." Mark's voice was grim. They were moving through the third floor's open center aisle as they spoke, heading, Jess realized, toward the far corner of the building, where, presumably, there was a staircase and elevator bank other than the central one. It was Friday afternoon, school had apparently just let out, and the rows of tall shelves were fairly well populated. A story session, complete with small chairs and a yellow-smocked librarian, was getting ready to get started in one corner, Jess saw as they reached a back hall, which held restrooms and an emergency exit.

"How did you know where the exit was?" Jess asked in a hurried whisper as Mark, holding her hand tightly, raced her toward it. Unspoken between them ran the knowledge that they had very little time; their pursuers would almost certainly come straight up to the computer room, realize immediately that their quarry had fled, and give chase. Remembering the open nature of the corner on which the library was situated, Jess realized they would be ridiculously easy to spot as soon as they left the building.

"I read the signs."

Before Jess could point out an alarm would probably sound if he opened the door—in her experience, emergency exits were like that—he flipped open the little plastic door on the small red rectangle set into the wall by the exit and pulled the fire alarm.

Immediately, loud, clanging peals filled the air. Jess's jaw dropped as he pulled open the door to the emergency exit—an alarm did sound, a tinny little one almost lost beneath the full-throated scream of the other—dragged her into the stairwell, picked her up, and ran down the stairs with her.

She didn't even protest.

"That was brilliant," she said, holding tight and regarding him with awe.

"Fuckin' A."

By the time they reached the ground floor, the stairwell behind them was clogged with people heading down. More people streamed out the exit at the bottom of the stairs. Emerging into the crisp spring air, looking desperately all around, feeling hideously exposed in the bright sunshine that had burned off most of the morning's chill, Jess saw that there were swarms of people pouring out of the building, milling around on the sidewalks, coming out of nearby businesses to stop and stare. Librarians tried to herd the kids into a group and keep them out of the street at the same time, with scant success. Patrons holding books and magazines blended into the growing crowd. This was an area of three- and four-story buildings, mom-and-pop-type stores, lots of foot traffic, and lots of vehicular traffic, all of which was slowing down and gawking and honking. Jess could hear the wail of sirens rushing to the rescue.

Putting her down, taking her arm, Mark pulled her out into the middle of the street at a near run. Trailing behind, Jess nearly got mowed down by a startled-looking mom in a minivan at approximately the same time that she saw a tall, dark-haired, granite-faced man in a black suit thrusting through the swirl of bystanders at the corner.

He was obviously looking for something. Jess felt a jolt of terror as she realized what—or, rather, who.

"Mark," Jess squeaked, as her eyes stayed glued to the man, who continued to wade through throngs of people and head in their direction without, she was sure, having yet seen them. "There's one of them."

Jess heard the quick intake of Mark's breath as he looked—at the exact same instant as the black-suited man saw them. Throat tightening with alarm, Jess watched the bad guy's gaze sweep over them, freeze, and come back. His face registered surprised recognition, and then he stuck his hand beneath his suit jacket. One word popped into Jess's horrified mind: *gun.*

Her heart leaped.

"Mark," she moaned in warning, but he had already seen, or maybe not; maybe the plan was already in motion and she had missed it, because he grabbed her and thrust her ahead of him.

"Get in."

Even as she gasped and refocused to see what was happening, he was cramming her inside an open car door. As her butt landed on a cracked vinyl seat, she realized that Mark had just stuffed her in a taxi that was being vacated by someone else.

"Scoot," he barked, but she didn't need to be told. She scooted like a dog with its tail on fire, and he jumped in beside her, slammed the door, and said, "Union Station, fast" to the cabbie, who sped off.

Jess's mouth was still hanging open as she glanced back. The black-suited man ran through the crowd, pushing people out of the way as he came after them, his hand still hidden beneath his jacket. She grabbed Mark's arm and tried to stutter out a warning, but nothing coherent emerged. Then the cab turned a corner and he was lost to view.

Jess thought she was going to melt into a little puddle of reaction right there on the seat.

"Friend of yours?" she asked. Her eyes rolled around to Mark, who gave her a warning look. Clearly this was something that was not to be discussed within earshot of the cabbie. Oh, yeah, she got why. Probably because the idea that murderous goons were chasing his cab with the idea of riddling his passengers with bullets might not go over so well. In fact, if his thought processes were anything like hers, the cabbie might well slam on the brakes and order them out on the spot. Good for him. Bad for them.

Thanks to near gridlocked Friday-afternoon locals-get-out-of-town traffic, progress seemed glacially slow. But no Dark Car appeared behind them, or beside them, or anywhere else. All vehicles moved in bumper-to-bumper unison.

As the Beaux Arts–style building that was Union Station came into view, Mark was already handing over a ten from their dwindling kitty. Jess spared no more than a passing thought for the money as the taxi stopped in front of the statue of Columbus and she scrambled out.

Some things were worth paying for. Like living.

Mark was right behind her. He grabbed her hand and towed her after him like a barge after a tugboat. Her legs and back had been bothering her earlier. Now, with the knowledge that a death squad was right behind them, the aches and pains were reduced to minor twinges that barely slowed her down.

"Did you recognize him?" she gasped out.

"No."

Hundreds of people were in and around the building. Jess barely registered the ornamental facade festooned with eagles, or the replica of the Liberty Bell. Instead, she concentrated on getting off the street and out of the sight of any arriving cars, and when they burst through the doors to join the teeming crowds inside the vast open space, she felt an overwhelming wave of relief.

"Unless they followed us"—she might be being overly optimistic here, but she was pretty sure the bad guys hadn't been able to get close enough to the cab to see where it went—"there's no way they can know where we are, right?"

Given the fact that Mark was still dragging her through the Main Hall, which seemed as long as a football field and boasted a 96-foot-high barrel-vaulted ceiling, she wasn't too surprised by the wry twist of his mouth, which told her that her optimism was sadly misplaced.

"Simple enough to find out where the taxi that just picked up passengers in front of the main library let them out. What we've got here is a few minutes' start." His eyes darted around, roaming over everything from the tourists munching pizza at the food court to the escalator that led to the movie theaters, with an occasional glance over Jess's head to survey the terrain behind her. As Jess had been casting frequent looks back herself, she knew what he saw: There were so many people that picking out black-suited goons with murderous intent would be impossible until the goons were practically upon them.

"This way," he said. Her pulse was now thundering so loud in her ears that she wouldn't have heard the words if she hadn't been looking right at him when he spoke. Pulling her with him onto an escalator, he looked like he wanted to push his way through the impassable lineup of people clogging the slow-moving thing. Instead, he stopped, seething with barely concealed impatience as the escalator leisurely chugged its way down.

Jess would have said something, but she was too busy catching her breath. After their life-or-death race from the library, she was sweating, she was exhausted, she was terrified, and her body ached like a losing prizefighter's. She'd swallowed a couple of pain pills along with her tacos earlier, but they were no match for the kind of day she was having.

Their destination, she discovered as they left the escalator and Mark dragged her through another set of doors, was the metro.

"Be right back." As soon as they were on the platform, he dropped her hand and strode away. Swallowed up in the milling crowd, she cast scared looks all around. Before she could totally succumb to panic he was back, thrusting a fare card into her hand. A moment after that, they were boarding a train.

Jess flopped down into one of the seats with relief. Taking a couple of deep breaths and straightening her glasses, which had gotten knocked crooked in their rush through the terminal, she cast a jaundiced eye at Mark, who dropped down beside her. She was glad to see that it wasn't just her—he was breathless and sweaty, too. He'd lost the baseball cap, and as she put a hand to her head in reaction she discovered she had lost hers, too. The bright sunlight streaming in through the windows showed up how bloodshot his eyes were, as well as the puffiness beneath them. More than a day's worth of stubble now darkened his cheeks and chin. His shirt was limp and had lost a couple of buttons, and he looked kind of like a bum. A sexy bum, which was the annoying thing, because she was fairly certain that sexy was one of the last words that anyone would use to describe her appearance at the moment. Questions about his calls to Davenport loomed large in her mind, but this was neither the time nor the place to confront him. Best not to upset the status quo with your protector until you were someplace safe.

"We can't just keep running," she pointed out between gulps of air as the train jolted out of the station. The car was almost full, so her voice was just loud enough to reach his ears. "We need a plan."

"We've got one."

She seemed to remember hearing that before. "Oh, yeah? Do tell."

"Trust me."

Her expression must have been something to see, because he laughed, picked up her hand that was lying curled on her lap, brought it to his mouth, and kissed it.

The sight of his handsome head bent over her hand, the feel of his warm lips on her skin, would have been enough to stun her into dazzled compliance at any other time. Even under the circumstances, for a moment there her heart did a little tap dance, and she teetered on the brink.

Then she got a grip, snatched her hand back, folded her arms over her chest, and scowled at him. "No."

"Guess you'll just have to wait and see, then."

He was still smiling a little. Mindful of their fellow passengers, Jess restrained herself. They sat in silence through two stops. By the time the train chugged into a third, she was breathing normally and her heartbeat had resumed its usual constant, steady rhythm. Then Mark stood up, pulling her up beside him, and her heart gave an automatic uneasy thump.

"Our stop," he said, and Jess almost groaned. She was worn-out, bone-tired, in pain, scared to death, and sick of it, filled with uneasiness and lack of trust toward her partner in flight, and in general ready for this to end.

Not that she said any of that. What was the point? Embracing her inner stiff upper lip, she left the station with Mark without saying anything at all. At least, she thought, as they hotfooted it across the street hand in hand, he was no longer walking as fast as he could, which seemed to argue that he felt they were relatively safe for the time being. Or maybe he was just being considerate of her still-much-less-than-optimum physical state. They were in Dupont Circle, the eclectic, primarily residential area with accommodations ranging from Civil War–era mansions, many of which had been turned into apartments or condos, to boxy new office buildings. There were numerous restaurants and quite a few art galleries and museums, and lots of people. Unfortunately, Jess was in no mood to appreciate the little bistros and boutiques that lined the streets. The people, however, she appreciated. Just in case the bad guys were using eye-in-the-sky technology to search for them right now, she wanted as many people around her as she could get.

She occasionally liked to try to solve the Waldo books

when she babysat her nephews. Now, she realized, she and Mark were Waldo, and the game had become *Where're Mark and Jess?*

Trying to keep her breathing from going haywire at the thought, she looked at Mark. "Now what?"

They had turned onto a quieter residential street with far fewer fellow pedestrians to get lost among, and then he pulled her into a narrow, grassy alley that ran between two identical four-story brick rectangles with colonial-looking white pedimented doorways and green shutters out front. There were no people at all in the alley. Glancing up, Jess saw a bright blue strip of sky above them and shuddered.

"Congressmen fly home on the weekends to make nice with constituents and see their families. They're required to maintain homes in their districts. Most of them—the honest ones—don't make squat. Therefore, they rent relatively cheap apartments to live in during the week when they have to be in Washington."

They reached the end of the alley, which opened out into a larger one with a lot more blue sky above it. A strip of blacktopped pavement ran down the middle and Dumpsters and trash cans lined either side. The slanting sunlight of late afternoon beamed down, but thanks to the buildings they were in deep shadow. She wrinkled her nose at the faint smell of garbage as she cast another worried glance up at the sky. Across the street, a calico cat watched them from inside a window two stories up. Other than that, there was no one around.

"Which means . . . ?" So far what she was hearing did not add up to anything helpful.

He pulled her around a brick retaining wall and let go of her hand. "We're going to borrow one for the night."

"What?" Jess's head snapped around. All thought of searching for bad guys was forgotten for the moment as her gaze riveted on Mark. He was standing on the stoop of the brownstone building beside the brick ones, punching numbers into a lock that hung from the back door-knob. He turned the knob and the door opened.

"The woman I was seeing is a Realtor. She rents out apartments in these buildings all the time. I know her code." He pulled her into a gloomy, hardwood-floored central hall as he spoke, and she realized that the lock he'd punched numbers into had been a Realtor's lock.

Glancing around as he closed the door behind them, Jess practically swallowed her tongue. A long row of flat brass mailboxes set into the wall lined the hall. She recognized some of the names as he pulled her past them and hit the elevator button: Sahlinger, Cristofoli, Urton, Guenther. Congressional representatives all.

"So we're going to let ourselves into an empty apartment?" Jess asked with a flicker of misgiving as they stepped into the elevator, the door closed, and it started its creaky ascent.

"I thought about that, but here's the thing: We've got to assume these guys know everything about us. So using an apartment she has access to is out. Sooner or later, when they can't find us, they'll probably think of that."

The elevator stopped on the fourth floor. Four doors, two on either side of the hall, bore the respective numbers 13, 14, 15, and 16. Beneath the numbers were affixed small brass plates with typewritten names inserted into the open centers.

"So . . . ?" Her voice trailed off as he stepped up to the door of apartment 14, knocked, and waited. Nothing.

"So we borrow one from Congressman Cristofoli."

Then he pulled a small Leatherman tool out of his pocket and applied one of the attachments to the lock.

Jess was still casting petrified glances all around in case somebody should come out of one of the other apartments and see what he was doing when he pushed open the door and grabbed her hand.

"Hurry up, I've got to turn off the alarm."

Still processing extreme dismay at the knowledge that they were breaking into a congressman's apartment as she scuttled in behind him, Jess felt her unease ratchet up to another level as she heard the warning beep leading to the earsplitting screech of a violated security alarm.

"This is so illegal. If we get caught, we could go to jail. I could lose my law license . . ."

"Baby, if we get caught that'll be the least of our problems."

Pushing the door shut behind her, Mark dropped her hand and disappeared into another room.

Facing the truth of what he'd said, Jess clasped her hands together and called after him in a wobbly voice, "Please tell me you know some way to shut off that damned alarm."

A moment later the ominous beeping ceased. Then Mark reappeared in the doorway between the two rooms and grinned at her.

"What did you do?" Wrapping her arms around herself, she was barely able to keep her teeth from chattering. And not from cold, either. From reaction. And fear. And way too much physical exertion. And exhaustion. And—everything. Her whole absolutely gone-to-hell-in-a-handbasket life.

"Took care of the alarm."

"How?" She asked the question before she realized she probably didn't want to know the answer.

"What can I say? I'm good." His gaze swept over her, and he frowned. "You look beat. Look, you can quit worrying for a while. I figure we've got a good twenty-four hours before we have to start thinking about moving on."

"Great." Which meant that a very uneasy day from now, they'd be on the run again—unless he was wrong and they got killed first. Still, as the prospect of even a nerve-racking respite began to seep through her system, she very slowly exhaled. She hadn't been aware of how tense she was until the worst of it started to ease.

"Are you hungry? Looks like there's food in the kitchen." He headed into the other room.

Jess was, indeed, hungry. She also realized that the solid core of trust she'd thought she'd established with her partner in flight was suddenly not so solid after all. They were all alone now in a place that was totally out of the public eye. What if he'd actually tipped somebody off to meet them here? What if . . . ?

She heard the sound of the refrigerator door opening and, as if in answer, her stomach growled. Firmly, she pushed all the terrifying *what if*s out of her head.

Unless something more concrete than suspicious phone numbers turned up, she wasn't about to rush back out into eye-in-the-sky-ville alone. Which meant she was on board with Mark.

She trailed after him through the small apartment. The front door they'd come in through opened directly into a living room, which connected to a single bedroom and a small kitchen in an open plan intended to make the place seem larger. The rooms were decorated in beiges and browns, and filled with furniture that she could only characterize as "early hotel." Inexpensive-looking beige carpet extended through the living room and bedroom to the kitchen. There was apparently a big window in both the living room and bedroom, because the drapes in both rooms, which were drawn, covered the entire outside wall. The only bathroom—which was also the only room with an actual door—was located between the kitchen and bedroom. She made quick use of the facilities, washing her hands and face, and emerged minutes later feeling a little better.

Mark was seated in one of the two bentwood chairs at the small glass-topped bistro-style kitchen table that sat in the middle of the tiny kitchen. A long, narrow window with its mini-blinds open ran the length of the far wall, making the kitchen, with its white cabinets, appliances, walls, and tile floor, the brightest room in the house. There was a paper plate in front of Mark, what looked like a heap of coleslaw on the paper plate, and a sandwich, which he had just taken a big bite out of, in his hands. A juice box sat beside the paper plate. Jess saw that another paper plate, complete with sandwich, coleslaw, juice box, and fork, waited across the table for her.

Swallowing, he nodded at her plate. "Made you a sandwich."

Jess looked from the plate to him. He was already taking another huge bite. His blue eyes met hers guilelessly.

"Thanks." Crossing the kitchen, she pulled two paper towels from the roll by the sink—she saw no sign of any napkins—and offered him one as she sank down opposite him.

The sandwich, she discovered as she bit into it, was ham. The coleslaw was spicy. And the juice was orange. Her stomach gave a little hiccup of delight.

Waiting and wondering was not her style, Jess discovered as she responded to some enthusiastic comment of his about the amount of food the congressman had on hand. So she put down her sandwich, looked him in the eye, and came out with it.

"Why did you call Mr. Davenport just a couple of hours before he tried to shoot me?"

Chapter 26

MARK CHOKED ON his ham sandwich. She knew right then she wasn't mistaken: Surprised guilt was there on his face, easy to read as a first-grade schoolbook.

He swallowed and coughed a little and drank some juice.

"What makes you think I did?" he asked at last.

Good try. Not working. "Mark."

He took another big bite out of his sandwich—a stall tactic if she'd ever seen one—chewed, and swallowed. Then he washed it down with a slurp from the juice box. All of which clearly gave him time to think.

She lifted her eyebrows at him, waiting.

He sighed and gave up. "I was authorized to make you a cash-settlement offer. Since it wasn't supposed to be known that it came through the Cooper family, we were funneling it through Davenport."

Jess's eyes widened as she remembered Marian telling her she would be getting a settlement. She never had learned how much it was going to be, which was probably just as well. No point in tormenting herself about its loss.

"We?"

"Well, actually they. The Cooper family."

"Why would the Cooper family give me a settlement?

They have no liability in the accident. The liability lies with the limousine company, its driver, and, to a lesser extent, Mr. Davenport and Davenport, Bascomb, and Kelly, because I was technically on the clock for them when the accident occurred."

"The settlement we were offering came with a secrecy agreement." He took another bite of sandwich.

"A secrecy agreement?"

"Would you eat?"

"Would you talk?"

Mark started in on the coleslaw. Before popping a forkful in his mouth, he said, "The President and his advisers thought you might have learned something detrimental to the First Lady during the course of your association with her. I was authorized to offer you enough money to make it worth your while to forget it."

Jess stared at him. "What did they think I might have learned? That she and her husband fought? That they'd had a fight?"

Mark's mouth twisted. "They fought, but that wasn't it. Mrs. Cooper had a drug problem, all right? The original feeling was that you might have been somehow connected with it, maybe somebody she was buying from. Certainly that you had learned of it."

"What?" Jess blinked at him. "She had a *drug problem? Annette Cooper?"*

"You know those pain pills you've been popping for the last week? It started out just like that for her, too. She broke her back in a horseback riding accident about eight years ago, had constant pain from then on, and started taking pills to deal with it. The whole thing just snowballed until she was a full-blown addict."

Jess goggled at him. "How do you know this?"

He shrugged. "I was head of her security detail."

"Wait. Hold on a minute. Are you saying that the

whole time they've been in Washington, Annette Cooper has had a drug problem?" Jess thought back to when she had first become aware of the Coopers as the new Vice President and his wife. That was almost five years ago. All she could remember of Annette Cooper from that period was stories featuring her working with children and charities. She'd seemed very much the traditional political wife, and completely devoted to her husband.

Mark nodded.

"*That's* why they killed her. Because of the potential embarrassment to her husband." Jess couldn't believe it. There it was, the motive. "If you knew she was addicted to drugs, you had to have suspected that was the reason she was killed. Why didn't you tell me?"

"You want me to talk, you're going to have to eat."

"Mark."

"Eat."

Jess realized he was right, realized she needed food, and took another bite out of her sandwich.

"At first I couldn't believe her death was anything but an accident," Mark said. "Even now that I know it wasn't, that it was murder, I'm finding it tough to believe that her drug problem was the reason. We were dealing with that. Dealing with it successfully."

"Dealing with it how?" Looking at him with fascination, Jess drank some juice.

"She was being weaned off them. We were keeping her away from her suppliers. In fact, we'd pretty much cut her off from the ones she'd always used, the ones she preferred. Occasionally, she would manage to meet with someone who wasn't on our radar and get some more. That's where Prescott and the others thought she might have been going when she slipped away from them the night of the accident. That's why no big alarm was raised and they just tried to round her up themselves. They were scared that the press might get wind of her buying drugs."

"Instead, she was running away from the White House." As Jess put them in context, the First Lady's words took on a whole new meaning. "We both saw Prescott looking for her. She didn't want me to wave to him and get his attention. She said, 'Don't you understand? I'm a fucking prisoner.'"

"Yeah, well." Mark polished off his sandwich. "It was for her own good."

Jess took another sip of juice. She couldn't eat another thing. Remembering the night of the accident had completely killed her appetite.

"So how long has this been going on?"

"The drug problem? I told you, pretty much the last eight years. It got gradually worse until the people around the President faced up to what was going on and came up with a plan to deal with it."

"What I meant was, how long had you been trying to keep the First Lady away from drugs?"

"They brought me on board last August. Up until then I'd been working on the outgoing President's detail, but I was asked to make the switch to Mrs. Cooper, and I did."

Jess frowned. "Why you?"

"I knew them. I'm from Texas, too, you know. Abilene. Actually, Lowell, Davenport, quite a few others that make up the inner circle—I know them, too. Known them for years. We're all from the same place. It was a tricky situation, and they felt they could trust me."

"You mean you knew the Coopers before you came to Washington?"

He nodded. "My mom worked as the elder Coopers'—Wayne and his late wife, Virginia's—housekeeper after my dad was killed on an oil rig when I was four. I pretty much grew up on their ranch in Abilene. David and his sister were gone by then—grown, with David working as a lawyer in Houston before he got into politics—but he came back to visit a couple of times a month. I got to know them all pretty well."

Jess looked at him with fascination mixed with more than a little bit of anxiety. This involvement with the Coopers—did it make him less trustworthy? If his ties to them were strong . . .

"Does your mother still work for them?"

He shook his head. "She remarried and moved to Florida. I go see her when I can. I'm her only child."

"Are you . . . close to them? The President and his family?"

"Depends on what you mean by 'close.' I know them. They know me. They knew they could trust me to do what I could to help with the situation they had." His gaze sharpened on her face. "If you're asking me would I conspire to commit murder for them, no. Would I keep my mouth shut if I knew they had conspired to commit murder? No. They know it, too. You need proof, all you got to do is cast your mind back to the bomb in my car."

Again with the bomb. But she had to admit, it was definitely reassuring.

"So how did you become a Secret Service agent? Was it because of the Coopers?"

"In a roundabout way, I guess. I played football in high school and college. Actually, that's all I ever wanted to do. I was good, too. Good enough to go pro. I got drafted by the Cowboys out of college and played for them for almost one full season. Second-to-last game, I got hit below the knee and something snapped: worst pain I ever felt in my life, and then I was on the injured list. At first I thought I was going to be able to come back. I had surgery, did physical therapy, the whole bit, but my knee was never the same. My speed was gone, and my agility was limited. It took me about a year to admit it, but then I knew I wasn't ever going to be able to play pro ball anymore. No matter how hard I worked at it, I wasn't going to be able to come back."

His tone revealed nothing but wry acceptance, but there was a flicker of pain in his eyes that told her how difficult it had been for him.

"That must have been terrible."

"Life happens."

Jess thought of his daughter. "You were married then, weren't you?"

He nodded. "Heather and I met in college. We got married our senior year, and Taylor came along soon after that. Heather was pretty, ambitious, loved the idea of being a pro football player's wife. When my career ended, so did our marriage. Of course, it took me a while to see that, too. Once everybody figured out I wasn't going to be playing pro ball anymore, Mr. Cooper—the old man, Wayne—helped me get on with the Secret Service. Knowing what I know now, it seems likely that he already had it in mind that David—he was in the Texas Senate at that time—would be going to Washington one day. So I moved up here with Heather and Taylor, worked round the clock trying to suck it up and get my new career on track, and in the process lost my marriage."

Jess looked at him questioningly. She didn't want to pry, didn't want to ask it outright, but she very much wanted to know what had led to the breakup. He must have seen the question in her eyes, because he grimaced.

"You want to know how it ended? It was classic, and I guess I should have seen it coming, but I didn't. I found out that Heather was sleeping around. With a guy I knew, Ted Parks, an FBI agent. A guy I thought was a friend. I couldn't get past that. Not even for Taylor, although I swear I tried my best. To be fair—and it's only in the last couple of years I've been able to be that fair—I was no piece of cake to live with after I figured out I was never going to be able to play football again. I had some down times. I drank too much. I spent a couple of years kind of cursing at fate, you know. Then I was working too much. The Secret Service is pretty much a twenty-four-hour-a-day, seven-day-a-week gig, and Heather was always the kind of woman who needed attention. Lots of attention. There were some rocky moments between us during and right after the divorce, but we're on good terms now. For Taylor's sake. Of course, Taylor plays us off against each other, which causes the occasional dustup. I just took her to Florida to see my mother for spring break. You know what she did while we were there? She got a tattoo on her butt. A butterfly, so I hear. I take her to the mall, she does it while she's supposed to be shopping, and then I don't know a thing about it until Heather calls me to blast me for letting her do it. A tattoo. At fifteen. Can you believe it?"

Mark looked so aggrieved, Jess had to smile. She hadn't even met his daughter, and she was liking her more and more. "It's the style. A lot of teenage girls have them."

Mark's eyes showed an unmistakable flare of interest. "Do you? No."

"No," Jess replied firmly. "I don't. And just for the record, I'm not a teenage girl. I'm twenty-eight years old, remember? But Maddie does."

Mark's eyes widened. "Jesus, that's just what I needed to hear. No worries there. First a tattoo, then she's pregnant. I'm going to have to lock her up till she's thirty."

Jess narrowed her eyes at him. She might not be thrilled to pieces about Maddie's pregnancy, but Maddie was her sister, and criticism of her from anybody outside the family was not allowed.

"You know what? Life happens." She threw his own words back at him with bite.

"I know, I know." Mark held up his hands in apology. "It's just—Taylor's my daughter. I don't want to even think about going there. She doesn't even date yet"—he frowned suddenly, looking uncertain—"I don't think."

That blatant manifestation of male cluelessness was so adorable Jess had to smile again.

"Anyway," Mark continued, with the air of someone getting back to the subject at hand, "I spent a good bit of time talking to Davenport about your settlement. Even though I never did think having you sign a secrecy agreement was a good idea. Almost as soon as you and I started talking, I realized you didn't know a thing about the First Lady and drugs."

"No, I didn't," Jess agreed.

"That's why I couldn't believe somebody was trying to kill you. There didn't seem to be any motive until you told me you thought the First Lady's death was murder. If you were right, and clearly you are, but hindsight's always twenty-twenty, the fact that you're the only witness to something that big would do it." He frowned. "But I'm willing to bet almost anything I own that Annette Cooper was not killed to keep her drug problem quiet. There's another reason. I guarantee it."

Jess was thinking about that when she realized he was looking at her intently.

"Back there in the library, you looked at my phone records, didn't you?"

Gulp. But there was nothing to do but fess up. "Yes."

"You know, you have some real trust issues."

That was so unfair, Jess could only blink at him in disbelief.

"I have trust issues? Well, gee, I wonder why. Let's see: Someone kills the First Lady in a car crash, which was also meant to kill me; then when they realized I survived, I was attacked in my hospital room; I try to tell people, including you, what's going on; you don't believe me, nobody believes me. I try to tell my boss, and he tries to kill me. I start trusting you, sort of, enough to let you take me to your house, where you promise I'll be safe, and while I'm there I hear the voice of the person who tried to kill me in the hospital. The person you called in, mind you. Your friend and fellow Secret Service agent. Not being stupid, I run, and you chase me down. I trust you again, sort of, until you start talking to another of your friends about bringing me in, which, we both know, means to be killed. I jump out, and your car blows up. Then I start trusting you again, sort of, because I really don't have a choice, and I find out, not because you told me but because I checked your phone records, that you have a prior relationship with my boss, the one who tried to kill me. You have an even stronger relationship with the President and his associates, one or several of whom are almost certainly behind the ongoing efforts to try to kill me." She took a deep breath and glared at him. "So if I have trust issues, is it any wonder why?"

Their eyes met. Then he smiled at her.

"Okay, point taken."

"*Point taken?* Is that all you can say?"

"What do you want me to say?"

"Something else."

"You're beautiful?"

Her eyes narrowed at him. That was the second time he had called her beautiful, and it made her feel as vulnerable this time as it had the first.

"Wrong answer." She stood up abruptly, gathering the remains of her meal and stalking away to dump them in the trash can.

"Jess. I'm teasing." He shoved back from the table, picked up his garbage, deposited it in the trash, and followed her into the living room, where she was in the process of sinking down on the couch. "Although you are. Beautiful, I mean. Actually, I think I'm developing kind of a thing here for petite girls with big greenish eyes and glasses."

He stopped walking, leaned a shoulder against the doorjamb, crossed his arms over his chest, and smiled at her. Smiled *dazzlingly* at her.

The look she sent him could have fried an egg in midair.

"If you're trying to distract me from everything you *didn't* tell me, you might as well give up," she said. She was suddenly supremely conscious of her disheveled state, her unstyled hair, her bruised, stitched and makeupless face, her ill-fitting, ill-matched, sexless clothes, her damned glasses. The problem was that she did not feel beautiful, never had, probably never would, and that, she discovered, was what was really ticking her off. "So you can just cut out the crap, pretty boy, because it isn't working."

His eyes widened. His smile widened. He straightened away from the doorjamb to grin at her.

"'Pretty boy'?" Instead of being stung, as she had intended, he was, she was incensed to see, starting to chuckle. "'*Pretty boy*'?"

"Oh, go away." She barely managed to control the impulse to chuck something at him. With studied indifference, she turned her attention to the coffee table in front of the couch, where today's paper lay folded and ready for reading.

"Fine," he said. She could feel him studying her, but she didn't look up. She picked up the paper and snapped it open, perusing the headlines, ostentatiously ignoring him. "I didn't get any sleep last night, and I'm starting to feel a little groggy. I'm going to go take a shower and see if that doesn't perk me up."

"Fine."

"Keep the TV on low if you want to watch it. And

don't answer the door. And stay off the damned computer. And the phone."

With that, he left her alone. A moment later Jess heard the click of the bathroom door closing. She thumbed through the paper—the front section was almost entirely devoted to coverage of the First Lady, and the luminaries who came in for the funeral, the size of the crowds, and the reactions of ordinary citizens, none of which she could bring herself to read—and listened to the muffled rush of the shower. Her skin tingled in atavistic response. She really, really wanted a shower. A long, steaming hot shower . . .

With Mark in it.

Do not go there, she chastised herself fiercely.

Scowling, she was scanning the pages for some mention of what had happened to Davenport or Marian— nothing, and no obituaries yet, either, and it would be too soon to even look for anything about Marty Solomon—when she heard the shower shut off. A couple of minutes passed before the bathroom door opened. That sound was followed by the soft pat of bare feet on carpet. Mark was heading for the bedroom. Probably wearing nothing but a towel . . .

She gritted her teeth, staring doggedly at the newsprint in front of her. And never mind that she was no longer taking in a word.

"You want to take a shower, it's all yours," he called.

She heard more footsteps followed by a rustle of plastic—the bag their clothes were in, she was guessing— followed a moment later by a long creak. Then nothing.

Finally, Jess couldn't stand it anymore. Folding the paper, she got up and went to check on him.

He was in bed, sprawled on his stomach with a white down comforter covering him to the waist. Thanks to the heavy drapes, the room was gloomy-dark, but she could see enough of him to know that his broad, bare shoul-

ders and wide, muscular back and brawny arms were—
the only word that came to mind was *fine*.

She was already mentally backing out when a snore
told her that he was sound asleep.

It was the only bed in the place. Right now, she was
tired but not particularly sleepy, certainly not ready for
bed. But later, sometime tonight, she had the option of
crawling into that supremely comfortable-looking bed
with him or grabbing a pillow, scrounging up some kind
of cover, and sacking out on the couch.

Couch, Jess told herself firmly. The other choice was
so dumb it bordered on self-destructive.

While Mark slept she took a shower, washed her hair
and blew it dry, brushed her teeth, smoothed on Chap-
Stick and a little face cream—thank God for the supplies
in her purse—and popped a single pain pill. Mark's re-
counting of the First Lady's troubles made her wary of
taking more than she absolutely had to. But the ones she
had swallowed earlier were wearing off, and her legs and
back were really starting to ache. So she compromised
on one and hoped for the best.

By ten o'clock Mark still hadn't awakened. His snores,
ragged but blissful-sounding, continually reminded her
that he was sacked out one thin wall away. She was on
the couch, dressed for sleeping in one of Mark's T-shirts,
so big on her it hit her at midthigh, and a pair of the plain
white cotton panties. Having stolen a pillow from the
bed and found a quilt folded on the bedroom closet
shelf, she had made herself as comfortable as possible.

To keep herself from dwelling on the possibility that
the black-ops death squad had discovered their hide-
away and was even now creeping up on it with guns
drawn, she turned the TV on. Low. So low, in fact, that
she had to strain to hear the *CSI* episode that wasn't really all that interesting anyway. Once she heard footsteps
in the hall outside and her heart went haywire and she

almost ran for Mark, but whoever it was went into another apartment, and after that silence reigned. Too nervous to turn on a lamp, Jess tried to read selected sections of the paper by the faint light of the TV. The comics, Ann Landers, and sports all provided a welcome distraction from the fear that seemed to have taken up permanent residence in her gut.

She was even starting to get sleepy until she turned a page and found a picture of herself in the paper. Actually, two. One as a little girl. Soaking wet, wrapped in a blanket, and staring big-eyed at the camera. The other as she was now. With contacts, not glasses, taken from her driver's license.

Death Car Survivor Had Previous Brush with Death, the headline read.

Chapter 27

JESS DIDN'T HAVE TO read the accompanying story to know what it said. Even as the paper fell from her fingers, she felt impossibly familiar waves of grief and pain. It had been so long now—she never thought of it anymore. Never, except maybe in the most secret depths of her deepest dreams. It was a tragedy of her past, long over. Long put behind her.

It could not make her feel this way anymore.

Standing up, she started to head for the bathroom and stubbed her toe hard on the coffee table.

"Ow! Shit! Damn it!" Clutching her injured foot, she hopped a couple of times, then sank back down on the couch, displacing more of the paper, which fluttered to the floor. Cradling her foot in her lap, rocking back and forth as she cursed under her breath now, she glanced down and saw the picture of herself looking up at her. Kicking at it with her uninjured foot, she closed her eyes.

She did not need this on top of everything else.

"Hey. I heard you yell. You all right?" Mark's voice made her jump. Her eyes flew open, her head jerked around, and she saw him standing there in the doorway, frowning at her, wearing only his boxers, with his gun in his hand. It was an indication of her state of mind that her gaze slid over him exactly once, and she didn't even flinch from the gun.

"Fine."

"Are you crying?"

To her horror, Jess realized she was: She could feel the warm, wet slide of tears trickling down her cheeks.

Turning her head away, she swiped at her cheeks with both hands. "No."

"What the hell?" Padding toward her, he put the gun down on the table at her elbow, then stopped in front of her. By dint of much blinking and sheer force of will, she got the tears under control. With her peripheral vision, she saw a very masculine-looking bare foot and a long, powerful-looking leg. A section of muscular stomach. A sliver of wide chest. A buff arm. "Did something happen?"

She wasn't quite ready to look at him again yet. "I stubbed my toe, okay?"

"Hard enough to make you cry? Let me see."

"It's fine. Don't worry about it."

She heard him sigh. Then he sank down beside her on the couch. Feeling the brush of warm, bare male flesh and realizing she couldn't order him to scoot over because of the pillow and blanket now piled on the rest of the couch, she looked at him with a forbidding frown. A well-muscled naked shoulder and a sculpted chest filled her vision as he reached for her foot, the one that rested in her lap. His hand slid around her instep, holding her foot still, his fingers long and strong. He leaned closer, peering at her toes.

"No blood. Can you move them?"

She jerked her foot from his grasp, put it on the carpet, and shot him a "back off" look. "I told you. It's fine."

But he wasn't looking at her. He was looking down.

"Is that you?"

She already knew what he was reaching for even as he bent forward. The light from the TV played over the rippling muscles of his bare back, and she watched it as if mesmerized, trying her best to hold off the moment she knew was coming. The rustle of the paper being picked up made her grit her teeth and look away. She realized in that split second that he was going to read the article and they were going to talk about it, nothing she could do to stop it at all, and she needed a moment to steel herself.

"It's too dark in here for me to read anything but the headline," he said a moment later, and Jess felt a tiny frisson of relief until he continued, "so we can do one of two things: You can tell me what it says, or I can turn on a light and read it for myself."

The idea of turning on a light, a light that would certainly be visible around the edges of the drapes and through the kitchen blinds and under the door, a light that could possibly lead to the killers that were certainly still hunting them finding them, made her shiver.

He was still holding the paper with the two photos topmost. She couldn't look at them.

"My father took my sister and me to the beach when we were little." Since there was clearly no help for it, she gave him the bare bones, her tone expressionless. "We got caught up in an undertow. He came out to try to save us. Courtney—my sister's name was Courtney—and my father drowned. I managed to make it back to shore."

For a moment her voice just seemed to hang in the air while the memories—the water closing over her head, her sister's tiny hands dragging at hers, the punishing waves forcing them apart—hit her.

"Jesus. I'm sorry, baby." Another rattle as he set the paper down on the coffee table. Then his arm came around her, bringing with it the smell of soap and warm male flesh. Jess felt the solid heaviness of it circling her shoulders, the comforting grip of his hand on her arm, the squeeze of a hug, and tensed. Until she got the memories corralled again, sympathy was the last thing she needed. She had to stay tough, stay strong, force them back. "I remember now. They ran all kinds of stories about you on TV this past week, and one of them said something about that. To tell you the truth, it kind of tore my heart out."

"It was on . . . TV?" Jess could hardly breathe at the thought of the whole world watching something so personal. He was looking at her. She could feel his gaze on her face, but she couldn't look back at him. She could only stare straight ahead, braced against the pain she knew would come if she didn't armor herself against it.

"Yeah."

Suddenly Jess remembered, while she was in the hospital, Grace saying something about the press wanting to talk to her because she was "the survivor." With an emphasis, like it had a special significance. And her mother saying, "Grace, don't worry your sister." This was what they must have been talking about. Grace, like Sarah and Maddie, the children of Judy's second husband, hadn't even been born at the time of the accident, so it wasn't much more than a curiosity to her, but their mother knew how deeply the tragedy was seared into Jess's soul.

She and Courtney had been inseparable.

"I don't ever even think about it anymore. It was a long time ago."

"You were five, weren't you? That's a tough age to lose people you love."

She remembered that he'd said his father had died when he was four.

"Were you close to your father?" she asked, barely breathing. It felt as if there was an iron band around her chest limiting the amount of air she could take in.

"Not really. From what I've been told, he was gone all the time, working." His hand tightened on her arm and he pulled her more firmly against his side. Jess refused to allow herself to relax against him. She was too intent on keeping the pain away. "To tell you the truth, I don't remember him at all. He's just somebody standing there with my mother and me in old pictures."

It wasn't so much sadness in his voice but regret, she realized. As if he wanted to remember and was sorry he couldn't. Jess took a careful breath.

"I can't really remember my father, either. My parents had split up, and he wasn't around a lot, so I guess that's why. But I can remember my sister."

"She was younger, right? Three, wasn't it?"

Jess nodded, surprised he remembered the details so well. He must have been watching the program closely, and the knowledge both touched and comforted her. What had he said? That watching had just about torn his heart out?

The thought made her dizzy. Some of the stiffness left her body. Hardly aware of her own softening, she let herself rest against him.

"Want to tell me about it?" His voice was almost unbearably gentle.

Her automatic answer, the answer she'd always given to anybody who had ever tried to probe her memories of the tragedy, was "no." But this was Mark. And, well, suddenly she just wanted him to know. For whatever reason.

She took another, deeper breath, and this time her lungs actually expanded to let in sufficient air.

"We were wading in the surf. My dad and his girl-friend were lying on towels on the sand, and I was supposed to be watching Courtney. She had those little floaty things on her arms, and she kept sitting down in the water and letting the waves carry her in. Only one of them pulled her out. She was laughing; she thought it was great because she was riding the wave. I was trying to catch her—I could swim a little—and I couldn't. Then one of her floaty things came off. I can still see it; it was clear with yellow-and-white fish on it, bobbing toward me. She went under, and I started screaming for help and dog-paddling toward her as fast as I could, only I couldn't see her anymore. Then she popped up right beside me and I caught her, caught her hands, and we both got dragged under again, and then she got pulled away from me. I came up and I saw her come up, too far away for me to grab her this time, but I saw her looking at me. She'd lost her other floaty thing by then and her eyes— she had blue eyes, like Mom, and dark hair like me— were big and wide and scared, and she was opening her mouth—I always thought it was to call to me, but I don't know for sure—when another wave broke over her. I think my dad went rushing past me about that time, but I don't really remember that. What I remember is Court- ney's eyes, and then a wave breaking over her and over me and me somehow winding up near the beach where somebody pulled me to shore." She broke off and closed her eyes. "The next time I saw her, she was lying in a lit- tle white coffin at the front of our church. I touched her—I thought if I touched her she would wake up—and she was cold. And still. And she didn't wake up."

The pain that engulfed her as she finished was so in- tense that it made her shudder. Bracing against it, refus- ing to cry, she did what she had learned to do over the years: endure it until it ebbed.

"Jess." Both Mark's arms were around her now. He must have felt her violent quiver because he shifted his grip on her, lifting her onto his lap, holding her close. She felt something brush the top of her head, and thought it might have been his lips. "That's a hell of a thing. I'm so sorry you had to go through that."

Jess took a moment to just breathe. Sure enough, the sharpness of the pain, the hard edges of it that cut like knives, went away. What was left was a dull ache that would recede, too, if left alone, burying itself deep within her subconscious until something called it forth again.

"It was a long time before I would babysit any of the others. My mom used to get so mad at me." She tried to smile, but it didn't quite work. Judy's steely determination not to let grief disable either of them had been hard on her until she had gotten old enough to recognize it for the courage it was.

"Baby, it wasn't your fault. You were five years old."

It was twenty-three years in the past, and the guilt was still there. Buried under layers of time and reason but still there. He'd gone right to the heart of what had tormented her most over all the intervening years.

"I know." Silently she added, *but still.* "I actually don't ever think about it anymore. Unless something reminds me."

"Like seeing an article about it in the damned paper." His hand rubbed up and down her arm in rough comfort. Relaxing as the pain slipped away just as she had known it would, Jess rested her head against his shoulder. "Jesus, I wish you hadn't gotten caught up in this."

That almost made her smile. She slanted a look up at him. "You and me both, believe me."

"'Course, we wouldn't have met."

Her brows twitched together. Her head came up again. Straightening her glasses, she gave him a severe look. "For the record, we met months ago. When you brought the First Lady to Mr. Davenport's office. You smiled at me. We talked. We talked several times after that, too."

"I don't remember."

"That's not exactly flattering, you know."

The look he gave her was almost surprised. Then he smiled.

"When I'm working I don't see anything except my principal and threats to my principal. Angelina Jolie could dance naked in front of me and I wouldn't notice."

Jess suddenly found herself looking at the history of their acquaintance in a whole new light.

"Really?"

"Yeah, really."

"That's good to know."

"Is it?"

She nodded thoughtfully. "You didn't see me—which is what I thought—but it was for a reason. That makes it much better."

"I'm not following you."

Jess smiled. "Never mind. It's not important."

She was suddenly acutely aware that she was sitting on his lap with his arms around her, and all he was wearing was a pair of boxers. Unbelievable that she'd registered the broad strokes of it but missed all the tiny details until now. The shirt she was wearing had ridden up, and her new panties were on the substantial side, but still she could feel the heat of him burning through them, and the solid muscularity of his thighs. Her bare legs lay on top of his so that the silkiness of her skin slid over the hair-roughened firmness of his every time one of them moved. Her shoulder butted into naked male chest. It was wide and buff and, she noticed with interest now that she was capable of noticing such things, sported a wedge of ash-brown hair that stretched from one flat male nipple to the other and tapered down over a trim abdomen and out of sight.

She glanced up to discover that he was looking at her. Looking at her looking at him, to be precise. There was something in his expression, a sudden sensuous glint to his eyes, a curve to his mouth that made her heart beat faster. His thighs felt harder, his arms around her more tense.

I want you so much. That's the thought that ran through her head as their eyes met, just as it had once before. Only this time, his eyes widened and blazed in response, and Jess realized to her horror that she hadn't just thought it but *said it aloud.*

It was all she could do not to clap a hand over her own mouth.

Her dismay must have been apparent in her face, because he smiled, a slow sexy curve of his mouth that made her stomach clench and her blood heat and her heart turn over.

"Good to know," he said.

Then he bent his head and touched his lips to hers.

Chapter **28**

IT WAS A GENTLE kiss, not hard or demanding at all, but the heat and thoroughness of it made her dizzy. Her lips parted. Her eyes closed. Her hands found his chest as her heart began to pound—and then he lifted his head.

"*Mmm.*" She made an involuntary sound of protest. Her lids rose to find that he was studying her face, his eyes dark and hot, his mouth almost tender.

"Talk about your coincidences." His face was still so close she could feel his breath on her lips. Her parted, damp, yearning lips. Her hands splayed over his rib cage in silent supplication. *Kiss me again.* . . . But this time she didn't say it out loud; she did have, she was thankful to discover, some control. "See, here I was thinking pretty much the same thing: I want you like hell."

"That *is* a coincidence," she managed, trying to keep some perspective, trying to keep from totally losing her head, and he smiled that sexy smile again.

Then he kissed her again, tilting her so that her head was tipped back against his hard-muscled upper arm, brushing his lips over hers, licking between them, tantalizing her until she shivered and closed her eyes and surged against him and put a stop to the teasing. Her mouth clung to his, greedily prolonging the contact, deepening it with a building urgency that sent fire shooting through her veins and melted her bones and made her pulse go crazy.

Forget perspective. Forget not losing my head—it's too late. Jeez, I'm in so much trouble here.

She knew it, recognized the future pain she was almost certainly storing up for herself, and she didn't care. Her hands slid up over his chest, luxuriating in the freedom to touch him, taking sudden intense pleasure in the warmth of his skin, the firmness of his muscles. His shoulders were broad and thickly muscled, and she loved touching them, too, loved sliding her hands along the brawny smoothness of them before surrendering to the need to wrap her arms around his neck and kiss him like she burned for him—which she did.

His arms around her tightened as he kissed her back with a torrid eroticism that sent her senses spinning. He was holding her so close now that she could feel every taut muscle and sinew of his chest and arms, feel the heat of him radiating through her shirt, feel the racing of his heart. Her breasts swelled and tightened and tingled at the contact. With a tiny, pleasure-filled sound, she undulated instinctively against him as the hot, rhythmic quickening in her loins intensified and spread, making her go almost mindless with anticipation, with need. Pressing her breasts harder against him, she squirmed deliberately in his lap, feeling his instant response with an upsurge of desire that made her shake.

"Jess." His mouth slid across her cheek to plant hot kisses down the side of her neck. His hand found her breast, fondling her, warm and strong as he tested the size and weight of the tender globe through the soft cotton before his thumb searched out her nipple, rubbing over it, pressing and playing.

Her lids lifted. Her gaze focused on how big and unmistakably masculine his hand looked against the white

T-shirt as it covered her breast. The sight was unbelievably sexy. Her tongue came out to wet her lips because her mouth went suddenly dry.

"That's . . . so good."

"Is it?" His voice was thick.

"Mmm."

He didn't stop, rubbing her nipples and caressing her breasts and tracing a burning path around the loose neckline of the too-big shirt with his mouth all at the same time. She clung to him, dizzy with wanting, pressing hungry, distracted kisses of her own along his bristly jaw, nibbling at the soft lobe of his ear. Then his mouth slid down the front of her shirt to close over the tip of her breast, suck at it, the sensation hot and wet and so unbelievably erotic that she moaned and tightened her grip on him and forgot all about his ear as her heart threatened to beat its way out of her chest. His tongue found her nipple through the cloth and played with it, teasing it until she was gasping and arching her back and basically doing everything except begging him to make love to her, which she was damned if she was going to do. Then he moved to the other one and did the same.

"Mark." When he lifted his head at last, though, she couldn't regain control quick enough to keep herself from clutching at his shoulders and breathing that small, instinctive protest.

"Hmm?"

More was what she wanted to say but she didn't; she bit it back even as it trembled on her lips. She didn't need more; what she needed, as any smart woman would surely recognize even at this, the eleventh hour, was less.

"Maybe this . . ."

Isn't such a good idea were the words that the tiny sliver of her brain that was still moderately cool and dispassionate tried to force her to say. But the rest of her rebelled. This was what she wanted. *He* was what she wanted.

"What?"

She was lying back in his arms, woozy with pleasure, breathing hard, flushed and quaking and dying to feel his mouth on her again, his hands on her again. She could feel him looking at her, feel the heat of his gaze touching her everywhere, she thought, so she opened her eyes to find that she was right, his eyes were all over her, taking in the slender length of her bare legs that were curled now toward the back of the couch, the curve of her body as she lay across his lap, the jut of her nipples against the T-shirt, the wet circles where his mouth had recently been.

He must have felt her looking at him, too, because suddenly their eyes met. His were dark and intent. His face was hard with desire.

"Kiss me," she said. Because it was just exactly what she wanted to say.

His eyes blazed. "How about we get you naked first?"

The hoarse undertone to his voice was enough by itself to make her heart lurch. The idea of getting naked for him—*for Mark*—sent a thousand fiery tremors racing over her skin. Her breathing got ragged and her pulse raced and the delicious throbbing that he had brought to life deep inside her body suddenly got a whole lot hotter and more intense.

She was *dying* to get naked for him. But that didn't seem like the thing to say, and given that her heart was beating like a jackhammer now and she was breathing way too fast to make intelligent conversation anything but a remote possibility and she was afraid to talk anyway, for fear she would blurt out something that was better left unsaid, she just didn't say anything at all.

What she did was sit up in his lap, trying to look several degrees less turned-on than she felt, trying to keep a modicum of cool, and took off her glasses and put them on the table behind her.

"Hey, I like those."

She shook her head at him. Not that she didn't feel sexy with her glasses on—with Mark, she now kind of, sort of, sometimes did—but she definitely felt sexier without them.

"They'll just get knocked off." At least, if she had anything to say about it they would.

The sudden gleam in his eyes made her go weak at the knees. "You think?"

"Yes."

His head rested against the back of the couch now, and his grip on her had loosened enough to allow her freedom of movement although his arms still encircled her waist. He watched her with what looked like lazy interest, and if she hadn't been close enough to see the hard restlessness in his eyes and the carnal set of his mouth, she might have started feeling a little uncertain, even shy. But she did see them, did feel the rock-hardness of his body beneath her legs, and so took his stillness for what she was almost certain it was: the calm before the storm.

"Let me see you, baby." His voice was low and husky. His eyes ate her up.

Taking a deep, shaky breath, she took hold of the hem of the T-shirt and lifted it over her head, then dropped it on the floor beside the couch. Even as the garment fell she had a flash of clarity in which she saw herself, sitting upright in his lap, naked except for a pair of plain white cotton underpants, the bluish light from the silent TV flickering over her small pert breasts with her nipples, already aroused, dark and erect and wanton-looking against the creaminess of her skin. She was small-boned and slender, with a narrow waist and slim hips. More boyish than voluptuous, actually, but in that moment, with his eyes on her, she felt incredibly female.

"Jesus, you're beautiful," he murmured. This time, when he said it, the look in his eyes made her believe it, too. Her heart slammed against her ribs. Her breath caught. Then his gaze slid down her body. Even as she leaned toward him, even as his head lifted and his back straightened and his arms tightened around her and he pulled her into an embrace, his hands moved down her back to slide over the smooth cotton of her underwear.

"Ah, granny panties. My favorite."

"What?" She almost frowned. The husky, sensuous-yet-satisfied-sounding murmur made no sense, but she was so dizzy with longing that she couldn't quite care.

"Forget about it."

By then his mouth was on hers and his hands were inside her panties, cupping her cheeks and squeezing and stroking and then pulling her astride him, so she did—forget about it, that is. She melted against him, her breasts burning and swelling against his chest, shuddering because his hands on her felt so good, kissing him back with a fierceness that shook her to her core. Rocking against him, feeling the heat and hardness of him pressing into her with only that thin layer of cotton between them, she felt as if her bones had turned to lava and her insides to flame.

He moved against her deliberately, holding her still for it, making her feel him, dropping his mouth to her breast and suckling it at the same time, and the sensation was so incredibly arousing she cried out.

"That's it. I'm going out of my mind here." His voice was so thick it was hardly recognizable. Then he stood up with her, kissing her with a hungry intensity that rocked her world as he carried her toward the bedroom. Curled against him, her arms around his neck, her mouth locked to his, she kissed him back, so hot for him she could have sworn the very air around them sizzled.

More than she had ever wanted anything in her life, she wanted this.

When he pulled his mouth away from hers, she made a tiny sound of protest and opened her eyes. Without her glasses the world was more of a blur, and the bedroom was dark except for the faint illumination provided by the distant glow of the television, but she could see him, see how heavy-lidded and hot his eyes were as they moved over her, see the chiseled planes and angles of his face set hard now as if he was trying to maintain control, see the sensuous line of his mouth.

Then he looked away and juggled her a little awkwardly. About the time she realized what he was doing—yanking the covers down—her back was making contact with the cool smoothness of the fitted sheet. But instead of coming down on top of her, which she wanted so badly now her teeth were clenched in anticipation and her hands clung to his shoulders, reluctant to let go, he pulled away from her, standing over her, looking down at her. With his back to the only source of light he suddenly looked very tall and strong. Very broad-shouldered above narrow hips and long, powerful-looking legs. Very big and fit, like the pro football player he had once been. Intimidating, even.

Except he wasn't, not to her.

"Mark . . ."

But his name died in her throat as he hooked his fingers in her waistband and pulled her panties down her legs, pulled them off and threw them on the floor. Suddenly she was naked and he was looking at her and she loved that he was, loved it so much that her breath caught and her nails dug into the mattress and her heart thundered.

Their eyes met. Electricity surged between them as

powerfully as a lightning bolt. She felt a rush of desire so intense that she shivered.

He was already shucking his boxers when she sat up, rolled onto her knees, and took him in her mouth.

She heard him inhale sharply. He stood stock-still for a moment. Then his hands found her head. His fingers threaded through her hair.

"Jess." It was almost a groan. She heard the shock in his voice, the deep pleasure, the mounting urgency.

His butt was high and round and tight, an athlete's butt. The feel of it in her hands made her insides melt, made the pulsing deep within spiral tighter. She was dizzy at the idea of what she was doing to him, at the intimacy of it, at the searing response she could feel radiating from him in waves.

When he pulled away from her she could do nothing but blink up at him, still dazed with sensation. Her hands slid down his thighs. Muscular, hair-roughened thighs . . .

"Mark . . ."

"Easy, baby. Wait."

She got the impression he was talking through his teeth, but she didn't really have time to think about it because he was already tumbling her onto her back and coming down on top of her, his weight and hardness heavenly against her, but only for a moment.

Pressing scalding wet kisses over every inch of her skin, he slid down her body until he reached the velvety delta between her legs. When he kissed her there, she moaned and writhed against him and went totally mindless with sensation. He knew just what to do, how to turn her on, how to make her shiver and pant and burn.

When he slid back up her body at last she was trembling like her insides were made of jelly, so hot and hungry for him that all she could do was clutch him and breathe, arching her back and moving in silent, compulsive invitation as he pressed lingering kisses to her breasts before claiming her mouth. Kissing him back as if she would die if she didn't, she wrapped her arms around his neck and surged against him, needy and wanting and absolutely on fire for him. He came inside her then, hard and fast and filling her to capacity, and it felt so good, so incredibly, mind-blowingly good, that she cried out. Murmuring something thick and throaty that she didn't catch, he pulled back, then plunged inside, deeper and harder than before, and she cried out again.

Wrapping her legs around his hips, drawing him in, she matched his movements with her own, lost in an urgent maelstrom of desire.

"Mark, oh, Mark," she gasped, burning higher and hotter as their tongues met with greedy passion and he pushed her down into the mattress, coming into her with such fierce need that she was driven to the brink, quaking inside, building . . .

"Oh, God, Jess," he groaned, and seemed to lose control, taking her higher and hotter with furious pounding thrusts that drove her out of her mind with passion, winding her tighter and tighter, making her wild.

Making her come.

In a shattering series of fiery explosions that was exactly what she wanted, what she craved.

"Mark, Mark, Mark, I love you so much, *Mark*," she cried at the end, breaking hard, shaking, clinging to him as she was swept away.

"*Jess.*" He buried his face in the tender hollow between her neck and shoulder and drove into her one last time and held himself deep inside her and found his own release.

Lost in bliss for a good minute or so afterward, Jess came crashing down from the heights of ecstasy to face the terrible reality of what she had said.

Maybe he hadn't noticed.

It had been so hot between them, so incredibly, indescribably good, and, like her, he'd been so caught up in it that maybe . . .

She remembered every word he'd said. Every groan and growl and indrawn breath, too.

What were the chances that he'd been so blissed out that he had missed her declaration of love?

In two words, not good.

Opening her eyes, she assessed the situation. Mark lay sprawled on top of her, deadweight and sweaty and heavy as a load of wet sandbags, his face still buried against her neck, his arms still wrapped around her, his legs still stretched between hers. Her hands rested on his back. His skin was hot and damp, and she could feel the rise and fall of his rib cage. His breath felt warm against her throat.

Much as she wanted to, she couldn't quite convince herself that he was asleep.

She quit breathing as he stirred.

A moment later he was propped up on his elbows, looking down at her. His eyes were sleepy-looking, and a smile just touched his mouth.

Their gazes met.

"Hey," she managed feebly, and felt color flood her face.

His eyes narrowed. His smile widened.

Then a sound—a metallic-sounding click—from the other room made him sharply turn his head.

Chapter 29

BEFORE JESS COULD SAY anything, before she could do anything, Mark clapped a hand over her mouth and shook his head warningly at her. Their eyes met, and she saw that his had suddenly gone diamond-hard.

Shh, he mouthed. When she nodded, he placed his mouth against her ear. "Get down behind the bed. Be as quiet as you can."

Then he slipped silently from the bed.

There was another sound—the faintest of rustles, like clothing brushing against something—from the living room.

Her heart gave a great leap. Her blood ran cold.

Somebody was out there, in the living room. She might be wrong—maybe the congressman was back—but the first thought that popped into her head was *bad guy with a gun.*

Oh, God, had they been found?

Holding her breath, watching Mark move soundlessly toward the door, she slithered off the far side of the bed, which—wouldn't you know it?—gave a slight creak. Her eyes widened. Her stomach clenched. As her knees hit the carpet, she shot a fearful glance toward Mark, toward the door, but nothing changed. Mark kept going. He didn't even glance around.

He was flattened against the wall by the door from the living room, his back pressed against it, his head turned toward the doorway, she saw an instant later, having scuttled on her hands and knees to the foot of the bed and peeped around the corner of it. Despite the darkness of the room, she could see the shape of him outlined against the white wall. Her hand touched crumpled cloth—the blue shirt he'd been wearing all day, she realized, as her fingers explored further. Hastily pulling it to her, pulling it on, fastening just a couple of buttons— naked was no way to confront a killer—she had a sudden flash of terrible memory: Mark had left his gun in the living room, on the table by the couch.

He was unarmed.

Oh, God, please let this be the congressman.

Without warning, a small white light—the beam of a flashlight, Jess realized with horror—shone into the short hall between the kitchen and the bedroom, moving from side to side, checking out the space.

A man appeared. Holding a gun. This she saw in an instant, as a dark silhouette against faint light, before he turned toward the bedroom and played his flashlight over the bed.

Light-headed with terror, heart pounding so hard and fast it sounded like a drumroll in her ears, she shrank back—and Mark exploded from the shadows, launching himself onto the man in a low, fast dive. The flashlight hit the carpet and rolled. The gun fired. There was no *bang*— it must have been equipped with a silencer, which made the sound more like a whistle—but Jess knew for sure because the bullet buried itself in the wall with a *thunk* just an inch or so past her head.

She yelped and ate carpet.

"Jess?" There was real fear for her in Mark's voice. The question was flung over his shoulder as he fought for his life, Jess saw as she looked up. He was in a desper-

ate struggle with the gunman. They were cursing and grunting and bouncing off the walls, careering through the doorway, through the hall, and into the living room.

"I'm okay." Scrambling to her feet, she raced to help, meaning to grab Mark's gun off the table and hand it to him. Or something.

The sound of blows came thick and fast. As she rounded the corner she saw that they were on the floor. Mark was on top—no, on the bottom—they were rolling around, trading punches, grappling for possession of the gun in the bad guy's hand. With the blue glow from the television flickering over them, it was like watching outtakes from an old movie—a violent and scary movie.

"You're a dead man, you son of a bitch," the stranger grunted as he locked an arm around Mark's neck and yanked him sideways.

"Eat shit, asshole." That was Mark, pounding his fist into the other's stomach with a sound like a pumpkin hitting pavement, and then rolling back on top.

"I have a gun! I'll shoot!" she cried, snatching Mark's gun off the table and dancing around the struggling men like she knew what she was doing.

"Damn it, Jess, no!" Mark punched the other man in the face while at the same time trying to rip his gun away.

Even with her glasses, she probably wouldn't have tried it: She had never fired a gun in her life. Without her glasses, both men were blurred. She could tell which one was Mark—he was naked, which helped—but where he ended and the other man began was a little fuzzy.

If she pulled the trigger, she might hit Mark. Clearly, clobbering the bad guy over the head with the handle was the way to go.

She had her back to the front door, the gun reversed (but carefully not pointed at herself) and her eyes on her target, still circling them, when the front door opened.

Just like that, no warning at all. There was a click, the sensation of air swooshing in behind her, a wedge of yellow light spilling over her.

Then somebody grabbed her from behind.

A man. In a dark suit. With a gun.

Jess squealed. She would have screamed, but the choke hold he instantly put on her was too tight. She dropped Mark's gun.

"Give it up, Ryan," the man holding her ordered. Writhing, fighting, Jess clawed at his arm—his jacket-protected arm—with her nails. Smacking her in the side of the head with his gun—she saw stars and her knees went wobbly—he pointed the gun at Mark.

Who shot him in the head.

Of course, it took a few seconds for Jess to realize exactly what had happened. One moment she was on her tiptoes seeing stars while a thug choked the life out of her and threatened Mark. The next there was a sharp *smack*— kind of like the sound of a hand slapping flesh—and then the man crumpled. Just crumpled like a discarded towel.

He didn't even make much of a thud.

Jess would have crumpled right along with him except, finding herself suddenly freed, she was too desperate to get away. She leaped out of reach, whirling to look at her attacker, who was lying on his side with a dime-size black hole in the left side of his forehead from which a trickle of black liquid—blood, she realized with growing comprehension—meandered toward his eye. She recognized him with a sense of shock: He was the man who'd chased them outside the library. Then she remembered the other bad guy, and leaped around to get a visual on him, too.

He was lying flat on his back on the carpet with his arms splayed out beside him. Unmoving. His eyes were wide open and staring at the ceiling. She was pretty sure he wasn't breathing.

Mark was getting to his feet beside him, the gun in his hand.

"You okay?" He sounded slightly winded.

"Yes. You?"

"Never better." His tone was grim.

"Is he dead?" She was referring to the man Mark had been fighting with, because there was no doubt in her mind about the guy with the hole in his forehead. Her eyes were still on Mark, running over him, checking to make sure he was in one piece. Now that it was past, she realized that as much as she had been terrified for herself, she had been equally terrified for him.

"Yeah." He sounded disgusted. "I was hoping to keep him alive. It would have been helpful if we could've asked him who he was taking his orders from. But when his partner showed up and grabbed you, I had to act fast. We would have been dead in another five seconds."

He had moved around her and was in the process of shutting the door as he spoke. The wedge of light vanished. The lock clicked shut.

They were left alone in the TV-lit living room with two freshly killed corpses. The smell of death hung in the air, thick and horrible.

She suddenly felt woozy. Her heart was slowing down, but her leg muscles were acting up. Or rather, giving up. She sank down abruptly in the nearest chair.

"That guy—he was at the library—knew your name. Do you know who he is?"

"Never saw either one of them before in my life."

"So what do we do now?" She meant about the bodies. Actually, the gore, too. On the wall by the door, a circle of black dots had appeared, the result of the gunshot that had killed the man holding her. The back of his head must have—she couldn't go further without wanting to gag.

"Get dressed. We're out of here. We've bought ourselves a little time, but when whoever sent these guys realizes they've gone offline, they'll come looking." Mark was bent over the dead men, going through their pockets.

"Oh, God." Forget being woozy. Forget spaghetti legs. Jess got up and stumbled toward the bedroom, grabbing her glasses off the table and putting them on as she went. Snatching up her clothes, she headed for the bathroom. She absolutely had to splash cold water on her face or pass out. Shedding Mark's shirt, she ended up giving herself what amounted to a quick, icy sponge bath, which helped a lot in banishing the wooziness, before dressing and snagging her purse from the shelf where she had left it. Mark was in the bedroom fastening his holster on over his pants as she emerged. Silently noting in passing how powerful his chest and arms were, she handed his shirt to him.

"Thanks." He pulled it on, buttoning it, then picked up the gun that lay beside him on the bed and thrust it into the back waistband of his pants. His other gun—Jess realized that he had taken one from their attackers—was in his hand.

Feeling the need for two guns was not a good sign.

"Find anything in their pockets?" She was gathering up their belongings and cramming them into the plastic bag that held their discarded clothes.

"Cash. ID—supposedly they're employees of Countrywide Exterminating—pretty funny, when you think about it." He was on the move, grabbing her hand as he went past, pulling her after him. "Car keys. Nothing useful."

They skirted the bodies, which, now that Jess could actually see them in focus, were really kind of pitiful-looking, in a terrifying way.

"Are we going to just . . . leave them?" She cast a haunted look back as he opened the door.

His voice dropped as they stepped into the hall.

"Whoever sent them will send along a cleanup crew as soon as they find out what happened. By the time the good congressman gets back, I guarantee you the bodies will be gone and there won't be a trace of this left." Dropping her hand, he closed the door quietly and they moved toward the far end of the hall, where the elevator and fire stairs were located. The light from the overhead fixture in the hall unnerved Jess. It made her feel horribly exposed. She glanced around anxiously. "His apartment will be good as new."

"You're kidding," Jess whispered, appalled. The elevator was on their floor, so they decided to, in Mark's words, "chance it," riding it down and exiting the building without incident. Mark kept his gun in his hand, which was both nerve-racking and comforting, and they both cast wary glances around the alley as the cold night air hit their faces.

Remembering the whole eye-in-the-sky thing, Jess drew her head into her shoulders like a turtle as they hurried through the alley. Fortunately, it was a dark night, with only a few stars and the smallest sliver of a moon. All she could do was pray that satellites didn't come equipped with night-vision goggles.

That spirit of optimism was dashed as soon as they were back on the street. Dupont Circle was hopping, so busy Mark immediately holstered his gun to avoid attracting attention. The restaurants were full, and the bars and social clubs were overflowing. Pedestrians crowded the sidewalks. Parked cars lined the streets. Music, talk, and laughter, plus the occasional honk from a car horn, filled the air.

"Oh my God, it's Friday night," Jess said under her breath. Weekend nights were big with tourists and college students alike.

"Saturday morning, technically. It's seventeen minutes past midnight."

They reached Massachusetts Avenue, which was even busier and more crowded. Jess cast anxious glances all around. The horror of the scene they had left behind stayed with her. The prospect of being dropped by a bullet where she stood had suddenly become horribly real. Mark was moving fast, but the massive doses of adrenaline that had to be pumping through her veins had given her legs new strength, and she was able to keep up.

"You see a cab, you let me know," he said.

"A cab? Not the metro?"

"We need to get out of here as quickly as possible. Time is what we don't have."

Jess felt her stomach plummet as she once again came face-to-face with the hideous truth that the hunters were closing in. Her heart picked up the pace. She rolled an eye at him. "Plan?"

He smiled. "Oh, yeah. We . . ." A yellow cab coming toward them caught both their eyes at the same time, interrupting. "Taxi!"

Once they were inside, Mark said, "The Hay-Adams," and the driver nodded and took off, swerving out into traffic. The bright lights and picturesque buildings of the area rolled past.

Jess turned to him. "We're going to a *hotel*?" she mouthed incredulously. Not that she didn't have faith in Mark's judgment, but taking a cab to the very public Hay-Adams, where one had to register and produce a credit card and jump through all kinds of hoops to rent a room, did not sound like a plan. At least, not a good one.

He shook his head at her. Clearly, carrying on any kind of substantive discussion with the driver listening in was impossible, so she let it drop, at least until they got out of the cab.

Mark picked up her hand and held it. He held her hand a lot, because dragging her from place to place required a lot of hand-holding, but this had a different feel to it. A little of her tension eased as her eyes met his. There was a warmth for her in his eyes that made her feel almost shy.

"Just for the record, that blew me away back there." His voice was low. She could tell from the way he said it that he wasn't talking about the epic battle with the dead men.

"Me, too." Okay, maybe as a response that was feeble. And maybe this wasn't exactly the best time and place for romance. But now was the only time and this was the only place they could be sure of, and that changed everything. Her eyes clung to his and her heart beat faster. The memory of how they had been together sizzled in the air between them, unspoken but as tangible as steam. He carried her hand to his mouth, kissed the back of it—jeez, just the touch of his lips on her skin was now enough to make her dizzy—then lifted his head again to look at her.

"That last thing you said—was it for real?"

Asking "What last thing?" was clearly not going to work. She knew exactly what he was talking about, and she could tell from the way he watched her that he was perfectly aware she knew.

She took a deep breath. "Kind of. Maybe."

His eyebrows lifted. His mouth curved with sudden amusement. "Way to lay it all on the line."

Still holding her hand, he leaned over and kissed her. A lush, deep, hot kiss that was nevertheless quick. Jess's head was still spinning and she was just getting enough of her senses back to glance away before he could read the embarrassing naked truth about how she felt about him in her bedazzled eyes, when her gaze hit on an advertisement pasted to the back of the seat.

Under a picture of a Learjet lifting off from a runway and the tagline *Remember when the skies were friendly?*

was the advertiser's name, *YourJets of Virginia*. Under the name was a phone number. It was the phone number that caught Jess's eye and caused her jaw to drop, but she recognized the company name, too.

"Mark." Her attention refocused just like that, she gave his hand an urgent tug and pointed to the ad, and never mind that he was still looking at her with heat in his eyes. "Do you still have those printouts?"

He followed her gaze. Frowning, he stuck a hand in his pants pocket and came up with the folded papers from the library. Jess scooted closer as he unfolded them, then took them out of his hands altogether, flipped through to the Aztec Limo sheets, and pointed wordlessly.

The three calls to the limo company immediately after Davenport's had been made from the YourJets number.

"Jesus," Mark said.

Mindful of the driver, Jess tried to keep her response cryptic. "That's where she was going. They operate out of a private airport in Richmond. Mr. Davenport used them all the time."

The cab pulled to the curb. A bright glow lit the inside of the vehicle, and Jess realized that they had reached the Hay-Adams.

Mark tucked the pages back into his pocket, handed over money, and they got out.

The doorman at the hotel eyed them with disfavor, and Jess realized that both she and Mark must be starting to look pretty seamy. A well-dressed couple walked past them into the hotel and a limo pulled slowly away from the front as Mark slipped a hand beneath her elbow and steered her away, into the safer shadows farther along the block.

"She really was running away. That explains the credit cards, too." Mark's tone was thoughtful.

"What?"

"Nothing."

He was looking across the street, toward the dark acres of Lafayette Park. It was much quieter here than in Dupont Circle. During the day, the area teemed with tourists. After dark, the homeless, druggies, hookers, thugs, and those locals attracted to such things, as well as the occasional too-brave or too-clueless tourist, mixed and mingled in the park. On the streets around it, at this time of night, a few pedestrians walked, a few cars glided by, and the hotels and a few bars were open. During the day, it was safe. At night it was one of those places Jess wouldn't want to visit by herself.

"Back to the plan," Jess said firmly, looking up at him. "Want to let me in on what it is now?"

"You don't think I have one, do you?"

"I'm hoping."

"O, ye of little faith." Mark stopped walking, turned her to face him, cupped her face in his hands, and kissed her again. A brief, hard kiss that nonetheless made her breath catch and her heart beat faster.

"Mark . . ." She curled her hands around his wrists.

"That conversation about whether you meant it about being in love with me? We're going to finish it. Later."

Then, taking her hand, looking both ways, he hurried her across the street and into the dark environs of the park.

Chapter 30

"SO WHAT ARE WE doing here?" Jess's voice was low.

It was stupid, she knew, considering that she had an armed federal agent by her side who had just proved himself lethal in the extreme when conditions warranted, and ordinary criminals were the least of her problems anyway, but the dimly lit paths and shadowy areas beyond them gave her the shivers. They weren't alone by any means, but only a few others—a trio of Goths with black everything, a hulking teenager with a blue Mohawk and a chain hanging from his jeans, a man in tattered clothing who was shuffling out of the light toward the tent city for the homeless that sprang up each night at the far end of the park—were visible. The rest lurked in the shadows, conducting their business under the trees, behind the bushes, in the lee of almost forgotten statues and monuments. Drunks sprawled on the grass, swigging from open bottles. A few teenagers made out. The heavy, sweet scent of pot wafted past in occasional drifts. The fact that the White House could be seen glowing like the proverbial beacon on a hill in the near distance didn't seem to discourage anybody from anything. It was there, a fact of D.C. life, and it was ignored.

"I thought of somebody who might've seen the First

Lady after she snuck out of the White House and before you picked her up at the hotel. Somebody she might have talked to."

"Who?"

"A woman she met when she was touring a halfway house. Her name is Dawn Turney. A real sad case, was an accountant before she got addicted to crack and crystal meth. She got arrested, lost everything, went to jail, then went into the halfway house, supposedly cured. She and Mrs. Cooper used to meet privately sometimes to talk about the woman's progress—one of her charity cases. Only we found out a few months ago that Dawn was also supplying her with drugs. We put a stop to the meetings—we thought—and then we found out that Dawn was hanging out here in the park, dealing and doing drugs. The First Lady found out, too, before we did. She would 'accidentally' run into her sometimes while she was out jogging at night and they'd do a drug deal with her detail looking on. Of course, they didn't know what the hell they were seeing. They just thought it was a harmless chat with some fringe person she somehow knew."

"You think she met this woman before going on to the hotel?"

Mark shrugged. "It's possible. She had drugs in her purse that night. I checked. We'd been weaning her off oxy, but when I looked inside the bottle she hid her pills in I saw she had some. Where'd she get them? My gut says here."

Jess felt like a thousand unseen eyes were watching them through the dark. Her skin crawled at the thought. Two members of the hit-man contingent were dead. That didn't mean there weren't more. In fact, the hard truth was that of course there were more. She tightened her grip on his hand.

"Mark. I think we need to get out of D.C. I think we

need to run away from here as hard and fast and far as we can."

"Yeah, I think so, too." The fact that he agreed with her scared her almost more than anything else had done. It told her that *he* thought the net was closing in, the situation was getting out of control, the odds of them being caught were ratcheting ever higher. "I want to talk to this woman first, see if she saw the First Lady that night and if she can shed any light on what was going on with her before somebody else tumbles to the fact that she might know something and gets rid of her. Then we'll get the hell out of Dodge while we try to figure out what to do." He hesitated, but from the expression on his face Jess didn't have any trouble divining the rest.

"I know that doesn't mean they'll quit coming after us." Her voice was flat. A deep tiredness that she recognized as the forerunner of despair was creeping over her, making her suddenly conscious of the renewed ache in her legs and back, her growing headache, her need for sleep. "They'll never quit, will they?"

"Not as long as they think we're a threat. The good news is, we're doing a helluva job outrunning them."

Jess shivered. "For now."

"Now's all we've got. It's really all anybody's got."

They had reached the statue of Andrew Jackson on horseback that dominated this section of the park. It was set in a concrete circle that was barely visible as a pale ring around the monument. The lights surrounding it were out, either from lack of maintenance or, more likely, from deliberate vandalism. Benches leading up to it were mostly occupied. People milled around the circle, moving in and out of the nearby bushes and trees. Jess couldn't see anyone clearly. They were dark wraiths weaving through darker shadows.

"Stay close," Mark breathed as they left the path for the concrete circle, and Jess did.

They were accosted immediately.

"You got a twenty you can give me, man?" The punk was one of a group that had been smoking dope near the bronze horse's raised forelegs. All Jess could see of him through the darkness was that he was under six feet tall and stocky, with long, stringy hair. He planted himself in front of Mark, still holding his joint, the tip of which glowed red. The smell of weed was strong.

"I'm looking for Dawn. She around?"

"You want to buy some shit, man? I got shit."

"I want Dawn."

"Who's that looking for me?" A woman pushed through the group and came toward them. Reed-thin, with teased black hair that fell down past her shoulders and a face so pale it seemed to float through the darkness like an oval moon, she was wearing skinny pants and an oversize sweatshirt. "Who wants Dawn?"

Mark didn't say anything, just turned his head to watch her approach. A few steps away, some of the swagger left her gait.

"Oh, it's you." It was clear from her tone that she recognized Mark and didn't like him. "What do *you* want?" Then in an aside to her stringy-haired friend, she added, "Get out of here, Daryl, he's a Fed."

"Oh, shit," Daryl said, and disappeared into the shadows.

"I want to talk to you," Mark said.

"About what?"

"Mrs. Cooper. Did you happen to see her a couple of hours before she died?"

Dawn crossed her arms over her chest and glanced away without saying anything. Jess could see the sudden tension in her body.

"I'm not looking to bust you or get you into any trouble. I just need some information."

Dawn's gaze fastened on Jess.

"Who's that?" Her voice was heavy with suspicion.

"Nobody you need to worry about."

"I ain't talking about nothin' in front of somebody I don't know." Her eyes rested on Jess.

"I'll just go wait for you over there," Jess said to Mark, nodding toward the nearby base of the statue. When he squeezed her hand, then let go, she took it to mean that he agreed with her assessment as to the best course of action and moved off. None of the shifting clumps of people eddying around them seemed to be paying her the least bit of attention, but still she didn't go as far as the statue's base, because that was where everybody seemed to be hanging out and because it was really dark there and it would be easy to lose sight of Mark. Instead, she stopped just a few paces away, out of Dawn's sight but close enough that when she turned around, she could still clearly see Mark. And, she thought, he could see her.

"So you saw Mrs. Cooper that night."

Folding her arms over her chest and doing her best to fight off the shivers that assailed her, Jess realized she could still hear their conversation. Mark's tone had made it a statement rather than a question.

"Maybe she bought some 'killers from me, I don't know." Dawn sounded sulky.

"Was she by herself?"

"If she was here, she was."

"She say anything or do anything to make you think she might be upset?"

Dawn hesitated.

"She was good to you, Dawn," Mark said. "It would mean a lot to her memory if you could help us out with this."

"Yeah, okay. She was real jumpy, said she needed the 'killers to help her calm down. Her hands were shaking when she paid me, you know? And she kept looking around, like she was expecting *you* to jump out of the bushes." She said that last with a touch of venom.

"She say anything about why she was upset?"

Dawn shook her head. "Only other thing she said was she asked me about e-mail. She asked me if I knew how to e-mail something. A video that was on her phone. I said, hell, no."

"A video—" Mark began, but broke off as the sound of footsteps pounding through the grass in front of the statue caused him to look sharply around. Pulse leaping, Jess took an automatic step back, her eyes widening as her gaze shot past him.

To discover what looked like an onrushing wall of men.

"Mark Ryan?" one of them called.

"Run," Mark barked in her direction as he whipped around, his hand diving for his gun.

Mark.

Jess screamed it in her head as she was almost knocked off her feet by Dawn's sudden dash away. Even as she regained her balance, even as her eyes found Mark again, there was a whistling sound and he groaned and staggered and then dropped, just dropped like a stone, falling to the concrete like he'd been shot.

A sudden unwanted vision of how the man Mark had shot dropped flashed into her head.

Mark had crumpled just like that.

Oh, no. Please, God, no.

Her heart gave a great thump. Her feet rooted to the spot. Her mouth opened to shriek, but her throat had closed up so tight no sound could escape. Then, without warning, she was hit by a wall of people, borne backward by the stampede of cursing, shouting bystanders fleeing the scene, and for a moment she could no longer see Mark.

Please, God, please.

She got knocked on her butt, and by the time she managed to scramble to her hands and knees and look again, there was a quartet of men in suits standing over Mark, three of them with guns drawn, one reaching down as though to check his vital signs.

Mark didn't move. Didn't make a sound. Just lay there facedown on the pale concrete around the statue. It was too dark and she was too far away to tell if he was breathing, to see if his chest rose and fell.

Everything in her wanted to go to him, run to him, fling herself down on top of him and do what she could to save him.

But there was nothing she could do.

Even as she faced that terrible truth, one of the suited men started glancing around, scanning the dark. As if he were looking for—what? Her?

They knew who Mark was—they had called him by name. That meant they almost certainly knew about her.

Jess rolled onto her hands and knees and started crawling away. The short, crisp grass was cold and damp beneath her palms. The scent of earth was strong. Bottles, cans, still-smoldering cigarette butts, all kinds of assorted trash that had been flung down in the mass exodus created what was basically an obstacle course in her path, and she did her best to dodge them. As soon as she judged she was far enough away so that they couldn't see her, she reeled to her feet and stumbled rubbery-legged into the dark.

It was only as her vision blurred that she felt the tears that were pouring thick and fast down her cheeks.

Chapter 31

JESS HAD NEVER BEEN so cold in her life. Her teeth chattered. She shivered like she would never stop. She felt like she was freezing to death from the inside out. Her throat ached. Tears rolled down her cheeks. Sobs racked her.

Please, God, don't let Mark be dead.

She was running, lurching, staggering, scrambling away from him as fast as she could go. Leaving him lying there like that was tearing out her heart. But to go back, to let herself be taken as well, would do him no good. If they succeeded in killing her, too, they would get away with it. The truth of who they were and the terrible things they had done would never be known.

And if Mark wasn't dead—please, God, please— maybe there was a chance that she could still save him.

If she could just come up with a plan in time. She latched onto the thought with a feverish urgency. It was all that kept her from going to pieces.

What she needed was proof that the First Lady had been murdered. Proof that she had been running from something and they had killed her before she could get away. Proof she could take to, say, the *Post*. She would go to their headquarters and tell everyone there what was happening, what she suspected, what had happened to

Mark, to their own Marty Solomon, Davenport, Marian—all of them. And show the proof.

Which she didn't have.

Without proof, would anyone listen? Yes. Would they believe? Hmm. Would they print her words, her claims, and at least get them out there for the public to judge for themselves? She thought so, given her status as "the survivor," but she couldn't be sure. Washington was a company town, and whoever was behind this had the kind of power and influence that could maybe find a way of making the story disappear. Just like they could make her disappear.

Maybe she should run straight to the police. The FBI. Somebody like that. But that might be an even faster route to disappearing. Unless she chose the right agency, the right cop or agent, she could be whisked away easily, never to be heard from again. No, she should go to the *Post,* tell her story, and have them call both the police and the FBI. Even if they took her away, even if they made her disappear, at least there would be witnesses. Lots of witnesses. Not even killers as ruthless as these could take out a whole newsroom, plus assorted innocent, uninvolved cops and FBI agents, too. Because there had to be more who weren't involved than who were. The trick lay in knowing which was which.

But whatever happened, whatever she did, it was probably going to be too late for Mark.

That conversation about whether you meant it about being in love with me? We're going to finish it. Later.

She could almost hear him saying it. The memory stabbed her like a knife to the heart.

Please, God, let there be a later.

The image of him dropping to the concrete replayed again in her mind, and even as she tried to block it out—to get anything done she needed a clear head, needed to be able to think—she found herself gasping for air. Her insides twisted into a knot. Her heart gave a great aching throb. The pain almost brought her to her knees.

Then she had a thought that galvanized her, that brought a blessed flood of adrenaline with it: They had to have known Mark was talking to someone, there at the statue. It probably wouldn't take them long to find out about Dawn. To find Dawn. Who, voluntarily or not, would tell them what questions Mark had asked, and about the video on the First Lady's phone.

Grieving, if grieving it had to be, would have to wait. Staggering through tent city, glad that there were now people around her even though they were paying her no attention, even though she knew they provided her with no protection at all, she realized that the thing she needed to do first was go get that phone.

She had an instant vision of the First Lady in the car, trying to make calls that wouldn't go through. Of her throwing the thing in frustration. Of herself on her hands and knees trying to retrieve it from under the seat.

Then thrusting it deep in her pants pocket as the accident went down. Where she thought there was a good chance it still was.

When her mother had returned her purse and phone to her in the hospital, she would have mentioned a second phone if one had turned up. Therefore, it probably hadn't. It was probably still in the pocket of her good black pants, which had been cut off her in the ambulance, wadded up with everything else she'd been wearing, and given to her mother later.

To be stored in a bag in the laundry room until Jess told her what she wanted done with them. Her mother had told her that, too.

The first order of business was to retrieve that phone, see what if anything was on it, and then, if it provided anything like the proof she desperately needed, convey it personally and at warp speed to the *Post*. Or even if it didn't. While calling a lawyer—George Kelly, Davenport's partner, sprang immediately to mind, but she hesitated even as she had the thought because of what had happened to Marty Solomon. But she needed an ally, lots of allies, as many as possible. Frowning, she thought of Davenport. Davenport had tried to kill her. Would Kelly be in the pocket of whoever was orchestrating this, too?

The bottom line was, now that Mark was gone, except for her immediate family, there was no longer anyone she felt certain she could trust. That left her with the old adage about there being safety in numbers.

She would pick up the phone and head straight for the *Post,* and ask them to summon every law-enforcement agency she or they had ever heard of after she told them her story.

As a plan, it was rough around the edges. And in the middle, and everywhere else. But it was the only plan she had. Even if she wanted to save only herself. Because just running wasn't going to work. They would catch her, just like they had caught Mark tonight.

Now's . . . really all anybody's got.

His words whispered through her mind. Suddenly they seemed terrifyingly prophetic. Oh, God, had he had some kind of premonition that he would die tonight?

Her heart bled.

Blocking him out of her thoughts wasn't possible, although for the sake of her ability to do what she needed to do, she had to try. Gritting her teeth, she focused on putting one foot in front of the other and getting safely away. She was so stunned she was having trouble getting her brain to function beyond that.

People were leaving the park like cockroaches fleeing a fire, she saw as she pushed through a low hedge at the shadowy corner of East Executive Drive and K Street. Punks and hookers and thugs and druggies and the homeless and everybody else with something to fear from the suits who had invaded the park were hot-footing it along the sidewalks and disappearing down side streets, making tracks for somewhere else. Nobody wanted to be involved. If asked, nobody would have seen a thing.

Didn't happen, wasn't there, don't know: It was the code of the streets.

Mark had been shot in front of at least a dozen witnesses, and it was almost a sure bet that not one of them would say a thing.

Jess pulled herself up sharply. She couldn't think of Mark again. Every time she did, she could feel herself falling apart inside.

A cab—she needed a cab. Her mother lived on Laundry Street, down at the very end of 16th Street, the part of the city that spilled over into Maryland. How much would it cost to get there? Jess realized she still had her purse, which meant she had some money. How much? Her share of the kitty: twenty-four dollars. They had never gotten around to actually pooling it.

At the thought, Jess's heart gave another of those horrible aching throbs. More tears leaked from her eyes. Wiping them away with determination, she sent one more heartfelt prayer winging skyward.

Please take care of him, Lord. Please.

Then she saw a cab coming toward her, and hailed it.

The ride to her mother's house was uneventful. Just to be on the safe side, she had the driver let her out on the next block over, and she cut through the alley. It was late now, well past one a.m. The chances that there would be anyone out and about in this slightly run-down residential neighborhood were slim. What worried her was that they—they, they, how she hated that terrifying, amorphous they—might have the place staked out, might be watching her even now.

Her steps slowed as she neared the two-story white house with its aging aluminum siding and black shingled roof. The family had moved here when Jess was a senior in high school, so her mother could be closer to her job. They'd all lived here until the last few years, when one by one they had started moving out. It was a working-class house, narrow and a little shabby, three bedrooms and a bath upstairs, living room, dining room, kitchen, and a half bath downstairs, and it had been crowded when they had all lived there together. Currently, depending on whether or not Sarah was still in residence with the kids, just her mother and Maddie lived there.

Jess stopped beside some garbage cans behind the house across the alley. Huddling against one of the rickety privacy fences that separated the tiny backyards from one another, she looked around—nothing out of the ordinary, nothing moving—and then back at her mother's house. Not a light on in the place. No cars in the graveled parking area that, when they were home, usually held her mother's Mazda and Maddie's Jeep.

Shivering, clenching her teeth to keep them from chattering, she hesitated, eyeing the house, almost ready to turn and walk away.

The very last thing she wanted to do was endanger her family. But it was the weekend, and Judy could often be found babysitting her grandsons while Sarah and her husband went out and then, if they got home late, just spending the night at Sarah's. (This was presuming Sarah's marriage was back on.) And Maddie might well be with Grace, or at a girlfriend's, or, more likely, with her boyfriend.

There was a good chance, then, that the house was empty. And it would take her only five minutes, tops, to slip inside, go down to the laundry room in the basement, and recover that phone if it was there.

If there was any chance, any chance at all, that Mark was still alive, for her to find evidence that the First Lady's death was murder and get it out to the public as fast as possible might be the only hope he had. After all, once the truth was out there, what was the point of killing anybody else? Of killing Mark?

She was probably kidding herself, and she knew it. There was no reason she could see that they would have kept Mark alive.

But she had to keep that slim hope. Otherwise, she was afraid she would just curl up in a little ball where she stood and cry and cry and cry.

Making up her mind, Jess took a deep breath and quickly crossed the alley. The familiar smell of home greeted her as she pulled her key from the lock and quietly closed and locked the back door. Something about just being inside the house was comforting. Her bedroom had been in the basement—as a teen, she'd made herself a whole lair down there—and knowing that her old bed and her old computer and everything else she'd left behind were still right where she had left them made her throat tighten with longing. But she couldn't stay. She couldn't even linger.

Holding her breath, listening hard as she crossed the well-worn linoleum floor, she heard nothing but the hum of appliances. The glowing numbers over the microwave announced the time: one twenty-three. She'd been wrong, she discovered as she glanced into the hall. The light was on in the half bath at the bottom of the stairs. It had no windows, so she hadn't been able to see the glow from outside. Now it showed her that there were no shoes kicked off in the hall—something that her whole family tended to do as soon as they entered the house—and so reinforced her belief that no one was home. And it was enough to light her way down the basement stairs.

Once away from the dim pool of light at the bottom of the stairs, the basement itself was dark as pitch. Fortunately, she knew her way like the back of her hand. The basement was separated by thin plasterboard walls into three rooms: the laundry room, which was in the far corner of the poured concrete rectangle; the utility-junk area, which the stairs led down into and which she was moving through at that moment; and her own former bedroom, which took up the entire area to the left of the stairs.

There were no windows, which had bothered Judy when Jess had insisted on moving down there. But Jess had liked the privacy and had compensated for the lack of daylight by plastering her walls with fluorescent posters.

The door to the laundry room opened with a creak. A faint mustiness and the scent of fabric softener hit her as soon as she stepped over the threshold. Once inside, with the door closed behind her, Jess turned on the light, blinking in the sudden brightness.

The washer and dryer were located against the far wall, a drying rack to the right. The ironing board and iron nestled in a corner. To the left were shelves that held everything from detergent to bug spray.

A brown paper grocery bag with the top folded over sat on one of the shelves. Jess was almost sure that it was the bag she was looking for as soon as she set eyes on it, and when she opened it she discovered that she was right. Thrusting her hand down into the jumble of clothes and finding her pants, she pulled them out. They had been slit up both legs, but that didn't bother her. Checking the right pocket, she drew out a phone.

Yes.

Her hand tightened around it. Then, frowning, she realized that it didn't look like her memory of the phone the First Lady had had with her in the hotel bar. It had been too dark inside the Lincoln to see the phone Mrs.

Cooper had tried to use without success just before the wreck, but Jess had assumed it had been the same one.

Now she saw that it wasn't.

Opening it, she pressed the button to turn it on, praying it still had power. It did. The Sprint logo flickered to life with a melodious beep that made her flinch. Quickly, Jess went to the menu, pressed another button, looked at the screen, and felt her stomach tighten as she realized that what she was holding in her hand was the President of the United States's personal cell phone.

His wife had obviously taken it. Why? Jess's heart knocked against her rib cage as she went to videos. Clicking on it, she watched what filled the tiny screen with stunned disbelief.

David Cooper had filmed himself in full bondage regalia being serviced by a leather-clad woman who was not his wife.

There were six similar videos.

The quality was not good. The film was grainy. But what she was seeing was unmistakable, as was the identity of the person she was watching.

Jess realized that she held the proverbial smoking gun in her hand.

Clearly, Mrs. Cooper had discovered the videos. Just as clearly, someone else had found out she had them and had been determined to stop her from showing them to anybody. They must have been going crazy searching for the phone ever since the accident. Or maybe they assumed it had burned up in the wreckage.

Now that she thought about it, Jess realized that Mrs. Cooper might have been trying to e-mail those videos in the final few minutes before the crash. That would explain why nothing was going through. That would explain her frustration.

Phone in hand, Jess was just turning toward the door when it opened.

She jumped a foot in the air before she realized that it was Maddie who was standing in the doorway staring at her.

"Jess? What are you doing here?" Maddie's hair was in braids and she was wearing a blue tank top, ratty sweatpants, and fuzzy pink socks, her typical sleepwear. Her pregnancy was only just beginning to show.

"I stopped by to get something." Jess brushed past her sister, already on the way to the stairs. Now that she knew somebody was home, she wanted to get out of there fast.

"Oh, my God, Mom's been so worried about you! When she heard that your boss killed himself, she started calling everybody she could think of, trying to track you down."

"I sent her an e-mail."

Maddie snorted. "That didn't even slow her down."

"So tell her you saw me and I'm fine, okay? I'll call her in a few days." Jess sought to turn the subject. "How did you know I was down here?"

"I was asleep on the couch upstairs. I thought I heard somebody in the basement." Maddie trailed her. "Are you leaving?"

"Yeah, I ..." Jess had a thought and stopped dead. Her head swiveled toward her old bedroom, and then she changed course and hurried toward it. "Is anybody else here?"

"No, just me. Mom's at Sarah's and—"

"I want you to get out of here." Jess pushed through her bedroom door and went straight to her computer. She still used it sometimes, and kept it up-to-date. Turning it on, she glanced back at her sister, who was just a few steps behind her. "Where's your Jeep?"

"Out front. What's going on?" Maddie's comprehensive glance turned to a frown. "Have you been crying?"

Mark was shot. . . .

But she didn't say it. Jess swallowed to try to dislodge the lump in her throat, and ignored Maddie's question.

"Go get in your Jeep and drive away. Go to Sarah's. Do you hear me? Right now."

She had turned on the small lamp beside the computer and was fishing in her desk drawer for the cable she needed as she spoke.

"Something's wrong, isn't it?"

"Yes. And I'm not going to tell you what." She found the cable and sat down in her chair to hook it up. "Go."

"Jess . . ."

Blood pounding in her temples, her eyes still blurry from the tears she had shed, working as fast as she could with fingers that were clumsy and cold from shock and grief, Jess didn't look around. "Go to Sarah's. Right this minute. Please, Maddie, I'm begging you. You know I wouldn't tell you to do it if it wasn't urgent."

"Okay." A lifetime of trust was in Maddie's reply. Without another word, she turned and left the room.

"Don't tell anybody you saw me until tomorrow at the earliest. Whatever you do, don't bring Mom or anybody back over here tonight," Jess called after her sister. Knowing how her family worked, she needed to be sure that was understood. "Promise me."

"I promise." Maddie's now frightened-sounding voice floated back to her.

"Hurry. Don't take anything. Just go."

She could hear Maddie's footsteps on the stairs. A moment later, as she listened to the front door open and close, she heaved a sigh of relief. At least her sister would be safe.

Then she got down to work. The process took a few minutes, but it wasn't hard, and it was helped along because she knew all the shortcuts. In fact, she was so engrossed in what she was doing that she didn't even realize she had company until she saw a shadow of movement in the still-open door and heard Maddie say, "J-jess."

She was just registering the wobbly tone of Maddie's voice when she glanced over her shoulder to see Maddie standing there watching her.

One of the dark-suited goons had an arm around her neck and a gun pressed to her temple.

Chapter 32

JESS'S HEART WENT INTO overdrive. Her blood ran cold. Her eyes collided with her sister's. Maddie looked scared to death.

Oh, God, what have I done?

"Hello, Ms. Ford." The goon flipped on the overhead light. He was maybe six feet tall, broad rather than lean, with buzzed black hair and an olive-skinned, harsh-featured face. Black suit, white shirt, black tie. One of *them.*

With nervous fingers, Jess immediately pressed a button on the computer and scooted her chair back a little to get out of the way.

"I had to . . . he made me . . ." Maddie stuttered. The arm around her neck tightened, cutting off her words, making her claw at his arm and gasp for air.

Jess knew she didn't have time to waste giving a useless command for him to let Maddie go.

"You're on a webcam. Millions of people are watching you right now," she said crisply, as the gun left Maddie's temple to point at her. Remembering how quickly Mark had been shot, how fast Mark had shot the guy in the apartment, her worst fear was that he would blow her and Maddie away before he even realized that he was on *Candid Camera.* Her heart hammered. Her pulse raced. But it was terror for her sister even more than for herself that helped her project an outward calm.

She could not bear to see another sister die before her eyes. She had lost so much tonight: the man she loved. She couldn't lose Maddie, too.

"What?" He frowned, looking from her to the computer. The camera mounted on it was small but unmistakable.

Smile, asshole.

"You heard me. You—and me and my sister, all of us—are on the Web right now. Live. Everybody out there is listening to this conversation. If you shoot us, they'll be watching. All those people will be witnesses."

"What?" He stared at the monitor, then looked closer, as if he suddenly realized that he, Maddie, Jess, the whole scene he was part of, was there on the screen for him to see, just like he was watching them as part of a TV show.

"Turn it off. I'll kill her." The threat was directed to Jess. The gun was once again pressed to Maddie's head.

"Jess." Mortal fear clouded Maddie's eyes. Jess watched her sister's face whiten until it was the color of chalk, and felt her stomach turn inside out. *I'm sorry, so sorry . . .* Maddie's hands were on her captor's arm, just resting there as if she was scared to try to pull it loose, scared to move. She looked like she was ready to faint. Jess felt herself breaking into a cold sweat.

"Too late, everyone already saw. It's already all over the Internet." She knew she had to lay all her cards on the table fast. Palms clammy, she clutched the armrests of her chair and projected confidence like she had never projected anything before. "Do you understand what I'm telling you? They've already seen you. They can identify you. They'll know you killed us. Everybody out there who's watching this right now."

His gun hand jerked. The computer exploded with a

bang as a bullet hit it. Jess jumped and squeaked as shards of glass and plastic flew past her to rain down everywhere in a shower of debris. Her heart lodged in her throat. Maddie's scream was immediately cut off, and Jess realized he had tightened his hold on her neck again.

A smoky, burning smell wafted beneath her nostrils.

"Fuck your camera, bitch." The gun pointed at Jess. In a split second her heart hit what felt like a thousand beats a minute. Trying not to cringe in terror, she tensed, feeling cold sweat pour over her in waves as she braced for the bullet that any second now was going to blast through her flesh.

Oh, God, would it hurt?

Desperately, she kept talking. "You can't erase what's already out there. Plus, you should probably know I found the phone. The President's phone. You need to call whoever you're working for and tell them that. Tell them I posted all those dirty videos of the President all over the Web. They're on YouTube. CNN's iReport. iWatch. Everywhere. If they haven't gone viral already, you can bet they will any minute. That means they'll be all over the world. Millions of people will see. There's no stopping it. Nothing anybody can do. It's over. You need to call and tell them that."

"She's t-telling the truth." Maddie wet her lips. "She's good at stuff like that."

Jess pointed at the phone that was now lying beside the shattered remains of her computer. The cable was still attached to it.

"See?" she said. "That's the President's phone. See the cable? I uploaded his videos to the Internet."

The goon stared at the phone.

"Nobody else home," a man's voice called from what sounded like the top of the stairs. "We got cleaners on the way, so hurry up."

Jess realized there was a second goon, and didn't know why she was even surprised. She should have learned by this time that they traveled in pairs.

"There's a problem," the goon called back. "Come down here."

Listening to the sounds of heavy footsteps on the stairs, Jess cast a cautious eye over the desktop, looking for anything she could use as a weapon. There was nothing. These guys were big, strong, well-trained professional killers. What was she going to do, staple them to death?

"What kind of problem?" The second goon was maybe an inch taller, twenty pounds lighter, and a little better-looking than the first. But in dress and manner, they could have been twins.

"Tell him." The first goon nodded at Jess. His gun was still aimed right at her. One squeeze of his finger and . . . even as the tiny hairs at the back of her neck prickled to life at the thought, she forced her mind away from it. But at least his grip on Maddie had eased. His arm was more around her collarbone than her throat now. Maddie still looked terrified, with her eyes big as plates and sweat beading her upper lip, but at least she could breathe. Jess could see her chest heaving from where she sat.

Heart hammering, doing her best to keep up a brave front, Jess told the second goon what she had done.

He walked over, looked at the President's phone, looked at the cable, looked at the dead computer, then looked back at the first goon.

"You better call," the second one said.

The first goon's lips compressed. Letting go of Maddie, he gave her a shove toward Jess.

"Get over there and behave."

Maddie stumbled toward her. Jess rose on unsteady legs to wrap her arms around her sister, whose breathing was ragged and who shook from head to toe. Maddie was several inches taller than she was and quite a bit bigger, but it didn't matter: In this time of extremis, her little sister looked to her for comfort and protection. Knowing that she had pretty much provided what protection she could by employing the webcam and the Internet, Jess tried to keep her own physical responses under control as she registered with an icy thrill of fear how both men watched them with nearly identical expressions: not hate, not even dislike, but cold indifference, which was more terrifying than either. They would clearly have no more trouble shooting her and Maddie than they would disposing of a piece of trash. Jess's insides churned at the thought, but she tried not to let it show. Seeing how terrified she was would only scare Maddie more.

Keeping his gun on them, his thick body blocking the door, the first goon pulled a cell phone out of his pocket and punched in some numbers.

"There's a problem," he said into the phone. Then he told whoever was on the other end what Jess had told him, said a few *uh-huh*s and *yeah*s and concluded with a terse, "Got it."

Then he hung up and waved his gun at her.

"You. Glasses. Get the phone. We're going for a ride. All of us. And if you give us any trouble, the first person we'll kill is baby sister."

THEY WERE HEADING NORTHEAST.

Maddie rode in the front seat beside the second goon, who was driving. Jess sat in the back beside the first one, whose gun rested casually on his thigh. Both women had their hands fastened behind them with plastic ties; seat belts secured them in place. The car was a black Lexus, comfortable and roomy, smelling of new leather—and fear. As the lights of the city gave way to the quiet rushing darkness of back roads that wound through the countryside, Jess's stomach cramped and her throat went dry at the thought of what might be waiting for them at the end of the journey. Having been ordered not to talk when she'd first asked where they were going, and having that order reinforced by a casual aiming of her seatmate's gun at Maddie, she sat silently behind the driver, watching her sister's pale face in profile. Maddie's lips trembled, and her breathing was ragged. Her shoulders slumped, and she kept glancing around and licking her lips.

My fault. I got Maddie into this.

Her already lacerated and raw heart felt like it was being shredded anew every time she looked at her sister's despairing face.

Their only hope was that someone had seen what was happening via the webcam and notified the police. Of course, it would take the police some time to track the broadcast to its source, and even when they did, they would have no idea where she and Maddie were being taken. She didn't even know that.

So her only hope wasn't a hope at all. It was more like wishful thinking. If she and Maddie were to survive, they needed something more concrete.

But before she could think of anything, the Lexus slowed, turned into a winding lane, and purred uphill.

Jess's heart began to pound as she realized their destination was at hand. The car slowed still more as it approached a wrought-iron fence that had to be at least ten feet tall. Equally tall bushes behind it formed a hedge that prevented Jess from seeing anything beyond it but curving treetops swaying against an inky-dark sky. They braked, and Jess saw that they had reached a tall gate complete with a small stone guardhouse and uniformed guard. The driver rolled down the window and waved. The guard, clearly recognizing him, nodded back and said something into a headset he wore. The gate opened inward. The Lexus rolled through.

"Where are we?" The question escaped her. There was no answer except the increasingly loud gasps of Maddie's breathing. The goon beside Jess gave her a single contemptuous glance then turned his attention forward. Jess was left to look out the tinted windows to try to make sense out of what was happening.

Acres of large trees; grass smooth and, so late at night, dark as black velvet; perfectly matched stones lining the driveway; then, finally, a glimpse of an imposing stone mansion—they were pulling up the driveway of an estate. An awesome estate, the kind that had to cost millions of dollars.

Jess's mouth went dry as she thought about who might own such a place.

Then she had no more time for speculation, because they had reached a large underground garage and a door was opening for them. As soon as the Lexus pulled inside, the door closed behind them.

Trapped. The word echoed through Jess's brain, chilling her to the bone.

A moment later they were out of the car and walking through a small door into the house. There was a tension in the air now; Jess could feel it, and her nerves stretched taut as piano wire. Her scalp prickled. Her pulse surged.

"Who lives here?" she asked, not because she expected an answer—she didn't. It was to break the increasingly oppressive atmosphere, to give Maddie, who was looking increasingly wild-eyed and terrified, a bit of heart.

"Shut up" was the growled response. The second thug, who was walking behind her sister, who was leading the way, gave Maddie a shove.

Maddie stumbled, regained her balance, and seemed to shrink. Feeling the welcome heat of building anger—welcome because it was an antidote to fear—Jess shut up.

As they were herded along a hall, Jess got the impression that they were still underground. The floor was stone, the walls seemed to be the real old-fashioned kind of plaster, and the air was quiet and cool. At the end of the hall was an elevator. They rode it up three floors in silence. The tension in that elevator was so thick it could have been cut with a knife.

When the door opened, Jess was pushed out first with a rough hand in the middle of her back. She found herself stumbling into what seemed to be an extremely large office, maybe thirty by forty feet, with a slate floor and bookshelves fashioned from some fine dark wood lining three of the four walls. The fourth wall, the one to the right of the elevator, had deep blue floor-to-ceiling curtains drawn over a pair of windows that flanked a white marble fireplace with a portrait of a woman over it. Scattered about were a number of gold-upholstered wing chairs positioned in pairs with a table between them. Jess could smell, just faintly, a mix of cigar smoke and lemon-tinged furniture polish in the air. A quartet of black-suited men, two on either side of the room, stood with their legs apart and their hands clasped behind their backs in the classic military at-ease position, their expressions impassive as they stared straight ahead, clearly on guard duty. Jess's heart pounded as she spotted them. *They*, *them*—those were the names she knew them by, and just the sight of them made her go all light-headed. A huge mahogany desk sat catty-corner across the far corner of the room. Two men were behind it, one standing, the other sitting. The sitting man rose as Jess stopped just beyond the elevator, looking at them.

Her breathing suspended as she recognized him: Wayne Cooper, the First Father.

"You've got yourself into a bad situation, I'm afraid, Ms. Ford." He sounded perfectly normal, if a little severe. He looked just like he did on TV, which was the only place Jess had ever seen him. But there was something about him, about the expression on his face, about the way his fingers tapped impatiently on the desktop, about the aura of power he exuded, that sent a chill racing down Jess's spine. "I need you to come over here, give me that phone of my son's, and tell me exactly what you've done."

He turned and pointed a bony forefinger accusingly at a computer monitor. The man behind him was absolutely ashen-faced as he looked at it, too. The reason was obvious: It was running one of the videos she had so recently uploaded.

"Free her hands," Cooper ordered over his shoulder. One of the goons must have had a knife, because he sliced through the plastic tie. Jess shook her hands, chafed her wrists, and glanced at Maddie, who had just been pushed down into one of the wing chairs.

Maddie's eyes clung to hers. Jess could see tears swimming in them. Her chest went tight.

"My sister?"

Cooper snorted. "Get the hell over here and give me that phone."

A goon pushed her forward. With her peripheral vision, Jess saw Maddie let her head drop against the back of the chair and close her eyes. She could feel her sister's terror, reaching out like icy fingers to clutch at her own heart. As she moved toward the desk, Jess swallowed, the taste of fear sour in her mouth.

She was horribly afraid they were just about out of time; even if she wanted to, even if they ordered her to at gunpoint, or with a gun to Maddie's head, what was done could not be undone.

Once they figured that out, would they kill them both?

Bubbling anger trumped the sick fear that threatened to turn her bones to water and her muscles to mush. These people were terrorizing and threatening her sister.

They had ripped her own life completely apart. They had killed so many people. They had shot Mark.

She was caught, with no way to escape them that she could see. And thanks to her, poor, innocent Maddie was caught along with her. But she refused to cower. No way would she give them the satisfaction of seeing how very frightened she was, of how helpless she felt.

Her head came up. Squaring her shoulders, she walked to the desk.

"Hand over that phone." He held out his hand. Jess pulled the President's phone from her pocket and put it in his palm. She had no further use for it, anyway. She'd taken what she needed from it.

"Now I want you to tell me just exactly what you did."

Ignoring her pounding heart, Jess looked Cooper in the eye.

"I uploaded those videos to every media outlet I could think of. I put them on YouTube. iReport. iWatch. Everywhere. They're all over the Web. And those goons of yours who broke into my mother's house and kidnapped my sister and me? That was captured on my webcam, too. It's all out there now. Millions of people are probably watching it as we speak."

His eyes bulged. His face slowly purpled with anger.

"God in heaven, young woman, you've done a bad day's work. A bad thing for your country. You—"

The phone on his desk rang, interrupting. Breaking off, fixing her with a fulminating stare, he snatched up the receiver.

"Yes," he said into it. Then, "It's about time. Send them on up."

Then he hung up.

"There's no fixing this, Mr. Cooper," the man at his side said. He looked absolutely ill as he glanced at the screen then away again. Jess thought there was something familiar about his round face and blond hair, but she couldn't quite place him and wasn't inclined to try. Instead, she was busy trying to think of anything, any sliver of a plan, that might save them. "Once it's out there on the Internet like this, there's no calling it back."

"There has to be."

A barely audible click and the whisper of the doors opening announced the arrival of the elevator.

Automatically, Jess glanced over her shoulder. Her eyes widened. Her heart wobbled. Her breath stopped. She turned, leaning back against the desk for support.

Mark walked into the room, a new, barely congealed gash in the left side of his forehead, his face tight with stress, tension apparent in the controlled way he moved, but very much alive. Their eyes met. Her soul sang hosannas. The icy grief that she'd been keeping so carefully isolated suddenly melted and turned into a rush of thanksgiving that surged through her veins.

It was only then, as her world righted itself on its axis and she drew a deep, cleansing breath, that she registered the identity of the man right behind Mark: Fielding. He was pointing a gun at Mark's back.

Chapter 33

"MR. COOPER. LOWELL." Mark nodded grimly at the two men behind the desk. Only then did Jess realize who the second man was: Harris Lowell, the President's Chief of Staff. With Fielding still behind him, Mark walked toward them. Guards and goons alike watched him carefully, but with Fielding's gun on him and outnumbered seven to one, he apparently wasn't considered a threat, because they let him come. Jess saw the sideways glance with which he took in Maddie's presence, as well as the subsequent narrowing of his eyes and thinning of his mouth. Maddie was sitting up now, tearstains on her face, looking at Mark with renewed hope.

Hoping was foolish, Jess told herself sternly as she caught herself hoping, too. The odds were so high—too high. Mark was still alive, yes, but he was in no better case than Maddie and herself: He was a captive, almost certainly slated to die.

"Mark." Cooper's eyes pinned him. His expression was unfriendly, to say the least. "If you'd kept a lid on Annette like I asked, none of this would have happened. How the hell are we gonna fix this?"

"Ms. Ford posted videos of the President all over the Web," Lowell said, gesturing unhappily at the monitor, where one of the films was playing. "It's bad. As bad as can be."

Mark reached the desk. He was so close his sleeve brushed hers, so close she could see how very raw and painful-looking the gash in his forehead was. It looked like the kind of thing that could have been gouged out of his flesh by a bullet. Had he been shot, as she'd thought, and that was the result? Even with Fielding and his gun behind him, Jess was so glad to see him that a warm little glow filled her. It must have shown in her eyes, because his eyes warmed in turn and he gave her a quick, intimate smile.

"It was the President's phone that I picked up right before the car wrecked," she told him. "Mrs. Cooper must have found it that night before she ran away from the White House. There were videos on it...." She gestured at the monitor. The graphic images spoke for themselves.

"My question is, how did you know Annette had it?" Mark asked Cooper. He was very calm, but she could feel his stress. He was wound tight, his edginess apparent in the hardness of his eyes and jaw, the tautness of his shoulders. Behind him, Fielding's face could have been carved out of stone.

"David called me and told me. He realized his phone was missing as soon as he got up to the residence from that damned dinner for whoever it was. He was panicking, because he knew what was on it and that she must have taken it. She'd been threatening him with divorce, you know. He guessed she was going to use those damned pictures against him. That boy always was a fool when it came to women."

"So you had Annette killed to stop her from using the videos against David in a divorce?"

Cooper grimaced. "Hell, no. I had her killed to save his Presidency. If they'd got out it would've been over.

Now that I've seen 'em, I know he wasn't exaggerating one bit about that."

"They are out," Jess pointed out. "They're everywhere. It's over, Mr. Cooper."

"Nothing's ever over, Ms. Ford." Cooper's eyes met hers. "If you'd died in that wreck like everybody else, none of the rest of this would've been necessary. But you didn't, you lived and you remembered and you talked and you put these damned pictures on the Internet, so that's where we are."

"You'll be charged with murder, Mr. Cooper." Lowell sounded like a man in shock. "Hell, they'll charge me as an accessory after the fact, even though I had nothing to do with killing the First Lady and just got on board later to try to clean up the mess. The President . . ."

"He was out of the loop," Cooper said. "He suspects some, but he doesn't know."

"He'll have to resign just on account of these videos, if nothing else," Lowell said.

"No." Cooper shook his head. "I've been thinking. We can claim the pictures are fakes—claim it's a look-alike and not David at all. There'll be some talk, maybe some things printed in rags like the *National Enquirer,* but they can't prove it's David, and we can face it down. There's no proof of anybody murdering anybody. Annette died in a car accident, pure and simple. Davenport committed suicide without anybody threatening to reveal that he'd been embezzling from his firm for ten years or more if he didn't kill himself and take this young lady with him—which the damned drunk failed to do. His secretary—hit-and-run. That reporter—car accident. It's all nothing. It can all be explained away. The only people who know otherwise are right here in this room." Jess knew what was coming. A thrill of fear shot down her spine even as Cooper looked around at his guards. "I want you—all of you—to take these three people here away and shoot 'em, then hide their bodies where they won't ever be found. Hennessey, I'm putting you in charge of that. We can't afford any screwups on this, you understand?"

"Yes, sir." Hennessey—the second goon—nodded and drew his gun.

"Oh, please, I'm having a baby! I don't want to die!" Maddie cried, bolting up from the chair and darting toward Jess. Jess's gaze shot to her. Her heart clutched. Her stomach turned over. Her arms reached out for her sister. . . .

Horror grabbed Jess by the throat as she realized Hennessey's gun was tracking Maddie.

"Maddie!" she screamed, lunging toward her.

"Please, please . . ."

"Get down!"

Mark dived on top of both of them. Even as she hit the stone floor hard, Jess realized Mark had a gun. He was rolling, coming to his feet, aiming . . .

And screaming into his sleeve, "Where the hell are you guys?"

A split second later a dozen armed men burst from the elevator, yelling, "Freeze, Federal agents!"

AN HOUR LATER, it was all over. Having taken Mr. Cooper and Lowell away first, the FBI was now loading the last of Cooper's private security personnel into vans. Put together from former federal agents, Cooper's team had all the skills of the real thing with none of the legal restrictions. Mark had been glad to learn that the men who had been trying to kill Jess and, later, both of them, had been Cooper's employees rather than Feds. The thought that he had killed two fellow agents had bothered him. Knowing that they were basically thugs for hire eased his conscience. It also saved him from the scrutiny, hearings, etc., associated with the killing, no matter how justified, of another operative.

"I'm so glad you came." Wrapped in a blanket, her hands freed, Maddie was in the backseat of Fielding's car, which Mark had "borrowed," if one wanted to use the term loosely, which he did. He was driving them—her and Maddie—back to D.C. Maddie to be dropped off at her sister's, and Jess—well, he had other plans for Jess. "I was *so* scared."

"So was I." Jess sat in the passenger seat beside him, smiling at him. She'd been smiling at him basically ever since he'd hauled her up off the stone floor in Cooper's house, with the occasional hug thrown in, and as soon as they got somewhere private he was going to demonstrate in a big way just how much he appreciated that. She shivered, looking at him. "I thought you were dead."

"Is that what was scaring you?" Maddie sounded indignant. "You thought *he* was dead? I thought *we* were going to die. That's what was scaring me."

Mark smiled at Jess. "Yeah, well, when I heard that Hennessey and Smith had caught up with you at your mom's house, my whole life flashed in front of my eyes. Their MO is to kill people on the spot."

"Jess talked them out of it," Maddie said. "With her computer stuff. It was probably the webcam that did it."

"So what happened after you were shot?" Jess asked. He had already told her that, just as she thought, the crease in his skull had been opened up by a bullet, which fortunately had ricocheted off his thick skull.

"I was knocked unconscious for a little while. When I woke up, two guys were carrying me through the park. I guess the other two had gone for the car or something. That made getting away from them fairly easy. I circled back to see if I could find you, but you were gone. Not knowing where you were or what was happening to you took a few years off my life there, I have to tell you, because I knew they would be coming after you hard.

So I tried to think how to wrap this thing up before they got to you. I was desperate, so I called Harvey Brooks—he's a lab guy I know. I had him run some tests on the Lincoln to see if some kind of impact had caused the crash, and lo and behold, when I called him he told me there was evidence that a bullet had been fired into the right rear tire, blowing the tire and probably causing the crash. Anyway, he came and picked me up, and while I was waiting for him I took the opportunity to go over those phone number printouts again. Know what I found?"

He looked at Jess, who lifted her eyebrows at him. "What?"

"Remember how Prescott called Fielding, Wendell, and Matthews right before the crash?"

"Yeah?"

"Right after Prescott called Fielding, Fielding placed a call to Wayne Cooper. To his private cell phone. I happen to have that number, too, so I recognized it. So much as I hated to think it, I knew from that Fielding had to be the one." He had already told Jess that Fielding was the man who had attacked her in the hospital, the man who'd said "sugar" downstairs in his house.

"Then what?"

"I had Brooks call Fielding and tell him he had some real sensitive information on the death car, as everybody was calling it, and could he come over so he could tell him personally. I knew that if Fielding was involved, that would get him, and it did. When he got there, I tackled him and, uh, basically got him to confess the whole thing." No need to tell Jess and Maddie that he'd been so terrified for Jess's life that he'd put a gun to his old friend's head and threatened to blow out his brains unless he told everything he knew. The thing was, he would have done it, too. By then he'd been sweating bullets worrying about Jess. If anything had happened to her, he had realized, it would have been a blow from which he would never have recovered.

"I'm sorry Fielding was involved." Jess's smile turned sympathetic. She reached over and patted his leg. Mark had to fight the urge to stop the car and take her in his arms. With her teenage sister in the backseat, though, he refrained.

"During the course of our conversation, I reminded him that there had never been a traitor in the Secret Service. You know what he said?" He glanced at Jess, who looked questioningly at him. "He said he wasn't a traitor. He said he was doing his job, protecting the President and the presidency. Of course, he was conveniently overlooking the fact that he was on Wayne Cooper's payroll, too."

"I guess he had to justify what he was doing some way," Jess said.

"I guess." Mark frowned out the windshield. They were back in D.C. now, cruising along the Beltway, which was thin of traffic at this time in the morning. "Once I knew the whole story, knew he was the only agent involved, I called up the chain. Arrangements were made, and Fielding was offered a sweetheart deal if he cooperated. See, by that time Fielding had gotten a buzz on his radio to let him know that Hennessey and Smith had captured you." He cast a glance back at Maddie. "And a sister. I didn't know which one it was until I got there."

"Glad to know I'm important," Maddie muttered. Jess threw her a quick grin.

"After that, we had to move fast." No need to mention how sick with fear he'd been that he'd get there, get to Cooper's house where they were taking Jess, and it would be too late. It had been at right about that time that he had realized just how crazy about her he really was. But that was something to go into with her later. In private. "The deal was, Fielding was going to get me in there so you'd have some protection. The others were going to wait until Fielding and I were inside before storming the place, just in case one or more of the guards managed to get off an alarm. What everybody wanted"— him most of all—"was to get you two out of there safely."

"Which you did." Jess's smile was bright enough to light up the inside of the car.

"I was never so glad to see anybody in my life," Maddie said. "Oh, wait, get off here, Sarah's house is two streets over. On Clay."

Mark pulled off the next exit. The streets of the quiet residential area in which he found himself were dark and deserted. Even the trees looked lonely. He looked for Clay.

"There's no chance Wayne Cooper can buy his way out of this or something, is there?" Jess asked.

Mark shook his head, found Clay, and turned onto it. "I was wearing a wire, so everything Cooper said—which was pretty much a thoroughgoing confession—is on tape. Add to that what you put on the Internet, and the whole gang is going down. Wayne Cooper is looking at spending the rest of his life in prison, and David will have to resign. Vice President Sears will wake up this morning to the happy news that he's going to be the new president."

"You know, Mrs. Cooper might not even have released those videos to the public," Jess said, as Maddie directed him to the third house on the left. It was a single-story brick ranch house with a bike lying in the driveway. Mark was glad he saw it before he ran over it. "She might just have used them to get what she wanted in the divorce."

"Clearly, that was a chance Wayne Cooper wasn't willing to take." Mark cut the lights and killed the engine. The house was completely dark, and he didn't want to wake everybody inside. "Having his son be president meant the world to him. He worked toward that his whole life."

"I have a key." Maddie unfastened her seat belt. "You all don't have to come in with me if you don't want to. In fact, if we're not supposed to talk about this to anybody, it'll be better if you don't."

In the interests of national security, Jess and Maddie had been asked to keep quiet about what had happened until the story could be officially released. They had agreed.

"I really don't feel like facing Mom and Sarah right now," Jess confessed. Mark didn't say anything, but he absolutely agreed with her there.

Maddie slid out. "This has been fun, guys, but . . ."

"I'll walk you in." Jess got out, too. They closed the doors, and Mark watched as the two of them walked side by side to the front door. They hugged, Maddie let herself in, and Jess headed back. She was small, he registered, watching her, and boyishly slim, and her beauty was the quiet kind. But it was definitely there. Along with so much more. Brains. Guts. A loyal, loving, kind heart.

She was, in fact, the kind of woman he'd been looking for all his life. Who knew he'd find her right under his nose?

She got back in the car then, and before he turned the motor on he leaned over and kissed her. Hard and long.

When he drew back at last he said, "Remember that conversation we were meaning to have later?"

"Yeah?"

"I'm crazy in love with you," he said, and kissed her again. Kissed her until he saw a light come on in one of the bedrooms inside the house.

Then he drew back, turned on the engine and lights,

and started backing out of the driveway. This was a moment he didn't feel like sharing with anyone but her, much less her whole clan.

She was looking at him with absolute stars in her eyes. Mark felt his heart kick into overdrive.

"Oh, yeah?" she said.

"Yeah." He backed into the street, shifted into drive, and headed toward the intersection. "If you want, I could take you home with me and prove it."

"Sounds like a plan," she said, and smiled at him.

Chapter 34

"TO MY DAUGHTER. And the young man she's going to marry." Judy was on her feet, glass in hand, delivering the toast with a broad smile.

The young man in question, the father of Maddie's baby and her new fiancé, turned bright red. Maddie glowed. Jess and Sarah and Grace beamed at her. Seated farther down the table in Pat's Steakhouse, where Jess's family had gathered en masse to celebrate Maddie's engagement, Mark saluted with everyone else and took a sip of wine. Beside him, Jess was looking lovely and so happy that her sisters had teasingly asked if she was sure she wasn't the one who was getting married, while casting sly looks at Mark.

"Don't be silly," she'd answered. But her flushing cheeks had told the real story: They were in love. Like Jess, Mark was happier than he'd ever been in his life, and he was sure it showed. The icing on the cake was that Jess liked Taylor and Taylor liked Jess. In fact, they got along so well that Mark suspected they would start ganging up on him any day now. For the present, though, he and Jess were taking it slow and just enjoying each other. After all, they had all the time in the world.

A month had passed since the night in Wayne Cooper's mansion. For the good of the country, no public question had been raised about the accidental nature of Annette Cooper's death, and the few who knew the truth had been asked to keep silent. David Cooper had been allowed to quietly resign, and President Sears and his family now occupied the White House. Wayne Cooper, Harris Lowell, and a number of Cooper's private security personnel had been killed in the crash of a private plane less than twenty-four hours after Mark had last seen them alive. Officially, the terrible accident had dealt the final blow to David Cooper's ability to govern. Unofficially, Mark was sure it hadn't been an accident at all. The shadowy forces whose job it was to make things that were bad for the country go away had once again performed with impressive efficiency. The videos that Jess had uploaded to the Internet had even been rendered harmless. The originals had been impossible to recall, but damage control had begun immediately. Mark had heard through the grapevine that they had copied the videos, digitally replaced David Cooper's face with that of the leaders of all the major nations, and uploaded those as well. The resulting uproar had been considerable, but all the videos, including David Cooper's, were subsequently proclaimed fakes and the public's attention had shifted elsewhere.

The wheels of government continued to turn without a hitch.

"So are you and Mark coming by the house?" Judy asked Jess when the meal was over and the group was saying their good-byes before leaving the restaurant.

"Not tonight. I start my new job tomorrow, remember?" It was a Sunday night, and Jess had to be in her new office at a law firm that had done business with her previous one by eight a.m. Monday. She'd been excited when the position had been offered to her, and since she was excited, Mark was excited for her. Just like she was happy for him when he got the transfer he wanted into the investigative arm of the Secret Service.

"You won't be so busy working you'll forget you're going with me to try on dresses Saturday, will you?" Maddie asked Jess as she came up to them, pulling her bashful fiancé by the hand. "I have to have my maid of honor with me."

"Wait a minute. I thought I was your maid of honor," Grace objected.

"You're all going to be my maids of honor. I'm having three," Maddie said, as Sarah, holding her sons by the hand and followed by her husband, joined them. "And you're all helping me choose my dress this Saturday. And so is Mom."

"Technically, I'll be your matron of honor," Sarah pointed out. "Your *only* matron of honor."

"Unless Jess . . ." Grace turned twinkling eyes on Jess.

"Not happening," Jess said firmly, and tucked her hand in Mark's arm. "Come on," she said to him. "We're going home now."

They were living together in his house. Jess had gone home with him that night a month ago and basically had never left.

"Sounds good to me," he answered, smiling.

"I'll see you Saturday," she called over her shoulder to her mother and sisters as she and Mark left the restaurant. It was dark, with a full moon just beginning to climb the sky, and the area around the restaurant was busy. Mark found himself struck by the exchange he and Jess had just had, and thought it over as he opened the door of his new car for Jess and she got in.

A moment later, he slid behind the wheel and looked at her.

"Just so you know, for a long time my house was just a house, a place where I slept and changed clothes. It wasn't a home."

"Are you saying it is now?"

"Yeah," he said. "Because you're in it. That's the difference."

He leaned over and kissed her. Then he drove her home.

May 1, 1981

"MOMMY, SOMEBODY'S WATCHING US from the woods again."

Five-year-old Marisa Garcia grabbed a handful of her mother's pale yellow cardigan sweater as she whispered the warning. The angora knit was fuzzy, and soft, and she hung on for dear life, bobbing along behind twenty-nine-year-old Angela Garcia like the tail on a kite as she stared fearfully at the dark shape she was sure she could see hiding in the undergrowth beneath the trees that crowded close to the gravel driveway.

A wind blew through the branches, making them whisper and creak. Marisa looked away, shivering, and tightened her grip on the sweater. There were no lights on in the house yet, no lights visible anywhere because the car headlights were off and they lived out in the country now, with no other houses nearby. Only the moon peeped at them over the swaying treetops, a pale sliver of light that looked thin as white tissue paper pasted against a dark purple sky.

"There's nobody in the woods, baby." Her mother's tone was of patience stretched thin. Her arms were full of groceries, and she was walking quickly through the grass, which was wet from the rain earlier in the day, toward the back door of their small brick house, without even bothering to look around at the woods. She thought Marisa was making things up. She always did, because Marisa did make things up. Sometimes.

But not now.

"Yes, there is." But Marisa said it hopelessly, because she already knew nobody was going to listen.

"Marisa's a baby. Marisa's a baby. . . ." That was her brother, Tony, who was almost seven. Swinging the grocery bag he was carrying over his head so that the Cheerios and hamburger buns and bag of potato chips inside threatened to fall out, he danced around, making faces at her.

"*Stop*, Tony." Her mother was grumpy tonight, because they were late getting home. It was already full dark out, which meant it had to be getting pretty close to seven, and her dad got home at seven, and if supper wasn't on the table when he walked in the door, he got mad.

When her dad was mad, he scared her.

Sometimes—she knew it was bad to think it, but sometimes—she didn't really like her dad.

"Here, Marisa, take this." Her mother thrust a grocery bag at her. Her mother didn't like her hanging on to her clothes. Marisa knew that because Angela was always telling her, so she knew giving her the grocery bag was supposed to make her turn loose. She did, letting go of the soft wool and taking the bag because her mother wanted her to, and she always tried to be good, even if she didn't always succeed.

"I got put in time-out today." Tony said it like he didn't care. He'd been getting in trouble at school *a lot*, and it worried Mommy. In fact, a lot of things seemed to be worrying Mommy lately. She didn't smile much anymore. Not like she used to.

"Oh, Tony, what did you do?"

Marisa tuned her mother and Tony out, and concentrated on carrying her grocery bag, which had the *eggs* in it, which was important because it meant her mother was trusting her not to drop it. Marisa's other arm was wrapped protectively around Gina, the nearly life-sized doll she had gotten for her birthday last week. Gina was so great, a My Best Friend doll that all the girls at home had, and she'd been wanting one so much but never expected to get one because they cost *a lot*. Gina even looked like her with the same black hair and clothes and everything, and getting her would have made it the best birthday ever, if they hadn't been living *here*. She hated this new house, hated her new school, hated the kids who called her fat even though she wasn't. She was *healthy*, Mommy said. And Marisa hated that Daddy was living with them all the time now, instead of usually being away. But most of all she hated the woods that rose up on either side of the house, looking like big black chicken-claw hands all winter and now that the trees had turned green casting a shadow over the house and yard so that even in the middle of the day it always seemed dark and scary. There were *things* in the woods: creatures with glowing eyes that she could see from her bedroom window at night, and lately there'd been people. She had never actually really *see* them, not as anything more than dark shadows hiding in among the trees, but she knew they were there. She knew they were mean. She'd tried to tell her mother and brother before, but they wouldn't listen. Now one of the shadow people was back again. She could feel the weight of eyes on her, feel the person's dislike even across the distance that separated them, and scrunched up her shoulders protectively as she hurried up the back stairs in her mother's wake.

As soon as the door opened, Lucy came bounding out, barking her head off and jumping on them all and then running around in circles because she was so glad to see them. Lucy was their dog. She was big and black and furry—a mutt, Tony said—and they'd had her for as long as Marisa could remember. They'd brought Lucy with them when they'd moved to Kentucky from Maryland last fall. Lucy didn't like Kentucky either, Marisa knew. They had to keep her locked up in the house all day because this new house didn't have a fence, and they didn't have enough money to put one up, and Lucy liked to chase the neighbor's cows. What kind of place had *cows* living next door anyway?

I want to go home, she thought as they all, Lucy included, piled into the small, ugly kitchen and the light was turned on and the door was safely shut and locked behind them, closing out the night and the woods.

Home was Maryland, a nice white house with lots of other houses around it and only one big tree in the yard. She missed it so much that whenever she thought about it, she felt like crying, so she tried not to. But tonight, because it was dark outside and they were late and her dad was probably going to be mad and there was someone in the woods, she thought about home again.

Her chest started to feel all tight, like it did sometimes when she remembered.

"Here, quick, let's get dinner going. Marisa, you can set the table. Tony, get Lucy's leash and take her out in the yard and put her on her chain." Her mother was already ripping the plastic off a package of hamburger and dumping it into the big silver frying pan on the stove. From that, and the red box sitting on the counter beside the burner, Marisa knew what they were having: Hamburger Helper.

It was okay, not her favorite.

"Be careful. There's somebody out there in the woods," she told Tony as she started to get some clean plates out of the dishwasher and he took Lucy, clipped to a leash now so she wouldn't go running off after any old cows, back out into the dark. She'd propped Gina in a corner so the doll could watch. She would have liked to have her sit at the table, but Tony would have made fun of her, and Daddy wouldn't have allowed it. Only her mother understood about Gina.

"There is not, turd brain," Tony said, and her mother sighed.

"I got an award today," Marisa told her mother when they were alone. She didn't like to tell things like that in front of Tony, because he would feel bad because he never got any awards, and that would make him *be* bad, and then he would get in trouble and that made *her* feel bad, so she just didn't do it. The award was a big silver medal that hung from a blue ribbon around her neck, and she lifted the metal disk for her mother's inspection. "For being a blue-ribbon reader. See, it has my name on it."

Her mother stopped stirring the hamburger stuff to look at the medal and then smiled at her. "Wow, Marisa. Good job. I'm really proud of you, baby."

Marisa smiled back. Sometimes, when she was alone like this with Mommy, it was almost like they were at home again. Like nothing had changed.

"Dad's home." Dragging a trail of mud in with him, Tony stomped into the kitchen, letting in a cool, damp-smelling breeze that fluttered the blue-checked curtains over the sink before he slammed the door. The kitchen was already smelling like cooking hamburger stuff with a whiff of gas from the leaky burner, so the outdoor scent just kind of mixed in.

"Oh." Looking harried, her mother grabbed a can of

green beans and a can of corn from the bags that hadn't yet been emptied and jammed the can opener into the top of the beans. The sound of it creaking around the lid joined in with the sizzle of meat and thud of Tony's muddy shoes as he kicked them off and, from outside, Lucy's barking. "Go put your pajamas on, Tony. You've got mud all over your jeans. And wash your face and hands while you're at it."

"Lucy kept jumping on me. She got me muddy."

Lucy didn't like being left outside all alone in the dark. She didn't like being fastened to a chain, either. Like Tony and herself and Mommy too, Marisa suspected, Lucy just wanted to go home.

The beans and corn were in pans, the pans were on the stove, Tony was nowhere in sight and Marisa had just picked up Gina when Michael Garcia came in through the back door. He was wiry, and he wasn't all that tall, but in his jeans and flannel shirt and boots, he looked enormous to Marisa. A baseball cap was jammed on his head, and beneath the brim, his mouth and eyes were tight.

Daddy's mad.

She could tell as soon as she saw him. Clutching Gina tight, sticking her thumb in her mouth, she sidled closer to her mother, and never mind that she'd been told time and time again not to get too close to the stove.

"God, I've had a hell of a day." Looking from Tony's muddy tracks to the grocery bags crowding the counter, shaking his head at what he saw, he shut the door, then walked into the middle of the kitchen to dump something on the table. Pressing back against the cabinet by the stove, close enough to her mother now so that she could smell the nice scent Mommy always wore to work, Marisa clutched Gina closer and sucked harder on her thumb. "Supper isn't ready yet? You've got to be kidding me."

"I just got home myself." Her mother never acted mad at her dad, never yelled. She just got quieter when he was around, like she was trying to stay very calm. Marisa guessed that sometimes her mother was afraid of him, too. "It'll be just a minute."

"What's that you're making?" He looked at the pans on the stove and frowned. "That crap again?"

"Money's tight, Mike."

"You blaming *me* for that?" He sounded so angry that Marisa's throat went dry. She would have clutched at her mother's skirt if she'd had a hand free. But she didn't, so she could only stand there and try to be invisible. "We moved down here to hicksville because of *you*."

"I know."

Trying to be invisible didn't work, Marisa discovered. All of a sudden, her dad's eyes focused on her. Marisa's stomach lurched. When he was in a bad mood, he had to take it out on somebody. Usually it was Tony, because Tony was so much noisier and bigger and harder to miss. But Tony hadn't come back from putting on his pajamas yet, probably on purpose. So that left Mommy and her.

"Get your thumb out of your mouth," he barked so loudly that Marisa jumped, and he drew back his hand like he was going to smack her. It scared her so much she almost wet her pants. She pulled her thumb out of her mouth, then stuck the hand with the wet, glistening, telltale thumb behind her back. She knew sucking her thumb was bad. He'd told her before.

"Supper's ready." Frying pan in hand, her mother turned away from the stove to start dishing the food out on the plates. "Marisa, go get Tony, would you please?"

Marisa nodded, edged around her mother, and, with a last, big-eyed look at her dad, fled the kitchen. Only she walked, because she knew seeing her run away from him would make him madder.

"Don't you start on her, Mike. I'm not going to stand for that."

She could just hear her mother's low voice as she

went into the hall that led to the three small bedrooms and their one bathroom one way and, the other, to the living room.

"You're going to stand for any damn thing I tell you to stand for—got that? After what you did, you owe me, and don't you forget it."

"I'm making up for it, aren't I? I'm here."

"You're here, all right. And we both know why."

None of that made any sense to Marisa, and she didn't hear anymore because she found Tony. He was in the living room, curled up in a corner of the couch, wearing his pajamas and watching TV with the volume turned down real low, because he didn't want to do anything that might attract their dad's attention unnecessarily.

"Supper," Marisa announced, then added in a confidential whisper, "He's mad."

"He's a dick," Tony said bitterly, and Marisa's mouth dropped open in horror. They weren't allowed to say bad words. But then Tony never seemed to care about what they weren't allowed to do.

"Tony! Marisa!" their mother called.

Tony got off the couch. "You better leave the doll in here. You know he doesn't like you to carry it around everywhere you go."

"Thanks, Tony," Marisa said humbly, because it was true. Daddy had already yelled at her about it, and he got really mad if he had to yell about the same thing too much. She carried Gina to her bedroom, propped her carefully against the wall by the door and went in to supper.

Nobody said anything much while they ate, and Marisa finished as fast as she could. When it was over, Daddy said he was going out and left, and the rest of them gave a big sigh of relief.

She helped her mother clear the table while Tony did his homework with them in the kitchen, and then her mother fixed her bath. She was just getting out of the tub and her mother was just wrapping her in a towel when they heard Lucy barking outside.

"Your daddy must be home," Mommy said with a sigh.

Marisa's stomach got a knot in it.

A moment later came the sound of the kitchen door opening and slamming shut.

"Angie! Angie, you get your ass in here!"

Her mother was still crouched down beside her, still rubbing her with the towel. Her hands stopped moving, and she went really still as she looked toward the kitchen. Then she stood up fast, but not before Marisa saw fear flash into her eyes.

"Get your nightgown on and get into bed. Tell Tony I said go to bed, too." Her mother's voice was quiet.

"Mommy." Marisa wanted to hold on to her mother, but she was already gone, her skirt swishing as she moved fast down the hall. By the time Marisa had her nightgown pulled on over her head she could hear her dad shouting, yelling loud, nasty things. Her heart started beating really fast. Goose bumps rose up on her skin with a prickle. Trying not to listen, she picked up her medal and hung it around her neck, then went to get Gina. Hugging the doll close, she started for Tony's room, to tell him to go to bed. His door was closed. She thought he probably had it locked, which meant she was going to have to knock, which meant Daddy might hear and come into the hall and see her.

She felt all shivery inside at the thought.

A giant crash from the kitchen made her jump. Then her mother screamed, the sound so loud and shrill it hurt her ears, and her dad shouted. Marisa's heart lurched as a terrible fear gripped her. There was a sharp bang, then another, like firecrackers going off in the house. An icy premonition raced down her spine.

"Mommy!"

She ran for her mother. A second later, Marisa found herself standing in the kitchen doorway, her eyes huge and her mouth hanging open as she looked at the most terrible sight she had ever seen. Her heart pounded so hard she could barely hear over it, and she had to fight to breathe. With one disbelieving glance she saw her dad lying facedown on the floor in what looked like a big puddle of bright red paint and her mother turning to face her with the front of her yellow sweater turning bright red, too, like something was blossoming on it, some awful flower that was getting bigger by the second as it gobbled her up from the inside out.

Mommy. But Marisa was so terrified now that, although her mouth opened and her throat worked, no sound came out.

"Run, Marisa," her mother shrieked, her face white and terrible. "Run, run, *run!*"

There was another person in the room, Marisa saw as beyond her mother something moved. Instantly she knew in her heart that it was one of the shadow people from the woods. Seized by mortal fear, she whirled around and ran like a jackrabbit with her mother's screams echoing in her ears, darting through the living room, bursting out through the front door as the cool night air whooshed past her into the house, leaping across the wet grass that felt cold and slippery beneath her bare feet, flying into the darkness as the shadow person gave chase.

There was nowhere else to go: sobbing with fear, she ran into the woods.

MIND-ATTACK!

About halfway, by Rissa's guess, across the shallow jungled bowl of valley, they saw the mountains come into view. Only their upper reaches showed above the cloud layer that hid the valley below...

Suddenly Tregare's face twitched and he fell silent; the scout jerked with the tremor of his hands. Rissa's head gave a stab of pain; her vision blurred...

From Stonzai came a groan. The Shrakken's sidewise-moving eyelids closed tightly, and the V-mouth made a triangle that bared clenched teeth. Words came.

"It—it the *Tsa* is!"

THE
ALIEN
DEBT

F. M. Busby

BANTAM BOOKS

TORONTO • NEW YORK • LONDON • SYDNEY • AUCKLAND

THE ALIEN DEBT

A Bantam Book / June 1984

ISBN 0-553-24176-1

Published simultaneously in the United States and Canada

Bantam Books are published by Bantam Books, Inc. Its trade-
mark, consisting of the words "Bantam Books" and the por-
trayal of a rooster, is Registered in U.S. Patent and Trademark
Office and in other countries. Marca Registrada. Bantam
Books, Inc., 666 Fifth Avenue, New York, New York 10103.

To Laura, *who sparked this book*

Contents

—THE—
ALIEN
DEBT

I. Lisele

*I*ntroduction to "A Short Study of How UET Gained and Lost Power Over the Planet Earth," a thesis for the 2nd Junior Degree by Liesel Selene Moray, ages 8-½ bio and 18 chrono, approx.

In this paper written for Professor Diebolt's history department in the Junior University at Sancia Leckaby Spaceport, I will try to cover everything important from when the United Energy and Transport conglomerate won the sixth corporate bidding election and its Presiding Committee took over the rule of North America, to the time when the space fleet headed by my father, Bran Tregare Moray, freed Earth and dissolved UET's government.

UET controlled most of Earth from 2004 to 2103, and those weren't good years to live here. UET's Committee Police were bullies and killers, and their Total Welfare centers were slave camps. Rissa Kerguelen, my mother, was put into a Center when she was five (since she'd never left Earth, she had only one age) and was there for eleven years, almost. Her brother Ivan Marchant, my uncle, was in there even longer. There are books that explain about Total Welfare, and I've read two of them. But all you really need to know is that when somebody was Welfared, UET took over everything that person owned and owed, and put the "client" into big barracks-type buildings where everybody wore jumpsuits and ate in messhalls. Male and female sections were separate, and each had three divisions: Pre-pube, Post-pube, and Adult. Those last two would be sent out in work gangs, but most of their pay went to UET; the clients did get a little bit credited to their Welfare accounts, and the idea was that they could someday earn their way out of Welfare. But the way UET had it set up, nobody really did. The way my mother got out was by

1

winning a big lottery prize. And the funny part was that she hadn't bought the ticket; her supervisor was doing a crooked trick with Post-pube clients' credits and it backfired. That's all I know about it because she doesn't like to talk about Total Welfare much.

Another thing that began in 2004 was star travel. I think everybody knows by now that UET didn't invent it. An alien ship came here, and UET killed the aliens and stole their ship and copied it. Then they sent out colonies and did other things. But some ships Escaped and set up their own colonies which were called the Hidden Worlds because UET didn't know where they were. When my father took *Inconnu,* the first armed ship ever to Escape, UET called him "Tregare the Pirate." But you've seen on the Tri-V, I expect, how on the planet Number One he got six ships together and went to take over UET's fortress world Stronghold, and made a bigger fleet there and came back and took Earth away from UET. My mother helped, too. I was born on Stronghold, which is why I have two ages and know firsthand what the Long View is all about.

The Long View has to do with relativity, when you ride a ship that gets up close to the speed of light. I don't know the math yet (I get that next year, I think) but I do know that when we came from Stronghold to Earth it took about six months by ship's time and close to ten years by any planet's time. So if you ride ships very much, you have to keep the Long View in mind.

Those aliens that UET killed are called Shrakken; my parents have met some of them but I haven't. Tregare, my father, captured a ship of theirs and made a deal to use it for a decoy when he went into Stronghold. He gave me some pictures of them, which I will put in the Appendix to this paper.

We don't know much about the Shrakken; they are very strange. Sometimes they kill people, but my mother says they don't do it on purpose, because they have to lay eggs in a living creature the same as digger wasps do, and she likes them anyway. But when they lay eggs in people it kills the people. Caused trouble, for a while.

I was too little to do any of it myself, of course, but my family and friends had a big part in getting rid of UET's slave system. That's why a lot of them are on the Board of Trustees of Earth. There's Rissa and Tregare, my parents. Then my dad's parents, Liesel Hulzein and Hawkman Moray. I'm named for Grandma Liesel and for my other grandma, Selene Kerguelen, that UET killed when my mother was five. And there's Mom's brother Ivan Marchant and his mate Ilse Krueger, and my great-aunt Erika Hulzein who is Grandma Liesel's older sister.

If you don't know about the Hulzein Establishment, which Erika merged with the rest of our government last year, it was based on a parthenogenetic dynasty that lasted five generations, and was one of the few power groups that managed to hold out against UET. Parthenogenetic means a mother having a daughter with no father. It's not the same as cloning which never worked out very well, because the Hulzein method fertilizes one intact ovum with the nucleus of another from the same person. I'm not sure why this works better, but the details are outside the scope of this paper, anyway. However, my mother did this to have my baby sister Renalle, who is enough younger than I am that we won't have to have sibling jealousy, since I'm practically a half-generation in between her and my mother. My Grandma Liesel explained to me about that, and I'm glad she did, because Renalle is really a very nice baby.

There are quite a few more Trustees but for most of the list I think I'll wait and tell about them when they come in the main thesis. Except for why they belong on the Board. It's not a hard and fast thing, but several were ship's captains for Tregare when he took Stronghold and then squadron commanders in the fight for Earth. Tregare goes with people who do good work.

That's true of the new Trustee; you saw on the Tri-V about the appointment, probably. Derek Limmer, with the scarred face—he and his wife Felcie Parager stayed behind to run Stronghold for Tregare and only came to Earth this year on one of the new Hoyfarul faster-than-light ships. Their son Arlen was my best friend on Stronghold and he used to be my same bio-age, nearly, but now he's nine years older because he stayed on Stronghold while Tregare's fleet chewed time. And then coming to Earth by FTL, Arlen didn't put much difference to his two ages. It seems strange, but that's the Long View for you.

There are a lot of other important people but as I said, I can tell about them when the time comes. Now I should end this introduction and get on with the main body of my thesis.

Note to Professor Diebolt: The main report, I'm afraid, will have to wait until we get back. I mean, the new armed FTL ship *Inconnu Deux* is going down-arm toward the galaxy itself, to help the Shrakken against some enemy that won't stop to talk; they only attack.

Some of the Board didn't see why we should go help the Shrakken, but Tregare says it's only common sense. That if these other aliens wipe out the Shrakken, we could be next. And Rissa, my mother, swung the Board vote by pointing out that if it weren't for the Shrakken we wouldn't even *have* star travel, because UET stole it from them. So we owe them, she says, and I think she's right. Also when she says that humans and Shrakken have killed each other, one way or another: "And that book is balanced; let us close it."

So *Inconnu Deux* is being readied to go down-arm. I don't know just when, but soon.

Rissa and Tregare aren't sure whether I'm going with them. But I am.

II. Rissa

*D*rying her long, dark hair, Rissa Kerguelen studied the tentative roster of *Inconnu Deux*. About a quarter the number she was used to: in a standard hull, Pennet Hoyfarul's FTL drive left much less room for quarters and supplies. Luckily, increased automation allowed the smaller crewing.

For a moment, Rissa frowned. It would be good to travel again with her brother, Ivan Marchant, but why wasn't his mate, Ilse Krueger, coming along? Trouble between those two? Since Ilse's disfigurement during the battle for Earth, her stability had sometimes been cause for worry.

No problem about the Kobolak twins, Anders and Dacia; those two had joined Tregare at Stronghold. Anders was bringing his wife, Alina Rostadt; Dacia remained persistently unattached.

Arlen Limmer: every time Rissa saw the young man she thought of how his father might look, without the terrible scars from UET's Space Academy. And Derek had incurred those scars when he was younger than Arlen was now.

Haskell Ornaway? Oh, yes! The ambush by misled cadets, when she and Tregare went to "civilize" the Academy. The boy who stood cradling a broken arm and asked the chance to redeem himself. Well, he'd made it.

She scanned down the list, finding no more familiar names. Two dozen adults, then, in all. Plus, despite Tregare's misgivings, young Lisele and her parthenogenetic half-sister, Renalle.

And, of course, Stonzai the Shrakken.

Hair coiled and piled high, Rissa stood and stretched. At the bio-age of twenty-eight, probably she could use more exercise, but she still looked and felt trim. If she'd changed much in the past five years, since the retaking of Earth, she couldn't detect it. Of course if she'd never *left* Earth, she'd be eighty now. Yes, there was something to be said for having two ages!

The door opened and Tregare entered. "Bran. You are home early." With their two decimeters difference in height, she was accustomed to stretching a little to kiss.

Lovemaking of late had been scarce. After Rissa's slow recovery from Renalle's difficult birth, pressure of work and social obligations had been intrusive. Especially now, with the preparations for *Inconnu Deux*'s mission. So Rissa did not misread the messages of Tregare's eyes and hands. "There is time?"

"Should be." And on this occasion came none of the vagrant pangs left over from parturition; Rissa's cry of triumph came unbidden, as though someone else had made it. Then she lay relaxed.

Sitting up, Tregare grinned. "Back to your best, eh?"

"Or near to it. And, Bran—thank you for your patience." As they dressed, she said, "Bran? Does Stonzai come here alone for your meeting tonight, or with other Shrakken?"

"One other. Her mate: Sevshen, I think the name is. Hasn't much English, Stonzai reports, but is working on it. Stonzai, now—she came onscreen for a minute when Dacia called from the port—Stonzai claims she's studied the tapes you gave her back on Stronghold. But she still piles all her verbs in one place a lot."

Rissa smiled. Yes, the Shrakken leader had always given English a rather Germanic syntax, not easy to understand. But still, Rissa looked forward to seeing the alien again, and this evening's gathering would provide the occasion.

In preparation for that planning session, Tregare left to check the computer terminal and holographic projector that were

newly installed in the dining area. Rissa went to see to her infant
daughter, and found Renalle just waking. The weaning medication would stop Rissa's milk soon, so while they could, mother
and daughter might as well enjoy the intimacy of feeding. Soon,
making little sounds of contentment, the baby nuzzled. When
she was satisfied, Rissa played with her until renewed signs of
drowsiness appeared, then called the nurse from the next room.
"Tonight it must be bottle feeding, for once the meeting begins I
cannot count on getting free of it."

The woman nodded, and Rissa decided to look in on her
older daughter. Entering Lisele's room, Rissa wondered why the
child's choice of furnishings gave such an unchildlike effect. At
any rate there would be no greetings or discussion now, for the
girl sat crosslegged before her biofeedback console, obviously in
the semi-trance "alpha state." Well, the regimen seemed to be
relieving tensions from the competitive pressures of the Junior
University. As Rissa watched, Lisele breathed evenly and deeply.

Her dark, wavy hair, currently rather short, set off her pale
skin well. Tall for her age, she'd grow to be taller—though not
so tall, Rissa hoped, as the twenty decimeters of Tregare's father,
Hawkman Moray. Tregare's eighteen, she decided, wouldn't be
too bad. . . .

Turning to leave, she saw a sheet of readout trailing from
Lisele's computer terminal, and gave it a quick look. Yes; the
child was revising her thesis-introduction. Rissa smiled, then
nodded: Lisele had her facts reasonably straight and clearly
stated.

She checked her chronometer. As she had expected, it was
time to rejoin Tregare.

She found him arranging potables at the small bar, set to
one side of the dining area. Across that room sat the electronic
gear he had come to inspect; presumably he was satisfied with it.

Now he glanced up and saw her. "Come have a drink.
There's time to talk a little." Since Renalle's birth she had only
recently resumed use of any alcohol at all; the mixture he poured
for her was quite dilute.

Sitting in adjacent, padded bar chairs, they clinked glasses
and sipped. "Thank you. Yes—the *Deux* roster. You list only
names, nothing of rankings or positions."

He nodded. "Well, you won't know the Engineering people; they're mostly new to space. All trained with Hoyfarul's
FTL group but only one of them has two ages." She waited, and
he said, "Control officers, then. You're my First Hat, of course,

and I like Anders Kobolak for Second." Rissa made to speak, but Tregare said, "Third, now—you remember a kid named Hask Ornaway?"

"Yes, after checking the name on computer. The ambush—and I am glad he has turned out well. But I do not understand—"

"You object to him?"

She shook her head. "No. But my brother Ivan—"

"What about him? He's coming with us; you agreed to that."

"Tregare! Ivan Marchant was Ilse's First Hat on *Graf Spee*, and then Coordination officer for Falconer squadron. Yet now you give him no Hat at all? Is he to serve as a rating, under an untried boy like Ornaway?"

"Easy." One hand warded off her urgency. "Ivan's my Gunnery chief, rank roughly equal to First Hat but outside the Hats' chain of command, answering directly to me. For the fancy turret setup you designed, I think that's a full-time job."

Her eyes narrowed. "Outside the command-chain, you say. Yet he will answer not only to yourself. Any Hat who happens to be watch officer can call him to account."

Tregare's fist thumped the bar. "As my representative, sure. Same as the Chief Engineer takes orders, no matter *who* calls from Control. I don't see any problem."

Rissa paused. "Why, Bran? And you know what I mean."

Slowly, he nodded. "All right. In the battle for Earth, Ivan broke. Cut loose from his duties and went all-out after Admiral Ozzie Newhausen."

"And got him. Do not forget that."

His hand sliced air. "Got him, sure. But dumped every squadron responsibility, right in the middle of combat, to do it. No, Rissa. I value Ivan and you know that—but I want him where his skills will help and any lack of discipline can't hurt." Briefly, he grinned. "For his backup, I've assigned Dacia Kobolak."

Anger ebbing, Rissa said, "I cannot argue, Bran—though I wish I could." Her other thought, that Ivan's willingness to leave Ilse behind might be a trouble sign, she did not mention.

The afternoon's first arrival was Dacia Kobolak's scoutship. These small spacecraft, ordinarily carried by the fleet's full-sized ships, did not have interstellar range but found use in and near planetary systems—or as emergency lifeboats. They were designed to accommodate twelve passengers—but from this one, only a pair of aliens followed Dacia down the ramp.

Reaching ground, the sturdy redhaired woman still led the way. Behind her the tall, thin Shrakken, each wearing only a sort of harness hung with bulging pouches, came with their toe-dancing gait. Unlike bears or humans, Shrakken were not planti-grade. As Tregare put it, "The heel is a hock; that's where the extra height is." And indeed they were tall—at least the equal of Hawkman Moray. The taller one, Rissa recognized—squinting against dust raised by the landing—as her old acquaintance Stonzai, commander of *Sharanj*, the ship Tregare had captured on Number One so long ago. Commander wasn't quite the correct term among Shrakken, Rissa knew, but close enough. Now she noticed that Stonzai's ocher skin was brighter than her companion's, its brownish clown-markings more clearly defined.

Closer now, Rissa saw eyelids blink horizontally across the black triangular eyes, each surmounted by a stubby pair of tendrils. The inverted-V mouth made what Rissa knew to be the equivalent of a smile. Passing Dacia with a quick, one-armed hug, Rissa moved to meet the Shrakken. "Stonzai!" and as when they had parted on Stronghold, each reached out fingers to touch the other's forehead.

Head moving in the Shrakken way that was neither nod nor shake, Stonzai spoke. "Again meet we; I to do so had not thought. But when in space we to Limmer talk, says he safe it is, us here to come; those here who Shrakken killed, now not rule. True, this is?"

"Yes, Stonzai. And—" She paused; it struck her that the other Shrakken had said nothing. And Tregare also stood quietly, as if uncertain. Rissa said, "Stonzai, do you remember Bran Tregare?"

"Remember, yes." Stonzai moved toward him, and without hesitation Tregare returned the forehead touch. Turning to her companion, the Shrakken said, "Sevshen, now also must you," and when the other did not move, spoke in their own language. Then Sevshen, too, came to both humans and exchanged the touch. Rissa's relieved sigh surprised her; she led the group indoors.

Surveying the dining area's golden-brown walls and glittering ceiling, Stonzai hissed approval. Tregare moved to the bar, and suddenly Rissa realized she had no idea whether Shrakken used alcohol. She opened a bottle and sniffed at it, then passed it to

Stonzai. Again she'd forgotten something; Shrakken had no visible nostrils. But Stonzai, holding the bottle near her open mouth, inhaled with a whooshing noise. Then she handed the liquor back. "I not this use."

Tregare shrugged. Before Rissa could think of anything to say, Stonzai pointed to the array of other bottles. "These, not have I try. Different, they be?"

With a grin, Tregare said, "Different flavors, same principle;" his gesture welcomed her to sample further, and she did, opening one bottle after another and whooshing at it. Three she set aside, but the next—a brandy—she handed to Tregare.

"This I use." But before he could pour from it she said, "Do you, wait," and methodically she worked through the entire lot, approving only a few. "These, good are." Curious as to the alien's criteria, Rissa peered at the bottles and found her answer: grape versus grain. Brandy, cordials and most wines, Stonzai approved; whiskeys, rums, rice wine, she rejected. Mentally shrugging, she watched Tregare do the honors; without asking, he added ice to the spirits and handed glasses to the two aliens. They sipped, and each gave a short hiss.

For Rissa and himself he set up bourbon and ice, lightening hers with water, then said, "Let's sit down, shall we?"

Human-built chairs did not fit Shrakken very well, but a low divan seemed to suit them. And now Rissa spoke. "Tell us, Stonzai, about your enemies."

From down the galactic Arm the Tsa came. How far? Stonzai didn't know. How long since they had first appeared? The Shrakken's considerable time in space, shrinking time near light-speed, did not help Rissa guess at the period involved.

When Tsa came upon Shrakken they killed them, or did their Tsa best in the attempt. After the first meeting, no parleys, only attack. Tsa ships, said Stonzai, were comparable to human or Shrakken: in size, power, acceleration, and turning ability. So with the Shrakken's "home field" advantage of shorter supply lines, the first and second waves of Tsa attacks had been beaten off. Losses, yes. "Ships where all Shrakken dead were, or lacking minds were." But no major damage to Shrakken planets.

Then, after a lapse of time indeterminate to Rissa if not to Stonzai also, a third and greater assault had come. And that one had nearly succeeded. "Whole worlds, dead are. Or, like blind animals, remaining Shrakken crawl, and for roots dig." Stonzai blinked. "For food, to find. More good, I think, dead to be."

"Yes," said Tregare. "From what you say, Stonzai, I have to agree." The temperature was mild, but sweat beads stood on his forehead.

To Rissa the point was clear. As Derek Limmer had reported, after meeting in space the Shrakken ship that then brought Stonzai to Earth, one more Tsa attack wave might well finish the Shrakken, might disrupt their civilization past rebuilding.

Tsa weapons? Tregare asked it. According to Stonzai, the Tsa's gunnery was more potent than Shrakken but less so than what she'd seen of Tregare's. At Stronghold he'd given Stonzai samples of the latter, for good will. But what with travel times—*the Long View*—the Shrakken could hardly have duplicated many by now.

The mind weapon, though—and now Rissa listened closely, for here seemed to be the crux of the danger. Leaning forward, holding the empty glass that Tregare wasn't alert to fill, Stonzai said, "Close enough the Tsa come, and like claws in the mind they reach. Of it, die, some do; others, to ship's danger, wrongly act. Tsa strikes, not the own self you be." She made a crooning groan. "What they do, to fight against, none can."

Frowning, Tregare asked, "*How* close, before their mind gadget gets to you?" In human-Shrakken communications, translation of quantities had never been a strong point, but after a time Rissa decided that the mind weapon's range had to be slightly greater than that of Tsa or Shrakken gunnery—somewhat less, therefore, than *Inconnu Deux*'s turrets could muster.

She said as much; Tregare shook his head. "The grade of approximation we have here, that's no real handle." At Rissa's frown, he added, "No, our one edge is FTL, the Hoyfarul Drive we're taking to Stonzai's people. Without that, considering the distances, we'd be pretty useless as allies." And thinking the matter over, Rissa had to agree.

Stonzai produced one other datum: Tsa was the enemy's own name for its species, not a Shrakken coinage. But how this fact had become known, Stonzai could not explain.

On that subject the discussion ended. And then other guests began arriving.

As house staff relieved Rissa and Tregare from bartending and serving duties, the two took station to greet—informally—the new arrivals. Many of these Rissa did not know; her work dealt with coordination, while some now present worked with other Board members in their own specialties. But in the greetings Tregare dropped hints to tell Rissa what those specialties were.

As her brother Ivan approached with Ilse Krueger, Tregare said, "That's about the lot. You want to go pump those two, and ease your mind, feel free."

Smiling her thanks, Rissa faced the newcomers. Ilse Krueger showed few visible signs of her old injuries; the small woman moved like a young girl. Her blonde hair, chin length and curly, hid most of the scar that ran from mouth corner past where her left ear had been, up into the scalp. The thin white line no longer pulled her mouth askew. But Rissa knew the hair covered scar tissue that closed the former earhole; Ilse was half deafened. One touch of a heat beam did it; her survival was sheer luck.

First the handshakes and polite words; then Rissa took each by a hand. "Come, let us have drinks, and talk."

Grinning, teeth glinting against his pale skin, her brother pushed back a lock of dark hair. "You mean, ask questions."

"That, too." And when the three found drinks and sat down, Rissa began. "*Inconnu Deux* will be out a long time. What is wrong, that you agree to such an indefinite separation?"

"Well, it's just—"

"The trouble is—"

Speaking together, then Ilse and Ivan smiled at each other and explained in turn. As the Board's trouble-shooter, Ivan was away from home more than not. But groundside, usually—whereas Ilse, in charge of combat training programs on the cadet ships, was in space quite often. "We're apart so much," said Ilse, "that we can never settle differences. All we do is tippy-toe around everything, to avoid argument." And Ivan nodded.

"So the answer," said Rissa, "is to be together not at all?"

"Trial separation," said Ivan. "Then maybe—"

"And meanwhile," Ilse put in, "it won't hurt either of us to be free people for a time."

Ivan shook his head. "No, Ilse. I've said it before; you be free if you wish, but it's not for me." He stood and walked to the bar. His stride, Rissa thought, would not encourage anyone to get in his way.

Ilse turned the talk to *Inconnu Deux* and kept it there. Well, the smallest person ever to survive UET's Space Academy *had* to be rather stubborn. Then it was time for dining—and the long discussions, buttoning up the needs of *Inconnu Deux*.

Hagen Trent, the ship's chief engineer, impressed Rissa. Young for his rank but balding early, his enthusiasm matched his obvious intelligence. He had studied directly under Pennet Hoyfarul, and after a tour in space he hoped to work in the improvement of FTL-drive design. His hand brushed the bulky curly fringe of his remaining hair. "We're still in the first phases. A few more years—" Then the man's female companion needed his attention, and he was led off toward the snack buffet.

Rissa's glass was empty; she strolled to the bar. A distinctive bottle attracted her attention—berry brandy from the planet Far Corner. She pointed, and the young attendant poured her three centimeters of the ruddy amber fluid. Sipping the tart flavor, she remembered—one-armed Bret Osallin, killed so long ago in Peralta's mutiny, had first offered her this drink. So long ago . . .

The lights blinked—Tregare's signal that business would commence—and Rissa brought her mind from Far Corner to Earth.

With considerable juggling of dials but less swearing than Rissa expected, Tregare got the holographic projector stabilized. Then, on the computer keyboard he punched combinations. In the dimly lit end of the big room a belt of white stars appeared.

His hand moved; one star turned green. "Us," he said. More movement, and a group of stars, spread among others that were unaffected, glowed a darker orange. "The Shrakken suns. Not entirely accurate, I expect, but the best info we have." Another touch, and two lights went red. One, the nearer to Earth, blinked. Tregare pointed. "Shaarbant, that one. Peripheral to the main volume of Shrakken space, and a good place to refuel on our way to Stenevo, their major world," and he pointed to the other red star.

"The distances we're talking about—well, more than half the width of our galactic Arm, and down it a little less than that. We and the Shrakken, both, have expanded more along the arm than across it. Shaarbant's closer to us than any other Shrakken world. So that's where we go first."

Beside him, Stonzai said something Rissa did not hear. Tregare nodded and made another adjustment; now several of the orange lights began to blink. "These, mostly toward the inner-arm side of Shrakken space, are the ones the Tsa have attacked." Nearly half, Rissa saw, of the Shrakken total. Tregare touched more keys, and four of the blinking stars dimmed. "Dead worlds," he said. "Killed by the Tsa."

He looked to Stonzai, but the alien gave no further sign.

Tregare stepped back from the terminal. "For now, I guess that's all the briefing." But then there were questions, and he answered them; the meeting lasted another hour.

Three days later, *Inconnu Deux* was on its way.

III. Elzh

*L*ong, now, since Elzh with seven ships left dear homeworld. Long enough to cross much of space shown on the Tsa-Drin chart, passing wide of mindbeast planets that knew the Tsa. Scouts had found new beastworlds; these the Tsa-Drin had charted for Elzh to study, and if possible, to destroy. As correct, as understood. To learn, then to obey.

From when Tsa first met beasts, Tsa must fight—Tsa ships against beastworlds, lest beast ships come to Tsa worlds. Since beasts gave Tsa no peace, then beasts must die—though the toll, in Tsa minds and Tsa lives, was frightful.

But, to obey. Seven ships and the Tsa-Drin chart, and only a few more cycles to the new beastworld. To obey.

But now, to gather. Freeing thought, Elzh began mindsay.

In the nest. Grouped with Idsath and Tserln, mindsay soft and murmurous, Elzh felt warmly indling. Nothing to hurt, as always between Tsa. Except—until their sex-progression stabilized, Elzh's incomplete maleness gave irritation, an itch without satisfaction. *No matter* (Idsath); *soon.* Fully ready as moderator, Idsath—to accept and blend Elzh's genes and Tserln's, and return them to Tserln for fruition. Had the Tsa-Drin plan allowed for increase, all of that would happen. Now, though, the first stages, in themselves ecstatic, could not go on to completion. Tserln, when wholly female, would bear that frustration of deep Tsa instinct.

As you accepted it (Tserln, to the unworded thought), *shall*

I, also. Touching as fully as now might be, the three shared warmth.

Then time to leave the nest, to share food instead, and with others of the crewing. Still, touching could be, but lesserly—as correct, as understood. Mindsay, with so many together, was slower—each giving much quiet between sayings.

Even so, dread of beastworld grew in Elzh's thought. To mindsay the fear would lessen it, but Elzh did not.

IV. Tregare

*E*ighty hours from Earth, the *Deux* passed light-speed; Bran Tregare shrugged in relief. It wasn't that he distrusted the Hoyfarul Drive, but after all, he'd grown up believing in Einstein. Not that the ship's ellipsoidal, coherent drive field, which shielded the *Deux* from the effects of a hundred gees or more, contradicted "Saint Albert"—not exactly. Velocity still built mass, but that mass appeared in parallel continua that held no other matter. "In fact," Doctor Hoyfarul had once said, "it's possible that the drive *creates* those extra universes. I can't vouch for the idea, either way."

And when Tregare insisted that mass was still mass, and required force to accelerate it, Hoyfarul's laugh shook the wattles at his throat. "In a continuum with all mass concentrated in one object," he said, "how do you define acceleration? Or, for that matter, motion?"

Tregare laughed too, then, and gave up the argument. Now, with all the *Deux*'s external sensors—except the gravitic detectors—showing zerch, the ship was unmistakably outpacing light. But it wasn't chewing time, or not by much; in FTL travel the "Long View," the passage of years while the ship experienced only months, was not a factor. Not much of one, anyway. There was still a residual second-order effect in the "home" continuum, but it was logarithmic and grew very slowly. At their top speed for this voyage—about 120 lights, Hoyfarul had estimated it—time-dilation would only briefly exceed three-to-one. As compared, Tregare reflected, to the twenty-to-one average for STL runs. No, this time—on a run of about one year, subjective—his two ages wouldn't diverge much farther.

Satisfied, he nodded to his watch officer, Anders Kobolak, and left Control. Boots clattering on the stairs, he headed downship. About now, he figured, Rissa would be feeding baby Renalle. In case she might like some coffee, after, he stopped by the galley. Ivan Marchant, sitting with Dacia Kobolak, waved a hand. "Bran! Have we passed light yet?"

"Surest thing you know." Tregare filled a small carafe with coffee. "I wonder if I'll ever get used to having most of my instruments go dead, this side of C."

"I know," said Ivan. "I was on Hoyfarul's first test flight; remember? But our inside sensors, the inertial ones, do integrate thrust measurements and give us valid course vectors."

"And speed and position, and maybe what's for breakfast next," Tregare said. "It all works; yeah. But still—" In his own voice he heard the plaintive note. "I do miss the hell out of my old *Inconnu*!" He held up the carafe. "I'll get this down to Rissa."

He found Rissa closing her blouse and beginning bottle-feeding. "I am nearly dry now, Bran, but still she likes to test me."

"Smart baby." Wordless signals set him to pouring coffee for Rissa and himself. He said, "You check the freeze-chambers lately?"

"Yes. Stonzai and Sevshen both seem stable; though Dacia felt unsure of dealing with the Shrakken metabolism, it appears she has done well." The problem had been the onset of Stonzai's ovulation. The ship carried no host animals for her voracious larvae, and now, after repeated use, the anti-ovulation drug caused increasing side effects. So freeze was the only reasonable answer—and since Sevshen understood little human speech, he joined his mate in cryogenic stasis rather than remaining awake and isolated.

"Right." Then Tregare had another thought. "Let's turn the freeze-chamber checkup over to the comm-tech of each watch, should we? I mean, with the outside circuits dead, up here above light, those people haven't much else to do." Rissa nodded agreement.

The *Deux*'s freezers had features new to Tregare; for one thing they could double as emergency acceleration tanks, with or without the freezing function. Sure as peace, he thought, progress sometimes did complicate things!

Hunger satisfied, the baby pushed the bottle aside. Rissa burped her, cuddled her, and put her down for sleep. As Tregare poured warmups for their coffee, Rissa sat. She said, "Our timing and position, Bran. Are there enough data yet, to check Hoyfarul's estimates?"

He spread his hands. "Not for certain sure. We have better accel than the earlier FTL ships. Time ratio, though—now we've passed light, there's no way to check it. But going by what we do have, I think the curve's flatter than the doc predicted."

Rissa nodded. "Then the difference between any person's two ages here will increase less than we had thought." Her brows raised. "As of now, how do the figures look?"

"Guessy." Too much coffee had Tregare's nerves on edge. A drugstick would have helped, but he and Rissa didn't smoke those when Renalle or Lisele were around to breathe the stuff. The sticks weren't harmful; a doctor at the Junior University had suggested Lisele use them for her tension problems. But Rissa and Tregare had misgivings about putting so young a child on a chemical crutch, and now, of course, she didn't need it. Too bad, Tregare thought, he couldn't make biofeedback work for *him*. Shrugging, he poured himself a short drink. *First today*.

He thought back to Rissa's question. "Our time to Shaarbant, maybe a subjective year. If our data's accurate—not to mention, if I figured it right—we use up about two-and-a-half years, groundside time, getting there."

Her eyes widened. "So many? Then, even without the shorter trip on to Stenevo, if that is needed, or any consideration of time spent groundside on either world, by Earth's clocks we shall be gone at least five years. Ilse and Ivan—she is not young, Bran!"

Tregare sighed. "If you don't know what makes those two tick, how could I? Maybe they're *pfft* and this is the polite way out."

"No. Ivan told her, she might consider herself free if she chose, but he would not do the same. I—"

Wanting out of a problem that gave him no handle on it, Tregare interrupted. "They married freestyle. What Ivan does, or doesn't, is his own business. But if he doesn't, I miss my guess." While he had the floor, he added, "Ilse isn't all that old.

Maybe eight years, she has on Ivan. You think a few more are going to bother him all that much?''

Obviously unsure, Rissa frowned. "When we were taken to Welfare I was five, and Ivan eight. But since then, it has been as though I were the elder, to worry about him."

A way out of this, maybe: "He had it rough. Any place in UET was a good place to keep your head down. *You* did, by instinct. Ivan was just at the age when he couldn't. And suffered for it."

She nodded. "Perhaps you are right. And in no case will it profit me, to worry so far into our subjective future years."

Well, now. Off the hook. And then Lisele came to tend her sister while her parents went to the galley for dinner.

Three weeks later Tregare reran Haskell Ornaway's astrogation figures through the computer. The tall young man, running fingers over his close-cut blond hair, looked anxious. "Did I get it right?"

"Seems so." However accurate the measuring systems were, they were all the ship had. In theory, inertial instruments measured thrust, along-course or lateral, and integrated the cumulative effect with respect to time. Tinhead, the computer, gave results in terms of velocity and ship's position.

There was a fudge factor: the frictional coefficient of the "interstellar gas." Either it varied or it didn't. But within limits of error, the *Deux*'s position as determined by inertial means checked with gravitic detection of landmark stars. So Tregare said, "We came out with the same answers, anyway."

Visibly, Ornaway relaxed. "Sir—Tregare, I mean—were you as nervous, your first trip, as I am?"

Tregare snorted. "Me? With Butcher Korbeith commanding, and every few days lining up all the cadets naked and maybe thumbing one of us to be spaced out the airlock? *Nervous?* I was scared shitless the whole time."

Face reddened, the boy's gaze dropped. "I'm sorry. I should have thought. It's only—"

Tregare gripped the other's shoulder. " 'sall right, Hask. Don't mind an old-timer's stories. And you're doing fine." He took one more scan of the monitors, decided they weren't telling him anything new, and left Control. Thinking: *Yes, the kid's shaping up into a good capable Third Hat.*

Ambling downship, Tregare mused. The trouble with FTL travel was no *input*, to keep the mind interested. On the ship's monitors, nothing from outside except the gravitic readings. No possibility of signals from another ship, not that any others were apt to be in this part of space. Why, it was almost as bad as riding cargo!

Heading for quarters he passed the galley and looked in. Seeing Rissa at a table with her brother Ivan, Dacia Kobolak and Arlen Limmer, he got himself a cold beer and joined them. "How's it shake?"

Looking a little tense, as he often did, Ivan Marchant shrugged. Rissa said, "Now that only the drive room has any real work to do, we are running out of diversions. I know the Shrakken data tapes by heart. If only Stonzai were not in freeze! Then we could talk, at least, in search of new information."

Arlen Limmer didn't look bored. At seventeen the swarthy youngster, still thin and gawky, had matched his father's height. He said, "I've got so much to learn, it keeps me busy. Navigation, comm-panels—for when there's someone to talk with—and next week I start learning gunnery."

Patting his hand, Dacia said, "You're lucky," and went on to detail her own boredom. Between her and Rissa and Ivan, the talk was working into a real gripe session.

Tregare quit listening; he almost had an answer. What had Arlen said? "Oh, sure! Gunnery practice."

"What?" At least three of them said it together.

"Gunnery practice. A contest. Maybe a series of them, if the idea catches on. Three teams, say, to share the six peripheral turrets." He thought back; yes, all six were rigged for computer simulation runs. "Now for team captains we want our three best gunners. Rissa and Ivan, I know you're tops, but who's next in line?"

Ivan laughed. "Dacia is. She's crowding the both of us."

"Not quite," said the redhead. "But I should, one of these days, with all the coaching you've given me."

Arlen Limmer frowned. Jealous, Tregare wondered, of the woman's headstart in gunnery? No matter; thoughts fully into the new project, he asked Rissa to set up the teams. "Spread the trained ones around as evenly as you can figure it. But *anybody* can enter as novices, assigned at random. Let's see; that's eight to a team, and—"

"Not exactly. *I* want to try, too." Tregare turned. He hadn't heard his daughter come in, but there she stood, and he knew the determined expression on her face.

"Why not?" said Ivan. "I'll bet you have the reflexes for it." The child waited until Tregare nodded and then Rissa, before she thanked them, got a glass of fruit juice, and left.

Looking after her, Rissa said, "Contesting with that one, novice or no, it may behoove all of us to sharpen our skills."

"I'm not worried," said Tregare. And he wasn't; he'd never been much in the gunnery line, anyway.

A day later, though, he climbed to Turret Two, to see how rusty he really was at converging a pair of laser beams on target and heterodying them to produce peak infra-red energy. "Melts a hull like going through cheese, if you're tuned right," was a fair description of the effect.

Working the turret controls against computer-simulated targets, Tregare felt sweat bead his hairline. His right-hand lever controlled an ellipse on the screen before him; when he tilted it straight, it became a circle, which meant he had his heterodyne right. To either side of the screen was an indicator light; the left one blinked and he moved the other lever to extinguish it. Both lights dead meant his convergence—his range—was also correct; within the screen's circle a dot appeared; signifying that he'd scored a hit. The circle tilted; he corrected; the simulated distance made a rapid change and his left hand moved again. When the computer run ended, his readout tape clunked out one number. Forty-eight. He grimaced; throughout the run he'd held destructive energy on target only 48% of the time possible. *Not too good—and that run was an easy one.* But at least he hadn't used the emergency override pedal, that doubled the combined range-heterodyne tolerance to let the gunner try desperation shots. And scored only half-value when hits *were* made on override.

Tregare stood. All right, he needed more practice. But now, time to check the watch log. First things first.

On the log, no problems. An anomalous blip where, above light speed, none should have been—but then a component-failure (and replacement) entry, initialed by Haskell Ornaway, that explained the discrepancy. Tregare nodded. Good mainte-nance—that was what kept a ship working. He headed down toward quarters.

On the galley landing he heard voices. "—that old man!" Arlen Limmer sounded like a bear with a sore ear; rounding a turn, Tregare found the youngster gripping Dacia Kobolak's arm.

"Four years older than I am," she said. "And you're nine younger, so that makes me an old woman, doesn't it? If I—"

"He's married!"

"Freestyle. Arlen, don't—" Limmer was the first to see Tregare; his hand squeezed the arm. Looking around, Dacia stopped talking.

Well. None of Tregare's business, likely. He said, "Hi, people," and walked past them and on his way downship.

After Rissa came off watch, she and Tregare ate together— his lunch, her dinner. Now, as she briefly nursed Renalle, they had time to talk. "—one problem, yes," she said. "Perhaps this ship is designed *too* efficiently. On the old ones we had nearly a hundred people; here we are only two dozen, and personal interactions may become overly important."

The baby fell into sleep, and Rissa put her to bed in the adjoining compartment. Now Tregare lit one of the small, black cigars he habitually carried but rarely smoked. When Rissa was back, he said, "How long's it been going on? And how far?"

Her hair hung loose; the headshake rippled it. "To both questions, I am not certain. Ivan spends much time with Dacia, and young Arlen—" Her smile was lopsided. "Not to make sport of him, but he *is* seventeen, and follows her like a puppy."

"You shipped on *Inconnu* at seventeen—and I was nearly the age Ivan is now."

"I have never allowed you, Bran, to apologize for your coercive behavior at that time. But if you continue to remind me—" She smiled, though, so he knew she wasn't really angry.

Still, he scowled. "So, are Ivan and Dacia into anything yet?"

Another headshake. "If they are, it is none of our concern. But Arlen thinks so, and he is infatuated and quite jealous."

Then Tregare got the point. "Yeah. If Arlen gets a bug up his nose and jumps Ivan, without giving your brother time to think before he moves—" He stood.

"Yes," Rissa said, "that is what concerns me." Her brows lifted. "Bran—where are you going?"

"To talk to somebody."

"To whom?"

"Whoever I run into first. I don't care which."

As it happened, he first came to Dacia Kobolak's quarters. Well, all right—it was her show, too. He knocked, and after a wait the door opened. Dacia looked a little mussed-up—and inside the room, so did Ivan Marchant. Ivan said, "Tregare, it's not what you think. I mean—"

"What I think, Ivan, makes no difference."

"Then why—?" Biting his lip, Ivan said nothing more.

"Yes, why?" said Dacia. "Because you've never been a nosy skipper."

"And I'm still not. Your business, the both of you, is your own. Young Limmer, though: he seems to think it's his, too." Tregare waited.

"Well, it's not." As she tried to pat her wavy red hair into order, Dacia's tone came cold. "I like Arlen, but his possessiveness gets annoying."

Before Ivan could speak, Tregare cut in. "What worries me is, if the kid blows up on Ivan. Because—"

Shrugging, Marchant said, "He's no danger to me; you know that."

"Hell, no!" Angered, Tregare said, "But you are to *him*!"

Ivan looked puzzled. "You think I'd hurt Derek's son, and Felcie's?"

"Course not, given time to *think*." Tregare saw Ivan's expression clear, and Dacia's. "But if he caught your kill-trained reflexes off-guard—you didn't break Ilse's wrist on purpose, Ivan, when she got a little rough on your honeymoon. But you still broke it. Y'see?"

Ivan's breath shuddered out. "I hadn't thought of that."

"Just so you do, now." Tregare's own sudden smile surprised him. "Well, that's all I had; see you." Turning, he left the room.

Back in quarters when he told Rissa, she said, "And shall you speak with Arlen also?"

"If the occasion suits. I don't think it's too important."

"But to arrange matters for him without his knowledge— that is to treat him like a child, not a man."

"Hmmm? Yeah, I guess you're right." So, first chance he got, Tregare sounded young Limmer out. The boy obviously had a real crush and a lot of jealousy, but his angry resentment of Ivan Marchant was not—it seemed—keyed to thoughts of violence.

What he said, glowering, was, "Dacia's not the only woman on this ship. I'll show her!"

Noticing a young comm-tech walk past, Tregare nodded in the direction of the slim, long-haired blonde. "Starting now, maybe?" The boy grinned, and turned to walk after her.

When Tregare reported to Rissa, she commented, "This young woman—Jenise Rorvik, I think? Is she unattached?"

Tregare shrugged. "I don't keep track. She's more the right age, though. A little older than Arlen, but not much."

Smiling, Rissa said, "And Arlen is not new to space; he has the cachet of two ages. I wonder if he knows how to make use of it."

The upcoming gunnery tournament, Tregare decided, did have the people interested. He'd run his own averages up into the high fifties including one fluke sixty-eight; he'd never be an ace gunner but at least he wouldn't let his team down.

Practice logs showed some novices making progress while others couldn't shoot fish in a barrel. Jeremy Crowfoot, the ship's computer expert, had an odd visual problem: he couldn't "see" the heterodyne circle and range lights simultaneously. So he had dropped out and would stick to programming the simulations.

But Lisele's entry evened the teams at eight members each. Noting his daughter's listed scores, Tregare chuckled. The child had speed and coordination, but her reach wasn't up to it yet; working with adult-sized gear she started well but tired quickly. She'd refused, though, the offer of an extension bracket to allow her to use the override pedal: "That's for your last chance, and uncle Ivan says none of the *good* gunners train with it."

Well, Tregare decided, she'd pull her weight on Dacia's team. Averages, nothing special, but surprisingly hot at the starts. He filed the logs away and took a summarizing look around Control. Everything running smooth, as usual.

No new input, also as usual.

Well, time for lunch.

V. Ivan

*H*e hadn't intended this. Nobody but Ilse, he'd told himself—not ever. Yet now as his pulse slowed again, it was Dacia his arms held. Red hair, not blonde, against his cheek—and a sturdy, full-bodied young woman instead of his tiny, wiry Ilse.

Perhaps his breathing changed, for Dacia said, "Ivan? Are you all right? You're not sorry, are you?"

"I—we shouldn't have, that's all. But—"

"You *are* sorry. Well, I'm not—except for how *you* feel. And surely you didn't plan to be some kind of monk the next two or three years?"

"I hadn't really thought it out." In his boyhood, years of UET's brutal "aversion therapy" had left him impotent. Later, under drug hypnosis, after Tregare had sprung UET's killer booby traps, Rissa had done something for his mind. So that the same day he met Ilse Krueger, he made love with her. And moved into her ship *Graf Spee*, working up to First Hat in short order. And never had any other woman.

He had now, though, and warm Dacia Kobolak looked unhappy. Trying not to be noisy about it, Ivan took a deep breath. "It's how I saw myself, you understand? All solid and permanent. Finding out I'm something different, it's a jolt. But no, Dacia—" A quick kiss, he gave her. "I'm not sorry. Just having a bit of trouble adjusting."

Her frown lines smoothed. "Then this won't be all of it?"

"You bet your little pink—I mean, sure not, Dacia."

"I'm glad." Up along his sides, to tickle, crept her fingertips. Slowly and gently, because he'd warned her of his reflexes and cited Ilse's broken wrist. So Dacia gave those reflexes due

23

notice that here was no attack. "Back on Earth, if you and Ilse are pair-closed, I won't argue. But now—"

Enough tickling; not harshly, he caught her hands. "Now? A little soon, wouldn't you say?"

"Not if you let me finish the sentence. Now, I meant, we can be together. And *right* now, aren't you hungry? I am." Pushing just enough, she rolled free of him and they dressed.

On their way up to the galley, Ivan tried to think. Ilse had *told* him to be free, hadn't she? But still . . .

They ate quickly, for Dacia was due on watch soon. As she was about to leave, Rissa joined them, and after a little talk, Dacia hurried away. Ivan stood also, but Rissa said, "Oh, stay a while; keep me company." Feeling somehow uneasy, he sat.

Eating slowly, Rissa asked no questions, but under her gaze his tension built. Finally he said, "All right, we're lovers. Just now, though; not before."

Her eyes moved slightly; that was all. "Ivan, I did not ask."

Even to him, his laugh sounded nervous. "No. You merely read me like a book."

"If so, a book I enjoy and respect. And what of this is my business? And what, that you think I might disapprove?" Rissa spoke softly, and in her face he saw no mockery.

He moved, not quite a shrug, and found himself telling Rissa his earlier thoughts. "I want it to be all right. Do you think it is?" And how had she come to be his arbiter?

Rissa pushed her empty plate away. "Ivan, our total experience shapes each of us. Yours has fixated you more upon Ilse than is—well, usual. More so than she could possibly be on you, for instance, since her life has been more varied." She smiled, then shook her head. "Between you and Dacia I see nothing wrong. Would it be better, on this ship, for you to share yourself only with your memories?"

While he was thinking that one over, she changed the subject, and Ivan found himself explaining his ideas, as Gunnery Officer, for best utilizing the seven-turret configuration Rissa had designed. Ordinarily a ship's nose carried eight turrets arranged in a circle, each with traverse and separate range and convergence controls. *Inconnu Deux* had a larger, much more powerful central turret, firing along the ship's axis only, without traverse capability, ringed with six traversible projectors that were also beefed up, somewhat, from standard. Considering the possibilities of the new setup, trying to adapt usual fire-control techniques, had cost Ivan more sleep than he'd care to admit. He did, though, have a few ideas.

"I've rigged some circuits. Tie all turrets to central control and fire strictly line-of-flight; in a tight spot you've got a lot of punch. Or hang the six peripherals together, traverse and all, under one gunner, and play 'Chopsticks' with 'em, against Big Baby in the middle. And—" He knew he sounded overly enthusiastic, like a kid, but what the hell? Until Rissa had to leave, they talked on.

Then Ivan went to his quarters—normally First Hat's billet, but of course Rissa shared captain's digs with Tregare. Pouring himself a mild drink, he sat to think a few things out.

First he tabled some questions. Whether he'd done right to agree to Ilse's desire for a separation, and to come on the *Deux*, made no difference. He was here; she wasn't. Case closed.

He hadn't realized, though, how much the trip would increase their biological age-difference. Let's see; he was thirty, and Ilse about thirty-eight. And if he had it right, she'd pick up seven or eight while he was adding maybe three. Well, that shouldn't matter, not really. *And Dacia was how old? Twenty-six.*

Dacia. Ivan had never minded the scars Ilse had from her brutal training at UET's "Slaughterhouse." But Dacia's unmarred skin—Ivan shook his head. Fixated, Rissa had said. Would he become fixated on Dacia's youth and beauty? To Ilse's cost? No, he must never let himself downgrade Ilse Krueger; she'd given him too much.

Which, for now, left him only one question. Should Dacia move into his quarters? Or rather, he realized, *when*?

A week before the gunnery contest, Ivan showed his file of combat-simulation tapes to Jeremy Crowfoot. "Your job now, Jere, to pick a good variety for competition. The coding on each run tells you whether it's a straight shot, skew curve, or whatever."

Tregare, sitting in, suggested leading off with easier runs, to help the novices get their feet wet. Crowfoot agreed. While the records showed him as part-Amerind, Ivan didn't think he looked the part: brown hair, ruddy skin, and freckles. Now the man said, "UET had these contests between ships' crews, right?" Tregare nodded. "What was the format?"

"Two ways," said Tregare, "depending on who ran the show. Butcher Korbeith liked one-hour sessions, nonstop. Wear everybody out and then call 'em quitters when their reflexes sagged."

"Whatever the other way was," Ivan said, "I like it better."

"Me, too," said Bran Tregare. "Okay—still an hour for each squad, but ten minute chunks, rotating between squads."

"Fine," Crowfoot said. "I'll do up six ten-minute sets, progressively harder but not predictable by pattern. All right?"

The session broke up. Checking practice logs, Ivan shook his head. Some novices had leveled off at their natural limits of skills, but a few had skimped practice. On Ivan's own team, for instance, Comm-Tech Jenise Rorvik.

Rorvik? Oh yes, the blonde that Arlen Limmer was chasing, lately. Except that he did it more when Dacia was there to see. When Dacia moved away, Arlen's gaze followed her.

Silently, Ivan groaned. Now, if he wanted to help his own team's scores, he had to spend time with Limmer's *new* girl friend. *Marchant—if you've got any tact, now's the time to use it!*

Finding Jenise and Arlen in the galley, Ivan approached them. Limmer looked up under lowered brows; the woman smiled. Well, say it right out. "How shakes it? Rorvik, with a week left before our shootout, you're short of practice. If you have time for a session now, so do I." And before the boy could react, "Like to come along, Limmer? Turret Six, plenty of room." He paused, then moved—knowing that if he'd timed it right, they'd follow. They did, and the three climbed to the turret.

Leading, Ivan took the gunner's seat. "I'll make sure everything's working right." He hoped for a complex run, a chance to show his skill, and that's what he got. He scored a sixty. "It's all on the money, Rorvik. Your turn."

Her first run was pathetic; she had the reflexes, but hadn't trained them. Ivan said nothing. Arlen looked at him, then turned to Jenise. "You have to coordinate your controls. Keep your eyes a little out of focus, to cover the screen and range lights both, without looking back and forth." She nodded. "Now imagine your left hand's connected to the lights; just move it toward the one that's lit, to put it out. No—not so *hard*!" Surprised, Ivan saw the boy was sweating. "And Jenise—imagine your right hand *on* that ellipse, and push just enough to straighten it up into a circle. Yes; and now—"

As he talked, her performance improved. At the run's end her score was still nothing to brag about, but most of the hits came toward the finish. Ivan punched the stop-button.

Arlen looked at him. "Did I do something wrong?"

"No. You did a lot of things *right*. Care to take over now, on your own? You don't need me, and I've got work piled up."

"Well, of course," said Limmer, "if you think I'm qualified."

"I think you are." Before leaving, Ivan turned back. "One hour. Ten-minute sessions, five-minute breaks. Agreed?" The two nodded. "And the same every day, from now to shootout?" Nods again. "Good. Thanks for helping, Limmer."

Arlen cleared his throat. "Glad to, Marchant."

A good line to end on, so Ivan went downship. By then he was hungry—and also a bit satisfied with himself.

First he went to quarters, to bathe and change clothing. Then to the galley, climbing fast—"on the high lope" as Tregare liked to say. And there he found the captain sitting with Dacia's brother, Second Hat Anders Kobolak. Lean and brown-haired, Anders didn't much resemble his fraternal twin. Ivan filled a tray and joined the two, half his attention on listening to the talk and half on eating. When he was down to coffee, laced with spicemix and sugar and something that pretended to be cream, he listened more.

"This awards setup, now," Tregare said. "To put a little zip in the gunnery contest. You tell it, Anders."

The way Kobolak put it, it sounded simple enough. Personnel scoring in the top third—except control officers and team captains—got graduated bonuses if they weren't in gunnery as a job, and points toward promotion if they were.

Ivan nodded. "Sounds good to me."

Tregare stood. "Me, too. Write up the skeds, will you, Anders, for the points and bonuses?" The Second Hat nodded, and Tregare walked away, leaving Ivan with Anders Kobolak and a fresh cup of coffee Ivan didn't really want. But now he could hardly leave without drinking it, and it was too hot to gulp.

His own cup dry, Kobolak sat silent. *What is he thinking?* Then, abruptly, the man said, "Is there anything we need to talk about?"

Ivan's sip scalded his tongue. "You're the one who asked."

Anders nodded. "Yes. Well—Dacia seems happier lately. To my mind, she's always been too much of a loner. I know that whatever happens here is temporary. But I hope she doesn't get hurt.''

Looking, Ivan knew the man didn't mean his statement as any kind of threat. "I hope the same," he said. "I'll try—"

"That's what I figured. But I'm glad you said it." The Second Hat stood, and left Ivan to drink the coffee or not.

That night, Ivan dreamed. A little girl was calling his name—a child with a red dress and long dark pigtails. He tried to go to her, but someone larger pulled him away. He shouted; they *had* to let him be with her. But between them the door closed. He woke, chilled but sweating, and realized that whatever the hour he was done with sleep. He got up, made coffee, and sat thinking.

The dream: the day, when he was eight and Rissa five, that they'd been taken to Total Welfare. It hadn't been quite that way, though. He couldn't remember directly, after the hashing his mind had taken from the Welfare Center's "discipline," but from Rissa he knew the Welfare agent had made them exchange their own clothes for grey-blue jumpsuits *before* taking them to the Center. So the red dress was earlier than the separation.

The dream still bothered him. By choice, he never looked back at the Welfare years. His insistence on wanting to see Rissa had hooked him into the punishment cycle immediately, and through all his twelve years in Welfare he'd never worked clear of that brutal routine. He didn't even remember meeting Rissa—after the lottery had sprung her loose and she in turn bought him free—at Erika Hulzein's, where the psych-techs had put his mind into somewhat better working order. He did recall the meeting, two bio-years later on the Hidden World called Number One, when Tregare's drug hypnosis defused his mind of UET's lethal booby traps. So then he'd joined Tregare, met Ilse, and . . .

His cup was empty. Filling it, he began scanning up, in the way he'd learned at Erika's, through his life from then to now. When he reached "now," he nodded and considered the dream again—but from outside it, not inside.

Whatever his subconscious was trying to say, he couldn't make the symbolism fit. Well, maybe the purpose was to do what he'd just done: review his entire past. But he'd found no new insights. *I could chew on this all night and get no place*.

Chew? Yes, now he noticed hunger, and nibbled slowly on some mixed-grain wafers, dunking each in his hot coffee first. Then he sat back and tried to let his thoughts float freely, toward whatever the dream's purpose might be. Relaxing, he almost dozed. Then a flash of violent memory brought him upright. *Why this?*

So clear, the visualization: almost as though he could scan it for details he'd missed at the time. The control room of *Graf Spee*, command ship for Falconer squadron when Tregare's fleet went from Stronghold to battle for Earth. Ilse at the controls, hell-bent for Ozzie Newhausen's UET ships. Good action, the gunners spiking targets, holding the missiles for later. Then crossfire—*the hits*—a turret blown, the beam slashing across Ilse's head! She sagged but her fingers moved on the board; *Spee* bucked and pulled free. Then another hit flung her sprawling to the deck; Ivan scrambled to the console and completed the ship's escape. Then heard himself yelling for the Second Hat to take over, so Ivan could go to Ilse.

The scene faded, but the rest of it he knew. Ilse dying, he thought, so only one purpose left. He called Tregare, removed *Graf Spee* from squadron command. And took that ship up the inside of Admiral Newhausen's cone formation and blew Ozzie to plasma.

And if Ilse hadn't come to consciousness and told him a better way to do it, Ivan fully intended to ram.

Memory ceased to grip him; he shook his head. *Why that?* Nearly half an hour he'd spent in a state close to trance; why? *It has to mean something.*

An answer came. He didn't like it, but all his pushing wouldn't make it go away. *I cling to blind impulse, and fail people.*

Maybe at age eight he had an excuse—scared and hurt, yelling at the Welfare goons and too stubborn to give up. Well, he'd paid, in years of pain and a messed-up mind. And was that mind back to "normal"? Or did he just think it was?

But his actions on *Graf Spee*, in the fighting—he tried to see them as Rissa might, or Tregare. Squadron coordination officer, a command ship's First Hat, sees his woman dying—so he pulls the ship out of pattern and goes for one-man revenge. Did he ask if the crew—nearly a hundred persons—wanted to die to avenge Ilse? No. Ivan Marchant was drunk on personal rage and desolation, so the rest of the ship could bloody well come along. And the *fleet*, Earth's fate hanging in the balance, could go hang.

The more he looked at it, the worse it got. *Tregare—what must the man think of me?* At this late date, he could hardly ask.

Tired, but curiously at peace, Ivan dressed and went upship. He had his answer: from now on, to put tighter rein to his fierce, sometimes berserk, impulses.

The dream had, after all, made sense.

Hungry again, he entered the galley. Rissa and Tregare sat with Anders Kobolak's wife, Alina Rostadt; Ivan filled a plate for himself and joined them. " . . . nearly to the point," Tregare was saying, "where a sub-light ship would be making turnover. Seems funny, not having to do the maneuver on this bucket."

"I've never understood that," Alina said, so Tregare explained how, on FTL ships, you ran most of the way on accel and then simply cut the Hoyfarul Drive, cold. Well, Ivan already knew that the excess velocity-derived mass, collapsing back into the ship's own universe, slowed it below light-speed _fast_.

"Then," Tregare added, "a few days' decel gets you down to zerch. If you've gauged your distance right, you're close to where you're going. That's the tricky part. Right, Ivan?"

"Right." Done eating, Ivan stood, took his empty tray to the disposal counter, and left the galley.

And found that Rissa had followed him. "Ivan—may we talk?"

He didn't want to, but paused while she caught up. "What about?"

"Whatever concerns you. Obviously, something does."

It was odd, he thought, that their childhood rapport had survived so strongly. After all, the Welfare system had separated them quite young—and then each had lived roughly thirteen bio-years until their next real meeting. During those years which had nearly crushed his own mind, Rissa's had been toughened instead. Disparate experience . . .

And yet, once they were together again, the reacquaintance took little time and the old bond of feeling grew as strong as ever. Often Rissa seemed to know what he was thinking before he said it. And sometimes this apparent link was comforting. Right now, though, he found it more of a nuisance. He'd already done his sorting of memories, his reevaluations; he didn't _want_ to hash through them all over again. Not now, anyway.

So he answered, "Trouble sleeping, is all. I'll catch up; I always do." Because she was wearing her worried look, he added, "Rissa—unless you have a time machine in your back pocket, to change the past, leave this one to me. I can handle it."

She frowned, but said no more.

VI. Lisele

As long as everyone else practiced gunnery an hour at a time, so did Liesel Selene—even though after fifteen or twenty minutes she got tired and her scores dropped. But when Tregare announced that the contest would be run in ten-minute heats, she changed to fifteen-minute sessions, with rests between.

Her average scores took a quantum jump. Now, two days before the shootout, she entered a sixty-three in the log—and pouted slightly, because it wasn't the best she'd done. Well, maybe on the last day of practice she could get in some extra time.

She was due back in quarters now, to take charge of baby Renalle when their mother went on watch. And while the infant slept, Lisele could get on with her studies. Checking to see that she was leaving the turret in good order, she turned and skipped down to the next level. Seeing grownups there, she slowed down and walked, but as soon as she was out of their sight she went back to a faster and less regular way of moving. Coming to the last stairs she drew a deep breath—could she take this flight *all* the way, three at a time? She launched herself and timed her leaps, and it was going fine—and then, below, someone entered from the side and started up to meet her. Lisele grabbed the handrail and stopped her plunge. "Oh, peace!"

"Lisele—are you all right?" It was Dacia, scrambling up toward her. Lisele caught her balance, and stood.

"Oh, sure." Dacia was good fun; she wouldn't scold. "I was trying threesies, was all, and didn't expect you."

Dacia snorted. "Not a very good place for it; this flight's blind at the bottom. Why not save threesies for farther downship, where there's openwork and you can see people coming?"

It made sense; Lisele nodded. "Sure. Thanks, Dacia." The woman patted her thin shoulder and went on up. Her dare-and-do mood broken, Lisele took the rest of the stairs one at a time, only clattering a little extra to make it sound better.

In quarters, Rissa had put the baby down to sleep and was ready to go on watch. She kissed Lisele and said, "If you have not eaten lately, Tregare stocked the coldbox this morning. And Ellalee will be here as usual, to relieve you at nineteen-hundred. Now—do you have any news for me?"

"Well, I'm doing better on the turrets." She recited her latest scores.

Rissa nodded. "Working in shorter periods, yes. Perhaps you will help Dacia's team win over mine." She laughed, and hugged the child. "If you do, I shall be most proud of you." Then she picked up her watch-officer's gear, and left.

Lisele went over to Renalle, saw that the infant wasn't asleep yet, and reached down to pat her cheek. She was growing, no doubt about that. Tregare claimed she was due to sprout teeth, but Rissa said he was thinking ahead of schedule. Still—gently, Lisele intruded a fingertip and felt along the baby's gums. There *was* something there. . . .

Renalle was clearly sleepy; time to leave her alone, and the next couple of hours would be a good time for Lisele to study. She got out her materials and sat at her mother's desk.

What did she most need to catch up on? She sighed; the calculus, probably. Not that she disliked math, but her project for Prof Diebolt had gotten so interesting that she'd skimped on the calc. By habit, she set out the filmtape unit and turned her calculator on; then she looked at the lesson assignment and put both units away. Because for the next three sections, Old Numberhead wanted everybody to practice using the older methods—books, sliderules, even the function-tables on paper. "Your math is no good to you," Old Numbers liked to say, "if a dead battery can put it out of business."

Lisele could see his point—but a few minutes later, frowning over a page of log-trig functions, she wished she didn't have to. Then she remembered how to follow his instructions, finally located the log-secant of 2.377 radians, and finished the problem. Well and good, as the old prof liked to say.

When she had worked through the first section, she felt hungry, and closed the books. As she fixed a snack for herself, her mind was still on the math. Differential-calc was clear enough; it made sense and you could work it out for yourself. Integral, though—using differentials instead of derivatives— well, she could see that it worked, when you looked at the tables and plugged values in, but how had anyone ever come up with those solutions in the first place?

The heck with it. She put more pickles and cheese on her sandwich, poured some fruit juice, and ate.

She'd finished the calc and a chapter of post-UET economics, and given the suddenly restive baby her bottle, when her relief sitter arrived. "Hi, Ellalee! I've just fed Renalle."

"That's good, Lisele. How are you?" Ellalee Ganelong's smile showed large white teeth against brown skin. Ellalee was Australian, half aborigine, with oddly heavy features. Maybe it was her pleasantness, Lisele thought, that made her seem pretty. But Rissa said she really was, in her own way.

"Studying hard tonight, have you been?" she said now. At Lisele's gesture toward the sandwich fixings, Ellalee shook her head, curly hair jiggling with the move. "I ate at midwatch. Heaps." She had a quick look at Renalle, then sat. Lisele seated herself again at Rissa's desk, and they talked. Ellalee was training for Drive-tech First, about halfway through the procedures that dealt with fine-tuning and lock control circuits. The funny part, Lisele thought, was that new drive-techs began by working with the heaviest power stages, because those controls weren't at all delicate, so it was hard to make any serious mistake. That job carried a Third rating, which Ellalee had held when the *Deux* lifted. And now going for First. Not bad!

Ellalee had a little driveroom gossip about her boss, Chief Engineer Hagen Trent. A little too fussy, Lisele had heard Tregare say of the man. Ellalee's opinion was: "No experience at being *boss*, I think—except in a lab, perhaps. But he's come quite patient now, unless someone makes the same mistake twice." She grinned. "Then he gets red and rubs knuckles in what hair he has left, and talks too fast. Not so often now, though." Imagining Trent that way, Lisele had to laugh.

Midway, the laugh turned to yawn. Ellalee said, "Long day?"

"Mmm—sort of." Lisele could, she decided, put her books away tomorrow. "Think I'll go to bed. Good night."

"Yes. Sleep comfy."

In her tiny bedroom and undressed, Lisele felt restless. Biofeedback, maybe? She hadn't used it much lately. Activating the machine, she plumped down on the mat and began the breathing exercises. Soon her mind floated, relaxed; she lost track of time.

When the machine turned off, its soft chime brought her awake enough to get into bed. But not awake for long.

Coming out of sleep, Lisele lay quietly and listened. Her chronometer indicated time for breakfast, so—considering the watch schedules, Rissa and perhaps Tregare should be here, and Ellalee gone. She got up, chose clothing, and went to see.

In the common room, nobody home. Probably in their bedroom, her parents. At this hour, awake and making love, maybe, or talking afterward. At school she'd seen holotapes about sex; it looked pretty funny but people seemed to enjoy it. Just as well, she thought, or maybe she wouldn't be here!

Renalle would, though; the parthenogenetic Hulzein process needed no man. Stowing study materials away, Lisele thought about her sister. Half-sister, really, and no kin to Tregare, at all—but he acted as if the baby were his own blood. Lisele sighed; she sure had a nice family!

Listening at the main bedroom's door, she heard nothing. Still asleep, maybe? So she wrote on the bulletin pad:

Have gone to breakfast. Last night caught up to sked on Calc and Econ. I bet my team (Dacia's) beats yours both! But what can we bet?

Lisele

Outside quarters, door closed softly, she charged up the stairs as fast as she could go. At the galley level, panting, she waited and walked slowly, to be breathing easily when she entered. At the door she paused and looked around. Arlen Limmer was sitting with the blonde, Jenise Rorvik. So Lisele filled a tray and went to a corner table, by herself. While she ate, she thought about Arlen.

On Stronghold as little kids, they'd been together all the time—like brother and sister, maybe even twins. She'd *loved* Arlen, and had missed him ever since. On Earth, other kids were all right, but not the same. Sometimes she'd pretend Arlen was with her, and tell him all her thoughts. She *knew* it was silly . . .

Then when the Limmers came to Earth, Lisele was thrilled. Because now she was a big girl, close to nine bio-years, and Arlen would be her best friend again, and maybe someday they'd get married or something. The details hadn't worried her.

Except that living slow on groundside while Tregare's fleet, coming to Earth, chewed time, Arlen was already grown up tall. And Lisele wasn't. So now he sat and smiled at that old harpy—at least *twenty*, she had to be—Jenise Rorvik, with her bright blonde hair that most likely wasn't even natural!

Wondering how she herself might look as a blonde, Lisele shrugged; Rissa probably wouldn't let her try it. Well, what else? How about the woman in the old filmtaped novel she'd scanned last month? So hopelessly in love that she wasn't even *eating*. Silly—but maybe not a bad idea for getting somebody's attention. Except, how could anyone do it with a straight face?

And besides, Lisele had already cleaned her tray.

Well, on her way out she'd say hello to Arlen; after all, she did still like him. But it wasn't fair, him grown up and her not.

The saying hello didn't work too well. Rorvik was smiling and friendly, and did most of the talking. Everything Lisele tried to say sounded more and more like a little kid, and she couldn't get the conversation off the subject of the gunnery match. Finally she saw Rissa and Tregare come in, and got away to talk with them a moment. Tregare gave her a hug, and a compliment on her studying; Rissa was glad her daughter wasn't skimping the biofeedback routines. But it seemed clear that both had other things on their minds, so Lisele went up to Turret Six for a practice run. It went well, and she headed downship again.

Approaching a landing, she saw Dacia Kobolak come out of Uncle Ivan's quarters, and waved to her. "Hi, Dacia!"

"Hi." Lisele wanted to talk, but Dacia hurried on past, so maybe this wasn't the time for it. Oh, well—she went on down to captain's digs; she needed a shower, anyway.

Drying herself, she stood before a mirror. When it came to looking grownup, she was pretty hopeless. Skinny like a boy, no butt to notice, no body fur at all, yet. It wasn't as if she was even interested in any sex stuff, at her age and with no real idea how people were supposed to *feel* about it—but it'd be nice if she *looked* like some competition for ol' Rorvik!

Squinting sidewise at the mirror, she squeezed the flesh around one pale nipple, to try to make a bulge. It didn't look like much of anything, and when she let go, right away it went flat again. Heck with it. She put the towel away and got dressed. Still thinking, though: in the old novel the woman was "flat-chested" and padded herself to look bigger there. Why? She was grown-up and functional; what difference did *sizes* make?

Anyway, if Lisele herself rigged stuff under her clothes to show up with her chest sticking out, who'd believe it? They'd just laugh and want to know what the joke was.

And then she'd be stuck. Because there wasn't any joke.

Later that day, Lisele managed two more practice sessions in the gunnery turrets. Then she sat with Renalle and covered the day's studies, did some biofeedback and went to bed early. When she woke, she felt up to tackling Ozzie Newhausen his own damn self!

Showered, dressed in her sloppiest and most comfortable jumpsuit, Lisele made a light breakfast. Full stomachs didn't go too well with competition. Climbing sedately to the turret deck, she found a crowd there—what Ellalee would call "a fair jam." The whole crew—except, Lisele supposed, for a skeleton watch.

Looking for her team captain, she found Dacia talking with Hagen Trent and Hask Ornaway. A visored cap made the balding Trent look a lot younger. Dacia greeted Lisele with a quick, one-armed hug. "For our team, you and Hask drew first round. All right?" Dacia was certainly sitting on lots of excitement.

"Sure." Why wait around? "When do we start?"

"Not long now," said Ornaway, grinning at her. So they waited for their assigned monitors to arrive—someone from another team, to observe and help keep score. And maybe, Lisele thought, have something to do while they waited for their own turns. Anyway, she'd drawn Anders Kobolak, and here he came. They greeted; then over the speaker Jeremy Crowfoot gave a quick recap of the rules. As he finished, Lisele turned to leave.

"Wait," said Dacia, and held out a small, firm cushion. "Here. Try sitting on this; it may help your reach."

Lisele took it. "Sure . . . thanks." But why now, with no time to practice and get used to it? Oh, well—it might help. And in the gunner's seat of Turret Six she found the cushion did give her a more comfortable angle on the control levers. So with the console's function switch on Test she applied power and confirmed that her controls were working: left hand on range lights and the other on her heterodyne loop. Returning the levers to neutral she switched function to Simulation; lights and screen image went dark. Her hands weren't sweaty; it was out of habit that she rubbed them on her jumpsuit. "Ready." Facing her, sitting where he couldn't see the indicators to get any possible

clues for his own turn, Anders Kobolak nodded. He'd call her
scores after each run; she wouldn't have to look.

Then Crowfoot began his countdown, and it all started.

First run came straight and closed slowly. *Nothing like
making easy points, while I can.* Next one had a swerve at the
middle, but she caught it fast and scored seventy-five. Then a
skew pass and an abrupt change of target: that's where fast
reflexes came in handy! "Fifty-eight."

It kept on; the ten minutes felt like thirty. Not physical
fatigue, though; the cushion did help. And when the eight-run
sequence ended, her overall score was sixty-seven.

"Nice going, there," said Anders Kobolak, and they went
out to the deck, to check team standings. And found that Lisele
and Ornaway had given Dacia's group a slight initial lead. "Now
if the rest of us can do as well—," Dacia said, and Lisele felt
good.

Ornaway touched her shoulder. "Quick galley break, partner?"

Lisele considered. Twenty minutes, before she was due to
monitor Rostadt. "Sure. *Real* fast, though." Their pace downship
could have cost them a few safety demerits if Tregare bothered
with such things. Ornaway had coffee while Lisele sipped fruit
juice, and they did get back on time.

Monitor work, except for watching Alina's concentration
and reactions, was dull. All Lisele could see was the numbers.
Final rating, overall, was sixty-two.

Mostly by Dacia's own skill, this set of runs helped her
team's lead. Then Ivan's shooting put his own group ahead, and
the first round was over.

Lisele's second session brought harder runs; she got a
fifty-nine total, and Rissa had brought her own team close to
Ivan's. "Dacia, we're behind!" Lisele hadn't expected to be so
anxious, but found herself sweating. "We have to *work!*"

"Sure." Dacia nodded. "But so does everyone else." At
the end of round two, Rissa led and Dacia came second. A
novice on Ivan's team had panicked and jammed the override
pedal down for most of his turn, cutting his hits to half-value.

Then Lisele got a bad run; a simulated hit crippled her
"ship's" drive and left her drifting, and she didn't adjust quickly
enough. A humiliating twenty-seven for the run, and forty-nine
for the round, overall. Avoiding Dacia and everyone else, she
wandered a lower deck where she wouldn't have to talk with

anyone. Maybe when this was all done with, she'd just lock herself in her bedroom and stay there!

In her bedroom! There wasn't time to go down there before she was due to monitor Alina's round, but—she stepped into a utilities locker, closed the door, and sat, breathing the way she should, paying attention to how she felt. With her eyes shut she could almost visualize the indicators of the absent biofeedback machine. She knew how much time she had, and she used it all, emerging with enough to spare so that she could reach her monitoring assignment without haste.

Alina scored well, and then Lisele found a nearer haven to use her next free time for further exercises in relaxation. As she headed, then, back to Turret Six, Dacia called to her. "Lisele! How are you feeling? I haven't seen you . . . "

The child grinned. "Best I've been all day." And when her first run began, she moved with confidence. It worked; she had a good fourth round, and her fifth wasn't bad, either. The final, though, was where she'd give it all she had!

Of course Crowfoot had saved his trickiest stuff for that one—but it was the same for everybody, wasn't it? So Lisele tried to balance concentration with relaxing, and while a few fast changes caught her by surprise, they didn't fluster her now.

At the end, Anders whistled. "Forty-seven. Jeremy was figuring nobody would do much better than forty on this series."

Lisele shrugged. "Rissa will, I expect. And Ivan, and Dacia. But whoever does what, I did the best *I* could." And found herself grinning. Later, watching Alina freeze on a tricky change and drop points, Lisele felt only sympathy, not gloating.

The end of action brought a letdown and a return of tension. Not even wanting to check team standings until final results were in, Lisele went to the galley—and suddenly found that her appetite had merely been lying in wait. She was finishing a second helping, and refilling her glass of synthetic milk, when the last group of contestants and monitors straggled in. Nervous now, as Jeremy Crowfoot began to announce the tournament results, she tried to keep her breathing slow and even.

Crowfoot didn't keep anybody in suspense. The ship's top five gunners, in order, were Ivan with an overall sixty-two, Rissa, Dacia, Anders Kobolak and Hask Ornaway. Rissa's team had won, with Dacia's second and Ivan's trailing. But all Lisele noticed was that Rissa won by less than twenty points—*if only I hadn't blown up in the third round!*

Tears wet her eyes; she couldn't look at Dacia, sitting next to her. But the woman squeezed her hand, and whispered, "Check the printouts. Nearly everyone had at least one bad round."

Jeremy still talked. "—novice category, placing seventh and ninth overall with scores of fifty-five and fifty-two. So a reasonable amount of cheering is in order, for Liesel Selene Moray and Jenise Rorvik."

Through the clapping, someone yelled "Speech!" Lisele shook her head; her throat wouldn't work. Finally, to Dacia, she choked out, "Tell 'em thanks," and Dacia did.

Then it was all right, except that someone had poured her empty milk glass full of wine. Sure, she'd had wine at dinner sometimes, but not *this* much. She looked across to where Tregare was sitting, caught his gaze, and touched the glass. Smiling, with thumb and forefinger he measured a vertical space.

About three centimeters. So over the next half hour, before the gathering broke up, that's how much she drank.

And left the rest of it.

Nothing was really wrong with her balance but it felt funny, so she walked slower than usual. Wine, she knew, was like that. Entering quarters she had a question on her mind, so she asked her parents, right out. "Up there, people acting like my shooting was the best thing since Uncle Ivan got Ozzie Newhausen. I know that's not real. How much *is*?"

Rissa put down her hairbrush and gave a hug. "You did very well. Not as well as some, or as you will do in future. The contest was a thorough success, so there will be more of them."

"I'm pretty good but I'm not wonderful?"

Tregare's special huff-and-puff hug should have crushed her, but somehow never did. "You're wonderful, all right, small potatoes. Not just your placing well; I saw your heat records, too. Partway through, you ran into trouble. Then you fought back and beat clear of it." He grinned. "That's what's wonderful."

All right; she could believe it. Going to her bedroom, she wondered if she needed the feedback machine. No, her mind felt just the way it ought to. She lay down and thought through her day, and never knew when thinking stopped and sleep began.

With gunnery off her mind for a while, Lisele spent more time studying. Another thing bothered her, though, and one day when she found Arlen Limmer sitting alone in the galley, she went and sat facing him. "Hi." She didn't know where Jenise Rorvik was and she didn't ask. "Hi, Arlen."

Mouth full, chewing, he nodded. And now, thinking of what she'd planned to say, it all sounded stupid to her. Still, here was her chance and she wasn't going to waste it. "Arlen—you remember back at Stronghold, when we were little?"

"Sure. Long time ago—for me, anyway. Why?"

She looked at him, nearly a man while she was only a child. "You were my best friend. I *loved* you. But now—"

His fork slapped down; food splattered, and he grabbed a napkin-tissue to wipe his tunic. "You keep acting as if it's *my* fault. When we came to Earth I really wanted to see you—I didn't think of you still being a little kid. All that about relativity and time-chewing—I knew it, but it didn't *register*." He looked as if maybe it hurt him, too, but his hurt didn't help hers any. She waited, and he said, "I'd even dreamed about you."

"You did? Dreamed what?" He shook his head. But he was on the run now, some way, so she said, "Just a dream—you can tell me."

His face had got awfully red. "Well—we were grownup and liked each other, and maybe we even got married." His glare hardly looked friendly, let alone loving. "But don't you tell anybody! Because now it's silly."

"I won't tell. But what's silly about it? I won't be a kid all my life; someday I'll be your age. Ever think of that?"

Her own words surprised her; Arlen's hands seemed to push at them, and he looked as if he'd swallowed the wrong way. "That's stupid. When you're my age I'll be nearly as old as your *mother*."

To Lisele, numbers were easy. She said, "You have nine years on me. Tregare has the same on Rissa. Doesn't seem to bother them."

Taking a deep breath she waited again, but Arlen shook his head and said nothing. All right, then! She stood. "I thought—but I don't *need* you!" She turned and ran out of the galley. Going downship she did threesies all the way and didn't miss once.

Feeling embarrassed, for the next few days she stayed clear of Arlen; the one time he tried to talk with her, she wouldn't answer. Then the new tourney took up her attention, and Dacia's team came in only eight points behind Rissa's. And in the third shootout Lisele made her best six-round score ever, and Dacia's team notched its first win. With that kind of action, who had time to think about Arlen Limmer?

One day when Lisele went with Tregare up to Control, all the outside sensors were working again! Tregare stopped cold. "Who the hell cut us below light? And *why*?"

"It's simulations, Tregare!" So Tregare cooled down, as Jeremy Crowfoot explained: the gunnery tourneys had given him the idea to rig some tapes for navigation training. "Above light, we've been stymied on that. So—"

"Sure." Tregare grinned now. "You could have told me, though; I practically had heart failure."

"Didn't want to bother you until I had the bugs out. Want to try it?" So Tregare took a control seat, and Crowfoot moved some switches. The screen showed a moving star field, and Lisele watched as one star, growing brighter, moved into the ship's path—though of course it would be the *ship* moving. Tregare punched a course change; the screen reflected the move. Other situations appeared, a lot closer together in time than could really happen. Sometimes Lisele saw what the problem was, but usually not.

After a few minutes, Tregare shut off the input. "Good job, Jere. You just earned yourself a bonus."

Headshake. "I don't need one. It was something to *do*."

"So's my giving you the bonus, so don't argue."

Before her father could get involved in his routine watch-log scan, Lisele asked, "Is that just for real navigators, or could I practice on it, too? Like with gunnery?"

Tregare looked at her, then toward Crowfoot. "If it's all right with you, Jere, let's announce that the facility's open to anyone who wants to learn. Nothing wrong with people knowing more jobs than one or two." Lisele got a quick hug. "You, now—you'll run a ship of your own someday, or I miss my guess. So you might's well start learning for it."

The simulations got only a few days' usage, though, because one evening, the whole family dining together in quarters for once, Tregare announced, "In about six hours we cut the Hoyfarul Drive and drop below light. I might as well stay up for the show; short naps never do me much good."

Lisele did nap, until Rissa woke her to go upship. In Control all the Hats were present—Rissa, Anders, Ornaway—as well as Crowfoot standing over the computer monitor and Jenise

Rorvik on the comm board. After a short wait that seemed longer, over the intercom Hagen Trent said, "Ready, down here. Give me the count?"

"Sure," and Tregare began it. This early, he didn't hesitate to interrupt with comment and advice. "Seconds four-twenty; mark. Now, Hagen—I'll tell you when we pass C going south, but don't turn ship for decel until I give you the office. Right?"

"Understood, Tregare." The count went on. At "Now!" came a pause, a second of nothing happening. Then the whole ship lurched, a shudder without sound, and yet Lisele's ears hurt. All the screens and indicators came alive—and this time, no simulation!

Tregare yelled. "Rorvik! Swing your input grids. Those blips—six? seven?—just going offscreen. What the hell *are* they?"

Jenise probably did her best—and like her or not, Lisele did admit she was competent—but the blips showed only briefly and wavering, and then were gone.

Lisele couldn't hear Tregare's muffled words, but by the look of him she knew he was swearing a blue streak. Then he said, "Those were ships; the speeds are right and they changed course. Whatever, they got away." He grinned. "Or maybe *we* got away. All right, Hagen; turn ship, and I'll feed you decel figures for Shaarbant." Lisele knew to stay strapped in during the zero-gee of turnover, but it sure *felt* funny. Then Tregare said, "Decel, point-six-seven of max. Should put us not quite four days from here to Shaarbant." A pause. "Make that four days on the nose, near as makes no difference. Because I'm aiming to hit orbital drift speed and go synchronous around that planet."

"You do not," said Rissa, "plan to land immediately?"

"Course not. Think about it—the odds are that this Shrakken colony never heard of Earth or humans. When they see we're not their own, likely they'd take us for Tsa, and—"

Rissa nodded. "Yes, I see. To our knowledge, only three Shrakken ships have had contact with our species. UET's Committee Police murdered the first's crew and took the ship." Counting by fingers, she moved her touch to a second. "Then Stonzai's *Sharanj* visited the Charleyhorse colony before going to Number One where you captured it."

Both those ships, Lisele knew, were now at Stronghold, for Tregare had sent Stonzai and her crew home with a UET ship and its superior armament, as a goodwill gesture. Where that ship had actually gone, no one on the *Deux* had any idea, for Stonzai had at a later time transshipped in space to a Shrakken ship. And then, in a chance meeting with Derek Limmer's FTL ship *Leapfrog*, just after Limmer cut drive to sub-light, received the guiding directions that took Stonzai to Earth. Or at least that was the way Rissa was telling it. It sounded right.

Dacia Kobolak had joined the group; Tregare turned to her. "Just saying we'll need to orbit awhile and exchange hails with Shaarbant, before it'd be safe to land. Stonzai and the other Shrakken: how long you think it'll take to get 'em up and around again?"

Dacia cleared her throat. "Eight hours or less. But you know Stonzai's problem. How long do you plan to stay in orbit?" Tregare scowled; looking uneasy, Dacia raised her voice. "Stonzai will be in the throes of the Shrakken compulsion to ovulate. How long, while we orbit, will she have to suffer it?"

Tregare shrugged. "Depends. On how long it takes her to talk the locals into letting us sit down peaceably." No one answered him. "Figure on having Stonzai awake and making sense when we're three-four hours short of making orbit. That's close enough to talk good, and sooner she gets contact, the sooner we can set her down safe."

Dacia's voice had an edge to it. "Our mission certainly depends on a lot of short-term considerations, doesn't it? And unplanned ones, at that."

Lisele saw Tregare change his mind and not get mad. "You've got a point, Dacia—and if you or I had designed the Shrakken biology, you might have a good one." Dacia's own scowl came and went, before Tregare said, "As is, though, we'll just play the cards we're dealt."

When Trent got his decel steady, the extra people relinquished Control to its regular watch crew. Lisele left her parents talking with others and went to quarters. There she had a snack, and took time for a brief biofeedback session before going to bed.

Before sleeping, her last thought was that she would be one of the first humans ever to land on a Shrakken world.

VII. Elzh

*B*ehind, now, lay the charted mindbeast planet. No close nearing had the seven ships made; when the most sensitive of the crewing felt mindpain, Elzh pulled back to study the beastworld at safe remove.

Beast minds never gave stillness; always and always came the fierce harsh jangling that brought pain and threatened madness. Tsa, unless mindsaying, always granted each other quiet. That these creatures did not, was what made them beasts. And never any answer to Tsa pleas, any notice of Tsa needs and Tsa pain.

So in grouping, mindsaying, Elzh decided. *The beasts die.* No Tsa protested; all thought was to end this beastworld, to put it behind and go toward the next—long far ahead, not soon—on the Tsa-Drin chart. As understood.

But now, of a sudden, a new thing—out of *nothing,* came a mindbeast ship. Not coming from distance, shown ahead by screen blinkings, as correct, as always, but impossibly there *now.* First and before, it was *not;* then it *was.* No nearing, as ships rightly did. And then gone turning to side, as Elzh turned also—away, it went, much soon, toward the mindbeast world. Too distant for mindpain, it had been, but not by great margin. A new thing; more dread?

To learn, the Tsa way—always to learn. But also to obey. Elzh thought, not yet mindsaying to any, and then decided. *Two ships go now, on to fulfill the Tsa-Drin plan. The rest stay, until we solve the riddle of the ship that came from nothing.* Elzh chose, then, the two ships to go, and sent the thoughts for parting, and waited in quiet while parting became done. As correct, as understood.

Other thoughts disturbed quiet; in fret, Elzh tried to keep

correct mind. But how, all indling together, could Idsath as
moderator forget the Tsa-Drin directive and return blended genes
to Tserln, as female, to give young? Yet it was happened, and
without death of Tserln, could not erase. Tsa-Drin or no, once
begun, the young would be. Fastly it had grown, in the Tsa way,
and Tserln gave it quite timely, and put about it the name Ceevt,
for all Tsa to know. A good young, thought Elzh, with tiny
mind-touch soft like blowing dust. But the Tsa-Drin—not to
obey, this was.

Parting ended. Mindsaying to the remaining ships, Elzh set
them to look for the ship from nothing.

Not on screen blinkings at all now, so too far to give
mindpain. And back toward beastworld it had to be, because
nowhere else. Mindsaying, Elzh turned the five ships.

Five Tsa ships and one beast ship. Yes. Dread, though, even
so—for how does a ship appear from nothing? But with mindbeasts,
no mercy—given or expected. Only dread and pain and death.

But for Tsa, to obey. *To the beastworld . . . yes.*

VIII. Rissa

*R*ecovering from freeze, Stonzai
took longer than Dacia Kobolak had predicted. Less than an hour
short of injecting *Inconnu Deux* into synchronous orbit, juggling
deceleration to give maneuverability if he needed it, Tregare
showed his impatience. "Rissa—if Dacia doesn't get that over-
grown woggle-bug up here pretty soon, we could be in trouble."

Standing behind the control seat, Rissa clasped his shoulder.
"She knows that, Bran. And is, I am sure, working as rapidly as
possible." Feeling the tension in him, she said, "If you like, I
will visit the recovery compartment and report back to you. But
you do *not* want to call again and interrupt her efforts."

"Right; go ahead." So Rissa left the control room and went
downship. Halfway to her destination she felt the ship lurch, and

barely caught herself from losing balance on the stairs. "All hands!" Tregare's voice; all-ship broadcast? "Shrakken ships rising from the planet. Took off from farside, I guess; coming fast, anyway. Get strapped down—or braced, at least—for maneuvering."

But Rissa had no time for precaution. Plunging down the stairs, one level and then the next, catching herself by grabbing handrail at each jump, she reached the room she sought. And a bit short of breath, went inside.

She looked. Stonzai, sitting upright, seemed alert; Dacia was feeding her. No sign of Sevshen, the other Shrakken. "Dacia! Is Stonzai ready to talk with her people? Because they have sent ships up, coming at us."

Dacia looked confused. "I think so. But getting her up to Control, with the ship bouncing this way—" For again the *Deux* had bucked.

What to do? *I must decide quickly, for no one else will.* Then she had her answer. "Dacia—down the corridor and across it—three doors along, I believe. A study room with an extension viewscreen." She turned to go there. "Bring Stonzai, and hurry! I will call Tregare, so that he can make the circuit arrangements."

Now she ran. The door she chose was the correct one, and as she had thought, it was not locked. She turned the lights on and looked around. The place was dusty, but that didn't matter. She activated the screen; it lit, but had no input signal. She hit the intercom switch.

"Tregare! I am in E-14. Connect its screen, two-way communication and of course you will interpose a hold circuit, to your offship channels. Stonzai will be here, to talk; Dacia says she is ready, but there is no time to—"

"Yeah, yeah—I get it, and thanks." Abruptly, half the screen showed Tregare, with Ivan and Hask Ornaway alongside him. The other half flickered; then Shaarbant, the planet ahead, appeared.

Behind her, Rissa heard sounds. She turned; Dacia came in, supporting Stonzai, both moving slowly. Rissa shifted chairs to give them all good position before the screen. A chair would not suit the Shrakken but on short notice it was the best Rissa could do, and Stonzai settled into it without complaint.

The screen had to be working both ways, because Tregare said, "Stonzai—we're near Shaarbant and your people are shooting ships up at us. You have to tell 'em we're here to be friends. I'm trying to get tuned for direct talk. Are you ready to help?"

Bewildered-seeming, Stonzai turned to Rissa. "Help, I would—but what is it he say, that to do I must?" Quickly, Rissa paraphrased Tregare's words, and looking to the screen, Stonzai said, "Yes. To Shrakken here, talk I will."

"Good," and Tregare's voice tone and angle of grin were as Rissa remembered, from the old fighting days. "We have speed on those ships," he said next, "and accel advantage. Come to crunch we could dodge, not have to shoot. But seems to me, running would set one lousy precedent. Better than shooting, but not by much."

On half the viewscreen, Shaarbant vanished and the image of two Shrakken appeared. One spoke and Stonzai answered, both speaking at length, and Rissa understood none of it. But then Stonzai turned aside to her and said, "That you are here to aid, I have told."

And a time later, after more talk, Tregare dispensed with orbital maneuvers and landed directly on Shaarbant—between two Shrakken ships, on a bare clearing at the junction of two rivers. The time of day, there, was not long past dawn.

Spaceport facilities, Rissa noted, were crude and of recent construction—but adequate. "Tregare—it seems we have accomplished the first of our mission."

"Sure. As long as Stonzai stays healthy, to interpret."

Sevshen's recovery was slower than Stonzai's. At a coffee break with Rissa, Dacia Kobolak shook her head. "The Shrakken metabolism—we simply don't know enough about it. We're lucky I didn't kill both of them by mistake."

"Where are they now?" said Liesel Selene.

"In their quarters," Rissa said. "Groundside, with host animals available for the resulting larvae, Stonzai can now safely ovulate and breed."

Lisele frowned. "I know a little about that. Tell me the rest."

Rissa explained. She had never seen Shrakken breed, but from Stonzai she knew the mechanics of it. The female ovipositor, which humans had first thought to be a male organ, entered the male's body and withdrew the sperm. The fertilized ovum—ovoid, about three centimeters long and two across—sprouted short tentacles and entered a larval phase. And at that stage a host animal was needed—for by fierce, uncontrollable instinct the female would seize on *any* available organism, even another Shrakken, and paralyze it with a naturally-produced "zombie gas'' and implant the voracious larvae. If she failed to do so, they would be her own death, instead.

Because, similar to the digger wasps of Earth, the larvae fed on their living hosts. Living and paralyzed, but not beyond feeling pain. Rissa knew that part of it first-hand; luckily, when the Shrakken female on the planet Number One had implanted her, a doctor had removed the larval parasite before it had time to attach itself to her tissues and begin to feed.

At this point, Lisele shuddered. ''I didn't know it was *that* bad. What terrible creatures!''

''No,'' said Rissa. ''Not so terrible. It is simply their biology, set by evolution, over which they have no control.''

''But every time there's a new Shrakken, something has to die!'' Grimacing, the child shook her head.

''Lisele,'' her mother said. ''We are not vegetarians, are we? Nearly every time we eat a *meal,* some creature has died to provide part of it.''

''But—''

''Adult Shrakken, Lisele, are largely vegetarian.''

''Oh?''

''Yes. I merely wished to put the matter into perspective.''

When the two Shrakken left the ship—hurriedly, for there was no time to waste—Tregare and Ivan escorted them. Rissa cut short her cuddling with baby Renalle, and went to Control. ''You'll have command,'' Tregare said. ''I think we're all right here, but just in case . . .''

''Yes. If need be, I lift ship and follow our contingent plans. Bran—be careful.''

''Sure.'' A quick hug, and he left.

Waiting, Rissa had both tension and boredom to fight; the two hours, while Tregare and Ivan were gone, seemed much longer. When her screen showed the two approaching without escort, she sighed in relief. To the watch crew, and via intercom to ramp guards and turret gunners, she said, ''Terminate special alert; return to normal alert procedures.'' Then, to Hask Ornaway, ''Your watch, Third Hat.'' He nodded, and she went to meet her husband and brother.

Halfway downship she saw them coming. Tregare waved. ''Let's talk in the galley,'' so she turned and climbed back, and went in. She poured herself tea; in a few moments Ivan brought coffee and joined her; Tregare found a beer and sat also. ''Stonzai deposited her young, all right, and then we got down to cases with the locals. If Stonzai's translations are accurate, we're in good here.''

Ivan filled in. ''Our stated intentions, plus delivering Stonzai and Sevshen in good shape, rate us a full refueling. As soon as their noon crew comes on duty. Then Stonzai's coming back here to brief us on this world.''

Rissa nodded. ''Good. And what else has been decided?''

Frowning, Tregare sipped from his glass. ''This port can't work directly with Hoyfarul's specs; it doesn't have facilities to build a groundcar, let alone rig a ship for FTL. There's a bigger installation, farside, that might be able to do the job. But the local admiral—well, 'he who speaks for Shaarbant', as Stonzai puts it—can't be sure. We'll have to go there and find out.''

''And if not?'' Rissa's brows were raised.

Tregare shrugged. ''Then we go on to Stenevo, after all—which is a trip I'd been hoping we could bypass.''

Rissa suppressed her frown. ''There is no nearer world, where the Shrakken have adequate means? One would expect their technology to be better distributed.''

Ivan said, ''It is. But not up-arm, *this* direction.''

''Then if that is the case,'' said Rissa, ''we go to Stenevo.''

''Yes, I guess we will.'' Her brother, Rissa thought, did not seem especially happy at the prospect.

Local time was still well before noon. Lisele wanted to go groundside and look around; Rissa could see no reason against taking the child offship for a bit of reconnaissance, and Ellalee was also interested: ''Stretch me legs some; it's been a while.'' Dacia was due for watch soon and had to beg off, so the three disembarked into warmish, sunny weather. An early morning haze had largely cleared but still kept the sky more pale than blue.

As they reached the ramp's foot, Rissa paused to look. The port's buildings weren't all that noteworthy; she saw wood and metal and concrete—or its equivalent, and plastic. The one noticeable difference from human architecture was that the Shrakken-built walls sloped slightly inward, not vertically. And so by the laws of proportion their doors and windows also tended to have a slight taper. As to colors, apparently the Shrakken had diverse tastes. Rissa found a few buildings, largely in tints of blue-green and reddish-orange, very much to her liking; others in drab shades reminded her all too strongly of UET and its Total Welfare centers.

The few Shrakken walking near *Inconnu Deux* and the
groundside party's path of march either ignored the humans or
made the Shrakken headbob that was neither nod nor shake, and
gave a brief curved wave of long fingers. Friendly enough, Rissa
decided; whoever had charge of this place must have spread the
information about the *Deux* both well and fast. *This is good,* she
thought, seeing Shrakken stride on their long toes.

Lisele pulled at Rissa's hand. "Let's get out of the port; it's
just about like any other, isn't it? Let's go see where they *live*."
Well, why not? Keeping in mind not to intrude, of course. So
she turned with the child's pull, and they left the port area by the
shortest route.

Outside it stood a random scatter of buildings, varying in
size but mostly of one or two stories; a few of the larger ones
had little third-floor penthouses atop them. As with the port
structures, walls were slanting, not vertical. Among and between
these structures, occasionally Shrakken moved, presumably on
their own errands, wearing pouch-hung harnesses similar to
those used by Stonzai and Sevshen. Remembering back to the
information Stonzai had given her, both verbally and on tape,
Rissa said, "They tend toward communal living groups. Within
those groups, some pair monogamously and others do not.
They—"

Lisele spoke. "Why aren't there any children?"

"A working base, this might be," Ellalee said, "with no
provisions for the young." She shrugged. "Like a camp for
miners or loggers, on Earth."

"If there were children here," said Rissa, "they would be
cared for by whatever group they lived in, as a whole. Stonzai—"
But then, as though Lisele's question had evoked it, a smaller
Shrakken emerged from a building and came to face them. Taller
than Lisele but with less height than either of the two women, it
wore only a simple belt with a pouch hung at each side. Now it
came within a pace of the three, and stopped, its triangular eyes
blinking slowly.

Lisele looked to Rissa. "What should we do?"

"I think—" Smiling, moving slowly, Rissa stepped forward. When she was within reach, still keeping her movement
slow, she put her hand out and touched fingers to the young
alien's forehead. The eyes blinked faster then, and the smallish
creature extended its own hand in turn; Rissa felt the hesitancy in
its touch as beside her she heard a gasp and turned to see an
adult Shrakken looming. Obviously a female, though the phalluslike

ovipositor was shrunken now, not extended. But the important thing, the first item Rissa noticed, was that the creature held a knife. At the ready.

"We will none of us react," she muttered quickly, and without haste withdrew her hand from the young one, turning to face the adult who had come to protect it. It made no move. Slowly again, Rissa reached for that one's forehead; first it flinched backward, then seemed to relax, and allowed the touch. Then, deliberately, it sheathed the knife and used the freed hand to return Rissa's touch. So she said, "Lisele, Ellalee—you see how it is done?" Only murmurs answered her, but as she stepped back, Lisele moved to exchange tactile greeting with the young-ster and Ellalee with the adult; then they changed partners and repeated the gestures. The adult said something in Shrakken, making the headbob Rissa could never interpret, then took the child's hand and escorted it away. The humans watched the two round the corner of a building and pass from sight.

"In a mite of trouble there, you think we could have been?" Ellalee's voice showed a residue of tension.

"Quite possibly, had we panicked or shown fight. But we did not."

"Right good thing you steadied me. A second more, I was ready to go for that knife."

"But you did not, and perhaps twenty or thirty Shrakken saw us all exchange peaceful greetings. I think it is not a bad thing we have done here, at all."

Lisele cleared her throat. "The young one's nice, anyway. Its fingers when it touched me—they seemed to vibrate, sort of. It felt good."

Rissa thought back. Had she felt any such thing? No, but perhaps the phenomenon was age-related. With a headshake she said, "Should we not return to *Inconnu Deux*? My stomach says that lunchtime is long past, and I think Tregare may be interested in the story of our experience here."

When they told him, aboard ship, his reactions proved Rissa correct.

Shrakken refueling gear was slow, but well before dusk *Inconnu Deux* was topped off. In quarters Tregare called council—his Control officers plus Ivan, Hagen Trent, Crowfoot and Dacia Kobolak. To one side—trying, Rissa thought, to look incon-spicuous—sat Liesel Selene. Briefly smiling, Rissa paid heed to the meeting.

"—and that," said Tregare, "brings us up to date. Next step, we go farside and check out Shtegel, the other Shrakken port."

"On an island, is it not?" said Rissa. "A largish one, in the middle of an archipelago?"

Tregare nodded. "Something like that. I guess you listened to Stonzai, this afternoon, closer than I did. Comes to place names, I even forget the two rivers alongside this port of Sassden."

"I remember," said Ivan Marchant, "but what's the point? The main thing, as I see it, is *how* do we check Shtegel out?"

Rissa looked to Tregare. When they had discussed this question, her own view had carried, but as captain it was his place to announce policy. He said, "This ship stays here; short hops waste fuel. We'll take one of the scouts, instead."

Ivan spoke again. "Good enough. Who goes, then?"

"Rissa and me, mostly," Tregare answered. "Stonzai, of course, to interpret. The rest, I haven't decided yet." He pointed a finger. "You stay, though, Ivan—in charge of the *Deux*."

Anders Kobolak stiffened; Tregare said to him, "Ivan ranks alongside First Hat; you know that. And he has seniority." He turned back to Ivan. "Your job is the ship's safety. In case of trouble—" He shook his head. "I've got nothing special in mind, but this is new country and anything can happen."

"Guidelines?" Serious now, Ivan spoke only the one word.

Tregare shrugged. "Like I said. Keep the ship safe, first, last and always. If that means lifting off like an ory-eyed bat, and worrying about groundside later, you do it." He looked around the group. "Questions?"

"Not exactly," said Hagen Trent. "But it's those unidentified blips that bother you, not the Shrakken. Now has anyone given much thought to special tactics an FTL ship might use? Such as getting up to C and then popping in and out of supra-light isolation?"

Yes. Rissa saw possibilities, and could tell that the others were also considering new ideas. She said nothing; later, she and Tregare could discuss whatever was suggested here. And now from the next room came sounds of an awakening fretful baby. Rissa excused herself and went to help Ellalee soothe Renalle. Certainly, for the next few days while she was away at the other Shrakken port, she would have no chance to enjoy her young daughter. But now she could do so. In a few moments, Lisele joined them.

* * *

When the others had gone, Rissa and Tregare and Lisele ate in quarters. Tiny Renalle dozed in a crib near them; Ellalee's shift was over and she had left.

After the meal, over coffee and wine, Rissa asked how the discussion had gone, concerning possible FTL ship tactics. Lopsidedly, Tregare grinned. "Oh, it went fine—until we plugged in some numbers. Y'see—if the *Deux* were nearly up to C and spotted some STL bogies, sure, we could pass light and effectively vanish. And then dead-reckon to drop into sub-light and appear right in front of 'em, and cut one peace-ripping swathe! But how often would we all the vectors be right, to pull that one off?"

"But we can change course," Lisele said. "Coming here we did, more than once. So why—?"

"Because when you start talking close quarters," said Tregare, "the numbers are different." Lisele looked as if she wished she hadn't spoken; he spread a hand toward her. "Don't feel bad; you're not the only one who got caught out—because going from Point A to Point B, the problem doesn't arise. But—" He thought, then nodded. "Use your calculator—I'll give you the same example that convinced Hagen Trent." She brought out the instrument, and waited. "All right—figure me the radius of a one-gee turn, at C, and keep in mind that halving the radius doubles the gees, and so on."

Rissa watched as Lisele worked out the problem, then looked up frowning. "Why, it's close to a light-year!"

Startled, Rissa said, "Truly?"

Tregare nodded. "Surprised me, too. Now one more, Lisele. Anders came up with a brainwave. A great way to *hide* an FTL ship would be, put it into a faster-than-light orbit. Dipping just below C at aphelion, so's to be accessible to communication periodically."

Wide-eyed, Lisele said, "That's a great idea!"

He sighed. "Plug in some numbers, honey. What's the radius of that orbit—around our own Sun, say?" After a time the child looked up and shook her head. "That's right," said Tregare. "Can't be done; you'd be inside the star. So—keep the primary the same size, orbit practically at the surface, and give me the surface gravity we'd need for the star."

This time the girl took a little longer, then canceled her results and tried a second time. Finally, in a low voice she said, "Something like twelve billion gravities. Is that right?"

"Close enough. I doubt you and Trent used exactly the same parameters, but you're in the same ballpark." For himself and Rissa he poured more coffee. "So, since I don't recall the data on black holes, and far's I know we don't have any around here close, we had to put the FTL-orbit idea back to bed."

Sated with coffee, Rissa sipped her wine. "And did you get any ideas that are usable?"

"If the *Deux* should have to skedaddle? Just one, and nothing fancy." Pantomiming with his hands, he said, "Put the pilot in a gee-suit and cocoon everybody else in the chambers, and get up past light as fast as the pilot can stand it. Then a few days out, drop to zerch and head back here." Again his hands demonstrated. "Homing in, don't figure to land on the first pass, but pop down below C to look the situation over. And maybe shoot the tail off somebody if you have the chance." He drained his cup. "Like it?"

For a time Rissa stayed silent; then she nodded. "Within the limits you cite, the plan has its merits. But yet—" Absently, she worried at a bit of food caught between two teeth. "Those numbers—I should like to study them a little further."

"Me, too," said Liesel Selene.

Next day at mid-morning—Shaarbant's day came to nearly twenty Earth-standard hours—Tregare readied the expedition. Rissa and himself, Stonzai and Sevshen and a ranking local Shrakken called Skandith. Or something like that; since that one and Rissa had no vocabulary in common, the name hardly mattered to her.

Then Hagen Trent and Jenise Rorvik, doubling as security people. Trent had little or no security training, but they would need his evaluation of Shtegel's technical facilities.

Half the *Deux*'s personnel, it seemed, were crowded outside the scoutship's launching bay to see the group off. Too many, Rissa thought, and some merely in the way. *But do not bother.*

Tregare and Ivan exchanged a few words, and the scout's crew boarded. Its airlock closed; Rissa followed Tregare to Control. Stonzai and Skandith came along; behind them, the others stayed to strap down in bunks. Scouts, Rissa had cause to remember, were not always smooth riding. Not in atmosphere, at least.

When all were ready—Rorvik acknowledged for the passenger compartment—the launching bay opened. Ivan confirmed that the launch area was clear of bystanders, and Tregare hit the power switch. When the drive's hum was up to pitch he lifted the

scout with a rush and took it high—but still within atmosphere—
then leveled off.

Navigation was simple; Skandith pointed and spoke, and
Stonzai translated for Tregare. Behind Sassden's river junction
the ground rose, mottled green and brown, into tree-covered
foothills that grew, as the scout flew above them, to be ridged
mountains. Only the upper reaches showed free of timber, and at
this latitude and season they held no snow.

"Rather pleasant terrain," said Rissa. "Is it not, Bran?"

"Nice enough." He chuckled. "Remember back on Number One, though? These mountains aren't a pimple on the Big
Hills there."

"I suppose not." But still, she thought, enjoyable to see.
Now the scout bucked as, below, the ground fell away again,
becoming a vast wide valley that looked like jungle. Well, they
were nearing the equatorial regions. Skandith pointed down to
large darker patches; if Rissa understood Stonzai's translation,
these latter were swamp.

For a time their course followed a river. Where it met with a
much larger one, Skandith wiggled a hand, making it clear
without words that Tregare should use the broad watercourse as
guide. And he did so until, ahead, shining in sunlight the sea
appeared.

From this angle it looked, to Rissa, greener than Earth's
oceans. And since Shaarbant had no large moons—though a
number of smaller ones—its major tides would be simpler,
following only the planet's sun. The scout passed the shoreline;
for a long time it flew over water, dotted with scattered islands.
Some were brown and bare, others wooded.

Skandith pointed ahead, to the left, and Rissa saw a fantastic stretch of islands—large and small, reaching at least to the
horizon. Like a hilly continent, partially flooded, she thought.
Tregare shifted course with the pointing, and for nearly an hour
the scout traversed this mix of land and water. And then Rissa
saw the largest land mass of all this archipelago.

Roughly elliptical, it had four irregular peninsulas spaced
around two-thirds of its shoreline. In the middle, inside a sort of
ringwall like those of Luna's craters, stood a body of water. To
Rissa's guess, its area was more than a quarter of the island's
total. Her intake of breath came louder than she expected.

"Yeah," said Tregare. "When *that* volcano blew, I bet it
made Krakatoa look like a wet squib." He squinted. "The
lake—it must be close to eighty kilos across."

"And it is old, Bran—very old."

"Right. I doubt the Shrakken can tell us much about it. I get the impression they arrived here fairly recently."

Before Rissa could answer, Skandith pointed ahead, where the largest peninsula met the main body of the island, and spoke rapidly. Rissa looked closely, and made out buildings and two ships. Stonzai said, "There, Skandith tells, land we do."

Tregare nodded. "Tell Skandith we're on our way." He slanted the scout down fast, spiraling around the installation below. This settlement was larger than Sassden, Rissa saw, and likely quite a lot older. Besides the construction, she saw that several thousand hectares of land were under cultivation—and in some areas the trees stood in orchard-like rows.

Tregare landed between the largest building and the two Shrakken ships that sat safely distant from it. He unbuckled and stood; the others followed him to where the passengers were also getting up.

"It was a nice ride, but I wish I could have _seen_ something."

"Liesel Selene!" Startled, Rissa found nothing more to say.

Tregare did, though. "Who told _you_ to come along?"

Looking troubled, Jenise Rorvik grasped the child's arm. "Wasn't she supposed to? I thought—"

Lisele looked defiant. "Nobody said I _couldn't_."

Suddenly Rissa could not help laughing. "So you followed aboard, bold as brass, and everyone assumed you had permission."

Looking down, away from them all, Lisele said, "I won't be any trouble. If you say so, I won't even go groundside. But I did so want to _see_ this place." No one spoke. "I—I'm sorry."

Moving quickly, Tregare went to hug her. "It's all right; you can come groundside, and all. But next time, ask."

"Yes, sure." For a moment the child's smile faltered. She looked at Rissa. "But if I'd asked this time, could I have come?"

Rissa paused, to visualize that asking and her response; then she nodded. "If Tregare had agreed, then so would I."

Lisele's gaze fixed on her father; he, too, took a moment to answer. "I'd have had misgivings—and then you two would have talked me out of them." He grinned. "Just like the question of bringing you on the _Deux_ in the first place."

"Then let's go groundside," said Lisele. "What are we waiting for?"

It was mid-afternoon; cruising at atmospheric speeds, the trip had been a long one. So today's schedule, Rissa gathered from Stonzai's translations, was to see only the facilities for starship repair and modification. "Well, that's what we're here to find out," said Tregare. "Hang on, while I set up communication relay to the *Deux*, via the Shrakken ground-to-ground terminals, and we can go."

So they trekked first through the largest building, pausing to hear explanations, and then through several others. When they had seen what Stonzai said were most of the important areas, sunset neared. Rissa expected that the humans would eat on the scoutship, but Stonzai relayed an invitation to dine with the Shrakken.

Tregare looked to Rissa. She shrugged, and he said, "I don't see why not. Stonzai, tell Skandish we accept with thanks."

Jenise Rorvik spoke. "Excuse me—but there's a risk, you know." Tregare's brows rose; Rorvik said, "The Shrakken can eat some of our foods, and some not; they get sick. We may have the same problem."

Yes—on the *Deux*, Sevshen had been ill. But he was recovering by the time Rissa heard about it, so she hadn't followed up the incident. "That some of the food here, you mean, may be dangerous to us?" Jenise nodded. Rissa thought for a moment, then felt her involuntary frown clear. "The testing kit in the scout. Scoutships have multiple uses; remember? And one of these is that of emergency lifeboat. And since even a marginally habitable world may be the survivors' only possible haven, food-testing kits are essential. So we may—"

"Afraid not," Tregare cut in. He had a sheepish look to him. "I let Ornaway borrow the kits. Off both scouts. He and young Limmer were hell-bent eager beaver on checking out local vegetation, and maybe animal life, for edibility. I couldn't see any harm to it, so I okayed the project."

"Of course." Rissa nodded. "But then how, and especially without offending our hosts, can we determine what is safe to eat?"

"Maybe I can help," said Jenise. "Back at university I studied exotic plants for a while, and the ways some primitives used to handle them. It's a little messy, but it usually works. The rule is, smell everything first and begin with very small bites of what you do try, and chew them well. At any stage, if something doesn't fit with what you *know* is all right—too strong or rank, or you're simply not sure—discard it. Spit it out, if need be." She pushed back her blonde hair. "You may miss some gourmet treats, but you'll have better luck avoiding a gut-ache, too."

Looking thoughtful, Tregare said, "Rissa, try to explain that to Stonzai, to pass to Skandish. So they'll know what we're doing, and why." Explaining, Rissa had to repeat and paraphrase, but finally Stonzai reported that Skandish understood.

"That you of care must be, accept we do." So, following Skandish into a sprawling, slantwalled, one-level building, the party trooped through a long corridor into the Shrakken equivalent of a galley. The color blue predominated, but walls and ceiling bore random abstract designs in green and yellow.

There were no tables, and if human chairs did not suit Shrakken, the converse was also true. Balancing a tray piled with steaming vegetation, Rissa tried to use the "chair" and found herself half sitting and half standing, like perching on the edge of a tall barstool. Lisele's legs were too short to reach the floor; she could not maintain balance, so she had to stand.

Her tray, Rissa learned, fit onto a prong that came up from the front of the device. She looked at her eating utensils—two, mirror images of each other, like shallow spoons with one edge sharpened, and ending in three short tines. And a thing like a small spatula riddled with holes. She shrugged—when in Rome, watch to see how the Romans do it.

The three Shrakken and five humans were in a circle; elsewhere in the room, Shrakken formed other circles, some eating already and some still arriving. Looking at her tray, Rissa could not decide where to start, and except for Rorvik, her friends seemed in like case.

Jenise said, "This green spongy stuff is all right; tasty, too. Stay off the leafy things with the dark-red veins—oxalic acid, I think, like in rhubarb leaves." She chewed something else, nodded and swallowed; then she set down her hardware. "Look, there's no point in you all trying each item for yourselves. Why don't I check out everything, and then if you're willing to go with my judgment—but of course if *you* don't trust something I okay, speak up and say so. All right?"

"Fine with me," Tregare said, so as the others watched, Rorvik sampled each offering and gave verdicts. Six items approved, four thumbed down, the rest doubtful and thus left alone.

Except for Lisele, who balked at an approved vegetable that reminded Rissa of broccoli, everyone followed Jenise's decisions. But then, the child hated broccoli, anyway.

Nobody got sick. And the spatula, Rissa learned, was for squeezing juice from a yellowish ovoid; small bits of something else were dipped in the juice as a sauce, and the squeezed yellow pulp left uneaten. All in all, Rissa liked Shrakken cuisine.

After dinner, other Shrakken joined the group and they all went to another room, this one colored a soft umber and decorated with curved line designs in black. Here, not unexpectedly, were drinks. Recalling Stonzai's tastes, Rissa expected wines and brandies, and was mostly right. As she had done for Stonzai, now the Shrakken offered open containers for the humans to smell or taste. One reddish fluid, brandy or no, smelled much like bourbon, so Rissa chose it. She would have liked some ice, but saw none.

Now Stonzai spoke. "All, to listen must." She stood with a Shrakken who was short for its kind and moved stiffly; its facial markings were paler and less distinct than most. Old? Possibly.

Being among her own people made Stonzai's English even less comprehensible than usual, but Rissa understood that this Shrakken was named Sharvil. And Sharvil was the one who "spoke for" the port of Shtegel, and for the entire colony on Shaarbant.

Well. It was *time* they got down to cases. Rissa listened and stayed silent, leaving it to Tregare to handle negotiations.

From the timing of some of Sharvil's responses, Rissa guessed the older Shrakken had already been briefed on Tregare's proposals; certainly, Stonzai had known of them. Yet Tregare had to tell the whole thing—through Stonzai—from the beginning. All about the Hoyfarul Drive, and his intention to give FTL travel to the Shrakken.

Then came questions, and Tregare paused to consider his answers. Finally he said, "Judging by what you showed us, here on Shaarbant you can adapt your ships for FTL. But not right away." He squinted past Stonzai. "What you have is the tools to make the tools to do the job. Two years, I'd guess, if you're lucky." Earth years, Rissa supposed he meant; she doubted that he knew the length of Shaarbant's. *She* did not.

"So we can talk your technical people through the specs, and leave you a few sets to work with. But then everybody's best bet is for us to go to Stenevo, as we'd planned—where we can get FTL conversions going in a hurry and on a big scale. That's—"

Now as Stonzai translated, Sharvil made shrill protest. Shaarbant did not *have* two years of safety, Stonzai relayed. No—the Earth ship must stay and be of aid!

With seeming patience, though Rissa saw the tension in him, Tregare went through it again. Two years, to accomplish anything, and so few ships here for conversion. Were more expected? When? And these here now—how many were scheduled to leave soon?

"No." Stubborn now, Tregare shook his head. All Shrakken life, not just Shaarbant, was at stake. To stay here might doom the species and still not save this world. And when he finished, Sharvil raised a hand. Head moving in the way Rissa could never interpret, Sharvil spoke. And Stonzai slowly relayed the words.

"Then to go, you must. But by your saying, as much help as can be, leave with us you will."

"Yeah, sure, Stonzai. And we *will* stay long enough to help you get started." He turned to Hagen Trent. "How long to get printouts of all the dope they'll need? I mean, you couldn't have brought all of it, this time."

Trent nodded. "I brought only the drive specs; they can have those now. The rest—first I had to know what they have, and what not."

"Right." Tregare explained to Stonzai, then said, "Tomorrow we go back to the ship, then soon as we can—two-three days, Hagen?" Again the man nodded. "—we'll bring you everything else we can. Then I guess we're off to Stenevo. Agreed?"

Sharvil complained no longer, but asked surprisingly germane questions. Rissa felt her anxiety ease. Then, soon, the meeting adjourned; the humans returned to the scoutship. All were invited to spend the night groundside but only the three Shrakken accepted. "Not that I don't trust them," was Tregare's comment as they entered the scout and Rissa sealed it, "but having tried Shrakken chairs, I'm not sure I want to risk what their beds are like!"

At least, thought Rissa, Shrakken beds might have had privacy; the scout's bunks did not. Oh, they were curtained off from one another—but sounds carried. So, while Rissa agreed with Tregare's desires, this was not the right time and place. She could not make love silently; neither could she allow herself to be heard by others. Well, Lisele was a different matter; from infancy she had often shared even closer quarters, and simply took things for granted. Jenise Rorvik, though, and Hagen Trent? No.

So, when Rissa was dozing off and a touch woke her, she felt brief anger. "Bran—no! I have told you."

For a moment, no answer; was this some intruder? But then he spoke. "Outside, the weather's nice. Like to take a little walk?"

Suddenly she giggled. "Why not?" She rummaged and found her robe, got up and put it on. Then, quietly, she followed Bran Tregare.

"Can I come too?" Lisele's voice was almost a whisper.

Rissa paused. Tregare squeezed her hand, leaned over to the curtain that hid the child, and whispered back, "For a few minutes, princess; then you come back inside. Because mainly we're going out to be by ourselves, a little while."

Barefoot, all three, they went to and down the ramp, then a few meters away from the scout. Tregare said, "Ground cover isn't damp, to speak of; let's sit, shall we?" When they did, he pointed upward. "See—two of the moons showing. Watch; you can see them move against the stars."

Neck craned, Rissa stared. Yes—one whitish disc and one orange, each slightly larger than a star's twinkling dot, inching across the starfield. "Are they as close together as they seem?"

"Not really," said Tregare. "On average, the orange one's half again as far out. Eccentric orbit, though, and near perigee right now." A pause. "The white one—if I remember right, it takes quite a slant from the ecliptic."

"It moves more," said Lisele, "than when we were at the ship."

Stellar light made vision ghostly; more than seeing, Rissa sensed Tregare's headshake. "Not the same moon; this one's a little brighter. The one you mean—from here, we can't see it."

Rissa chuckled. "Bran, I had no idea you kept such a close check on this planet's satellites."

"The one we just mentioned? Special case—it's practically in synchronous orbit. Takes years to go around the planet. Right now it's somewhere above that big jungle valley we flew over."

They talked longer, Tregare pointing out his guesses of stars known on Earth. Rissa offered to bet against two of his choices, but he didn't take the wagers. Then Lisele said, "I'm getting cold," so her parents kissed the child goodnight and sent her back inside.

Tregare reached for Rissa. She responded, but said, "The chill is *not* entirely comfortable."

He laughed. "Almost forgot; I brought this big fat quilt."

He wrapped it around them; they snuggled together. And a little later, if stars or moons heard Rissa's cries, she did not care at all.

An hour past dawn, everyone on the scout was up and dressed. Lisele poured fruit juice, and Tregare made coffee, but said, "We shouldn't eat yet, in case somebody wants to invite us out." When no one did, after a time he heated and served a round of standard rations. Then, after Hagen and Jenise did a quick job of cleanup duty, the group waited. An hour, before Tregare stood, and said, "I don't know protocol around here, but I think it's time we go look people up."

First, relaying through the Shrakken comm-net, he called *Inconnu Deux*. At the ship, Ivan reported, all was well. "Okay," said Tregare, "I guess we can get on the march."

Only Tregare and Rissa went. Hagen Trent's digestion was giving him delayed reactions to last night's dinner, so he stayed aboard, nominally in charge. Jenise and Lisele wanted to explore a little. "All right. But stay within sight of the scout."

Once outside, Tregare headed for the building where they had met Sharvil. The Shrakken galley held only a few attendants, making slow work of tidying the place, so Tregare and Rissa went to the other room they knew. And found six Shrakken, including Sharvil, plus the three who had come in the scout. Rissa spoke greetings; Stonzai relayed them. Sharvil answered, and Stonzai said to Tregare, "Back to ship now, today, we go?"

He nodded. "I'd thought so. Expected you on the scout, though, earlier. We waited quite a while."

"Sharvil *here*, to talk, waits." So, thought Rissa—the Shrakken leader stood on form. But why had not Stonzai told them?

At any rate, now Tregare and Sharvil negotiated. At first, rather than moving the scout back and forth, Sharvil wanted him to bring the *Deux* to Shtegel—and offered to replace the fuel wasted in such an inefficient short hop. But Tregare refused; aside, to Rissa, he said, "I wouldn't like to *tempt* these nice folks."

Equally soft-voiced, she said, "I think the problem would not arise—but if we are to misjudge, let it be on the side of caution."

Then Sharvil wanted a firm time for the scout's return, bringing the FTL conversion data. Tregare shrugged. "Two-three days was my engineer's guess. He's not here, and I can't commit him to a definite time when he knows the answers better than I do." And after several rephrasings, Sharvil eventually accepted that answer.

Then came the forehead-touching ceremony, and they left— Rissa, Tregare, Stonzai and Sevshen. Skandith would remain at Shtegel. Outside, Rissa saw Lisele and Jenise near a grove of trees. Tregare gave a piercing whistle, startling the Shrakken so that each gave a little jump; he pointed to the scout, and everyone began running toward it. Rissa overtook Tregare, and wondered if he were losing stamina, but he winked at her, and she also slowed. The Shrakken passed them, making whuffling noises that could have been laughter as they moved in their toe-dancing lope. Jenise, Rissa saw, was not overtaking Lisele very rapidly.

Stonzai and Sevshen reached the upramp first, with the four humans in a near-tie. Tregare picked up Lisele. "The champ."

Laughing as they went up the ramp, she said, "Someday I really will be."

There was time, Tregare said, to get back to the ship before mid-afternoon. "Especially since we're going *against* the planet's rotation. Over more than two radians of longitude, the time differences add up." Mentally, Rissa converted the figure—yes, about a third of the world's circumference.

"Well, then," she said. "Shall we strap in for liftoff?"

"Can I sit in Control this time," asked Lisele, "so I can see everything?" Hagen Trent had started in that direction; now, smiling, he shrugged and went toward a bunk instead.

Tregare said nothing, so Rissa answered. "All right. Come along, and let us make sure of your safety harness."

While she did so, Tregare called the *Deux*. Anders Kobolak had the watch; he patched the intercom through to Ivan's quarters. "Marchant here. All's calm so far. You coming back soon?"

"Preparing to lift," Tregare said. "See you by mid-afternoon, or close to it. Tregare out." He cut the circuit and activated his drive; when its hum built to suit him, he nodded and hit the power lever. Vibrating under thrust, the scout rose. As the ground fell away and swooped to one side, then further as Tregare set his climb angle, Rissa saw Lisele grip the arms of her seat. And realized that the child *hadn't* ridden a scout this way before.

The ring-shaped island slipped over the horizon behind;

soon the entire archipelago followed it, and after a time the mainland lay ahead. Not obviously, though; their earlier trip had been under mostly clear skies; but now, below, cloud layers hid much of the shoreline and the land beyond. The great river's mouth was hidden. Rissa turned to Stonzai. "The river?"

The alien pointed left, where cloud masses covered all surface features. "There, should be it."

Tregare grinned. "Doesn't matter. The course-and-speed integrator in this bucket's little computer isn't calibrated for fine detail, but it'll do. Because if things are socked-in at the far end, we can home on the *Deux*'s beacon."

About halfway, by Rissa's guess, across the shallow jungled bowl of valley, ahead they saw the mountains come into view. Only their upper reaches showed above the cloud layer that hid the valley below, but Lisele smiled and pointed to them. "Yeah," Tregare said, "something to see, finally. Too bad you weren't up here yesterday, when—" Then his face twitched and he fell silent; the scout jerked with the sudden tremor of his hands. Rissa's head gave a stab of pain; her vision blurred; then the moment passed.

"Bran! Did you feel—?"

"Something—as if—I don't know. It's all right now."

From Stonzai came a groan. Rissa looked; if the Shrakken agreed with Tregare, her appearance did not show it. The sidewise-moving eyelids closed tightly, and the V-mouth made a triangle that bared clenched teeth. Words came. "It—it the *Tsa* is!"

"Stonzai!" Rissa touched her. "Is it still hurting you?"

Strangely, unreadably, the Shrakken's head moved. "Attacking now, they not. But for pain to ease, a time takes."

Rissa turned. "Lisele—did *you* feel anything?"

Squinting upward, at the sky, the child said, "For a second, everything flickered, was all. But I saw—up there, some dots moving." She shook her head. "Gone now."

Cursing, Tregare threw a switch. Beeps sounded, and on a sidescreen five blips appeared. "Stupid!" he muttered. "Flying with topside detectors off, just because—" Swiftly the blips moved offscreen; he twiddled dials to no effect as the beeps died away. "Well, that does it!" He pointed the scout steeply down; the speed indicator showed a rapid increase.

"Bran. Are you sure?"

"Enough. The Shrakken don't *have* five ships here, and

weren't expecting any, just yet.'' He shrugged. "Doesn't prove anything, I know. But let's get home like a bat!''

They sat, tense, as Tregare drove the scout, bucking at the limits of stability in atmosphere, across the great valley. Skimming the cloud layer, occasionally they passed through its upper promontories. After ten minutes, then twenty, Rissa saw her husband begin to relax. Even Stonzai, except for the way she gripped the seat's arms, looked normal again.

Then the detector alarm sounded; Tregare reached for the screen controls. "No, Bran," Rissa said. "I will do it. Flying this low, you need all your concentration." Her third try gave results—five blips, homing from above and behind. Homing *fast*.

Tregare's first choice of words showed little imagination. Then, "All right—we can't outrun that lot, or outmaneuver. Not in a scout. But maybe we can outslick 'em!" Abruptly they dropped into cloud, and kept dropping. Then the scout was braking, *hard*. "If I can set down before they get here, and cut drive—''

"The jungle! Bran—''

"Landing blast should clear the ground; let's hope so." The scout lurched; Stonzai made a shrill bleat. "In my head again!" Tregare shouted. "You feel anything?''

"I—I am not certain." Had she? Rissa could not be sure.

With forward motion almost stopped, Tregare pointed the nose up; the craft began to settle. From below, Rissa heard rumblings— then pain clutched her mind, and shook it. Stabs of light came; she fought to see and think; nausea struck. Tregare's fist beat the control panel; he screamed. Lisele cried, "Oh, make it *stop*!''

A crashing jolt as the scout hit dirt; then it tipped. Power came on in a great surge—by Tregare's purpose, or a random swipe of his hand? To Rissa's left, something dealt the scout a staggering blow, then another. Pain shattered her thinking; the next impact came directly facing her, and her safety harness cut cruelly. Tregare's tore loose, and he was thrown against the controls.

Teeth clenched, Rissa batted at the power switch—and again, until she got it. Then the pain flowered so brightly that she saw nothing more, and heard only the dying cough of the scout's drive.

To feel her consciousness leaving was total relief.

Rissa woke to pain—of mind and of body, and for a time she could not separate the two. But her mind cleared, and she found herself hurtfully suspended by her harness. The scout, then, lay on the side she faced. Carefully she tested arms and legs; each moved, not pleasurably. After a moment she decided how to free herself safely; one hand on each side's harness release, she pushed them, and fell bruised and sprawling against her control panel.

Normal lighting was gone; the dim glow of the emergency system lit the place. She looked; Tregare lay still, but he breathed. His face was turned away; blood smeared the part she could see. And his left leg bent wrongly. She crawled toward him.

But above her, once and then again, she heard a faint gurgling gasp. Something spattered on her neck. Rissa looked up.

Horror! Half in her harness and half out, one strap across her chest and another cutting into her throat, Lisele hung. The child's face was purple and blackening; one bleeding hand was inside the strap at her neck, and the other clawed feebly at it.

Adrenaline struck; time slowed. Clambering to her feet, Rissa reached for Lisele's harness to pull herself up; the task took seeming hours. With one foot in a loop of her own loose-hanging harness, her left hand reached for the catch that would free Lisele's throat—but from where she hung, she had no leverage. And the child swung there, barely making any sound.

Panting, Rissa let go the catch, bent her leg and jumped—with only one arm and leg to propel her. Now the time-stretch helped—in mid-air she lunged, with both hands, for the catch.

And got it. Falling, unable to protect herself from impact, she saw the strap fly loose, and Lisele suspended only by her chest. Then the edge of the control panel crashed against her kidney. Agony shot through her and blanked her mind.

When she could think, she found herself again trying to reach Lisele. This time the climb was almost impossible, but at its end, the task was not. She rigged her own harness to hold her—swaying, semi-upright—wrapped her left arm through Lisele's restraints and around the child, and carefully released the final strap. Lisele's weight unbalanced her, but she managed to hold. Then, figuring each move carefully, it took long minutes to get the child down safely.

At any rate, Lisele was breathing. Had she needed resuscitation she would have died, for Rissa could not have given it in time. She lowered her daughter past the control consoles to a bare section of forward bulkhead, and laid her down with limbs straight. None was broken; good; the mouth was free of blood or phlegm. And now normal color was returning to the small face.

Rissa stood, and climbed back onto the now-horizontal control panel. It was time to see to Tregare.

The panel was not quite level; the scout, she decided, was lying a bit nose-down. She considered the matter longer than need be, so that she would not have to think of what must be done—or of what *could* be done, which might be very little indeed.

Surprising her, Tregare had his eyes open. "She all right?"

"Bran! How long have you been awake?" She shook her head. Her coiled hair had come loose; part of it fell across her face. Irritably she pushed it back. "No—first, how badly you—?"

His hand made a small motion; he winced and flexed it, then shrugged, and winced again. "You see the leg. When we have time, you'll have to set it." At her start of protest, "You know how; you trained at Erika's." When she nodded, he said, "Still more than half deadhead, I was, dizzy with hurting, when something fell and jarred me. You?" Again she nodded. "I'll ask later. Next I knew, you were climbing up. Toward Lisele, hanging there, face all purple. Didn't say anything; why distract you?"

How could he look so calm? "So I waited. *Is she all right?*"

"By great luck, perhaps a miracle. Her harness slipped somehow; she was hanging—Bran, for a time I did not think I could free her!"

Her left hand was near enough that he could clasp it. "You did, though. Peace be thanked, Rissa—you did!" He squinted past her, up where Lisele had dangled. "And from here, I can't think how you managed." He tried to turn his body; she saw his teeth clench. "Ugh! We can't move me until that leg's set. First, though—you've had no chance to check on anyone else, yet. For starters, how about Stonzai?"

She had not thought—she had not *thought* of any others. Not Stonzai, nor of those who had suffered the crash in isolation, strapped in bunks and knowing nothing of the peril. "Oh, Bran! Wait—I will go and see."

Again she climbed, this time not in frantic hurry. She reached Stonzai and found the Shrakken female hanging against her safety harness as Rissa had done when she woke, and breathing evenly though not yet conscious. From the alien's mouth trickled bright orange blood. Judging by the puddle below, the stream had been larger and was dwindling; in itself, the blood loss should not be serious. At this point Rissa could do nothing helpful; she climbed past Stonzai's seat position and found footing to stand. And from here she could see the hatch that gave access to the bunkroom.

The hatch was slightly ajar. At what was now its lower edge, something dark moved, and grew. Even in the dim light, Rissa could see that it had to be blood. Not a great lot, here—but at the source?

And it was not bright orange. The stuff was dark red.

IX. Elzh

Again now the beastworld—near! Too soon, with Elzh in fret for Tserln and Ceevt. Idsath had projected that itself and Tserln, indling, could fill the young with warm thought to turn mindpain away, and Elzh followed that hope. Still, though—two less Tsa to strike at mindbeasts. Of five ships, only.

And now, beastworld. Twice around it, so near to mindpain range as to brush that world's gases, Elzh's ships curved.

Only two places, distant from each other, showed mindbeast sign. Two ships at the larger; at the smaller, three. But there, the third was the ship that came out of nothing!

To decide—as correct, as understood. Pain and dread would be, but Tsa-Drin law gave no choice. Mindsaying the need and regret, Elzh directed the five ships to descend. Gases tugged at the speed of Elzh's ship; it shuddered, almost as Elzh did.

But ships cannot feel dread.

Down toward beastworld, within mindpain distance, and slowing. But nearing surface *between* mindbeast places, the curve of beastworld itself shielding Tsa from pain. To now, then, success for Elzh. And time for thinking. But always, to obey.

Then, below, the *small* ship—and in it, some mindbeasts not the same. At first, no mindpain—never deadly it came, Elzh knew, until the beasts detected Tsa. So—to strike first! Yes.

Quickly, Elzh mindsaid, and with agony the Tsa threw attack. At first, no seeming effect—then the small ship faltered, but soon recovered course. As mindpain struck! To evade! Up and up, to observe at safe distance while Tsa healed from mindbeasts' return attack. Then turn and pursue. Mindsaying and mindhearing with all crewmates, Elzh exulted. Even with two kinds of mindbeasts, this small ship was no match for the Tsa!

Now down again, nearing the tiny thing—strike! Below the opaque gases it went; Elzh's mind ranged there without finding. But strike again! And more, and more!

Soon then, no more feel of mindbeasts. Up again, the Tsa ships now. Mindsaying, as near to indling as can be over distance, Elzh spoke the ships. Finding hurt, as expected, but fastly healing. And from Tserln the thought that Ceevt, the young, had felt no pain.

So. As the Tsa-Drin wills. But the ship from nothing, that still waited, was not small. Best to strike it at speed, so that if mindpain built into death-risk, Elzh's ships would be soon away to safe distance.

Then, no matter how strong the ship might be, that had come out of nothing, Elzh's five ships would wait. High above this beastworld, so that the strange ship could have no chance to leave it.

Elzh's mindsaying ended. Toward the place where the ship from nothing stood, the Tsa fleet turned.

X. Ivan

*A*fter Tregare signed off, Ivan resumed his meal with Dacia Kobolak—his breakfast, her after-watch dinner. "So we'll see them about mid-afternoon," he said, and told her of Tregare's agreements with the Shrakken leader at Shtegel. "Soon as I check the watch logs, I'll get on the computer and start coding out the Hoyfarul Drive data. Maybe I can give Hagen a head start." Done eating, he stood. "If I save a day or so, we can lift for Stenevo that much sooner."

Standing also, Dacia said, "Are you in a hurry, Ivan?"

He shrugged. "The Shrakken seem to be. Maybe they're right."

They went to First Hat's quarters. While Dacia prepared for bed, Ivan riffled papers until he found what he needed. He gave Dacia her goodnight kiss; then, impatient, he climbed to Control.

The watch logs held no surprises; Ivan initialed acceptance and Anders Kobolak nodded in acknowledgment. Then, at the primary computer terminal, Ivan ran his data search. Jeremy Crowfoot interrupted, suggesting a coffee break, and in the galley the two men discussed the scope of what the Shrakken would need to know. Afterward, upship again, Crowfoot helped with the data retrieval and finally said, "That's really all I can think of. I'd run it through once again to cut redundancy, and leave it for Trent to check."

"Right. Thanks for sitting in, Jere." Crowfoot left. Ivan punched directions for pruning the data, and the new readout began. He nodded; this version came out shortened by nearly a third.

By his chronometer, more time had passed than he'd realized. Dacia would have had her refresher nap and might be in a mood for company. No need to check out with Anders Kobolak ...

But as Ivan reached the door, the Second Hat said, "Blips—something upstairs. Look quick!" Ivan turned to peer. On the topside screen five dots moved. Anders moved dials, trying to follow them, but in seconds they were gone, offscreen.

Ivan frowned. "What kind of a track does Tinhead show?"

"Just a minute; I'm on it." Impatient, Ivan waited until Kobolak looked up and said, "They weren't on screen long enough to be sure—but roughly, at the edge of atmosphere, and too fast for orbit. Using power to hold such tight curvature. Marchant—do you think—"

Ivan shook his head. "It doesn't matter what I think. We have to assume—" Scowling, he nodded. "Sound general quarters; everybody groundside, get aboard fast. All projector turrets and missile controls manned until further notice." He paused. "And get the drive warmed up. Now."

Kobolak relayed those orders, then turned back to Ivan. "You're thinking of lifting off? With Tregare out there still?"

Ivan didn't like the man's expression. "You heard Tregare: keep this ship safe at all costs. *That's* what I'm thinking."

Anders didn't meet his glare. "Of course. But for a minute there—"

"You thought I'd use his orders as excuse to abandon him, and keep command." He leaned forward; Kobolak flinched. The man was no coward; Ivan wondered what his own face showed. Trying to relax it, he shook his head. "My sister's out there, too—not to mention my niece, Lisele. Rissa and Tregare—I owe them my life, and more."

Now Kobolak looked up. "I'm sorry. Don't know what got into me."

"*I* know. You're chuffed that I have command. But that's all right—so long as you're sure you've got it out of your system."

He raised his eyebrows, and Kobolak nodded. "I'm sure."

What else to say? Nothing. Ivan clapped a hand to the other's shoulder. "Continue alert procedures; keep gunnery and drive informed. I'll be back soon—before those ships can get around the planet, let alone spiral in close enough to worry." For in atmosphere, projector range was drastically reduced.

"All under control, then," Anders said, "until you return."

Turning away, Ivan paused. "Not much chance, with the scout's antennas pulled in so they won't break off, plowing air, but try calling Tregare, anyway. To let him know what we're up against."

Now Kobolak could smile. "Right away." He spoke to his comm-tech. After a moment, Ivan nodded and left Control.

Fast, he went downship. Not enough time, probably, for him and Dacia—but at least, for a little while, they could talk. And suddenly he needed to be with her.

There was time, Dacia insisted, for both talk and love. But plagued by the distraction of the ship's danger, Ivan could not reach completion. Finally, though, lying with her and giving up that particular goal, panting and sweating he felt better, anyway.

He checked the time. "A fast shower; all right?" They took it together, and dried themselves quickly. He said, "Time for a short drink? *Very* short." And sipping from the ice-tinkling glass, he muttered, "If we have to lift—"

"You've planned for that?" How could she look so unworried?

"I have to." He felt his scowl but couldn't release it. "We're groundside. Hoyfarul Drive or no—any ship upstairs, with speed on, has us by the knockers."

She squeezed his hand. "But you've thought of an answer?"

"No. Tregare did. I'm just trying to figure the best way to use it." And then it was time for him to get back upship.

Lower than before but not by much, again the five ships passed above. This time, aided by the computer's track of the earlier contact, the *Deux*'s screens followed from horizon to horizon. "At the last, there," said Anders, "they changed flight angle, and slowed. They're coming down."

Ivan nodded; the statement was obvious. More important—on high-mag, with time to tune reception, the screens had caught the ships on visual. The picture wavered, but there was no question—those five weren't Shrakken. Nor, of course, human.

"So," he said, "that leaves the Tsa." Arlen Limmer's face showed excitement; the boy suggested a possible unknown alien species. Ivan shook his head. "The point is, it wouldn't matter. We have to assume the worst case." Without speaking, Arlen nodded.

Ivan had never seen the control room so full of people, some in the extra seats and others standing. With intercom circuits open to gunnery turrets and the drive room, effectively the entire crew was present. Yet the talk went slowly. Kobolak hadn't been able to reach Tregare; that fact seemed to put a damper on everyone. A thought nagged at Ivan, and finally he recognized it.

He rapped knuckles on the control panel. "One moment,

please. Something that needs doing—if we have to lift, we should leave Tregare a supply cache." He looked around. "Third Hat?"

Ornaway stood. "Orders?"

"Yeah. You test-flew Number Two scout, when we broke it out to sit groundside. In top shape, is it?" The young man nodded. "Then that's our cache. Is it fully stocked?" Another nod, and Ivan returned it. "Let's do better—beef up the stores a little." He paused to think. "Two one-hand energy guns, plugged in to stay at full charge, and one of the big portables, too. Plus three-four extra needlers with plenty of ammo." And what else, now?

He asked, and Anders said, "Communication. To let Tregare know where the scout is. I mean, we'll have to hide it."

Of course! Damn! Ivan realized he was letting worry cloud his thinking. He punched for screen display of a local terrain contour map. "Where's a good place? And Kobolak—about the communications?"

Anders' ideas made sense: automatic timing for the scout to transmit, at intervals, short bursts of recognition signals on frequencies Tregare could receive. And receipt of a proper answer would key the sending of the scout's location code. "Good enough," said Ivan, and turned the group's attention to the screened map. "So where do we hide the scout?"

Crowfoot liked a low island, out in the river-junction delta. "The wooded part, with all those irregular clearings." The problem was that reaching the spot would involve crossing water, which might be difficult for Tregare, later, or might not. Ivan picked a dry flat-bottomed gully, angling off the lefthand river about two kilos upstream. Narrow, it looked, and partly overhung by tall trees up the high banks.

"Not perfect cover," Ivan said, "but usable if Hask sets the scout in without burning much foliage. Vote?" The gully won. "Ornaway? You think you can be gentle with the shrubbery?"

"I'll pick a fair-size opening, and at the last, throw side-drift."

Ivan grinned. "Good enough. Two things, now. One is, I know we took hell and forever to decide, but now do it *fast*. Push comes to lift, we don't want to be leaving you behind." Ornaway waited. "The other thing. You won't have to walk back; I'll send you a ride."

The Third Hat left, with two persons to help him stock the scout. Ivan looked back and forth among the assembled group. "Limmer!"

Arlen stood. "Yes?"

"You're good with aircars. Go take one up. Until Ornaway moves the scout, stay downriver, out of his way. Then follow. Forget the map; just land near where he does, and bring him back. Got it?"

At first the boy looked unbelieving; then his chest swelled and his grin stretched wide. "Yes. I'll be careful about the trees, too." Ivan suppressed a smile and waved a half-salute; in any case, the aircar wouldn't leave noticeable marks. Limmer waved back, and left.

So far, so good, thought Ivan. *But what have I overlooked?*

On the screen Scout Two and then the aircraft hopped over the ridge of hills and sank out of sight. The wait, then, was too long—in the gully, what was happening?

"Ivan," Dacia began; then her face twisted and she screamed. "The Tsa!" The screen bloomed with five ships, coming low at first, then starting to rise. To Ivan came recognition and then adrenaline and then pain that put his hands to his head to keep it from bursting. His vision blanked; then it worked again.

Pain or no pain—and he heard his own voice whimper, and didn't know when it had begun, and couldn't make it stop—he reached for the screen's tracking controls. And—one thrust, was all he could make—set them to follow those ships. If he could have seen better, held purpose against the pain—but everything *hurt*. He felt himself sliding down out of the control seat, fingers scrabbling to no avail.

Then he welcomed the blackness.

"Ivan!" Dacia's voice. "Oh, peace—my *head*. Ivan?"

What with the urgent voice, and being shaken by the shoulders, Ivan forced himself awake. In two tries he pulled himself up into his seat. Shaking his head was a mistake and opening his eyes was worse; light stabbed like swords and the lids clamped shut again. More cautiously, he blinked them open a little at a time, absorbing the hurt in increments. "Dacia?"

She tried to hug him. "You're all right?"

"Maybe." No time, now, for hugging. He shrugged away, looked at the screen and saw nothing. "What's upstairs?"

As she leaned across him he saw tears following the little channels from her eyes and dropping from her cheeks. "Those ships?" she said. "Gone now. And now we know what the Tsa are, don't we? Clawing into our minds!" All her body, that Ivan could see or feel, trembled. "The screen's blank; they're gone. But what can we *do*?"

"I think—" He came upright and bore the pain of it, and leaned forward to the controls and hurt more, and yet knew he was past the worst of it. "If I got the right switch when they attacked," he said, "then we have them on tape. What they did, where they went."

Leaving the main screen watching upstairs in real time, he put the tape on an aux viewer, and carefully noted what he saw. And thought about it. "They made a hedgehop pass here, and then turned straight up, tight as they could. Dacia—when they hit us, hurting, how close do you think they were?"

"I saw them top the horizon." Now her voice was steadier. "I started to tell you, when the attack came. Only a second or two—"

"Just long enough for them to spot us," said Anders Kobolak. Rubbing his neck, he grimaced as he moved it.

Ivan kept his cursing unvoiced. "So we still have no idea what their range is." Looking round, he shrugged, then wished he hadn't. Some people were sitting up and some not. The one man—was he even breathing? To Dacia he said, "Well, first things first. You're in charge of casualties. See how bad everybody was affected; maybe we can find some correlations." Then a thought came. "The baby! Peace take me, what would that mind-clawing do to Renalle?"

He hit the intercom for captain's quarters. "Ellalee—are you there? Is Renalle all right?"

After a pause, the woman's voice said, "When it happened, she was asleep. Near as I can tell, she didn't even notice."

Dacia leaned forward. "And yourself?"

"I—all right if I come upship, and bring Renalle? I don't fancy being alone just now."

"Sure." And soon the young aborigine came in, carrying her charge. She looked well, but Ivan asked, "How bad did it get you?"

Sitting, settling the sleepy baby comfortably, Ellalee said, "Not so badly as some, looks as though. It hurt like all billy, and googled my eyesight, but I kept control, right enough. Just couldn't *do* much of anything. It was like—" She frowned, then nodded. "I'm from the Outback, you know—a big place, and in our part a white man was something rare, something to stare at. I was the only half-breed in the tribe. Children ran the bush and desert, naked. Come puberty, the old men cut away at your private parts with their dirty knives, so's you wouldn't enjoy sex much."

One side of her mouth smiled, then didn't. "I ran away. I wasn't the first. Off to the west was a white men's dig—the building of Lena Hulzein's Aussie branch HQ, though we didn't know that at the time—and several young boys and girls had fled there." Again she grimaced. "You should see what the old men do to the boys. The penis gives so *many* opportunities for surgical cleverness."

Ivan shook his head. "And cruelty perpetuates itself. If it was good enough for daddy, it's good enough for sonny." And wasn't that the way it had been for him, too, in Welfare? Not quite, but bad enough. He said, "You ran. And the old men chased you?"

"Too right; I saw my turn coming, and lit out. A week, ten days, from the installation; one water bag and about half the dried meat I could have used." Ellalee muffled a cough. "The old men—not old in your terms. Life's short in the Outback, for abos. But old enough to be past resenting their own mutilation, and be good hunters. If they'd caught me, I was stonkered for sure."

He had to keep attention on the topside screen, and certainly they weren't going anywhere just now, but still her story was running long. "I know you have a point to make, Ellalee."

"Right. 'pologetics and all. Three days I ran—really ran, much as I could manage—and behind me they were never in sight, but I knew." She shuddered. "Some they'd caught and brought back, you understand. Boys and girls both. None of them good for much, afterward, except scavenging."

Ivan looked hard at her, and she talked faster. "The third night, no food left and little water, and I knew they were close behind. If they kept on I'd be done, and for that day my legs were gone; I needed to go farther but I couldn't. So I buried into the lee of a sand dune and breathed through a hollow stalk of weed."

Her eyes widened; Ivan wondered what she saw. "Near asleep, when I heard the muttering. Not far off, but I couldn't hear words. Pointing the bone, though, they had to be. Their way of setting a curse; if they still have a claim on your mind, it kills you."

"But you'd rejected them. Is that it?"

"Thought I had. But I could still feel it on me. Lay there, and fought the death pushing at me. If they'd seen me and come, I couldn't have moved. But they didn't; a long time they chanted, and then went away. Gone in the morning—but their curse wasn't. All I could do to walk, early that day, but by noon I was mostly free. Then, only two days' walk without food, and the last with no water."

Her eyes came into focus; incredibly, she laughed. "And the Hulzein people taught me English and numbering, and about clothes and such, and there I was with the great luck to be in the right time at the right place, later, to come into space training."

His brows raised; she spoke quickly. "The point is, that what those aliens did to us—well, it felt of a muchness to what the old men did, when I lay under the sand. And if I fought it then—?"

Ivan looked up; the screen was still clear. "Then maybe you can resist the Tsa, better than most. All right; when there's time, you start learning how to fly this ship, and gunnery, too, I think."

Ellalee shook her head. "But I have *no* such training. I—"

"You're the one person aboard that the Tsa can't put out of control." The statement, Ivan realized, might be prematurely optimistic. All he really knew was that the Tsa hadn't done it yet.

Scout Two didn't answer—and the aircar hadn't returned. On sidescreen Ivan scanned toward the gully, and saw no wreckage. Impatient, starting to jitter, he wanted a drink or drugstick. Not now, though . . .

Then at the edge of the forest, two dots moved. "Anders!" Kobolak looked, also. "Ornaway and Limmer?"

"Let's hope so. They're a long way off, though."

Nothing to do but wait. Dacia came to report: one man had died of the Tsa attack, and two others were still too weak to function. Everyone else, she said, was recovering. "More or less. A few are still disoriented, but improving fast." Suddenly, she sobbed once. The second sound might have been a hiccough.

Giving her a quick, one-armed hug, Ivan turned to her brother. "Anders, have the dead man put in freeze. Not all the hookup; just for preservation. No time now for the courtesies; they'll have to wait. Not forever, though." As Anders relayed the order, Ivan looked back to the screen. Too far to recognize the approaching men, but the sizes were right. The Ornaway-sized one cradled one arm in the other. Well, until they reached the ship, no way to know what had happened.

"Look!" Anders pointed at the topside screen. One blip flashed across, while another drifted to a halt. "What—?"

Squinting, Ivan punched computer keys and had an answer. "Synchronous orbit, or close to it. Directly on top of us—or rather, on our meridian but at the equator." His laugh, he knew, sounded more like a snarl. "They've set us a watchdog."

"And what else?"

"We'll have to wait and see."

What they saw, eventually, was Tsa ships going over at regular intervals, with less time between passes than the *Deux* would need to reach the watchdog ship. Ivan was still considering the situation when Ornaway and Limmer entered Control.

He said, "Welcome back. Glad you made it." Young Limmer had a bruised face and bloody nose, but he moved well enough. Ornaway, though, still cradled one arm in his other hand, and his pale face held taut with pain. Ivan went to him. "Sit down. What happened?"

Ornaway sat. "If it was the Tsa thing, then you know how it hit us. All I've got here is a busted collarbone. Arlen was awake more than I was; let him tell it."

Arlen Limmer swallowed once. "Lucky, compared to what could have been. Haskell sat the scout down with barely a mark on the trees. I landed beside, and he got into the aircar and I lifted. Then—" His face convulsed into lines of pain.

"Then," said Ivan, "the Tsa ships came, and something clawed in your head so you couldn't hold onto a spoon if you were starving to death! That about right?" Limmer nodded. "Don't fret; we all got it, and at least you lived. One man, here, didn't. All right, Arlen; then what?"

Again the young man made a gulping sound. "I'd lifted out of the gully fast, the way you said to, and was slanting over the ridge, when it hit." If ever a face showed incomprehension, Limmer's did. "I don't *know*. Everything hurt and I couldn't see right. Tried to gun the car topside where at least we wouldn't hit anything, but my hands went numb; I couldn't feel what I was doing." For a moment he put his face into those hands, then looked up again. "The car spun out on me and we crashed. Upside down, I think, but we could have rolled, afterward, to get that way. Hask was thrown out of his seat; harness failed, maybe." The boy shook his head. "I don't think I was ever knocked out all the way. But for a long time I couldn't break past the pain and *move*. When I could, I climbed down to Hask. He was awake by then, but I was shaking too bad to try to set the fracture; all the way here, walking, he just had to hold it." The voice was plaintive. "We did the best we could."

Ivan nodded. "No blame; you did well, both of you." He

looked to where Jeremy Crowfoot was tending Ornaway's shoulder. "Congratulations, in fact."

"But the aircar's a total loss." Sullen, the boy sounded.

Shrugging off irritation, Ivan said, "Aircars we can spare; people, we can't. You had some luck and I'm glad you did. Now, are your guts unchurned enough, you can eat something? I expect you need to. So why don't you hit the galley?"

He nudged Dacia; she moved to escort the two men. Nursing, Ivan Marchant reflected, wasn't his best skill. Or even close.

With no word from Tregare, mid-afternoon came and passed. Ivan assigned Jeremy Crowfoot as ad-hoc watch officer and called an executive session. "Captain's quarters; my place is too small." He watched everyone's reactions. Anders didn't protest, and no one else seemed concerned. *All right.*

As soon as the group assembled, Ivan began. "We don't know what's happened with Tregare. If he ever got Scout One high enough for line-of-sight, I expect he'd have called. Or answered—we've had a call-tape on his frequencies, and no response. So it looks as if we're on our own."

Half standing, Alina Rostadt raised a hand. "Ivan—you're not writing Tregare off yet, are you? And Rissa?"

Because he liked the woman, he didn't shout. "Course not. But unless we hear from them, we have to be ready to act, all by ourselves. I hope there's no need for that." His gaze scanned the room. "Now does anybody have a really good idea, here?"

Silence; then Dacia said, "There aren't any. Except to wait."

No one contradicted her. Ivan smacked one fist into his other palm. "Then let's do the waiting up in Control. I've been too long away from there." Going upship, his pace ran him short of breath.

In Control the screens showed him nothing new. The watchdog still sat in synchronous orbit; another Tsa ship crossed below it. He turned to Crowfoot. "The pattern still holding?"

The man nodded. "No change. I'd have called you."

"Right. And thanks." Crowfoot moved over; Ivan took the primary control seat. Again he checked the scout's frequencies; a coded tape was sending, and no response came. He bit his lip, and told himself once more that worry wasn't going to help anything.

*   *   *

Dacia's cry brought his attention back to the screen. "The synchronous ship. It's moving!"

Squinting, Ivan tried to evaluate the blip's drift. Outside, day neared to dusk, but the screen was not affected. Checking his chronometer, Ivan estimated the next pass of the Tsa orbital patrol. Soon. And coming down, maybe? It came into view, and he was right. "Dacia! Get *everybody* in the cocoons, for acceleration. Anders, first bring out my gee-suit; if I have to fly this kite out through the roof, it might be kind of nice to survive." *Babbling.* Ivan shook his head. He checked the screen; as yet, the ships' approach was slow.

Dacia said, "I have Alina and Ellalee prepping the cocoons."

"Good." But what if—? Ivan changed his mind. "Make it full plug-ins, all around."

"For *freeze*?"

"Just in case, Dacia. *All* the options." He saw her shrug and turn away, and wished his hunch were solid enough to explain.

After she helped him with the gee-suit, she went below. Still tasting her kiss, Ivan strapped solidly into the main control seat and watched the Tsa ships descend. He waited.

No place to go but up; the only questions were how and when. In the control room Ivan sat alone; everyone else was below, being tucked into an acceleration/freeze cocoon or else doing the tucking. Eventually Dacia called. "All secured but me; give me three minutes." He acknowledged, and waited that time out, and a little more.

More comfortable than he had expected, still the gee-suit hampered movement and vision; he really didn't like it much, though he was grateful for Dacia's help in adjusting it. At the moment, though, he felt more lonely than grateful. Once more he tried to call Tregare, and again got no response.

On screen the Tsa ships still came. Ivan gave a ragged sigh. He could do it or he couldn't, and either way, the time was now. His voice said, "I got Ozzie Newhausen, didn't I?" But the saying gave no comfort; that crisis was long past and not the same. "Rissa?" he murmured. "This time we can't say goodbye."

Left hand on his centralized gunnery hookup, Ivan used his right to put the *Deux* into liftoff. Not at the normal red-line limit. Not this time. At full-out max, the *Deux* went up.

Even in the gee-suit, pressure had him close to blackout. He couldn't risk it; his too-heavy hand cut the power back a notch, then another. For if he had to turn ship, he'd need some margin.

More awake now, he noticed something else—*Inconnu Deux,* the whole mass of it, was rasping with vibration. Should he cut power further? No; he shook his head. Or tried to; his neck didn't seem to care for the idea. But plowing air under this kind of accel, he decided, would make *any* ship shake your teeth loose.

Above, coming nearly on a head-to-head course, the Tsa watchdog ship was closing. From the side, slanting, faster but not yet so near, came the other one. Ivan's jaw clenched; for the first ship his projector range would be right, within seconds now. Turning the *Deux* directly toward it, he fired a missile—and wasn't surprised when the Tsa projectors picked it off at a safe distance. Then, all seven turrets aimed line-of-flight, he set heterodyne for peak heat, and fired.

Two seconds, three, he held the switch down—and in the suddenly black sky the Tsa ship bloomed like fireworks. *Out of atmosphere now!* Switch off, he swung ship to miss the wreckage. One down . . .

Then the pain licked at him, ebbed and came again—worse than back on groundside! One last, pre-planned order his muscles executed; the last thing he felt, that was not pain, was the power lever moving to its final notch.

When he could next see and move, Ivan eased the power back. Three notches—but even out of atmosphere, the *Deux* still shook. He checked the chronometer; this time he'd blacked out for less than two minutes. Extra accel got him out of range fast? Must be. His rear screen showed the other ship following, but losing ground. The planet looked larger than he would have expected by now, but as he watched, it shrank visibly in perspective.

He wasn't home free. The Tsa had three other ships—and sure enough, here came two of them. One from either side, higher than on their patrol beats and with better speed, too.

Automatically he shook his head again. His neck allowed it, this time, but he paid in stabbing ache. No time to coddle himself—the trick was, don't let both those ships near him at once, if he could help it. Gauging distance, he upped power a notch and turned *Inconnu Deux* toward the nearest Tsa, to pass behind it. But as he expected, it slowed and began to turn, also. "All right, you brainburners! Let's see you figure *this* move."

He adjusted his projectors' heterodyne; the three seconds of firing would have drifted it some. On the controls he separated the six peripheral turrets from the central one, and set them for coordinated traverse within their mutual limits.

Still outside effective range, Ivan put his central turret on continuous fire, fishtailing the *Deux* to flick the beam toward the Tsa ship and then away again, so he could menace it while still holding course to clear it safely. Meanwhile he tried another missile. He didn't expect a hit and didn't get one, but a little confusion couldn't hurt.

He was wasting heterodyne but he didn't care; the Tsa wouldn't know his beam had lost peak heat capacity, and they'd think—well, with luck, maybe what he *hoped* they'd think.

Range closing—so before their weapon could reach him, *make the move*. Grinning, snarling, at the first touch of pain Ivan screamed like a banshee—not from hurt, but a war cry. Holding course to pass the Tsa ship at one side, he cut the central projector, fired the other six and traversed them to meet that ship.

Twice it bloomed fire—first the air of it and then, a greater burst, the ship's drive. Concentrating now, to get the *Deux* safely past the molten debris, Ivan lost track of his other foe. When the pain struck, it broke his barriers totally. He needed full-max accel but couldn't see the switch, or feel what his hands did. He *willed* to do it right, and now he screamed because he couldn't stop. Finally he didn't hear it any more.

Ivan woke to agony and darkness. For a time he lay back, first merely trying to stay conscious, then working through the exercises of breathing and nervous system, that he had learned at Erika Hulzein's. And when he could stop groaning, then he could think.

The lights out? Even the emergency backups, and the control panel indicators? But with no power at all, the air wouldn't circulate. And certainly the vessel wouldn't be vibrating to the high acceleration that held him flat.

With great effort he reached to feel over the control panel, seeking by touch to get some clues to the ship's condition. With care, identifying each switch before he moved it, he began a slow, halting checkout procedure. At first he didn't learn much.

He hadn't managed full-max accel; that lever still sat three notches back. No need, now, to spend fuel at such a rate; gently he notched back until he heard the "sping" of the red-line clip, then backed off two more, just for luck.

He touched a switch and, for a moment, couldn't recall its function. Then the memory came; it was an added frill that was seldom used, though it had seemed like a good idea in theory. But right now he could use it—he pressed, and a voice-tape from the ship's chronometer announced the current date-time group.

Nearly three days, I was out! Two thoughts came, then. One, it was a flaming miracle he hadn't fouled himself with excrement; that one set him to clawing free of the gee-suit and then feeling his way to the nearest latrine. His relief was considerable. While he sat, the protoplasmic computer in his mind considered the other idea, taking time and acceleration, and rendering them to him in terms of velocity and distance. When he had the figures, he whistled. In the small booth, the sound rang.

"At *that* accel we passed light in hours, not days." In the darkness, speaking aloud made him feel less lonely. "We must be—" He shook his head; the movement sent dim green glows across the black of his vision. For seconds he thought the backup lights had flickered, then realized the phenomenon was internal.

He went, slowly and sometimes bumping into things, back to his control seat. Now he ignored switches that gave only visual response. Memory clearing faster now, he found the detector indicators; as expected, the sub-light instruments gave no bleeps. He tried the gravitics, and the gentle sounds told him there were stars out there, all right—and none dangerously close. So the *Deux* was well above C. How far above? Since there was no way to get audible confirmation of his own guess, he'd have to stand on it, as is.

Tregare's plan—to go a week maybe, before cutting Hoyfarul Drive and starting turnaround—should he stay with it, now? Ivan scratched his head. Maybe, for this, he needed to talk with someone.

He fumbled at the controls for the acceleration cocoons; when he found them, he paused. *This one?* Something was wrong—or was it? He thought again, and was certain. He knew that under Tsa attack he'd failed to get accel up to full-max. And what his hand had done, instead—that switch had put the whole ship's force into freeze!

He was halfway downship—and still without lights—before he wondered what he was going to do, anyway. He knew resuscitation procedures, of course; all officers did. But in the dark? He stopped, holding the railing for balance, and thought, "Three days. A little less, really. Just turning the thing off, waiting for the signal and opening the cocoon, should do it." *If I'm lucky.*

Inside the compartment, feeling his way among the cocoon positions, he had to face the next question. *Who?* Since he knew the assigned location of only one person, he had two choices. Someone at random—or Dacia. *How bad is the risk? I wish I knew.*

He chose Dacia. Because, he told himself, she was the freeze expert; if she came through all right, everyone's chances were better. But his real reason, he knew, was that he needed her.

He checked thoroughly, counting his way row by row, leaving his keys on the selected cocoon and then counting rows to the back wall and to the ones on either side. Until he was sure he was right. He pulled down the small seating-shelf that made the control assemblies easier to work with, and sat, and groped among the switches. He needed only to turn the thing off and let it cycle down; he moved, and the switch made the proper click. Now there'd be an hour or so before the cocoon announced, with a blinking light and audible tone, its readiness to be opened.

Might as well spend the time up in Control. He might learn something. But he didn't expect to enjoy that learning.

Back upship he sat at his console, fingering switches and occasionally trying one. Nothing new, and Ivan had used up all his ideas. Except for one, and the result of that one could kill all hope.

But finally he had to test it; he couldn't hide forever. He pulled up the right-hand arm of his seat. More than not, he hoped to find the small compartment empty. Occasionally Tregare smoked a cigar, but so seldom that he didn't carry a lighter. He kept one here, though, and one in his work desk. Ivan reached, and there it was.

Holding it in front of him, his arm bent slightly, Ivan pushed the operating stud. No light; maybe the thing was out of energy. *Quit kidding yourself!* His other forefinger reached and felt the heat.

Well, now you know! Cursing at the slight burn, mumbling past the finger he sucked to soothe the scorch, helped ease the pain of knowing.

*   *   *

The chronometer's voice-tape was blithe and perky. Though Ivan waited, each time, as long before consulting it as he could manage, he got decidedly tired of its perkiness. When finally it told him his hour's wait was nearly over, he stood and made his way again downship. He felt his way past the cocoons and found his keys. He sat, and while he waited, made sure of the next control he needed. When the tone sounded—and of course the damned light would be blinking, too—Ivan's breath was not steady.

Here it goes. He moved the switch that would let the cocoon open. It made the right sound—which was to say, the tone stopped. He put his hands to the lid, not to hold it but to feel it move, and at first he thought it wasn't working, but then it began to lift. Not quickly—never fast, these devices—but not hesitating, once begun.

When it was up all the way, Ivan stood and reached into the open tank, fingers outspread to find Dacia but cautious of the connections that needed care to terminate.

Brushing past her hair, he touched her face. Cool but not chill; her throat had a good pulse and he heard breathing. A little slow, in the normal range for sleep. He stroked her cheek and squeezed one hand, waiting. Her head moved; her lips touched his hand. "Dacia?"

"Mmm. Yuh—Ivan?" Her head raised, then fell back.

"Dacia. Lie still; don't move. Stay as you are, until you're all the way awake. Because—I'm sorry, but I can't help you; you'll have to make all the disconnects yourself. So wait; wait, Dacia—"

He talked on, pausing only now and then, until he knew she heard and understood. Finally she said, "All right, Ivan. But why?"

He knew what she meant, sure. But for a time he couldn't say it. Then he did. "Because there's no light."

She didn't understand immediately; then she gasped, and he felt her sit up and try to hug him. "Dacia! The connections—"

"It's all right; I didn't break any. But, *Ivan!*"

Gently he pulled her hands free of him. "You'd better see to yourself first. And be careful." When she was done, and had climbed out—he reached to help, but fumbled and was no use at all, that he could tell—they stood and hugged properly.

"Ivan—you can't see *anything*?" He shook his head, and felt tears leaking from his useless eyes.

XI. Lisele

Lying on something hard, feet higher than her head, Lisele came awake. Her throat hurt. Staring upward, she wasn't sure where she was. Then she looked to one side—and seeing from that angle, began to recognize things. The control room was tipped over, was all—so the whole scout was, too.

She tried getting up, and found she could. Tipping her head back she looked at the seats above her; from one, Stonzai hung by her harness. From the alien's mouth fell a drop of blood, then another.

"Lisele! You're all right?" Tregare's voice. She turned and saw him lying across the control panel, level with her eyes. Gasping, she spoke his name, then said, "Yes. I think so."

She'd have to climb up to him. His foot stuck over the edge; she reached for it. "No!" Startled, she pulled her hand back. Gently, he said, "The leg's broken; touching the foot wouldn't be a good idea. Can you climb some other way?"

She looked. "Sure." She reached for her mother's harness, hanging from the seat, and pulled herself up. Then, stepping across to the control panel, careful not to step where she shouldn't, she squatted beside her father. "Those Tsa crashed us, didn't they? Can you fix it?"

Once, falling out of a tree, Lisele had broken her arm; she remembered how it felt. But if Tregare was tightened up with the hurt of his leg, she couldn't tell it. He said, "Fix the scout, you mean? To lift-off again?" She nodded. "I can't think how. The scout itself won't be hurt much—but we're tipped over. And out here with no equipment, that's a lot of kilos to hoist." He shook his head. "Our best bet is to yell for help, to get us out of here. If we can raise anybody. Then, if it seems worth it, come back

86

and clear a landing pad. A ship's crane, that's what it takes to roust this baby up again.''

She frowned. "If we can raise anybody? Why couldn't we?"

"Well, we don't know yet, how Ivan made out with that Tsa fleet. Or the Shrakken, for that matter. So—"

"But what if we *can't* get help?"

Now in his face she saw the tension, but all he said was, "Then, princess, we'll just have to think of something else."

Sitting at the edge where she could hang her feet over, she considered what he said. She heard a noise and looked up to see her mother climbing down through the deck hatch. "Lisele!" Rissa dropped what she was carrying, and came down fast; for a moment they held each other. "Thank peace you are not injured." But Rissa's hand, touching her throat, brought pain.

"Ow! I remember now; I was choking. What—?"

"Your mother got you down," Tregare said. "Good job, too—*I* couldn't have." Then, staying clear of the hurt leg, she and Rissa were over by Tregare, all talking at once, and hugging.

Finally Rissa said, "I should report. I have freed those in the accel bunks, and we have laid the pads on the bulkhead where they can be of use. Sevshen is still unconscious—as I note Stonzai is, also. I detect no serious physical damage to either, but—" She shrugged. "Mental injury? We can only wait and see."

Now Rissa looked as if something hurt. "Hagen Trent is only bruised. But Jenise—" Shuddering, she said, "When we struck, somehow her left hand had slipped between the inner and outer frames of her bunk. Bran—the wrist, and more—*crushed*."

Inhaling, Tregare's breath whistled. "What's been done for it?"

"Not enough. I stanched the bleeding and operated the transfusion kit. Then Trent took over, and began sewing tendons back together. But the *bones*—like assembling a puzzle, with pieces missing!"

Tregare patted his wife's shoulder. "Yeah—no fun. I had to try to do something like that, myself, once."

"Is there anything you have not done?" Now, at least, Rissa could smile—though not, in Lisele's view, very well. "At any rate—I plundered a lifeboat kit for organic bone cement, enough anti-infectant to obviate extreme sanitary precautions, and surgical tools. And of course we put Jenise out of pain. Not out of consciousness—we needed her cooperation, her reactions.

But having to watch us deal with that mangled wrist—" Her face twisted. "She cried so much!"

Feeling a little sick, Lisele still had to know. "But what did you *do*?"

Rissa ruffled her daughter's hair. "We tried to put together those shattered fragments of bone; there was not enough left, to do it right. Not without a real surgeon and a kit of plastic laminate."

"How did you leave it?" said Tregare. "What's the prognosis?"

Rissa shook her head. "Even if she does not lose the hand, it will retain little function. As of now the mangled parts are covered, with synthetic dermis filling the gaps in the remaining skin. We determined size and contour for the flexicast; when I left, he was fitting it. The fingers will protrude slightly; if they turn color, of course, the hand comes off." She sighed. "At least Hagen has volunteered for that chore, if it is necessary."

She freed herself from Lisele's embrace and Tregare's, and retrieved the bundle she had dropped earlier. "We are not doing things in proper order. Here, Bran, is the flexicast kit for your leg. That, at least, I do know how to use. And first, of course, before setting the fracture, the injection to free you of pain."

Tregare sighed. "I was hoping you'd get around to that part, pretty soon."

The setting didn't work; Rissa couldn't apply the flexicast and keep the broken ends in place at the same time, and Lisele simply wasn't strong enough to hold traction by herself. So Rissa sent her to fetch Hagen Trent. "—when he's free to come, of course."

Not as sore or stiff as she'd been a short time earlier, Lisele climbed to the deck hatch. Passing Stonzai, she saw the Shrakken's eyes were open, and called the news down to Rissa. "We'll get you out of there in a minute," Lisele said, and went to look through the hatch opening.

What she saw, relieved her. Sitting up, Sevshen drank from a cup Hagen Trent held. And Jenise Rorvik lay breathing evenly—either asleep or doped out.

Trent looked around. "How's Tregare's leg? Need any help?"

"Yes. We do need help. Can you come now?" As he followed her down, she looked back and saw Sevshen coming, also. Moving not too well, but being careful, at least. At Stonzai's level he paused; the two Shrakken spoke in their own language, and began fumbling at the harness that held Stonzai.

"Wait!" Lisele gestured at them. "You'll fall, if—" She shook her head. "In a minute, Hagen can do it." So Stonzai stopped trying, and pushed Sevshen's hands away, too. Lisele went on down to where Tregare lay.

Trent and Rissa talked for a moment; he put traction to Tregare's leg and she felt for the broken part, pushed a little and then nodded. "This is correct; hold steady, please." Face sweating, Tregare grunted as she wrapped the sheath—several layers— and sealed it. "There!" she said. "Now, Bran, we can get you off this uncomfortable roost."

And when he was down, seated on a purloined cushion and leaning against the bulkhead, Rissa and Trent climbed up and freed Stonzai.

The Shrakken said only, "Trouble, we have. But loose of those straps to be, good is."

The first thing, Tregare said, was that no matter what worked out later, certainly they'd all be in the scout for a while. So Lisele and the rest of the able-bodied went back to the bunkroom and took loose the rest of the accel pads, to make more comfortable beds. They carried some down to Control, too, and arranged them so Lisele could sleep at one side of the console that now lay flat on its back, and Rissa and Tregare on the other.

Moving under his own power, Tregare edged over to his new bed and stretched out. "Not half bad. Thanks." Then his face took on an expression Lisele knew, the one that meant he was planning ahead. "Rissa? You want to check the control panel and see if it's got any news for us?"

Rissa seemed preoccupied, but she nodded. "I am afraid I have allowed myself to fall into worry about the *Deux*—and our little Renalle aboard. But first things first, as you say. And I agree that at this stage we need outside data." She climbed to perch on hands and knees over the console, and began to check the indicators and call out the results.

"Drive is operative—were we not pointed into the planet itself."

"Lucky, there," Tregare said. "It could've blown."

"But it did not. Power reserves, fuel, near full capacity. Comm gear in working condition, but no incoming signals, because—"

"Yeah," Tregare put in. "Antennas retracted. Unretract?"

Rissa moved switches, turned a dial, then scowled and shook her head. "They are jammed; they do not move."

"Plowed into the dirt, you think?"

"Probably. When I apply power, the servos overheat and disconnect."

Tregare shrugged. "Well, skip it. What else is on the board?"

Straightening, balanced on knees and shins, Rissa shook back her loose hair, then bent forward again. A viewscreen lit, and Lisele saw a dim picture: dense growth of trees, afternoon light reflecting on water. Rissa sighed. "Not the best of luck, eh, Bran?"

Lisele didn't understand. "What do you mean?"

Tregare's laugh came harsh. "Jungle, I was braced for. What we're down in, though, is *swamp*."

Tregare had no more interest in the control board's information, and showed it, but Rissa stayed where she was and read off what she found. Finally she said, "That is all," and jumped down, knees bending as she landed. She turned to Tregare. "Now, until something new occurs, I am done with that uncomfortable position. Another thing, though—how long since any of us has eaten?"

Shaking his head, Tregare grinned, and Rissa said, "Our mini-galley now sits at the upper far corner of this space—and on its side, too." She looked across to Trent. "Hagen, if you will get a tool kit from under the console, perhaps you can take loose one of the cooking units and remount it—" She scanned the place, and shrugged. "—oh, in some way that it can be used."

Trent chuckled. "Right side up, you mean. Sure; I'll try." As he rummaged for the tool kit, Lisele followed Rissa's climb to the small galley, and helped sort the food packets her mother handed out from the upended cabinets. Trent's relocation job, when he finished it, looked pretty slapdash—but it worked, and after a time, everyone was fed. Except Jenise Rorvik—Rissa carried food up to her, but the injured woman wasn't awake yet.

Even fed, Tregare was restless. "There's still daylight left," he said. "Rissa, couldn't you and Trent take a quick look around, outside, before it's dark? Give us some idea what we're up against, out there?" He moved a hand. "No big safari—just a quick scan."

Rissa nodded. "Of course. To reduce our uncertainties. Hagen?"

The man agreed, and then Lisele knew she wanted to do something, too. "Can I go with you? I'll be careful."

After a moment, Tregare said, "You both watch out for her, though. All right?"

So Lisele—feeling as much scared as important, but the other way around, too—went with Trent and Rissa. The man had a needlegun at his belt, and Rissa a holstered energy weapon. Climbing first up and then down, walking the side walls of staircases and bent over because the stairs were built so narrow, Lisele followed them to the airlock.

At first it wouldn't open. Rissa frowned, tapped the pressure gauge and punched the override button. Noise came, a groaning shudder and with it a burnt smell; then the airlock door, lying on a slant now, gave two feeble jerks and slid partway open. Through the lower third of the opening oozed thick, grey mud topped with a layer of green slime. It smelled pretty bad, but Lisele gulped and kept her dinner down.

Rissa and Trent looked as if the stink had got to them, too. Lisele said, "Are we still going outside?"

Both hands busy with her long dark hair, tying it up around her head, Rissa Kerguelen said, "I am, because I told Tregare that I would. You need not; it might prove dangerous. If—"

"I *told* you I'll be careful."

Face relaxing, Rissa squeezed Lisele's shoulder. "Of course. Come with us, then." Together, all three waded out through the mud.

Outside, a breeze blew, so the stink wasn't too bad. The heat was, though. A little away from the scout, which lay with its nose buried in mud as Tregare had guessed, was some solid ground; they waded over to it and scrambled up. Lisele had mud most of the way up her legs; the others, taller, hadn't quite so much.

It wasn't a good place for walking. There was more mud and water, as far as Lisele could see, than solid groundside. But Rissa squinted against the low sunlight, and pointed. "There, just under the water. A kind of path, I think."

The man bent and looked. "I don't see it. What do you mean?"

Rissa's smile didn't look very relaxed. "It is a thing I have seen, in swamps, on another world I have visited. Under a little water, when that water comes and goes with time, animal trails retain their firmness and can be utilized.'' She turned. ''Briefly, only, for this day, let us explore.'' And she began wading again.

It was fun at first, following Rissa and hearing Trent slosh along behind. With the sun at the horizon to one side, the slanting light outlined everything Lisele saw. But then, almost like someone ducking under water, the sun went away—leaving only sky glow, grey water, and a whitish moon that hung low where the sun had gone. Lisele faltered. ''Are we going much farther?''

Ahead, Rissa turned and came back. ''No. In fact we had best move quickly, while the light holds.'' In passing she gave Lisele a quick handclasp; in turn the two moved past Hagen Trent, who again brought up the rear. Slower now, they moved along the underwater path.

Squinting ahead in the dim light, Lisele looked for the scoutship—tipped over or not, it was still *home*. For a long time she couldn't see it, and peering ahead so much, twice she missed her step and floundered in mud to her waist before someone caught her wrist and pulled her up again. Feeling ashamed, each time she said, ''Sorry. Thanks,'' and made up her mind to watch closer.

But she didn't see the thing leap out of the water. From her left came a big splash that knocked her down, then the huge grey beast loomed—but it fell short, and made a greater splash. When she stood and could breathe again, snorting water out, she saw only the splash-waves spreading.

Only Trent had kept his feet; now he put away his unfired gun and helped Rissa up. Sputtering, mud-covered, she tried to wipe slime from her face. Her hair hung sodden, clotted with mud. She spit out swamp water, and said, ''Thanks, Trent. What *was* that creature?''

Lisele, fingers trying to comb mud from her own hair, shook her head. Hagen Trent said, ''It's like nothing I ever heard of. Big, certainly—I'd guess three meters long and a half-meter thick—'' He raised his brows and Rissa nodded. ''What I thought I saw, in this dim light—hadn't we better get moving again?'' Rissa turned and began walking; the others followed.

Lisele spoke. ''What *did* you see?''

Trent hesitated. ''Only an instant, I saw it head-on. I expected a huge gaping maw, lots of teeth. But instead there were—I *think* there were—a lot of sucker mouths, all grouped at the snout.''

Over her shoulder, Rissa said, "It is some sort of huge leech?"

"In its way of feeding, yes. If the light didn't fool me."

Even in the heat, Lisele shivered. Walking, careful to follow Rissa exactly, she peered from side to side. But no monster appeared, and soon they reached the scout.

In the airlock, standing above the intruding water, they tried to get some of the mud off themselves. The stuff hardened quickly, to a damp rubbery toughness that clung. She could work lumps of it loose, Lisele found, but still a thin layer coated her skin.

And as it dried, it began to make her itch.

Pulling at the heavy globs caught in her hair, Rissa muttered a curse. Lisele said, "What's the matter? The mud'll wash out."

Rissa gave a snort. "Wash out? How? The shower is horizontal, with the drain halfway up one wall." She shrugged. "Oh, we will improvise something—but it will take some thought, to do so in a way that will still conserve our water." Now Rissa sighed. "And each extra effort we must make, to cope with these conditions, slows our real task—which is to get ourselves out of this place." Rissa started toward the control cabin. Following, Lisele didn't say anything.

First they told Tregare what the outside was like, and about the water beast. Lisele mentioned the white moon, and Tregare said, "If it's the synchronous one, we can sight on it and fix our location."

Then they talked about the mud.

The shower wasn't too much of a problem; with the stall's door now on top, they didn't have to do any cutting or welding. Tregare had the answer to draining and recycling; Rissa arranged a spare fuel pump unit and some hose, from emergency stock, to suck water from the stall's bottom corner into the drain. Hagen Trent wired power to the pump, and broke a thumbnail getting the drain's grill out so the hose could go in past the first bend that pointed down.

Still, the result wasn't a total success. Even pointing the spray up pretty well, people had to squat or kneel or go on hands and knees to use it. Scrubbing wasn't easy, unless someone else was there to help, and the mud took a lot of scrubbing. Even on skin, let alone trying to get it out of hair.

Kneeling, Rissa worked at Lisele's hair—painfully, but

hearing Rissa mutter, Lisele didn't feel like complaining. Finally Rissa said, "Oh, this is impossible!" and turned the water off.

Not bothering to dry, Rissa pawed through the jumble of a wall cabinet that lay on its side. She picked up, then discarded, a pair of scissors. "Altogether too much work." Next an electric trimmer; she pushed the button and the thing buzzed. Turning the adjustment dial, she motioned Lisele to sit. "We will not mind looking a little funny, will we? Because the mud will not allow us the luxury of looking any other way."

Following Rissa toward Control, Lisele thought that her mother's ears weren't really all that big. But with no hair to frame them, only stubble you could hardly see, they did seem to stand out a lot. She supposed her own ears did, too, now.

Seeing the two of them, Tregare's eyes went wide. "Peace take me—*why*?" He shook his head. "Couldn't you have just washed that gloop out?"

Rissa's voice held a sharp edge. "Over a matter of hours, perhaps. And how many times, working outdoors in that slippery mess, would we need to repeat the tiresome process? Saying nothing, as yet, of the problem if we must leave here and travel on foot."

Tregare looked stubborn. "A plastic hood, you could wear."

"Not in the heat of day. Even clothing may be too much. No." Her eyes narrowed. "Bran, I do not make decisions lightly."

Tregare and Rissa hardly ever got mad at each other; now they were, and Lisele didn't like it. Quickly she said what Rissa had told her about looking funny, and the luxury part, and all. "*I* don't mind looking funny," she finished, "so what's so important?"

Tregare glowered, and at first she thought he was going to say something loud, but then the expression broke. "All right, princess. Rissa, you win." He touched his own black, curly hair. "And I guess the rest of us need shearing, too, to work outside any."

"It would appear so." Rissa's voice still sounded chilly.

"Okay," said Tregare. "I'm at a disadvantage, though." Lisele waited, and he said, "You two, you have pretty-shaped skulls. Me, though—I remember from my year as a snotty, at the Slaughterhouse." He meant, Lisele knew, UET's old Space Academy.

"I had the lumpiest head in the whole peace-forsaken place!"

Rissa and Tregare didn't stay sore at each other, because that night when Lisele was barely asleep, from the far side of the console Rissa's cries woke her again. And they never did that unless they felt good together. So Lisele smiled, and as soon as things quieted again, she went back to sleep.

Next morning she woke to hear their voices. "—as worried as you are, Bran! Renalle, poor infant! How can she know why I do not come to her? But I cannot, so Ellalee will simply have to do her best. And at least, the child is weaned."

"Rissa—you sure this isn't bothering you, more than you let on?"

"*Of course* it is! But brooding on the matter will do no good, when there is so much else we must plan and do. So, please, Bran—" Then they were quiet, and pretty soon it was time to get up and eat.

A little later, Lisele went outside with Rissa and Trent and the two Shrakken, to have a better look at how the scoutship lay. What with the mud and heat, they didn't wear any clothes except foot-protectors. Hagen Trent's head wasn't sheared; he said that while they stayed with the scout, he got to keep what was left of his hair until it came up full of mud. "And it's not fair to trip me!" Hairless by nature, the Shrakken didn't have the problem.

Mud covered most of the scoutship's nose. "The projector turret," Rissa said, "must be nearly two meters under," and Trent nodded. "But the antenna systems—how far buried?" Leaving the Shrakken to probe that area, the two went back inside. Lisele, standing on a solid hummock, studied the swamp around her. She stood in shade; even early in the day, the sun shone hot.

The trees looked strange. The smaller ones grew straight up from mud or water, the trunks rising several meters before branching. She noticed something; there were three branches, or five, or seven. Always an odd number, always slanting steeply upward. And there the main trunk stopped; above, each branch divided in the same way. She thought about it, then shrugged; a *lot* of things happened, that she didn't understand, that made no difference either way.

The leaves weren't anything special; if she'd seen them on Earth she wouldn't have noticed they hadn't grown there. But the trunks—as a tree grew bigger, it put out branching roots from above the water, down into the swamp. Then—looking around, she could see the various stages—the original, central root dwindled and rotted away. The biggest trees stood on spider legs, with nothing under the main trunk.

She ought to make notes, she thought—this stuff might be

good for a term paper when she got back to the Junior U. But she didn't have anything with her, to write on.

Rissa and Trent came outside again. Each carried a crude shovel, and on the tools Lisele saw fresh weld marks. "You made those, just now?"

Smiling, Trent nodded. "Rissa said we need some digging done, so I rousted material out from ship's stock and took the torch to it." He held his shovel up. "Like it? Want to do some digging?"

Lisele shook her head. "Too heavy for me, looks like."

Rissa went over and spoke to Stonzai and Sevshen, who were cautiously pawing mud away from one area of the scout's nose. She gave Stonzai her shovel, and Trent handed his to Sevshen. Still carefully, the two Shrakken began to dig. "Now," said Rissa, "let us appraise the lie of this vessel, how it balances." One hand touching the scout's hull, she picked her way among the hummocks, back from the airlock toward the drive nodes. Trent and Lisele followed.

About halfway, Rissa paused and pointed. "Close, this, to our center of gravity—the pivot point. And note the crushed and splintered wood, quite a mass of it, protruding from under the scout, just forward of us. It might be possible—" Then she moved on.

Trying to hurry, Lisele slipped, and scrabbled up out of the mud. "*What* might be possible?"

Trent reached to catch her before she slipped again. "To tilt the scout, Lisele. Enough to free the nose and extend the antennas. Or maybe—no, I'm not that much of a mindreader."

At the scout's tail, Rissa stopped and the other two caught up. This end was a good three meters above ground or water—partly due to the hull's taper. "This section, though," said Rissa, "is the heavier." Trent seemed to know what she was talking about, so Lisele kept quiet. "But already the drive fills most of it. What else could be moved back? Or unloaded altogether?"

Trent frowned. "If you'd tell me just what you're planning, maybe I could help." She didn't speak; he touched her shoulder. "Come on, say it—what is it you're thinking to dare?"

Lisele saw her mother relax. "Why, perhaps merely to free the nose, so we could call for help without rigging new antennas in the trees. Or possibly—if we could get even a slight upward tilt—" Her breath came shuddering. "There is a chance that I could lift us."

She shrugged. "Or, of course, kill us all in the trying." And Lisele wondered how her mother's face, her strange new face that no longer stopped at the forehead, could look so calm while she said those words.

Near sun's noon they all went inside. Without the complications of clothes or hair, cleaning up didn't take so long; then, clothed except for the Shrakken, everybody gathered in Control. Trent had installed a cooking unit down near the control console and Rissa had stocked some food there; now Tregare, up and about on plastic crutches, surprised them with lunch cooked and ready. Her father, Lisele thought, wasn't the greatest cook she knew—but still she had seconds.

Rissa had made coffee; Lisele got up to pour it, remembering that Stonzai liked coffee but Sevshen refused to sample it. Then she sat again, as Tregare said, "Well, Rissa—how do our prospects look?"

Rissa looked up from her plate. "If we try to tilt the scout, there is a fulcrum of sorts, barely forward of our center of gravity. A mass of crushed timber. Not entirely solid, most likely, but—"

"Better than trying to pivot on a sea of mud," said Tregare.

"Yes." Rissa nodded. "My thought, now, is that a little planning may save much work, in affecting this vessel's balance. One kilo moved from nose to tail will have more effect than ten moved some short distance. And many things will be best off-loaded, since space behind is so limited."

"Yeah, right," Tregare said, scowling but not looking angry, and named some items that could be moved. "Hell of a job, with everything lying sideways. How's the digging going, by the way?"

Stonzai had begun climbing to the deck hatch; she paused, and motioned to Hagen Trent. He said, "Our Shrakken friends have been doing most of it, so far. No sign of the antennas yet. The trouble is, we know the two sets are 180° apart, and how far back, but nobody remembers their orientation—with respect to the airlock, say. I wish to hell we had some blueprints."

Tregare grinned. "We have them, all right. On the *Deux*."

Loading a tray for Jenise Rorvik, Rissa turned to head off Trent's protest. "Aboard here we have the manuals and drawings needed to operate or repair this craft. Since scoutships normally function *above* the surface, it never occurred to anyone that we might need help in locating our own antenna systems."

After a moment, he laughed. "Yes, of course. All right, the word is dig. I think I'll go out and have a turn at it."

As he left, Rissa started up toward the deck hatch. She was having trouble, Lisele saw, climbing and balancing the tray at the same time. "Can I help?" And without waiting for an answer, Lisele scrambled up past her mother; from there, one climbed while the other held the tray. At the third exchange they reached the hatch.

Jenise Rorvik, lying with her injured arm across her chest, didn't look good. Her head moved slowly back and forth; her eyes stared upward. Rissa put a hand to the woman's forehead. "Feverish. Jenise . . . can you hear me?" At least the exposed fingers, sticking out the end of the cast, hadn't begun to turn dark.

Jenise blinked; her head stopped moving and her eyes seemed to focus. "I think I'm better. Hungry, even. If it didn't *hurt* so—"

Rissa checked the time. "Yes. You are overdue for an injection. Just a moment." The medical kit lay on the bulkhead, in a corner; from it, Rissa brought an ampoule and spray can. She sprayed Jenise's arm above the cast, and gave her the shot. Then, while Rissa fed the other woman, she told of their situation, and what they hoped to do about it.

Only then did Jenise register their changed appearance. "Your hair! What happened?" Rissa explained, and Rorvik's good hand went to her own sweat-soaked hair. "I'm so *hot*—this fever. I'd be joining the fashion soon, anyway, I guess; why don't you do it now?" So Lisele fetched the trimmer and Rissa did the job quickly. One of Jenise's ears stuck out more than the other, but Lisele didn't mention it.

Then Rissa helped with the bedpan, and dumped it; as with the shower, the scout's position didn't make things easy. The latrine cubicle was now in a lower corner. Pretty soon, Rissa said, they'd have to take off the top wall and set the toilet upright. Meanwhile, with the pumps working and the lid tight, the thing could be drained without making a mess. The one off Control wasn't set so handily, but could be reached, all right, for bedpan dumping.

And for those who could go outside, about a hundred meters down the flooded path sat a handy log.

Starting to leave, Rissa turned back. "Jenise—how soon do you think we can move you? You should not be alone, and yet we can spare no one to stay with you."

Rorvik hesitated, "With the shot fresh in me, I could almost take it right now." She moved a little, and winced. "No—not on a full stomach. But next time, maybe. Just so nobody drops me!"

"We shall be as careful as possible."

"Sure, I know." Jenise made an odd, lopsided smile. "Truth is, I'll be glad to be out of here. I know the Shrakken are our buddies, and I do like Stonzai, but they give me the willies." Her voice lowered. "Maybe I was delirious. But last night, those two got in the same bed—and Stonzai's the female, but I'd swear she was screwing Sevshen!" She looked at Lisele, and her good hand went to her mouth. "I'm sorry—I shouldn't—"

"Lisele knows about sex," Rissa said, "as much as she needs to know at this time—and is not embarrassed by it. It has not always been feasible for her to be in a room separate from Tregare and myself." Lisele thought her mother sounded angry, a little, but her face didn't show anything. "And if she did not know, as apparently you do not, that with the Shrakken it is the female ovipositor that enters the male body, then it is time she learned."

Now Rissa frowned. "But Stonzai has only recently ovulated—and we have no host beasts at hand. I must ask her . . ."

Suddenly Lisele knew what was wrong—but it wasn't, really. "No," she said. "Dacia found out; she talked with Stonzai a lot. They—" She struggled for the words, then nodded. "When they ovulate, it's all instinct, like animals in—rut?—yes, that's right. But between times they have sex just like people do."

"Well, not quite," said Jenise, but now she smiled.

"Very well," said Rissa. "At any rate, when you have had your next injection, Hagen Trent and I will undertake to move you down to Control. And your bed, also. You will have dinner with us."

"Fine." Hair or no hair, Lisele thought, Jenise looked a lot better than she had a little while ago. "One thing, though."

Rissa's brows raised. "Yes?"

"I need a bath; I don't like smelling me. But how—?"

"Indeed." Rissa nodded. "You can hardly utilize our horizontal shower. Nor can Tregare. We shall need some kind of bathtub—but where? One of the corridors, perhaps; there is no room in Control. Somewhere, at least, where hoses can reach to provide water and drainage.'' She sighed. ''I hope this scout stocks another pump in working condition.''

Then she and Lisele did go down to Control, talked with Tregare about ways to rig a bathtub, and went groundside.

They found Trent and Sevshen shoveling mud away. Stonzai, with a slab of wood, pushed back the crest of the pile so it wouldn't ooze down again. All in all, Lisele saw, they'd moved quite a lot of gumbo, and to one side a growing hummock sat where a pond had been.

Trent looked up to greet them. He was mud all over, but it didn't mask his smile. ''We found one antenna feed. A stub, rather; it's broken off. About a radian off the vertical, clockwise as you face upship. So the other feed's too far down to bother with.''

Rissa's face took on the look of concentration. ''The stub— what is its condition? Can we connect to it?''

Trent rubbed a muddy wrist across his brows; the result wasn't much improvement. ''First we dig out some more; no point in trying to work too close to the ooze. Then I'll disconnect the broken part at the fittings, and hang an extension on, and spray a good seal against any mud that seeps back. Then—'' He shrugged. ''Tregare's the communications expert. I'll get with him, and try to scrounge up stuff to build antennas to his design.''

He looked up. ''We can hang it in one of these trees. I hope our instruments still tell direction right, lying slaunchwise.''

''I would think so,'' said Rissa. ''And now, if Stonzai will spell you at that shovel, shall we look closer and see if any reasonable amount of digging, behind our fulcrum, might let us tilt this scout?''

Lisele wanted to do something useful, but what was there? She watched Rissa and Trent move back along the scout, looked at the two Shrakken working against the mud, and turned away. She walked along the sunken path away from the little ship, careful to stay on the slippery ridge under the stinking ooze. Here the water was too shallow to hold monsters, so she felt safe. In the patches of sunlight the heat came like a blast from an oven; when she reached a patch of shade, she paused a moment.

She looked aside, toward the afternoon sun. In a tree she saw movement—but not what moved; the leaves gave too much cover. Whatever, it had to be pretty small.

Exploring, on such a precarious route, wasn't much fun. Lisele sighed; might as well go back to the scout. Placing her feet carefully at every step, she began her return.

Suddenly, about twenty meters short of the scout's buried nose, under the water Lisele saw a branching path. It went to the other side of the scoutship, away from the airlock. Might be nothing new to see there, either, but at least she could be the first to walk it. And maybe come all the way around the scout's tail, and surprise Rissa. Why not?

This trail, too, was slippery, but Lisele took care and didn't fall. She went nearly two-thirds of the scout's length, and there the path petered out. She squinted down into the water. Actually, she decided, the timber knocked down by their crash had torn out the path's ridge. So now what?

A tree was down, pushed over and slanting. With not too much of a jump she got onto it and began to climb its slope. Maybe there'd be a branch, back among the heavy leaves that smelled like some spice she couldn't quite name, that would let her get down to where the path started again. If it did. No harm, trying . . .

Off to the side, again she saw movement, and looked quickly, and decided it was bugs. Not quite like Earth insects, but not too different, either. Or bigger. One fell back and floundered, its three wings flailing; she grabbed it, to have a look. The small thing struggled while she stared at its color patterns—the orange and green and purple and . . .

It came to her that she could be stung or bitten; and with a gasp she tossed the bug free, and it flew away. Then she thought, *if it wanted to sting me, it had time to.* Behind bunched leaves, it vanished.

Until she heard the voices, Lisele didn't realize how high she'd climbed. "No, Hagen!" Looking down, she saw Trent hugging Rissa, who stood with one arm braced against the scout. "I said no."

The engineer breathed so hard, Lisele could hear it. "Why not? You and Tregare, you're not exclusive. And now that he's crippled—"

With a ragged laugh, Rissa pushed him away. "Now, perhaps he needs me even more. But the point is, I do not *want* you."

There was movement—Lisele couldn't tell just what

happened—and Rissa said, "I do like you, Hagen. Let that be enough."

"Oh, no. Oh, no!" He reached to pull her to him; she said something Lisele didn't hear, and then—

Lisele wasn't sure how it went. Rissa turned her back on Hagen Trent, and then he was up off the ground, and Rissa turned again. And Trent flew out into the mud and landed on his face. He went almost under water but not quite; when he scrambled up, he was sputtering. "Peace take you, woman! I'll—"

Quite still, Rissa stood. "Please. No one is harmed."

Gradually, the man stopped shaking. "All right." He climbed out of swamp, back onto the path. "Are you going to tell Tregare?"

Rissa shrugged. "No, if you prefer. Though if I did— Tregare, you must understand, trusts me to make my own decisions."

The man sagged as if someone had hit him. "But what *I* want, how I feel, makes no damned difference."

Lisele saw her mother frown. "Not entirely true, that. But—*nobody*, Hagen Trent, commands Rissa Kerguelen against her will." As he turned away, Rissa added, "If you had spent eleven years in UET's Total Welfare, as I did, you would feel as I do."

Over his shoulder, Trent looked back. "Maybe so; I don't always understand you two-ages people who lived so long before I was even born." He shrugged. "I'm sorry, Rissa. This mess here—I guess I let it wiggle my mind too much." He faced her. "Can you still like me?" She nodded. "Then that *is* enough." Sloshing away, he turned at the scout's tail and went out of sight.

Until Lisele called down, "Mother?", Rissa stood looking after the man. Then she glanced up, and after a moment, laughed.

"I suppose you can clamber down safely?" She waited while Lisele worked her way down to the tree's trunk, then inched over and jumped down to the path. Landing, she braced hands against the scout and avoided slipping. Then Rissa came to hug her. "And how much, my daughter, did you observe? And what do you think about it?"

Lisele looked up. "You told him to leave you alone and then you made him do it." She made a face. "Some people sure have to learn things the hard way. I didn't think he'd be like that."

After a pause, Rissa said, "Basically, Hagen is a good person. The circumstances here—he got a bit overwrought." Lisele thought for a few seconds, and then nodded.

They sloshed their way around the back of the scout—past a gap where Lisele waded waist high through murky water—and toward the airlock. Rissa gestured. "This section is bedded solidly. Digging, to tilt the ship, would be a forbidding task. Let us hope we do not have to try."

"You think we can call for help, then, and somebody will come?"

"As matters stand, that possibility is our best chance."

Past the airlock, they reached the digging site. Stonzai tossed a shovel of mud, then stuck the tool in the ground. "I think, enough is." And Sevshen laid down his own shovel.

Looking at the exposed antenna fitting, Rissa said, "You are right. Once Hagen fits a new connection and seals it, ooze should do no harm." She suggested a break, and they all headed for the airlock.

Inside, Tregare and Hagen Trent were talking; the engineer had bathed, and was now clipped near-bald. On a folding table he was fitting pieces of apparatus together. "Today I'll install and seal the new signal-feeds. Tomorrow—" He gestured toward a rough drawing. "Tomorrow, Tregare, I'll scrounge up parts and start building an antenna array to this design of yours." Then, seeming quite at ease, he greeted Rissa and the rest.

Rissa and Lisele went up to the horizontal shower; after the two Shrakken were done with it, they washed clean of mud and slime. Jenise was awake when they looked in on her; for a few minutes they visited. Returning to Control they found Tregare alone. "Hagen's out rigging the new feed; should be back, pretty soon." His smile, then, looked a little smug. "Meanwhile I think I've figured the easiest way to fix us a bathtub."

It *was* simple; when Rissa saw it, she laughed. At the right of Control was a closet, only a few decimeters above the bulkhead now serving as deck, and the closet held a working sink. "We take the door off," said Tregare. "The closet's solid metal, leakproof, so we get the junk out and rig a pump for drainage, and we're in business."

Trent came in and reported the new antenna feed shipshape. He wasn't too muddy; soon he and Rissa and the two Shrakken emptied the closet and dismounted the door, which they laid across two folding tables as a workbench. "Could double as dinner table, too,''Tregare said, ''if we take some of those seats loose from the deck and bring 'em down here.'' But that job had to wait; people were hungry. First, Trent and Rissa brought Jenise Rorvik down to Control; Lisele and Sevshen carried the accel pads down, and Jenise's bed was laid out alongside Lisele's.

Then they ate. Lisele was getting a little tired of Tregare's cooking, but she didn't think she'd better say so.

Later, Jenise and then Tregare tried out the new bathtub. Rissa hadn't located another spare pump yet, so Trent swung the sink to a vertical position, and drainage was bailing with a bucket and using towels to sop up the last of the water.

That job was slow but not really difficult. The hard part, earlier, was someone having to stand and hold Jenise's arm, then later Tregare's leg, clear of the water. ''We'll have to put up hooks,'' Tregare said, ''so we can hang slings to support us cripples.''

Then they all sat around and talked, sipping brandy—except for Lisele, who had a small glass of wine. It made her sleepy; as soon as she finished it, she went to bed. And even with the lights and the talk, almost at once she felt herself dozing off.

Thinking, *at least we're getting a start made....*

XII. Ivan

*F*or a time, not long, Dacia cried against Ivan's chest. Then she sat up, and he heard her sniffing the tears away. When she spoke, her voice was steady. ''How long has it been?''

''In freeze, you mean? Three days, nearly.''

She gasped. ''Why did you leave me in there so long?''

Almost but not quite, he had to laugh. ''Because until just about two hours ago, I was still knocked out from the Tsa attack. So—''

She touched his lips. "You must be starving—*weak*." He felt her moving. "If you help a little, I can walk. Let's get up to the galley, and I'll feed us something."

Quite suddenly, he *was* hungry. "Sure. Let's go."

Between his support and her guidance, they got upship fast. At the galley level she tried to turn, but Ivan said, "First you should check Control out, tell me what I missed." So they went up.

He had to give her some of the computer codes; her work hadn't included them. When the answers came, they fit his own guesses of speed and distance a lot closer than luck would allow.

"Ivan? We're a long way from Shaarbant."

"I know. And staying below redline, a long *time*, too." He paused. "Is it just my imagination, or is the *Deux* shaking a lot?"

"It's shaking, all right. Do you know why?"

Headshake. "Not sure. We plowed air at top max accel, though—'way past redline. I hope I didn't bust something."

Her brief laugh sounded nervous. "Me too. But—shouldn't we cut the Hoyfarul Drive, slow down? Get ready to turn back?"

He tried to think. "Maybe. Tregare said—I don't know." Of a sudden, again his hunger came real to him. "Before we change anything, I need full readings, all the instruments. Let's eat first."

They went to the galley; if Dacia hadn't been with him, he could have found it by the faint odors. He sat, and soon she fed him—literally, cutting the food and bringing bites to his mouth. After a little experimenting, he could handle the coffee by himself. *Thank peace for small favors*.

"Ivan?" Her tone implied a slight, puzzled scowl.

"Yeah? Hey—good meal, Dacia. Thanks."

"And welcome. But, Ivan, we have to talk. Your eyes—you don't see anything at all?" He shook his head. "Then why is it that you keep them closed so tightly?"

He hadn't noticed, but she was right; his eyelids were clamped shut so hard they hurt. He tried to relax and open them; pain stabbed sharper and the lids squeezed shut again. He grimaced, and Dacia asked what was happening. "I'm not sure; it hurts to open them, is all. Hold on a minute, while I try something." Deliberately he forced his lids open; the pain made him close them. Again, and the same result. On the third try he endured the hurt, and gradually it left him. "I don't see a thing, Dacia. But are they open now?"

"Yes." Her voice was near; his face felt her breath. "Ivan—whatever's happened, there is no visible damage to your eyes."

"Visible" nearly threw him into laughter he couldn't have stopped. He took a deep breath. "Well, that's something. But, now what?"

She paused. "Keep them open—that's right. And now move them, up and down, and side to side." He pretended to look in those directions, and thought he felt movement. Dacia said, "Yes. Those muscles work, all right."

Those muscles tired quickly, too. Ivan let himself "look" straight ahead, but forced his eyes open after each involuntary blink; the pain, now, was minor and lessening. "Just a moment," Dacia said; he heard her get up, move away, come back and sit again. Her breath moved air against his face. "Ivan, I want to try something. Just keep your eyes open." His cheeks and forehead felt warmth.

"What's that all about? What did you do?" In his ears, his pulse beat fast; his breathing came rapid and shallow.

Sure, he trusted Dacia—but he couldn't *see*.

Until she spoke he didn't know he'd said it out loud. "Ivan—I'm sorry. I should have told you." The sound she made, then, didn't quite qualify as a laugh. "Testing the pupillary reflex. Shine a light, see if the pupils contract. Yours do, Ivan."

He couldn't understand. "What's that supposed to mean?"

Her hand clasped his shoulder, then moved up to cup his cheek. "Whatever it was the Tsa did to you, your eyes themselves still work."

"Then why the hell can't I *see*?" He knew he'd snarled it—but her hand on his face told him he needn't apologize.

"I don't know. Their clawing, in our minds—it blocked synapses, so we couldn't act. Froze us, like a muscle cramp. So perhaps—"

Wrist to elbow, he stroked her forearm. "A cramp in my optic nerves, somehow? Or even the visual center itself? What do you think?"

She had no idea. "Too sketchy, what I remember about the pupillary reflex arc. But it still operates, so whatever they did to you has to be farther back, past the arc's extent."

Slowly, he considered what she said. "And will I—what are the chances that I'll ever see again?"

With a rush, she came and held him. Her tears wet his face. "All I can do—the same as you, Ivan—is *hope* you will!"

*   *   *

They went back up to Control. There, sitting in the watch officer's position, Ivan felt more like a ship's commander than like a helpless cripple. He tapped fingers on the panel's edge, and said, "It's time we woke more people. Not too many. Who?"

The first answers were easy. Jeremy Crowfoot. Anders Kobolak, because the *Deux* needed a ranking officer who could see, and Haskell Ornaway for backup. Alina Rostadt because Anders would want his wife with him. The two top engineers and a couple of good drive techs. Who else, though?

Ivan snapped his fingers. "Ellalee. If she gets training, how to fly the ship, and shooting, her ability to resist the Tsa could make a difference." Dacia agreed; in turn she suggested Arlen Limmer, both for training and as a general handyman, and after a moment's pause, Ivan nodded.

Downship they went, to start the resuscitations. Ivan wasn't sure why he went along, when he couldn't even see what was happening, let alone help. By the time they got there, he decided it was because he'd rather be with Dacia than alone.

When she began opening the cocoons, though, he felt he was in the way, and found his own dark passage to the galley. The big pot still had coffee in it; after he spilled one cup all over himself, he was more careful how he drank it. The stuff was getting stale, but what else was there to do?

After a time he heard people coming upship, talking. He couldn't get the words, and as they came up onto the galley level, everybody shut up. He heard them walk in, and said, "Everybody okay?"

"Yes." "Sure." "Just fine." "Hungry, though."

He could sort out some of the voices, but not all. "Do we have all ten, Dacia, that we agreed on?"

"Yes, Ivan."

"And no others?"

"That's right."

"Then while everyone gets fed, we should decide who else we need to wake up. If anyone."

He waited, and Anders Kobolak said, "First thing, we ought to get the ship squared away. The way it's shimmying, it needs some work."

"I'm not hungry." Rance Peleter, First Engineer under Hagen Trent, spoke softly. "I'll go down to Drive and have a look." The man's walk, when he left, was as quiet as his voice.

Someone's fingers drummed the table. Ivan's bet was Anders Kobolak, and when he spoke the man's name, the sound stopped. Ivan said, "We have to change some procedures, I guess Dacia's told you."

Kobolak cleared his throat. "Yes, I was waiting for someone to mention the obvious. You're right; Dacia told us you're blind. So what you mean, I guess, is that you want me to take command."

Ivan bit back his first angry response, and took a breath. "That wasn't exactly what I had in mind." He needed Kobolak's eyes, sure—but Ivan intended to keep making the decisions. Now, though, he paused. Maybe Anders was right. Ivan cleared his throat. "I want to be fair. Given your full cooperation—all of you—I think I'm fit to command this bucket. But if a majority thinks otherwise—" He shook his hand. "Vote by show of hands. Dacia, tell me just the numbers, no names. Question, yes or no—do I keep command? All in favor." Pause. "Opposed?" Again he waited. "Results, Dacia?"

"Nine yes, two no. Ivan, you retain command."

A hand grasped his. "I voted no, of course," said Anders Kobolak. "I still don't think a blind man should try to run a ship. But my word on it—I'll do my best to prove myself wrong."

"Thanks." Ivan's voice was less steady than he wanted it, but he went ahead, anyway. "As I started to say, before, the command function has to change a little, now. What I keep is control of *policy*. Operationally, Anders, you're in charge of how that policy gets carried out. Clear?"

There was more talk, spelling things out. At the end, Ivan was as satisfied as he could expect to be—the way things were.

With the *Deux* still outrunning light, watch officers had little to do. So Ivan scheduled all Control people to train on Crowfoot's computer simulations. Three watch teams—Anders and Alina, Ornaway and Crowfoot, and Arlen Limmer with Ellalee. He'd switch the teamings around later, he said, to give everyone a shot at working with everyone else. And because young Limmer was the weakest instructor—but that part, he didn't say.

Dacia stood no watches; he needed her with him. That wasn't how he put it, but he didn't figure he was fooling anyone.

At evening, by ship's time, he and Dacia went to captain's quarters. Ivan was nervous; when it came bedtime, he stalled. Finally she asked what was wrong, and he had to tell her.

Sitting, his blind stare aimed where he'd last heard her, he explained.

What if the impotence of blindness reflected in other ways? "When I came out of Welfare, remember, not even Erika's psych-techs could fix it so I was any good. And now—"

Dacia came to sit on the arm of his chair, and held him. "Ivan. It'll be all right. Come—you'll see." She gave an embarrassed giggle. "Well, that too, I bet, sometime. But tonight—"

In the bed with her, at first he thought his fear was rightly based, or that the fear itself would prevent him. But she told him, while she did warm, gentle things, "We're not in a hurry; just wait."

And finally, when he relaxed and simply enjoyed what was happening, the rest of it happened, too.

Except for Hagen Trent, Ivan hadn't known the Drive people too well. Talking with Rance Peleter, next day, he remembered him as a short, cheerful black man who did his job with a minimum of fuss.

Now, across the galley table, the soft voice didn't sound cheerful. "I've never seen a drive act this way, skipper. I mean, the continual shaking. Under overload, sure." Remembering Peleter more clearly now, Ivan visualized a quiet shrug. "I don't have Trent's theoretical background, of course, or his FTL experience. But—"

"But we have to go with what you do know. So, would you suggest we cut the Hoyfarul Drive now?" He sipped a beer Dacia had brought him.

"Cut it dead? Anything sudden—hard to tell what might happen." Judging by his voice, Peleter had leaned forward. "I've tinkered, refining the balance; it helped. To a pretty minor extent, though, worse luck. I'd say, cut FTL drive back a notch at a time, with me down there rebalancing after each change." Ivan heard him sigh. "I'm sorry—I know that's not much to offer. But it's my best guess."

Ivan nodded. "So we'll go with it." He checked the time with Dacia, and said, "At ten hundred hours; nearly half an hour. Right?"

"Sure, skipper. I'll be ready." Ivan heard feet scuff, then only the first few steps as the man walked away.

Ivan turned to Dacia. "Anders has the duty. Let's go up."

In Control the Second Hat greeted them; Dacia steered Ivan to the seat beside him, and Ivan told him what was planned.

"Sounds reasonable," said Anders, and reported the ship's speed and position. "We won't get back soon, you know."

"I know." Kobolak's tone was factual, not complaining; so was Ivan's. "We haven't wasted time. Peleter needed leeway to check the drive. Now we're ready to make changes."

"Sure." Now Kobolak gave data from the gravitic detectors; space ahead was clear. Then they sat quietly until Anders said, "Ten hundred coming up." The intercom switch clicked. "Ready to cut, Peleter. Twelve seconds." And he counted down.

"Go!" Still shaking, the ship bucked hard. The vibration eased, grew again, and finally settled to a steady pitch.

"It's worse, isn't it," said Ivan, "than before the cut?"

The intercom must have been live; Peleter's voice answered. "Instability, a few percent increment I can't balance out. If it's a resonant point we should be able to get past it. Ready if you are."

Again the *Deux* shuddered, and again the residual vibration was worse. Ivan waited, but no one said anything. Well, somebody had to decide, and he'd asked for the job. "Give the count, Anders, and hit it another one!"

Four notches later—two short of FTL cutoff, if Ivan hadn't lost track—the *Deux*'s lurch flung him so hard against his safety harness that he nearly blacked out. Getting his breath and rubbing bruised ribs, he said, "Anders—Dacia—you all right?" They gave him brief assurances. "Peleter! What's happening down there?"

The answering voice wasn't Peleter's. "Sir—Mr. Peleter, he's knocked out. Not strapped in good enough. Scraped up a little, but breathing okay. I don't—" The voice stopped; the *Deux*'s shuddering came in great waves; nausea rose in Ivan's throat.

Now he knew what was happening, and waited for it to end. But it seemed *long*, until the sub-light detectors bleeped, and told him that the *Deux* was safely below C. Anders gasped. "We're down, Marchant. Under light-speed, I mean."

"I know. Like our very first test run, way back when, with old Hoyfarul himself. The drive blew." Ivan raised his voice. "Drive room! Anybody there know how to reset the circuit breakers, in the right order, so we can start putting on some decel?"

The intercom distorted the sound of someone clearing his

hroat. "I know how. But sir—we blew a hell of a lot more than breakers."

Ivan fumed, an hour later, with a coffee cup in one hand nd the other held by Dacia. If he could *see* what was going n . . .

"Any more news yet?"

"No. Peleter said he'd come up and report, as soon as he ould."

But it was nearly another hour before the man came to the galley. He had a small bandage on his head, Dacia whispered to van, but seemed to be all right. And all he could say, basically, was that the Hoyfarul Drive was down, with a number of components burned out, "—and *maybe* enough spares to fix it. The lock circuits—they didn't cause the trouble but they took the backsurge. I don't know—"

"What's being done?" Ivan frowned. The only way to fight he discouragement in Peleter's voice was to focus on what *could* be accomplished. "What orders did you leave?"

"Well—without the lock circuits we can still build an incoherent field, a standard sub-light drive, and get decel for urnaround. Nowhere near as quickly, of course. And keep working on the Hoyfarul units—they'll be out of circuit, dead, and safe to tinker with—and hope to restore a coherent FTL field later."

Ivan nodded. "Makes sense. Keep your people on it. Don't short anybody on rest, though; it's not that urgent. And—good work."

"Thanks, skipper. I guess I'll get back to it now."

And not much later, Ornaway on watch announced deceleration coming up. "Point-eight of max." Redline-max, he meant, not full-out. On the count, it came, and held steady. Peleter, Ivan decided, must be a good man. But was he good enough for this situation?

XIII. Lisele

Things at the crash site didn't happen very fast, the next few days. Trent had more trouble building Tregare's antenna, than he seemed to expect. Metal in stock was too long or too short; he had to cut and splice a lot. But the framework, leaning up against the scout, did grow.

Rissa's sightings on the white moon—it was the synchronous one, all right—gave the party's comparative longitude. Tregare shook his head. "Well over a radian, we are, from Sassden and the *Deux*—maybe one-and-a-half, at worst. I'm not sure, exactly; didn't record the angle, as seen from there."

"How far in kilos?" Lisele asked.

Tregare's mouth turned down at the corners. "One hell of a lot."

As long as Jenise stayed still, she could make do without pain shots. But the cast wasn't right; any attempt at using the hand jarred the crushed wrist, and she went pale. And the end of the middle finger was the only part she could wiggle at all.

Tregare, though, improved fast. Rissa said he was trying to overdo, but usually he didn't fail too badly. The day he insisted on going outside, with a heavy plastic wrap around his cast, Lisele watched. And sure enough, two steps from the airlock, his crutch slipped and he went flat! When he rolled over and sat up, he was streaming mud. Laughing, though, when his face stopped showing pain.

Her father, Lisele decided, was a stubborn man. He worked a long time trying to get the mud out of his hair before he let Rissa shear it away. Seeing his bare head, Lisele gasped—*the scars!* Rissa touched one. "This is from Stronghold, when Korbeith's UET diehards ambushed you."

"Trying to break max-secure detention, no less." Looking

oward Trent and Rorvik, he nodded. "Next day I cut their
hroats."

Lisele's eyes widened. "Their *throats*?" Her own father...?

Rissa spoke. "Not for the attack on Tregare. He executed
hose men for killing innocent hostages, out of spite and terror-
sm."

"And to show Butcher Korbeith's gang," said Tregare,
"that I meant business." Lisele nodded. Dealing with UET, she
supposed, people had had to do a lot of things they'd rather not.

Rissa's fingers spanned other scars. "These, I do not
know—"

Looking up, Tregare grinned. "Me either. Well, the jagged
one I got at Escape, when we first took my old *Inconnu*. The
rest—mostly from the Slaughterhouse, I expect. Easy to get
marked up, there."

"Yes. A bad place, that must have been." Rissa smiled
then. "Bran, you misled us. Your skull is nowhere near as lumpy
as you gave us to believe. Hardly at all, in fact."

Later that day, Lisele got a new job. If it happened, Jenise
said, that they had to leave the scout, they'd need to live off the
country. "To some extent, anyway. So we'd better know what's
safe to eat. Why don't you bring me some samples of local
vegetation, and I'll try to check it out."

So with several plastic bags looped under her belt, Lisele
set out looking. She didn't remember much about the native
foods they'd eaten at Shtegel, and supposed they'd look different
cooked, anyway. So she had to start from scratch.

She hadn't much noticed what grew in the swamp; now she
did. On the hummocks were bushes with pale green berries; she
took a handful. A water plant's leaves looked like something she
could have seen in a salad on Earth; all right, she gathered some.
And the same plant had a fat root; broken open, it smelled like
raw potato. That went into a bag, too.

She ran out of land-clumps; near the edge of deeper water,
where the great beast had jumped at them, she turned back. She
still had empty bags so she went on past the scout, saying hello
to Hagen Trent who was cussing a piece of metal that kept
slipping as he tried to clamp it, and continued to the path behind
the vessel.

Approaching a thick stand of tall trees, she found that it sat
on a real rise of solid ground. The middle was at least two
meters above water level and the surface was dry. How big was

it? She looked and made a guess. Thirty meters wide, maybe, and nearly a hundred long—though dense growth hid the far end from her.

Here the underbrush grew thick, and the ground cover included plants she hadn't seen in the swamp. She took samples until she ran out of empty bags, and left specimens of what she'd taken, laid out in a row beside a tree, so that next time she wouldn't duplicate anything. Then she went back to the scout.

One thing, she was bursting to tell somebody: if half the stuff on that island was safe to eat, rescue wasn't urgent. Not that she didn't want to get back to *Inconnu Deux*—but if they had to, they could all *live* here.

"Yes." Listening to Lisele's story, Rissa nodded. Jenise was busy looking through the samples Lisele had harvested. Rissa said, "This scout is stocked to feed six people for as many months, Earth reckoning." She looked away; Lisele knew she was figuring. "Or—assuming, Lisele, that you eat at adult capacity, which I doubt—we have food for perhaps one hundred ninety of this world's shorter days." She shrugged. "Make it two hundred."

Lisele scowled. "But if we can eat what grows *here*, too?"

"Only up to a point," said Jenise. She used her cast to hold a bag stationary; with her other hand she picked out shreds of vegetation. She smelled them, looked through a magnifying glass, then either bit off a tiny piece to chew and taste or else set the item aside. Now she chewed one, and nodded. "Good, that." She laid the bag over with others she'd approved, wrote a line on her notepad, and reached for the next sample. Lisele noticed that up to now, the approved and rejected piles were running about even. "But the problem is," Jenise said, "we can't take all our diet locally, no matter how much we find good. Trace elements, specific amino acids, all that—we'd be risking deficiencies. Plus, total vegetarianism, without expert guidance, carries its own risks."

Maybe. Lisele said, "What if we find meat, too?"

Rissa made a snort, and Lisele saw her mother hiding a smile. "Your pardon, Liesel Selene—but *what* meat? The water beast that leaped at us, or the small scuttling things we hear but never see?"

Jenise shook her head. "It doesn't matter. Even if we caught something, meat's trickier to judge, for safety. We don't have lab facilities and I wouldn't know how to use them, anyway. So somebody would have to eat the stuff and see what happened. Too risky.''

"True," said Rissa, "unless the alternative is to starve." She reached to touch Lisele's cheek. "Even so, my daughter, you may be doubling our effective food supply, and that is no mean feat. Now—I believe you said you have brought only a fraction of the types of plants available on your island?" And Rissa winked.

"Oh, yes; sure. I can find more." She found extra bags, rigged them at her belt, and headed back to the island. Once there, again she took care to lay a specimen of every new sample with her treeside museum. The first lot was quite a help to her, so she wouldn't bag a sample she'd already taken in. Well, a couple of times she did that, but then checked against her display and threw the extras out.

When she had no bag left empty, she decided to walk all the way around the island. She couldn't always follow the waterline, because some places the brush was too thick to plow through. So she detoured, but kept as near the water as she could.

And coming around a large, dense thicket, back toward the shoreline, across a clearing she saw the animal.

It was big, was her first thought—like a very large dog, but built high and narrow. Pink, mostly, but splotched with black and white spots, and patches of pale bristles. It looked to be leaning over something it had mostly swallowed, all but the legs that stuck out of the gaping mouth and reached to the ground. The thing's own legs curved back from where its body split to form them; they were board-thin sidewise and board-wide the other way, ending in heavy-clawed toes. Then it reared up on those legs, and the two things in its mouth reached out and wiggled, and it came at her.

And she simply stood there, and watched it come.

Time slowed and nearly stopped. Lisele found part of her mind watching the rest of it decide whether to be scared, and what to do about it. The creature's eyes sat wide on the sides of its head; she couldn't see both the tiny reddish organs at once; the head swung back and forth, showing her first one eye and then the other. She could see all the teeth, though—a lot of them. Big ones. They could take her arm off and hardly notice. But if they did, they'd bite off the thing's own tentacles, or front legs, or whatever they were. Tongues, maybe?

Until her foot caught on something behind her, she hadn't noticed she was dancing backward, staying ahead of the beast. Catching balance, she glanced down to see what she'd stumbled against. A stick, a good thick one, and long as her arm.

Behind, now, was heavy brush—hardly any room to move back. She picked up the stick; it was heavier than it looked, and she had no idea what she was going to do with it.

Why wasn't she afraid? Lisele shook her head; without thought she aimed the heavy stick at the creature's mouth, and held it steady. The animal still came directly at her; its mouth opened to take the piece of wood, and the tentacles grasped it. The tip of one of them touched her hand; *it burned!* Gasping, she stepped back and to the side; the beast stopped, and reared up. The clutching tentacles retracted; she could hear the teeth grinding at the wood. Still the head moved, peering at her first with one eye and then the other. And now again, with half the stick's length taken into its mouth, and tentacles reaching, the thing bent forward and came toward her.

Straight at the end of the stick, she kicked her hardest. Suddenly it was nearly all the way inside the mouth, and around it a blue-brown fluid gushed out. Lisele stepped farther aside; the creature shuddered, and made noises like something coughing itself to death. Once more the tentacles retracted; then the beast fell forward, and they came out again and pushed it up, body almost level. It turned to face her; she began to circle it. Trying to follow, its tongue-legs stumbled and it fell over.

For a long time she stood, her own legs shaking, until it no longer breathed. By then, she was too tired to bother with crying—and what was the point?

Tregare, on the scout, wanted to go view the beast, but Rissa insisted he couldn't. When Lisele said that probably nobody could carry it all the way along the slippery path, he settled for Rissa's taking a holocamera. "Shoot from every angle," he said. Rissa agreed to do so, and to bring samples of flesh, stomach contents and the tip of a tentacle, so Jenise could try to analyze them.

First, though, she washed Lisele's sore hand, and applied salve and a light bandage. Then she and Lisele and Hagen Trent went to the island. At least the creature hadn't gone anywhere.

Seeing it lying flat on one side, Trent gave a low whistle. "Such a thing—in my craziest nightmares, I couldn't have dreamed it. But if Lisele could kill it, it can't be too dangerous."

Rissa turned on him—and if a tone of voice could bite,

Lisele thought, the man's ears would be hurting. "We do not know yet, exactly *how* she did it. Now, I would ask." She did, and when Lisele told how time slowed and she *watched* herself do things, Rissa nodded. "I thought as much. The ability is not rare, but hardly common, either. The suspension of time is subjective, largely; while adrenaline does speed the reflexes somewhat, it is the subjective time for *deciding* that makes the real difference." She coughed slightly, then cleared her throat. "I have had the reaction many times; to a lesser extent, Tregare has the trait also. I had wondered whether Lisele would inherit it; apparently, to her benefit, she has done so."

Lisele shook her head. "It's so *strange*. I'd never—" She didn't know what to say next, so she stopped.

Trent said, "Then the beast is more dangerous than I thought?"

Rissa shrugged. "If there are more, I suppose we shall find out." Then she used the holocamera. Trent helped her turn the animal this way and that, to give the different views Tregare wanted. She cut meat from the flank, and opened the abdomen. Half-digested material went into one of Lisele's bags.

Rissa turned away to leave. Lisele said, "Jenise wanted some of the leg, or tongue, whatever it is, too." She took out her pruning knife and knelt beside the dead thing. Then she paused; she couldn't touch the part she needed, without burning herself some more. All right; she had one sample bag left. Sliced down the middle, it made a pair of protective mitts. In a few moments she had her sample, and wrapped it. Then she stood. "Let's go."

Back in the scout, Tregare exclaimed over the holo-pics and Jenise analyzed Lisele's specimen. Finally she said, "I'm not sure of all of it, but a main component is formic acid."

After a moment, Lisele nodded. "Oh, sure. Ant bites."

Next, Jenise opened the bag of stomach contents. Using tongs, she sorted the material into little piles, leaving several disgusting-looking lumps to one side. After a while she looked up. "Most of the vegetation is things I've already cleared as edible. More important, there's nothing here that I've figured to be unsafe for us. Some are new to me; maybe Lisele will find samples of them tomorrow. But for now—"

Lisele said, "You think we can eat meat from this animal?"

Jenise shrugged. "I don't know yet. We don't have the equipment for all the tests I'd like—to check the aminos, say. I

can test for metallic poisons, that sort of thing. But first, will
someone put a small piece to boil, with a lid over it?"

Rissa's eyes narrowed. "Of course. As the volatile components boil out, the odors will give us clues." Soon she had the
setup heating.

"If it smells all right," said Jenise, "I'll sample the broth."

Rorvik's limited chemistry and the "sniff test" gave the
meat, tentatively, a clean bill of health. But the spoonful of broth
she sampled stayed down only about fifteen minutes. Pale-faced,
Jenise insisted on trying a bit of meat, anyway, and an hour later
her digestive system hadn't made any protest.

"Whatever's toxic, then, boils out," said Tregare. "Which
means we don't ever roast or broil or fry the stuff." Rissa
suggested boiling the meat in several successive waters, to get
rid of as much poison as possible. After a second boiling,
Tregare insisted on trying a sample, and it gave him no trouble.

"Where'd you get that idea?" he asked Rissa.

She paused, brow wrinkled; then she nodded. "Browsing in
an old book, at Hulzein Lodge on Number One. The method was
applied to kidneys, which otherwise have a rather ammoniac
smell."

"Sure." Tregare smiled. "I used to hate the things, until
you served up bushstomper kidney at the cabin there, across the
Big Hills from the Lodge. That's how you did it, huh?"

"That is how, yes." Rissa stood. "Now, should we go and
harvest more bounty from Lisele's kill? Hagen?" The engineer
got up, too. Rissa hadn't said that Lisele couldn't come along, so
Lisele did—and helped cut meat from the back and sides, then
carried her share into the scout, where much of it was wrapped
and frozen.

At dinner, Stonzai and Sevshen tried portions of the new
stuff—vegetables and meat, both—and showed no ill effects.

Next, with help from Rissa and the two Shrakken, Trent got
his new antenna system up among the trees, oriented, and
connected to the scout. Inside, Tregare had to admit there was no
way he could perch to operate the up-ended comm panel. So
Rissa took over.

"Try the *Deux* first," he said, settling into one of the
relocated seats. "With the mountains in between, the odds aren't
good—even if the ship's still on Shaarbant. But worth a try."

The *Deux* didn't answer. Nor, when Stonzai spoke, did the

Shrakken bases at Sassden or Shtegel. Nearly an hour, they kept trying. Finally, crouched over the panel, Rissa turned and said, "I find no coherent signals whatsoever. But this does *not* prove that the Tsa have wiped those bases out."

Tregare nodded. "Curvature of the planet, yeah. Ground-to-ground equipment, we don't have. The Shrakken have relay satellites that accept our frequencies, but damned if I know how we'd spot one, from here." He rubbed his chin. "I was hoping this place had enough ionosphere to give us the chance of a freak skip condition." Now he grinned. "Maybe somebody *did* hear us, but the skip just isn't working in both directions. Well, short of that—since we can't get upstairs ourselves, our best shot is if somebody flies over. You want to make a loop-tape, Rissa, and leave it transmitting? And Stonzai—will you make one, too, for raising *your* people, just in case? We can set the receivers to give audible alarm, and to record, if anyone does call back."

"As you say, I do." And not long after, she and Rissa finished their jobs and climbed down. Rissa stretched and grimaced, but the Shrakken showed no sign of being uncomfortable.

"And what, Bran, do we do now?"

"Wait. Well, go ahead with the food-gathering project, and all—except that from now on, that's a job for two, and with guns. But mostly, just wait."

It was another week before Tregare, after dinner, said, "We're not going to get any answer. Folks, it's time we figured out our next move."

XIV. Ivan

Inconnu Deux slowed, and "stopped," and headed back toward Shaarbant. Over a drink in captain's quarters, Anders and Alina visiting Ivan and Dacia, Anders Kobolak asked, "Did everybody get the word, how many light-years we are, out from Shaarbant?"

Ivan had guessed, but at the figure Anders gave, he whistled. Translating distance into travel time, he whistled again. "Something more?" Dacia asked; he shook his head. But—without the Hoyfarul Drive, the *Deux* had real trouble. Its food supply was based on FTL travel times. Some folks might have to go back into freeze. . . .

Without stirring up alarm, Ivan checked on the matter. After all, if the captain wanted an inventory, he got one. He was relieved to find that things weren't urgent yet—but he made a point of getting Peleter's reports as soon as possible. If he had to hand his people a bombshell, he wanted to pick his own time for it.

Crowfoot knew Hoyfarul's theories, the math part, and Peleter knew the hardware. Their expertise didn't quite meet, let alone overlap. But working together, as the *Deux* built speed toward C, they began to understand each other better. Sitting in as they talked, lounging in captain's quarters, Ivan could tell that they were nearing a conclusion. He thought he knew what it would be; he hoped he was wrong.

But nothing stinks as bad as dead hopes. Tregare had said that once, and now Ivan knew how right his brother-in-law had been. "Our parabolic, acoherent drive field," said Crowfoot, "is solid as a rock, for sub-light speeds. But locking it into coherence, closing the field into ellipsoidal form for FTL—" He clicked his tongue. "The thing's not stable enough. And given what we have aboard to work with, I don't think it's going to be."

Accepting, Ivan nodded. "You'll both keep trying, of course?"

"Sure," said Peleter. "But, skipper—don't expect too much."

Ivan's sigh came from tension, not relief; he hoped he kept it quiet. Turning to Dacia beside him, he said, "We need a meeting. Everybody. Drive and Control can attend over the intercom."

She asked no questions; she called and set things up, putting Ellalee on the comm and Peleter on driveroom duty. After he heard several people come in, Ivan said, "Is everyone here, that should be?"

"Just a minute." Then, "Yes, Ivan."

"All right." He ranged his stare, that meant nothing now, around the room. One thing he'd learned—even though he couldn't see, pointing his eyes at people had an effect on them. *So use it.*

No one spoke. Ivan cleared his throat. "I'll make this quick. What we have is slower-than-light drive and faster-than-light food supplies. That means, some have to go back into freeze and sleep their way to Shaarbant." He paused. "Comments?"

"I have some." An unfamiliar voice. "Why did we have to wait until now, to hear this?" A woman, and an angry one.

"Because until now I didn't know for sure. Who are you?"

"Melaine Holmbach, Drive-tech First. Nobody asked me to get frozen, or thawed out later, and now you don't ask, either. You just *tell* us. Don't I have *anything* to say about it?"

First she angered him; then he felt pity; finally, only command was left to him. He unclenched the fist he'd nearly slammed on the table, and said, "Yes, of course; everybody gets to speak their piece. But you have to know the ground rules—Melaine, is it? We have twelve of us up, awake and eating and breathing. The way things are in your Drive room, we don't have food enough to keep that many alive, all the way to Shaarbant. And I'm speaking of short rations." He blinked, ignoring the pain that had become trivial, and tried to scowl in Holmbach's direction. "Can you understand that much?"

A hand touched his own; close to his ear, the woman's voice came then. "You mean it, don't you?" Ivan nodded. "I thought it was a scash—but it isn't?" He shook his head. On his hand, hers squeezed hard. "Then say what you need, Captain."

He found the numbers hard to say. "Four back to freeze, at least; more later, maybe. Without the Hoyfarul Drive, eight is the outside that our stores can support. And I'm not certain of that many—but that's how we'll start."

The yelling, then, didn't surprise him. Ivan stayed shut up; let them get it off their chests, and then maybe they might start making sense. A man—*who?*—shouted, "Just for a start, blind man, who the hell needs *you?*"

Ivan's voice caught in his throat; he couldn't answer. Then he heard Anders Kobolak say, "*I* do."

To know what happened then, Ivan didn't need vision. Someone was scuffling; then Haskell Ornaway said, "What we're all going to do now is sit down, while Captain Marchant tells us the rest of it."

Ivan wished it could be that simple. Quickly he assessed what he knew of those present. Then he made up his mind, and spoke. "First off, dump the idea that freeze is second-class treatment. I once paid through the nose to ride that way, Earth to Terranova and then to Number One. Fourteen ship's months, which came to something like twenty-six years, objective time."

He listened; no one's breathing sounded like getting ready to interrupt, so he didn't hurry. "Freeze spares you a lot of boring routine—and *you don't age,* not enough to notice. Think about it."

He looked to where he remembered Dacia being, and she said, "You're making your point, Ivan. Go ahead."

His held breath came out faster than he liked. He said, "All right; priorities, now. I'm staying up, myself, because Bran Tregare gave me responsibility for this ship—to keep it safe for him. And I *owe* that man." He blinked; the pain tweaked at him. *And now who?*

He had to do it fast. "Those I'm keeping up with me, you'll be the ones I need most." He didn't want to laugh, then, but couldn't repress a snort. "The hell of it is, any choice I make is going to have holes in it." They were holding better than he'd expected; no one spoke. *Damn it!*—he couldn't list the ones for freeze; he didn't know all the names. He'd have to do it the other way.

All right. "For starters—" Peleter for Drive, and Crowfoot for there and Control both. For reasons he didn't give, both the Kobolaks—and Alina. "Ellalee Ganelong resisted the Tsa attack better than any of us; that ability might be the most useful of all." *And . . . ?*

Ornaway and young Limmer broke the silence, each giving reasons to claim the eighth spot. Pointing his blind stare at each voice in turn, Ivan waved a hand. "No. Your thinking's valid, and given any leeway I'd go along with you. But I don't have that leeway. So—"

Who? "One more for Drive." And what was the woman's name? Oh, yes. "Melaine Holmbach."

Her voice came hoarse. "Me? Why, captain?"

"You don't want the assignment?"

"Sure I do. But *why*?"

Because you know how to change your mind; I heard you do it.

But he couldn't say that. "Luck of the draw. Somebody has to take the hard jobs."

*   *   *

Embarrassing, Ivan found it, to shake hands and send people off to freeze, where Dacia and Alina would do the final trundling. The ones he hardly knew didn't bother him, but Hask and Arlen—he felt he should say something and didn't know what. Finally he did find words. "You'll be up and doing when we come to Shaarbant. It's only the dead time, you're missing."

They left, and so did others—until, if Ivan had heard and counted correctly, only Anders Kobolak sat with him. He cleared his throat, and knew it was only a nervous reflex. "Anders. I'd like to thank you for backing me, when the man called me useless." He found he was straining to *see*, and made himself relax. "I don't mean to push anything, you understand—but *why*?"

Ivan heard knuckles cracking, and guessed the Second Hat was frowning, also, before he said, "I spoke the truth, was all. As soon as that idiot insulted you, I had this picture—of me with the *Deux* to keep safe, and you not there to turn to." He made a small cough. "I'm not much for false modesty, and in most circumstances I believe I'm capable of running this ship. Or any other."

"Yes." Ivan nodded. "I'd agree with that."

"But now—going back to face the Tsa again, with the Hoyfarul Drive out—I need that brain of yours. You make good decisions; you have the combat-type mind, like Rissa's, and Tregare's." Very briefly, Anders laughed. "I'm working on it. But I don't think I'm quite there, yet."

Ivan had to smile. "We deserve a drink. Want to pour?" He waved toward the corner where the little bar-console sat. "Bourbon on ice, for me."

Slowly, compared to what a coherent drive field could have done, the *Deux*'s speed built. Peleter and Crowfoot, with Melaine Holmbach working extra hours as "gopher" for them, spent long days working over the Hoyfarul apparatus. But despite improvisations that sounded ingenious to Ivan, the FTL drive stayed dead.

Ivan's original job on the *Deux* had been Gunnery Officer, but Dacia was the ship's best remaining gunner; he set her to instructing Ellalee and Alina. He didn't have enough people for separate operation of each turret, so he had Crowfoot rearrange the controls—the pilot handled the central turret and two "side gunners" each had charge of three-turret groups, set to traverse together. Heterodyne and convergence couldn't be synchronized

perfectly, but after a little practice Dacia said the system seemed
to work pretty well.

Ivan wasn't satisfied, though; he wanted to be able to *do*
more. It should be possible, he thought, for a gunner to work
from auditory signals. So, in one side-position, Crowfoot rigged
the circuitry to feed a set of headphones.

The trouble was that even with different signal patterns,
Ivan couldn't sort out the heterodyne indications at his right ear
from the range checks at his left. Finally, swearing, he found the
"Stop" switch and got up. "Come on, Jere. Maybe coffee will
liven up my thinking." In the galley Ivan talked of other matters,
not consciously considering the gunnery problem. He knew how
his mind could work, sometimes, and finally—

"Got it!" He snapped his fingers. His mistake, he decided—
but didn't say so—was going with Crowfoot's lead, when Crowfoot himself had never been able to work a turret. How to put it?
"I think we went wrong, Jere, working one function into each
ear."

Crowfoot's tone was mild. "How else would you suggest
we do it?"

Quickly, gulping his coffee, Ivan told his idea. Then they
went upship and Crowfoot made some changes. When he was
ready, Ivan—hands on his control levers—said, "Feed me heterodyne," and for a few minutes he worked with it. A steady
tone now, fed to both ears equally; when it rose in pitch, it meant
the circle on the screen was tilting to the right; and vice-versa
when the pitch lowered. When it was exactly "on," the tone
was pure; any deviation distorted the waveform and threw in
extra harmonics. "Well, *that* part works."

The range indicator was different. When either range light
came on, a different, higher tone beeped into the corresponding
ear. The farther off correct range, the faster the beeping.

Very quickly, Ivan got the hang of it. "Now for all the
marbles. Both signals at once." The sounds came, and for a
few moments he couldn't sort them out. And then he could.
When the simulation run ended, Crowfoot patted Ivan's
shoulder.

"I think you have it whipped. Your score's not outstanding,
but after all, it was your first run using this method."

An hour later, Ivan's performance was within a few points
of what he'd done when his eyes worked. Tired, he stretched
and stood. "I'll need more practice, but it does work. Thanks,
Jere."

When he told Dacia the results, over dinner, he tried to keep his voice casual. But of course he couldn't.

In gunnery and pilot training, people began to level off at their own natural grades of skill—for the most part, the results pleased Ivan. His own shooting, he realized, was more useful to his ego than to the ship's safety. Nearly everybody else could do much the same as he could, in that line—and see what they were doing, as well. And most could do something he couldn't at all—operate the ship itself, guide it. He considered adding audible indicators to more of the ship's instruments, then realized the sheer number of signals he'd need, and growled to Dacia, "It'd sound like fifty cats fighting. Nobody could sort heads or tails out of it."

And meanwhile the *Deux* built speed to as near light as fuel economy allowed, and pushed ahead, chewing time.

XV. *Tregare*

*T*regare waited until evening to call council. Things were a mess, he knew, but he still felt good. For dinner he'd tried a really good-sized slab of tonguewalker haunch; he was coming to like the stuff, and so was his digestion. Now he sat back with a glass of brandy and waited for people to be ready to talk, and to listen.

His leg, in the cast, itched where he couldn't scratch—but except for twinges, the ache was gone. He wished Jenise was doing as well; she still took pills, and couldn't wiggle her fingers much.

She looked pretty good, though, except that Tregare wasn't used to everybody's bare scalps showing through short stubble. Of course, with *his* ears, who was he to talk? Setting down his brandy, he lit one of his few remaining cigars. "All right, folks?"

Talk stopped; he had the floor. Everybody knew the situation but he skimmed it anyway. "So for now, we have to figure we're on our own. Except, if the *Deux* got offworld, and I don't see why not, Ivan should have it back here in a week or two. And if he circles down to spot us, which seems reasonable, he should catch our signal."

Sipping more brandy, he blew a smoke ring—and remembered when a younger Lisele always laughed and poked her finger through the hole. "But even if he does hear us," Tregare said, "what he can do about it depends on the Tsa—whether they're still around or not."

"And now, Bran," said Rissa, "you have a point to make?"

"No. A question to ask." He shrugged. "Goes without saying, we wait here as long as the *Deux* might still come looking—and a bit longer. Question is, if they *don't* come, what's our best bet?"

"What's your own guess?" said Hagen Trent. "You must have one."

Tregare grinned. "You first. Chairman gets the wrapup spot."

Shrugging, Trent said, "I see three choices, none good. Camp here indefinitely, undertake to raise this scoutship to launching attitude, or pack up and hike out. I'd like another alternative."

So would I. Tregare gave the nod to everyone in turn—Rissa, Jenise, Lisele and the two Shrakken. Sevshen didn't say anything; he rarely did. Tregare knew the alien understood human language, now, but he seldom used it. Stonzai said, "Not our world, this is. It we not know." Haltingly, then, she tried to explain something that at first Tregare didn't understand. It took some repetition.

After a time, though, he stopped her. "Stonzai—you say the swamp's drying up, farther out from here?" She signed assent. "And faster, as time passes?" The same sign: Tregare looked around the group. "Does that click, now, with anything else we know? Anybody?"

Rissa spoke. "This latitude gives rainy and dry seasons, only—the latter with much heat. The *Deux*'s computer could inform us as to how orbital eccentricity and axial tilt affect those seasons. But I recall that at this time the planet is nearing its primary, not receding. So we must be entering a hotter, drier period."

"Yeah." It sounded right. "So pretty soon we could move out with a fair chance of making it to the mountains ahead of the next rains. The foothills, rather, where the jungle ends. Though maybe—'' Tregare grinned. "Jungle, outside this swamp, might be fit to live in. For a while, anyway.''

Jenise Rorvik raised her good hand. "What we really want is to get back to Sassden, where we left the *Deux*. Clear across the mountains, though—too far, probably.'' She chewed her lip. "But wouldn't we have to be out of the jungle, to have much chance of sighting anything flying over, and being seen in return?''

"Even jungles have open spaces," Tregare said. "Usually, I mean; I can't vouch for this one yet.''

Rissa cleared her throat. "Then you feel we should prepare ourselves, waiting for the swamp to become passable, against a trek toward the mountains? In case no rescue comes?''

"That's about it. We can't go yet, of course; I'm in no shape to hike on this leg, especially toting a pack. Jenise needs more time, too. But we might's well start getting ready. Including an exercise program, if we want to be in marching condition.''

Hagen Trent looked about as annoyed as he ever got, so Tregare caught his gaze and nodded. The man said, "You're not even considering the chance of getting the scout upright, and flying out?''

"No.'' Pausing, Tregare thought how to say it. "Last time I was outside, I took a hard look and made a time estimate on that job.''

"I'd like to hear it.'' Trent sounded obstinate.

"All right. Given solid ground, so the drive nodes wouldn't sink in the mud and blow us to plasma when we tried to lift, and given a moratorium on the next rains, so our work wouldn't be washed away when we were half-finished, my guess was four hundred days. And that was everybody working double shifts.'' He spread his hands. "And since we don't have solid ground and we do have to expect the rains again—''

Hagen's mouth puckered like a hurt child's. "Say no more; you're already into overkill. But how can you be so sure? I thought *I* was the engineer in this crowd.''

"In a drive room, you are. But I built me a spaceport once. Not fancy—you remember it, Rissa. But I did learn how much work it takes to move dirt. Mud, I don't even want to find out about.''

The water level did lower; the exposed path slowly dried. As hiking became feasible, everyone took daily workouts. Tregare discarded his crutch and nagged Rissa until she peeled the cast off him; then, face pale and teeth gritted, he practiced until he could walk without limping. It hurt like hell at first, but peace take him, he was going to be ready when the time came!

Occasionally, Hagen Trent bagged a tonguewalker. Now they boiled the sliced portions free of toxins, irradiated the meat to sterilize it, and packed it into sealed containers—that way it would keep without refrigeration.

"The hardest part," Tregare said, one day, "is figuring what to take along and what to leave." He waved a hand. "The scout's loaded with things we need, but we're limited to what we can carry." He scowled. "It's the choosing that drives me nuts."

He showed Rissa his list, marked with scribbled changes until it was barely legible. Running a finger down the page, she nodded. "A good start, Bran. From our food stores, mostly concentrated items, and nothing that duplicates what we can expect to find as we go." The finger stopped. "This second energy gun. A large one? But—"

"I thought about that a lot." Once discharged, the thing would be useless. And it weighed twice as much as the smaller ones—but it held nearly five times the charge, and could be set to discharge at the smaller-gun rate.

At his explanation, she nodded again. "Yes. But in the long run we shall have to depend on the needle guns. And the ammunition for those, in quantity, is heavy."

Tregare spread his hands. "*Everything's* heavy, when you add up enough to last us. But what choice do we have?"

The scout stocked backpacks, since its emergency function was as a lifeboat, and survivors can't count on coming groundside in settled country; drawing a habitable world at all would be a bonus.

Tregare found a dozen packs, lightweight and sturdy. Leafing through the instruction sheets he saw how they hooked together so a person could carry one in front and one aft. It didn't look comfortable but he guessed it would work. In this heat, though . . .

Considering the number of packs they could take and the capacity of each, he checked down his list. The list far outran the capacities. Too discouraged to curse, he stood. Rissa called to him. "Time for lunch, Bran!" Realizing he'd been hungry for some time but hadn't noticed, he turned and followed her to the control room.

The rest were already eating. Nobody talked much, and that suited Tregare. When he was done—irritable, he skipped coffee—Rissa said, "Bran, I would like to show you something. Outside."

Again he followed her. Now, except for scattered daubs, the airlock was free of mud, and outdoors the footing was solid. She pointed forward, where a metal framework leaned against the scout.

"See?" He looked, and it didn't make much sense. A kind of ladder, more than two meters long and about three decimeters wide. But with rungs and diagonal braces both curved, convex downward, the way the thing was leaning. The sidepieces' upper ends were bent down to form handles; there, and spaced along the sidebars, eyebolts were fastened.

At the bottom the sidebars fastened to a metal sheet that curved up, as the bars did, in an arc of about a radian. Of sturdy weight, the sheet was corrugated, grooves parallel to the framework's length, and rounded at the free end. And the whole thing was put together with bolts and rivets, not welded.

Rissa's face had an expectant look. Puzzled, Tregare said, "I'll bite. What is it?"

"A travois, Bran. As used by the aborigines of North America. They lacked the wheel, you see, but a person or draft animal can drag a much greater load than could be carried. So I—"

"Peace be kept!" Turning, he grabbed and hugged her. "Rissa, I think you just put this outfit on a paying basis!" Now he inspected the device more carefully, asking questions and making an occasional suggestion. "At the shoulder harness we'll need a quick release, some kind of ripcord. So if a tonguewalker charges, for instance, a person can get out of the way fast."

Rissa agreed, and marked down a note. Hagen Trent came over to join them; Rissa said, "Tregare approves our work. Bran, Hagen designed the bracing, for best strength with least weight. And all the riveting is his work."

Tregare shook the man's hand. "Good on you, friend." He raised an eyebrow. "One question. *Why* the bolts and rivets?"

"Magnesium," said Rissa. When he still scowled, she added, "We are not on *Inconnu Deux*, with access to an inert-gas environment for welding." Tregare's palm slapped his forehead, and he laughed.

"Of course!" he said. "A nice big flare and a lot of smoke." Then he got down to business. First the three of them loaded packs, helter-skelter with whatever came to hand, to reasonable carrying weights. "Now," said Tregare, "we're going to test this out scientifically. Maybe not very, but some."

So each, carrying a pack, walked along the path to where the deep water began, and back. After resting, they all tried the travois over the same course with various loads, for comparison. The results—ratio of burdens for roughly the same effort—disappointed Tregare, and he said so.

"You're not looking at the whole picture," said Trent. "We figure on three of these gadgets. Consider *that* ratio, to six individuals playing packhorse, and see how it looks."

Tregare did, and he nodded. "It's better, all right."

"And the adults form two reliefs, Bran," said Rissa. "As well matched for strength as we can manage. While one team drags the travoises, the other can walk unhampered."

"Yeah," Tregare said. "Everybody works only half the time. I like it." He grinned. "As of now, we all practice with this thing."

Back in the scout, reworking his list, Tregare felt better. He still couldn't take everything he'd like—not even a lot of things he was sure they'd need. But then he'd never really expected to. And at least the percentage had gone up now.

In case a travois broke—*take along extra bolts!*—or had to be abandoned, they'd still need the packs. So use them, on each travois, as stowage units. Of course there'd be extra stuff to be bundled separately; that was all right, too.

Loading. Heavier things at the rear, the bottom of a travois; let the ground, not the person, argue with gravity. On level terrain and solid footing, anyway; crossing submerged patches it might be better the other way around. And don't forget some inflatable buoyancy bags; crossing water, they'd make all the difference.

The bottom skid, smooth curved metal, grooved in the direction of travel, should help with friction and slippage. Good enough; for the first time, Tregare felt that things might actually *work*.

So at dinner he was in a mood for conversation. Lisele obliged him, telling how a tonguewalker had got away, and what its escape had shown to her and Stonzai. "She hit it good with the needlegun; she really did. And we dodged, one to each side the way we do now, so it couldn't make up its mind. But it kept going somehow—plowed through all that thick brush and into the water." Looking exasperated, the child sighed. "Almost ten meters out, before it sank. The water's too deep there; we couldn't get it.''

But from the water's edge, the girl and the Shrakken saw a part of the island that was new to them. "A little ridge that goes out from the far end. Never saw it before, because you'd have to cut through some really heavy bush to get there. I bet it's above water all the time; there's lots of stuff growing on it. But anyway—''

The thing was that this ridge curved off to the right, toward the mountains. Whereas the trail they knew, forward of the scout, began parallel to those mountains and slanted away from them.

"Good observation, Lisele . . . Stonzai," Tregare said. "Tomorrow we'll go hack some brush and take a better look.''

Leading his daughter and Stonzai past the scout toward the island, Tregare decided his leg was almost serviceable. When he told Lisele, though, she wanted to race, and he had to pass the offer.

Once they passed the high point of the island's low ridge, he dropped back and let the child lead. "Which way, now?''

She pointed ahead, into a dense thicket. "It's that direction, the ridge. But off here to the left is where we can see it from.''

The tonguewalker's plunge had pushed the brush aside; they shoved their way through the narrow passage. Short of the waterline, Tregare turned and saw the ridge Lisele had mentioned. He stopped, and she bumped into him from behind. "Just a minute, princess.''

"But we're not there yet.''

"I can see from here." He looked back, then ahead again. "Trying to figure the shortest way to cut through this jungle and get to that ridge." After a moment, he shrugged. "Here's as good a place as any. Stay behind me now, both of you.''

He pulled out his energy gun, the smaller model, and crouched down. Level with the ground and close to it, he burned a swathe through the brush ahead. Thick, it grew; even cut off at ground level, the bushes hung in place. Stepping forward, Tregare lifted the severed plants and tossed them aside. A few meters along, he had to stop and crouch again, and do another burn. And another, a little later, that got them down to where the narrow ridge left the island.

Looking along that ridge, Tregare's gaze followed past the next grove of trees and caught the line beyond, curving to the right. Toward rising ground, too, as far as he could see in this morning's haze. And over there, the foliage looked to be a lighter color. Remembering what Skandith had said, riding the scoutship on its way to Shtegel, Tregare made a guess: that within about two kilometers, this patch of swamp gave way to ordinary jungle.

Of course, he reminded himself, this was only the first patch.

Turning, he told Lisele and Stonzai his thoughts. The girl said, "Then we won't have to fight mud all the way, and worry about water monsters?"

Tregare chuckled. "Well, I'd hope not. And with jungle terrain being higher than swamp, maybe we can spot swamp country coming up and try to avoid it."

They began walking back. As they reached the island's crest, from a cloudless, hazy sky the thunder came. Just ahead was a small clearing; ignoring stabs of pain from his leg, Tregare ran there, and looked up. Something, he saw—high and fast, too far away to name, and for an instant his vision blurred. Shaking his head, he turned. Lisele stood, eyes wide and blinking slowly. Stonzai lay huddled, arms around her head. He went to her.

"You all right?" She moaned, and said something in her own language. The only word Tregare recognized was "Tsa."

"Yeah. That's what I thought." Kneeling, he tried to work her arms free; she moaned again, then let him straighten them. Her face turned upward; the triangular eyes opened. "You hurt, Stonzai?"

"Hurt, yes. But get up, can." Lisele helped him get the Shrakken to her feet. Her first steps were shaky, but she said, "Walk now, can." Still, Tregare decided to keep a slow pace.

He looked to his daughter. "You haven't said—did you feel much of anything? Except that things blurred, a second, I didn't."

The girl frowned. "I'm not sure. Something—like fingers touching me and pulling back. Only in my *head*." She shook that head, and gave a little skip. "But it didn't hurt. Not any."

"Me either. I wonder—" And back at the scout, he got everyone together and took a poll. Trent and Jenise, outside for travois practice, had seen the ship a longer time than Tregare had—and both felt pain as well as disorientation. Rissa, inside, wasn't sure she'd felt anything at all. "I was concentrating. By the time I noticed the sound, it had nearly gone."

Stonzai and Sevshen talked; then she reported. He too had been inside, but the sound made him think of Tsa, and pain struck. Unlike Stonzai, though, he hadn't been knocked off his feet.

Tregare related his group's experiences, then said, "Do the differences give us any ideas?" And after a pause: "Jenise, Hagen—did the pain begin as soon as you saw the ship?"

Not exactly, it turned out. Their first reactions had been like those of Tregare and Lisele; then one of them had said, "The Tsa?" "And as soon as I got scared," Jenise said now, "the pain hit. It didn't last long, though." Trent's report was similar, except that his reaction had been anger, not fear.

"All right," said Tregare. "The Tsa have to be some sort of telepaths, and it looks as if it pays not to notice them, to think of them *as* Tsa when they're in range. And especially, not to have any kind of hostile reaction."

"But how can we help it?" Jenise's face showed strain.

Rissa shook her head. "I have no answer. It is impossible, normally, to *refrain* from thinking of something by act of will."

Trent leaned forward. "Look—think of dealing with a mean dog. If you act—movements, tone of voice, all of it—as if the dog's going to behave itself, like as not, it will." He looked around. "I've done it. Has anyone else, here?"

Tregare said, "Sure. Same with people, too, sometimes." Elbows on the table, he steepled his fingers. "What you're saying—if we think of the Tsa mental touch as harmless, maybe it will be?"

Above Stonzai's eyes the stubby tendrils quivered. "The Tsa, not to fear, not to hate? *How* do I that?"

"That," said Rissa, "is the difficulty. In a group, if only one falters and succumbs, the Tsa strike will likely reach all, if contact lasts any time. The Shrakken are most vulnerable; having suffered Tsa attacks for so long, the fear and hate are reflex to them."

"Where we've only had it twice," said Tregare. "But I think that reflex wouldn't take much reinforcement, to set in solid. Today I didn't have the problem; the Tsa were gone before I had time to guess what they were. But in the general case—" He shrugged. "Trent, I think this is a meaner breed of dog than what we're used to."

Before dinner, Trent announced that it was time to remove Jenise's cast. "If you're going to need a brace on that wrist,

Rorvik, we want some time here—before we leave—to experiment and find out what works best for you.''

So with Rissa helping, he took the casing off. Tregare knew he wasn't going to like what he saw, and he was right. Wrist and lower palm were discolored and misshapen, with lumps and hollows that didn't belong there, and ridged with angry-looking scars. Looking, Jenise Rorvik whimpered.

"Try moving it," said Trent. Tregare watched; together, like a mitten, the fingers moved slightly. The thumb flexed better, but without strength. Trying to bend the wrist itself, Jenise went pale.

She tried moving a light object along the table, and stopped. "No!" At Trent's urging she pushed from a different angle, but no bending stress on that wrist was bearable to her.

Tears ran down her face. "You should have taken the hand off!"

Softly, Rissa spoke. "That is not, I believe, what you wanted at the time. And if we ever rejoin *Inconnu Deux*—"

"We never will! You can't believe that, still?"

The two faced each other, Jenise glaring from tear-filled eyes while Rissa's stayed wide and solemn. "I have to believe it."

Tregare cleared his throat. "She needs a brace, all right. Trent, can you make something that's light and strong, and can be taken off fairly easy, for washing up? What's in the kit?"

Rummaging through the supplies, Rissa brought out several items. "This, Hagen, and—"

"Right." The man set to work. When he was done, the layered bracing had a slim contour. Jenise's fingers were left bare past the knuckles, and the thumb entirely free, but the wrist was held rigidly. "See how that works. And exercise those digits."

Now, at least, she could apply pressure with the hand, without wincing. "That's a lot better; thanks, Hagen. And I *will* try to get more use of my thumb and fingers."

At dinner, though, the thumb wasn't strong enough to hold a fork or spoon firmly.

The last day passed, that the *Deux* should have shown up if Tregare's plan had gone well. They waited ten more. Supplies were packed, except that people kept thinking of something else they needed, and Tregare had to make choices. He stepped up the exercise program. His own leg wasn't fully back to strength yet, but he figured he could keep up well enough. Sure as peace, he'd try.

Regarding stores to be left behind, economy went by the boards. At meals they gorged on the choicest tidbits. "Might's well live it up while we can," Tregare said. "Later we'll get our fill of concentrates and local weeds and boiled tonguewalker." He poured himself more wine; none of that was going with them, either. Two liters of medicinal alcohol, but no wine.

Tregare sighed. He *liked* wine.

The group was quiet tonight, absorbed in thought or in last-minute preparations. Tregare looked again down his thrice-recopied list, and hoped they'd get out of here before he made it illegible enough to need a fourth copying. He checkmarked some items he'd added today. Spare micropile for the water purifier . . . right. Double the allowance for Stonzai's anti-ovulation pills; take all of them along, not just half. Because the more Tregare thought about it, the more it struck him that the last thing they needed, out in the boonies, was an instinct-maddened Shrakken breathing out zombie gas and needing a nice fat human grub to feed her larvae!

Maybe just a *few* kilos of goodie-foods. Question mark. Well, why not? The stuff would be used up in the first few days, lightening the load. He erased the question mark.

Checking further, he paused twice, then decided to stick with what he'd written. At some point, he reflected, you had to quit shuffling, and firm things up.

Their last night on the scout Tregare looked around. By now, the upended control room seemed positively like home.

He caught Rissa's gaze and raised one eyebrow; she nodded. Saying nothing, they got up and climbed into the dorm area and past it to the drive room. This, now that Jenise lived in Control with them, was the only place Rissa and Tregare could have privacy. Two acceleration pads helped. He held her. "Let's spend all night here."

"Bran—we do need some sleep."

"Sure. But not all that much."

She laughed. "Yes. I think the need will regulate itself."

When pre-dawn glow tinged the edge of sky, the group set out. Tregare looked once at the open airlock, no way to close it. Then he turned ahead, and didn't look back again.

They crossed Lisele's island to the low, narrow ridge she'd found. First they walked with water on each side; Tregare kept glancing one way and then the other, wondering if the stuff was deep enough to harbor the huge leech-beasts. Then, skirting a grove of swamp-rooted trees, the ridge turned "west" toward the mountains. Now it ran fairly straight, into the light-colored area, ahead in the haze, that Tregare guessed to be jungle.

He was right; about three kilos from the scout, the ridge merged into a larger version of Lisele's island. How much larger, they weren't sure; by noon they were still climbing. Not for the highest part, but to avoid the thicker shoreline growth. They tried to follow a sort of path, but it kept dividing into indistinct trails that sometimes petered out. Tonguewalkers—or what else? Tregare shrugged, and made sure his gun was free in the holster.

So far, the travois system worked fine. Tregare traded his off with Hagen Trent, Rissa with Jenise, and Stonzai with Sevshen—while Lisele carried a light pack. Rissa had the hardest of it; Jenise, it turned out early, couldn't handle her full shift. Tregare thought he had an answer. Trent, Rissa and Sevshen had just done their stints; now, after a rest pause, Tregare, Jenise and Stonzai would take over. Well, if Rissa was stronger than Jenise, Tregare—bad leg or no bad leg—had weight and muscle on Hagen Trent. He looked down at Rissa's travois and began to unfasten one carrier pack.

"Bran—what are you doing?" Rissa sat up straight.

"Lie back, honey. Just equalizing things a little. You can haul more than Jenise, and I can tote more than I've got, no sweat. So every stop, we'll just shift this pack back and forth."

"Why bother?" Lying back, hands behind his head, Trent drawled the words. "If you can haul it, I can, too."

Tregare wasn't so sure, but he caught Rissa's scowl. "All right; we'll try it." *Peace take people who always have to prove something!* He thought fast, and said, "Come to think, there's no reason we can't shift load components any time somebody turns up a little tired or off the feed. I mean, nobody's going to have *all* good days." And he saw Trent relax.

Time to move again; quicker than Tregare expected, everyone was ready. Following their same general route, after a time they passed the highest ground. But through the trees, Tregare couldn't see ahead much. Stopping, he raised a hand, and pointed. "I'm going up there. Try to get a better look, see what's ahead." He unhooked the travois, set it down, and walked slowly up the hill.

He still couldn't see much—too many trees. He walked to one, thinking to climb it, but his first effort stabbed at the leg.

He cursed under his breath, and turned downhill. "Anybody want to come up and climb a tree for me?"

Lisele shed her pack and came running. Tregare told her what he wanted to know, and added, "Be careful, princess."

"Yes. All right." She went up that tree like a squirrel; soon, among the thick branches, she was out of sight. Finally, nearly as fast as she'd gone up, she descended. Catching her breath, she pointed. "That way." A bit to the right, Tregare noted. "Another kilo or so, then it's all swamp except one narrow part, light-colored like jungle. There's some thick haze out there a way, so I can't tell for sure—but *looks* like maybe the good part goes all the way through to another piece of high ground. Lots bigger than this one."

Not solid data, maybe, but the best he was going to get. Tregare nodded. "Good work, Lisele; thanks." Then they walked back down—Lisele skipping ahead sometimes—and rejoined the others. And got moving again.

The winding ridge did go all the way through, but daylight failed before they reached the next land mass. The unburdened used their handlamps to help guide the travois-haulers and watch for dangers to the sides. Once off the ridge, climbing through dense brush, Tregare stopped. "This heavy thicket, to the right. Let's clear a space and make camp." Using the lighter energy gun, as he'd done on Lisele's island, he carved a small clearing. The cutdown bushes were packed around the perimeter and into the entrance, to block it. "Not much of a stockade," Tregare said, "but better than nothing." And once Rissa and Trent had built a cookfire, the group settled in cheerfully enough.

One day, thought Tregare, after dinner and before sleep. *How many hundreds more?*

XVI. Ivan

*T*he problem with the Hoyfarul Drive, said Jeremy Crowfoot, was a lack of components to beef up the lock circuits, and hold the drive field coherent. But one day he had another idea. "Feed all the exciters from one source, using power stages for isolation. Nobody's ever done it that way, but let's try." So Ivan followed him down to Drive, and listened while he and Peleter and Melaine Holmbach worked to haywire the place.

Afterward—after something blew up and left the drive room stinking of burnt insulation—Ivan got up from where the blast had sent him diving, reflexively, for safety, and brushed at himself. Other hands were there to help. Ivan said, "Is the normal drive still working all right?"

"Uh, yes." Crowfoot sounded embarrassed. "It's still a good idea, Ivan. Simply—well, the time delays on the different feeds seem to need finer tuning." His voice trailed off. "If we have enough spares left, to rebuild that configuration."

Reaching out, Ivan found the man's shoulder and gripped it. "Nice try, anyway, Jere." He turned away. "I think I'll go lie down for a little while. Explosions give me a headache."

Declining help, he groped his own way to quarters. Dacia wasn't there; he remembered she'd planned a little extra simulation work. Tired, discouraged after the drive-room fiasco, Ivan showered, had a heavier drink than he usually allowed himself, and lay down to nap.

Some fairly aggressive cuddling woke him. He yawned, and mumbled, "Dacia? Maybe you have a good thought there." He turned to hold her, and no clothes were in the way. He managed a kiss.

"Mmmmm?" Well, if she didn't need words, neither did he. More quickly than usual, skipping their ordinary rituals, he joined with her. That part went faster, too; why were they in such a hurry?

When it was done, she nudged him gently to one side and moved away across the room. Already dozing again, he heard her in the bath-cubby. Her touch brought him nearly awake again. "Very good," she whispered, and then she was gone. Or else he was . . .

Next time he woke, Dacia was kissing him, and this time she used words, too. "Miss me? I've missed you, and I think it's about time." Her hands moved on him.

Suddenly he sat up. "Dacia—isn't it a little too soon?" He laughed. "After all, I'm only superhuman!"

Her hands stopped. "Too soon? Nearly three days?" A pause. "Well, I know you've been working hard, but I thought—"

"Dacia, what time is it?" She told him; thinking back, he made a quick estimate. "Less than an hour ago you were here, and we—"

Her hands left him; when she spoke, he knew she was standing. "I was *not* here. Except for galley breaks, I've been in Control the past nine hours!" She sounded angry, but not very.

Ivan shook his head. "Then who was it? Because I—"

And then Dacia began to giggle. "That's a good question, isn't it?"

Maybe Dacia was amused, but Ivan wasn't. There was something humiliating about having his blindness used to deceive him.

"Well," said Dacia, still chuckling now and then no matter how he frowned, "you do have to take the incident as a compliment."

"Maybe." He grudged the word. "*Who*, though?" Not Alina, surely; she and Anders favored a fairly strict grade of monogamy. But still—no, Alina's hair was long. He'd stroked that woman's, and noticed no difference from the shortish cut Dacia wore. With Ellalee he wouldn't have, probably; curlier, maybe, but not by much. The other one, though. "Dacia. The woman down in Drive, Holmbach. What's her haircut like? How long, I mean?"

"Oh—" Dacia paused, then said, "You've eliminated Alina, then, on that basis? Well, I'd say Holmbach's still in the running."

He sat up, feet over the side of the bed to rest on the floor. "Get her up here, will you?"

"Why? What do you want to say to her?"

He shook his head. "I don't know."

"Then until you do, why don't you leave it alone?" She sat and hugged him, head on his shoulder. "I know what bothers you—being *fooled,* that way. But it's not as if she did something *mean,* whoever it was." She nibbled at his ear. "Is it, now?"

"I guess not." He hated the whiny way his voice sounded, then, so he tried to change it. "Let's go up and eat, shall we?"

"All right. I think it's Jeremy's stint as chef."

Ivan shrugged. "Who cares? We can cook our own."

The next couple of days he considered putting himself into one-to-one situations with his suspects, asking clever questions and getting one of them to betray guilty knowledge and give her game away. Dacia laughed him out of the idea. "She'll be two jumps ahead of you, if she wants to be. If she doesn't, she'll likely come and tell you of her own accord."

They were both wrong. For over a week nothing happened, and every time Ivan was in company with either woman he felt foolish and ineffectual. Then one day, hurrying too much, on the stairs he slipped and fell, and bruised one hip. Getting up, he limped off to quarters. And heard someone behind him, following.

He pretended not to notice; inside, he didn't lock the door. He stripped, and turned the shower as hot as he could stand it, to soak the ache loose. Out and dried, when he clambered into bed he wasn't surprised to find somebody else there. Somebody female.

He touched a specific part of her body, and because of a certain thing Dacia had done and this woman hadn't, he knew she wasn't Dacia. His hand moved; he gripped one shoulder and held her down. "All right. Who? And why?"

Her breathing sounded calm enough. Her voice, a whisper, gave away no identity. "I came to tell you. Any time we talked, lately, you seemed nervous. And that's not what—I mean, all I wanted, before, was to do something nice. Because you picked me, Captain."

It took him a minute to remember; then he eased his grip on her, and nodded. "Melaine Holmbach, then?"

"Yes." Two almost silent breaths; then she spoke in a voice he could recognize. "You still sound angry. Why?"

"Because—look! To use a blind man's darkness, to fool him, makes him *feel* like a fool, and helpless." She moved; her hair brushed his arm and he knew she was shaking her head. Without intention his lips found her forehead, and suddenly he felt that somehow he was in the wrong. He kissed her. "It's all right now."

"Then can we, again, Captain? Let's!"

Well, it wasn't as if Dacia had shown resentment, the other time. But after, when Melaine was ready to leave, he said, "I understand, now, and I'm glad we've pleasured each other. But the way things are, here on the ship, I think this had better be all of it."

Against his fingers beside her head, he felt Melaine nod. "If you say so, Captain." Under his wrist her shoulder moved. A shrug? Probably. "I suppose I may as well take up Rance Peleter's offer. He's a kindly man—and I don't really mind that he's shorter."

By intent, he was up and dressed when Dacia came in. Waiting, he'd thought about the inevitable pairing process. When he chose people to stay awake he hadn't thought about a balance of sexes; now he was a little surprised to realize that everything came out even. He'd paid even less heed to his people's off-duty doings; unable to see, he observed no clues to draw his interest. Now he wondered, and grinned at himself. "Nosy!"

"Who?" His voice had covered the sound of Dacia's entrance.

"Hi. Oh, nothing important. Except, Melaine visited me again."

"Again? Then the mystery's solved?"

She sounded interested but not concerned, so he said, "I told her, this is the last time," and mentioned the remark about Peleter.

"You were considerate, Ivan, not to turn her away." He heard no sarcasm, and now she hugged him. "You didn't have to end it with her, you know—but I'm glad you did. I'm not horribly possessive, but I am a little bit." She left him and took a fast shower. When she came back, she said, "And who were you calling 'nosy', Ivan?"

Grinning, he said, "Melaine got me curious. As to how our four unattached peas are rattling around in this pod. That's all."

"Well—" Pausing, she clicked her tongue twice, then began. The duty situation governed, she thought—Peleter and Holmbach in Drive, Ellalee in Control, Crowfoot working both places. "I don't know about the drive room, but topside Jeremy hasn't given Ellalee much of a play." Cloth rustled; she was probably dressing. "And Ellalee herself—if her eyes are on anyone, it's usually you."

She chuckled. "That's why I wasn't making any bets about your mysterious visitor."

Why he should feel embarrassed, Ivan wasn't sure. But he did. "My stomach says it's time to eat. Shall we go?"

"If that's the best offer I'm going to get, let's do."

Dacia no longer needed to feed him. She cut the meat for him, then he'd locate each bite between knife and fork before spearing it with the fork. No doubt there were better ways, but he couldn't think of one and nobody here had any ideas for him.

Vegetables were chancier and salads impossible, until he thought of using tongs. They might have been handier for meat, too, but he'd mastered the fork and stubbornly stayed with it. As for "spoon vittles," his skill left something to be desired, but with a big napkin tucked into his collar he used the spoon anyway. He was finishing a bowl of stew when Jeremy Crowfoot greeted him. "Join you?"

"Sure, sit down. Coffee? Or have you eaten yet?"

"Nothing right now." With his schedule about a radian out of phase with Ivan's, the man was between mealtimes. "Business," he said.

"Let's have it," and Crowfoot began. The gist was that he and Peleter had scrounged up enough parts for one more try at activating the FTL drive. But if it blew again . . .

"We'd be short on spares for *normal* drive. And this far out, we can't afford the risk."

Ivan shrugged. "So we don't try it. Right?"

"Not right." Because there was more to the situation. On the last FTL try, the haywire had held together for more than thirty seconds. "And the monitors show that for at least twenty, we were beating light. Running so close already, it didn't take much to put us over. Ivan—why didn't the watch mention that?"

Ivan thought back. "They said the instruments blinked out briefly, but then came the explosion, and the ship bucking—I guess nobody thought to evaluate what really happened." Ellalee would have had the duty then—or Alina, maybe. Neither of them had enough training to figure something like that, coming unexpected.

Sighing, Ivan leaned forward. "Okay; let's hear the new idea."

"We go ahead and rebuild the setup—with tighter synchronization of the time-delay paths—but we don't test it."

Puzzled, Ivan said, "If we don't even know it works, what good is it?"

"Ace in the hole, at Shaarbant. Meanwhile, if we need any

of the spare components to repair normal drive, we have them. If we don't have to use them, we still keep the FTL option open."

Slowly, Ivan nodded. Crowfoot went on. "At Shaarbant, all we need is to get above light. *Barely* above light, and we can do it by running the FTL section in short bursts, too short to allow instability to build to blowup. I can key that control to the instruments that monitor the vulnerable stages. That way, you see—"

"It shuts down before it blows, yeah. So we lose FTL for *then*, but not the capacity for it later." Then Ivan frowned. "One thing you may have missed. Switching the drive field between coherent and acoherent phases very much—won't that heat up the circuits that feed the shaping nodes?"

Silence, then Crowfoot said, "Damn it, you're right." His feet moved on the deck; his voice came from higher up. "Back to the old drawing board; I'll have to add more safety interlocks, to shut off the Hoyfarul circuitry at *any* overload. Or—" He sounded hesitant. "Would you rather I drop the whole project?"

"Hell, no." Ivan didn't have to think twice; Crowfoot's morale depended on this thing; so did Peleter's, maybe. "Go ahead." He laughed. "Somehow, Jere, I don't think you're done having good ideas."

But when the man had gone, Ivan felt depressed. It must have shown; Dacia patted his hand. By reflex his head turned back and forth, to see if anyone was in eavesdropping distance. Feeling sheepish, he asked Dacia. "No," she said. "No one's near. Why?"

"Sooner or later I have to announce this, but I prefer later. Dacia—I've hoped, like everybody else, that we'd get back to FTL. Well, we won't, except maybe briefly at Shaarbant, a tactical gimmick."

"So?" He imagined her brows arching.

"You forget your earlier training? No—I'm sorry. Look, though. The other day, Alina ran me some calculations. Just the numbers and instructions; I didn't say what they were about." She squeezed his hand; he turned his blind stare away from her. "We're making a good clip now, in STL terms. In weeks we'll be back. *Our* weeks."

She gasped, and he said, "Yeah. At twenty to one, roughly, we're chewing time. Any idea how long this trip's taking, by Shaarbant's clocks?" He told her, and again her breath made sound.

"But then—?" She didn't say any more.

"That's right, Dacia. It's *years*, we're talking about. Whatever is happening on Shaarbant, win or lose, by the time we get there it'll all be settled."

She was only sniffling a little, not crying aloud, but he had her lead him to their quarters where she could do it in privacy. He resented Melaine Holmbach a little, then, because lovemaking would have been the best comfort, and he simply wasn't ready again, yet.

XVII. Lisele

*I*t was the growing heat that slowed them down. Lisele wasn't bothered too much; one day Hagen Trent, feet shuffling as he pulled the travois, half-cuffed and half-caressed her head, saying, "Kids! They could live in hell and have fun."

Jenise Rorvik, gaunt and hollow-eyed, turned and said, "Where do you think we are *now*?" Then Rissa made a mild joke; everybody else laughed a little, but Jenise didn't.

Shaarbant was still coming closer to its sun; that's what Tregare said. Nobody was sure how long before it began moving away again, but for now the heat kept getting worse. At first they'd been able to move all day, with rests. But pretty soon they began stopping well before sunset, cutting brush for shade and lying quiet. They tried moving by dark, but the third night something jumped on Hagen Trent and clawed him some before Tregare got a clear shot at it against moonlight. Nobody got a good look at the thing; it leaped into the dense brush and got away. Tregare said it probably didn't get very far, but the undergrowth was too heavy; next morning even Trent said it wasn't worth wasting energy charges to find the beast. With the bandages, and limping, he didn't look too good that day. He kept up, though.

After another week or so they only walked until mid-afternoon, and a time later they were stopping at noon, and now they could barely keep going until mid-morning. If it got much worse . . .

Early on, they tried to avoid swamp except to hunt

tonguewalkers, but now swamp was usually the only place to find extra water. The little dew-stills gave nearly enough for drinking, but not quite. The plant stems helped, if you could stand the taste, but the stems unconstipated you too much, if you chewed very many.

The only good time for walking, now, was from false dawn to when the sun got high enough to "turn on the furnace," as Tregare said—and every day the furnace came on earlier. Twilight was no good; the heat stayed long after dark closed in. So each day they made less distance.

One morning, Jenise just lay there. "Leave me and go on. I'm going to die anyway; why put myself through any more of this agony?" Sounding quite sane, Rorvik pointed out that here she had shade and water, " . . . and you can spare me a *few* days' food, can't you?" When she said that, she smiled.

Tregare looked as if he was going to hit her, but Rissa caught at his arm. "Bran—she cannot help it. She is worn down, below the level of sustaining purpose."

Scowling like a man ready to kill, still Tregare looked down and patted Rissa's hand. Sprouting beard masked the lines of his face, but Lisele saw how his mouth was set. "All right. We'll do it another way."

They left the camp too late to benefit from any cool at all. Drugged into quiet, Jenise lay strapped to the travois Tregare hauled. Part of its former load was on Stonzai's. And in place of Jenise, Lisele struggled under the burden of the third travois.

Including pauses to rest and trade off loads, they pushed ahead for over an hour before the heat reached the level that usually stopped them. Panting, sweat running from his face, Tregare said, "We're done; we can't do much more of this." He looked around; Lisele looked, too, and wondered if he saw everyone the same as she did. Hagen Trent seemed shrunken, as if something had sucked the juices out of him. Tregare himself might have had fires inside, raging to burst out. Days ago, Rissa's face had gone tight; it showed nothing of what she might feel. And the two Shrakken—there was no way to read their expressions, and there never had been.

Until her father squinted at her, it didn't occur to Lisele to wonder how *she* looked. She was tired, sure, and hot—if she let her legs tighten up at all, they began to shake. Her body's hunger for strength had nothing to do with her stomach. But she'd kept up, hadn't she? Nobody had to wait for her!

"No, princess; nobody did." Then she knew she'd said it

out loud, and felt silly. But Tregare managed a kind of grin. "After today, though, we can't go on. Not until this damned planet passes perihelion and starts cooling off."

"Here?" Rissa said. "Without water?" From her voice, she might have been asking if he wanted another piece of meat.

He shook his head, moved his shoulders. "Course not." He pointed ahead, to the slope they were rounding. "Swamp ahead. Not more than two kilos, likely. Saw it when we crossed the high part. That's where the water is—so that's where we go. Now, today—no matter *how* peacetwisting hot it gets! And then, there we stay."

Staring at him, Rissa shrugged. "If you have a kilo of travois-pulling left in you this day, then so do I."

Trent looked as if he'd been kicked in the gut, but he clambered to his feet. "My turn, Tregare, to pull that thing."

In the worst heat Lisele had yet known, they set off. She couldn't get her breath, and twice felt herself half-fainting, beginning to fall. If she did, though . . .

No! She saw Trent stagger, and forced her own shaking legs to take one firm step after another. When she did fall, for seconds she thought she was still walking. In red haze, she couldn't tell where anything was, except the ground against her.

She knew she wasn't crying, but her face was wet. Her eyes opened; she saw Rissa, a damp rag in one hand, looking down at her. Her head lay in her mother's lap. "I'm sorry; I—I slipped, I guess."

"You wore yourself down to a nubbin, Lisele; that's what you did. I should have watched you more carefully." For the first time in days, Lisele saw Rissa smile. "Basically you are all right; your pulse is good and your breathing is normal for this heat. When we continue, however, Stonzai will take the travois, while Sevshen relieves her on the heavier one."

Lisele tried to sit up. "*I* can do it!"

"Not today, duckling. Working yourself to collapse—for now, once is enough. Later you will have other chances—many of them."

Past Rissa, Lisele saw Tregare's face; his expression didn't show his thoughts. He shook his head, and said only, "I guess you get it from both sides of the family."

In a little while the group was up and moving again. Even without the travois, now, Hagen Trent had trouble keeping pace. Lisele angled over to walk beside him. He looked at her without seeming to see her, until he stumbled and she grasped his elbow; then he glared and pulled away. "What you doing? *I* don't need help."

"Please, Hagen. If you fall, somebody's got to pick you up. Like they did me."

He muttered a curse; then his arm went around her shoulder, and he said, "Know something? One thing I can't stand, it's a smart-off kid—but sometimes you make a lot of sense."

He tried not to put much weight on her; she could tell that. But before they got down to the water, he was leaning about as heavily as she could handle.

Twenty meters back from the water—a little more, maybe— a steep bank rose. A gully cut the bank, and that's how they went down. To their left a big tree stood, with some of its roots buried in the cliff and some arching down in air, making a shallow cave under the main trunk. "Not perfect," said Tregare, "but it'll do for bivouac until things cool off." He checked his chronometer. "I'll take first watch. You next, Stonzai. Two hours; all right?"

Even with the heat stifling her, once Lisele lay down it didn't take her long to go to sleep.

Rissa's touch woke her; she blinked at the red sun, just grazing the horizon. The smell of food, cooking, brought her more awake. Stretching stiff muscles, she got up to have dinner with the rest, sitting around a fire of small wood. Everybody sat well back from its heat, but after the dark closed in, the fire's light let her see far enough to feel reasonably safe.

Evenings had been quiet, lately; nobody had energy for talk. But now Rissa said, "Bran? We have as much relief from heat, tonight, as we can expect. Perhaps you should now announce your plan."

"Sure. Why not?" Looking almost like his normal self, Tregare stood. "We built us a kind of little fort, here. You see—" He pointed, and shone his handlamp; Lisele began to see what he meant.

Then he said, "Rissa's right; it's cooled off as much, tonight, as it's going to. So now's a good time to start building."

By the light of handlamps, Lisele saw branches and entire trees cut by Tregare's energy gun and come crashing down. Too heavy to move, those fallen things, until Tregare or Hagen cut them smaller. But then, everybody helping, a respectable barricade was built. "Not high enough," Tregare said, "but it will be."

Two days later he was satisfied. Then they put the roof on—mostly heavy-foliaged branch-ends, but those lay over a lattice of strong boughs spaced close enough that no tonguewalker could squeeze through. Or anything else, big enough to cause much trouble. That's what Tregare said, and Lisele thought he probably had it right.

Waiting miserably through Shaarbant's perihelion, the group had a few nasty surprises. No one had thought that tonguewalkers might come in smaller sizes, but they did. When a clutch of them squeezed down through the roof, nearly everybody got burned by the acid tentacles before the things were killed. Then Rissa and the two Shrakken wove thinner, pliant branches into the ceiling, leaving no opening big enough to let the creatures through. The irony was that once the place was secure, no more of the animals turned up. "Migrating, maybe," Tregare said.

The heat was worse than ever, but if you didn't have much work to do, you could get used to it. Especially if, as Lisele, you practiced alpha-state meditation a lot. Besides helping with normal camp chores, Lisele's only job was to go scouting—with Stonzai's gun to guard them both—for plants to eat. Every morning they set out at false dawn, using handlamps until true dawn came.

As time passed, they had to range farther for good forage, and one morning they crossed a point of land and heard a gurgling sound. Pushing ahead through a thicket, Lisele came to a running stream, about two meters across—the first water she'd seen since the scout crashed, that wasn't swamp and didn't *smell* like swamp.

Lisele was tired of smelling like swamp, herself, from bathing in a stagnant pool while somebody stood by with a gun. Mostly, everyone scrubbed off with fine sand—but sometimes, to feel halfway clean, they just had to bathe in water.

The stream was cooler to her hand than she expected. Cupping her palm, she scooped up a little water; it tasted fine. Quickly, as Stonzai approached, Lisele slipped off the light slacks and blouse she wore against scratchy brush, kicked loose her sandals and stepped into the stream. It felt so *good;* with a splash, she sat down, and then lay flat. She ducked her head under for a moment, then sat up and began rinsing her short hair.

Grown out from stubble now, it was almost long enough to need a comb.

She ducked under again, came up, and rubbed some more. Stonzai, looking down at her, suddenly pointed, yelling words Lisele didn't understand. Then something struck her thigh. It felt like fire, and without meaning to, she shrieked—shrieked, and tore with her hands at a grey thing that flopped in the water and sent agony up her leg.

A hand gripped her shoulder; she was yanked up and then she landed on dirt, flat on her back with the wind knocked out of her. Stonzai's gun gave a ripping hiss; something clawed at her right thigh where it hurt worst, and then the pain eased a little.

Struggling to get up, she managed to prop herself on one elbow and could see what was happening. Not flopping now, burned nearly in half, the grey thing lay to one side. She looked at her leg. Dark blood ran from a cluster of wounds at the front of her thigh, toward the inside, a handsbreadth from the groin. And as she watched, the area began to swell and darken.

With a high, keening wail, Stonzai put her mouth to the bleeding punctures, spat discolored blood and repeated the act. A half-dozen times, until the blood that came, looked normal. Slowly the darkened patch of flesh began to clear at the edges; the swelling didn't leave but it stopped spreading. Pain settled down to throbbing ache; Lisele found she was biting her lip, and that now she could stop doing it.

She took a deep, ragged breath. "Thanks, Stonzai. What *was* it?"

"Poison out, to get," the Shrakken said.

"Yes—yes, I know, and I thank you. I meant, the creature—?"

Stonzai gestured; on her hands and one knee, the hurt leg trailing, Lisele moved to see. The grey thing was about a meter long, and as thick as the thigh it had attacked—wormlike, with a sort of flipper at the tail. At the front she saw no eyes, only a cluster of leechlike sucking mouths. She nodded, and said, "Yes. Stonzai, remember the big water beast we told you about, our first day in the swamp?"

"Remember, yes. See, though, not."

"Well, you have now; this is just like it, only smaller. We'd better take it back, to show everybody."

Stonzai touched the injured leg. "Walk, you can?"

"I think I ought to try." Being helped up, she couldn't hold back a moan. Then, standing, she held still and the pain ebbed.

Not in her face, but somehow in the way she stood, the Shrakken looked concerned. "Carry you, must I, yes."

Lisele was tempted, but shook her head. "You need your gun hand free. Wait a second." Leaning on Stonzai and keeping her leg stiff, even the hipjoint, she took one step and then another.

It wasn't as bad as she'd feared. "We can do it. It'll be slow; I may have to stop a lot." Sweat ran down her forehead, and the furnace wasn't even on yet. "Some sticks for crutches would be good, but here there's nothing big enough." Now she felt feverish; maybe there wasn't much time to spare.

She asked Stonzai to fetch her clothes, and to fill two plastic bags with stream water. Then she said, "We'd better start."

The trip back was longer than she'd realized. She had to pause often, and sometimes the pain wouldn't let her keep silent. The day's heat built; usually they were home by this time. But some of her own heat, she knew, was fever.

Things she saw wouldn't hold still, and once in a while she forgot where she was and who Stonzai was. She wanted a drink of water, but had a vague idea there was some reason she couldn't have one. The one thing she never forgot was to keep that leg straight.

Finally she saw the "fort" ahead, and for a moment everything came clear to her. Rissa, eyes wide, ran toward them. "What happened? Are you all right?"

Hot, reddish blackness was closing in, but now it was all right if it did. Except that first she had to *tell*. "We found some real water, a little river. And something bit me—like the big thing in the swamp, only a little one. And Stonzai sucked the poison out, and—and I *did* walk."

There was more to say, but the blackness wouldn't wait. As the leg crumpled under her, the last she felt was its stab of pain.

Something felt good; after a while she knew it was the wet cloth that lay over her head, leaving only nose and mouth exposed. When she figured that out, she reached and pushed it back, so she could see.

Rissa sat watching her. "Are you feeling better now? The fever is gone, and most of the swelling from your leg."

Her thigh wore a bandage, but through it Lisele felt no

rigid, painful lump. She tried moving the leg; it was plenty sore, but nothing worse. "I feel pretty good, I guess."

Across from Rissa, Tregare said, "The fever and swelling, all of it—some kind of venom reaction, strictly chemical. Lucky thing Stonzai could get most of it out. The rest, your system just took a while to clear up." He leaned and touched her forehead. "Princess, you had us scared. Welcome back."

Then he kissed her, and so did Rissa, and Lisele told them everything that had happened, in case she'd missed something before. Tregare said, "There has to be a safe way to bathe in that good water. Tomorrow I'll go check it." And with the look that meant he was enjoying figuring something out, he talked about making some kind of hand-pumps, and screens, and maybe filters, too. . . .

Lisele smelled dinner cooking. When Rissa brought a plateful, she was hungry, all right. Well, it was her first meal of the day. And then she was sleepy again.

For a few days the leg bothered her some, but she got around well enough. And now the furnace wasn't turning on so early. Shaarbant, Tregare said, had definitely passed perihelion and was moving farther from its sun. Every day, and faster than Lisele expected, the time grew that they could stay outside and be active. "Well," said Tregare, "I think we're all acclimated better, now. This time, when we get moving again, we should do better."

They'd been a long time inactive, though, so he set everybody practicing with the travoises again. Lisele found the work easier than she remembered. When she told Rissa, her mother said, "After all, you *are* growing, you know." The haul to Tregare's "bathtub" at the stream, and back, was just about right for a practice stint.

With a sharpened stick for a spear, Hagen Trent caught one of the leeches. But even after boiling in several waters, it stank, and had to be thrown away.

When the heat ebbed enough that they could work outside past noon, the group in council decided to move on. Choosing what to take or leave, and then repacking, took another day.

Next morning they ate by handlamps, and left at true dawn.

A week they traveled, a little longer every day, before they ran out of solid ground. A kilo ahead, maybe, they saw a wooded rise, but in between was pure total swamp. Tregare turned and hiked back up the last hill, and this time climbed a tree himself. He came back shaking his head. "If there's any kind of route to either side, it's a long way around."

Jenise Rorvik pointed down at the scummy water. "You want to go through *that*?"

Tregare shrugged. "No more than you do. But we have to." Before she could answer, he added, "There'll be more like this. We might as well start learning how to handle it."

Lisele poked a long stick into the water; even at the edge it was over her head. She could swim some, sure—but a *kilo*? Then Tregare began opening a pack, and talking; she listened.

"We inflate these flotation rigs, they'll carry the travoises with buoyancy to spare. We'll hang on, using safety lines, and propel them as best we can. I don't know how high things will ride; we can't guarantee to keep it all dry. So we better look at our loads and see what needs waterproofing." He squinted up toward the sun. "Lucky we've got more than half the afternoon to do that."

Lisele had a question, but Hagen Trent beat her to it. "How about the leeches—like the one that got Lisele, or even a big one?"

Rissa smiled. "We shall all smell very badly, but I do not think any life form will consider us edible." She looked from pack to pack, rummaging, and brought out a spray container. "This repellant was developed on Earth. I understand that among other things it is effective against sharks, Alaskan mosquitoes, piranha and the tsetse fly."

There wasn't enough brush at hand to make a decent stockade, so at nightfall Tregare set one-hour watches. "Me, Trent, Rissa, Jenise, Stonzai, Sevshen, then repeat." Lisele scowled—Tregare should know she was big enough to stay awake when she had to, and he did know she wasn't afraid to use a gun—but he didn't notice, so she picked a place and lay down to sleep.

Near to dawn, Rissa woke her. Everyone ate last night's leftovers, cold. Rissa and Trent rigged flotation units to the travoises and Tregare inflated them. Then Rissa had everybody strip, and spread the clothes on the ground, and she sprayed them. "As advertised," Tregare said while he dressed, "we don't stink pretty, at all." Fumes from her blouse stung Lisele's eyes, and she saw why Rissa wanted the clothes off when she sprayed them.

Then they got into the water, gear and all, and began the longest day Lisele had ever lived. Behind a travois she kicked, swimming style, until her legs ached—and then, because she had to, kept doing it. Breathing so near the surface, the swamp stench knotted her stomach. She kept her breakfast down, though, because she was pretty sure she was going to need it.

They must have been moving nearly an hour before there was any sign that other life shared the water with them. Then something moved, ahead, and made the surface swirl. Tregare signaled for everyone to hang quiet, and they waited. The thing, whatever it was, came to within about five meters—still under water, only a shadow there, but a big one—then turned, throwing a wave of water, and went away. Tregare whistled. "Your stuff works, Rissa!"

After that, once in a while they'd see some disturbance in the water, but nothing came very close and they just kept moving.

Lisele began to wish they wouldn't be quite so brave; to keep going at all, she had to hold her mind on the time when she could rest. The least-loaded travois was buoyant enough to let a person lie on it. One out of seven, and by Tregare's schedule, soon it would be Lisele's turn.

When that turn came, she opened her mind to relaxation. She wasn't certain whether she slept, but when Jenise nudged her to slip back into the water, for a while her legs were strong again.

More than Tregare's guess of a kilo, the distance had to be. But by sun's noon the land ahead was nearer than that behind, so Lisele could rid herself of the notion that this hell would never end. Especially when they paused to sip broth and water from plastic bags.

Past mid-afternoon she wasn't so sure. The water went shallow—still too deep for her to find footing on the muddy bottom, but shallow enough that water plants entangled her feet and made her leg movements futile. Tregare, Hagen, and of course the two Shrakken, were tall enough to stand up and push. Tregare told the others—except Jenise, who was having her turn at rest—just to hang on and let their legs dangle. Eyes closed, Lisele hung limp.

When her trailing feet dragged bottom, she looked to see Tregare in water not much above his knees. Now she stood up. Everybody else was bending over, pushing a travois. So she did, too.

Even more shallow, the water got, and the less of it to balance against, the easier it was to slip and fall, and get smeared with sticky, itchy mud. When the water deepened again, they paused and tried to scrub that mud off each other. But without much luck, and Tregare said, "Hell with it; let's go. We don't want to be caught out here when it gets dark." So, back to the swim-kicking. Lisele was getting hungry; dawn was a long time ago, with no food but broth. Rissa had figured a way to eat, even in the middle of wet swamp. But then she'd shaken her head. "No. We cannot risk exposing anything that smells edible." They could sip from the bags, only.

Lisele knew the afternoon couldn't really be longer than the morning, but it sure felt like it. She quit paying attention to anything; she put her head on her arms that held onto the travois, and she knew her legs still kicked because she could hear the splashes.

When her feet began hitting bottom, and Tregare yelled, "We're here! We made it!" at first she thought she was dreaming.

On the shore, away from the mud, she sat with head down and arms hanging. Tregare and others deflated the buoyancy units and dragged the travoises up to safety. She knew she should help, but couldn't make herself move, or even keep her eyes open. When she smelled food cooking, at first she didn't care. Until Rissa came with two trays, and sat beside her. "Lisele! You did well today. I would have come to you sooner, but you were resting, and there was so much to do. Here; eat." And once she'd forced the first bites down, Lisele found she did have an appetite, after all.

Halfway done with her tray, she began to feel she could do things again. She looked over to Rissa. "How hard was it, for you? Today, I mean."

Her mother gave her a quick, one-armed hug. "Damned peacetwisting hard, your father would say. And I am sorry I found no time to see to your own well-being, during that ordeal. But—"

Swallowing a lump of meat that could have used more chewing, Lisele said, "You had your own job to do." She thought back, to things Tregare had said. "If I can't pull my weight, what good am I?"

Arms squeezed her, hard. Rissa's cheek touched hers, and she knew the tears she felt were not her own. "*Much* good, my dear. To pull weight, as you say, takes time. We must give you the chance to learn how.''

Then through growing dark they walked over to where the rest of the group sat, well back from the cooking fire that lit the area. ''Watch-schedules again tonight, I'm afraid,'' Tregare said. ''Start from where we left off last night, and same rotation. All right?''

''No.'' Lisele hadn't known she was going to speak. ''How about me?''

Looking not quite angry, Tregare said, ''What you mean, princess?''

She took a moment, to think. ''You say people should pull their weight; I want to pull mine. You know I can shoot.'' She paused. ''First watch; okay?''

His look puzzled her; then he smiled. ''Good enough. Here's my gun; you start on the hour.'' He looked around. ''Everybody else goes in the same order as before.''

The energy gun was heavy; in practicing, she was more used to the lighter needle weapons. But when everybody else lay down—sleeping, or maybe not—she checked her handlamp and pointed her gun here and there at the edges of vision, and decided she could handle it.

Staying awake was easy; she was tired, not sleepy. When Stonzai relieved her she was still alert; lying down, she had to use the alpha techniques before she could relax enough to sleep.

In the morning, after eating, Rissa scratched her head. ''I cannot abide the itching of this residual mud. I had not thought to bare my scalp again—but, Tregare, if that trimmer is handy—?''

He looked into packs and found the thing, and cut Rissa's hair to stubble that—against a good scrubbing—wouldn't hold mud at all. Then the rest of the humans took the same treatment. Lisele thought the Shrakken, lacking the problem, might be amused—but as usual, their faces showed no reaction. She herself didn't care about ''looking funny''; her hair had been flopping into her eyes, and she'd have had to do something about it soon, anyway.

With Jenise Rorvik bald on top but still shaggy around the edges, the trimmer threw sparks and quit working. Tregare looked disgusted. ''Water got into it, maybe.'' He finished the job by scraping with a sharp knife, and the same for Hagen Trent. Now and then he drew blood. ''Looks like a cat clawed you; sorry." But Jenise didn't fuss as Lisele expected, and Trent only shrugged.

Then they moved out; with a cloth over Lisele's head, the sun wasn't too bad.

For a time they found mostly dry land—with only a few wet stretches, shorter than the first they'd swum, that they couldn't detour around. And as Shaarbant receded from its sun, slowly the days cooled. Soon they could travel all day, and Tregare judged they were making pretty good time. His sightings on the angle of the synchronous moon, though, didn't show much change yet.

Her legs, Lisele thought, were getting stronger. Now she handled the lighter travois as well as Jenise did—or nearly.

They came to a range of hills. At first Lisele thought they'd reached the edge of the mountains, but Tregare pointed out that on these, trees went all the way to the summits. "Still a long haul, I'm afraid." And when they topped the crest and could see the real mountains in the distance, she knew he was right.

Then down into low country, and more swamp. They were used to it now, but one day came to a vast area that made Tregare shake his head when asked to guess its extent. The only sure thing was, on the far side they could see dry-land trees. "That's no one-day crossing," he said. "Two, if we're lucky."

He cut and trimmed straight sticks, nearly two dozen of them, thick as his thumb and nearly his height, and lashed them to the lightest travois. Rissa cooked up a thick soup, the meat shredded finely and the vegetable matter pureed, so it could be swallowed directly from a plastic bag, exposing no attractive odors to whatever lived in the water ahead. She filled six bags.

Next morning, clothes sprayed with the repellant, they set out. Swamp crossings, though not pleasant, were old stuff now; the only new things were eating en route and the prospect of being in the water overnight. At the "lunch" pause, the group emptied the first bag; Lisele found the cold soup most welcome.

A little before dusk, they stopped. "At least," said Rissa, "the land ahead is nearer than that behind." She passed "dinner" around until the second bag was empty. Then everybody helped line up the three travoises, and Tregare got his sticks loose, and he and Rissa lashed them across to form one framework, the three units parallel and about four decimeters apart.

"Not the last word in comfort," Tregare said, "but let's see how many people can lie up out of the water while the rest sleep wet, hanging from their harnesses. Then we'll set the shifts.''

The thing held two without sinking too deeply into the water. Tregare didn't want to try for three, but Hagen Trent got a stubborn look on his face. "It floated you and Stonzai, Tregare. Rissa and Jenise and Lisele, all together, don't weigh much more. And that would make three shifts, instead of three-and-a-half."

Tregare looked to Rissa; the half-set sun glared red on her face as she nodded, and he said, "You're right, Hagen. Let's try it."

It worked—so every ninety minutes, all night, some people climbed out of the water while others went back into it, for three hours of resting in harness. When morning came, Lisele decided she'd had more sleep than she expected. She was still tired, though.

After breakfast Tregare began to unlash the framework, but Jenise said, "What for? The way it is, we can all push on it together, and won't have to go with the slowest team." She grimaced. "Which is usually the one *I'm* on."

In careful tones, Hagen Trent said, "Pointed straight ahead, the water drag won't be any different, together or apart."

Tregare's frown smoothed out. "Hell, yes; why didn't I think of that?" He looked, and said, "In that case, the travoises need straightening up. The middle one has a cross-slant to it."

Not long after, they were moving again. At noon, stopping to pass the lunch bag around, they could see land not too far away. And before mid-afternoon they slipped and slogged through mud—separating the travoises now—and reached dry ground.

Scrubbing herself in a slimy pool, Lisele was glad they'd taken care of the hair problem recently. Much more of this kind of country, though, and it might be nearly time to do it again.

But after a few more days, with no swamp crossing of more than half a day, the land began to rise. They found a fair-sized river and followed its course upward; largely it ran placid, but sometimes they detoured above canyons that rang with the sound of rapids.

There had been no tonguewalkers past the first range of hills. The first nights along the river, they heard shrill howlings, and in the mornings found disturbingly large footprints where the dirt lay soft. Then for a time, no signs of animal life, and Tregare had discontinued watch-schedules. Now, though, came chitterings in daylight, and occasionally some small grey-brown thing would streak across their path. Lisele was the first to kill one.

The shrill, timid-sounding calls woke her early, still in near-dark. Squinting against dim light she saw the small, pudgy shape. Her instinct was to *like* the little creature—but they were running awfully short of meat. She aimed and sighted, best she could in the dimness, and fired. Squealing, the animal pitched backward; it kicked once and lay still. As she walked over to see what she'd shot, other people sat up. "What was that?" "What happened?"

Then Tregare's voice. "Who fired? Speak up!" He was crouching, Lisele saw, and his energy gun scanned the area.

"It's all right," she said. "I—I shot a little animal that might be good to eat. That's all."

Seeing her kill up close, she felt sorry for it. But it dressed out at two kilos, and was good eating—safe, even, *without* boiling.

Lisele didn't shoot any more of the fuzzy little beasts; Tregare knew how to set snares and Hagen Trent learned fast. Meat went off the short-rations list. Some of the other animals around had to be predators, in the nature of things, but those stayed out of range, seen only as small quick blurs, and never bothered anybody. After a time, even Tregare relaxed and decided that maybe, for a change, they were in safe country. Except for some scratchy plants that raised blisters on bare legs, he seemed to be right.

Farther along, when the small animals became scarce, Jenise got Trent to help her make nets out of monofilament line. She said she'd seen things swimming in the river, and she was right. The first five-kilo catch looked like a small, furry whale— and with only one boiling the meat was edible. Tasty, too.

Once a ship passed overhead, not very high. Out of sunrise came the rumbling thunder; then the ionized drive wake blazed across the sky. Tregare turned to face the others. "*We don't know who it is*. Keep thinking that way." Lisele tried to do what he said, and everybody else must have, too, because the ship passed and nobody felt any hurt. So maybe the Tsa hadn't noticed them.

The ground leveled off into plains; the jungle thinned. Often they came to large clearings that lacked even bushes, with only knee-high ground cover. The stuff looked like grass at first, until you noticed its branching structure. Lisele became used to the sound of it, swishing against her legs.

Nothing bloomed; she'd seen no flowers on this world, and outside the swamp, no equivalent of flying insects. One kind of airborne creature first appeared when they reached the plains and soon showed up in greater numbers. Smallish, it was, and its flight swooped like that of bats or swallows. Tregare wanted to see one at close range, but the erratic movements were too much for anybody's marksmanship. Then one day they came upon a crippled one, dragging a wing as it tried to hobble away through the tall "grass." Hagen Trent took his shirt off, and caught the thing in it.

It didn't look appetizing, and it smelled awful. From its bare skin, Rissa guessed it might be something like a reptile, but Trent shook his head. "From the body heat and pulse rate—I can feel both through the cloth—it's obviously warm-blooded."

The toothed, beaklike snout opened wide as it hissed, then snapped shut in a try for Trent's hand. The eyes, facing neither forward nor to the sides but about halfway between, blinked rapidly. Trent hefted its weight. "Not over a kilo, if that." It snapped at him again and nearly connected. He said, "Does anybody want it for anything?" No one spoke; he dropped the shirt and stepped back, and the creature made its hobbling escape.

He picked up the shirt and sniffed at it. "Might be useful, at that—if we ever hit any more swamp, and run out of repellant."

After one of Tregare's nightly readings on the synchronous moon, he announced they'd reached its meridian. "So we've covered maybe a quarter of our trip. Or—" He shrugged. "—maybe only a fifth. Like I told you, I don't remember, for sure, the reading from Sassden and the *Deux*." Well, Lisele thought, a fifth was better than nothing—and Tregare *had* said it could be more.

A week later, they reached a fork in the river; the two tributaries were about the same size. One branch started off northwest; the other went roughly west-southwest. "That one's ours," said Tregare, "because I make us a little north of Sassden's latitude. We'll keep checking, and hope it doesn't take us too much out of our way."

He got only two more moon sightings, because on the third day the rains began. Not gradually, but all at once. Under clear sky they went to sleep; they woke to thunder, and then the torrent fell.

Getting things together was a miserable scramble. With their fire drowned, they ate breakfast cold. And as soon as possible, sloshing through the downpour, they got under way.

One good thing, Lisele thought, feet slipping on the wet ground, was that the rain was cool. Not cold—just right to ease the heat of exertion. But that was the only good thing. Well, maybe that this mud wasn't sticky like swamp mud, but only slippery.

They took lunch cold, too, but toward dusk they came to a stand of bushes. Tregare and Trent cut brush up with bolos and only used the energy gun to light the fire. Hot food felt good—but even sitting painfully close to the fire, their wet clothes were only heated, never dried. After a time, Rissa said, "Bran—there is plastic sheeting, such as you used to line the bathtub at the fort. And we still have the poles that helped us sleep through the night in the swamp. So—"

"A tent?" said Tregare. "Okay, sure; we can have a go at it."

The first two designs didn't work very well, but the third try made a shelter that stayed up and covered all of them. Water still leaked in under the edges, but they and the ground were already wet, so what did *that* matter?

"Tomorrow," Tregare said, "we'll scrounge up something for a floor, too." But with the dark coming so quickly, this night, there hadn't been time to do that much rummaging.

Three more days they slogged along, the rain beating harder all the time. Around noon, the fourth day—though the sun barely made a lighter spot in that drenching sky—they came alongside a fair-sized hill that rose from the river to a thick grove of trees.

Tregare stopped, slipped and almost fell under the weight of the travois. Water ran from his eyebrows down into his eyes; with the back of one hand he brushed it away. Looking uphill, he said, "I vote a stopover—camp and dry out. Anybody else in favor?"

Several—Lisele was one—mumbled, "Yes." Jenise Rorvik, looking too tired to do anything more, nodded.

"Motion carried." Tregare turned to plod up the hill—not directly, but slanting around its side. The others followed.

About halfway up, Lisele looked toward the summit and

saw the little cliff, and the cave. "Tregare!" She pointed; he looked, also.

"Now that's luck!" For the first time in days she heard him laugh. "I doubt it's big enough, as is, but we can do some digging. And maybe build out some, in front of the hole. Lisele, I think you've saved us one big lot of work!"

Leaving his travois, he scrambled up; she followed, until they stood at the foot of a minor talus of clods and gravel, looking into the cave's mouth. A roughly-squared oval, over two meters tall, with the bottom perhaps a meter above where they stood. As far as she could see inside, the passage continued. Five meters, anyway, and maybe more. Looking around to her, Tregare said, "Not too much building, we'd have to do." He gestured at the loose rubble. "Clear this away, cut steps in the solid dirt. Wouldn't have to be wide, especially."

His gaze was on her but she sensed he was looking beyond. "Lots of edible plants around. Small animal tracks leading in and out of this hole, but nothing big. We could live here for a time." He faced downhill. "We *can* keep moving in this slop— but in terms of wear and tear on all of us, I'm not sure it's worthwhile." He shrugged. "After a dry night's sleep, we can talk about it."

Twenty days later the rain still poured and the group showed no intention of leaving. Instead, one project at a time, they worked to make the place more comfortable. The loose talus was cleared, and the dirt-cut steps floored with wood slabs. Two thin tree trunks—one found fallen, the other cut down and trimmed— leaned against the cliff at either side of the cave. The slanting roof built across them, not quite leakproof but close to it, was made of heavily-leafed branches. Above the raised fire-pit, scraped together from talus debris, a hole let smoke escape; most of the heat, though, was deflected into the cave. At the front, the roof ended well above ground level, at moderate stooping height for Tregare; it shielded a drier-than-not area about five meters wide and three deep. All in all, Lisele thought, a comfortable arrangement.

Inside, the cave went back nearly eight meters at a slight leftward curve, then narrowed fast, and at the same time shallowed and dropped away toward the vertical. A projection of rock blocked further exploration; lying against it, from far below Lisele could hear faint sounds of rushing water. Stonzai tried letting down a plastic bucket, but after a few meters it caught on an unseen obstacle and the line went slack. So they had to bring water from the river, perhaps a hundred meters down the hill. That was all right; Jenise and Hagen went there to ply their nets, anyway.

Now, Jenise was nearer her old self than any time since the scout had crashed. The wetness inflamed the skin of her wrist, so Trent took the cast off. The damaged bones, they found, had knit into an apparently solid mass—with the fingers half-curled, only slight flexure to them; the left hand was a rigid club. But now the thumb could grip against those fingers, and she could exert pressure with the hand as a whole. Freer of pain, and rested, Jenise became more lively and talkative—no longer sitting gaunt-faced and silent, in seeming reproach to the others' efforts to raise their spirits. And one evening—and then another, and afterward quite often—she and Hagen went in the cave while the rest sat outside, and Lisele heard sounds much like those Rissa made with Tregare.

Was the rain still getting heavier? Tregare thought so; others disagreed. Rissa noted a cyclic pattern, slacking off at night for a time and pouring harder in the mornings. Since outdoors was wet *all* the time, Lisele didn't see what difference the details made.

She was slogging back from the latrine to the cave. The facility itself was roofed, but not the twenty meters of path leading to it. The thing was set downhill from the cave and a little to the right—downriver, to avoid polluting their water supply.

Reaching the lean-to, Lisele turned before the fire until she was fairly dry, before putting her clothes back on. Being naked in the rain was chilly now, but skin dried faster than clothes did.

Near one of the lean-to's outer corners, a plastic vat sat open. As Rissa came out of the cave, Lisele wrinkled her nose at the vat's stench. "I know it'll help, if you can tan the skins from those little whales, but it doesn't smell like this batch is working."

Rissa shrugged. "I hoped this type of bark contained enough tannin, but apparently not. Next I will try the outer layers from the roots Sevshen gathered." She covered the vat. "When someone is here to help, I will take this past the latrine and dump it."

Rissa wasn't hinting; they both knew Lisele could barely lift one end of the thing, let alone help carry it. The girl said, "Where is everybody?"

"The Shrakken are with Tregare, gathering firewood. Hagen and Jenise went to the river to check their nets."

"How's the vegetable supply? Should I go look for more?"

"Not today. I have put the present store to cooking, before it molds, and that will last us two or three days."

"Then I guess I'll go inside for a while. Unless there's something else I could do." Smiling, Rissa shook her head, so Lisele climbed the steps and went to sit on her pallet. She might as well practice alpha meditation; it would help pass this boring time.

A time came when everyone agreed the rain was really easing off. Rissa, using the roots she had mentioned, did produce usable leather. It smelled awful, but didn't rot or crumble. With plastic thread, Lisele sewed herself a pair of moccasins and then measured everyone's feet and made each person a gift pair. The humans, that was—the toe-walking Shrakken didn't use footwear.

Almost as abruptly as it had begun, the rain stopped; one night, Lisele woke to silence. Next day's rain was light and intermittent; the group began sorting stores, and packing. On the following day, they saw the sun.

At dinner, Hagen Trent said, "Do we start off tomorrow, if we're ready by then, or give the footing more chance to dry?"

Brows raised, Tregare looked around the circle. Rissa said, "Not tomorrow, I would think. For two days, perhaps three, let us observe how quickly the ground dries. When the improvement looks good to us, is time enough to go."

Rorvik nodded, her short blonde hair flopping with the motion. "If we try to move too soon, I think we'd lose more in the long run. That slippy-sliding on mud takes it out of you, fast."

Tregare nodded. "I think you're both right. So that's how we'll do it." And on the fourth morning, they set out.

Descending the hill, rounding its flank to go upriver, Lisele stopped and looked back at the lean-to, hiding the cave's entrance. From the morning's fire, smoke still rose. She sighed.

Pausing beside her, Tregare said, "Something the matter?"

"Not really. But we lived there—how long? And, you know—except for being so *wet* all the time, it wasn't such a bad place."

He laughed. "With the right people, and a little work to make things comfortable, no place is. Let's go."

XVIII. Ivan

Nobody liked Ivan's announce-
ment much, when he made it. The idea that on Shaarbant years
were passing while the *Deux* spent mere weeks in space—by its
own clocks—dampened spirits. But as Ivan said, "You can't
argue with Einstein. Nobody can, except maybe Pennet Hoyfarul,
and he's not here." He heard Crowfoot's laugh, and a snicker
that sounded like Melaine Holmbach, so maybe he'd broken the
tension a little. He said, then, "Everybody's doing the best they
can. That's good enough for me." Clinking sounds indicated that
Dacia was breaking out drinks for the group; a cold glass came
against his knuckles and he picked it up and sipped from it.
Bourbon, a little ice. "Thanks, Dacia."

"Welcome."

He sipped again. Talk buzzed around him: nothing important, so he quit listening and retreated mostly into his own mind.
Where the worries ahead awaited him—but he couldn't afford to
wrangle with them, not yet. And the worries behind, the past
ones, were over and done. ("Unless you have a time machine in
your back pocket, Rissa . . .") Suddenly he laughed, bringing the
discussion to momentary halt, until he said, "A chance thought;
don't heed me."

But the mood was broken; the group began to disperse. Ivan
heard the leave-takings and departing footsteps; when he figured
that only Dacia remained with him in their quarters, he spoke her
name. She said, "Yes, Ivan. They're gone now."

"Then—" *Is there time for us?* he wanted to ask, because
somehow lately there hadn't been much.

"Ivan," she began. But then the alarms rang, the extension
from Control, and they had to hurry upship.

By now he didn't need a great deal of guidance, but to make speed it did help.

Anders had the watch; Ivan knew that, and on entering Control was greeted by Kobolak's voice. "It's a ship, Captain. Passing at an angle, not in the same plane with us. No possibility of intercept, either way." Skew meeting, yes.

Ignoring the question of which side of ninety degrees the courses converged—because it didn't matter—Ivan said, "Whose?" No answer. Irritated, he raised his voice. "Damn all, Anders! Out here, that ship can't be human. Is it Shrakken or is it Tsa?"

Low-voiced, Kobolak answered. "I—I can't be sure. I never got a good look at either."

Ivan bit back his response. Hell, the man was right! He said, "Estimate closest approach?"

"Yes. One moment." And shortly the First Hat read off numbers that brought relief to Ivan Marchant. Whoever might be on that passing ship, it couldn't come close enough to affect the minds aboard *Inconnu Deux*.

No point in hiding his relieved sigh, so he didn't. "Thanks, First Hat. This time, whoever's out there, we're safe enough."

He turned toward the soft sound of Dacia's breathing, then thought of something else and put his blind gaze to Kobolak's position. "That ship's course. Any clues where it came from, where it's going?"

Sounding calm now, Anders said, "Nothing connected to human space. The course is nearly right-angled to the way we came out here."

Ivan shrugged. "Then I guess we can forget it." Well, it made sense. Nothing said that everything in space had to relate to *Inconnu Deux*. And some things wouldn't. "Thanks."

Again he turned to Dacia. "All that bourbon calls for a little coffee. Join me?" She came and grasped his arm, and they went down to the galley, where she left him at their usual table and brought the coffee plus a few light rolls. Relaxing, Ivan nibbled the yeasty biscuits, now and then dunking the edge of one into hot coffee. Lacking sight, he was learning to make the most of other senses. *Might as well*, he thought.

He still had on his mind the same idea as before the alarm had rung. So when he declined Dacia's offer of a second refill on coffee, Ivan said, "Your next watch is some hours away? You suppose we might have time for *us*?"

Her indrawn breath sounded a bit shocked. "Ivan! Can't we discuss these things in more privacy?"

"I didn't hear anyone sitting around close." And he hadn't.

"That's not the point. I—"

"You're right," said Ivan. "Let's go downship."

Descending, holding Dacia's arm for quick guidance, Ivan wondered whether maybe he had his head on backwards. Because the problem with sex, lately, had very little to do with Dacia; it was that he, Ivan, was so wound up with worries and couldn't seem to unload them. They would go to bed, the two of them, and begin all the nice playing around, and then when it came to cases he'd find that his mind had betrayed him. His thoughts would be back to Shaarbant and his body might as well be there, too, for all the good it was doing him—not to mention Dacia's feelings.

But for better or worse, this ship's day had brought a diversion, and bourbon wasn't all that bad an idea, and Shaarbant could *wait*.

So when they entered captain's digs he held onto Dacia's arm and said, "Can we skip all the niceties? Just make love? Please?"

Her voice trembled, a little but not much. "I guess so, Ivan."

"Good." And the clothes came off, seams ripping a little with the force of Dacia's help. *Peace take me, it's all working!*

And for both of them, apparently. Ivan hadn't known that Dacia could talk and bite at the same time, but she certainly could.

Ivan had never understood that *triste* stuff; sex didn't sadden him, it energized him. He'd have liked to nap with Dacia for a time but felt too restless; after a parting kiss he dressed and went up to Control. He arrived just in time to hear Ellalee relieving Alina at the comm-panel, so by the roster in his mind he knew that Crowfoot would be taking over from Anders Kobolak. Ivan spoke a general hello, heard the four answers and then the departures of Anders and Alina.

He found his way to the backup pilot's position, sat, and turned to face Ellalee. "How's the pilot training coming along?" He knew she'd begun the learning program, using Crowfoot's simulations, but he hadn't checked on it recently.

"I'm none too certain," and something in the voice made

him visualize her shrug. "To start me off easy, Jeremy rigged sims in the scout, too, I suppose you know." He hadn't. "So when he decided I had those simpler controls down bonzer, he moved me up to trying the ship itself. Those programs, you'll recall, are rigged to where you're sitting now. But as to how I'm doing at it, Jeremy hasn't truly said yet."

Ivan turned toward Crowfoot. "Any problems, Jere?"

"None at all," and in the answer Ivan detected no hesitation. "Sorry if I haven't given enough feedback, Ellalee. You learn well, make few mistakes and are gaining in proficiency. All you need now, I'd say, is to keep practicing."

"And I surely will."

"What's she best at, now?" Ivan asked. "And what *not*?"

After a pause, Crowfoot said, "Good fast reactions, good judgment in choosing and executing maneuvers. That's the strong part."

"And the weak?"

"Just what you might expect, I suppose. The things a trainee can't really master without some experience in actual ship handling, to get the feel of a vessel." For a moment, Ivan thought he'd have to ask again, to get a solid answer. But then Crowfoot said, "Well, simulated landings, of course."

With a brief laugh, Ivan relaxed. "Then that's all right. Nobody would expect a green hand to do a landing without actual flight training—and whatever else happens, a landing while we're under Tsa attack won't be one of them. And Ellalee's ability to resist the Tsa is *why* she's training."

The woman's chuckle indicated release of tension. "Since it's not been tested all that much, let's hope we don't need it."

Confiding in no one else, Ivan considered Dacia's reports of the dwindling food inventory. With only a rough guess as to the ship's clock-time remaining before they could reach Shaarbant, he tended to think conservatively. Eventually, after one confab with Dacia, he called assembly and put the question.

"For obvious reasons, we need a food reserve. At our current rate of chow down, with eight of us eating, we won't have that reserve."

Melaine Holmbach's voice. "You want some of us back in freeze?"

He shook his head. "Not really. We're few enough now, for company, and our human need of it."

"Then what?" Rance Peleter: not sounding belligerent, just asking.

"A choice," said Ivan. "Majority rules. Either two go into freeze, or we cut rations by twenty-five percent. You choose which we do."

"That's fair," said Jeremy Crowfoot. "For freeze, though—who do you have in mind? Or have you made that decision?"

He had. Crowfoot himself, for one. And the other—Anders wouldn't like it, but Alina was next most expendable to the ship's operation. But, grinning, Ivan shook his head. "You're asking me to influence the vote. I won't do that."

So he got the result he wanted: eight-to-zerch, the group voted for the short-rations option.

One more passing ship, they spotted—on Crowfoot's watch, this one, and much too far away for identification. Its course, nearly parallel to the *Deux*'s but diverging slightly, gave no clue to origin or destination. The two ships' velocities were so nearly matched that the vague, flickering dot hung on the main screen for more than half a day, drifting too slowly for the motion to be seen. Consensus was that due to the relative course angles, the other probably hadn't spotted the *Deux* at all. "Which suits me just fine," said Ivan Marchant.

Then, once again, space around the ship was empty except for stars, none of them near enough to show a disk. How far, still, to Shaarbant? Ivan wished he knew.

XIX. *Lisele*

*F*or a long time the country stayed pretty much the same. By the time the heat got bad again, they were nearing the mountain range—or its foothills, anyway. The river branched once more, and then again, until it wasn't much more than a large stream they followed.

The underbrush thinned, and the trees; it became safe to travel for a time after dark and before daylight. As the ground rose, they found that while the heat increased as badly as ever in the afternoons, at night the air cooled drastically.

Stonzai was the first to see one of the big reddish-brown animals; by the time the rest looked to her pointing, they saw only a patch of color disappearing behind a ridge. Not long after, though, they saw another, drinking from the stream. It had long, powerful legs and a heavy tail; its head, except for the large, upright ears, reminded Lisele of a bear's. As it left the stream, it picked up something in its mouth and carried it away.

"A dead animal, it had," said Tregare. "Carnivore, is it, or scavenger?" But the next beast they saw was grazing, and he shrugged. "Sooner or later, I guess we'll find out." Two days later, Stonzai surprised one of the creatures; after pausing and making a trumpeting noise, it charged her. So she shot it. Stomach contents were a mix of animal and vegetable matter. "Omnivore," was the verdict.

At any rate the meat was edible without boiling, though a little strong to the taste. But as Rissa reminded the others, "Because we eat these native plants and animals without apparent harm, it does *not* mean that we may not be accumulating trace poisons, over a period of time."

Tregare made a mock frown. "You trying to spoil my appetite? You don't have to; there's plenty of dinner to go around."

The heat grew to fill more of each day, shortening travel. When they were barely into the mountains, far short of the higher parts and now forced to stop moving before noon, Tregare called halt.

"We won't make it over the top, not on this run. So we'd better look for a place to set camp." He waved toward the stream, here less than two meters wide, though still better than knee-deep. "We go much higher, pass another fork or two, maybe we're stuck with a trickle that dries up altogether when the heat does its worst." He looked around. "Comments?"

"A stop place find we, yes," said Stonzai, and asked if Tregare meant right now, this very day.

"Soon as we can, I'd say. Judging from last year, once the heat turns up this far, it gets unbearable in a real hurry."

"But the water," said Rissa, "must govern. Bran—suppose we continue a day or two—until we find a good site, or the stream branches, or becomes too small for us to depend upon."

"And if we don't find a good place?" said Hagen Trent.

Jenise pointed downstream. "Yesterday, we passed one that might work." She turned to Bran Tregare. "Where the pond was, under a clay bank with overhang? We could claw out a fair-sized cave there."

Lisele saw he was thinking about it. "Let's don't backtrack if we can help it. We can keep that spot in mind, though."

But next day before mid-morning, the question was settled. Beside a flat expanse of hard-packed soil the stream branched, and the smaller part dropped from a narrow-gated box canyon with steep walls and a surprising thick growth of trees. At its upper end the water came down in a fall that dissipated almost totally into spray. The slope below it held a lush growth of grey-green vegetation, and from that delta of damp ground the water seeped to become again a current that filled its narrow channel.

Standing, hands on hips, just inside the canyon's gate, Tregare looked up at the feathery waterfall and then back toward the stream's junction. "I don't see how we could ask for better." No one disagreed. "Now then—let's figure how to bar off the neck of this canyon, here. Make it our own exclusive private entrance."

Here, Lisele thought, was the best place they'd had since the scout crashed. Some days of hard work gave them shelter and reasonable security. Tregare designed living huts the easiest way, using four trees for corner posts—except in one case where he used two, and laid cut-off branches over to the adjacent rise of stone, to make that enclosure. At the canyon's bottom the exit gate was framed strongly in wood, and the gaps between that frame and the narrow natural exit filled with steeply piled clay, blasted down from the nearby cliff wall. "Anything that comes over that pile," said Tregare, "has to be bigger than I've seen on this world—and with a pretty good running start."

Vegetation was easy to gather; under the spray of waterfall it grew in lush profusion, and most was edible. Meat was more of a problem; as time passed, the mounting heat made hunting expeditions shorter, until Rissa suggested that the foraging parties take along improvised shelters and wait through until next morning before they came back. Since the large omnivores were the major prey, it took at least three persons to carry a kill home.

The parts not eaten immediately were cut into thin strips and sun dried for storage; the searing heat, and lack of flying insect scavengers, made the process easy.

As perihelion neared, they worried about the water supply. The stream outside the canyon looked about the same, but the little one that sprayed from above was shrinking enough to notice. "If we have to," said Tregare, "we can haul up water for ourselves. But irrigating our natural-born garden up there—" He looked, and shook his head.

So far, though, the plants seemed to be doing well enough.

Lisele wasn't sure how Tregare knew just when perihelion came, but one day he announced it. The day after, she woke to find blood on her thighs. She knew what it meant, of course; back on Earth Rissa had explained the whole business, when Arlen Limmer's younger sister Helene had made such a big mystery about her own first period, before the Limmers hosted Helene's menarche party. But Lisele hadn't expected it so soon, for herself; her lower belly wasn't showing much more than fuzz, and whether the flesh around her small nipples was beginning to bulge or not, she couldn't be sure. Sometimes she thought it was; other times she decided it was just wishful thinking.

Finding nothing else close to hand, to wipe herself with, she used a clean sock; she could rinse it later. She went looking for Rissa, and found her in the work hut at her latest project of trying to make some sort of cloth from plant fibers. From her expression, Rissa wasn't having much luck. Jenise and Hagen were there, too, sewing whaleskin reinforcements to the worn plastic straps of a travois. Lisele nodded toward those two and went to Rissa. "I just started menstruating, I think. Do you have any extras, of those things you use to keep it from getting on your clothes?"

For a moment Rissa's eyes widened; then she looked at her personal chronometer and nodded. "Time! I had not thought about it, but in Earth bio-years you are past twelve, nearer thirteen. So I should not be surprised." She looked closely at Lisele. "Is there any discomfort?"

Lisele checked her internal sensations and shook her head. "Just hungry, like always in the mornings." And Rissa laughed.

"Then your development is sound, despite the strains from our environment, and I shall not worry." Her brow wrinkled; then she said, "Yes, we have enough of the reusable inserts to go around, and I believe you have seen how I recycle them." Lisele nodded. "One caution, only; these items are non-expendable; the supply here is limited."

"Well, sure!" What shocked Lisele was that since the scout had crashed, she hadn't thought much of *anything* was expendable.

"Well, then; let us go and equip you." Rissa stood, and for the first time Lisele realized that she and her mother were so near the same height as made no difference. She followed to the hut her parents shared, and waited while Rissa searched through a pack of miscellany. Pushing some of it aside, she brought out four of the foam plastic devices, and shook her head. "I had not thought, when we planned a brief trip to Shtegel—so there are none of these in the smaller sizes. I hope you will have no difficulty."

Lisele took one, and sat down. "Maybe I'd better try it now."

It was first awkward and then painful; she knew where to start but not which way to go. She didn't want to ask for help but finally had to. Then for a few seconds it still hurt, but once the thing was in place, the pain stopped. "Thanks. It's all right now, I think." Getting to her feet made her wince one time, but she realized that was soreness from her own try, pushing in the wrong direction. She took a couple of steps forward, then back. "Yes. I'm fine."

"Good." Rissa gave a few more instructions, ending with, "And if you need help again, of any sort, do not hesitate to ask."

"Course not." Hearing herself speak in mimic of Tregare's tones, Lisele had to smile.

When she got back to her own hut, she remembered to wash the sock.

When she saw Tregare a little later, he grinned and said, "Welcome to puberty," so she knew Rissa had told him. Jenise asked how she felt, and she said all right. When she and Trent were up gathering food plants, he seemed awkward with her, and she asked why.

He paused, then shrugged. "I don't know. It's just that you've been a kid all this time, and now you're not."

"But you must've been around a *lot* of kids that grew up."

His brow wrinkled. "Not like this, the few of us living so closely, and no one else. It makes it—embarrassing, somehow."

She patted his shoulder; his flinch surprised her. She stiffened, and finally said, "After all, I'm not going to *molest* you."

"No, that's not—" His face reddened, and then Lisele

remembered, back at the scout when Rissa had thrown him down into the mud.

She shook her head. "And not the other way around, either. Because we all *know* each other now—and I trust you, Hagen."

He took a deep breath, and nodded, and let her pat his arm. Then in his usual tone of voice he began talking about whether the little stream was still shrinking. And after that one awkward time, they were friends again, all right. No problems.

The upper stream lasted long enough, just barely, to save them a lot of hard work. As the heat ebbed, they began sorting and packing, getting ready to leave the canyon at the right time. Heading into the mountains now, with steeper parts coming up, they'd want half the day fit for travel before it would pay to start out at all.

Two or three days before the start—they hadn't quite decided— Stonzai couldn't get up. The next day, Sevshen couldn't either. Nobody knew what to do; the humans hadn't seen a Shrakken ill before.

The visible symptoms didn't tell much, and Rissa detected no chill or fever—only some shivering and an obvious lack of strength. And Stonzai seemed to have lost all grasp of human language.

Treatment? "Food and water," said Rissa, "and more covering if they seem to need it." So they took turns sitting with the sick aliens, feeding them, offering water more often than they seemed to want it, and tending their other needs. But none of it helped.

Jenise had sickbay watch; the others grouped in the common hut. "Nearly fifty days," Tregare said, "and we still don't know what the trouble is."

"It could be a natural thing," said Hagen Trent, "something that happens at periodic intervals. How can we know?"

Tregare frowned. "Damned odd, that individual cycles would coincide. Disease, though—in all of space I know of only three cases where humans came down with infection from an alien world."

"Now four, perhaps," said Rissa, "though not of humans, this one." She shook her head. "Besides worrying over Stonzai and Sevshen, I cannot forget the *time* this is costing us."

"And effort," Tregare said. "Packing twice as much water from below, so we can water the up-valley garden at night."

Lisele sat upright. "We can't leave them! They've been so good, and loyal—and now Stonzai can't even *talk* with us."

Tregare waved a hand. "Nobody said anything about deserting our friends. And nobody's going to. Rest easy, princess."

Rissa touched her daughter's arm. "Even if we wished to, we could not. Without Stonzai fully recovered, when we reached a Shrakken outpost there would be no way to communicate."

"But it'll be a load off my mind," said Tregare, "when those two get healthy. Load off our feet, too—all that peacewasting *water*."

And when the Shrakken were up again, for many days they still lacked strength. Able to talk again, Stonzai had no explanation for the illness. "Something, not before happen did," was all she said. And as Tregare put it, there was no way to argue with that.

"The long and short of it is," he said in council, "now we're so close to rainy season, it's not worth moving." There was argument, but he wouldn't budge and Rissa backed him. Twenty-three days later, when the rains struck, the rest admitted he was right. At this height the season wasn't as drastic as down in swamp country—but nobody claimed it was fit to travel in.

Jenise worried that the little canyon might flood. Tregare pointed out some high-water marks and called her worry needless. Neither, it turned out, was wholly right. The highest water covered the dirt floors of two huts. Jenise and Hagen moved into the work hut, against the canyon's west wall, and the common hut was out of business—so when any partying spirit could be aroused, Rissa and Tregare now hosted. The maturing of Trent's leaf-bulb wine sparked one such occasion. Lisele thought the stuff didn't taste too bad, but next day Tregare went around surly, and told Trent, "I've got a name for that booze of yours. 'Old Head-Splitter'."

Hunting became impossible, so it was lucky they'd stored so much dried meat—and at the rain's onset, wrapped and sealed the stores against damp and mold. Hagen and Jenise sometimes braved the rain to net the small whalethings from the swollen lower stream, except during the peak of flood when it simply wasn't safe to do so—but those gleanings were mere tidbits to break the monotony. Still, Lisele appreciated even that much change, and said so.

Up here the change of seasons was less abrupt. The rain eased off, the streams slackened, but gradually. Lisele found the process interesting—watching the plant life change from day to day, while the ground firmed for better walking.

Getting ready to move again was confusing, because their adjustments for high water had been hurried and unplanned. Now they had to look around to find things, because who remembered where they'd moved this or that, all in a rush when the water rose? But eventually they got everything more or less in order, and when the ground dried enough for decent walking they were ready to go on up farther into the mountains.

While the steep crests still rose high before them, the stream they followed became a trickle. One night, sitting in dark around cooking-fire embers, they talked. "Unless we get high enough to find snow patches, we're seeing just about the last of the water."

"From this view, I see snow only on the peaks. In valleys we cannot see from here—when we flew over, so long ago, I do not recall noticing."

"I didn't see, of course. Well, we have to carry as much water as we can manage. Because aside from snow, what is there?"

"Lakes, maybe. Ponds. But yeah, Jenise—you're still right."

"Food, too. When's the last time anyone brought down some meat?"

"I could've, today. But these up here, they're so *little*."

A hand, touching. "Sure, princess. But while we can still spare water for boiling, we'd better sample some, just in case. So tomorrow, if you get the chance, throw a needle or two."

"Sure. Course I will, Tregare."

"But the main point. We must open all packs, and discard those things so necessary in the low country but not now— perhaps even a travois or two—and proceed with what we *now* need."

Silence, then a gruff laugh. "You called it, Rissa."

Keeping only one travois and six of the unit packs, they continued. The travois carried mostly water, and only Tregare and Hagen and the two Shrakken took turns hauling it. Lisele worried, thinking of things left behind that might be needed—but in this steep country they were carrying all they could manage. Enough? Who knew? Maybe even the few lightweight luxuries would prove to be too much.

She wished that when she was making moccasins she'd made herself some larger ones; hers were too small now, and her stretch shoes were wearing out, right where her weight came down the hardest.

Far behind, and off their necessary course, lay the last trickle of stream. Now as they climbed steep ravines and crossed jagged ridges, the only water lay in small, stagnant pools. What they found, they used—Tregare had elected to keep the light-weight purifier—but it was only minor aid.

They shot and ate three of the small animals; then they saw no more.

The heat, when it began, wasn't the burden it had been at lower altitudes. Hot, yes, but bearable far past the point at which they'd been forced to stop, down below. They kept moving.

When they topped the final highest gap and looked down the long rugged slope of ridges that hid the coastal plain, Tregare laughed—high-pitched, in the thin air. "That's it, people. If we can last until we get down to water, we'll make it the rest of the way, all right."

He didn't sound, though, as if it was going to be easy.

The first of the descent was steep, over bare rock and down graveled gullies. Almost at once, as soon as they were a few hundred meters below the crest, Lisele felt the change. The air was cooler, and from the distant ocean came a steady breeze. Of course, as Tregare pointed out, they were farther from the equator now, heading toward where he guessed Sassden to be. But still the coastal slope had a different feel to it than the inland bowl.

They spent one night in the open. They'd seen no animals except something like a spotted, hornless goat, but Tregare set watches anyway. Next day they reached timberline and walked in partial shade, on a sparse blanket of dead foliage that gradually became thicker as they progressed. And now there was water— mere seepage at first, but then true springs that fed tiny streams. Jenise wanted to refill some water bags, but Tregare said to wait until the streams grew. Meanwhile they dipped the fresh cool liquid up in cups, to drink it. It was *so* good!

Once Rissa stopped and pointed, and Lisele caught a glimpse of a medium-sized animal that moved like a carnivore as it vanished into underbrush. Later they saw others like it; each time the beast skulked rapidly away. Even so, they stood watches that night, too.

*   *   *

The fourth day of descent they came to a lateral valley with a large creek running through it. Longingly, feeling the itch of her skin, Lisele asked, "Do you think it might be safe to swim?"

Tregare stroked his beard. "We weren't around this side of the mountains long enough to learn much. And after that leech that got you, last time you played guinea pig—"

Rissa gestured downstream. "The bend, there. The pool, that an eddy has formed? The sandbar nearly encloses it. Perhaps—"

They walked over, and looked. The pool *was* almost isolated; only a shallow passage joined it to the current, and the meter-deep water was clear as crystal. Hagen Trent said, "Just a minute," and went to timber's edge, then brought back a fair-sized log. From the redness of his face, it was about as heavy as he could manage, but when he plunked it down beside the sandbar, it blocked the passage. "There! And I'll be your guinea pig." He began to undress.

"Wait." From her pack Rissa took a strip of dried meat, then moved to the pool and dropped it in. Nothing happened. After a time she shrugged and picked it up, impaled it on a stick and held it in the current outside the pool. A small fishlike creature nosed at it; then several more came.

"They're nibbling," Tregare said, and Lisele saw one of the little decimeter-long things jerk and tug, and pull away a minuscule shred. Tregare knelt on the sandbar, motioned for Rissa to bring the meat nearer, and cupped his hand. On the third try he caught one of the tiny swimmers, and held it up for all to see. The mouth opened and closed; Tregare explored it with a finger, and grinned. "Not much bite," he said. "About like a young trout, on Earth."

So the humans undressed. Hagen and Tregare went in first; there was room for both, but not much left over. They ducked their heads under, scrubbed themselves with bare hands and then with sand, and came out laughing. Then, with Rissa and Jenise, Lisele had her turn. The feel of the cold water was *delicious;* even when her teeth chattered, she stayed until Rissa called a halt, and came out reluctantly.

"Wash us also, will we," said Stonzai. The two Shrakken shed their usual harnesslike garb and entered the pool. Side by side they lay; then, slowly and in unison, they submerged their heads and began to roll over in the water. Each time their faces came uppermost, they raised them for a quick breath. For washing they used their hands not at all, but merely let the water lave them as they turned. After what seemed a long time, both sat up, looked at each other and made hissing noises. Then they got out, and walked through the trees and out of sight into the brush. Except for Stonzai's picking up her needle-gun, they were unencumbered.

Well, *there's* a new ritual," said Tregare. "New to us, I mean."

Trent chuckled. "I think they're off on a date."

"Do we have to hold lunch for them?" asked Jenise. She was smiling, and it struck Lisele how different the woman was, from the whining cripple who had left the scout with them. Without paying close attention, it was hard to notice any difficulties with the maimed hand. Now she gestured with it. "I'm really hungry!"

"Since we're cold-snacking," Tregare said, "I wouldn't think we need to wait. I hope they don't stay out too long, is all. On account of it'd be nice to make a lot more distance today."

Before the two returned, he was fretting, but Lisele used the time for another dip in the pool. When the aliens had eaten, the group donned packs and waded the creek at a shallow run of rapids. By nightfall they were well into the next, lower range of foothills.

In the next few days, before the coastal plain came fully into view, they surmounted two more such ranges. They reached the crest of the last one shortly before sunset, and decided to camp there. While dinner cooked, Lisele noticed a steep knoll, the nearest high ground, topped by a tall straight tree. Nudging Tregare, she pointed. "From up there I could get a good scan. Anything special you'd like me to look for?"

For a moment he looked startled; then he nodded. In the soft bare dirt he drew lines. "Two rivers that come together about like this; Sassden's at the junction. We'd see it, here, from about *this* angle, I think." She watched his gesture and nodded. Then, checking her needle-gun for full load, she set out to climb the knoll.

At the top she paused for breath—the slope *was* steep—and surveyed the tree. To catch the lowest branch she had to jump, but then she swung up and climbed with fair ease. She didn't look away yet—time for that, when she was as high as she could go.

She got higher than she expected; twice she had to halt and get her breath. Then the trunk and branches thinned enough that

her movements made the whole thing wobble. All right; far
enough. Time to do some looking.

She knew, from riding aircars, that seeing a piece of country
at a slant was different from looking straight down on it. Now
she squinted at a flat angle to the far terrain, into the setting sun,
and tried to make out any features at all, let alone Tregare's two
rivers. She saw red glare of sun, soft green foliage brilliantly
backlit at this hour, shadows she couldn't interpret. And far out
on the plain, a great patch of mist. Past it, something now
glittered and then didn't, the pattern repeating. Ocean? From
Sassden they hadn't seen it, but this place was higher, with
nothing much in the way. Yes, she decided finally. She couldn't
judge the distance, but sure as peace that was ocean sparkling
at her.

She brought her gaze back to the mist; nothing definite,
there. Nearer, she looked—and briefly two bright curving lines
flashed at her, then disappeared. She slitted her eyes, fixed on
that area and waited. Again the flashes came, and then—maybe
due to cloud movement—steadied to a lesser brightness but
remained. Yes—Tregare's rivers, and for a moment she saw
where they met. His direction-guess had been a little off, but not
badly.

With thumb and forefinger she gauged the angle between
that junction and the sun's setting point; to clinch it she measured the separation on her other hand. All right; she wouldn't
lose it now.

She looked again, over the entire oddly-angled landscape.
More shadows grew; the sun was close to gone; she saw no new
features. Time to get down, while the light held. For the first
time she looked to the ground below, and was surprised at the
height she'd reached. Slowly, she began her descent.

It seemed longer than the climb had; hunger always made
her tired, and fatigue fostered carelessness. This was no place for
sloppy work. So with slow caution she made her way to the
ground, and then downhill to the night's camp.

Trent was serving a hot stew. His cooking had improved a
lot, since the scoutship days. Lisele took her kit and sat between
Tregare and Rissa, and told them what she'd seen.

Tregare had her demonstrate the finger-angle, duplicated it
with his own hand, and measured off from the spot where
sun-glow made twilight brightest. Then he nodded. "The notch
across there, with the clump of trees in it. That's our line of
march." Making the same test, Lisele agreed. Then, while the

others talked, she ate in silence. Thinking, *he didn't compliment me any.* She smiled. *Because he knows I don't need it.* Then his arm hugged her shoulders, and she decided that a little appreciation didn't hurt, after all!

Later, in full dark except for stars and two tiny moons, with the fire down to embers, Lisele lay breathing deeply, and sleep came.

Terror woke her—thunder above and nearing, coming down on them. Someone keened a wail that hurt her ears—Stonzai? No human, surely. A thick curse; she couldn't tell if the mumble was Tregare or Hagen. Rissa, sharply: "Do *not* know who it is. Do *not*! As Tregare said—" The voice trailed into a moan, and pain clawed into Lisele's head.

Up and running downhill, unable to see, she grazed a tree and caromed off another, fell and rose and ran through brush that raked skin as the other thing raked inside her mind. She heard little noises from her mouth but couldn't stop making them. Sensing, now, rather than seeing obstacles, she avoided them; she knew they were there in the same way she knew something hunted her. She kept running, while part of her mind wondered how and why she could do it.

The thing found her! Her sensing failed; a great blow came as she crashed into something and tasted blood and fell flat and rolled aside, curling up small so there'd be less of her to hurt. Inside her head blazed agony; outside, a crashing impact shook the ground.

She couldn't take any more. With one deep breath she sought escape, mind-stop, the nirvana of the alpha state.

Near the edge of consciousness she felt the claws hesitate and leave her mind. Without volition her slow, trained breathing continued—not enough, after that exhausting headlong run, to give her full awareness. Suspended between sleep and waking she lay without thought. In her mind, pictures flashed, and feelings—but before she could recognize them, they vanished.

After a time she calmed, near to normal sleep but still able to maintain the alpha state that had saved her. Hours passed; she stayed unmoving. She knew she should get up, find her way back—but she couldn't, yet.

It was when she'd decided she had to try, that she heard the shuffling and felt the mind-touch. She froze her thought—deep breaths, no cognition—and waited. Then something picked her up, something warm and dry. And she felt herself carried farther down the hill.

XX. Elzh

Long away now, the ship from nothing, with Elzh left to mourn the two Tsa ships the thing had killed. Only three remaining, Elzh had, and one damaged, not able to rise to follow Tsa-Drin directive. For long it sat, far around planet-curve from mindbeast places, while Tsa worked to make it again useful. Elzh with two good ships could not leave hurt one behind; Tsa-Drin or no, Tsa would not abandon Tsa on mindbeast world. As correct, thought Elzh—understood, or not understood.

Two ships, able. Not enough to give this beastworld death. To wait, then. Heal third ship and follow those gone to next world of Tsa-Drin chart. To wait—and to learn, always.

And face mindbeasts in some and other time. One beast ship came from distance, defied Tsa for short time only and went chased away without chance to bespeak this world. And from ground here, beastships made bid to rise—once, twice and again. But dropped back when met by Elzh's two. And the way one dropped, it would not rise more.

Healing of Elzh's third ship was slow and slow. Other two, except for now and ever landing to add supplies, kept orbit several world-cycles, to use least fuel. Then joined the third, on ground, to use none at all. Drone tankers, orbiting outer planet, must be conserved. If beastships rose, though, or came from distance, Tsa ships lay ready. As correct, as understood.

And now again, from distance, came beastship.

XXI. Ivan

On *Inconnu Deux*, time passed—
roughly, one day for twenty of Earth's or two dozen of Shaarbant's. Finally, watching the far-range detectors, Jeremy Crowfoot spotted Shaarbant's sun ahead.

In Control, Ivan called council; from his drive-room post,
Peleter attended by intercom. "Let's get to it," Ivan said.
"Tregare's plan hinged on our getting out and back in a hurry,
with FTL-drive working fully. Seeming to escape, then flashing
back out of super-C when the Tsa didn't expect us. Instead
we've been gone for several Shaarbant-years, and can't be sure
how many—and we're sub-light and limping. So it's a whole
new ball game." He caught himself thumb-twiddling, and stopped.
"Open for good ideas."

Alina Rostadt said that without the Hoyfarul Drive working,
if they followed Tregare's plan they'd be three months, objective
time, getting back again. Anders Kobolak said that if they
slowed to a quarter-C, maybe even an eighth, they could make
the intended punitive pass and still be too fast to catch. Dacia
pointed out that any sub-light approach to Shaarbant left the
Deux detectable, going in. Jeremy Crowfoot didn't consider
that problem too serious; the Tsa might get ships up to
intercept, but how much could they do against something
passing at a quarter-C?

Fine discussion, Ivan thought—until Dacia had to shoot it
down. He'd left that part to her, and was glad she didn't wait too
long before speaking up. "Let's forget all the fly-by options,"
she said, "because we can't afford any of them."

Ivan wished he could see how people took Dacia's words,
because this was only the first of several jolts the group would
get, soon. He also wished he could remember who knew what,

but he couldn't. Now Alina said, "You're saying we're low on fuel?"

No such thing, Dacia assured everybody; if necessary, the *Deux* could get itself back to Earth. "Not us with it, though—not alive. That's the crunch, shipmates. We're low on food."

Protest was loud; Ivan lost patience and outshouted everybody. "Doesn't *anybody* on here, besides Dacia, monitor the inventory readouts?" Silence; Ivan nodded. "Then listen to her."

What Dacia told was what she and Ivan had agreed on, and all true. "We have to have a plan," she said, after much talk, "that lets us land on Shaarbant now, or—"

"Or *what*?" Ivan couldn't identify the voice.

He spoke, anyway. "Or get us somewhere else, safely."

New discussion; in this one, Ivan had more to say. "Tregare, he's holed-up somewhere on Shaarbant. I hope." *And Rissa, and Lisele,* yes. "If we can get down there and find him, in touch with the Shrakken if *they've* survived, maybe we can put something together, to fight the Tsa." He heard murmurs, and spoke up to override them. "The Tsa aren't automatically invincible; from what little we know, numbers count, too." He banged a fist down. "I blew two Tsa ships out of space. Escaping Shaarbant. If we can hook up with the Shrakken on that world, through Tregare, maybe we've got a chance here."

"I'm not sure this is a good question, but it puzzles me." Peleter's quiet voice. "Why didn't we try that the first time?"

"Because we didn't know enough," Ivan said. Peleter was a good man, he reminded himself; no point in getting exasperated. "Tregare wanted the ship safe at all costs; his idea sounded good and it *was* good. We'd never been under Tsa attack, and what did happen was something nobody could have predicted. But now we're stuck with it, and have to work with what we've got."

"Plus the rest of the crew," said Melaine Holmbach, but her voice trailed off. "Oh—of course. If we're short of food..."

"Right." Ivan nodded. "If we *knew* we could land and resupply, we'd rouse them. As it is—" He shrugged. "Too many question marks." And if they couldn't land, if the Tsa were too strong and drove them off? Ivan knew that answer, too—everybody into freeze, including himself, except for Anders. And leave it to the First Hat to get them to Stenevo, and hope the Shrakken there would parley instead of shooting them out of space.

He knew the answers, yes. That didn't mean he liked them.
He smiled toward Dacia. "Let's just hope we *can* land."

They talked longer. Ellalee referred back to the Tsa mental
attack. "They caught me cold, before—it was like running a
footrace with my knickers down around my ankles." Her quick
cough hinted of shyness. "But y'know—if it fits the planning
any way, I wouldn't mind another go at those blokes."

Ivan said he'd think on it; certainly, nothing else new was
coming out of the discussion. A vague idea worked in the back
of his mind, but wouldn't come clear. Finally Anders said, "I
think we've got all of it. What's your decision, Captain?"

Ivan turned his blind stare toward the voice. "Tactically? To
think, a time longer; there has to be more to it. How soon must
we set decel, to choose our course and our approach speed?"

He heard readout tape click out. "Two days, a little less,"
said Kobolak. "When I get firmer distance readings I'll give you
the time more exactly."

"Right; thanks." He swung to face the entire group in turn.
"Thank you all, in fact. When I reach a decision, you'll be
advised."

He stood, went to the galley and dished up some soup. He
heard Dacia follow, but he no longer needed guidance. When he
ate, he used the spoon without spilling. Learning such things had
been hard, and though he knew it might be a little childish of
him, he thoroughly enjoyed showing that he could do them.

Later, in quarters, as he sipped beer and talked with Dacia,
his vague idea took form. Instead of a straightforward approach
to Shaarbant, what if they went diving in as if for a sling turn?
"Set to point us toward Stenevo's coordinates, if it comes up we
have to go through with it."

"Why Stenevo?" Then, "Oh, of course. We came here to
help the Shrakken, so—"

He nodded. "If we can't do it here, we'll do it there. But if
the odds look good, or we can improve them any, we go decel
and land." The tension was getting to him, though—all the
waiting, and now the need to decide. He had some time, yet, to
reconsider. But to use it well, he'd have to be more relaxed.

Dacia suggested they go to bed for a while; he said she must
have been reading his mind. When they got up, without asking
his preference she poured him bourbon over ice in place of the
beer he'd been nursing. Tasting it, he smiled. "Don't know what

I'd do without you." And somehow it no longer hurt him to admit it.

They talked late, coming back to old ideas when new ones turned out to be blind alleys. Then, in the middle of discussing a variation on the sling approach, Ivan stopped. "Wait a minute. I think—" Then he nodded. "As far as the Shrakken know, the Tsa don't have scoutships. We still have one aboard."

"Ivan! You have a way—?"

"Not yet. But it's a wild card, the only one I can think of. I don't know just how to use it, but there's time to figure something."

He drained his glass and held it up. "Pour me another?"

Waking, Ivan decided he hadn't drunk enough to hang him over. He felt good. Hearing no sound of Dacia, he got up and lumbered to the intercom, and called the galley. She was there.

"I haven't eaten yet, Ivan. Jeremy and I are drinking coffee, working up an appetite. Shall I bring two trays down?"

"No, thanks—but if you want to fill them, that's fine. Heavy with the eggs on mine, please. I'll be right up." His shower was sketchy; he put on the first shirt and trousers and sandals he happened to find. He hadn't worn his skipper's hat for some time and he didn't bother with it now, either. Going upship he practiced taking the steps two at a time, fingers on handrail for guidance.

At the galley he paused. "Over here," said Dacia. With hands outstretched to detect obstacles he walked quickly to her and sat; a moment's listening spotted his target for a good-morning kiss. Only one other person breathed nearby. "Morning, Jeremy." At the man's intake of breath, Ivan laughed. "Dacia said you were here."

Chuckling, Crowfoot said, "One on me, that." While they ate, Ivan told his ideas for tactics at Shaarbant. When he mentioned the scoutship, Crowfoot asked, "Are you thinking of it as a major factor, or some sort of decoy?"

Ivan leaned forward. "So far, I'd figured on the *Deux* drawing attention so maybe the scout could slip past and land first. I admit, I haven't considered all the angles. Or I wouldn't be asking."

Later, in Control, he talked with Ellalee. Concerning the scoutship, she said, "I wouldn't try landing that thing, but I'm

bloody sure I could fly it, elsewise. So if—'' She took a deep
breath, as though preparing for exertion, then continued. ''Riding copilot, say I was, and the flamin' Tsa do their mind-clawing
trick. Well, you see, if I *could* hang onto control of me, might be
I could get us out of range, what with the planet's curvature and
all. You see?''

"Maybe." Ivan nodded. "And then what?"

"And then, given time and safety, the real pilot would be
recovered, and could land us, wherever."

Ivan felt himself smiling. "That's not bad, Ellalee. Dacia—
you've got it noted?" He heard her stylus on the paper, and
nodded as he spoke.

Crowfoot thought the scout should be an unmanned weapon, its drive hyped past red-line to max, and set to blow on
impact. Ivan shook his head. "In a big operation, yes. In fact
that's the way—on Ilse Krueger's advice—I got Admiral Ozzie
Newhausen, in the battle for Earth. But here we have just the
ship and the scout, and neither's expendable on a one-shot
gamble."

It all came down to Ivan's own decision, and now he'd
made it. In quarters, over after-dinner tea. He got up and went to
the intercom; from Control, Anders Kobolak answered. "Any
orders?"

"Yes. For now, red-line max decel. When we know our
distance better, we can adjust from that."

Silence. Then, "Right, Captain. You've chosen your plan?"

"I've made the choice that gives the most options. That's
all."

Kobolak sounded hesitant. "If you say so."

"After your watch, we'll talk. Marchant out." Feeling the
wall to get his angle right, he made his way back to his chair.
Dacia asked if he wanted anything; he settled for a beer. Then he
talked, and the more he explored the sling idea, the better he
liked it. "The dead sling, they won't spot us early, with luck.
When they do, we have—" On his fingers he ticked the options.
"Go to a power sling; tighter in, that would be." If need be, use
the accel to boost them off toward Stenevo. "Or with real luck,
get Shaarbant between us and the Tsa, pour on decel and sit
down. Dive and plow air. Have to spot Sassden and Shtegel first,
though; once we hit air there won't be time to find our ass with
both hands. Not with the Tsa chasing us."

"And do you think there's any chance we *can* land?"

Through his tension, Ivan tried to smile. "I purely hope so."

Ivan was in no mood for sex, but Dacia was, and when he went along with her wish he was surprised how well things went. It was odd, he thought; sometimes they'd leave each other alone for days, and then it'd be *all* the time. Well, now might be their last chances, ever—so why not?

Then, sitting up, she asked more questions about Shaarbant. He was tired; his most recent sleep was long hours ago. But he knew she wanted to help, so he tried to concentrate. And it paid off—because suddenly he knew how he was going to use the scoutship.

"Whatever move the *Deux* makes, Dacia, that looks crucial—" Ivan blinked; there was no pain to it now. "—that's when the scout drops free. To land, or play decoy, or whatever—we can't know yet."

She touched his cheek and said, "There's one thing you know, that you haven't told me. Ivan—*who goes on that scout*?"

Well, he hadn't expected to fool her; he sighed. "Ellalee rides copilot, as we discussed, in case she can get the scout through any Tsa attack. For the rest—the scout's detectors have auxiliary audible alarms, and of course, the landing sensors have to work that way. In case of dust, and all. So—" He waited; she made no protest.

He reached, fumbled, and then held her. "Yes, of course, Dacia. When that scout leaves the *Deux*, I'll be on it."

One hand gripped his shoulder; the nails of the other dug into his neck. "You said—you said you had to keep this ship safe, for Tregare. And you haven't—not yet. Ivan—"

Her nails drew blood; he shook his head, and she moved the hand away. He said, "Once I commit the ship to its best choice of action, my job's done. Anders can do the rest, and I couldn't. But what I *can* do, then, is choose options for the scout, to help give *Inconnu Deux* its best licks."

"No—Ivan, you're trying to take too much on yourself. You—"

Both his hands found her head, running fingers through her hair and fondling one ear. "*Think*, Dacia! When the scout drops away, the ship's committed but the scout isn't. So where does *command* lie?"

Three breaths she took, before speaking. "Yes, Ivan—you

have to go where the choices are. Of course." One more breath.
"I agree—so long as I go with you."

His answer came unthought. "I figure the scout's odds
about 50-50. If that's good enough for you—well, the ship's
chances are much the same, come to that. In the long run."
Dacia hugged him, and Ivan decided he'd made a deal.

Next morning, before he and Dacia had breakfast, they and
Ellalee moved their "landing kits" to the scout. Then it was time
to announce the decision.

Anders Kobolak didn't like it. Alina had had breakfast with
Ivan and Dacia before relieving her husband; now while the two
drank coffee, he had his off-watch meal. For Ellalee it was
lunch.

Ivan repeated his arguments but Anders still disagreed.
"You say you'll have given your last possible decisive command
before the scout leaves the ship. How can you be sure of that?"

Ivan shrugged. "The last big one, I said. And likely the last
I *could* give effectively, being unable to see the situation directly.
In a fast crisis, Anders, my command presence could kill
you—if you waited for answers instead of making your own
choices."

"He's right and you know it." Dacia sounded irritated at
her brother. "We've been over all the variations we could think
of, and this looks like everybody's best chance."

Ivan cleared his throat. "If you come up with anything new,
Kobolak, we'll certainly give it a hearing. But otherwise we'll
use the scout the way I said."

The dead sling around Shaarbant was Ivan's initial choice—
and its vector requirements the touchiest. With that approach,
though, they could switch to another of the alternatives at any
point. Anders kept Ivan informed of their speed and distance;
they were close enough to Shaarbant, he said, that from this
angle the planet showed a lopsided disk. And so far, neither
screens nor emission detectors showed any sign of Tsa ships.

The orbit Crowfoot gave them, to arc around Shaarbant,
was a cometary—a hyperbola with asymptote-angle of about a
radian. "And cutting air just enough, I hope, to let us bend our
path wherever we need it." This far out, they couldn't insert
yet; most of the time, comets and other debris travel slowly.
Crowfoot gave them a least-time course to meet orbit outside

estimated Tsa detector range. "With a twenty percent margin, of course."

"And even cutting it that fine," said Ivan, "we'll be a long time to Shaarbant." Couldn't be helped, though. Simulating a dead object in natural orbit—that's what Ivan was betting on.

"Just so they don't take too close a look."

Ivan sweat it all the way, but they did reach orbit safely. Crowfoot took readings and made adjustments, then gave Anders the okay to cut the drive, and all ship's power except maintenance and control functions. The rest was keyed to the drive switch; if the ship was brought to life, it would wake all at once, driving at red-line max. The computer chewed viewscreen data and spit out the thrust angles for changing, at any moment, to the power sling maneuver. Right now, there was nothing more anyone could do.

Well inside estimated detector range, instruments registered the first search beam. One blip and no repeat—and twice more, hours apart, the same thing happened. "Automatic scanners?" No one knew; Ivan shook his head. The fourth beam passed but then returned, and for several seconds wavered back and forth across the *Deux*'s position. Until the blip disappeared, no one spoke; then they could relax.

"Nobody home but us comets," said Ellalee. "Absolutely nobody."

"Let's hope they believe that," Ivan said. Shrugging tension from neck and shoulders, he was surprised it went so easily. Now that they were committed—to a fixed set of alternatives, at least—somehow the waiting bothered him less.

Until Crowfoot told him, he hadn't considered that no comet could orbit a planet; anything doing a cometary around a moving world could only be sheerest coincidence. But if the idea had fooled him, maybe it'd get past the Tsa, too.

One thing for sure; he couldn't afford to worry about it.

Their orbit bent; curvature grew as Shaarbant's gravity took firmer hold. Ever faster, *Inconnu Deux* fell toward the calculated near-miss. and still no sign from the deadly, waiting Tsa.

"You're sure?" said Ivan. If he could *see* the damned screens—!

"Not a peep, not a glimmer," said Ellalee. "Don't fret you, Captain. First pop, I'll have Anders up here to take over, before there's time to say squat."

Ivan chuckled; Dacia, beside him, squeezed his hand. He said, "Time-distance readings again, please, to closest passage on this orbit." Ellalee read the figures; he nodded, then sighed and turned to Dacia. "Too long and far to sit up without sleep. Too soon and near, though, to chance sleep in quarters and maybe get caught out. Time we moved to the scout, do you think?"

"Probably," she said. "Shall we check quarters once more first, to see if we've left anything we really should take along?"

"Why not? And, Ellalee—soon as you're off watch, you move in, too. If action happens before that, come *running!*"

"Sure as you know." So they left, gathered a few items from quarters, and began settling in on the scout. The left-hand screens were tandemed through to Control; Dacia checked with Ellalee to make sure the hookup was working. It was.

Ivan sat in chief pilot's position. He put his board on test status and began to feel it out, to familiarize himself again with the controls he might need to operate. Twice he made errors, but kept his curses down to a mumble. He stayed with the chore until he felt he knew the board as well as he ever would, and put it operational again. "If I have to," he said, "and it's not unlikely, I can land this thing. Especially if somebody watches the back screens for me and picks a good place to set down."

Dacia touched his shoulder. "That's good. I landed a scout once, but a long time ago. And Ellalee never has."

They hadn't eaten, so now they did. Then they laid the seats back, and not bothering to undress, they slept.

A noise woke Ivan. He sat up, and in moments remembered where he was. Quietly, Ellalee said, "Sorry, skipper; bumped my kitbag against the airlock hatch. I'll go backship now, and doss down."

"Wait a minute." He spoke as softly as she had. "You're off watch? What's our situation?"

"Closing in, going faster." She sounded excited, a little. First giving the time, she said, "About four hours until our tight pass starts, and still not the sign of any Tsa intercept."

"Good. All right, Ellalee; get some rest." She left; the rear door closed gently; he lay back again, and dozed. Between sleep and waking, his mind searched the chances ahead. But he must have slept, because when he smelled coffee he had heard no sounds of whoever made it.

Abruptly, he sat up. "The time! How long before the sling turn starts?"

"Seventy minutes, a little more." Dacia's voice. "I've been keeping tabs, Ivan. I'd have woke you soon."

Reassured, he said, "Yes, I know. Ellalee still sleeping?"

"She's aboard?" Dacia sounded surprised. "Oh, of course; she's off watch, long since. I didn't wake up when she came in, though, so—"

"I did." He was getting the seat up straight again. The smell of coffee came closer, and when he had the seat properly upright, Dacia handed him a cup. "Thanks. Well—still waiting, are we?" He opened the intercom circuit. "Anders? Ivan. What word?"

"Crowfoot here. Anders had to take a little walk. Should be back in a minute. He—"

"*Who's got the con?* Jeremy—you're no pilot!" Alina was, some—but not for *this*. He turned aside—should he have Dacia roust Ellalee out and get her up there? But damn it all, she was needed *here*. . . .

Mildly, Crowfoot said, "There'll be time, Ivan. To start the power-sling, all I'd have to do is push the button; the computer's feeding the proper angle constantly, you know that. Then Anders would come running and take over."

Ivan had to work at calming himself, but he did it. Crowfoot's view of the situation was ridiculously optimistic; yelling wouldn't help, though. All he said was, "Kobolak better hurry it up."

Alina's voice came. "I'll go tell him." Fingers drumming, Ivan waited, and finally Anders Kobolak said, "All right, I'm back. And I think my guts will let me stay put, now. What was the emergency?"

Ivan choked back the first answer that came to mind, and said, "The idea, I think, is not to have one. Report?"

Anders read off speed, distance and approach-angle. "Do you still want to drop, if possible, at point-two radians short of perigee?"

"The computer likes it," said Ivan, "so I won't argue."

"All right," said Crowfoot. "I'll put the readout on your screen, with an audio countdown on the pickup button."

"Good enough." Checking that button, Ivan heard the faint tones of the numerical series, counting off the seconds.

Not long now. "Okay, thanks. Marchant out."

And Dacia said, "I'd better get Ellalee up."

While the Australian woman ate, Dacia got the downviewer on her right-hand screen, and kept Ivan informed. "We're coming in over the side of Shaarbant we don't know. There's a subcontinent, of sorts, at the rear horizon. Some speckles at the far one—maybe the archipelago where Shtegel is, the port Tregare went to.''

"Then Sassden, where *we* were, is farside of the planet?"

"Has to be," said Ellalee Ganelong. "Billy-o hiding out on us."

Ivan grinned. "You sound cheerful enough."

"So do you," she said—and he had to laugh, and wondered why. Then he knew. The Tsa had blinded him—how, he didn't know—and crippled his ship and cost it years of planets' time. But now, if those devils were still here, something was going to *happen*. His death, it could be; he knew that. But either way—long enough, he'd waited blind.

All he said was, "A glum mind wouldn't help much, would it?"

Before she could answer, the intercept alarm shrieked.

"Two ships rising." Kobolak's voice. "Tsa, I'd expect. Coming around from darkside, and with fair speed up already."

Ivan leaned forward. He shook his head. *Words*—all he could get now, and they weren't enough to tell him what he needed.

"Can they intercept the dead-sling turn? Jeremy—what's the computer's guess?"

He heard Crowfoot and Kobolak talking, low-voiced, but couldn't make out what they said. Before impatience made him shout for an answer, Anders spoke. "No physical intercept possible. But they can get within mind-attack range, or close to it."

"What if we go into the power sling?"

"A moment." Crowfoot. Then, "Close, still, but I think we can keep safe distance, just barely."

Ivan's seconds stretched. No time to think, though—and, he decided, no reason to, either. "Drop us. Drop us and hit the power sling." He paused; another idea came. "Anders, Jeremy—are we slow enough that you could bend a tight loop, crabwise acceleration, clear around Shaarbant, and catch them from where they don't expect?"

"Hey!" Kobolak sounded startled. "Might, at that. Should I?"

If Anders wouldn't decide, Ivan would. "Yes! Now drop us."

Shuddering, the scout plunged; the peeps and trills of its sensors drowned in the ionic roar of the *Deux*'s drive, raging into full blast. Ivan waited until sound and motion quieted; then he said, "Reports?"

For moments, only, the scout's drive fired. Dacia said, "There. We were a little too high and too fast. I gave a touch of back-vector, to get us into air sooner, while the ship's drive still masked ours."

"Can you see the Tsa ships?"

"Right pouring it on, they are," said Ellalee. "Trying at intercept, but the *Deux*'s out for showing them a clean pair of heels."

Ivan turned up the audio on the detector circuits, but with three ships to scan, the signals were so much hash. He shook his head, and cut the sound to the edge of audibility. "Soon as they're out of sight, get us downstairs fast. Hedgehopping's the slow way to get around Shaarbant, but we're less apt to be detected."

"Yes, Ivan." The scout felt the first tugs of atmosphere, and made a little bounce. "Still too fast; we skipped. Wait, though—"

"Sure." It couldn't be too much longer, now.

Then she said, "There goes the *Deux*—past the horizon, I mean, out of view. And the Tsa—*no!* They're swinging around, coming back."

Now the bleeps were easier to read, and his hearing told him the story. Two ships, close together as sensed from such a distance, slowly approaching at an angle that crossed the scout's path. Not a collision course, but passing within easy detector range. "Ivan—what shall we do?"

The trouble was, he didn't have the faintest idea.

As he waited, the sounds changed. "Those ships—Dacia, are they separating?" Nearly an hour, it had been, since the *Deux* vanished.

"Yes. One's moving off to our left. The other, though— now it's headed almost straight at us."

As much to himself as to the others, Ivan said, "They've got a lot of accel on us, but we can turn quicker. For what that's worth, here. I mean, once they spot us in mind-range . . ."

The indicator noises wavered. "Now that's odd." Ellalee sounded puzzled. "Why the circling?"

"Both of them?" he asked.

"Just the one ahead of us," said Dacia. "It keeps turning. The other's headed straight away, and climbing."

"Climbing? What for?" What kind of tactic was that?

Ellalee spoke. "To get a wider view, would you suppose?"

"Maybe." The nearer ship stayed in its turn. The scout touched air again; no bounce, this time. "Now we'll start slowing." Ivan waited. Ahead the Tsa ship completed a circle and straightened its course—roughly toward the scout, but now high above it.

And the other Tsa turned and dove headlong, swooping back toward the scout's course but pointing behind it. The sounds told Ivan only part of this, but the women kept him informed. Then, almost shrieking, Ellalee cried, "On the back screen—it's the *Deux*!"

Ivan felt his mouth hang open, and shut it. Then he snapped his fingers. "The Hoyfarul Drive! Anders—or Jeremy, more likely—figured how to get some advantage out of it. All that extra accel—even if they can only use short bursts, to keep from blowing it up. Come on, *Deux*!" He gripped Dacia's arm. "I can't make anything out of the sound indicators now. What's happening?"

As she told him, minute by minute he tried to visualize it. The Tsa above made for *Inconnu Deux*, which opened fire at a slant—"All six of the traversing turrets, probably." —and swung ship to improve the angle. Still short of effective range, but that range closed fast, and—

"They got the bugger!" Ellalee shouted it.

"Its drive, they got," Dacia corrected her. "The ship's still there, but drifting. Slight outbound vector." And above and behind the scout, the *Deux* hurtled toward the remaining Tsa.

Then the human ship faltered. Its drive field flickered and vanished, then after long seconds, reappeared. Paler now, though, and less intense. Hearing that, Ivan nodded. "Blew the Hoyfarul setup again, once and for all. Now—"

"Wait! Something—" Dacia paused. "They've fired a missile—the *Deux*, I mean. I thought you said you'd used them all up."

"No, just two. And no luck with either of them." He waited; missiles were high-gee *fast*, but still they took time, to travel.

Ellalee gasped; Ivan heard her clap her hands. "Some luck *this* time, I'll tell you. They holed her. The Tsa drive field—it's flickering like a wet squib."

But now the *Deux*'s field died completely; projectors silent, that ship drifted on toward its enemy. And with only the two ships ahead, the sound indicators clearly showed Ivan their movements.

He cursed. "The mind attack! They'll slide right into it. Helpless!" Only one thing to do. "Ellalee, I'll take the controls."

The only question was, could he do it, when the Tsa attack came? And if he couldn't, could Ellalee? And *would* she? Quietly, guiding the scout by sound as he eased its drive up to full power, he talked to the two women.

"The *Deux*'s a sitting duck; the Tsa can kill everyone who's awake, then board her. They can do away with the freeze-riders at leisure, and have the ship—and the Hoyfarul Drive. The *Deux*'s is blown, but the plans are aboard, and clear enough. So the Tsa, not the Shrakken, will have FTL capability."

As the scout left atmosphere, Ivan said, "They'll have the ship's star charts, that show Earth and most of our colonies. They won't know our computer coding but they must know the principles or they wouldn't be here. So they'll figure it all out, eventually—and come after humanity as they've gone after the Shrakken."

Ellalee interrupted. "Why all this, Ivan? We both know it."

"Because if their attack stops me, Ellalee, then it's up to you. So I have to be sure you understand how important it is that the *Deux* isn't captured."

"Jolly right I do. Look here, Ivan Marchant! Ramming that ship, with the drive to blow on impact, isn't my first choice of a way to sign out. But that's what you mean, and I see the need as well as you, and if it comes to me I'll do it. Anything more?"

"Just, I'm proud to know you." He listened as the scout, building speed, arced up toward the Tsa ship. For the moment it didn't need him; he pulled Dacia to him and kissed her. "Sorry, love. Sometimes things can't be helped." The worst of it was, pain was the last thing she'd ever feel.

He got closer than he'd expected, the beeps told him, before mind-touch came. Dacia took a shuddering breath; Ellalee whispered, "I'm blanking my mind, hiding. Wish me luck."

At first it didn't hurt, exactly. Exploring? Then he adjusted course, and as he acted with intention, the pain struck. Teeth gritting, Ivan held on, and vaguely sensed something different this time. It was *pushing* him, and when he let it, the pain eased. But the push was to sheer off, to miss the Tsa ship. He brought the scout back on line, and the pain *clawed*. Dacia whimpered, then screamed. From Ellalee he heard no sound.

The push reversed; he overcontrolled and fought to recover. Again it changed, and again—back and forth, shaking him. He was tiring fast, and there was still a long way to go. He fought for breath to speak and said, "Ellalee? Take over for a spell?"

She must have nodded, forgetting he couldn't see, because after a moment she said, "Sorry. Yes," and he felt the controls move against his hands. He relaxed his own grip and let her have dominance, his own hands merely following the moves she made. He felt the pressure fade in his mind, and at the same time he heard Ellalee groan.

Now, breathing deeply while he could, Ivan listened to the bleeps that told him the scout's course. She was doing well, he decided—overcontrolling at first but then adjusting to the Tsa pummeling. Ellalee's breathing, though, came ever harsher, and faster and more shallow—and in the background Ivan heard a quiet, muffled sobbing from Dacia, as though her face were buried in her hands. He reached, fumbled and found her shoulder, but when he squeezed it, she flinched, so he let go.

It seemed a long time that he had partial respite, before the scout's movements became jerky and the tones showed it mostly off-course. Ellalee tried to say something—half groan, half shout—but no clear words came. The controls, though, shuddered against Ivan's hands, so he knew what she meant. "All right," he said. "I'll take it." And as he resumed control and set his intention, pain struck again, trying to push him aside from his target. Stubbornly, with renewed strength after his breather, he horsed the scout back on line.

Briefly he wished he could thank Ellalee, congratulate her for a good job. Because she'd bought him time and distance he couldn't have managed on his own; her hunch, about her ability to resist the Tsa, had paid off. If they'd been out to escape rather than attack, her effort would have got them free. But he couldn't thank her; he had no control of his voice. He heard himself sobbing, and he couldn't stop. It was all he could do to keep bringing the scout back on course, and now he began to wonder if his strength would hold out long enough, for what he had to do.

He threw the autopilot on circuit; it wasn't fast or accurate enough for this job, but it could do part of the work, and his own motions still overrode. The pain peaked, not pushing now, then leveled back. With bitten lips he grinned; he could stand it! He felt a numbness, a level beyond which the pain no longer grew.

In the back of his head, a fumbling; a clenched thing opened, stabbing flame across his mind. Light seemed to flash, then vanished, then came again. He tried to ignore it, to concentrate on the sounds that told him his course. But then—

The screens, the control panel! The light wasn't inside his head—he was seeing! And he saw that the sound indicators were off mark; their heading would have him miss the Tsa ship. He corrected course, and blackness replaced the burst of vision.

Minutes still to go, but not many now. Again the light came, dimly this time—and with it the push of pain. Against his will he let the scout veer; the pain eased and his vision returned. He corrected course; more pain, and again darkness. Pain, push, flicker of light—Ivan was off course as often as on it, but always he brought the scout back on aim, and always pain and blindness rewarded him.

Maybe another relief spell? He let the scout drift, so that he could ask Ellalee, but in a quick flash of vision he saw her shake her head. "I can't! When I hide I can't move, now, and if I move the pain stops me. Ivan—I'm sorry!" As soon as she spoke he wrenched at the controls again, so he couldn't answer; he literally couldn't form words and keep control of what he did. Pain and push varied at a stepped-up rate; his muscles jerked and his heart raced toward fibrillation. The scout swung far aside; as he paused, shaken, gauging the course correction, the pain stopped and his vision came bright and clear.

Then he knew—*somebody's trying to make a deal!* How to find out for sure, though? Mind-touch, without pain, pawed at him. He checked his speed and distance; time was short, but he still had some. Deliberately letting the scout stay off-course, slowing a bit, he spoke aloud. "Our ship. Leave it alone. And the planet—our people there, and the Shrakken, too. Or else—" He twitched the scout's course toward the Tsa ship, then away; mind-touch came and went and came, then dwindled to a sensation he could barely feel. *Agreement?* Briefly he had time to wonder why *seeing* didn't thrill him, but no emotion came.

The Tsa ship turned; weak and fitfully its drive field bloomed, moving it away from *Inconnu Deux*'s drifting approach and nearer to the scout's path. Mind-touch strengthened, but short of pain. Still slowing, Ivan guided the scout away a little more, and the touch lessened further.

He looked aside; Dacia sat with eyes wide and cheeks

tear-streaked. Beside her Ellalee lay back, her eyes closed, breathing slowly. Ivan motioned and said, "She looks peaceful enough. Came through pretty well in the clutch, too."

"Ivan! You can *see*?" She hugged him, clung to him.

"Yeah. Something *they* did." Quickly he told her what he thought had happened, was still happening.

"Then it's peace, Ivan? We don't have to—"

While he thought about it, he let her talk. It would be nice to believe the easy answer, but he wasn't sure he could manage that.

It was the Tsa *power*, like UET's in the old days, like UET's Total Welfare center that had so nearly destroyed him. People like Colonel Osbert Newhausen, who had offhandedly killed a lot of folks including the parents of Ivan and Rissa. And Newhausen's grandson, Ozzie the admiral—well, Ivan had gotten *him*, all right. . . .

But all of them—they could do to you what they wanted, when they wanted, and there wasn't bloody hell you could do about it. He had the Tsa on the hook right now, and they knew it—they'd tried to push him off *and by God they couldn't do it*.

But once he let the hook loose, who was to say what the Tsa would do? *You can't trust power.* To save *Inconnu Deux*, for sure, this one handle was all he had.

And he'd promised Tregare.

Dacia was still saying how nice it all was; his kiss stopped her. Then he said, "I'm sorry. I do love you." *And you, Ilse!* He threw the switches; the scout swung and accelerated.

At this range, even the autopilot couldn't miss.

The Tsa must not have sensed his intention. Ivan Marchant felt no pain at all.

XXII. Elzh

Screenblinks marked beastship's coming. Elzh's ships, both, rose. Soon screens showed the other clearly—and Elzh saw it to be the ship that had come from nothing! Now, though, it came from distance, like any ship.

A trick? (Tserln). *No matter* (Idsath); *it lacks speed for tricks.* Indling, the two aided Elzh to soothe Ceevt, the growing young, so Elzh's mind could go free to probe when beastship neared more.

Pain, and pain! Beastship's speed escaped Elzh's ships; then the thing came back before anything *could*, and struck. Elzh's driving-forces dead, his other ship weakened—but the beastship floating helpless, also! Mindsaying, Elzh planned.

But then of sudden, *small* ship, like the one Elzh attacked before. Not from nothing, this thing—only not seen until it rose from cloud and neared other Tsa ship. Elzh's mind reached there, sensed pain and effort between Tsa and mindbeasts in small ship. From sub-commander in other Tsa ship, came mind-touch: *It almost understands! Great Elzh, I try further!* But only instants more, and small beastship hurtled to implode itself and Tsa to gases.

Effort now, frantic to give driving force to Elzh's ship before beastship can again move; ion-flickers showed that mind-beasts worked to bring their own ship alive. *They must not be first, or we die.*

With Tsa and beasts drifting apart, no mind-touch and no pain. But as Elzh felt drive-force return, beastship's drive flared more bright, then died. Elzh made decision and gave command— before beastship had power to follow, Elzh's ship to go away

199

around planet-curve, and land, and not be killed by beast-madness. For if small ship would kill all in it, to kill Tsa, what might the ship from nothing do?

Landing came not well; drive forces waned, left little margin from all-death. Moments from grounding, thrust from mindbeasts below blurred control of the Tsa making land-touch. Once assuring of the ship—down with safeness but damaged not to rise again, for longtimes—Elzh saw to Ceevt, that the young had wellbeing. And then left ship, went to ground. Asking no Tsa—not Tserln, not Idsath. But carrying a firepiece that could kill Tsa *or* mindbeast.

Down ground and up, Elzh walked long and long. Mind kept away from beast-touch ahead, though pain came random, pouring and rolling and then away gone. Came feeling of a mind holding itself closed. Caution, Elzh used in reaching. Very gently, not to disturb—and Elzh found that mind. And walked to it, where it lay. Seeing not with light, only with mind, Elzh tried to know. To learn—as always, as correct, as understood.

And, as needed, *decision*. To take this mind-closed beast to Tsa ship. *To learn*. Dread, pain, danger, death! Yes. But if need came, Elzh could use firepiece, long enough to kill *any* mindbeast.

XXIII. *Lisele*

While the thing carried her, moving with its strange, slow rolling gait, Lisele kept her mind still. First she felt descent, then there was the wading of a splashing stream, then a slow climb and another dip—this one to level ground. Finally she was borne up a steep slope and heard metal ring underfoot, and then tiny echoes told her she was inside a ship. Still her eyes and mind stayed closed, because she didn't know what else to do.

Listening, she sensed differences between corridors and ramps and open spaces. Her feet brushed against something and she heard a door close; then she was set down on something partly soft and partly firm, shaped like a shallow bowl. It felt like plastic, but smelled different—spicy, a little.

Sound of feet shuffling; the thing that had brought her was moving back now. But its mind-touch came—not hurting, or not very much, just twinges now and then. Strange feelings came—a hunger not for food or drink, urgency that had nothing to do with anything she knew, a brief sense of peace and then a disgust that recalled every rotten stench she'd ever smelled. And pain struck!

She tried for calm and was failing; she slowed her breathing but it wouldn't stay that way. Then footsteps again, retreating, and she heard the door close.

Now her mind quieted. No doubt about it, the thing had gone.

It was some time before Lisele dared open her eyes. She found herself in a beige-walled room, a perfectly ordinary-looking place with straight surfaces and square corners. The bowl she lay in was bright yellow; it and a sort of beanbag stool of the same color were the only furniture. The lighting was a soft white from panels in the ceiling. The room could have been built by humans.

She started to sit up, then heard sound at the door and lay back as she had been, eyes closed. Again came footsteps, but softer than before; she heard the door shut again. Holding to the alpha-state breathing pattern she awaited mind-touch, but when it came she hardly recognized it—like feathers brushing under her scalp, and a tinkle of tiny chimes. She opened her eyes.

This thing couldn't have carried her—it was too small! The body was robed; all she could guess was that the creature was built hefty for its height, several decimeters less than her own. The head was like some human-animal caricature, neither handsome nor ugly, that a cartoonist had drawn. The skull rose to a pronounced central ridge, and the ears sat high and well forward. Except for short, rippling fringes around nostril holes set below the ears, no hair was visible, and the skin reminded Lisele of soft, dark leather. Forehead and brow ridges were the most human features; the wideset eyes, large and round, never seemed to blink. If there were pupil and iris, both were black; only thin pale rings of yellow showed around the edges.

There were cheekbones of sorts, and a nose that on next

look turned into all the rest of the face, for no mouth or jaws lay below it. The "nose" was a long hanging muzzle that lay against the neck but could be raised. When it opened slightly, it was the upper jaw that moved. Did the Tsa have teeth? She couldn't be sure.

The feathers and chimes still came, now with other feelings that had to be from the other, not her own mind. But much more gently than from the first Tsa; had they sent an expert? For no reason she felt a twinge of fear, and that brought the first pain this creature had given her. It made a jumpy motion, and now the eyes did blink; the lids closed diagonally.

On a hunch, she spoke aloud, concentrating only on the words themselves. "Please don't hurt me. Why do you do that?"

A flood of images she couldn't sort out, and again the feel of something soft in her head. Like fur, this time. But it all moved too fast; she couldn't follow. She said "Slower, slower," and spoke the words themselves ever more slowly. And the flow did slacken, but still she couldn't recognize much of anything. A flower, there? Maybe; not one she'd ever seen, though. "I'm sorry; I still don't understand."

Now the chimes had a questioning tone. "Not yet," she said. "Keep trying." And something impelled her to start talking a blue streak, about anything and everything. Startled at first, then she relaxed and let the words spill out. Excitement grew, and brought another dart of pain until she heeded her breathing rhythm and kept closer to the alpha state.

Then, in her head, words came. "Are you mindbeast?"

There was no hostility to the question, only curiosity. Through her surprise, almost shock, Lisele realized that *her* mind made the words, out of whatever the other was doing. But she listened as though her ears heard, while the question was repeated. Then she said, "I'm just me—Lisele. Who are you?"

"Ceevt, of the Tsa. Tsa kill mindbeasts. What do you do?" The thing spoke of killing, but its tone was light and friendly. Puzzled, not afraid now, Lisele tried to think what to say next. But before she decided, the door opened again.

The robed Tsa who entered then was bigger, almost Lisele's height and much heavier. Its mind-touch rasped at her once and then faded; she could still feel it, though. Enough to know that here was the one who had brought her. And the thing it held in one hand looked an awful lot like an energy gun.

Her control began to slip; fear surged and pain hit her. She sensed something from the two Tsa minds but this time it made no words for her, and then the small one scuttled out and the big one closed the door. Struggling for calm, she shut her eyes again, and waited. She heard feet move toward her, and then stop.

Her only chance was to speak; she knew that, and after a time she managed it. "You don't have to hurt me. Why *do* you?"

Brief stab, then a "voice," fumbling at first. "You hurt *us*, you mindbeasts. The Shrakken first, but your kind too, though not as bad. We only protect ourselves." The creature paused. "But you did not hurt Ceevt, our young, who could not have protected itself. That is why you still live. Why did you spare Ceevt?"

Hard it was, to stay calm then; Lisele gave it her best try. "We never tried to hurt *any* of you. We were trying to stay clear of you, and you came down after us and crashed Tregare's scoutship. And tonight we were minding our own business, didn't even know you were anywhere around, when you began hurting us so awful. We—"

Pain struck, then eased; she drew ragged breath and fought again to calm her mind. "Did you do that, just now, on purpose?"

Confusion. "When you give hurt, what can we do except attack in return, force you to stop? It is reflex, almost instinct."

"Does it work? Do the Shrakken stop?"

Not while they lived, the Tsa admitted. Which made the Shrakken so deadly a menace, that the Tsa-Drin had dedicated the entire next Great Era to—

"Killing them? Wiping them out?" Pain twinged; Lisele made herself feel detached, as if the whole thing was hypothetical. It worked. She nodded; the rules of the game took a little getting used to, but she was learning. She didn't open her eyes, though.

"But the Shrakken haven't gone looking for you; all they want is to stay away from you. If you'd only leave them alone—"

"They came to us first, those mindbeasts. At start we thought no harm. Then one injured itself and blamed Tsa for the hurt—and threw the pain at all minds, its fear and rage and hate. Long ago, this was; I have only been told. But on both sides, much pain and many dead—all, on theirs. And at the end of it, Tsa and Shrakken cannot both live. When we meet, they give us agony—so we give them death. Though the giving costs *us* pain and deaths—or loss of sanity, which is worse to fear."

The creature paused. "You humans are not so ready to hurt, but you have the same power. And you have not answered me. Why did you spare Ceevt, our young?"

She wasn't quite sure what he meant, but she answered anyway. "Because Ceevt didn't hurt *me*. Ceevt's mind-touch—it was nice. Soft and friendly and pleasant. And then we could talk. I thought maybe Ceevt was a communication expert."

"No. Only a young, not yet trained in defense."

Suddenly Lisele knew something she couldn't define. "You, though—the Tsa, among yourselves—don't you ever hurt each other that way?" And from the flood of images, she had her answer.

Carefully, she spoke. "Then normally you have control over what your minds send, but never over what you receive." *Agreement*. "We humans, and the Shrakken, don't even know we're sending anything, so we have no idea of controlling that." *Skepticism*. Hurriedly she said, "What I'm doing is something different. Most people don't even know about it. Some could learn, though. And then maybe—"

She knew she didn't know enough to do a good job of what she was trying to say, but it was a place to start, so she did. If the Tsa would leave the Shrakken alone, the Shrakken would stay away from Tsa worlds. Humans could ferry any needed data back and forth, and if necessary the exchanges could be done without personal contact. "A mail drop." An uninhabited satellite, was the idea the Tsa finally understood.

The creature wasn't convinced, though; she could tell. It asked questions; those she understood, she tried to answer. Then came a feeling of purpose, and the thing said, "Your humans would agree? And persuade the Shrakken? I am Elzh, once called Great Elzh of the seven ships—" She felt a pang of loss. *Why?* "I have right to speak for Tsa-Drin; my saying would bind."

The breath Lisele drew then was out of the rhythm she tried to hold. After all, what authority did *she* have? Not doodly! So she said, "I can propose it. I'll have to find my people—" *If you haven't killed them*, but by main force she kept that thought carefully hypothetical and without feeling. "—and we'll need to talk with the Shrakken leaders. *You* mustn't be anywhere around then, of course. So—"

What else? *Inconnu Deux!* "There was a human ship here. It—"

"It escaped. Destroying two of ours, as it went. And now has come back, with a small one that killed another Tsa ship." Again the pang of loss, and now Lisele understood it.

But then what—? "I'm sorry. That's all part of what we need to stop. But if another human ship comes here, you mustn't attack it. You see?" So the *Deux* was back! But where, and in what condition? Never mind, for now; stick to cases, as Tregare would say. "We humans can't help, if we're stuck here on Shaarbant."

A slow thought, then. "True seeming. And I cannot help you largely, either. Except guide you, to return where I found you."

Lisele shook her head. "You can do better than that. Lift this ship and scout the area, in case my people have moved on. Then, I'm not sure how to work this, yet, but maybe you could fly us all over near the Shrakken headquarters." If the humans would agree to be doped asleep so everybody could stand each other? She winced at the idea of trying to persuade Tregare to any such arrangement, but...

A sad note in Elzh's thought. "That, I wish could do. But at landing, human mind-thrusts affected our pilot, and the ship did not land well. At now, it cannot lift again."

"You're sure about that?"

"Very sure. I am Elzh, I said. I command, and I know my ship."

"What about your scoutships?"

"Scoutships? Like the little things we saw, once cycles ago, and again now? We have no such."

Nothing to say to that; why should Elzh lie? Then she felt the Tsa's new thought in her mind, and decided to say it first. "Yes; I'll open my eyes. It was just—I didn't dare risk any disturbing stimulation, before." Her eyes opened; she blinked a couple of times, to get focus. Elzh's features were more pronounced, more emphasized than Ceevt's had been, and the skin was a little darker. Otherwise the adult Tsa looked pretty much like the young.

Through her mind went a ripple of wry amusement; not hers, she knew, but Elzh's. The Tsa must have caught her puzzled feeling; it said, "I see how you see me. I would not like to see me that way." A picture came—of herself, Lisele, but seen through some distorting screen that made her look . . . no, not ugly, but utterly ludicrous. How could such a contrived, flimsy creature *work*?

Involuntarily she laughed, then forced herself to stop.

"What did you do?" Elzh seemed puzzled. "Can you do it at will?"

"Show me that picture again," and when it came, she laughed, and this time didn't try to stop until she'd finished.

"You can send pleasure, also! We had not known that."

"Hey." She leaned forward. "Maybe we *can* get along."

Later, though, eating the mushlike foods the Tsa commander offered her, she wasn't quite so sure. Heartburn played hob with the alpha state. But Lisele managed.

She was tired to the edge of collapse; before sleep, though, she needed a bathroom. She had a time finding words that meant anything to Elzh; when she did, the Tsa opened a sliding panel and showed her various fixtures that used water in one way or another. Then the creature demonstrated how to work the lights, and left her. She tried the door; it wasn't locked, but she was in no hurry to go anywhere. Not until morning, at least.

Back to the bathroom, she studied the fixtures. They weren't like anything she was used to, and she couldn't decide which was what. Finally she made a guess and hoped she was right; the gadget cycled out looking clean, at any rate. Then she turned the lights down, and looked at the big soft yellow bowl. The temperature was comfortable; she could use her clothes for a pillow. She undressed, crawled into the bowl, and slept.

She woke feeling cheerful, and looking around the alien room didn't break that mood. After all, hadn't she *talked* with Tsa? But that step, Lisele knew, was only a start; now she had to follow through. And a few minutes later, she was ready to begin.

She found no intercom or signal system she could recognize, so she opened the door and went out, into a bright-lit blue-green corridor. Tsa walked past her in both directions; she tended to her breathing and wondered how she'd recognize Elzh. The aliens looked at her, and she felt very light mind-touches. *Elzh told them about me; that's why they're not startled.* Speaking to all of them in general, she said, "I'd like to find Elzh, please."

She received the same kind of impression-flow, and a little of the chime sounds that she'd first had from Ceevt and the commander. Then from someone—she couldn't tell which, and they all looked alike: "Elzh." One made a kind of beckoning move, so that had to be the one who'd responded. It turned, looking back, and she followed. Upship, passing other Tsa and now not at all nervous about them, she followed her guide and wasn't surprised to come into the Tsa equivalent of Control. Everything was different, of course—but she bet she could learn the setup pretty quick.

"Elzh," said the guide, and from a central control position, one rose and came to her. Now, by a round notch in its left ear, that she hadn't consciously noticed before, Lisele recognized Elzh. In the Tsa way, the words came to her. "You are all right?"

"I'm fine. Hungry, though. And then somebody should help me find my people. Or do we need to talk some more, first?"

"Eat and talk, same time. With two others, if agreed. In mindsay and indling, very close to me."

Indling? Maybe the meaning would come clear in the talk, without her asking. "All right."

"Tserln. Idsath." And as Lisele followed the Tsa commander out of its control room, two others joined them.

She expected they'd go someplace like the *Deux*'s galley, but found herself entering a cramped cubicle with a small, low table and several of the bean-bag stools. Dull green, these. Elzh sat; so did Lisele and the other two. All well and good, but where was the food? Last night, someone had brought the trays in with the little dishes of various-tasting mush. Now Elzh reached and opened out the table top both ways from center, doubling the thing's area. And in the central opening thus revealed, rose first one tray and then three others stacked beneath it—each legged to stand, one above the next, about a decimeter. Elzh handed her the top one and she repressed a sigh. The same dishes of vari-colored mush, the same clumsy spoon to eat with. No liquid to drink. Oh, well...

Of the seven dishes, this time she thought she knew how to choose the digestible ones by smell and taste. Last night she'd been too tired to pay heed until her stomach complained, and that had been too late. Now she found four things she liked, and wondered how she'd managed more than one bite of any of the others. After the exploratory tastes and decisions she ate slowly. And when, she thought, would the talk begin?

The Tsa, she noticed now, finished one dish at a time, and each in the same order. Too late for her to try to conform to that game of protocol—and the grey-pink mixture they were just beginning was one she'd had to discard, anyway. Ulcer bait, that stuff!

Elzh paused in feeding. "You surprise those who see you today; you keep your sendings smooth. Do the Tsa treat you well, also?"

"Yes, sure." She nodded. "I asked them to find you for me, and one brought me along to you. That's pretty good."

Elzh's sending, then, came quick and rich, confusing her. Similar flashes came from the others; she realized they must be talking together. Then Elzh said, "Time now, meet Tserln and Idsath." Each in turn moved a hand, and Lisele thought she knew which was which—but looked closely, trying to see how to tell them apart.

Finally she thought she had it—not enough to spot either of them in a crowd, but to distinguish one from the other, and from Elzh. Tserln had lighter skin and narrower ears; Idsath's muzzle was wider. Enough of that; waiting, she listened.

Hesitantly, one "spoke" to her; from eye movements, Lisele guessed it was Tserln communicating. "—that we have not to harm each other, your and my people. And the Shrakken, also?" The Tsa went on, playing back what she and Elzh had said, the night before. "Is true?"

She nodded. "I think it can be done; I'm going to try." Then the third Tsa, Idsath, went through the whole same routine. Lisele wondered if the Tsa were a little slow in the brains, and then decided it must be hard for people used to multipoint telepathy, to deal one-on-one with an outsider. A different way, was all, so she stayed patient. And considering the alternative, she'd better!

When Idsath was satisfied, again the three Tsa began their flickering interchange of images, too fast for Lisele to recognize. Definitely *not* slow in the brains! Now, without the need to concentrate on talking, her mind began to slip into worry—what had happened to Rissa and Tregare and the rest? But she felt the Tsa getting disturbed, and caught a flicker of almost-pain; determinedly, she put her worries back on automatic hold, where she'd been keeping them. And could feel the Tsa mind-touches relax. But how, she wondered, did they manage to handle their own worries?

Then Elzh said, "When you feel ready, I take you to the place where I found you. There is nothing else there, though—

your people or anything of them. Will the taking be of the help you need, to find them?''

She thought, then said, ''I think so. When your—'' No, she mustn't say attack. ''When I left our camp I ran downhill. In daylight now, I think I can find my way back.''

''Then if you are fed enough, do we go there now?''

''Yes, I guess so.'' Then a wish came to her. ''Elzh—could I see Ceevt again, before we go? Because we might never have been able to talk without hurting, you and I, if it hadn't been for him.''

All three Tsa blinked once, and Elzh said, ''You and Ceevt to greet parting, is correct; the young will meet us here. But Ceevt is not a him. Nor a her—as you, I think. Nor yet a—'' The image made no word she knew. ''Grown to fullness, Ceevt will be those things. But not as a young. With you, this is not so?''

Explaining puberty to the Tsa was more than Lisele wanted to tackle, especially since it sounded like their own biology was pretty complicated. All she said was, ''I'm a her; yes.''

They were all getting up now; Elzh opened the door and they followed him out. The three Tsa were much of a height; Lisele could look over the tops of their heads, but just barely. As they turned to go along the corridor, rapid footsteps came from behind, and Lisele turned to see a smaller Tsa approaching. ''Ceevt?''

''Yes,'' said Elzh. ''Our young.'' The way Elzh said it, Lisele caught two meanings. *Our*. Elzh and Tserln and Idsath. Well, maybe so. The other meaning was that Ceevt was the *only* young around here. If she had it right, and she wasn't betting much on that.

Ceevt came closer to her, slowed and stopped within touching distance. The small Tsa stood breast-high to her; it looked up and blinked once. ''*You* aren't mindbeast!'' And the touch of its thought was like soft laughter.

On total impulse and no thought at all, Lisele knelt and hugged the young Tsa. Seconds later, she realized she'd taken a terrible risk, for she felt the adult minds reach to crush her—and then draw back. Elzh's thought came: ''Made a saying first, you should have. But it is all right.''

The young Tsa smelled like spice, up close at nuzzling range—like the bowl she'd slept in. It was heavy, all right; she could feel that. And its arms were strong, hugging her in turn. Something warm and wet stroked her ear; Ceevt was licking it. Well, if that's the way they did—she stretched to return the caress. Then a hand patted her shoulder, and Elzh said, "Enough. Stand now." She did; she and the young Tsa released each other. Elzh spoke again. "Not the power to decide, has Ceevt, but I bind it now. The young has made you Tsa. One of us." And her ear got wet again.

A little later, when Tserln and Idsath had gone somewhere with Ceevt, Lisele and Elzh left the Tsa ship and set out walking. Quickly she decided that Tsa weren't much for hiking; if she moved faster than a stroll, Elzh fell behind. She wondered if the alien was used to a lesser gravity. Then she chuckled— after all, it hadn't walked a quarter of the way around Shaarbant, as she had!

"You send pleasure. Why?"

"Nothing important. I'm enjoying our walk, is all." The mind-touch had an uncertain feel to it, and withdrew.

The Tsa ship sat in a flat clearing; when they topped the small surrounding ridge, Lisele looked across a wide, steep ravine. Stopping, she gazed at the far side in search of the knoll she'd climbed the day before. She saw one, a bit down from the crest as seen from this perspective, but wasn't sure it was the right place. With her fingers she measured its angle from the sun. At least, she could try it for starters.

Elzh, watching, asked what she did. "Trying to figure where I have to go, on the far side of this gulch. I think I have it now." She turned to face the Tsa. "You'd better go back. You mustn't meet my people before I have a chance to explain to them."

"You think that with your telling, they can do as you do?"

"Meet with you, talk, without setting off mind-pain?" She shook her head. "I don't know. Some can, maybe. We need to find a way to test, that doesn't hurt a lot or even kill somebody, maybe. Do you have any ideas?"

Slow, the Tsa's thought came. "Only that *I* must do the meeting of these others, and singly—and you, to help, should be there."

It wasn't much: far as it went, though, it made sense. "All right." But the way Elzh walked, the humans had better do most of the traveling. "Keep watch on this spot. When I can, I'll bring somebody back here. And you come out by yourself; right?"

"Not far enough." The meaning wasn't clear, so she

waited. "Here, if a human sends fierce pain, it would reach my ship, and all Tsa there might react, and kill it." Elzh pointed. "Below, there, where rock will shield. By that outcrop?" Sure; the way the boulder jutted, she could recognize and find it again.

"All right. I'll come here; the other can wait down there."

"It suffices. I will have watch kept for you."

She couldn't think of anything else that needed saying, so she gave a good-bye gesture, a sort of wave, and turned and started down the steep slope.

The valley held no breeze; heat soon had her thirsting. No matter; at the bottom, she remembered, a stream ran. Climbing down became automatic, as Lisele's mind centered on what had happened to her, and what would happen *now*.

For openers: did she trust Elzh? She guessed so. But why? Puzzling at the question, she found an answer. It was because people can lie with words but the Tsa didn't *send* words, only feelings and intentions that her own mind somehow translated. She tried to think how she might convince Tregare of her certainty, and shrugged. He shouldn't be the first to meet Elzh, anyway; he'd need some examples before he could shed his own wary mistrust. If he could do that, at all. Well, obviously, not everybody should even try to speak with the Tsa. Certainly the Shrakken couldn't—not yet, anyway.

Rissa, she decided, was her best first bet. Lisele knew some of her mother's history, and had seen how she operated under stress, enough to have that confidence. Rehearsing what to say, how to explain, Lisele was still at it when she reached the stream. The water tasted fresh and clean; when she'd had enough of it, she splashed some over her head and face. Refreshed, she began the long uphill climb.

She thought of her own experience; how had she and Elzh managed it, breaking through the reflexes of pain and retaliation? Well, they hadn't, of course; not by themselves. Without the lucky accident of Ceevt's coming, the young who knew nothing of attack and defense, maybe they never would have. Elzh hadn't been carrying that energy gun for nothing! Lisele shivered for a moment, then shook free of feeling spooky. It *had* worked out, and that was that!

The slope's curve, above, hid the knoll that was her destination. She rechecked the sun's angle; it would have arced away from the position she'd sighted, but in this short time, not by much. When, panting more than a little, she came in sight of that knoll, she wasn't far off course. And it was the one she wanted, all right.

She didn't have to climb all the way to it; the camp had been a little farther down. Estimating her direction, she turned toward it, and in a few minutes she found where it had been.

Nobody was there. Nobody, and only scattered remnants of their gear, stuff they hadn't bothered to take along.

She turned back. Before she pushed on toward Sassden—because, thinking her lost, that's where they would go—she might as well let Elzh know he needn't bother keeping watch.

XXIV. *Rissa*

When the Tsa attack ended, Rissa found herself still on her feet, leaning against a tree. Breathing deeply, she relaxed most of the pain from her head. A patch of light moved; she saw Tregare stumbling along, shining a handlamp here and there. "Bran?"

He turned; light flashed in her eyes and then he pointed the beam lower. "Standoff, Rissa! I felt how to throw it back at them. The pain leveled off; maybe I gave as good as I got." He staggered, but caught his balance. "Takes it out of you, though." He came to the tree and sat against it; Rissa knelt and gave him a brief hug.

She said, "I am not certain what I tried to do—block the mind attack, negate it? For a time I thought I succeeded, but—" The handlamp slipped from his grasp; she picked it up, brushing her hair out of her eyes with the other hand. "Bran—are you all right?"

"I'll live." His voice came bitter. "That's more than I can say for Sevshen. And Stonzai's in some sort of fit, or coma."

Indrawn breath whistled through her teeth. "And the others?"

"I don't know yet. Haven't found them. *Lisele*—"

"I know, Bran. I had best go search." Getting up on her feet was hard, but she did it. "You will be all right here?"

His hand touched her leg. "Go ahead. For Lisele, look downhill. The last I saw or heard of her, she was headed that way."

Rissa looked at the dark sky, then along the short distance the handlamp lit. "I will look for her, and call. But another light, as a beacon, might help her find her way back. If you can locate one."

Tregare sighed. "Right; I'll try." She patted his shoulder and moved off, shining the light back and forth ahead of her.

She found Stonzai first. The Shrakken lay stiff and twisted, back arched, writhing; the triangular mouth gaped and the eyes were closed so tightly that wrinkles showed around them. Breath came in irregular, shuddering gasps. Rissa bent to put a hand on the heaving chest. "Stonzai?" No response. Futilely, Rissa tried other words and touches to reach the alien; finally she shook her head and went on.

Across the clearing, Sevshen looked like a still-picture of Stonzai—the same distortions, but no movement or sound. Grimacing, Rissa turned away, and tried to decide where next to search.

At the edge of level ground, where the slope dropped away, she paused. In the quiet she heard muffled sobs below, and turned the light that way. Motion caught her eye; a closer look showed her a foot, sticking out of underbrush and moving. She hurried down in time to help Jenise Rorvik get free of the clump of bushes. "Jenise?"

"Oh, Rissa!" The woman's lunge to hug her almost knocked Rissa off her feet. "I thought they'd—I thought they were killing me!"

Rissa's instinctive surge of sympathy died on a practical note. "Did you fight their attack? And to what effect?"

"Fight it? *How?* I—"

"Never mind. Let us get you to the camp." With an arm around Jenise, Rissa helped her climb to the clearing. At its edge, Rissa heard noises to their right, and turned the lamp to show Hagen Trent getting to his feet. Blood streaked his face, but it was caked and clotted, not flowing.

He squinted into the light; Rissa turned it briefly toward her own face, then at the ground between them. She could still see him, though dimly, as now he grinned. "Hi! That damned onslaught set me running, and while I was still trying to stop, I ran me into a tree or something and got knocked cold as a pickle.''

Under the circumstances his good humor was contagious. ''Well,'' said Rissa. ''You seem to have survived in good order. Have you seen Lisele? Or have you, Jenise?''

Two negatives—and Tregare, approaching now, added a third. So, using other working handlamps he'd found, he and Rissa and Trent searched downslope for Lisele. Jenise stayed to tend Stonzai, though no one had any idea how to help the alien.

Down the hill, Tregare pointed out a trail of bent and flattened ground-cover. But it petered out in naked ground, with no continuation on the far side of the bare patch. Further search, and shouts, brought no success. So finally, choking on the words, Rissa called a halt. ''This task needs daylight—and some rest, if not sleep, for all of us.'' They climbed back to the camp. Rissa did not expect to sleep, herself, but only for a brief time did she lie awake.

In the morning Stonzai was more or less aware—able to walk and to eat, but not talking. Aside from seeing she was fed, there was nothing the others could do. In any case, their attention centered on two things: Lisele's absence, and the tip of a spacecraft that showed above forest growth, across the valley. The Tsa? ''Who else?'' said Tregare. But enemies or no enemies, the group made a sweeping search of the valley slope. No sign of Lisele, though; the girl simply was not there. So everyone straggled back up to camp.

It seemed to Rissa, fighting the sick ache of her daughter's loss, that the group was waiting for someone to make a decision. Looking across to the Tsa ship, she said, ''Bran Tregare—what is it that we do now? Wait here, for the Tsa to strike again? Cross this great ravine and attack their ship, *and their deadly minds*, with handguns? Go to ground somewhere, and try to hide?'' He said nothing, and now her voice rose. ''Do you decide, or do I?''

Answering, he sounded like a man trying to be patient and reasonable. ''You don't give very good choices, do you?''

''Because there *are* none.'' For the first time, she wondered if marrying this man had been a mistake. But then she saw him grin.

''*I* know that. I'm just trying to think through, what we do have.'' His hand raised to halt her answer. ''What's hanging us up is that we haven't the faintest clue how to find Lisele.''

Frowning, he paused for Rissa's nod. "We've hit our best licks and struck out. Well, what I say is, if the princess is on her own, she'll make it; she'll head for where we were all going. If she's caught by the Tsa, or—" He gulped. "—or dead, we can't do any good, anyway." He looked like someone expecting to be hit with an axe. "So I say we pick up and go on—get to Sassden, like we intended." His mouth twisted. "I'm sorry, Rissa. That's the only move that makes sense."

"Of course it is, Bran." Now, through her hurt, she tried to smile. "I was afraid you would not see it."

Tregare dug the hole, in the shade of a large tree but far enough away to avoid striking major roots. After Rissa stripped the dead Shrakken's harness of all useful gear and supplies, Tregare and Hagen Trent gently lowered Sevshen into the grave. Tregare looked over at Stonzai, who had watched briefly and then gone to sit a few meters distant, facing away. "D'you think, Rissa, we should do some kind of ceremony?"

"Just a moment." She went to Stonzai, called the Shrakken's name. "We must bury Sevshen now. Is there anything your people do at such a time?"

"Cannot do. Not the things or people have, here. Not the sounds or scents. No. Over him the dirt put." Stonzai would say nothing more, so Rissa went back to Tregare and explained.

"In shock, that one," he said. "Well, we plain don't have time to wait around for her to snap out of it." He put the shovel to dirt, then paused. "*Something* should be said. So I'll say it." He cleared his throat. "Sevshen, we never did get to know each other. But I'll say this: you pulled your weight."

Packing and loading-up didn't take long. They chose a route that led far down the valley, away from the Tsa ship, toward the farside gap that looked easiest to scale. But once they had started, Rissa felt an urge to have a closer look at the enemy. "Bran—I am going to make a side trip, a reconnaissance. If I do not catch up before dark, camp beside the stream so that I can find you."

He protested, but she would not change her mind, so they kissed and she headed back up the valley. "Peace save you, be *careful*!" he called after her, and she waved in reply.

Orienting herself by the knoll above last night's camp, she climbed the valley's opposite side. She thought she knew the approximate direction of the Tsa ship, and when she peered over a minor ridge and saw the thing, she hadn't missed her aim by much. She ducked back behind the ridge's crest and moved to her left, where she would be nearer the ship. Then she belly-crawled through undergrowth, as far as she could go without running out of cover, and looked.

Her mini-binocs had seen better days; the right barrel was cracked, and had been full of swamp water more than once. Residual sediment blurred the image to that eye, and the left-hand objective lens was marred by scratches and a tiny, jagged impact crater.

But out of the ship that differed subtly from those she knew, she saw the robed creature waddle down the ramp and come toward her.

Straight, directly toward her.

No mind-touch yet; subvocally, Rissa thanked peace for that much blessing. She wriggled backward, until the edge of slope masked her from the approaching alien. Then she turned and ran downhill, heedless of footing, trying to gauge how long she had before the Tsa reached the edge, and could look down and see her.

A place to hide! At one side of vision was a jagged rock; she turned toward it. Her mind's clock said she was running out of time; plunging down through brush and gravel she slid sidelong, to stop behind the jutting crag and slightly under its overhang. Breathing hard, not daring to peep around the rock's edge, she waited. But took time to check her handgun, wishing it were an energy weapon, not a mere needle-gun. Then she tried to blank her mind, to be non-existent. Looking at the rock before her, in her thoughts she *was* rock.

The creature must have held its mind well. Very near, she heard its movements, before any mind-touch came. And what she felt, then, was a sense of question, and a faint ghost of chime-sounds. Puzzlement broke her concentration. Image came, of a Shrakken, and without intent she saw dead Sevshen, and—*you killers!* And the Tsa struck with pain.

Rissa whimpered; her hand lost the gun. Now she set her mind to give nothing, built a mental wall and felt acid lick it, like fire. An inert wall, then—one that wouldn't react! But the pain came and went, and so did her control of her own mind.

Not by her choosing, her eyes opened; she found she was standing, not hiding behind the rock at all. And she saw the robed creature she'd seen before; only its head was exposed with part of a real face but not all. Not moving, it stood there, throwing agony. Groaning, Rissa shook her head and reached for the gun she no longer had. She couldn't find it.

All right! She concentrated on *how* her mind hurt, and pushed back in the same fashion. Suddenly the alien made a jerking, backward move, then stood still again. Mouth drawn wide in agony, Rissa felt her face pull into a predatory grin. "How—" She gasped it. "How do you like some of your own medicine?"

And how was she doing it? She did not know—only that repeated exposure to Tsa attacks had created responses in her. Her pain ebbed, then grew again. Hearing her breath make a snarl, Rissa forced her mind to *push*—and felt something, outside her, begin to crumble. *"Now!"*

"No! This is not necessary!" *No real voice said that.*

"No, please stop! You don't have to; it's all right!" And that voice, Rissa knew from somewhere. But the Tsa mind-attack then, with a strangely gentle power, shoved Rissa off the edge of awareness.

She did not let go; as she tumbled, she felt the other falling with her.

XXV. Lisele

*I*f she hadn't taken the wrong trail, deep in the ravine where she could see no landmarks, Lisele would have been there sooner. As it was, she came breathless around a switchback to see Rissa point a gun at Elzh, then drop it as the Tsa's mind-touch struck. Pain came to Lisele, but it came diffused, not concentrated.

She tried to call out, but no sound emerged. She stood, frozen, and managed one outcry before her mother and the alien, almost in unison, slowly collapsed. She ran, then, and knelt beside Rissa.

"Are you all right?" No answer; Rissa was certainly knocked out. Breathing, though, and Lisele saw her eyelids flutter. She looked uphill toward Elzh; the Tsa hadn't moved yet. She went to it, and saw the nostril-fringes flutter rhythmically.

Now what? If they both woke up, the whole thing would happen all over again, for they lay in plain sight of each other. *But what if—?* Moving Elzh was out of the question, but Rissa wasn't all that heavy, and the nearest hummock lay downhill from her. Getting her mother up into a fireman's carry wasn't easy, and Lisele's legs quivered with strain, but she made it down and around the hummock without falling, and managed to dump her burden on the ground fairly gently. And now the mound of dirt shielded Rissa and the Tsa from each other.

Rissa showed no signs of wakening, but Lisele looked uphill and saw Elzh begin to move. She hurried up toward the Tsa, but a few meters away, mind-touch stopped her. Mind-touch with more than a hint of pain, as Elzh sat up, eyes blinking. "You said you would explain to your humans. Instead you sent that one to kill me. Why should I not end you now?"

Shocked, Lisele gasped, fighting to quiet her mind. "But I didn't! I didn't even *find* my mother until just now, when you were—and I tried to get you both to stop. I—"

"Mother?" Pain ceased; Lisele felt curiosity replace the Tsa's anger. "Yes. I see the concept. You are that one's young."

"Yes, and I've got to go down there and be with her when she wakes up, so I *can* explain. And you stay here, Elzh, and if Rissa slips a little when she tries to talk with you—" *If she will, at all!* "Please try not to hurt her."

Without waiting for an answer, Lisele ran back downhill.

Rissa woke slowly, her head in Lisele's lap. "What—?"

"Now *listen*!" Lisele said. "Elzh didn't want to hurt you, and he won't if you're careful, and keep your thoughts calm. You can't afford to get mad, or scared, so don't *let* yourself. Start breathing deep, now, and think how *nice* it'd be to have peace with the Tsa."

Frowning, Rissa shook her head. "What are you talking about?"

"Weren't you paying attention at all? Here's what happened." She told it as quickly as she could, from the time Elzh had carried her away, to the present moment. "The little one did it, you see—talked to me without hurting, so I knew to try it with Elzh. And Elzh is up there right now, willing to give you another chance." Rissa's brows raised, but Lisele didn't want to take time to explain all that. "Just remember—he's friends as long as we are."

Rissa smiled like a pale ghost of herself. "I do not have the *energy* to muster anger; in fact, you had best help me clamber up this hill. But if you can talk with those creatures, I can do no less than try."

It really went pretty well, Lisele thought; the lapses into disturbance and pain were few, and after a time, stopped altogether. Slowly, color returned to Rissa's face, and her quick understanding jumped past the need for long explanations. Watching and listening, Lisele decided she'd certainly guessed it right, the best choice of someone to lead off the discussions. Rissa had some improvements on the ideas Lisele and Elzh had put together; once again, Lisele admired the way her mother adapted to new situations.

When it came time to leave, Rissa introduced the Tsa to the human custom of shaking hands, and said, "We have our children to thank, for this peace we begin. Let us keep it well."

"The young, yes," said Elzh. "I will say to Ceevt, for you."

Later, following down the ravine toward the place where Tregare would choose a camp, Rissa said, "It will work, I think, Lisele. Some will be able to treat with the Tsa, and some will not. But I do not look forward to the task of convincing your father."

XXVI. *Tregare*

*H*e still couldn't manage Lisele's alpha-state trick on his own hook, and maybe he never would. But for the purpose at hand, being able to talk with Elzh the Tsa, light hypnosis worked well enough; with a couple of dopy-pills to help, Rissa had been able to make the suggestions stick. "Friend" was the key-word; any time the Tsa mind-touch rubbed his nervous side the wrong way, he repeated it until the mental irritation eased. For a man who had lived on the raw edge of adrenaline as much as Bran Tregare had, he felt he was adjusting pretty well.

He looked past Elzh, across to Rissa. Her grief for her brother was still new and she made no attempt to hide it. For hours he'd held her, as—for the first time since he'd known her—she cried so hard he feared she'd hurt herself.

"If only he could have known," she said now. "The Tsa *cannot* lie. But poor Ivan, unable to trust . . ."

Tregare cleared his throat. "He's not the only one, might've made that mistake. The trouble was, Rissa—well, the way things stood, best we can know from what the *Deux* overheard at the last, he must have felt he couldn't take the *chance*."

"It is not understood," said Elzh, "how your colleague failed to recognize truth, and destroyed my other ship and himself. It is hoped that no such thing shall again occur."

Yeah, sure. "Friend," he subvocalized before speaking, because in the back of his mind, claws flexed, and he knew he couldn't afford them. "Ivan didn't know you," he said. "He couldn't. Until Lisele found out how to talk with you, nobody ever did. Don't downgrade Ivan Marchant." Again, for calm, he whispered the key-word.

Rissa's hand stroked his arm. "They do not, Bran. Be easy, as we must, here." He knew she was right, but still the easing was a struggle, before Tregare controlled his thought enough that the mind-touch gentled. Then behind him he heard sounds, and turned to see Lisele approach.

"The *Deux*'s landed," she said. "At Sassden. Hagen spotted her coming down, and Tserln set him up a relay, to talk. Anyway, there's a scoutship there, that Ivan left, that can come pick us up. As soon as everybody's out of freeze, and Anders says that won't be long."

"Out of freeze?" But side-issues couldn't hold Tregare's attention; one question governed. "What's the ship's condition?"

Lisele shook her head. "Anders doesn't know, for sure. A lot of work, he thinks, and we need some parts. But no permanent damage, he's pretty certain."

"All right," Tregare said. "We'll see when we get there."

Ready to leave, he stood, but Rissa caught his arm. "The

Tsa, Elzh, is not at ease. Because you are not, and Elzh knows you command. So say again the words of peace. *Say* them, Bran, and *mean* them.''

With the past flooding him—*Ivan, Dacia, Ellalee, Sevshen*—Tregare found the saying hard. But he set his mind and he did it.

Waiting in their new camp, the crater ridge giving insulation from accidental mental interplay with the Tsa ship, Tregare thought things over. The truce functioned—the truce that young Lisele had cobbled together, talking with Elzh and playing by ear. Well, he'd never thought his daughter, and Rissa's, was stupid!

Judging by Stonzai's reactions, the Shrakken wouldn't be able to shed fear of the Tsa, and mistrust. Not for a long time, anyway. But with humans working as go-betweens, and no direct meetings of Tsa and Shrakken—yes, the kid had called that one right, on the first bounce.

The Tsa, now. Once Tregare had been able to put his own fierce instincts under control, his natural curiosity took over—for here was a whole new intelligence to get to know! At Lisele's suggestion he learned the trick of putting his emotions at distance when talking with Elzh—and it did ease matters a lot. He not only got to know the former ''admiral,'' but came to like him (well, he assumed Elzh was still male, though he didn't understand the Tsa sex-sequence).

Near as Tregare could tell, the Tsa chieftain was sincere. The whole mess was because Tsa couldn't shut off telepathic reception, and gave hurt for hurt by sheer reflex, while Shrakken and humans hadn't known they were *sending* pain.

Well, it was going to be tricky; no help for that. But if all parties pulled their socks up and paid some attention . . .

Tregare grinned. ''Peace be primed, it can *work*!''

XXVII. Lisele

There wasn't any way the Tsa and Shrakken could meet in person; not yet, anyway. Lisele had seen Stonzai try it, and two others in test situations, and they'd all had to dive for shielding cover. And Elzh said, "No more, Lisele. *I* do not want their pain. We must avoid, they and we."

So at Sassden, where the *Deux* waited repairs, the Tsa delegation kept to itself in a riverside camp behind hills, at the place where Ivan, so long ago, had left the scoutship.

Some humans could deal with Tsa and others couldn't. Hagen Trent seemed to have no trouble at all, but Jenise Rorvik wouldn't even try, and Lisele couldn't blame her much. Jenise was hurting enough already, with her bad wrist healing from an attempt at corrective surgery. Maybe the plastic-laminate "bones" would restore movement and maybe not; Lisele was sure that Trent and Jeremy Crowfoot had done their best, but would it be good enough?

Another who avoided the Tsa was Anders Kobolak. Bewildered and resentful of his sister's death, the Second Hat took to his quarters and would see no one but his wife, Alina. Normally a temperate man, he stayed drunk for three days; then, a day later, he joined a group in the galley. Rissa said, "Are you better now, Anders?"

Looking well, Lisele thought, for a man just done with a binge, he nodded. "It needed some time, Rissa—for me to understand why it had to happen. But Ivan saw no choice, and Dacia wanted to be with him." Now he smiled, sort of. "I heard the tape this morning. The last thing he said was, he loved her."

After one meeting with Tsa, Tregare came back to the *Deux* and said, "I was talking with the young one; Elzh said I could. He's a cute little blob."

"Not a he," said Lisele. "Or a she, either, or even a something I don't quite understand. Not yet. But Ceevt will be—all of them, if I have it right."

Tregare shook his head. "Well—whatever works."

Acting as go-betweens, the humans negotiated a firm agreement that Tsa and Shrakken would stay clear of each others' worlds. Only then did Tregare announce that both species would be given the FTL drive. "To spread word of the truce, as soon as possible." Actually the Shrakken had one ship fully converted to Hoyfarul specs, and now that Elzh no longer barred the way, that ship lifted from Shtegel port, to take word—and the specs—to Stenevo.

Also from Shtegel, where the Shrakken had their main labs and fabrication facilities, came components needed to repair *Inconnu Deux* and Elzh's two crippled ships, and modify those latter for FTL. The Shrakken had two other ships, but one was under repair and the other in process of FTL conversion, so that left the scoutship to do all the ferrying.

Sometimes Tregare flew it, and sometimes Rissa, when she wasn't busy getting reacquainted with baby Renalle. Lisele nagged until she was let to fly it in trajectory, later to do liftoff, and finally to land the thing. The landing wasn't the best she'd ever experienced, but she looked defiantly at her mother. "I *told* you I could do it. And next time I'll do it better." Rissa only shrugged. But the next chance they gave her, three trips later, Lisele made the promise good; she set the scout down, level-solid, with hardly a jar. And Rissa said, "Congratulations, Lisele. You do seem to have the makings of a good pilot." *Told you so!*

Then they all carried several loads of Shrakken-made electronic components over and up into *Inconnu Deux*. What with all the things that needed doing, Lisele hadn't been on the ship much, yet. Now, sweating after effort, she stopped off at the galley for a cool drink of fruit juice. What she got was the squeezings from local berries; it tasted good, though.

Looking for a place to sit, she met Arlen Limmer. She'd seen him at a distance once or twice, since he came out of freeze, but never to talk with. Now she looked at the tall, dark young man—not as tall, of course, as she recalled him—and said, "Hi, Arlen. Remember me? Come and sit down a minute."

With one eyebrow cocked, he looked at her. "You have to be Lisele. Aren't you? But you're older. I—"

She laughed. "You froze your butt while I didn't, is all. Come on; let's talk."

"Sure." They sat; while Arlen ate, she sipped juice. He said, "You and Tregare, all of you, you really walked halfway around this planet? I heard you did." He grinned at her. "Hey, that must have been a real adventure. Lots of excitement, I'll bet."

"You could say that. It wasn't halfway around, though. More like a fourth, I think."

He shrugged. "It's still quite a way. Say—I notice your mother doesn't have long hair now. Why'd she cut it?"

Almost, Lisele smelled swamp mud; she felt the urge to scratch a scalp itch she didn't really have. "Oh, it got to be too much bother."

"Yes, sure." Finished with eating, Arlen sipped his coffee. "Y'know, the other day I had a chance to talk with a Tsa. What I can't see is why everybody thought they were such monsters."

Lisele looked at him. "Didn't they attack you in the *Deux*, when it lifted from Shaarbant?"

"I guess they did. I hadn't time to feel much of anything, though, before *zap*—I was in freeze. Your uncle Ivan—"

She felt uncomfortable. "My uncle Ivan did the best he could. He didn't freeze you on purpose, I understand, but—" Her turn to shrug. "Believe me, you were a lot safer that way."

"I guess you're right." He leaned forward. "Hey, Lisele— how old are you now? Bio-years, I mean?"

She wasn't certain. "Fifteen, maybe." She was stretching it, probably, but if *he* didn't know the difference . . . and he was still eighteen, of course. She felt herself frowning. "Why did you ask that?"

His cheeks reddened. "Well, you used to say—*you* know. And now you're not a kid. I thought maybe we could go walk up the river a way, where we could be by ourselves a little while, and—"

She shook her head. "Not now. There's a conference in about an hour, some people who haven't met with Tsa yet, and Elzh needs me to sit in. So I'm flying an aircar over with them, and—"

He laughed. "Oh, come on, Lisele. They don't need *you*. Tregare can handle it, he and Rissa. So why don't we—?"

"If Elzh says he needs me, he needs me."

Arlen grinned again. "All right. Why don't we take our walk tonight, then? That'd be even better, wouldn't it?"

Now she thought she understood. He wanted sex with her.

Well, she could, if she chose; she was old enough. Just in case, maybe she should get a contraceptive implant from Rissa; it couldn't harm. And then, how many days was it, before the implant "took"? She didn't remember. It hardly mattered yet, though, because she didn't *know* Arlen well enough to want to be lovers with him. And he didn't know her, either, or what she'd done and survived, and what it meant to her.

He waited for her answer; she said, "Let's just get acquainted for a while, Arlen. Talking, like we are now."

"Well, all right; sure." He looked a little disappointed, she thought. But now it was time for her to leave, so she did.

Arlen was a nice kid, but he sure had a lot of growing up to do.

XXVIII. Elzh

*W*atching humans board aircar, Elzh mindsaid gratitude to Lisele, the human young who would control it. Meeting with new humans, changing them to *not*-mindbeasts, had held danger. But Lisele had said, "Elzh? When the mindspeak starts to turn harsh, send them *pleasure*." More, that young said, for his better understanding. A new thought, never tried with mindbeasts, but Elzh mindspoke Tserln and Idsath for gathering and aid, and they three agreed: to learn, as always. As correct, as understood.

At later, Lisele sent the three Tsa pleasure. "It worked, didn't it? I could feel you doing it, every time anyone got edgy. And it *worked*."

Into aircar now, Lisele, and the small construct rose with no jarring and little sounding of air. Until a ridge came between, Elzh watched its leaving. Much thought, Elzh had.

To follow two Tsa ships sent ahead. To mindsay the *changes* Elzh knew, so no need to attack mindbeast worlds. But long and long, to reunite with those two ships. If only Elzh could ride the ship that had come from nothing! For now he understood that coming; the Tregare human had told how the ship outpaced its own radiation, as no Tsa ship could ever do. "But one could, Elzh, once we give it the Hoyfarul conversion. And since you couldn't possibly ride the *Deux*—"

No. Too many humans still mindbeasts; too much effort, no rest from it, to keep their minds from sending pain. But Tregare told of time and time—that Elzh could wait cycles while his ships were made like to Tregare's, and still find forereaching Tsa ships sooner than by leaving without changes. Could overtake them before they approached next beastworld.

Tregare mind was harsh but gave truth. So Elzh would wait.

But not with those ships, would Elzh go. No; to Tsa-Drin, instead, his ship only. Not safe, for Elzh, but needed to do. Because—always to learn, as correct, as understood. But also *to obey.* And this that Elzh now did, speaking and learning with mindbeasts—*not* to obey Tsa-Drin, this was.

To human female Rissa, who mindfought as Tsa could do but not again since first meeting, Elzh told dilemma. A day and day ago, but still Elzh thought of her saying. "As Tregare might put it, bucking your brass beats hell out of burning your brains." Odd thought, but with clear meaning.

Now Elzh approached warm nest, mindreaching to feel where Tserln and Idsath waited—and Ceevt! Stopping, not to enter before this thought ripened, he heard his mind.

A time comes, when Tsa-Drin itself must obey. For this new way is better than all the deaths and madness.

And if Tsa-Drin would not hear? Elzh's mind quirked; he felt it sending pleasure to himself.

Against ships that come from nothing, what can they do?

About the Author

F. M. BUSBY's published science fiction novels include *Rissa Kerguelen*, the related *Zelde M'Tana*, *All These Earths*, and the now-combined volume *The Demu Trilogy* (*Cage a Man*, *The Proud Enemy*, and *End of the Line*). Numerous shorter works, ranging from short-shorts to novella length, have appeared in various SF magazines and in both original and reprint anthologies, including *Best of Year* collections edited by Terry Carr, by Lester Del Rey, and by Donald A. Wollheim. Some of his works have been published in England and (in translation) Germany, France, Holland and Japan.

Star Rebel, the first of two books concerning the early life of Bran Tregare, is set in *Rissa*'s universe.

Buz grew up in eastern Washington near the Idaho border, is twice an Army veteran, and holds degrees in physics and electrical engineering. He has worked at the "obligatory list of incongruous jobs" but settled for an initial career as communications engineer, from which he is now happily retired in favor of writing. He is married, with a daughter in medical school, and lives in Seattle. During Army service and afterward he spent considerable time in Alaska and the Aleutians. His interests include aerospace, unusual cars, dogs, cats, and people, not necessarily in that order. He once built, briefly flew and thoroughly crashed a hang glider, but comments that fifteen-year-olds usually bounce pretty well.

JITTERBUG
by Mike McQuay

2155 A.D.: America is ruled by a fanatical Arab dictator with life-and-death power over every human being on earth. His weapon of control: the Jitterbug—a devastating plague used as an instrument of genocidal extermination. In the cities, the only refuge, millions of people struggle for survival while a ruthless cabal of amoral executives battle each other for the remnants of power. Out of the Southwestern desert comes Olson, an outlaw and outsider. Aided by blind chance, and a woman who knows the corporation's darkest secrets, he dares to challenge its corrupt rule. Only his strength can stand against the tide of destruction. Only his courage can make a better world out of the chaos of the old.

Read JITTERBUG, on sale July 15, 1984, wherever Bantam paperbacks are sold, or use the handy coupon below for ordering:

*Read the Powerful Second Novel in
an Exciting New Future History*

FAR STARS AND FUTURE TIMES

FLIGHT
OF
HONOR

by Richard S. McEnroe
author of THE SHATTERED STARS

Richard McEnroe has created a compelling, dramatic tale of three
people caught in a destructive quest for honor. One must sell
himself into mercenary service to stake a claim in his world.
One's virtue has caused him to be used as a pawn in an interstellar
struggle. And one can only find salvation in a final act of
murder. Their confrontation is at the heart of this stirring novel of
danger, intrigue and war.

☐ FLIGHT OF HONOR (24121-4 • $2.50 • on sale June 15, 1984)
☐ THE SHATTERED STARS (23853-1 • $2.50)

Read both of these fine *Far Stars and Future Times* novels,
on sale wherever Bantam paperbacks are sold, or use the handy
coupon below for ordering.

SPECIAL MONEY SAVING OFFER

Now you can have an up-to-date listing of Bantam's hundreds of titles plus take advantage of our unique and exciting bonus book offer. A special offer which gives you the opportunity to purchase a Bantam book for only 50¢. Here's how!

By ordering any five books at the regular price per order, you can also choose any other single book listed (up to a $4.95 value) for just 50¢. Some restrictions do apply, but for further details why not send for Bantam's listing of titles today!

Just send us your name and address plus 50¢ to defray the postage and handling costs.